PETERSBURG

ANDREI BELY was the pseudonym of Boris Nikolayevich Bugayev: a novelist, poet and critic, he became a leading figure amongst Russian Symbolist writers. Born in Moscow in 1880 he studied mathematics, zoology and philosophy at Moscow University, simultaneously interesting himself in art and mysticism. He began to publish in 1902 while still a student, adopting his pseudonym to spare his father, an eminent professor of mathematics, the embarrassment of public association with the still scandalous Symbolists. In 1914 he joined a Rudolf Steiner anthroposophical community in Switzerland. Returning to Russia in 1916 he welcomed the Revolution, but with the increasing restrictions placed upon artistic expression he became disillusioned. After making a forlorn attempt to revive the Symbolist aesthetic through the journal *Zapiski mechtateley*, he emigrated again in 1921. Bely returned to Russia in 1923 and was left relatively undisturbed during his last years. His work continued to be published in small editions but was largely ignored; nevertheless the influence of his style and ideas upon other Soviet writers was considerable. On his death in 1934, Evgeny Zamyatin wrote of him: 'Mathematics, poetry, anthroposophy, fox-trot – these are some of the sharpest angles that make up the fantastic image of Andrei Bely . . . [he is] a writer's writer.'

His first prose works were four short pieces which he designated 'symphonies'. In 1909 he published a more conventional novel, *The Silver Dove*; other works include *Kotik Letayev* (1922) and a series of novels, published during the 1920s and 1930s, under the generic title *Moscow*. *Petersburg* was first published in book form in 1916 and was immediately recognized as a work of major literary importance.

DAVID MCDUFF was born in 1945 and was educated at the University of Edinburgh. His publications comprise a large number of translations of foreign verse and prose, including poems by Joseph Brodsky and Tomas Venclova, as well as contemporary Scandanavian work; *Selected Poems* of Osip Mandelstam; *Complete Poems* of Edith Södergran; and *No I'm Not Afraid* by Irina Ratushinskaya. His first book of verse, *Words in Nature*, appeared in 1972. He has translated a number of twentieth-century Russian prose works for Penguin Classics. These include Dostoyevsky's *The Brothers Karamazov, Crime and Punishment, The House of the Dead, Poor Folk and Other Stories* and *Uncle's Dream and Other Stories*; Tolstoy's *The Kreutzer Sonata and Other Stories* and *The Sebastapol Sketches*; and Nikolai Leskov's *Lady Macbeth of Mtsensk*. He has also translated Babel's *Collected Stories* for Penguin Twentieth-Century Classics.

ADAM THIRLWELL was born in 1978. He has written two novels: *Politics* and *The Escape*. In 2003 he was chosen as one of *Granta*'s Best Young British Novelists. *Miss Herbert*, an essay on international novels, was published in 2007 and won a Somerset Maugham Award. His work has been translated into thirty languages. He lives in London.

ANDREI BELY

Petersburg

A Novel in Eight Chapters

With a Prologue
and an Epilogue

Translated by
DAVID MCDUFF
and with an Introduction by
ADAM THIRLWELL

PENGUIN BOOKS

PENGUIN CLASSICS

UK | USA | Canada | Ireland | Australia
India | New Zealand | South Africa

Penguin Books is part of the Penguin Random House group of companies
whose addresses can be found at global.penguinrandomhouse.com.

Penguin
Random House
UK

First published in Russian 1916
This translation, made from the 1916 edition, published in Penguin Books 1995
This edition first published in Penguin Classics 2011

017

Translation and Notes copyright © David McDuff, 1995
Introduction copyright © Adam Thirlwell, 2011
All rights reserved

The moral right of the translator and author of the introduction has been asserted

Set in 10/12pt Postscript Monotype Garamond
Typeset by Jouve (UK), Milton Keynes
Printed in England by Clays Ltd, Elcograf S.p.A.

ISBN: 978-0-141-19174-4

Contents

Introduction

*First-time readers should be aware that details of the plot
are revealed in this Introduction.*

SIGNS NAMES WORDS NOVELS SYSTEMS!

Moscow

The novelist Andrei Bely died of a stroke, in the Moscow of Soviet
Communism, in 1934. He was fifty-four. He had been born in the same
city: when it was the Moscow of Tsarist Autocracy. It was the ordinary
sad story of History. But the more detailed story of his death is even
sadder.

> His book of memoirs, *Between Two Revolutions*, had just appeared, with a
> preface by Lev Kamenev in which all of Bely's literary activities were
> termed a 'tragi-farce' acted out 'on the sidelines of history'. Bely bought up
> all the copies of the book he could find and tore out the preface. He con-
> tinued visiting the book shops until he suffered the fatal stroke.[1]

The sidelines of history!
  Bely's epilogue took place in 1934. But this epilogue was also Kamenev's. It's true that, with Stalin and Trotsky, Kamenev had once been at
the centre of history – the pure Communist impresario. But then the
machinations of politics had begun. In 1927 he had been expelled from
the Party. He was soon readmitted, but was expelled again in 1932, and
then readmitted a year later. This was the context of his terrified preface
to Bely's book. Historically, Kamenev was disappearing. In December
1934, after Bely had died, Kamenev was again expelled from the Party;
this time, he was also arrested. Sentenced in 1935 to ten years in prison,
he was retried in the first Moscow Show Trial in August 1936. He was
found guilty and immediately shot.

This epilogue, however, is only a prologue. It is only Moscow – and so it is only the political version of reality's multiple forms of disappearance. Whereas the more important story of Andrei Bely and his investigation into reality takes place in another Russian city, Petersburg – the city where Bely became famous. Petersburg was the pretext for his intricate novel called *Petersburg* – the city that Bely converted into a portable experiment with words.

Petersburg

But then, Petersburg was already an experiment. Before Bely, it had been invented as a problem by another great novelist: Nikolai Gogol. 'Passing as it were through Gogol's temperament,' wrote Vladimir Nabokov, who loved both Gogol and Bely, 'St Petersburg acquired a reputation of strangeness which it kept up for almost a century . . .'[2] In the mid-1830s, Gogol published a series of Petersburg stories: 'Nevsky Prospekt', 'Nose' and 'Portrait', followed in 1842 by 'Coat'. In them, he developed the idea that this city called Petersburg was an experiment in what was real. It was built between land and water, its climate was fog, the water was undrinkable: and in this fluid atmosphere it was therefore difficult to tell what was real and what was not: 'Oh, do not trust that Nevsky Prospect! I always wrap myself more closely in my cloak when I pass along it and try not to look at the objects that meet me. Everything is a cheat, everything is a dream, everything is other than it seems!'[3]

Petersburg – an exercise in unreality! Pure surface!* This was the city that Andrei Bely invented once again, in his novel called *Petersburg*.

In this melting greyness there suddenly dimly emerged a large number of dots, looking in astonishment: lights, lights, tiny lights filled with intensity and rushed out of the darkness in pursuit of the rust-red blotches, as cascades fell from above: blue, dark violet and black.

Petersburg slipped away into the night. (p. 198)

This was how to describe the city as a landscape: an abstract metamor-

---

* The city, after all, had been founded as St Petersburg, but it was known as Petersburg, or even Piter: from 1914 it would be Petrograd, and from 1924 it would be Leningrad, until eventually, in 1991, it would become St Petersburg again.

phosis of dots. But maybe even this was too definite; maybe it only existed as a sign – a creation of cartographers:

> ... two little circles that sit one inside the other with a black point in the centre; and from this mathematical point, which has no dimension, it energetically declares that it exists: from there, from this point, there rushes in a torrent a swarm of the freshly printed book; impetuously from this invisible point rushes the government circular. (p. 4)

A city as a point, or dot: this is Andrei Bely's initial act of revolution in his novel *Petersburg*. It is an invention with multiple effects. And the most important is outlined in this novel by a hallucinating terrorist, who is suddenly possessed by the knowledge that

> 'Petersburg possesses not three dimensions, but four; the fourth is subject to obscurity and is not marked on maps at all, except as a dot, for a dot is the place where the plane of this existence touches against the spherical surface of the immense astral cosmos . . .' (p. 409)

In other words: everything in this city is on the brink of meaning; everything in Petersburg is potentially a sign.

Names

Even, for instance, a novelist's name. For Andrei Bely is a pseudonym. (Andrew White!) His initial name was Boris Bugayev.

The reason for this new name was sweetly chic. At the beginning of the twentieth century, Bely was avant-garde. And the avant-garde he belonged to was Symbolism. The Symbolists believed in renewing literature through a renewed description of the real, and this description would encompass sound coding, synaesthesia, hieroglyphics: the whole alphabet of esoteric craziness. And so naturally a poet could not use his own name. The hipster had to hint at a purer truth. So Bely invented his oddly abstract pseudonym. To the bourgeoisie who knew his parents – like, for instance, Marina Tsvetayeva's aunt – it only sounded uncouth:

> '. . . the worst of it is that he comes from a respectable family, he's a professor's son, Nikolai Dmitrievich Bugaev's. Why not Boris Bugaev? But

Andrei Bely? Disowning your own father? It seems they've done it on purpose. Are they ashamed to sign their own names? What sort of White? An
angel or a madman who jumps out into the street wearing his underwear?[4]

Tsvetayeva herself, however, adored Bely's abstract example. But then,
Tsvetayeva was a young poet, who loved Bely's bravura. Bely, writes
Tsvetayeva, was always trying to escape the ordinary real: he 'was visibly
on the point of take-off, of departure' – and his 'basic element' was
'flight': 'his native and terrible element of empty spaces'.[5] His pseudonym, therefore, was just another way of turning things upside down.

Every pseudonym is subconsciously a rejection of being an heir, being a
descendant, being a son. A rejection of the father. And not only a rejection
of the father, but likewise of the saint under whose protection one was
placed, and of the faith into which one was baptized, and of one's own
childhood, and of the mother who called him Borya and didn't know any
'Andrei', a rejection of all roots, whether ecclesiastical or familial. *Avant moi
le déluge!* I – am I.[6]

The self was an invention, and so was a city. Everything was fictional.
This was the premise of Petersburg, at the start of the twentieth century.

Petersburg

Andrei Bely's novel called *Petersburg* appeared in three issues of the
magazine *Sirin* in 1913 and 1914: in 1916 it appeared as a book.

As for its plot: its plot is about a plot. Roughly, this plot takes place
over a week or so in Petersburg at the beginning of October in 1905 –
just before the General Strike.

A senator, called Apollon Apollonovich Ableukhov, has a son: Nikolai
Apollonovich Ableukhov. Nikolai, unhappy in love, unhappy in life and
a student of the philosophy of Kant, has promised to help the revolutionary cause. An obscure adherent to this revolutionary cause delivers
to him a package, wrapped in a cloth printed with a design of pheasants,
for safe keeping. It turns out that this package is a sardine tin, and the
sardine tin conceals a bomb – which Nikolai is then ordered to throw at
his own father.

This is the basic plot. It follows the ordering and possible execution of a revolutionary conspiracy. This conspiracy links the various islands of Petersburg: the dive bars and the mansions. But really, of course, these facts are not important. For Petersburg is a city whose true form is infinity: its streets are endless.

> There is an infinity of prospects racing in infinity with an infinity of inter-secting shadows racing into infinity. All Petersburg is the infinity of a prospect raised to the power of n.
> While beyond Petersburg there is – nothing. (p. 19)

And so the real investigation of this novel cannot be into the contours of a plot. The plot recedes in the infinity of the city. The real plot is the movement of Bely's sentences. Or, in other words, the plot is simply a pretext for Bely to investigate how language might determine what we habitually, and mistakenly, think of as the real.

Reality

According to *Petersburg*, reality is multi-levelled: like an infinite car park. Yes, this novel is set within the perspective of the infinite; and so its style flickers between the almost-mystic and the almost-materialist – so that this is how a man is described, standing in a candlelit room:

> Lippanchenko stopped in the middle of the dark room with the candle in his hand; the shadowy shoals stopped together with him; the enormous shadowy fat man, Lippanchenko's soul, hung head down from the ceiling . . . (p. 531)

There is the world of sensation, true: but behind this is everything else. '". . . one must admit that we do not live in a visible world . . .",' a hallucination tells a character. '"The tragedy of our situation is that we are, like it or not, in an invisible world . . ."' (p. 408). And so the visible world can suddenly dissolve, within a sentence, into another world entirely – 'a world of figures, contours, shimmerings, strange physical sensations' (p. 181).

'Like a race of people divided into those with long heads and those with short heads,' commented the revolutionary critic Viktor Shklovsky, in the city that was now Leningrad, writing on Bely, 'the Symbolist movement was split down the middle by an old controversy. Essentially, it involved the following question: Was Symbolism merely an aesthetic method or was it something more?': 'All of his life, Bely championed the second alternative (i.e., that Symbolism is much more than just art).'[7]

But I'm not quite sure that Shklovsky is accurate. Because it's true that in his frenetic and haphazard career Bely took up with the Symbolists, and then with the spiritualists, and even the anthroposophists. He was into Kant, and Schopenhauer, and Rudolf Steiner. But this list is only a list of crazes. It indicates a roving interest in flight, in emigration from the ordinary categories: not a sustained mystical vision. The philosopher Nikolai Berdyayev, who was a genuine mystic, was one of Bely's mentors. And Berdyayev had his doubts about the thoroughness of Bely's thinking. 'Bely knew very little,' wrote Berdyayev, 'and what he knew was confused and incoherent.'[8]

Rather than the detail of the temporary visible world, Bely preferred its more permanent abstractions: the Cube, the Sphere and the Swarm. With these categories, he described the fluid transitions of reality. But there's no need to be a mystic to believe that reality is fluid. Even the most empirical of philosophers has been unable to prove that an objective world exists. Our knowledge of reality is never direct. There is an idealism hidden in every realism. And this fluidity of the material world is what Bely loved exploring.*

If a sardine tin can also be a bomb, for instance, then all objects are revealed as potentially ambiguous. Their solidity evaporates: '"they're what they are – and yet different . . ."' This is one effect in *Petersburg* of the panic of a revolutionary conspiracy. Another conspirator tries to offer a rational explanation: this slippage in reality is only a 'pseudo-hallucination': '"a kind of symbolic sensation that does not correspond to the stimulus of a sensation"' (pp. 359, 360).

And I think: but this is really a description of language! That is the coded subject, after all, of Bely's novel. Language is what creates a sym-

---

* Just as Lenin loved denying it. In 1909, the exiled Lenin published his strange work of philosophy: *Materialism and Empirio-Criticism*. In it, he wanted to prove a total positivism, the absolute objectivity of the world: 'The "naïve realism" of any healthy person who has not been an inmate of a lunatic asylum or a pupil of the idealist philosophers consists in the view that things, the environment, the world, exist *independently* of our sensation, of our consciousness, of our *self* and of man in general.' The mad italics are Lenin's.

bolic sensation that doesn't correspond to an actual sensation. Language is what constitutes the disturbing fragility of the real.

In an essay of 1909 called 'The Magic of Words', Bely wrote that the 'original victory of consciousness lies in the creation of sound symbols. For in sound there is recreated a new world within whose boundaries I feel myself to be the creator of reality.'[9] The new reality of language is Bely's constant subject. For he was expert at dissolving the binary oppositions of ordinary philosophy. Everyone knows, say, that a sign is made up of a signifier and a signified: an outer form and an inner content. Only Bely would think that in constructing a sign he might 'surmount two worlds' – the inner and the outer. 'Neither of these worlds is real. But the THIRD world exists.'[10]

This extra world of the sign is what is investigated in *Petersburg* – and I mean investigation. This novel is a system of parallel investigations into the minute moments where words materialize as a version of reality.

Words

In Paris, twenty years earlier, in his text called 'Crise de vers', the French poet Stéphane Mallarmé had outlined the inverted reality that language could produce:

> I say: a flower! and, beyond the oblivion to which my voice consigns any outline, being something other than the known calyxes, musically rises an idea itself and sweet, the one absent from every bouquet.[11]

And Bely knew about this philosophy of the poetic word. But a novel offered more complicated demonstrations. And so in Petersburg he closed the first chapter of *Petersburg* with a small essay in literary theory. So far, the reader only knows that there is a man called Senator Apollon Apollonovich Ableukhov; and that in this city he is perturbed by a mysterious stranger – one of the novel's revolutionaries. At the moment the stranger is only a 'shadow': he exists only in the Senator's consciousness. But, adds Bely: 'Apollon Apollonovich's consciousness is a shadowy consciousness, because he too is the possessor of an ephemeral existence and is a product of the author's fantasy: a superfluous, idle, cerebral play' (p. 67). He is just a character. And with this moment of metafiction, Bely pauses. If he is only the inventor of illusions, then the novelist might as well abandon his novel. But, writes Bely, just because they are illusions doesn't mean the characters aren't real. There Ableukhov is: and there we are – reading.

> Once his brain has come into play with the mysterious stranger, that stranger exists, really does exist: he will not disappear from the Petersburg prospects while a senator with such thoughts exists, because thought, too, exists.
>
> And so let our stranger be a real live stranger! And let my stranger's two shadows be real live shadows!
>
> Those dark shadows will follow, they will follow on the stranger's heels, in the same way as the stranger himself will directly follow the senator; the aged senator will pursue you, he will pursue you, too, reader, in his black carriage: and from this day forth you will never forget him! (pp. 67–8)

You only need to name something, and it is real: even if it is imaginary. It exists, now, in the consciousness of the reader. The real is produced by and produces writing. This is Bely's artistic premise. Just as from the abstract dot of Petersburg, wrote Bely, rushes the government circular, so the real dissolves into writing – even when you sharpen your pencil: 'the acutely sharpened little pencil fell on the paper with flocks of question marks' (p. 483).

This infiltration and contamination of signifiers and signifieds represents the mobile process of Bely's novel. So that a character's childhood memory of a fever where a bouncing elastic ball became a man called Pépp Péppovich Pépp, with its bouncing consonants, drifts in a new delirium to become associated with a bomb: so that by the end of the novel the bomb has appropriated this nonsense name as its own, as if it is a character itself. Or a nonsense word *enfranshish*, which haunts a revolutionary in his nightmares, suddenly inverts itself to become the name of a hallucinated character: '"Shishnarfne, Shish-nar-fne . . ."' (p. 410).

The history of the world as a history of phonetics: that is the wild aim of Bely's absolute novel.

Phonemes

Writing in Petrograd, in 1923, Bely's friend Ivanov-Razumnik recounted a moment of conversational acrobatics from Bely:

'I, for one,' says Bely, 'know that *Petersburg* stems from l-k-l-pp-pp-ll, where *k* embodies the sense of stuffiness and suffocation emanating from the *pp-pp* sounds – the oppressiveness of the walls of Ableukhov's "yellow house" – and *ll* reflects the "lacquers", "lustre" and "brilliance" contained within the *pp-pp* – the walls or the casing of the "bomb" (Pépp Péppovich Pépp). *Pl* is the embodiment of this shining prison – Apollon Apollonovich Ableukhov; and *k* in the glitter of *p* with *l* is Nikolai Apollonovich, the Senator's son, who is suffocating in it.'[12]

The phonic and metrical line of the whole novel, added Ivanov-Razumnik, was drawn in the names of the leading characters.

To invent a world, it turned out, you don't even need a word: phonemes will do. But this wasn't quite Bely's invention. Once again, this is also an effect first discovered in Gogol's Petersburg stories.

It was another revolutionary critic, Boris Eikhenbaum, who in 1919 wrote an essay, 'How Gogol's "Overcoat" is Made', where he noticed that the repeated *ak* sound in the name of that story's protagonist, Akaky Akakiyevich Bashmachkin, was also repeated in his constant use and overuse of minute Russian words: like *tak* and *kak*. The real and the linguistic began to merge, so that Gogol's text was 'composed of animated locutions and verbalized emotions'. Gogol's *ak* phoneme, a minute melodic unit, was just another aspect of the story's emphasis on the overlooked, the minor, the forgotten.

But Bely's theory of phonemes was odder. In his prose, the Gogolian method was shadowed by a complicated, esoteric theory – and it is visible in his reported conversation with Ivanov-Razumnik. The sound of a signifier, thought Bely, has its own meaning separate from the ordinary signified.

In 1922, when Bely was living briefly in Berlin, he published a poem called *Glossolalia*, subtitled *A Poem on Sound*. In it, he offered a detailed theory of what phonemes mean: *k* is suffocation, death and murder; *sh* and *r* are the sensations of the etheric body. Twelve years later, when Bely had returned to the Soviet Union, in his final book, *Gogol's Craftsmanship*, he revised this theory. In the Soviet Union, the meanings were more prosaically revolutionary: he emphasized *pl*, *bl* and *kl* – as all sounds of bursting pressure. While *sh* represents the expansion of gases, and *r* represents explosion.[13]

In *Petersburg*, Bely wanted to saturate prose with repeated sounds: even the phonemes would be part of the pattern's meaning. Bely had once rearranged the hierarchy of Russian vowel sounds: putting *u* at the bottom of the series and *i* at the top.* And as he began his novel called *Petersburg*, Bely would later write, he suddenly heard 'what seemed like an "u" sound; this sound permeates the whole length and breadth of the novel . . .'[14] The *u* sound is a sad lament throughout his revolutionary, anxious novel. It is there implicitly: in the constant choice of words with the stress on *u*; or the exploitation of the fact that Russian nouns and adjectives in the accusative case include that *u* sound, necessarily. But he also states it, explicitly – in his descriptions of Petersburg at night: 'have you ever gone out at night, penetrated into the god-forsaken suburban vacant lots, in order to listen to the nagging, angry note on "oo"? Ooo-ooo-ooo: thus did space resound . . .' (p. 97). The *u* sound is the sound of impending revolution: of catastrophe. It is a concealed prophecy.

And of course: this theory that a phoneme is meaningful, Bely's habit, as Shklovsky put it, 'of using every word as a springboard for the Infinite . . .'[15] – this habit is craziness.

Signs

I am not the first person to notice this.

In Petersburg, between 1914 and 1916, when Bely was writing *Petersburg*, a group of linguists and literary critics, including Viktor Shklovsky, Boris Eikhenbaum and Roman Jakobson, founded the avant-garde group Opojaz – a jazzy Russian acronym for the Society for the Study of Poetic Language. This was their official name, but their real name – the name they became known by in the various battles of the avant-garde – was the Formalists. In Petersburg, of course, at that time, the ruling avant-garde was Bely and the theory of Symbolism. And so, remembered Eikhenbaum in a retrospective essay in 1927 called 'The Theory of the Formal Method', the first argument they picked in the formation of their avant-garde was with the Symbolists: 'in order to wrest poetics from their hands . . .'[16]

The Symbolists still believed that words were agents of esoteric

---

* With this dislike of the sound *u*, Bely was again echoing Mallarmé's 'Crise de vers': 'what disappointment, faced with the perversity that confers on *jour* as on *nuit*, contradictorily, here obscure tones, there clear.'

inquiry. This was why they so adored their sound-effects, their phonemes. Whereas the 'basic motto uniting the original group of Formalists was the emancipation of the poetic word from philosophical and religious biases to which the Symbolists had increasingly fallen prey . . .'[17] Their allies in this fight were the Futurist poets, who included Velimir Khlebnikov and Vladimir Mayakovsky. And what they loved were the Futurists' exuberant experiments with nonsense: which they called, in their mania for definitions, transrational language: or, *zaum*. With their poems in invented languages, even the possible language of birds, the Futurists in their cabaret performances discovered the autonomy of a word when used in poetry. Or, as Khlebnikov put it, in his essay 'About Contemporary Poetry': 'the principle of sound lives a self-spun life, while the portion of reason named by the word remains in shadow . . .'[18]

This self-spun life of sound – so gorgeous! – meant that language in poetry was pure event: a linguistic sign was a delirious airborne shimmer. And in the buoyancy of Futurist poetry the Formalist critics found a proof that language in literature was not a form of access to any higher reality. In this 'trend toward a "transrational language" (*zaumnyj jazyk*)', wrote Eikhenbaum, it was possible to define the poetic sign: not as a route to the mysteries, but a total playfulness: 'the utmost baring of autonomous value'.[19] Or, as Roman Jakobson put it many years later, in 1933, in his essay 'What is Poetry?' – poetry was when 'the word is felt as a word and not a mere representation of the object being named . . .'[20]

Bely's orchestrations of sound, like his other formal tricks, were always subordinate to the work's content. The meaning of words had billowed out acoustically with the phonemes. The Symbolists, argued Shklovsky and his friends, had thought that form and content in literature were inextricably linked. Whereas the truth was that a novel or a poem was a rickety machine: there was nothing special about its linguistic elements: the interest was in the outlandish ways these elements were combined. A poem, or a novel, was just a system. And so, wrote Eikhenbaum, in departing from the Symbolist view, 'the Formalists simultaneously freed themselves from the traditional correlation of "form-content" and from the conception of form as an outer cover or as a vessel into which a liquid (the content) is poured'.[21]

The problem with the ordinary ways in which novels had been read was that they had always been viewed as a poem: and a poem, according to Bely's theory, was an expanded sign, whose form and content minutely overlapped. Whereas, argued the Formalists, a novel is too long for this kind of hopeful analysis. It absolutely disproves the ordinary ideas of form and content. A novel is a system that is constantly patching itself up.

And yet the strange thing, I want to add, the lovely thing is that Bely's novel called *Petersburg* was nevertheless – against all Bely's obvious intent – one of the most intricate places where this new way of reading could be proved.

Novels

Writing in Leningrad, as he remembered the minutiae of that city's avant-gardes, Eikhenbaum went on to describe how the sidestep of the ordinary terms like form and content had led to new ways of analysing the machinations of novels: especially in 'the distinction between the elements of a work's construction and the elements comprising the material it uses (the story stuff, the choice of motifs, of protagonists, of themes, etc.)'. A novel was really a series of structural devices, 'subordinating everything else as *motivation*'. But no novel fully integrated these devices: the fit was never absolute. This is why, according to Eikhenbaum, Shklovsky's emblematic novels were *Don Quixote* and *Tristram Shandy*. Both novels were zanily broken-down: there was no true fit between these novels' devices and their motivation. In *Quixote*, this was not deliberate: it was just the result of Cervantes's delighted mania for interpolating more and more material. In *Tristram Shandy*, Sterne 'deliberately tears away motivation and bares its construction'.[22] But the effect was the same: a novel was a rickety construction.

And it was with this idea in mind that Shklovsky, in his own book *Theory of Prose*, went on to consider the prose of Andrei Bely's novels.

Bely, wrote Shklovsky, was a mystic. He believed in the multi-level reality. (And of course, I am not so sure of this: I'm not sure that Shklovsky was quite accurate about Bely's intuitions about this abstraction called reality.) But in fact this didn't mean that his vision and his novels formed a perfect whole. Because, wrote Shklovsky, 'the particular elements constituting literary form are more likely to clash than to work in concert. The decline or decay of one device brings in its train the growth and development of another device.'[23] A novel is a series of devices, true: but there is no reason why these devices will run happily in parallel.

The devices invented by Bely never quite proved what he wanted them to prove.

In Shklovsky's summary, Bely's invention was a novel that operated on two levels. There was a rudimentary plot, and on this foundation, wrote Shklovsky,

> . . . the author has erected metaphor leitmotivs that serve as superstructures, as high-rise buildings. These structures – let's imagine them as buildings – are connected to each other by means of little suspension bridges. As the story moves along, it creates pretexts for the creation of new metaphorical leitmotivs which are connected, the moment they come into being, with the leitmotivs already in place.[24]

But this superstructure, added Shklovsky, then took over from Bely's mysticism. The pursuit of leitmotivs and patterns distracted Bely from his esoteric aim. And so Shklovsky came to his conclusion: there was no such thing as a unified novel. And I like Shklovsky's general conclusion: I am just not sure that he is right about why Bely's prose is so lavishly ornamented. For the shimmer of devices, of phonemes and fictional games, in *Petersburg* is part of Bely's absolute refusal of conclusions: his rickety investigation into how a rickety reality might be put together.

Words in a novel don't function like ordinary words. A novel is a chaotic system. In this kind of system, everything is potentially meaningful. And this is deliberately exploited by Bely in his novel called *Petersburg*: his strange construction of phonemes and shadows. He invented a novel that was also a conspiracy – where motifs signal to each other, throughout the novel, from one part to another.

Systems

In Bely's system, a novel, like a city, is made up of millions of minute units. Sometimes, these units blossom into motifs: sometimes, motifs dissolve into random detail.

Like, say, sardines . . . First, they are randomly offered by a landlord in a dive bar, and randomly refused: '"No, landlord, I don't want the sardines: they're floating in a yellow slime"' (p. 279). Then it turns out that the bomb is in a sardine tin, and so sardines become a crucial unit in the plot. Yet the motif of sardines then continues, at random – in the terrorist's bedsit: which has a 'sink and a sardine tin that contained a scrap of Kazan soap floating in its own slime' (p. 330). Except, this isn't quite random: because the Russian word for soap – мыло – has the sound ы in it, a kind of English 'ugh', which Bely thought was symbolic of formlessness, of evil . . . and so the pattern continues.

The overlapping systems of Petersburg and *Petersburg* are a swirl of fragments, a jigsaw of surface. Information is occluded: and its genetic unit is therefore the overheard, impenetrable conversation:

> 'Cra-aa-yfish . . . aaa . . . *ah*-ha-ha . . .'
> 'You see, you see, you see . . .'
> 'You're not saying . . .'
> 'Em-em-em . . .'
> 'And vodka . . .'
> 'But for goodness' sake . . . But come now . . . But there must be something wrong . . .' (p. 30)

And this is why Petersburg is a city of conspiracy. It is a melodrama of hidden details: a system that is never quite unified. Meaning might take the form of a pattern; but the pattern is a flicker: it shimmers in and out of focus. At one point, Bely interrupts himself with an abstract summary: 'The heavy confluence of circumstances – can one thus describe the pyramid of events that had piled up during these recent days, like massif upon massif? A pyramid of massifs that shattered the soul, and precisely – a pyramid! . . .' This is the form of Bely's novel. 'In a pyramid there is something that exceeds all the notions of man; the pyramid is a delirium of geometry . . .' (pp. 448–9).

And this abstract pyramid is an accurate description of how the minutiae of his plot's conspiracy functions. It is a miniature farce. Nikolai, this serious, sweet scholar of Kant, only found himself giving a revolutionary group a promise of help because of 'a failure in his life; later that failure had gradually been erased'. Nikolai, the poor schmuck, was unhappy in love: and now he was over the girl: but the promise remained. It 'continued to live in the collective consciousness of a certain rash and hasty circle, at the same time as the sense of life's bitterness under the influence of the failure had been erased; Nikolai Apollonovich himself would undoubtedly have classed his promise among promises of a humorous nature' (p. 92). Humorous! This is how politics is depicted in *Petersburg*: it is shadowy; it is uncertain; its ideology is tremulous. And of course, Bely was right. You only have to think of the sad epilogue of Bely and Kamenev. It is so difficult, finding the seriousness of history, and politics. It is so much easier to see the structure of farce.

But there is another way of interpreting invisible patterns. This could be a form of pure poetry, true – or it could be a form of revolutionary politics. But it could also be a form of the mystical. This is the final investigation of Bely's network of details. A revolution overlaps with the mystical in the idea of conspiracy – a hidden network of controlling details, a code present on the surface that is only legible to illuminati. But then, in Petersburg there had always been a connection between the theory of hidden meaning and the theory of revolution. They were both theories of the real, and they both derived from the abstract principles of Hegel – and his diagram of the progress of the Spirit.

And I think of another émigré from Petersburg, Alexandre Kojève – whose seminars on Hegel in Paris in the 1940s were attended by Raymond Queneau; and were admired by Saul Bellow . . . But no: the story of those seminars is part of another story, another confluence of circumstances; and I don't want – not now – to write the secret history of the art of the novel.

Koktebel

The year before Bely died, in 1933, the poet Osip Mandelstam and his wife Nadezhda went to Koktebel, in the Crimea, on the shores of the Black Sea, for a vacation at the Writers' Union rest home. Andrei Bely and his wife were there at the same time. In Nadezhda Mandelstam's autobiography, she records how Bely and Mandelstam 'enjoyed talking with each other. M. was writing his "Conversation About Dante" at the time and read it out to Bely. Their talk was animated, and Bely kept referring to his study of Gogol, which he had not yet finished.'[25]

A decade earlier, it was very different. In the 1920s, Mandelstam loved attacking Bely and the Symbolists. Mandelstam had grown up in Petersburg; he had been taught by one of Bely's Symbolist friends. And so in the ordinary way, from within his own avant-garde, he had attacked the older avant-garde – 'the glorious traditions of the literary epoch when a waiter reflected in the double mirrors of the restaurant in the Hotel Prague was regarded as a mystical phenomenon, as a double . . .'[26]

But now, everything was different.

In Koktebel, Mandelstam was writing his 'Conversation About Dante'. It is called a conversation. But no one else is mentioned in the text. And I think that the real person to whom this conversation is addressed is Bely. For Mandelstam is writing about Dante's *Commedia*: but really he is continuing the investigations of his former city of Petersburg – the constant probing of how to turn language into art. The *Commedia*, writes Mandelstam, is 'a power flow, known now in its totality as a "composition", now in its particularity as a "metaphor", now in its indirectness as a "simile". . .' With this idea of a power flow, Mandelstam rejects all ideas of form and content: 'form is squeezed out of the content-conception which, as it were, envelops the form.' Instead, writing is pure performance: 'Poetic material does not have a voice. It does not paint with bright colours, nor does it explain itself in words. It is devoid of form just as it is devoid of content for the simple reason that it exists only in performance.' Or, in other words: 'In talking about Dante it is more appropriate to bear in mind the creation of impulses than the creation of forms . . .'[27]

Constantly, Mandelstam laments the lack of vocabulary: 'Again and again I find myself turning to the reader and begging him to "imagine" something; that is, I must invoke analogy, having in mind but a single goal: to fill in the deficiency of our system of definition.'[28] And so, since 'this poem's form transcends our conceptions of literary invention and composition', Mandelstam doesn't offer theories, but improvised metaphors:

We must try to imagine, therefore, how bees might have worked at the creation of this thirteen-thousand-faceted form, bees endowed with the brilliant stereometric instinct, who attracted bees in greater and greater numbers as they were required. The work of these bees, constantly keeping their eye on the whole, is of varying difficulty at different stages of the process. Their cooperation expands and grows more complicated as they participate in the process of forming the combs, by means of which space virtually emerges out of itself.[29]

Yes, I think that Mandelstam is talking to Bely. Indirectly, he is offering a precise description, in fact, of Bely's strange invention in *Petersburg*. For Mandelstam rejects the idea that Dante was an obscure mystic. Instead, he argues, Dante's investigations into the meaning of what happens were part of his investigations into the art of composition: 'the inner illumination of Dantean space derived from structural elements alone'.[30] The illumination was an effect of art. Just as a third term, a sign, had emerged as the only true form of the real, in Bely's investigations into words.

Tsvetayeva thought that Bely was a man in flight. And now – by chance – Mandelstam projects this flight into the structure of Dante's composition, based on the principle of 'convertibility or transmutability':

> . . . just imagine an airplane (ignoring the technical impossibility) which in full flight constructs and launches another machine. Furthermore, in the same way, this flying machine, while fully absorbed in its own flight, still manages to assemble and launch yet a third machine.[31]

The self-assembling flying machine: this fantastical metaphor seems to me to be the best description of what Bely invented in *Petersburg*: a process of metamorphosis and reversal, a multiple escape . . .

> One must traverse the full width of a river crammed with Chinese junks moving simultaneously in various directions – this is how the meaning of poetic discourse is created. The meaning, its itinerary, cannot be reconstructed by interrogating the boatmen: they will not be able to tell how and why we were skipping from junk to junk.[32]

Adam Thirlwell, 2011

NOTES

1. Emma Gerstein, *Moscow Memoirs*, translated and edited by John Crowfoot (London: Harvill Press, 2004), p. 58.
2. Vladimir Nabokov, *Nikolai Gogol* (New York: New Directions, 1961), pp. 10–11.
3. Nikolai Gogol, 'Nevsky Prospect', in *The Complete Tales of Nikolai Gogol*, edited by Leonard J. Kent and translated by Constance Garnett, vol. 1 (Chicago: University of Chicago Press, 1985), p. 238.
4. Marina Tsvetayeva, 'A Captive Spirit', in *A Captive Spirit: Selected Prose*, edited and translated by J. Marin King (London: Virago, 1983), p. 100.
5. *ibid.*, pp. 102 and 154.

6. *ibid.*, pp. 151–2.

7. Viktor Shklovsky, *Theory of Prose*, translated by Benjamin Sher (Champaign, IL: Dalkey Archive Press, 1990), p. 188.

8. Nikolai Berdyaev, *Dream and Reality*, translated by Katherine Lampert (London: Godfrey Bles, 1950), p. 196.

9. Quoted in Steven Cassedy, *Flight from Eden: The Origins of Modern Literary Criticism and Theory* (Berkeley: University of California Press, 1990), p. 48.

10. *ibid.*, p. 53.

11. Stéphane Mallarmé, 'Crise de vers', in *Igitur, Divagations, Un Coup de dés* (Paris: Gallimard, 1976), p. 251, my translation.

12. Ivanov-Razumnik, *Vershini* (*Summits*) (Petrograd: Kolos, 1923), p. 110: quoted in Ada Steinberg, *Word and Music in the Novels of Andrey Bely* (Cambridge: Cambridge University Press, 1982), p. 93.

13. Andrei Bely, *Masterstvo Gogolia* (*Gogol's Craftsmanship*) (Moscow: 1934), pp. 306–7.

14. Andrei Bely, 'Vospominanija' ('Memoirs'), in *Literaturnoe nasledstvo*, nos. 27–8, p. 453.

15. Shklovsky, p. 187.

16. Boris Eikhenbaum, 'The Theory of the Formal Method', in *Readings in Russian Poetics*, edited and with a preface by Ladislav Matejka and Krystyna Pomorska (Champaign, IL: Dalkey Archive Press, 2002), p. 6.

17. *ibid.*, pp. 6–7.

18. Quoted in Cassedy, p. 55.

19. Eikhenbaum, p. 9.

20. Roman Jakobson, *Selected Writings*, vol. 3, *Poetry of Grammar and Grammar of Poetry*, edited by Stephen Rudy (The Hague and Paris: Mouton, 1981), p. 750.

21. Eikhenbaum, p. 12.

22. *ibid.*, pp. 18, 19 and 20.

23. Shklovsky, p. 171.

24. *ibid.*, p. 176.

25. Nadezhda Mandelstam, *Hope Against Hope*, translated by Max Hayward (London: Harvill Press, 1999), p. 155.

26. Osip Mandelstam, in *The Collected Critical Prose and Letters*, edited by Jane Gary Harris, translated by Jane Gary Harris and Constance Link (London: Harvill Press, 1991), p. 212.

27. *ibid.*, pp. 402, 408 and 442.

28. *ibid.*, pp. 439–40.

29. *ibid.*, p. 409.

30. *ibid.*, p. 411.

31. *ibid.*, p. 414.

32. *ibid.*, p. 398.

PETERSBURG

PROLOGUE

Your excellencies, eminences, honours, citizens!

. . . .

What is our Russian Empire?

Our Russian Empire is a geographical entity, which means: a part of a certain planet. And the Russian Empire comprises: in the first place – Great, Little, White and Red Rus; in the second – the realms of Georgia, Poland, Kazan and Astrakhan; in the third, it comprises . . . But – et cetera, et cetera, et cetera.[1]

Our Russian Empire consists of many towns and cities: capital, provincial, district, downgraded;[2] and further – of the original capital city and of the mother of Russian cities.

The original capital city is Moscow; and the mother of Russian cities is Kiev.

Petersburg, or Saint Petersburg, or Piter (which is the same) authentically belongs to the Russian Empire. While Tsargrad,[3] Konstantinograd (or, as is said, Constantinople), belongs by right of inheritance.[4] And on it we shall not expatiate.

We shall expatiate more on Petersburg: there is Petersburg, or Saint Petersburg, or Piter[5] (which is the same). On the basis of the same judgements the Nevsky Prospect is a Petersburg prospect.

The Nevsky Prospect possesses a striking quality: it consists of space for the circulation of the public; numbered houses delimit it; the numeration goes in the order of the houses – and one's search for the required house is much facilitated. The Nevsky Prospect, like all prospects, is a public prospect; that is: a prospect for the circulation of the public (not of the air, for example); the houses that form its lateral limits are – hm . . . yes: for the public.[6] In the evening the Nevsky Prospect is illuminated by electricity. While in the daytime the Nevsky Prospect needs no illumination.

The Nevsky Prospect is rectilinear (speaking between ourselves) because it is a European prospect; and every European prospect is not simply a prospect, but (as I have already said) a European prospect, because . . . yes . . .

Because the Nevsky Prospect is a rectilinear prospect.

The Nevsky Prospect is a not unimportant prospect in this non-Russian – capital – city. Other Russian cities are a wooden pile of wretched little cottages.

And Petersburg is strikingly different from them all.

If, however, you continue to assert a most absurd myth – the existence of a Moscow population of one and a half million – then one must admit that the capital is Moscow, for only in capitals are there populations of one and half million: while in provincial towns there are no populations of one and a half million – have not been, and will not be. And in accordance with the absurd myth it will be seen that the capital is not Petersburg.

But if Petersburg is not the capital, then there is no Petersburg. It only seems to exist.[7]

Whatever the truth of the matter, Petersburg not only seems to us, but also does exist – on maps: as two little circles that sit one inside the other with a black point in the centre; and from this mathematical point, which has no dimension, it energetically declares that it exists: from there, from this point, there rushes in a torrent a swarm of the freshly printed book; impetuously from this invisible point rushes the government circular.

CHAPTER THE FIRST

in which the story is told of a certain worthy personage,
his intellectual games and the ephemerality of existence

> It was a dreadful time.
> Of it fresh memory doth live.
> Of it, my friends, for ye
> I here begin my narrative –
> Melancholy will my story be.[1]
>
> A. Pushkin

Apollon Apollonovich Ableukhov

Apollon Apollonovich Ableukhov came of most respected stock: he
had Adam as his ancestor. And this is not the main thing: incomparably
more important here is the fact that one nobly-born ancestor
was Shem, that is, the very progenitor of the Semitic, Hessitic and
red-skinned peoples.[2]

Here let us pass to ancestors of a less distant era.

These ancestors (so it appears) lived in the Kirghiz–Kaisak
Horde,[3] from where in the reign of the Empress Anna Ioannovna[4]
the senator's great-great-grandfather Mirza Ab-Lai,[5] who received
at his Christian baptism the name Andrei and the sobriquet Ukhov,[6]
valiantly entered the Russian service. Thus on this descendant from
the depths of the Mongol race does the *Heraldic Guide to the Russian
Empire*[7] expatiate. For the sake of brevity, Ab-Lai-Ukhov was later
turned into plain Ableukhov.

This great-great-grandfather, so it is said, was the originator of
the stock.

. . . .

A lackey in grey with gold braid was flicking the dust off the writing
desk with a feather duster; through the open door peeped a cook's cap.

'Watch out, he's up and about . . .'

'He's rubbing himself with eau-de-Cologne, he'll be down for his coffee soon . . .'

'This morning the postman said there was a little letter for the *barin* from Shpain: with a Shpanish stamp.'

'I'll tell you this: you'd do well to go sticking your nose into letters a bit less . . .'

'So that must mean that Anna Petrovna . . .'

'And that goes for "so that must mean", too . . .'

'Oh well, I was just . . . I was – oh, never mind . . .'

The cook's head suddenly disappeared. Apollon Apollonovich Ableukhov stalked into his study.

. . . .

A pencil that was lying on the table struck Apollon Apollonovich's attention. Apollon Apollonovich took a resolve: to impart to the pencil's point a sharpness of form. Swiftly he approached the writing table and snatched up . . . a paperweight, which for a long time he twiddled in deep reflectiveness, before he realized that it was a paperweight he was holding, not a pencil.

The absent-mindedness proceeded from the fact that he was at this moment visited by a profound thought: and at once, at this inopportune time, it unfolded into a runaway sequence of thought (Apollon Apollonovich was in a hurry to get to the *Institution*). To the *Diary*, which was to appear in periodical publications in the year of his death, a page was added.

Apollon Apollonovich quickly noted down the sequence of thought that had unfolded: having noted down this sequence, he thought: 'It's time to go to work.' And went into the dining-room to have his coffee.

As a preliminary he began to question the old valet with a kind of unpleasant insistency:

'Is Nikolai Apollonovich up?'

'On no account: his honour is not up yet, sir.'

Apollon Apollonovich gave the bridge of his nose a rub of displeasure:

'Er . . . tell me, then: when does Nikolai Apollonovich, tell me, so to speak . . .'

'Oh, his honour gets up rather latish, sir . . .'

'What does that mean, rather latish?'

And at once, not waiting for an answer, stalked in to coffee, having glanced at the clock.

It was exactly half past nine.

At ten o'clock he, an old man, left for the Institution. Nikolai Apollonovich, a young man, rose from his bed – two hours later. Every morning the senator inquired about the hour of his awakening. And every morning he frowned.

Nikolai Apollonovich was the senator's son.

In a Word, He Was the Head of an Institution

Apollon Apollonovich Ableukhov was notable for acts of valour; more than once were the stars that had fallen on his gold-embroidered chest: the star of Stanislav and Anna, and even: even the White Eagle.

The sash he wore was the blue sash.[8]

And recently from a small red lacquered box the beams of diamond insignia, or in other words, the decoration of the Order of Alexander Nevsky, had begun to shine on the abode of patriotic feelings.

What then was the social position of the person who had arisen here out of non-existence?

I think that the question is rather misplaced: Russia knew Ableukhov by the excellent expansiveness of the speeches he gave: these speeches did not explode, but flashing without thunder spurted a kind of poison on the opposing party, as a result of which the party's proposal was rejected in the appropriate quarters.[9] When Ableukhov was established in a senior post the Ninth Department[10] became inactive. With this department Apollon Apollonovich waged a constant battle both in documents and, where necessary, speeches, in support of the importation of American sheafing machines into Russia (the Ninth Department was against their importation). The senator's speeches flew around all the districts and provinces, some of which are not, in a spatial respect, the inferior of Germany.

Apollon Apollonovich was the head of an Institution: oh, *that* one . . . what is it called, again?

In a word, was the head of an Institution which is, of course, familiar to you.

If one were to compare the cachectic, utterly unprepossessing little figure of my respected man of state with the immeasurable vastness of the mechanisms he controlled, one might, perhaps, for a long time give oneself up to naïve astonishment; but after all, decidedly everyone was astonished at the explosion of intellectual energy shed by this cranium in defiance of all Russia, in defiance of the majority of departments, with the exception of one: but the head of that department[11] had, for what would now soon be two years, fallen silent at the will of the Fates beneath a gravestone.

My senator[12] had just passed his sixty-eighth birthday; and his face, a pale one, recalled both a grey paperweight (in solemn moments) and a piece of papier mâché (in hours of leisure); the senator's stony eyes, each surrounded by a black-green concavity, seemed in moments of tiredness both more blue and more enormous.

For our own part, let us also say: Apollon Apollonovich was not in the slightest agitated upon surveying his completely green ears, enlarged to massive dimensions, against the blood-red background of a burning Russia. Thus had he recently been depicted: on the front page of a humorous little street journal,[13] one of those little Yid journals, the blood-red covers of which multiplied in those days with shocking speed on the prospects that seethed with humanity . . .

North-East

In the oak dining-room the wheezing of a clock was heard; bobbing and hissing, a small grey cuckoo was cuckooing; at the signal from the time-honoured cuckoo Apollon Apollonovich sat down in front of a porcelain cup and broke off warm crusts of white bread. And over his coffee Apollon Apollonovich would remember his former years; and over his coffee – even, even – he would joke:

'Who is more respected than anyone else, Semyonych?'

'I suppose, Apollon Apollonovich, that a real privy councillor[14] is more respected than anyone else.'

Apollon Apollonovich smiled with his lips alone:

'Well, you suppose wrongly: a chimney sweep is more respected than anyone else . . .'

The valet already knew the answer to the riddle: but of this, out of respect, he said – not a word.

'But why, *barin*, may I be so bold as to ask, such honour to a chimney sweep?'

'In the presence of a real privy councillor, Semyonych, people stand aside . . .'

'I suppose that is so, your excellency . . .'

'A chimney sweep . . . Before him even a real privy councillor will stand aside, because: a chimney sweep makes people dirty.'

'Precisely so, sir,' the valet interjected deferentially . . .

'Yes indeed: only there is a post that is even more respected . . .'

And at once added:

'That of lavatory attendant . . .'

'Pff! . . .'

'The chimney sweep himself will stand aside before him, and not only the real privy councillor . . .'

And – a mouthful of coffee. But let us observe: Apollon Apollonovich was after all himself a real privy councillor.

'Oh, Apollon Apollonovich, sir, there was another thing: Anna Petrovna was telling me . . .'

At the words 'Anna Petrovna', however, the grey-haired valet stopped short.

. . . .

'The grey coat, sir?'

'Yes, the grey one . . .'

'I suppose it will be the grey gloves, too, sir?'

'No, I want suede gloves . . .'

'Try to wait a moment, your excellency, sir: you see, we keep the gloves in the wardrobe: Shelf B – North-West.'

Apollon Apollonovich had entered into life's trivia only once: one day he had made an inspection of his inventory; the inventory was registered in order and the nomenclature of all the shelves established; the shelves were arranged by letters: A, B, C; while the four sides of the shelves assumed the designations of the four corners of the globe.

When he had put his spectacles away, Apollon Apollonovich would mark the register in fine, minute handwriting: spectacles, Shelf B, NE – North-East, in other words; while the valet received a copy of the register, and learned the directions of the appurtenances of the precious toilet by heart; at times during bouts of insomnia he would flawlessly scan these directions from memory.

. . . .

In the lacquered house the storms of life passed noiselessly; but ruinously did the storms of life pass here none the less: not with events did they thunder; they did not shine purifyingly into hearts like arrows of lightning; but like a stream of poisonous fluids from a hoarse gullet did they rend the air: and some kind of cerebral games whirled in the consciousness of the inhabitants like dense vapours in hermetically sealed boilers.

The Baron, the Harrow

From the table rose a cold, long-legged bronze: the lampshade did not flash with a violet-pink tone, subtly painted: the secret of this paint had been lost by the nineteenth century; the glass had grown dark with time; the delicate pattern had also grown dark with time.

The golden pier-glasses in the window-piers devoured the drawing-room from all sides with the green surfaces of mirrors; and over there – a golden-cheeked little cupid crowned them with his little wing; and over there – a golden wreath's laurels and roses were perforated by the heavy flames of torches. Between the pier-glasses a small mother-of-pearl table gleamed from everywhere.

Apollon Apollonovich quickly threw open the door, leaning on the cut-crystal handle; his steps rang out over the radiant tiles of the parquetry; from all sides rushed heaps of porcelain trinkets; they had brought these trinkets from Venice, he and Anna Petrovna –

some thirty years ago. Memories of a misty lagoon, a gondola and an aria sobbing in the distance flashed inopportunely through the senator's head . . .

Instantly he transferred his eyes to the grand piano.

From the yellow lacquered lid the minute leaves of a bronze incrustation shone resplendently; and again (tiresome memory!) Apollon Apollonovich remembered: a white Petersburg night; in the windows a broad river flowed; and the moon was out; and a roulade of Chopin thundered: he remembered – Anna Petrovna had played Chopin (not Schumann) . . .

The minute leaves of the incrustation – of mother-of-pearl and bronze – shone resplendently on the boxes and shelves that came out of the walls. Apollon Apollonovich settled down in an Empire-style armchair, on the pale azure satin seat of which garlands wound, and with his hand he reached for a bundle of letters from a small Chinese tray: his bald head inclined towards the envelopes. As he waited for the lackey with his invariable 'The horses are ready' he absorbed himself here, before leaving for work, in the reading of his morning correspondence.

Thus did he act on this day, too.

And the small envelopes were torn open: envelope after envelope; an ordinary, postal one – the stamp affixed lopsidedly, the handwriting illegible.

'Mm . . . Yes, sir, yes, sir, yes, sir: very well, sir . . .'

And the envelope was carefully put away.

'Mm . . . A petition . . .'

'A petition, and another petition . . .'

The envelopes were torn open carelessly; these were things to be dealt with in time, later: this way or that . . .

An envelope made of thick grey paper – sealed, with a monogram, no stamp and the seal done in sealing-wax.

'Mm . . . Count Doublevé[15] . . . What's this? . . . He wants to see me at the Institution . . . A personal matter . . .'

'Mm . . . Aha! . . .'

Count Doublevé, the head of the Ninth Department, was the senator's adversary and an enemy of separated farming.

Next . . . A pale pink, miniature envelope; the senator's hand gave a start; he recognized this handwriting – the handwriting of

Anna Petrovna; he studied the Spanish stamp, but did not unseal the envelope:

'Mm . . . money . . .'

'But the money was sent, wasn't it?'

'The money will be sent!! . . .'

'Hm . . . I must make a note . . .'

Apollon Apollonovich, thinking he had got his pencil, pulled an ivory nailbrush from his waistcoat and was preparing to make a note to 'Return to address of sender', when . . .

'? . . .'

'The horses are ready, sir . . .'

Apollon Apollonovich raised his bald head and walked out of the room.

. . . .

On the walls hung pictures, suffused with an oily lustre; and with difficulty through the lustre one could see French women who looked like Greek women, in the narrow tunics of the Directoire of former times and with the tallest of coiffures.

Above the grand piano hung a small reproduction of David's painting *Distribution des aigles par Napoléon Premier*. The painting depicted the great Emperor wearing a wreath and an ermine purple mantle; the Emperor Napoleon was extending one hand to a plumed assembly of marshals; his other hand clutched a metal sceptre; on top of the sceptre sat a heavy eagle.

Cold was the magnificence of the drawing-room on account of the complete absence of rugs: the parquet tiles shone; if the sun illumined them for a moment, one's eyes screwed up involuntarily. Cold was the drawing-room's hospitality.

But with Senator Ableukhov it had been exalted into a principle.

It impressed itself: in the master, in the statues, in the servants, even in the dark, tiger-striped bulldog that lived somewhere near the kitchen; in this house everyone became disconcerted, giving way to the parquetry, the paintings and the statues, smiling, being disconcerted and swallowing their words: obliging and bowing, and rushing to one another – on these noisy parquets; and wringing their cold fingers in an access of fruitless obsequiousness.

Since Anna Petrovna's departure: the drawing-room had been

silent, the lid of the grand piano closed: the roulade had not thundered.

Yes – with regard to Anna Petrovna, or (to put it more simply) with regard to the letter from Spain: hardly had Apollon Apollonovich stalked past than two nimble lackeys quickly began to jabber.

'He didn't read the letter . . .'

'Oh well: he will read it.'

'Will he send it?'

"Course he will . . .'

'Such a stone, the Lord forgive . . .'

'I'll say this to you, as well: you ought to observe the verbal niceties.'

. . . .

When Apollon Apollonovich came down to the hallway, his grey-haired valet, who was also coming down to the hallway, looked at the respected ears, clutching a snuffbox in his hand – a gift from the minister.

Apollon Apollonovich stopped on the stairs and searched for a word.

'Mm . . . Listen . . .'

'Your excellency?'

Apollon Apollonovich looked for the right word.

'How, as a matter of fact, – yes – is he getting on . . . getting on . . .'

'? . . .'

'Nikolai Apollonovich.'

'Passably, Apollon Apollonovich, his honour is well . . .'

'And what else?'

'It's as before: his honour is pleased to shut himself up and read books.'

'Books, too?'

'Then his honour also paces about the rooms, sir . . .'

'Paces about – yes, yes . . . And . . . And? How?'

'Paces about . . . In a dressing-gown, sir!'

'Reading, pacing . . . I see . . . Go on.'

'Yesterday his honour was waiting for a visit from someone . . .'

'Waiting? For whom?'

'A costumier, sir . . .'

'What costumier?'

'A costumier, sir . . .'

'Hm-hm . . . What was that for?'

'I suppose that his honour is going to a ball . . .'

. . . .

'Aha – so: he's going to a ball . . .'

Apollon Apollonovich gave the bridge of his nose a rub: his face lit up with a smile and became suddenly senile:

'Are you from the peasantry?'

'That's right, sir!'

'Well, so you – do you know – are a baron.'

'?'

'Do you have a *borona*,[16] a harrow?'

'My father had one, sir.'

'Well, there you are, you see, and yet you say . . .'

Apollon Apollonovich, taking his top hat, walked out through the open door.

A Carriage Flew into the Fog

A sleety drizzle was pouring down on the streets and prospects, the pavements and the roofs; it hurled itself down in cold jets from tin-plated gutters.

A sleety drizzle was pouring down on the passers-by: rewarding them with grippes; together with the fine dust of rain the influenzas and grippes crawled under the raised collar: of gymnasiast, student, civil servant, officer, ordinary chap; and the ordinary chap (the man in the street, so to speak) looked around him in melancholy fashion; and looked at the prospect with a grey, washed-out face; he was circulating into the infinity of the prospects, crossing infinity, without the slightest murmur – in the infinite stream of others like himself – among the flight, the hubbub, the trembling, the droshkys, hearing from afar the melodic voice of the motor cars' roulades and the increasing rumble of the yellow-and-red tramcars (a rumble that decreased again), and the incessant cry of the loud-voiced newspaper sellers.

From one infinity he fled into another; and then stumbled against the embankment; here everything came to an end: the melodic voice of the motor car roulade, the yellow-and-red tramcar and the man-in-the-street of every kind; here were both the end of the earth and the end of infinity.

And over there, over there: the depths, the greenish dregs; from far, far away, seemingly further than ought to have been the case, the islands[17] frightenedly sank and cowered; the estates cowered; and the buildings cowered; it seemed that the waters were going to descend, and that at that moment over them would rush: the depths, the greenish dregs; while in the fog above these greenish dregs rumbled and trembled, fleeing away over there, the black, black Nikolayevsky Bridge.

On this sullen Petersburg morning the heavy doors of a well-appointed yellow house[18] flew open: the windows of the yellow house looked on to the Neva. A clean-shaven lackey with gold braid on his lapels rushed out from the entrance porch to give signals to the coachman. The dappled horses started with a jerk towards the entrance; they drew up a carriage on which an old aristocratic coat of arms was depicted: a unicorn goring a knight.

A dashing non-commissioned officer of the police who was walking past the porchway looked foolish and stood to attention when Apollon Apollonovich Ableukhov, in a grey coat and a tall black top hat, with a face of stone that recalled a paperweight, swiftly ran out of the entrance porch and even more swiftly ran on to the footboard of the carriage, putting on a black suede glove as he did so.

Apollon Apollonovich Ableukhov threw a momentary, confused glance at the police inspector, at the carriage, at the coachman, at the large black bridge, at the expanse of the Neva, where the foggy, many-chimneyed distances were drawn so fadedly, and from where Vasily Island looked in fright.

The lackey in grey hurriedly slammed the carriage door. The carriage flew swiftly into the fog; and the chance officer of the police, shaken by all he had seen, looked for a long, long time over his shoulder into the grimy fog – there, where the carriage had impetuously flown; and sighed, and walked on; soon this police-man's shoulder, too, was concealed in the fog, as was every shoulder, every back, every grey face and every black, wet umbrella. In that direction, too, did the respected lackey look, looked to the right, to the left, at the bridge, at the expanse of the Neva, where the foggy, many-chimneyed distances were drawn so fadedly, and from where Vasily Island looked in fright.

Here, right at the outset, I must break the thread of my narrative in order to present to the reader the place of action of a certain drama. As a preliminary, an inaccuracy that has crept in ought to be corrected; the blame for it belongs not to the author, but to the author's pen: at this time tramcars were not yet running in the city: this was 1905.[19]

Squares, Parallelepipeds, Cubes

'Hey! Hey! . . .'

That was the coachman shouting.

And the carriage sprayed mud to every side.

There, where only a foggy dampness hung suspended, first lustrelessly appeared in outline, then descended from heaven to earth – the grimy, blackish-grey St Isaac's; appeared in outline and then completely took shape: the equestrian monument of the Emperor Nicholas;[20] the metal emperor was dressed in the uniform of the Leib Guards; by its pedestal a Nicholas grenadier peeped out and withdrew back into the fog like a shaggy fur hat.

The carriage, meanwhile, was flying to Nevsky Prospect.

Apollon Apollonovich swayed on the satin cushions of the seat; he was separated from the street scum by four perpendicular walls; thus was he detached from the crowds of people flowing past, from the drearily sodden red wrappers of the cheap journals that were being sold at that crossroads over there.

Planned regularity and symmetry calmed the senator's nerves, which were stimulated both by the roughness of domestic life and by the helpless circle of the revolution of our wheel of state.

By a harmonic simplicity were his tastes distinguished.

Most of all did he love the rectilinear prospect; this prospect reminded him of the flow of time between the two points of life; and of one other thing, too: all other cities are a wooden pile of wretched little cottages, and Petersburg is strikingly different from them all.

The wet, slippery prospect: there the houses fused like cubes into a line of life in only one respect: this row had neither an end nor a beginning; here what for the wearer of diamond insignia was only the middle of life's wanderings turned out for so many high officials to be the ending of life's way.[21]

The senator's soul was seized by inspiration every time his lacquered cube cut across the line of the Nevsky like an arrow; there, outside the windows, the numeration of the houses was visible; and the traffic moved; there, from there – on clear days from far, far away, flashed blindingly: the gold needle,[22] the clouds, the crimson ray of the sunset; there, from there, on foggy days – nothing, no one.

And there were – the lines: the Neva, the islands. Probably in those far off days, when from the mossy marshes rose the high roofs and the masts and the spires that pierced with their merlons the dank, greenish fog –

> – on his shadowy sails the Flying Dutchman[23] flew towards St Petersburg from there, from the leaden expanses of the Baltic and German[24] Seas, in order here to erect by illusion his misty estates and to give the wave of amassing clouds the name of islands; from here the Dutchman lit the hellish lights of the drinking dens for two hundred years, and the Orthodox folk flocked and flocked into these hellish drinking dens, carrying a foul infection . . .

The dark shadows floated off a little. But the hellish drinking dens remained. For long years the Orthodox folk caroused here with a ghost: a mongrel race arrived from the islands – neither human beings nor shadows, – settling on the boundary between two worlds that were alien to each other.

Apollon Apollonovich did not like the islands: the population there was industrial, coarse; a human swarm of many thousands plodded its way in the mornings to the many-chimneyed factories; and now he knew that the Browning circulated there; and a few other things as well. Apollon Apollonovich thought: the inhabitants of the islands are numbered among the population of the Russian Empire; the general census has been introduced among them, too; they have numbered houses, police stations, fiscal institutions; the island resident is a lawyer, a writer, a worker, a police clerk; he considers himself a citizen of Petersburg, but he, a denizen of chaos, threatens the capital of the Empire in a gathering cloud . . .

Apollon Apollonovich did not want to reflect any further: the restless islands must be crushed, crushed! They must be riveted to the ground with the iron of the enormous bridge and transfixed in every direction by the arrows of the prospects . . .

And now, as he looked pensively into that boundlessness of mists, the man of state suddenly expanded out of the black cube in all directions and soared above it; and he desired that the carriage should fly forward, that the prospects should fly towards him – prospect after prospect, that the whole spherical surface of the planet should be gripped by the blackish-grey cubes of the houses as by serpentine coils; that the whole of the earth squeezed by prospects should intersect the immensity in linear cosmic flight with a rectilinear law; that the mesh of parallel prospects, intersected by a mesh of prospects, should expand into the abysses of outer space with the planes of squares and cubes: one square per man-in-the-street, that, that . . .

After the line of all the symmetries it was the figure of the square that brought him the most calm.

He was in the habit of giving himself up for long periods of time to the insouciant contemplation of: pyramids, triangles, parallelepipeds, cubes, trapezoids. He was seized by anxiety only when he contemplated the truncated cone.

As for the zigzag line, he could not endure it.

Here, in the carriage, Apollon Apollonovich took pleasure for a long time without thought in the quadrangular walls, residing at the centre of the black, perfect and satin-covered cube: Apollon Apollonovich had been born for solitary confinement; only a love for the planimetry of state clothed him in the polyhedrality of a responsible post.

. . . .

The wet, slippery prospect was intersected by a wet prospect at a right angle of ninety degrees; at the point where the lines intersected, a policeman stood . . .

And exactly the same houses loomed there, and the same grey human streams moved past there, and there was the same green-yellow fog. Concentratedly did the faces move there; the pavements whispered and shuffled; were rubbed briskly by galoshes; the nose of the man in the street sailed solemnly on. Noses[25] flowed past in large numbers: aquiline, duck-like, cockerel-like, greenish, white: here also flowed the absence of any nose at all. Here flowed ones, and twos, and threes-and-fours; and bowler hat after bowler hat: bowlers, feathers, service caps; service caps, service caps, feathers; a cocked hat, a top hat, a service cap; a kerchief, an umbrella, a feather.

But parallel with the racing prospect was a fleeting prospect with the same row of boxes, numeration, clouds; and the same civil servant.

There is an infinity of prospects racing in infinity with an infinity of intersecting shadows racing into infinity. All Petersburg is the infinity of a prospect raised to the power of n.

While beyond Petersburg there is – nothing.

The Inhabitants of the Islands Strike You

The inhabitants of the islands strike you with the vaguely thievish ways they have; their faces are greener and paler than those of any earth-born beings; the islander will get through the keyhole – some kind of *raznochinets*:[26] he will have a small moustache, perhaps; and I fear he will try to get some money out of you – for the arming of the factory and mill workers; your room will begin to mutter, to whisper, to giggle: you will give; and then you will be unable to sleep at nights any more: he, the inhabitant of the island, will be a stranger with a small black moustache, elusive, invisible, there will be no trace of him; he will already be out in the province; and if you look – the rural distances will be muttering, whispering there, in the expanse; there, booming and muttering in the rural distances will be – Russia.

It was the last day of September.

On Vasily Island, in the depths of the Seventeenth Line, out of the fog looked a house enormous and grey; from the small courtyard a black, rather dirty staircase led away into the house: there were doors and doors; one of them opened.

The stranger with the small black moustache appeared on its threshold.

Then, having closed the door, the stranger slowly began to descend; he came down from a height of five storeys, cautiously treading the staircase; in his hand there evenly swung a not exactly small, yet not very large little bundle tied up with a dirty napkin with red borders that showed discoloured pheasants.

My stranger behaved with exemplary caution in his treatment of the little bundle.

The staircase was, needless to say, black, strewn with cucumber rinds and a cabbage leaf that had been repeatedly crushed by a foot. The stranger with the small black moustache slipped on it.

With one hand then he gripped the staircase railing, while his other hand (with the bundle) confusedly described in the air a nervous zigzag; but the description of zigzag actually applied to his elbow: my stranger evidently wanted to protect the bundle from a vexatious accident – its precipitate fall on to the stone step, because in the movement of his elbow there truly was manifested the skilful stunt of an acrobat: the delicate cunning of the movement was prompted by a certain instinct.

And then in his meeting with the yardkeeper, who was coming up the stairs with an armful of aspen wood slung over his shoulder, the stranger with the black moustache again concentratedly began to display a delicate care about the fate of his bundle, which might catch on a log; the objects contained in the bundle must have been objects especially fragile.

Otherwise my stranger's behaviour would not have been comprehensible.

When the momentous stranger cautiously descended to the black exit door, a black cat that was near his feet spat and, tucking up its tail, cut across his path, dropping at the stranger's feet a chicken entrail: my stranger's face was distorted by a spasm; while his head jerked nervously back, displaying a soft neck.

These movements were peculiar to young ladies of the good old days when the young ladies of those days were beginning to experience a thirst: to confirm with an unusual action an interesting pallor of face, imparted by the drinking of vinegar and the sucking of lemons.

And precisely these same movements sometimes distinguish those of our young contemporaries who are worn out by insomnia. The stranger suffered from this kind of insomnia: the tobacco-smoke-filled nature of his abode hinted at that; and the bluish tint of the soft skin of his face bore witness to the same thing – such soft skin that had my stranger not been the possessor of a small moustache, I think you would probably have taken the stranger for a young lady in disguise.

And so there was the stranger – in the small courtyard, a quadrangle that had been entirely covered in asphalt and hemmed in on every side by the five storeys of a many-windowed colossus. In the middle of the courtyard damp cords of aspen wood had been piled; and even from here one could see a piece of the Seventeenth Line, whistled round by the wind.

Lines!

Only in you has the memory of Petrine Petersburg remained.

The parallel lines in the marshes had once been drawn by Peter;[27] those lines had become coated now with granite, now with stone enclosures, now with wooden ones. Of Peter's straight lines in Petersburg not a trace remained; Peter's line had been converted into the line of a later era: the rounded line of Catherine, the Alexandrine formation of white stone colonnades.

Only here, amidst the colossi, the small Petrine houses had remained; there a house built of logs; there a green house; there a blue one, single-storeyed, with a bright red sign reading *Stolovaya*.[28] It was exactly houses such as these that were scattered here in ancient times. Here also, one's nose was struck directly by various smells: there was a smell of salt, of herring, of hawsers, of leather jacket and pipe, and shore tarpaulin.

The Lines!

How they have changed: how these grim days have changed them!

The stranger remembered: in that window of that lustrous little house on a summer evening in June, an old woman chewed her lips; since August the window had been closed; in September a silk brocade coffin had been brought.

He reflected that life was going up in price and that soon the working people would have nothing to eat; that from there, from the bridge, Petersburg came stabbing here with the arrows of its prospects and a band of stone giants; that band of giants would soon shamelessly and brazenly bury in their attics and basements the whole of the islands' poor.

From the island my stranger had long hated Petersburg: there, from where Petersburg rose in a wave of clouds; and the buildings hovered there; there above the buildings someone malicious and dark seemed to hover, someone whose breathing firmly coated with the ice of granite and stone the once green and curly-headed islands; someone dark, terrible and cold, from there, from the warring chaos, fixedly with a stony gaze, beat in his mad hovering the wings of a bat; and lashed the islands' poor with official words, standing out in the fog: skull and ears; thus not long ago had someone been depicted on the cover of a little journal.

The stranger thought this and clenched his fist in his pocket; he remembered the circular and remembered that the leaves were falling: my stranger knew it all by heart. These fallen leaves were for many the last leaves: my stranger became a bluish shadow.

. . . .

For our part, however, we shall say: O, Russian people, Russian people! Do not let in the crowds of gliding shadows from the islands! Fear the islanders! They have a right to settle freely in the Empire: it is evidently for this purpose that black and grey bridges have been thrown over the waters of Lethe to the islands. They ought to be pulled down . . .

Too late . . .

The police did not even think of raising the Nikolayevsky Bridge; dark shadows began to throng over the bridge; among those shadows the shadow of the stranger began to throng, too. In its hand evenly swung a not exactly small, yet all the same not very large little bundle.

And, Having Caught Sight, Widened, Lit up, Flashed

In the greenish illumination of the Petersburg morning, in the saving 'apparently', a customary phenomenon also circulated in front of Senator Ableukhov: a manifestation of the atmosphere – a human stream; here people grew mute; their streams, accumulating in an undular surf, thundered, growled; but the accustomed ear could in no way detect that that human surf was a thunderous surf.

Welded together by the mirage the stream was disintegrating within itself into the elements of a stream: element upon element flowed by; perceptibly to the mind each was withdrawing from each, like planetary system from planetary system; neighbour was here in the same approximate relation to neighbour as that of a pencil of rays from the celestial vault to the retina of the eye, conveying to the centre of the brain along the telegraph of the nerves a troubled, stellar, shimmering message.

The aged senator communicated with the crowd that flowed before him by means of wires (telegraph and telephone); and the shadowy stream was borne to his consciousness like tidings that calmly flowed beyond the distances of the world. Apollon Apollonovich thought: about the stars, about the inarticulateness of the thunderous stream that was hurtling by; and, as he swayed on a black cushion, he calculated the intensity of the light that was perceptible from Saturn.

Suddenly . . . –

– his face winced and was distorted by a tic; his stony eyes, surrounded by blue, rolled convulsively; his wrists, clad in black suede, flew up to the level of his chest, as though he were defending himself with his hands. And his torso leaned back, while his top hat, striking the wall, fell on to his knees below his bared head . . .

The uncontrolled quality of the senator's movement was not subject to the customary interpretation; the senator's code of rules had not foreseen anything of this kind . . .

As he contemplated the flowing silhouettes – the bowlers, feathers, service caps, service caps, service caps, feathers – Apollon Apollonovich likened them to points in the celestial vault; but one of those points, breaking loose from its orbit, rushed at him with dizzying speed, assuming the form of an enormous and crimson sphere, or rather, what I mean is:

– as he contemplated the flowing silhouettes (service caps, service caps, feathers), Apollon Apollonovich saw on the corner among the service caps, among the feathers, among the bowlers, a pair of furious eyes: the eyes expressed a certain inadmissible quality; the eyes recognized the senator; and, having recognized, grew furious; perhaps the eyes had been waiting on the corner; and, having caught sight, widened, lit up, flashed.

This furious stare was a stare consciously thrown and belonged to a *raznochinets* with a small black moustache, wearing a coat with a turned-up collar; subsequently going more deeply into the details of the circumstance, Apollon Apollonovich more concluded than remembered something else as well: in his right hand the *raznochinets* was holding a little bundle tied with a wet napkin.

The matter was so simple: squeezed by the stream of droshkys, the carriage had stopped at a crossroads (the policeman there was lifting his white baton); the stream of *raznochintsy* that was moving past, squeezed by the flight of the droshkys towards the stream of the ones that were racing perpendicularly, cutting across the Nevsky – this stream now simply pressed itself against the senator's carriage, breaking the illusion that he, Apollon Apollonovich, as he flew along the Nevsky, was flying billions of versts away from the human myriapod that was trampling the very same prospect: rendered uneasy, Apollon Apollonovich moved close to the windows of the carriage, having seen that he was separated from the crowd by only a thin wall and a space of four inches; at this point he caught sight of the *raznochinets*; and began calmly to study him; there was something worthy of notice in the whole of that unprepossessing figure; and no doubt a physiognomist, encountering that figure in the street by chance, would have stopped in amazement: and then in the midst of his activities would have remembered that face he had seen; the peculiarity of that face consisted merely in the difficulty of classifying that face among any of the existing categories – no more than that . . .

This observation would have flickered through the senator's head had this observation lasted a second or two longer; but last it did not. The stranger raised his eyes and – on the other side of the mirror-like carriage window, removed from him by a space of four inches, he saw not a face, but . . . a skull in a top hat and an enormous pale green ear.

In that same quarter of a second the senator saw in the stranger's eyes – that same immensity of chaos from which by the nature of

things the foggy, many-chimneyed distance and Vasily Island surveyed the senator's house.

It was precisely at that moment that the stranger's eyes widened,
lit up, flashed: and it was precisely at that moment that, separated
by a space of four inches and the carriage wall, quickly on the other
side of the window hands were thrown up, covering eyes.

The carriage flew past; with it, into those damp spaces, flew
Apollon Apollonovich; to where from where – on clear days rose
splendidly – the golden needle, the clouds and the crimson sunset;
to where from where today came swarms of grimy clouds.

There in the swarms of grimy smoke, as he leaned back against
the wall of the carriage, in his eyes he still saw the same thing: the
swarms of grimy smoke; his heart began to thump; and expanded,
expanded, expanded; in his breast there came into being the sensation of a growing, crimson sphere that was about to explode and
shatter into pieces.

Apollon Apollonovich Ableukhov suffered from dilatation of the
heart.

All this lasted an instant.

Apollon Apollonovich, automatically putting on his top hat and
pressing a black suede hand to his galloping heart, again devoted
himself to his beloved contemplation of cubes, in order to give
himself a calm and sensible account of what had taken place.

Apollon Apollonovich again looked out of the carriage: what he
saw now blotted out what had gone before: a wet, slippery prospect;
wet, slippery flagstones shining feverishly in the miserable September day!

. . . .

The horses stopped. A policeman saluted. Behind the glass of the
entrance porch, behind a bearded caryatid that supported the stones
of a small balcony, Apollon Apollonovich saw the same spectacle as
usual: a heavy-headed bronze mace gleamed there; the dark triangle
of the doorman had subsided on an octogenarian shoulder there.
The octogenarian doorman was falling asleep over the *Stock Exchange Gazette*. Thus had he fallen asleep yesterday, and the day
before yesterday. Thus had he slept for the past fateful five years[29]
. . . Thus would he sleep for the next five years to come.

Five years had now passed since Apollon Apollonovich rolled up to the Institution as the junior head of the Institution: over five years had passed since that time! And there had been events: China had been in a state of ferment and Port Arthur had fallen.[30] But the vision of the years is immutable: an octogenarian shoulder, gold braid, a beard.

. . . .

The door flew open: the bronze mace banged. Apollon Apollonovich carried his stony gaze into the wide open entrance porch. And the door closed.

Apollon Apollonovich stood and breathed.

'Your excellency . . . Please sit down, sir . . . Look at you, how you're panting . . .'

'You're forever running as though you were a little boy . . .'

'Please sit down, your excellency: get your breath back . . .'

'There now, that's it, sir . . .'

'Perhaps . . . a little water?'

But the face of the distinguished man of state brightened up, became childish, senile; it dissolved entirely in wrinkles:

'But tell me, please: what is the husband of a countess, a *grafinya*?'

'A countess, sir? . . . But which one, may I be allowed to ask?'

'Oh, just any old *grafinya*.'

'The husband of a *grafinya* is a *grafin*, a decanter!'

. . . .

'Hee-hee-hee, sir . . .'

. . . .

And the heart that was disobedient to the mind trembled and thumped; and because of this, everything all around it was the same and not the same . . .

Of Two Poorly Dressed *Coursistes* . . .[31]

Among the slowly flowing crowds the stranger was flowing, too; and more precisely, he was flowing away, in complete confusion, from that crossroads where by the stream of people he had been squeezed against the black carriage, from whence had stared at him: a skull, an ear, a top hat.

That ear and that skull!

Remembering them, the stranger hurled himself into flight.

Couple after couple flowed past: threesomes, foursomes flowed past; from each one to the sky rose a smoky pillar of conversation, interweaving, fusing with smoky, contiguously moving pillar; intersecting the pillars of conversation, my stranger caught fragments of them; from those fragments both phrases and sentences formed.

The gossip of the Nevsky began to plait itself.

'Do you know?' came from somewhere to the right and expired in the accumulating rumble.

And then to the surface again came:

'They're going to . . .'

'What?'

'Throw . . .'

There was a whispering from the rear.

The stranger with the small black moustache, turning round, saw: a bowler hat, a walking stick, a coat; ears, a moustache and a nose . . .

'Who at?'

'Who, who,' came an echoed whisper from afar; and then the dark suit spoke.

'Abl . . .'

And, having spoken, the suit moved on.

'Ableukhov?'

'At Ableukhov?'

But the suit finished what it was saying somewhere over there . . .

'Abl . . . oody wish you'd try to splash me with a . . . cid . . . just you try . . .'

And the suit hiccuped.

But the stranger stood still, shaken by all he had heard:

'They're going to? . . .'

'Throw? . . .'

'At Abl . . .'

. . . .

'Oh no: they're not going to . . .'
. . . .

While all round the whisper began:
'Soon . . .'
And then again from the rear:
'It's time . . .'
And having disappeared round the crossroads, there came from another crossroads:
'It's time . . . *pravo*, indeed it is . . .'
The stranger heard not *pravo* (indeed) but *provo-* and himself completed the word:
'Provo-cation?!'
Provocation began to go on a spree along the Nevsky. Provocation altered the sense of all the words that had been heard: with provocation did it endow the innocent 'indeed'; while it turned 'I bloody wish' into the devil knew what:
'At Abl . . .'
And the stranger thought:
'At Ableukhov.'
He had simply of his own accord attached the preposition 'at': by the appendage of *the letter a and the letter t* an innocent verbal fragment had been changed into a fragment of dreadful content; and what was most important: it was the stranger who had attached the preposition.
The provocation, consequently, lay in him; and he was running away from it: running away – from himself. He was his own shadow.
O Russian people, Russian people!
Do not admit the crowds of flickering shadows from the island: stealthily those shadows penetrate into your corporeal abodes; they penetrate from there into the nooks and crannies of your souls: you become the shadows of the wreathed, flying mists: those mists have been flying from time immemorial out of the end of the earth: out of the leaden spaces of the wave-seething Baltic; into the fog from time immemorial the crushing mouths of the cannons have stared.
At twelve o'clock, in accordance with tradition, a hollow cannon

shot solemnly filled Saint Petersburg, capital of the Russian Empire: all the mists were broken and all the shadows were scattered.

Only my shadow – the elusive young man – was not shaken and was not diffused by the shot, completing his run to the Neva without hindrance. Suddenly my stranger's sensitive ear heard behind his back an ecstatic whisper:

'It's the Elusive One!'

'Look – it's the Elusive One!'

'How brave he is! . . .'

And when, unmasked, he turned his island face, he saw steadily fixed on him the little eyes of two poorly dressed coursistes . . .

Oh, You Be Quiet! . . .

'*Býby . . . byby . . .*'

Thus did the man at the small table thunder: a man of enormous dimensions; he was stuffing a piece of yellow salmon into his mouth and, as he choked, shouting out incomprehensible words. He seemed to be shouting:

'*Vy–by . . .* (You should . . .)'

But what was heard was:

'*Bý–by . . .*'

And a company of emaciated men in lounge-suits was beginning to squeal:

'A-*ah*-ha-ha, *ah*-ha-ha! . . .'

. . . .

A Petersburg street in autumn permeates the whole organism: chills the marrow and tickles the shuddering backbone; but as soon as you come from it into some warm premises, the Petersburg street runs in your veins like a fever. The quality of this street was experienced now by the stranger as he entered a rather dirty hallway, stuffed tight: with black, blue, grey and yellow coats, devil-may-care caps, lop-eared ones, dock-tailed ones and every possible kind of galosh. One felt a warm dampness; in the air hung a white vapour: the vapour of pancake smell.

Having received the numbered metal tag for his overcoat, a tag that burned the palm of his hand, the *raznochinets* with the pair of moustaches at last entered the hall ...

'A-a-a ...'

At first the voices deafened him.

. . . .

'Cra-aa-yfish ... aaa ... *ah*-ha-ha ...'

'You see, you see, you see ...'

'You're not saying ...'

'Em-em-em ...'

'And vodka ...'

'But for goodness' sake ... But come now ... But there must be something wrong ...'

. . . .

All this threw itself in his face, while behind his back, from the Nevsky, behind him in pursuit ran:

'It's time ... indeed ...'

'What do you mean indeed?'

'Cation – acacia – cassation ...'

'Bl ...'

'And vodka ...'

. . . .

The restaurant's premises consisted of a small, rather dirty room: the floor had been rubbed with polish; the walls had been decorated by the hand of a painter, depicting over there the remnants of a Swedish flotilla, from the elevation of which Peter was pointing into space; and from there flew spaces with the blue of white-maned rollers; but through the stranger's head flew a carriage surrounded by a swarm ...

'It's time ...'

'They're going to throw ...'

'At Abl ...'

'Indee ...'

Oh, idle thoughts! ...

On the wall there was a splendid display of curly spinach, depicting in zigzags the *plaisirs* of Peterhof's nature[32] with spaces, clouds and a sugar Easter cake in the form of a small, stylish pavilion.

. . . .

'Do you want picon[33] in it?'

The podgy landlord addressed our stranger from behind the vodka counter.

'No, I don't want picon in it.'

But wondered all the while: why there had been a frightened gaze – behind the carriage window: why the eyes had bulged, turned to stone and then closed; why a dead, shaven head had reeled and vanished; why from the hand – a black suede one – the cruel whip of a government circular had not dealt him a blow on the back; why the black suede hand had trembled there, impotently; why it had not been a hand but . . . *a wretched little handie* . . .

He looked: on the counter the snacks were turning dry, under glass bells some kind of limp little leaves were going rancid, along with a pile of overdone meatballs from the day before yesterday.

'Another glass . . .'

. . . .

There in the distance sat an idly sweating man with a most enormous coachman's beard, in a blue jacket and blacked boots on top of grey trousers of military colour. The idly sweating man was knocking back glasses; the idly sweating man was summoning the mop-headed waiter:

'What are you yelling for?'

'I want something . . .'

'Melon, sir?'

'To the devil: your melon is soap with sugar . . .'

'A banana, sir?'

'An indecent sort of fruit . . .'

'Astrakhan grapes, sir?'

. . . .

Thrice did my stranger swallow the astringent, colourlessly shining poison, the effect of which recalls the effect of the street: the oesophagus and the stomach lick its vengeful fires with a dry tongue, while the consciousness, detaching itself from the body, like the handle on the lever of a machine, starts to revolve around the whole organism, making everything incredibly clear . . . for one instant only.

And the stranger's consciousness cleared for an instant: and he remembered: jobless people were going hungry over there: jobless people were begging him there; and he had promised them; and taken from them – yes? Where was his little bundle? Here it was, here – beside him, here . . . Taken the bundle from them.

. . . .

Indeed: that encounter on the Nevsky had knocked out his memory.

'Some watermelon, sir?'

'To the devil with your watermelon: it just sticks in your teeth, and there's nothing in your mouth . . .'

'Well, some vodka then . . .'

But the bearded man suddenly fired off:

'I'll tell you what I want: crayfish . . .'

. . . .

The stranger with the small black moustache settled down at the small table to wait for that person who . . .

'Won't you have a glass?'

The idly sweating bearded man merrily winked.

'Thank you, but . . .'

'Why not, sir?'

'Well, I've already been drinking . . .'

'You ought to drink some more: in my company . . .'

My stranger put two and two together: suspiciously he gave the bearded man a look, grabbed hold of the soggy little bundle, grabbed hold of a torn sheet of paper (newspaper); and with it, as if casually, covered the little bundle.

'Are you from Tula?'

The stranger tore himself away from his thought with displeasure and said with sufficient rudeness – said in a falsetto voice:

'I'm certainly not from Tula . . .'

'Where are you from, then?'

'Why do you want to know?'

32

'I just do . . .'

'Well: I'm from Moscow . . .'

And with a shrug of his shoulders he angrily turned away.

. . . .

And he thought: no, he did not think – the thoughts thought themselves, expanding and revealing a picture: tarpaulins, hawsers, herring; and sacks stuffed full of something: the immensity of the sacks; among the sacks, with a bluish hand, a workman dressed in black leather was shouldering a sack, standing out clearly against the fog, against the flying watery surfaces; and the sack fell dully: from his back into a barge that was laden with girders; while the work-man (a workman he knew) stood above the sacks and pulled out a pipe with his clothes dancing most absurdly in the wind like a wing.

. . . .

'You here on business?'

(Oh, Lord!)

'No, just – here . . .'

And he said to himself:

'A police spy . . .'

'Is that so: well, I'm a coachman . . .'

. . . .

'My brother-in-law's a coachman for Konstantin Konstantino-vich . . .'[34]

'Well, and what of it?'

'What of it: nothing – no strangers here . . .'

Obviously a police spy: wish the *person* would come soon.

Meanwhile the bearded man fell into hapless reflection over a plate of uneaten crayfish, crossing his mouth, and giving a pro-longed yawn.

'Oh, Lord, Lord! . . .'

. . . .

Of what were his thoughts? Of Vasily Island? The sacks and the workman? Yes – of course: life was going up in price, the workman had nothing to eat.

Why? Because: *over the black bridge Petersburg comes lunging here;*

over the bridge and the arrows of the prospects – in order to crush the poor under heaps of stone coffins; he hated Petersburg; above the accursed regiments of buildings that rose up from the opposite bank out of a wave of clouds – someone small soared out of the chaos and floated there like a black point: there was a constant screeching and weeping from there:

'The islands must be crushed! . . .'

Only now did he realize what had happened on Nevsky Prospect, whose green ear had looked at him from a distance of four inches – behind the carriage wall; the small, trembling, dead little fellow had been that same bat which, as it soared – tormentingly, menacingly and coldly, threatened, screeched . . .

Suddenly –

But of 'suddenly' we shall speak – in what follows.

The Writing Desk Stood There

Apollon Apollonovich was taking aim at the current working day; in the twinkling of an eye there arose before him: reports from yesterday; he envisaged clearly the folded documents on his desk, their sequence, and on those documents the markings he had made, the form of the letters of those markings, the pencil with which carelessly in the margins had been entered: a blue 'set in motion', with a little tail on the final *n*; a red 'inquiry' with a flourish on the *y*.

In a brief moment, Apollon Apollonovich transferred the centre of his consciousness by willpower from the departmental staircase to the doors of his office; all his cerebral games retreated to the edge of his field of vision, as did those whitish patterns over there on the white background of the wallpaper: a little heap of parallel-placed dossiers was transferred to the centre of that field, as was that portrait that had just fallen into the centre.

And – the portrait? That is: –

And he is not – and Rus he has abandoned . . .[35]

Who is 'he'? The senator? Apollon Apollonovich Ableukhov? But no: Vyacheslav Konstantinovich . . .[36] But what about him, Apollon Apollonovich?

And it now seems – my turn has come,
My Delvig dear doth summon me . . .[37]

Order – order: by turn –

And o'er the earth new thunderclouds have gathered
And the hurricane them . . .[38]

An idle cerebral game!

The little heap of papers leapt up to the surface: Apollon Apollonovich, having taken aim at the current working day, addressed the clerk:

'German Germanovich, please be so good as to prepare a dossier for me – that one, what is it called? . . .'

'The dossier on deacon Zrakov with the enclosure of material evidence in the form of a tuft of beard?'

'No, not that one . . .'

'The one on the landowner Puzov and the hotel room? . . .'

'No: the dossier about the potholes of Ukhtomsk . . .'

No sooner was he about to open the door to his office than he remembered (he had almost completely forgotten): yes, yes – the eyes: they widened, were astonished, grew enraged – the eyes of the *raznochinets* . . . And why, why had there been that zigzag of his hand? . . . It had been most unpleasant. And he thought he had seen the *raznochinets* – somewhere, at some time: perhaps nowhere, never . . .

Apollon Apollonovich opened the door of his office.

The writing desk stood in its place with the little heap of case documents: in the corner the fireplace crackled its logs; preparing to immerse himself in work, Apollon Apollonovich warmed his frozen hands at the fireplace, while the cerebral game, restricting the senator's field of vision, continued to erect there its misty planes.

He Had Seen the *Raznochinets*

Nikolai Apollonovich . . .

At this point, Apollon Apollonovich . . .

'No, sir: wait.'

'? . . .'

'What the devil?'

Apollon Apollonovich stopped outside the door, because – how could it be otherwise?

His innocent cerebral game again spontaneously rose into his brain, that is, into the pile of documents and petitions: Apollon Apollonovich would have considered as a cerebral game the wall-paper of the room within whose confines the projects ripened; Apollon Apollonovich treated the spontaneity of mental combinations as a plane surface: this plane surface, however, moving apart at times, let through a surprise into the centre of his intellectual life (as, for example, just now).

Apollon Apollonovich remembered: he had once seen the *raznochinets*.

He had once seen the raznochinets – *imagine – in his own home.*

He remembered: one day he had been coming down the stairs, going in the direction of the exit; on the stairs Nikolai Apollonovich, leaning over the banisters, had been talking to someone animatedly: the statesman did not consider himself within his rights to inquire about Nikolai Apollonovich's acquaintances; a sense of tact then naturally prevented him from asking straight out: 'Kolenka, tell me, who is it who visits you, my dear fellow?'

Nikolai Apollonovich would have lowered his eyes.

'Oh, it's nothing, Papa, I just receive visits from people . . .'

And the conversation would have been broken off.

That was why Apollon Apollonovich was not in the slightest interested in the identity of the *raznochinets* who was looking out of the hallway in his dark topcoat; the stranger had that same small black moustache and those same striking eyes (you would have encountered just such eyes at night in the Moscow chapel of the Great Martyr Panteleimon,[39] by the Nikolsky Gate: – the chapel is famed for the curing of those possessed by devils; you would encounter just such eyes in the portrait appended to the biography of a great man; and, what is more: in a neuropathic clinic and even in a psychiatric one).

On that occasion, too, the eyes had; widened, begun to glitter, gleamed; in other words: that had happened once, and, perhaps, that would be repeated.

'About everything – yes sir, yes sir . . .'

'It will be necessary to . . .'

'Obtain the most detailed information . . .'

The man of state received his most detailed information not by a direct, but by a circuitous route.

. . . .

Apollon Apollonovich looked out of his office door: writing desks, writing desks! Piles of dossiers! Heads inclined over the dossiers! Squeaking of pens! Rustling of pages being turned! What a seething and mighty production of papers!

Apollon Apollonovich calmed down and immersed himself in work.

Strange Qualities

The cerebral play of the wearer of diamond decorations was distinguished by strange, highly strange, exceedingly strange qualities: his cranium became the womb of mental images that were instantly incarnated in this ghostly world.

Once he had taken into consideration this strange, highly strange, exceedingly strange circumstance, it would have been better had Apollon Apollonovich not cast from himself one single idle thought, continuing to carry around idle thoughts, too, in his head: for each idle thought stubbornly developed into a spatio-temporal image, continuing its – by now unchecked – activities outside the senatorial head.

Apollon Apollonovich was in a certain sense like Zeus: out of his head flowed gods, goddesses and spirits. We have already seen: one such spirit (the stranger with the small black moustache), coming into being as an image, had then quite simply *begun to exist* in the yellowish expanses of the Neva, asserting that he had come – precisely out of them: not out of the senatorial head; this stranger proved to have idle thoughts too; and those idle thoughts possessed the same qualities.

They escaped and acquired substance.

And one such escaped thought of the stranger's was the thought that he, the stranger, really existed; from the Nevsky Prospect this thought fleeted back into the senatorial brain and there strengthened his awareness, as though the stranger's very existence in that head had been an illusory existence.

Thus was the circle closed.

Apollon Apollonovich was in a certain sense like Zeus: hardly had the Stranger–Pallas, armed with a small bundle, been born out of his head, than out clambered another Pallas exactly like it.

This Pallas was the senator's house.

The stone colossus has escaped from his brain; and now the house opens its hospitable door – to us.

. . . .

The lackey was going up the staircase; he suffered from breathlessness, though we are not concerned with that now, but with . . . the staircase: a beautiful staircase! And it has steps – as soft as the convolutions of the brain. But the author does not have time to describe to the reader that same staircase, up which ministers have climbed more than once (he will describe it later), because the lackey is already in the reception hall . . .

And again – the reception hall: beautiful! Windows and walls: the walls somewhat cold . . . But the lackey was in the drawing-room (we have seen the drawing-room): We have glanced over the beautiful abode, guided by the general characteristic which the senator was in the habit of allotting to all objects.

Thus: –

– when, once in a blue moon, he ended up in the flowering bosom of nature, Apollon Apollonovich saw the same thing here as we did; that is: he saw – the flowering bosom of nature; but for us this bosom instantly disintegrated into characteristics: into violets, buttercups, dandelions and pinks; but the senator reduced these particulars once more to a unity. We, of course, would say:

'There is a buttercup!'

'There is a forget-me-not! . . .'

Apollon Apollonovich said simply, and briefly:

'Flowers . . .'

'A flower . . .'

Let it be said between ourselves: Apollon Apollonovich for some reason considered all flowers to be bluebells . . . –

He would even have characterized his own house with laconic brevity, a house which for him consisted of walls (forming squares and cubes), cut-through windows, parquets, chairs, tables; after that – the details began.

The lackey entered the corridor . . .

And here it will do no harm to remember: the things that fleeted past (the pictures, the grand piano, the mirrors, the mother-of-pearl, the incrustation of the small tables), – in a word, everything that had fleeted past, could have no spatial form: it was all of it a mere irritation of the cerebral membrane, if not a chronic indisposition . . . perhaps, of the cerebellum.

The illusion of a room took form; and then it would fly apart without trace, erecting beyond the limit of consciousness its misty planes; and when the lackey slammed behind him the heavy doors to the drawing-room, when his boots hammered along the small, resonant corridor, it was only a hammering in the temples: Apollon Apollonovich suffered from haemorrhoidal rushes of blood.

Behind the slammed door there turned out to be no drawing-room: there turned out to be . . . cerebral spaces: convolutions, grey and white matter, the pineal gland; while the heavy walls, that consisted of sparkling spray (caused by the rush of blood) – the bare walls were only a leaden and painful sensation: of the occipital, frontal, temporal and sincipital bones belonging to the respected skull.

The house – the stone colossus – was not a house: the stone leviathan was the senatorial head: Apollon Apollonovich sat at the desk, over dossiers, depressed by migraine, with the sensation that his head was six times larger than it ought to be, and twelve times heavier than it ought to be.

Strange, highly strange, exceedingly strange qualities!

Our Role

Petersburg streets possess an indubitable quality: they turn passers-by into shadows; while Petersburg streets turn shadows into people.

We have seen this in the example of the mysterious stranger.

He, having arisen like a thought in the senatorial head, was for some reason also connected with the senator's own house; there he had surfaced in the memory; but most of all he assumed substantial form on the prospect, immediately following the senator in our modest story.

From the crossroads to the little restaurant on Millionnaya Street we have described the stranger's route; we have described, further, his sitting in the little restaurant until the notorious word 'suddenly', which interrupted everything; suddenly something happened to the stranger there; some unpleasant sensation visited him.

Let us now investigate his soul; but first let us investigate the little restaurant; we have a reason for doing so; after all, if we, the author, mark out with pedantic exactitude the route of the first person who comes along, the reader will believe us: our action is justified in the future. In the natural investigation we have undertaken we have merely anticipated Senator Ableukhov's wish that an agent of the Secret Political Police Department should steadfastly follow the stranger's steps; the good senator would himself take up the telephone receiver in order by means of it to convey his thought to the proper quarters; fortunately for him, he did not know the stranger's abode (while we do know that abode). We shall go and meet the senator; and for the time being let the light-minded agent kick his heels in his Department – we shall be the agent.

But wait, wait . . .

Have we not gone and put our foot in it? I mean to say, what kind of agent are we? There is an agent already. And he is not asleep, my goodness, no, he is not asleep. Our role has proved to be an idle role.

When the stranger vanished through the doors of the little restaurant and we were seized by a desire to follow there too, we turned round and caught sight of two silhouettes that were slowly cutting through the fog; one of the two silhouettes was rather fat and tall, clearly standing out by his build; but we could not discern the face of the silhouette (silhouettes do not have faces); all the same, we did make out: a new, opened, silk umbrella, dazzlingly shining galoshes and a semi-sealskin hat with earflaps.

The mangy little figure of a short-statured little gentleman constituted the principal content of the second silhouette: the silhouette's face was visible enough: but we did not manage to see this face either, for we were astonished by the hugeness of the wart on it: thus did facial *substantia* screen from us the insolent *accidentia* (as it is fitting that it should act in this world of shadows).

Making it appear as though we are looking into the clouds, we have let slip the dark couple, in front of the restaurant door that dark couple stopped and said a few words in human language:

'Hm?'

'Here . . .'

'Just as I thought: precautions have been taken: that's in case you didn't show it to me by the bridge.'

'And what precautions have you taken?'

'Well, I've placed a man there, in the little restaurant.'

'Oh, you've no business to go taking precautions! Why, I've told you, told you: told you a hundred times . . .'

'Forgive me, I did it out of zeal . . .'

'You ought to have consulted me first . . . Your precautions are fine . . .'

'You say so yourself . . .'

'Yes, but your fine precautions . . .'

'Hm . . .'

'What? . . . Your fine precautions will make a mess of it all . . .'

. . . .

The couple went five paces, stopped; and again said a few words in human language.

'Hm! . . . I'll have to . . . Hm! . . . Wish you success now . . .'

'Well what doubt can there be of it: the undertaking has been set like the mechanism of a clock; unless I stop this deed now, then, believe me as a friend: the deed is in the bag!'

'Hm?'

'What are you saying?'

'Damned head cold . . .'

'But I'm talking about the deed . . .'

'Hm . . .'

'The souls are tuned like instruments: and make up the concert – what are you saying? It remains for the conductor to brandish his baton from the wings. Senator Ableukhov must issue a circular, while the Elusive One is in for . . .'

'Damned head cold.'

'Nikolai Apollonovich is in for . . . In a word: a concert trio, where Russia is the pit. Do you understand me? Do you understand? But why do you still say nothing?'

'Listen: you ought to take a salary . . .'

. . . .

'No, you won't understand me!'

'I will: hm-hm-hm – you definitely don't have enough handkerchiefs.'

'What?'

'But your cold! . . . And the wild beast – hm-hm-hm – won't go away?'

'Well, where is there for him to . . .'

'Well then, you should draw a salary . . .'

'A salary! I don't work for a salary: I'm an artist, do you understand – an artist!'

'Of a sort . . .'

'What?'

'Nothing: I'm curing myself with a tallow candle.'

The small figure took out its snot-covered handkerchief and again made a squelching sound with its nose.

'But I'm talking about the deed! Make sure you tell them that Nikolai Apollonovich has given a promise . . .'

'A tallow candle is a marvellous remedy for a cold . . .'

'Tell them all that you heard it from me: this deed has been set . . .'

'In the evening you smear it on your nostrils, in the morning you're as right as rain . . .'

'The deed has been set, I tell you again, like the mech . . .'

'Your nose is cleared, you breathe freely . . .'

'Like the mechanism of a clock!'

'Eh?'

'The mechanism, the devil take it, of a clock.'

'My ear's blocked: I can't hear.'

'The-me-chan-ism-of-a . . .'

'Achoo! . . .'

Under the wart the handkerchief again began to ply: the two shadows were slowly flowing away into the dank murk. Soon the shadow of the fat man in the semi-sealskin hat with the earflaps appeared again out of the fog and looked absent-mindedly at the spire of Peter and Paul.

And went into the little restaurant.

And Moreover the Face Glistened

Reader!

'Suddenly' is familiar to you. Then why, like an ostrich, do you hide your head in your feathers at the approach of a fateful and inexorable 'suddenly'? Start talking to you about an alien 'suddenly', and you will probably say:

'Dear sir, excuse me: you must be an out-and-out decadent.'

And you will probably expose me as a decadent.

You are even now before me as an ostrich; but in vain do you hide — you know me perfectly well: you also understand the inexorable 'suddenly'.

Then listen . . .

Your 'suddenly' steals up behind your back, indeed sometimes it precedes your appearance in the room; in the first case you are made horribly uneasy: in your back an unpleasant sensation develops, as though a gang of invisible beings had begun to throng into your back, as through an open door; you turn round and ask the hostess:

'Madam, will you permit me to close the door; I have a peculiar nervous sensation: I cannot abide sitting with my back to an open door.'

You laugh, she laughs.

But sometimes upon entering the drawing-room you will be greeted by a general:

'But we were just talking about you . . .'

And you reply:

'I expect heart gave the tidings to heart.'

They all laugh. You also laugh: as though here there were no 'suddenly'.

But sometimes the alien 'suddenly' will look at you from behind the shoulders of your interlocutor, wishing to get your own 'suddenly' by scent. Between you and your interlocutor there will take place something that suddenly makes your eyes flutter, while your interlocutor will become drier. Afterwards there will be something he will not forgive you all his life.

Your 'suddenly' is nourished by your cerebral play; the vileness of your thoughts it devours gladly, like a dog; it swells up, you melt like a candle; if your thoughts are vile and a trembling takes possession of you, then 'suddenly', having gorged itself with all forms of vileness, like a fattened but invisible dog, it will everywhere begin to precede you, provoking in a casual observer the impression that you are screened from view by a black cloud invisible to the gaze: this is the shaggy 'suddenly', your faithful *domovoi* (I knew an unfortunate fellow whose *black cloud* was very nearly visible to the gaze: he was a literary man . . .)

. . . .

We left the stranger in the little restaurant. *Suddenly* the stranger turned round impetuously; it seemed to him that a certain nasty slime, penetrating under his collar, had seeped along his backbone. But when he turned round, there was no one behind his back: gloomily, it seemed, gaped the door of the restaurant entrance; and from there, from the door, thronged *the invisible*.

At this point he pondered: up the staircase was coming, of course, the *person* he had been waiting for; in a moment or two he would come in; but he did not come in; in the doorway there was no one.

And when my stranger turned away from the door, through the doorway immediately walked the unpleasant fat man; and, as he went up to the stranger, he made a floorboard creak; the yellowish face, shaven, very slightly inclined to one side, floated smoothly in its own double chin; and moreover the face glistened.

Here my stranger turned round and started: the *person* was cordially waving a semi-sealskin hat with earflaps at him:

'Aleksandr Ivanovich . . .'

'Lippanchenko!'

'Yes, it's me . . .'

'Lippanchenko, you are making me wait.'

The person's shirt collar was tied with a necktie – satin-red, loud, and fastened with a large paste jewel, a dark yellow striped suit enveloped the person; while on his yellow shoes gleamed brilliant polish.

Taking a seat at the stranger's table, the person exclaimed contentedly:

'A pot of coffee! . . . And – listen, some cognac: my bottle's there, registered under my name . . .'

And around them was heard:

'You – did you drink with me?'

'I did.'

'Did you eat? . . .'

'I ate . . .'

'Well, with your permission, let me tell you that you're a pig . . .'

. . . .

'Be more careful,' cried my stranger: the unpleasant fat man, called Lippanchenko by the stranger, was just about to put his dark yellow elbow on a sheet of newspaper: the sheet of newspaper covered the little bundle.

'What?' Here Lippanchenko, lifting the sheet of newspaper, caught sight of the small bundle: and Lippanchenko's lips trembled.

'Is that . . . that . . . it?'

'Yes: that's it.'

Lippanchenko's lips continued to tremble: Lippanchenko's lips recalled little pieces of sliced-up salmon, – not yellow-red, but buttery and yellow (the kind of salmon you have probably eaten with *bliny* in a poor household).

'How careless you are, Aleksandr Ivanovich, may I observe to you.' Lippanchenko stretched out his coarse fingers towards the little bundle; and they shone, the fake stones of the rings on his swollen fingers with their bitten nails (the nails actually showed dark traces of a brown dye that corresponded to the colour of his hair; an attentive observer could draw the conclusion: the person dyed his hair).

'I mean, one movement (just put your elbow on it), and there might be a . . . catastrophe . . .'

And with especial caution the person moved the small bundle to a chair.

'Well, yes, with both of us there would be . . .' the stranger joked unpleasantly. 'We would both be . . .'

He was evidently enjoying the confusion of the person whom – let us say for our part – he hated.

'I'm concerned, of course, not for myself, but for . . .'

'Of course, of course you're not concerned for yourself, but for . . .' the stranger agreed with the person.

. . . .

While around them was heard:

'Don't you call me a pig . . .'

'But I don't mean it like that.'

'Yes you do: you're annoyed for having paid . . . So what if you paid; you paid that time, I'll pay today . . .'

'All right, my friend, I'll smother you with kisses for this good deed of yours . . .'

'Don't be angry about the "pig": but I'll eat and eat . . .'

'All right, go on and eat, eat: it's more proper that way.'

. . . .

'Here now, Aleksandr Ivanovich, sir, here now, my dear chap, take this little bundle' – Lippanchenko looked sideways – 'to Nikolai Apollonovich, immediately.'

'To Ableukhov?'

'Yes: to him – for safe keeping.'

'But let me look after it: the little bundle can reside at my place . . .'

'Inconvenient: you may be arrested; whereas *there* it will be in safe hands. One way or the other, the house of Senator Ableukhov . . . By the way: have you heard about the old fellow's latest crucial pronouncement? . . .'

Here, leaning over, the fat man began to whisper something into my stranger's ear:

'Shoo-shoo-shoo . . .'

'Ableukhov?'

'Shoo . . .'

'To Ableukhov? . . .'

'Shoo-shoo-shoo . . .'

'With Ableukhov? . . .'

'No, not with the senator, but with the senator's son: if you're at his place, then do me a favour and give him along with the little bundle – this little letter: here it is . . .'

Straight to the stranger's face did Lippanchenko's narrow-browed head lean; in their sockets the gnawing little eyes hid searchingly; his lips quivered imperceptibly and sucked the air. The stranger with the small black moustache listened closely to the fat gentleman's whispering, attentively trying to make out the contents of the whisper that was being drowned by the voices in the restaurant; the voices in the restaurant covered Lippanchenko's whisper; something was imperceptibly rustling from the repulsive lips (like the rustle of many hundreds of arthropodal ants' legs above a dug-up anthill) and it seemed as if that whisper had terrible contents, as if what was being whispered about here was worlds and planetary systems; but one had only to listen closely to the whispering in order to realize that the terrible contents of the whispering were actually humdrum contents:

'Give him the letter . . .'

'Oh, is Nikolai Apollonovich in special liaison, then?'

The person screwed up his small eyes and gave a click of his small tongue.

'Why, I thought all liaison with him was through me . . .'

'Well, you can see that it isn't . . .'

. . . .

Around them was heard:

'Eat, eat, friend . . .'

'Get me some beef jelly.'

'In food is truth . . .'

'What is truth?'[40]

'Truth is tooth . . .'

'I know.'

'If you know, that's fine: move up a plate and eat . . .'

. . . .

Lippanchenko's dark yellow suit reminded the stranger of the dark yellow colour of the wallpaper of his abode on Vasily Island – a colour that was connected with insomnia and white spring nights and September sombre ones; and, so it must be, that cruel insomnia had suddenly evoked in his memory a certain fateful face with narrow little Mongolian eyes; that face had looked repeatedly at him from a piece of his yellow wallpaper. Examining this place by day, the stranger had only been able to make out a damp spot, over which a woodlouse was crawling. In order to distract himself from memories of the hallucination that had tormented him, my stranger lit a cigarette, to his own surprise, becoming garrulous:

'Listen to the noise . . .'

'Yes, they're making a fair old noise.'

'The sound of the noise is an *i*, but you hear an *y* . . .'

Lippanchenko, torpid, was immersed in some thought.

'In the sound *y* one hears something stupid and slimy . . . Or am I mistaken?'

'No, no: not in the slightest,' not listening, Lippanchenko muttered and for a moment tore himself away from the computations of his thought . . .

'All words with an *y* in them are trivial to the point of ugliness: *i* is not like that; *i-i-i* – a blue firmament, a thought, a crystal; the sound *i-i-i* evokes in me the notion of an eagle's curved beak; while words with *y* in them are trivial; for example: the word *ryba* (fish); listen: *r-y-y-y-ba*, that is, something with cold blood . . . And again *my-y-y-lo* (soap): something slimy; *glyby* (clods) – something formless: *tyl* (rear) – the place of debauches . . .'

My stranger broke off his discourse: Lippanchenko sat before him like a formless *glyba*: and the *dym* (smoke) from his cigarette slimily soaped up (*obmylival*) the atmosphere: Lippanchenko sat in a cloud; my stranger looked at him and thought 'Pah!, what filth, Tartar stuff . . .' Before him sat quite simply a kind of *Y* . . .

. . . .

From the next table someone, hiccuping, exclaimed:

'You big *Y*, you big *Y* . . .'

. . . .

'I say, Lippanchenko, you're not a Mongol, are you?'

'Why such a strange question? . . .'

'Oh, it just occurred to me . . .'

48

'Well, but Mongol blood flows in every Russian . . .'

. . . .

Against the next table leaned a fat paunch; and from the next table a paunch rose to greet it . . .

'To the slaughterer Apofriev! . . .'

'Regards!'

'To the slaughterer of the city abattoirs . . . Take a seat . . .'

'Waiter! . . .'

'Well, how are things with you? . . .'

'Waiter: put on "The Negro's Dream" . . .'

And the horns of the machine bellowed to the slaughterer's health, like a bull under the slaughterer's knife.

What Costumier?

Nikolai Apollonovich's lodging consisted of the rooms: bedroom, working study, reception room.

The bedroom: the bedroom was taken up by an enormous bed; it was covered by a red satin spread – with lace covers on the fluffily plumped-up pillows.

The study was furnished with oak shelves that were tightly packed with books, before which silk lightly slipped on brass rings; a careful hand could at one time completely conceal from the gaze the contents of the shelves, at another reveal rows of black leather bindings that were speckled with the inscription: Kant.

The study's furniture was green-upholstered; and there was a handsome bust . . . of Kant, of course.

For two years now Nikolai Apollonovich had not risen before noon. For two and a half years before that he had woken up earlier: had woken up at nine o'clock, at half past nine appearing in a tightly buttoned-up uniform jacket, for the family imbibing of coffee.

Two and a half years before, Nikolai Apollonovich had not paced about the house in a Bokharan robe; a skullcap had not adorned his Oriental drawing-room; two and a half years before, Anna Petrovna, Nikolai Apollonovich's mother and Apollon Apollonovich's spouse, had finally abandoned the family hearth, inspired by an Italian

artist; and after her flight with the artist Nikolai Apollonovich had
appeared on the parquets of the cooling domestic hearth dressed in
a Bokharan robe: the daily meetings of father and son over morning
coffee were somehow curtailed of themselves. Coffee was served to
Nikolai Apollonovich in bed.

And Apollon Apollonovich was inclined to partake of coffee
considerably earlier than his son.

The meetings of father and son took place only over dinner; and
even then, only for a short time; meanwhile in the mornings a robe
began to appear on Nikolai Apollonovich; Tartar slippers, trimmed
with fur, were acquired; while on his head a skullcap appeared.

And the brilliant young man was transformed into an Oriental.

Nikolai Apollonovich had just received a letter; a letter written in
unfamiliar handwriting: some kind of wretched doggerel with an
amorous-revolutionary tinge and the striking signature: 'A Fiery
Soul'. Wishing for the sake of precision to acquaint himself with the
contents of the doggerel, Nikolai Apollonovich began helplessly to
rush about the room, hunting for his spectacles, rummaging among
books, quills, pens and other knick-knacks and muttering to
himself:

'A-a . . . But where are my spectacles? . . .

'The devil take it . . .

'Have you lost them?

'Tell me, please.

'Eh? . . .'

Like Apollon Apollonovich, Nikolai Apollonovich talked to
himself.

His movements were impetuous, like the movements of his
eminent papa; like Apollon Apollonovich, he was distinguished by
an unprepossessing stature, a ceaselessly smiling face with an anxious
gaze: but when he immersed himself in the serious contemplation of
anything at all this gaze slowly turned to stone: drily, sharply and
coldly protruded the lines of his completely white countenance, like
one painted on an icon, striking the observer with an especial kind
of aristocratic nobility: the nobility in his face was manifested in a
notable manner by his forehead – chiselled, with small, swollen
veins: the rapid pulsation of these veins clearly marked on his
forehead a premature sclerosis.

The bluish veins coincided with the blueness around his enormous eyes, which looked as though they had been pencilled in some dark cornflower colour (only in moments of agitation did his eyes become black from the dilation of the pupils).

Nikolai Apollonovich was arrayed before us in a Tartar skullcap; but had he taken it off – there would have appeared a cap of white flaxen hair, softening this cold, almost stern exterior with an imprinted stubbornness; it was rare to encounter hair of such a colour in a grown man; this hair colour, unusual for adults, is frequently encountered in peasant infants – especially in Belorussia.

Carelessly abandoning the letter, Nikolai Apollonovich sat down before an open book; and the thing he had been reading a day earlier arose before him (some kind of treatise). Both chapter and page came back to him: he recalled even the lightly traced zigzag of a rounded fingernail; the convoluted passages of thoughts and his own notations – in pencil in the margins; now his face grew enlivened, remaining both stern and clear: it was animated by thought.

Here, in his room, Nikolai Apollonovich truly grew into a self-appointed centre – into a series of logical premisses that predetermined thought, soul and this very desk: here he was the sole centre of the universe, both conceivable and inconceivable, cyclically elapsing in all zones of time.

This centre made deductions.

But scarcely had Nikolai Apollonovich succeeded this day in putting away from him the trivia of day-to-day existence and the abyss of all kinds of obscurity, called world and life, and scarcely had Nikolai Apollonovich succeeded in going into his study than obscurity again burst into Nikolai Apollonovich's world; and in this obscurity consciousness of self got shamefully stuck: thus does the untrammelled fly, running along the rim of a plate on its six legs, suddenly get inextricably stuck leg and wing in a sticky sediment of honey.

Nikolai Apollonovich tore himself away from the book: someone was knocking at his door:

'Well . . .?

'What is it?'

From the other side of the door a hollow and deferential voice was heard.

'There, sir . . .

'They're asking for you, sir . . .'

Concentrating himself in thought, Nikolai Apollonovich was in the habit of locking his work room: then it began to seem to him that both he and the room and the objects in that room were instantly transformed from objects of the real world into the intelligible symbols of purely logical constructions; the space of the room blended with his body, which had lost sensitivity, into a general chaos of existence, called by him the 'universe'; and Nikolai Apollonovich's consciousness, separating itself from his body, united itself directly with the electric lamp on his writing desk, which he called 'the sun of consciousness'. Having locked himself in and reviewing the tenets of his system which was being, step by step, reduced to a unity, he felt his body being poured into the 'universe', that is, into the room; while the head of this 'body' was displaced into the electric lamp's pot-bellied lightbulb under the coquettish shade.

And having displaced himself thus, Nikolai Apollonovich became a truly creative being.

This was why he liked to lock himself in: the voice, rustle or step of an intruder turning the 'universe' into a room, and 'consciousness' into a lamp, shattered Nikolai Apollonovich's whimsical sequence of thought.

So it was now.

'What is it?

'I can't hear . . ..'

But from the distance of space the lackey's voice responded:

'A man has arrived out there.'

. . . .

At this point Nikolai Apollonovich's face suddenly took on a pleased expression:

'Ah, this will be someone from the costumier's: the costumier has brought me my costume . . .'

What costumier?

Nikolai Apollonovich, gathering up the skirts of his robe, strode off in the direction of the exit; by the staircase balustrade Nikolai Apollonovich leaned over and shouted:

'Is that you? . . .

'The costumier?

'Are you from the costumier?

'Has the costumier sent me the costume?'

And again we repeat to ourselves: what costumier?

. . . .

In Nikolai Apollonovich's room a cardboard box appeared; Nikolai Apollonovich locked the door; fussily he cut the string; and he raised the lid; further, pulled out of the box: first a small mask with a black lace beard, and after the mask Nikolai Apollonovich pulled out a sumptuous bright red domino cape with folds that rustled.

Soon he stood before the mirror – all of satin, all of red, having raised the miniature mask over his face; the black lace of the beard, turning away, fell on to his shoulders, forming to right and left a whimsical, fantastical wing; and from the black lace of the wings from the semi-twilight of the room in the mirror looked at him tormentingly, strangely – it, the same: the face, – his, his own; you would have said that there in the mirror it was not Nikolai Apollonovich looking at himself, but an unknown, pale, languishing – demon of space.

After this masquerade Nikolai Apollonovich, with an exceedingly pleased look on his face, put back into the cardboard box first the red domino cape, and after it the small black mask.

A Wet Autumn

A wet autumn was flying over Petersburg; and cheerlessly did the September day glimmer.

In a greenish swarm shreds of clouds rushed by out there; they thickened into a yellowish smoke, pressing themselves against the roofs like a threat. The greenish swarm rose unceasingly above the irreparable distance of the Neva's spaces; the dark watery depths beat at the boundaries with the steel of their scales; into the greenish swarm stretched a spire ... from the Petersburg Side.

Having described a funereal arc in the sky, a dark stripe of soot rose high from the funnels of steamboats; and fell like a tail into the Neva.

And the Neva seethed, and cried desperately there with the whistle of a small steamboat that had begun to hoot, smashed its shields of water and steel against the stone bridge-piers; and licked the granite, with an onslaught of cold Neva winds it tore away peaked caps, umbrellas, capes and service caps. And everywhere in the air hung a pale grey mould; and from there, into the Neva, into the pale grey mould, the wet statue of the Horseman continued to hurl his heavy, green-turned bronze.

And against this darkening background of tailed and drooping soot above the damp stones of the embankment railing, his eyes fixed upon the turbid, bacillus-infected water of the Neva, the silhouette of Nikolai Apollonovich distinctly stood out, clad in a grey Nikolayevka and a student's peaked cap worn at a slant. Slowly did Nikolai Apollonovich move towards the grey, dark bridge, did not smile, presenting a rather ridiculous figure: tightly wrapped in the greatcoat, he appeared stooping and rather awkward, with a wing of greatcoat dancing most absurdly in the wind.

By the large black bridge he stopped.

An unpleasant smile flared for an instant on his face and died; memories of an unsuccessful love had seized him, gushing out in an onslaught of cold wind; Nikolai Apollonovich remembered a certain foggy night; on that night he had leaned over the railing; turned round and seen that there was no one there; raised his leg; and in a sleek rubber galosh brought it over the railing, and ... remained like that: with raised leg; it seemed that consequences ought to have ensued; but ... Nikolai Apollonovich continued to stand with raised leg. A few moments later Nikolai Apollonovich had lowered his leg.

It was then that an ill-considered plan had matured within him: to give a dreadful promise to a certain frivolous party.

Remembering now this unsuccessful action of his, Nikolai Apollonovich smiled in a most unpleasant manner, presenting a rather ridiculous figure: tightly wrapped in the greatcoat, he appeared stooping and rather awkward with his long wing of greatcoat dancing in the wind; with such an aspect did he turn on to the Nevsky; it was beginning to get dark; here and there in a shop's display window gleamed a light.

'A handsome fellow,' was constantly heard around Nikolai Apollonovich.

'An antique mask . . .'

'The Apollo Belvedere.'

'A handsome fellow . . .'

In all probability the ladies he encountered spoke of him thus.

'That pallor of his face . . .'

'That marble profile . . .'

'Divine . . .'

In all probability the ladies he encountered spoke of him thus.

But if Nikolai Apollonovich had wished to enter into conversation with the ladies, the ladies would have said to themselves:

'An ugly monster . . .'

Where from an entrance porch two melancholic lions place paw on grey granite paw, – there, by that place, Nikolai Apollonovich stopped and was surprised to see behind him the back of a passing officer; tripping over the skirts of his greatcoat, he began to catch the officer up:

'Sergei Sergeyevich?'

The officer (a tall, blond fellow with a little pointed beard) turned round and with a shade of annoyance watched expectantly through the blue lenses of his spectacles as, tripping over the skirts of his greatcoat, clumsily towards him trailed a diminutive and student-like figure from a familiar place where from an entrance porch two melancholic lions with sleek granite manes mockingly place paw upon paw. For an instant some kind of thought seemed to strike the officer's face; from the expression of his trembling lips one might have thought that the officer was excited; he seemed to be hesitating: should he *recognize or not?*

'Er . . . hello . . . Where are you going?'

'I have to go to Panteleimonovskaya,' Nikolai Apollonovich lied, in order to be able to walk along the Moika with the officer.

'Let's go together, if you like . . .'

'Where are you going?' Nikolai Apollonovich lied a second time, in order to be able to walk along the Moika with the officer.

'I'm going home.'

'That's on our way, then.'

Between the windows of the yellow, official building, above both of them, hung rows of stone lions' faces; each face hung above a coat of arms that was entwined with a stone garland.

As if trying not to touch on some painful past, they both, interrupting each other, began to talk concernedly to one another: about the weather, about how the disturbances of recent weeks had affected Nikolai Apollonovich's philosophical work, about the cases of swindling that the officer had uncovered in the provisions commission (the officer was in charge of provisions somewhere out there).

Thus did they talk all the way.

And there was the Moika already: the same bright, three-storeyed building of the Alexandrine era; and the same stripe of ornamental stucco above the second storey; circle after circle; and in the circle a Roman helmet on crossed swords. They had already passed the building; there after the building was a house; and there – windows ... The officer stopped outside the house and for some reason suddenly flushed; and, having flushed, said:

'Well, goodbye ... are you going further? ...'

Nikolai Apollonovich's heart began to thump violently: he was getting ready to ask something; and – no, he did not ask; now he stood alone in front of the slammed door; memories of an unsuccessful love, or more correctly – sensual attraction – these memories seized him; and more violently did the bluish veins at his temples begin to throb; now he was considering his revenge: outrage at the emotions of the lady who had wounded him and who lived through this entrance porch; he had been considering his revenge for about a month now; and – for the moment about this not a word!

The same bright, five-columned building with a stripe of ornamental stucco; circle after circle; and in the circle a Roman helmet on crossed swords.

. . . .

In the evening the prospect is suffused with a fiery murk. Regularly in the centre rise the apples of the electric lights. While along the sides plays the variable lustre of signs; here, here and here rubies of lights suddenly flare; there – emeralds flare. An instant: the rubies are there; while the emeralds are here, here and here.

In the evening the Nevsky is suffused with a fiery murk. And the walls of many houses burn with a diamond light: words formed from diamonds brightly scintillate: 'Coffee House', 'Farce', 'Tate Diamonds', 'Omega Watches'. Greenish by day, but now effulgent, a display window opens wide on the Nevsky its fiery maw: everywhere there are tens, hundreds of infernal fiery maws: these maws agonizingly disgorge on to the flagstones their brilliant white light; they spew a turbid wetness like fiery rust. And the prospect is gnawed to shreds by rust. The white brilliance falls on bowlers, top hats, feathers; the white brilliance rushes onwards, towards the centre of the prospect, shoving aside the evening darkness from the pavement: and the evening wetness dissolves above the Nevsky in glitterings, forming a dim, bloody-yellowish lees made of blood and mud. Thus from the Finnish marshes the city will show you the site of its mad way of life as a red, red stain: and that stain is soundlessly seen from the distance in the dark-coloured night. As you journey through our immense motherland, from the distance you will see a stain of red blood rising into the dark-coloured night; in fear you will say: 'Is that not the place of the fires of Gehenna over there?' You will say it – and will go trudging off into the distance: you will try to avoid the place of Gehenna.

But if, reckless reader, you dared to walk towards Gehenna, the brightly-bloody brilliance that horrified you from the distance would slowly dissolve into a whitish, not entirely pure radiance, surround you with many-lighted houses, – and that is all: in the end it would disintegrate into a great multitude of lights.

And there would be no Gehenna.

. . . .

Nikolai Apollonovich did not see the Neva, in his eyes he still saw that same little house: the windows, the shadows behind the windows; behind the windows, perhaps, merry voices: the voice of the Yellow Cuirassier, Baron Ommau-Ommergau; of the Blue

Cuirassier, Count Aven and *her* − *her* voice ... Here sits Sergei
Sergeich, the officer, inserting into his merry jokes perhaps:

'Oh, I've just been out walking with Nikolai Apollonovich
Ableukhov ...'

Apollon Apollonovich Remembered

Yes, Apollon Apollonovich remembered: he had recently heard a
certain good-natured joke about himself:

The civil servants said:

'Our Bat[41] (Apollon Apollonovich's nickname in the Institution),
when he shakes the hands of petitioners, behaves not at all like one
of Gogol's civil servants; when he shakes the hands of petitioners,
he certainly does not run the gamut of handshakes from complete
contempt, through inattention, to non-contempt: from collegiate
registrar[42] to state ...'

And to this they observed:

'He plays only one note: contempt ...'

Here defenders intervened:

'Gentlemen, please stop: it's caused by haemorrhoids ...'

And everyone agreed.

The door flew open: Apollon Apollonovich came in. The joke
was timidly curtailed (thus does a young, quick-moving mouse
swiftly fly into a crack as soon as you enter the room). But Apollon
Apollonovich did not take offence at jokes; and, moreover, there
was a degree of truth in the assertion: he did suffer from
haemorrhoids.

Apollon Apollonovich went over to the window: two children's
heads in the windows of the house that stood there saw opposite
them behind the pane of the house that stood there the facial stain
of an unknown little old man.

And the heads over there in the windows disappeared.

. . . .

Here, in the office of the lofty Institution, Apollon Apollonovich
was truly growing into a kind of centre: into a series of government
institutions, studies and green tables (only more modestly furnished).

Here he was a point of radiating energy, an intersection of forces and an impulse of numerous, multi-constituent manipulations. Here Apollon Apollonovich was a force in the Newtonian sense; and a force in the Newtonian sense is, as you probably do not know, an occult force.

Here he was the final authority – in reports, petitions and telegrams.

He did not relate this authority in the state organism to himself, but to the centre he contained within himself – his consciousness.

Here consciousness detached itself from valiant personality, spilling around between the walls, growing incredibly clear, concentrating with such great force in a single point (between the eyes and the forehead) that it seemed an invisible, white light, flaring up between the eyes and the forehead, scattered around sheaves of serpentine lightnings; the lightning thoughts flew asunder like serpents from his bald head; and if a clairvoyant had stood at that moment before the face of the venerable statesman, he would without doubt have seen the head of the Gorgon Medusa.

And Apollon Apollonovich would have seized him with Medusan horror.

Here consciousness detached itself from valiant personality: while personality, with an abyss of all possible kinds of agitations (that incidental consequence of the soul's existence), presented itself to the senator's soul as a cranium, an empty, at the present moment voided, container.

At the Institution Apollon Apollonovich spent hours in the review of the document factory: from the radiant centre (between the eyes and the forehead) flew out all the circulars to the heads of the subordinate institutions. And in so far as he, from this armchair, cut across his life by means of his consciousness, so far did his circulars, from this place, cut the patchwork field of everyday life.

Apollon Apollonovich liked to compare this life with a sexual, vegetable or any other need (for example, the need for a quick trip through the St Petersburg prospects).

When he emerged from the cold-permeated walls, Apollon Apollonovich suddenly became an ordinary man in the street.

Only from here did he tower up and madly hover over Russia, in his enemies evoking a fateful comparison (with a bat). These enemies were – all to a man – ordinary folk; this enemy without the walls was himself.

Apollon Apollonovich was particularly efficient today: not once did his bare head nod at a report; Apollon Apollonovich was afraid to display weakness: in the discharging of his official duties! ... To tower up into logical clarity he found particularly difficult today: God knew why, but Apollon Apollonovich had come to the conclusion that his own son, Nikolai Apollonovich, was an out-and-out scoundrel.

. . . .

A window permitted one to see the lower part of the balcony. If one went over to the window one could see the caryatid at the entrance: a bearded man of stone.

Like Apollon Apollonovich, the bearded man of stone rose above the noise of the streets and above the season: the year eighteen twelve had freed him from his scaffolding. The year eighteen hundred and twenty-five had raged beneath him in crowds; the crowd was passing even now – in the year nineteen hundred and five. For five years now Apollon Apollonovich had seen daily from here the smile sculpted in stone; time's tooth was gnawing it away. During five years events had flown past: Anna Petrovna was in Spain; Vyacheslav Konstantinovich was no more; the yellow heel had audaciously mounted the ridges of the Port Arthur heights; China had been in a state of ferment and Port Arthur had fallen.

As he prepared to go out to the crowd of waiting petitioners, Apollon Apollonovich smiled; but the smile proceeded from timidity: something was waiting for him outside the doors.

Apollon Apollonovich had spent his life between two writing desks: the desk of his study and the desk of the Institution. A third favourite place was the senatorial carriage.

And now: he – quailed.

But already the door had opened: the secretary, a young man, with a small medal liberally throbbing somewhere on the starch of his throat, flew up to the elevated personage, with a deferential click of the overstarched edge of his snow-white cuff. And to his timid question Apollon Apollonovich honked:

'No, no! . . . Do as I said . . . And knowest thou,' said Apollon Apollonovich, stopped, corrected himself:

'Dyouknow . . .'

He had meant to say 'do you know', but it had come out as: 'knowest thou . . .'

About his absent-mindedness legends circulated; one day Apollon Apollonovich had appeared at a lofty reception, imagine – without a tie, and stopped by a palace lackey he had got into the greatest confusion, from which the lackey had extricated him by suggesting that he borrow a tie from him.

Cold Fingers

In a grey coat and a tall black top hat Apollon Apollonovich Ableukhov, with a stony face that recalled a paperweight, quickly ran from the carriage and ran up the steps of the entrance, taking off a suede glove on his way.

Quickly he entered the vestibule. The top hat was with caution entrusted to the lackey. With the same caution were surrendered: coat, briefcase and muffler.

Apollon Apollonovich stood before the lackey in meditation; suddenly Apollon Apollonovich turned to him with the question:

'Please be so kind as to tell me: does a young man often come here – yes: a young man?'

'A young man, sir?'

An awkward silence ensued. Apollon Apollonovich was unable to formulate his thought differently. And the lackey could not, of course, guess what young man the *barin* was asking about.

'Young men come seldom, your exc'cy, sir . . .'

'Well, but what about . . . young men with small moustaches?'

'Small moustaches, sir?'

'Black ones.'

'Black ones, sir?'

'Well yes, and . . . wearing a coat . . .'

'They all arrive in coats, sir . . .'

'Yes, but with a turned-up collar . . .'

Something suddenly dawned on the doorman.

'Oh, you mean the one that . . .'

'That's right, yes: him . . .'

'A man like that did come one day, sir . . . he was visiting the young *barin*: only it was quite a long time ago; you know how it is, sir . . . they come and pay a call . . .'

'What did he look like?'

'How do you mean, sir?'

'Did he have a small moustache?'

'That's exactly right, sir!'

'A black one?'

'He had a small black moustache . . .'

'And a coat with a turned-up collar?'

'That's the very man, sir . . .'

Apollon Apollonovich stood for a moment as though rooted to the spot and suddenly: Apollon Apollonovich walked past.

The staircase was covered by a grey velvet carpet; the staircase was, of course, framed by heavy walls; a grey velvet carpet covered those walls. On the walls gleamed an ornamental display of ancient weapons; and beneath a rusty green shield shone a Lithuanian helmet with its spike; the cross-shaped handle of a knight's sword sparkled; here swords were rusting; there – heavily inclined halberds; a many-ringed coat of mail lustrelessly enlivened the walls; and there bowed: a pistol and a six-pointed mace.

The top of the staircase led on to a balustrade; here from a lustreless pedestal of white alabaster a white Niobe raised her alabaster eyes to heaven.

Apollon Apollonovich sharply flung open the door before him, resting his bony hand on its faceted handle: through the enormous hall that stretched excessively in length, resounded the cold step of a heavy tread.

It is Always Like This

Above the empty Petersburg streets flew barely illumined dimnesses; fragments of rainclouds outran one another.

A kind of phosphorescent stain, both misty and deathly, rushed across the sky; the heights became misted by a phosphorescent sheen; and this made the iron roofs and chimneys gleam. Here the green waters of the Moika flowed past; on one side towered that same three-storeyed building with its five white columns; on top there were projections. There, against the bright background of the bright building, one of Her Majesty's cuirassiers was slowly walking. He had a golden, gleaming helmet.

And above the helmet a silver dove had extended its wings.

Nikolai Apollonovich, scented and shaven, was making his way along the Moika, wrapped tightly in furs; his head had sunk into his greatcoat, while his eyes shone somehow strangely; in his soul – tremors without name were rising there; something sinister and sweet was singing there: it was as though within him Aeolus' bag of winds had flown to pieces and the sons of foreign gusts were cruelly chasing him away with whistling lashes to strange and incomprehensible lands.

He thought: was *this* also – love? He remembered: one foggy night, running headlong out of that entrance way there, he had set off in flight towards a cast-iron Petersburg bridge, in order there, on the bridge . . .

He started.

A shaft of light flew by: a black court carriage flew by: past the bright window recesses of *that same* house carried its bright red, as if bloodshot, lamps; on the black flood of the Moika the lamps played and shone; the ghostly contour of a lackey's tricorne and the contour of the wings of his greatcoat flew with the light out of the fog into the fog.

Nikolai Apollonovich stood for a while before the house, reflectively: his heart was hammering within his breast; stood for a while, stood for a while – and suddenly he disappeared into a familiar entrance porch.

In former times he had come here every evening; but now it was more than two months since he had crossed the threshold; and he crossed it now as though he were a thief. In former times a maid in a white apron used to open the door cordially; would say:

'Good day, *barin*,' with a sly smile.

But now? No one would come out to meet him; if he were to ring, the same maid would blink her eyes at him in fright, and would not say, 'Good day, *barin*'; no, he was not going to ring.

Then why was he here?

The entrance-porch door flew open before him; and the entrance-porch door struck him in the back with noise; darkness enveloped him; as though everything had fallen away behind him (this is probably what the first moment after death is like, when the temple of the body comes crashing down from the soul into the abyss of putrefaction); but Nikolai Apollonovich was not thinking about death now – death was far away; in the darkness, evidently, he was thinking about his own gestures, because in the darkness his actions took on a fantastic stamp; on the cold step he sat down near one of the entrance doors, his face lowered into the fur and listening to the beating of his heart; a certain black emptiness was beginning behind his back; a black emptiness was in front.

Thus did Nikolai Apollonovich sit in the darkness.

. . . .

And as he sat, the Neva still went on revealing itself between Alexander Square and Millionnaya; the stone curve of the Winter Canal showed a whining expanse; the Neva rushed from there in an onslaught of wet wind; the soundlessly flying surfaces of its waters began to shimmer, furiously returning to the fog a pale sheen. The smooth walls of the four-storeyed palace flank, speckled with lines, mordantly gleamed with moonlight.

No one, nothing.

Here the canal went on, as ever, pouring the same cholera-infected water into the Neva; and the same small bridge curved as ever; the same nightly female shadow kept running out across the bridge, in order to – throw itself into the water? . . . Liza's shadow?[43] No, not Liza's, but simply – a Petersburg woman's; a Petersburg woman ran out here, did not throw herself into the Neva: having cut across the Winter Canal, she quickly ran away from some yellow house on the Gagarin Embankment, below which she stood every evening, looking long at a window.

A quiet lapping remained behind her back: before her spread the square; endless statues, greenish ones, bronze ones, revealed themselves from everywhere above the dark red walls; Hercules and Poseidon[44] went on surveying the expanses in the night as ever; on the other side of the Neva a colossus rose – in the contours of the islands and the houses; and sorrowfully cast amber eyes into the fog; and seemed to be weeping; a row of riverside street lamps dropped fiery tears into the Neva; its surface was burned through by simmering gleams.

Higher up, ragged arms mournfully stretched some kind of vague outlines across the sky; swarm upon swarm they rose above the Neva's waves, racing away towards the zenith; and when they touched the zenith, then, impetuously attacking, from the sky the phosphorescent stain hurled itself upon them. Only in one place that had not been touched by chaos – there, where by day the heavy stone bridge threw itself across – enormous clusters of diamonds showed strangely misty.

The female shadow, face set into a small muff, ran along to the Moika to that same entrance porch from which it had run in the evenings and where now on the cold step, below the door, sat Nikolai Apollonovich; the entrance-porch door opened before her; the darkness enveloped her; as though everything had fallen away behind her; the little lady in black thought for a while in the entrance porch about simple and earthly things; in a moment she would give instructions for a samovar to be brought; she had already stretched out her hand to the bell, and – then saw: some kind of outline, a mask, it seemed, rose before her from the step.

And when the door opened and a shaft of light illumined the darkness of the entrance porch for a moment, the exclamation of a frightened chambermaid confirmed it all for her, because in the open door there first appeared an apron and an overstarched cap; and then from the door shrank back – both apron and cap. In the bright flare of light a scene of indescribable strangeness was revealed, and the little lady's black outline rushed out of the open door.

Behind her back, out of the murk, rose a rustling, dark crimson clown with a small, bearded, trembling mask.

One could see from the murk how soundlessly and slowly from the satin-rustling shoulders slid the furs of the Nikolayevka,[45] how two red hands painfully stretched towards the door. At this point, of course, the door closed, cutting through the shaft of light and throwing the entrance-porch staircase back into complete emptiness, darkness: crossing the threshold of death, thus do we throw back our bodies into the darkened abyss that has just shone with light.

. . . .

A second later Nikolai Apollonovich leapt out on to the street; from under the skirts of his greatcoat dangled a piece of red silk; his nose tucked into his Nikolayevka, Nikolai Apollonovich Ableukhov raced in the direction of the bridge.

. . . .

Petersburg, Petersburg!

Falling like fog, you have pursued me, too, with idle cerebral play: you are a cruel-hearted tormentor; you are an unquiet ghost; for years you have attacked me; I ran through your dreadful prospects and took a flying leap on to the cast-iron bridge that began from the limit of the earth, leading into the limitless distance; beyond the Neva, in that other-worldly, green distance there – the ghosts of islands and houses arose, seducing with the vain hope that world is reality and that it is not a howling limitlessness that drives the pale smoke of the clouds into the Petersburg street.

From the islands trail restless ghosts; thus the swarm of visions repeats itself, reflected by the prospects, driving one another way down the prospects, reflected in one another, like a mirror in a mirror, where the very moment of time itself expands in the boundlessness of zones: and as you plod your way from entrance porch to entrance porch, you experience centuries.

Oh, great bridge, shining with electricity!

I remember a certain fateful moment; over your damp railings I too leant on a September night: a moment – and my body would have flown into the mists.

O, green waters, seething with bacilli!

Another moment and you would have wound me, too, into your shadow. The restless shadow, preserving the aspect of an ordinary man in the street, would have ambiguously begun to loom in the draught of the damp little canal; over his shoulder the passer-by would have seen: a bowler, a walking-stick, a coat, ears, a nose and a moustache . . .

He would have gone further . . . to the cast-iron bridge.

On the cast-iron bridge he would have turned round; and he would have seen nothing: above the wet railings, above the greenish water that seethed with bacilli would have merely flown past into the draughts of the Neva's wind – a bowler, a walking-stick, ears, a nose and a moustache.

You Will Never Forget Him

In this chapter we have seen Senator Ableukhov; we have also seen the senator's idle thoughts in the form of the senator's house and in the form of the senator's son, who also carries his own idle thoughts in his head; we have seen, finally, another idle shadow – the stranger.

This shadow arose accidentally in Senator Ableukhov's consciousness and received there an ephemeral existence of its own; but Apollon Apollonovich's consciousness is a shadowy consciousness, because he too is the possessor of an ephemeral existence and is a product of the author's fantasy: a superfluous, idle, cerebral play.

The author, having spread out scenes of illusions, ought to clear them away as soon as possible, breaking off the thread of the narrative if only with this sentence; but . . . the author will not act thus: he has sufficient right not to.

Cerebral play is only a mask; behind this mask the invasion of the brain by forces unknown to us is accomplished: and even if Apollon Apollonovich is woven from our brains, he will none the less be able to frighten with another, stupendous existence that attacks by night. Apollon Apollonovich is endowed with the attributes of this existence; all his cerebral play is endowed with this existence.

Once his brain has come into play with the mysterious stranger, that stranger exists, really does exist: he will not disappear from the Petersburg prospects while a senator with such thoughts exists, because thought, too, exists.

And so let our stranger be a real live stranger! And let my stranger's two shadows be real live shadows!

Those dark shadows will follow, they will follow on the stranger's heels, in the same way as the stranger himself will directly follow the senator; the aged senator will pursue you, he will pursue you, too, reader, in his black carriage: and from this day forth you will never forget him!

END OF THE FIRST CHAPTER

CHAPTER THE SECOND

in which the story is told of a meeting
fraught with consequences

> I myself, though in books and words
> My confrères level mocking chat,
> I am a philistine, as well you know,
> And in that sense a democrat.[1]
>
> A. Pushkin

The Diary of Events

Our respectable citizens do not read the newspapers' 'Diary of
Events'; in October of the year 1905 the 'Diary of Events' was not
even read at all; our respectable citizens were probably reading the
leading articles in the *Comrade*,[2] unless, that is, they were subscribers
to the most recent, thunder-bearing newspapers; these latter kept a
diary of rather different events.

However, all the other real Russian men-in-the-street, as though
it were natural, rushed to the 'Diary of Events'; I too rushed to the
'Diary'; and reading this 'Diary', am splendidly informed. Well,
who, in fact, actually read all the reports of robberies, witches and
spirits in the year 1905? Everyone read the leaders, of course. The
reports quoted here will probably be recalled by no one.

It is a true story ... Here are some newspaper cuttings from that
time (the author will be silent): alongside notification of robberies,
rape, the theft of diamonds and the disappearance from a small
provincial town of some literary man or other (Daryalsky,[3] I
believe) together with diamonds worth a respectable sum, we have
a series of interesting news items – sheer fantasy, perhaps, that
would make the head of any reader of Conan Doyle spin. In a word
– here are some newspaper cuttings.

'The Diary of Events'.

'*First of October*. According to the account of a *coursiste* of the higher medical assistant courses, N.N., we publish a report concerning a certain exceedingly mysterious event. Late on the evening of the first of October, the *coursiste* N.N. was walking near the Chernyshev Bridge.[4] There, near the bridge, the *coursiste* observed a very strange sight: above the canal, in the middle of the night, against the railings of the bridge a red satin domino was dancing; on the red domino's face was a black lace mask.'

'*Second of October*. According to the account of the schoolmistress M.M. we notify the respected public of a mysterious event near one of our suburban schools. The schoolmistress M.M. was giving her morning lesson in O.O. municipal school; the windows of the school looked on to the street; suddenly outside the window a pillar of dust began to swirl with violent force, and the schoolmistress M. M., together with her sprightly youngsters, naturally rushed to the windows of O.O. municipal school; but great was the confusion of class and class preceptress when a red domino, situated in the centre of the dust he had raised, ran up to the windows of O.O. municipal school and pressed a black lace mask to the window! In O.O. municipal school lessons ceased . . .'

'*Third of October*. At a spiritualist seance that took place in the flat of the respected Baroness R.R. the amicably assembled spiritualists formed a spiritualistic chain; but hardly had they formed the chain, when in the midst of it a domino was discovered who, while dancing, touched with the folds of his cape the tip of titular councillor S.'s nose. A physician at the G. Hospital has ascertained that there is a most violent burn on titular councillor S.'s nose: the tip of the nose is, according to rumour, covered with purple spots. In a word, the red domino is everywhere.'

And finally: '*Fourth of October*. The inhabitants of the suburb of I. have unanimously fled in the face of the domino's appearance: a number of protests are being drawn up; the U. Cossack Hundred has been called to the suburb.'

This domino, this domino – what can it mean? Who is the *coursiste* N.N., who are M.M., the class's preceptress, the Baroness R.R., and so on? . . . In the year 1905, reader, you did not of course read the 'Diary of Events'. Then blame yourself, and not the author: but the 'Diary of Events', believe me, ran all the way to the library.

What is a newspaper contributor? He is, in the first place, a functionary of the periodical press; and as a functionary of the press (of a sixth of the world) he receives for a line – five copecks, seven copecks, ten copecks, fifteen copecks, twenty copecks, reporting in a line all that is and all that never was. If one were to put together the newspaper lines of any newspaper contributor, the single line formed of their lines would entwine the terrestrial globe with that which took place and that which did not.

Such are the respected characteristics of the majority of contributors to extreme right-wing, right-wing, centrist, moderate liberal and, last but not least, revolutionary newspapers and, combined with a calculation of their quantity and quality, these respected characteristics are simply the key that opens the truth of the year 1905 – the truth of the 'Diary of Events' under the headline 'The Red Domino'. This is what it was all about: a certain respected contributor to an indubitably respected newspaper, receiving five copecks, suddenly decided to make use of a certain fact that was told to him in a certain house; in that house a lady was the mistress. What it was all about, then, was not the respected contributor who was paid by the line; what it was all about was the lady . . .

But who is the lady?

Very well, we shall start with her.

A lady: hm! And a pretty one . . . What is a lady?

The chiromancer has not revealed the properties of the lady: lonely stands the chiromancer before the riddle that is headed 'lady': how, in that case, is the psychologist – or – pah! – the writer – to tackle the enigma? The enigma will be doubly enigmatic if the lady is a young one, if it be said of her that she is pretty.

So it was like this: there was a certain lady; and out of boredom she attended the courses for women; and again out of boredom sometimes in the mornings she substituted for a schoolmistress at the O.O. municipal school, provided that in the evening she was not at a spiritualist seance on days that were vacant of balls; it goes without saying that the *coursiste* N.N., M.M. (the class preceptress), and R.R. (the spiritualist baroness) were simply a lady: and a pretty lady. The respected newspaper contributor spent evenings at her home.

One day this lady laughingly told him that she had just encountered a red domino in an unlighted entrance porch. Thus did the pretty lady's innocent confession end up in the columns of the newspapers under the heading 'Diary of Events'. And having ended up in the 'Diary of Events', it unravelled into a series of occurrences that never were, and that threatened the peace.

What actually did happen, then? Even rumoured smoke rises from a fire. What then was the fire from which this smoke of a respected newspaper proceeded, smoke about which all Russia read and which, to your shame, you probably have not read?

Sofya Petrovna Likhutina

That lady ... But that lady was Sofya Petrovna; we must at once devote many words to her.

Sofya Petrovna Likhutina was distinguished, perhaps, by an excessive *chevelure*: and she was somehow unusually lissom: if Sofya Petrovna Likhutina had let down her black hair, that black hair would, covering her entire figure, have fallen to her calves; and Sofya Petrovna Likhutina, to be quite honest, simply did not know what to do with this hair of hers, which was so black that there was, perhaps, no object any blacker; because of the excessiveness of her hair, or because of its blackness – whatever the reason: above Sofya Petrovna's lips a fluff appeared, one that threatened her with a real moustache in her old age. Sofya Petrovna Likhutina possessed an unusual facial colour; this colour was simply that of pearl, marked out with the whiteness of apple petals, or else – with a delicate pink; but if anything unexpectedly agitated Sofya Petrovna, she would suddenly turn completely crimson.

Sofya Petrovna Likhutina's sweet little eyes were not sweet little eyes at all, but eyes: were I not afraid of lapsing into a prosaic tone, I should call Sofya Petrovna's sweet little eyes not eyes, but great big eyes of a dark, blue – a dark blue colour (let us call them orbs). These orbs now sparkled, now grew dim, now seemed vacant, somehow faded, immersed in sunken, ominously bluish sockets: and squinted. Her bright red lips were lips that were too large, but her little teeth (ah, her little teeth!): her pearly little teeth! And in addition – her childlike laughter ... This laughter imparted to her protruding lips a kind of charm; her lissom figure also imparted a kind of charm; and again it was excessively lissom: every movement of this figure and of its somehow nervous back was now impetuous, now languid – almost outrageously clumsy.

Sofya Petrovna often wore a black woollen dress that fastened at the back and invested her luxurious forms; if I say *luxurious forms* this means that my vocabulary has dried up, that the banal phrase 'luxurious forms' signifies, one way or the other, a threat to Sofya Petrovna: a premature plumpness by the age of thirty. But Sofya Petrovna Likhutina was twenty-three.

Ah, Sofya Petrovna!

Sofya Petrovna Likhutina lived in a small flat that looked on to the Moika: there from the walls on all sides fell cascades of the brightest, most restless colours: brilliantly fiery there – and here azure. On the walls there were Japanese fans, lace, small pendants, bows, and on the lamps: satin lampshades fluttered satin and paper wings as though they were butterflies from tropical lands; and it seemed that a swarm of these butterflies, suddenly flying off the walls, would spill with azure wings around Sofya Petrovna Likhutina (the officers she knew called her Angel Peri,[5] probably fusing the two concepts 'Angel' and 'Peri' quite simply into one: Angel Peri).

Sofya Petrovna Likhutina had hung up on her walls Japanese landscapes, every single one of which depicted a view of Mount Fujiyama; in the hung-up little landscapes there was no perspective at all; but neither was there any perspective in the little rooms, which were tightly stuffed with armchairs, sofas, pouffes, fans and live Japanese chrysanthemums: perspective was a satin alcove, from behind which Sofya Petrovna would come fluttering out, or a reed curtain that fell down from the door, whispering something, through which she would again come fluttering, or else Fujiyama – the motley background to her luxuriant hair; it should be said: when Sofya Petrovna Likhutina flew through from behind the door to the alcove in the mornings, she was a real Japanese woman. But perspective there was none.

The rooms were – small rooms; each was occupied by only one enormous object: in the tiny bedroom the bed was the enormous object: in the tiny bathroom it was the bath; in the drawing-room it was the bluish alcove; in the dining-room it was the table-cum-sideboard; in the maid's room the object was her maid; in her husband's room the object was, of course, her husband.

Well, so how could there be any perspective?

All six tiny rooms were heated by steam central heating, which meant that in the little flat you were suffocated by a humid, hothouse heat; the panes of the windows sweated; and Sofya Petrovna's visitor sweated; both maid and husband eternally sweated; Sofya Petrovna Likhutina was herself covered in perspiration, like a Japanese chrysanthemum in warm dew. Well, so how could any perspective be established in such a hothouse?

And there was no perspective.

Sofya Petrovna's Visitors

The visitor to the hothouse of Sofya Petrovna, Angel Peri (he was obliged, incidentally, to purvey chrysanthemums to the angel), always praised her Japanese landscapes, adding in passing his opinions on painting in general; and knitting her small black eyebrows, Angel Peri would at one point authoritatively blurt out: 'This landscape belongs to the pen of Hadusai'[6] . . . The angel decidedly confused all proper names and all foreign words. The visitor who was a painter would take exception to this; and after that he would not address Angel Peri with any more lectures on painting in general: even so, with the last of her pocket money this angel went on buying landscapes and would admire them in solitude for hours, days and months.

Sofya Petrovna did not entertain the visitor in any way: if he were a young man of polite society, devoted to amusements, she considered it necessary to laugh loudly at all the joking, not-at-all joking and most serious things he said; she laughed at everything, turning crimson with laughter, and perspiration covered her tiny nose: the young man of polite society would also then turn crimson for some reason; perspiration covered his nose, too: the young man of society would admire her young, but far from politely social laughter; admire it so much that he classed Sofya Petrovna Likhutina as belonging to the *demi-monde*; meanwhile on the table appeared a collection box with the inscription 'Charitable Collection' and Sofya Petrovna Likhutina, Angel Peri, laughing loudly, would exclaim: 'You've told me another "fifi" – now you must pay.' (Sofya Petrovna Likhutina had recently founded a charitable collection for the benefit of the unemployed, into which payments were to be made for each social 'fifi': 'fifis' were what she for some reason called any intentionally-uttered stupid remark, deriving this word from 'fie' . . .). And Baron Ommau-Ommergau, one of Her Majesty's Yellow Cuirassiers, and Count Aven, one of her Blue Cuirassiers, and Leib Hussar Shporyshev, and a clerk of special assignments in Ableukhov's office, Verhefden (all young men of polite society) uttered 'fifi' after 'fifi', putting twenty-copeck piece after twenty-copeck piece into the tin box.

But why did so many officers visit her? Oh my goodness, she danced at balls; and while she was not a lady of the *demi-monde*, she was pretty; lastly, she was an officer's wife.

If, however, Sofya Petrovna's visitor turned out either himself to be a musician, or was a music critic, or simply a music lover, Sofya Petrovna explained to him that her idols were 'Duncan' and 'Nikisch';[7] in enthusiastic expressions which were less verbal than gesticulatory, she explained that she herself intended to study meloplastics,[8] so as to be able to dance 'The Ride of the Valkyries' neither better nor worse than it was danced in Bayreuth; the musician, music critic or simple music lover, shaken by her incorrect pronunciation of the two names (he himself said Duncan and Nikisch, not Duncan and Nikisch), would conclude that Sofya Petrovna Likhutina was quite simply an 'empty little female'; and become more playful; meanwhile the very pretty maid would bring a gramophone into the little room: and from its red horn the gramophone's tin throat would belch forth 'The Ride of the Valkyries' at the guest. That Sofya Petrovna Likhutina did not miss a single fashionable opera, this circumstance the guest would forget: he became crimson and excessively familiar. Such a guest was always shown the door of Sofya Petrovna Likhutina's flat; and for this reason musicians who performed for polite society were rare in the little hothouse; while the representatives of polite society, Count Aven, Baron Ommau-Ommergau, Shporyshev and Verhefden, did not permit themselves unseemly escapades in relation to a woman who was, after all, an officer's wife who bore the name of the old noble family, Likhutin: and so Count Aven, and Baron Ommau-Ommergau, and Shporyshev, and Verhefden, continued to visit. For a time there had also been a student who had quite often moved among their number, Nikolenka Ableukhov. And then suddenly disappeared.

Sofya Petrovna's visitors somehow fell of their own accord into two categories: the category of guests from polite society and 'guests so to speak'. These guests-so-to-speak were not really guests at all: they were all welcome visitors . . . for the unburdening of her soul; these visitors had not made efforts to be received in the little hothouse; not in the slightest! The Angel dragged them to her flat almost by force; and, having dragged them there by force, at once returned their visit: in their presence the Angel Peri sat with compressed lips: did not laugh, did not indulge in caprice, did not flirt at all, displaying an extreme shyness and an extreme muteness, while the guests-so-to-speak stormily argued one with the other and one heard: 'revolution-evolution.' And again: 'revolution-evolution.' They only argued about one thing, these guests-so-to-speak; they were neither golden nor even silver youth: they were poor, copper youth who had obtained their education on their own work-earned farthings; in a word, they were the studying youth of the higher educational establishments, sporting an abundance of foreign words: 'social revolution'. And then again: 'social evolution'. Angel Peri unfailingly got those words mixed up.

The Officer: Sergei Sergeich Likhutin

Among the rest of the studying youth there was a certain respected, radiant person in that circle who was a regular visitor to the Likhutins: the *coursiste* Varvara Yevgrafovna (here Varvara Yevgrafovna might from time to time encounter *Nicolas* Ableukhov himself).

One day, under the radiant person's influence, the Angel Peri illumined with her presence – well, imagine it: a political rally!

Under the radiant person's influence, the Angel Peri placed on the table her very own copper collection box with the nebulous inscription: 'Charitable Collection'. This box was, of course, intended for the guests; while all the persons who belonged to the guests-so-to-speak had been once and for all exempted by Sofya Petrovna Likhutina from the requisitions; but requisitions were imposed on Count Aven, and Baron Ommau-Ommergau, and Shporyshev, and Verhefden. Under the radiant person's influence Angel Peri began to go to the municipal school of O.O. in the mornings and repeated Karl Marx's *Manifesto* over and over again to no purpose whatever. The point was that at this time she received daily visits from a student, Nikolenka Ableukhov, whom she could without risk introduce both to Varvara Yevgrafovna (who was in love with Nikolenka) and to Her Majesty's Yellow Cuirassier. Being Ableukhov's son, Ableukhov was, of course, received everywhere.

As a matter of fact, ever since the time that Nikolenka had suddenly stopped going to visit Angel Peri, that angel had suddenly, in secret from the guests-so-to-speak, gone fluttering off to the spiritualists and to the baroness (oh, what is her name?) who was preparing to enter a nunnery. Ever since, on the table before Sofya Petrovna lay in splendour a magnificently bound little book, *Man and His Bodies* by some Madame Henri Besançon or other (Sofya Petrovna was again confused: it was not Henri Besançon,⁹ but Annie Besant).

Sofya Petrovna assiduously concealed her new passion from both Baron Ommau-Ommergau and Varvara Yevgrafovna; in spite of her infectious laughter and her tiny little forehead, the Angel Peri's secretiveness attained improbable proportions: thus, not once did Varvara Yevgrafovna meet Count Aven, nor even Baron Ommau-Ommergau. On one occasion only did she accidentally catch sight in the hallway of a Leib Hussar's fur hat with a plume. But to this Leib Hussar's hat with a plume no reference was thereafter made.

There was something behind all this. God knows!

Sofya Petrovna Likhutina had yet one more visitor; an officer: Sergei Sergeyevich Likhutin; as a matter of fact, he was her husband; he was in charge of provisions somewhere out there; early in the morning he left the house; reappeared no earlier than midnight; equally meekly greeted the ordinary guests and the guests-so-to-speak, with equal meekness said a 'fifi' for the sake of propriety, dropping a twenty-copeck piece into the collection box (if Count Aven or Baron Ommau-Ommergau were present at the time), or modestly nodded his head at the words 'revolution-evolution', drank a cup of tea and went to his little room; the young men of polite society privately called him 'the little army fellow', while the studying youth called him 'the Bourbon officer' (in 1905 Sergei Sergeyevich had had the misfortune to defend the Nikolayevsky Bridge from the workers with his half-company). As a matter of fact, Sergei Sergeich Likhutin would have been best pleased to abstain both from 'fifis' and from the words 'revolution-evolution'. As a matter of fact, he would not have been averse to going to the baroness's for a little spiritualist seance; but he made absolutely no attempt to insist on his modest wish by using his rights as a husband, for in absolutely no way was he a despot in relation to Sofya Petrovna; he loved Sofya Petrovna with all the strength of his soul; moreover: two and a half years earlier he had married her against the wishes of his parents, very rich landowners in Simbirsk; after that, he had been cursed by his father and deprived of his fortune; after that, to everyone's surprise, he had entered the Gregorian Regiment.[10]

There was yet another visitor: the crafty *khokhol*-Little Russian,[11] Lippanchenko;[12] this was an individual of thoroughly voluptuary temperament who called Sofya Petrovna not an angel but ... *dushkan*;[13] to himself, however, the crafty *khokhol*-Little Russian Lippanchenko called her quite plainly and simply: *brankukan, brankukashka* or *brankukanchik*[14] (there are some words, for you, then!) But Lippanchenko kept within the bounds of propriety: and so he was received in that house.

Sofya Petrovna's most good-natured husband, Sergei Sergeyevich Likhutin, a second lieutenant in the Gregorian Regiment of His Majesty the King of Siam, took a meek attitude towards the revolutionary circle of his better half's acquaintances; the representatives of the polite society circle he regarded merely with emphasized good humour; while the *khokhol*-Little Russian he only barely tolerated: this crafty *khokhol* did not at all, incidentally, resemble a *khokhol*: he sooner resembled a cross between a Semite and a Mongol; he was both tall and fat; this gentleman's yellowish face floated unpleasantly in its own chin, which was pushed out by a starched collar; and Lippanchenko wore a yellow and red satin tie, fastened with a paste jewel, sporting a striped dark yellow suit and a pair of shoes the same colour; but on top of this, Lippanchenko shamelessly dyed his hair brown. Of himself Lippanchenko said that he exported Russian pigs and was preparing to get rich once and for all on this swinishness.

Be that as it may, it was Lippanchenko, he alone, for whom second lieutenant Likhutin had no especial liking. But why ask whom second lieutenant Likhutin did not like: second lieutenant Likhutin liked everyone, of course: but if there was one person he had liked especially at one time, that person was Nikolai Apollonovich Ableukhov: after all, they had known each other since the earliest years of their adolescence. In the first place, Nikolai Apollonovich had been best man at Likhutin's wedding, in the second, a daily visitor to the flat on the Moika for a period of almost one and a half years. But then he had disappeared without trace.

It was not Sergei Sergeyevich, of course, who was to blame for the disappearance of the senator's son, but the senator's son, or even Angel Peri herself.

Ah, Sofya Petrovna, Sofya Petrovna! In one word: a lady . . . And from a lady what may one ask?

The Slim and Handsome Best Man

Even on the first day of her, so to speak, 'ladyhood' during the accomplishment of the ritual of marriage, when Nikolai Apollonovich held above her husband, Sergei Sergeyevich, the most solemn crown, Sofya Petrovna Likhutina had been tormentingly struck by the slim and handsome best man, by the colour of his unearthly, dark blue, enormous eyes, the whiteness of his marble face and the godlike quality of his blond flaxen hair: for those eyes did not look, as they often did later, from behind the dim lenses of a pince-nez, and his face was supported by the gold collar of a brand new uniform jacket (not every student has such a collar). Well, and . . . Nikolai Apollonovich started visiting the Likhutins at first once every two weeks; later it became once a week; two, three, four times a week; in the end he came daily. Soon Sofya Petrovna noticed under the mask of these daily visits that Nikolai Apollonovich's face, godlike, stern, had turned into a mask: the little grimaces, the aimless rubbing of his sometimes sweaty hands, and ultimately the unpleasant froglike expression of his smile, which proceeded from the play of every conceivable type that never left his face, obscured that face from her for ever. And as soon as Sofya Petrovna noticed this, to her horror she realized that she was in love with *that* face, *that* one, and not this. Angel Peri wanted to be a model wife: and the dreadful thought that, while yet faithful, she had already fallen for someone who was not her husband – this thought completely shattered her. But more, more: from behind the mask, the grimaces, the froglike lips, she unconsciously tried to call forth her irrevocably lost being-in-love: she tormented Ableukhov, showered him with insults; but, concealing it from herself, dogged his footsteps, tried to find out what were his aspirations and tastes, unconsciously followed them in the constant hope of finding in them the authentic, godlike countenance; so she started to put on airs: first meloplastics appeared on the scene, then the cuirassier, Baron Ommau-Ommergau, and finally Varvara Yevgrafovna with the tin box for the collection of 'fifis'.

In a word, Sofya Petrovna began to grow confused: hating, she loved; loving, she hated.

Ever since then, her real husband had become no more than a visitor to the little flat on the Moika: began to take charge of provisions somewhere out there; left the house early in the morning; reappeared at around midnight: said a 'fifi' for the sake of propriety, dropping a twenty-copeck piece into the collection box, or modestly nodding his head at the words 'revolution-evolution', drinking a cup of tea and going off to his room to sleep: for he had to get up as early as possible in the morning and walk to somewhere out there in order to take charge of provisions. Sergei Sergeich had only begun, somewhere out there, to take charge of provisions because he did not want to hamper his wife's freedom.

But Sofya Petrovna could not endure freedom: after all, she had such a tiny, tiny little forehead; together with the tiny forehead there lay concealed within her volcanoes of the most profound emotions: because she was a lady; and in ladies one must not stir up chaos: in this chaos ladies keep concealed all manner of cruelties, crimes, degradations, all manner of violent furies, as well as all manner of heroic actions such as have not been seen on the earth before; in every lady a criminal is concealed: but let a crime be committed, and nothing but holiness will remain in the truly ladylike soul.

Soon we shall without doubt demonstrate to the reader the division that also existed in Nikolai Apollonovich's soul into two independent values: a godlike ice – and a simply froglike slush; this duality is a typical characteristic of all ladies: duality is in essence not a masculine, but a ladylike property; the number two is the symbol of the lady; the symbol of the man is unity. Only thus is the triality obtained without which it is questionable whether the domestic hearth would be possible.

We have noted Sofya Petrovna's duality above: a nervousness in her movements – and an awkward languor; an insufficiency of forehead and an excessive profusion of hair; Fujiyama, Wagner, the faithfulness of the female heart – and 'Henri Besançon', the gramophone, Baron Ommergau and even Lippanchenko. Were Sergei Sergeich Likhutin or Nikolai Apollonovich real unities, and not dualities, there would have been a triality; and Sofya Petrovna would have found life's harmony in a union with a man; the gramophone, meloplastics, Henri Besançon, Lippanchenko, even Ommau-Ommergau would have flown to the devil.

But there was not just one Ableukhov: there was Ableukhov number one, the godlike one, and Ableukhov number two, the little frog. It all happened because of that.

But what happened?

In Sofya Petrovna, Nikolai Apollonovich-the-little-frog fell for her deep little heart that was raised above all the fuss and bustle; not her tiny little forehead or her hair; while Nikolai Apollonovich's godlike nature, despising love, was cynically intoxicated by meloplastics; *both* argued within him about whom they should love: the little female or the angel? The angel, Sofya Petrovna, as naturally befitted an angel, loved only the *god*: while the little female got confused: at first she was indignant at the unpleasant smile, but subsequently she came to love precisely her own indignation; then, having come to love hatred, she came to love the nasty smile, but with a strange (everyone would say, depraved) love: there was in all this something unnaturally burning, unfathomably sweet and fateful.

Had the criminal awoken within Sofya Petrovna Likhutina then? Ah, Sofya Petrovna, Sofya Petrovna! In a word: a lady and a lady . . .

And from a lady what may one ask?

The Red Buffoon[15]

As a matter of fact, in recent months Sofya Petrovna Likhutina had been behaving extremely provocatively with the object of her affections: in front of the gramophone horn that belched forth 'The Death of Siegfried', she had studied body movement (and how!), raising almost to her knees her rustling silk skirt; moreover: from beneath the table her foot had, more than once or twice, touched Ableukhov. It was not surprising that the latter had more than once endeavoured to embrace the Angel; but then the Angel had slipped away, first showering her admirer with cold; and then again resumed her old ways. But when one day, defending Greek art, she proposed to form a nudist circle, Nikolai Apollonovich could hold out no longer: all his hopeless passion of many days rushed to his head (Nikolai Apollonovich dropped her on the sofa in the struggle) . . . But Sofya Petrovna agonizingly bit to blood the lips that sought her lips, and as Nikolai Apollonovich went out of his mind with pain, a slap to his face resounded in the Japanese room.

'Ooo . . . Freak, frog[16] . . . Ooo – red buffoon.'

Nikolai Apollonovich replied calmly and coldly:

'If I am a red buffoon, then you are a Japanese doll . . .'

With exceeding dignity did he draw himself erect by the door; at that moment his face took on precisely that remote expression that had once captivated her, and remembering it, she imperceptibly fell in love with him; and when Nikolai Apollonovich left, she crashed to the floor, both scratching, and biting the carpet as she wept; suddenly she leapt to her feet and extended her arms through the doorway:

'Come to me, come back – god!'

But in reply to her the exit door banged: Nikolai Apollonovich fled to the large St Petersburg Bridge. Later on we shall see him take by the Bridge a certain fateful decision (upon the completion of a certain act, to destroy his own life). The expression 'Red Buffoon' had wounded him in the extreme.

Sofya Petrovna Likhutina did not see him any more: in a kind of wild protest against Ableukhov's passion for 'revolution-evolution' Angel Peri involuntarily flew away from the studying youth, flying instead to Baroness R.R. for a spiritualist seance. And Varvara Yevgrafovna began to call more rarely. On the other hand, frequent visits were once again made by: Count Aven, Baron Ommau-Ommergau, Shporyshev, Verhefden, and even ... Lippanchenko: and Lippanchenko's visits were more frequent than those of the others. With Count Aven, Baron Ommau-Ommergau, Shporyshev, Verhefden, and even ... Lippanchenko she laughed without growing tired of it; suddenly, breaking off her laughter, she would ask perkily:

'After all, I'm a doll – am I not?'

And they replied to her with 'fifis', poured silver into the little tin box with the inscription 'Charitable Collection'. And Lippanchenko replied to her: 'You are a *dushkan*, a *brankukan*, a *bran-kukashka*.' And brought her a small yellow-faced doll as a present.

But when she said this same thing to her husband, her husband made her no reply. Sergei Sergeich Likhutin, second lieutenant in the Gregorian Regiment of His Majesty the King of Siam, went off as though he were going to bed: he was in charge, somewhere out there, of provisions; but going into his room, he sat down to write Nikolai Apollonovich a meek little letter: in the letter he made so bold as to inform Ableukhov that he, Sergei Sergeyevich, second lieutenant in the Gregorian Regiment, most humbly requested the following: while not wishing to meddle for reasons of principle in Nikolai Apollonovich's relations with his preciously beloved spouse, he none the less urgently requested (the word urgently was thrice underlined) to cease visiting their home for ever, as the nerves of his preciously beloved spouse were upset. As far as his behaviour was concerned, Sergei Sergeyevich resorted to concealment; his behaviour did not change one iota; as before, he left very early in the morning; returned towards midnight; said a 'fifi' for propriety's sake if he saw Baron Ommau-Ommergau, frowned ever so slightly if he saw Lippanchenko, nodded his head in most good-humoured fashion at the words 'evolution-revolution', drank a cup of tea and quietly disappeared: he was in charge – somewhere out there – of provisions.

Sergei Sergeich was tall of stature, had a blond beard, possessed a nose, a mouth, hair, ears and wonderfully shining eyes: but unfortunately he wore dark blue spectacles, and no one knew either the colour of his eyes or the wonderful expression of those eyes.

A Vileness, a Vileness and a Vileness

In those frozen days of early October Sofya Petrovna was in an extraordinary state of agitation; upon being left alone in the little hothouse she would suddenly begin to wrinkle her little forehead, and grow flushed: turn crimson; go over to the window in order to wipe the sweating panes with a small handkerchief of delicate transparent batiste; the pane would begin to squeak, revealing a view of the canal with a gentleman in a top hat walking by – no more; as though she were disappointed in her presentiment, Angel Peri would begin to pick and shred the dampened handkerchief with her little teeth, and then run to put on her black plush coat and matching hat (Sofya Petrovna dressed most modestly), in order, pressing her fur muff to her little nose, aimlessly to wander from the Moika to the embankment; she even once looked in at the Ciniselli Circus[17] and saw there a wonder of nature: a bearded lady; but most often she called by at the kitchen and talked in whispers with the young chambermaid, Mavrushka, a very pretty young girl in an apron and a butterfly cap. And her eyes crossed: thus always did her eyes cross at moments of agitation.

Then one day, when Lippanchenko was there, with loud laughter she snatched a pin from her hat and stuck it into her little finger:

'Look: it doesn't hurt; and there's no blood: I'm made of wax . . . a doll.'

But Lippanchenko did not understand at all: he burst out laughing, and said:

'You're not a doll: you're a *dushkan*.'

And flying into a rage, Angel Peri drove him away from

her. Seizing from the table his hat with earflaps, Lippanchenko retreated.

And she rushed about the little hothouse, wrinkling her brow, flushing, wiping the pane; a view of the canal with a carriage flying past came into view: no more.

What more could there have been?

The fact of the matter was this: several days ago Sofya Petrovna Likhutina had returned home from Baroness R.R. At Baroness R.R.'s that evening there had been table-tapping; whitish sparks had run across the wall; and on one occasion the table had even jumped: no more; but Sofya Petrovna's nerves were stretched to the limit (after a seance she wandered about the streets), and the entrance porch to her house was not lit (the entrance porches to blocks of cheap flats are not lit): and inside the black entrance Sofya Petrovna very distinctly saw a spot even blacker than the darkness staring at her – it looked like a black mask; something showed dimly red beneath the mask, and with all her strength Sofya Petrovna tugged at the bell. And when the door flew open and a stream of bright light from the hallway fell on the staircase, Mavrushka uttered a scream and threw up her hands: Sofya Petrovna saw nothing, because she impetuously flew past into the flat. Mavrushka saw: behind the *barynya*'s back a red, satin domino stretched forward its black mask, surrounded from below by a thick lace fan that was of course black, so that this black lace fell towards Sofya Petrovna's shoulder (it was a good thing that she did not turn her little head); the red domino stretched out to Mavrushka its bloody sleeve, from which a visiting card protruded; and when the door slammed in front of the hand, Sofya Petrovna, too, saw the visiting card by the door (it had doubtless flown through the crack in the doorway); but what was drawn on that visiting card? A skull and crossbones instead of a nobleman's coronet and also the words, set in fashionable script: 'I await you at the masked ball – at such-and-such a place, on such-and-such a date'; and then the signature: 'The Red Buffoon'.

Sofya Petrovna spent the whole evening in a dreadful state of agitation. Who could have dressed up in a red domino? Of course, it was he, Nikolai Apollonovich: after all, she seemed to remember she had once called him by that name . . . And the Red Buffoon had arrived. In that case what name was one to give to such a piece of behaviour with a defenceless woman? Well, was it not a vileness?

A vileness, a vileness and a vileness.

She wished her husband, the officer, would hurry up and come home: he would teach the insolent fellow a lesson. Sofya Petrovna blushed, squinted, bit her handkerchief and became covered in perspiration. If only someone would come: Aven, or Baron Ommau-Ommergau, or Shporyshev, or even . . . Lippanchenko.

But no one appeared.

Well, so in that case suddenly it was not he? And Sofya Petrovna felt distinctly upset: she felt somehow loath to part with her thoughts about the buffoon being him; in these thoughts together with anger was interlaced that same sweet, familiar, fateful emotion; she must have wanted him to prove to be a most complete scoundrel.

No – it was not he: so he was not the scoundrel, not the naughty boy! . . . Well, but what if he really were the Red Buffoon? Who the Red Buffoon could be, to this she could not offer any coherent answer to herself – and yet . . . And her heart fell – it was not he.

She at once ordered Mavrushka to say nothing: but she went to the masked ball; and in secret from her meek husband: for the first time she went to a masked ball.

The fact of the matter was that Sergei Sergeich Likhutin had most sternly forbidden her to attend masked balls. He was a strange fellow: valued his epaulettes, his sword, his officer's honour (was he not a Bourbon?)

Meekness upon meekness . . . to the point of eccentricity, to his officer's honour. He would say only: 'I give you my officer's word of honour – this will happen, and this will not.' And – would not on any account be moved: a kind of inflexibility, cruelty. When, as he usually did, he raised his spectacles on to his forehead, became cold, unpleasant, wooden, as if carved out of white cypress, he would bang his cypress fist on the table: at such times Angel Peri would fly out of her husband's room in fear: her little nose wrinkled, teardrops fell, the bedroom door would be bitterly locked.

Among Sofya Petrovna's visitors, one of the guests-so-to-speak who talked about 'revolution-evolution' was a certain respected newspaper contributor: Neintelpfain; black-haired, wrinkled, with a nose that was bent from top to bottom, and with a little beard that was bent in the opposite direction. Sofya Petrovna revered him dreadfully: and in him did she confide; he it was who had taken her to the masked ball, where some kind of buffoon—harlequins, Italian maidens, Spanish maidens and oriental women flashed the hostile pinpoints of their eyes at one another from behind black velvet masks; on the arm of Neintelpfain, the respected newspaper contributor, Sofya Petrovna modestly walked about the halls in her black domino. And some kind of red, satin domino kept rushing about the halls, kept looking for someone, stretching before him his black mask, below which swished a thick fan made of lace – also black, of course.

At this point it was that Sofya Petrovna Likhutina told the faithful Neintelpfain about a mysterious event, well, of course, hiding all the threads; the little Neintelpfain, the respected newspaper contributor, received five copecks per line: ever since that time it had invariably, invariably been the case that each day without fail there appeared in the 'Diary of Events' a note about – a red domino, a red domino!

People discussed the domino, grew dreadfully excited about him and argued about him: some saw in him revolutionary terror; while others merely said nothing and shrugged their shoulders. Bells rang in the Secret Political Department.

People talked of that appearance of the domino on the streets of Petersburg even in the little hothouse; and Count Aven, and Baron Ommau-Ommergau, and Leib Hussar Shporyshev, and Verhefden made 'fifis' in this connection, and a ceaseless rain of twenty-copeck pieces flew into the little copper collection box; only the crafty *khokhol*-Little Russian Lippanchenko seemed crookedly to laugh. While Sofya Petrovna Likhutina, beside herself, turned crimson, turned pale, became covered in perspiration and bit her handkerchief. Neintelpfain had quite simply proved to be a beast, but Neintelpfain did not show himself: day after day he assiduously teased out his newspaper lines; and the newspaper rigmarole dragged on and on, covering the world with the most utter nonsense.

A Completely Smoked-up Face

Nikolai Apollonovich Ableukhov stood above the staircase balustrade in his little multicoloured robe, scattering in all directions an iridescent gleam, forming a complete contrast to the column and the small alabaster pillar from which a white Niobe raised heavenward her alabaster eyes.

'Nikolai Apollonovich, I expect you took me for someone else . . .'

'I am – I . . .'

There at the bottom stood the stranger with the small black moustache and the coat with the raised collar.

At this point Nikolai Apollonovich bared his teeth in an unpleasant smile from the balustrade:

'Is it you, Aleksandr Ivanovich? . . . Most pleasant!'

And then hypocritically he added:

'I did not recognize you without my glasses . . .'

Overcoming the unpleasant impression of the stranger's presence in the lacquered house, Nikolai Apollonovich continued to nod his head from the balustrade:

'To tell you the truth, I've only just got out of bed: that's why I'm wearing my robe' (as though with this chance remark Nikolai Apollonovich wanted to give the visitor to understand that the latter had inflicted his visit at an inopportune time; on our own part we shall add: every night of late, Nikolai Apollonovich had been missing).

The stranger with the small black moustache presented in his person an exceedingly pathetic spectacle against the rich background of the ornamental display of ancient weapons; none the less the stranger summoned up his courage, continuing with heat to calm Nikolai Apollonovich – half mocking, and half being the most utter simpleton:

'It does not matter at all, Nikolai Apollonovich, that you've just got out of bed . . . The most utter trifle, I assure you: you are not a young lady, and I am not a young lady either . . . Why, I myself have only just risen . . .'

There was nothing for it. Having mastered within his soul the unpleasant impression (it had been evoked by the stranger's appearance – here, in the lacquered house, where the lackeys might be thoroughly puzzled and where, at last, the stranger might be greeted by his papa) – having mastered within his soul the unpleasant impression, Nikolai Apollonovich conceived the design of moving downstairs in order with dignity, in the Ableukhov manner, to lead into the lacquered house the punctilious guest; but, to his annoyance, one of his fur slippers jumped off; and the naked foot began to stagger from under the skirts of the robe; Nikolai Apollonovich stumbled on the steps; and in addition he let the stranger down: in the assumption that Nikolai Apollonovich, in an access of his usual obsequiousness, was rushing down towards him (Nikolai Apollonovich had already manifested in this direction all the impetuosity of his gestures), the stranger with the small black moustache rushed in his turn towards Nikolai Apollonovich, leaving his muddy footprints upon the velvet-grey stairs; but now my stranger stood bewilderedly between the hallway and the summit of the stairs; and as he did so he saw that he was besmirching the carpet; my stranger embarrassedly smiled.

'Please, take off your coat.'

The delicate reminder that it was on no account possible to penetrate into the *barin*'s chambers wearing a coat, belonged to a lackey, into whose hands with despairing independence the stranger shook off his wet little coat; he stood now in a grey, checked suit that had been nibbled by moths. Seeing that the lackey intended to stretch out his hand for the wet bundle, too, my stranger flared up; having flared up, he became doubly disconcerted:

'No, no . . .'

'But please, sir . . .'

'No: *this* I shall take with me . . .'

The stranger with the small black moustache trod with his worn-through boots the shining slippery parquetry with the same doggedness with which he rushed at everything; surprised and fleeting were the glances he cast at the sumptuous perspective of rooms. Nikolai Apollonovich, with particular mildness, gathering up the skirts of his robe, walked ahead of the stranger. To both of them, however, their silent peregrination through these shining perspectives seemed irksome: both were sadly silent; to the stranger with the small black moustache Nikolai Apollonovich presented with relief not his face but his iridescent back; for that reason, doubtless, the smile had also vanished from his hitherto unnaturally smiling lips. For our part, however, let us observe directly: Nikolai Apollonovich was afraid; in his head quickly spun: 'It's probably some charitable collection – for a victimized worker; at the very most – for arms . . .' And in his soul drearily began to whine: 'No, no – not this, or what will happen?'

Before the oak door of his study, Nikolai Apollonovich suddenly turned sharply round to face the stranger; across the faces of both a smile slipped for a moment; both suddenly looked each other in the eye with an expectant expression.

'So please . . . Aleksandr Ivanovich . . .'

'Don't be uneasy . . .'

'Welcome . . .'

'But no, no . . .'

Nikolai Apollonovich's reception room stood in complete contrast to his severe study: it was as multicoloured as . . . as a Bokhara robe; Nikolai Apollonovich's robe, so to speak, extended into all the appurtenances of the room: for example, into the low sofa; it sooner recalled an oriental tapestry couch; the Bokhara robe extended into the wooden stool of dark brown colours; the stool was incrusted with fine bands of ivory and mother-of-pearl; the robe extended further into the Negro shield of thick hide from a rhinoceros that had fallen once upon a time, and into the rusty Sudanese arrow with its massive handle; for some reason it had been hung up on the wall here; lastly, the robe extended into the skin of a multicoloured leopard, thrown to their feet with a gaping maw; on the stool stood a dark blue hookah and a three-legged censer in the form of a sphere pierced with openings and a half moon on top; but most surprising of all was a multicoloured cage in which from time to time green budgerigars began to beat their wings.

Nikolai Apollonovich moved up the multicoloured stool for his guest; the stranger with the black moustache sank on to the edge of the stool and pulled from his pocket a rather cheap cigar case.

'May I?'

'Please do!'

'You don't smoke yourself?'

'No, I don't have the habit . . .'

And at once, growing embarrassed, Nikolai Apollonovich added:

'As a matter of fact, when others are smoking, I . . .'

'You open the small window?'

'Oh come, come! . . .'

'The ventilator?'

'Ach, but no . . . quite the contrary – I was trying to say that smoking rather affords me . . .' Nikolai Apollonovich hurried, but his guest, who was not listening to him, continued to interrupt:

'You yourself leave the room?'

'Ach, but no, I tell you: I was trying to say that I like the smell of tobacco smoke, especially cigars.'

'You shouldn't, Nikolai Apollonovich, you really shouldn't: after smokers . . .'

'Yes? . . .'

'One ought to . . .'

'Yes?'

'Quickly air the room.'

'Oh come, come!'

'Opening both the small window and the ventilator.'

'On the contrary, on the contrary . . .'

. . . .

'Do not defend tobacco, Nikolai Apollonovich: I tell you that from experience . . . Smoke penetrates the grey matter of the brain . . . The cerebral hemispheres become clogged: a general inertia spreads into the organism . . .'

The stranger with the small black moustache gave a familiarly meaningful wink: the stranger saw that the host still doubted the permeability of the brain's grey matter, but because of his habit of being a courteous host he was not going to dispute with his guest: then the stranger with the small black moustache began vexedly to pluck at that small black moustache:

'Take a look at my face.'

Unable to find his spectacles, Nikolai Apollonovich brought his blinking eyelids right up to the stranger's face.

'You see my face?'

'Yes, your face . . .'

'A pale face.'

'Yes, a little on the pale side,' – and a play of all kinds of civilities and their nuances spread over Ableukhov's cheeks.

'A completely green, smoked-up face,' the stranger interrupted him, 'the face of a smoker. I will smoke your room for you, Nikolai Apollonovich.'

Nikolai Apollonovich had long been experiencing an uneasy heaviness, as though what were spreading into the atmosphere of the room were not smoke but lead; Nikolai Apollonovich felt the hemispheres of his brain becoming clogged and a general inertia spreading into his organism, but now he was thinking not about the properties of tobacco smoke but about how he was going to get out of a ticklish incident with dignity, about how – he thought – he would act in the risky eventuality if the stranger, if . . .

This leaden heaviness was in no way related to the rather cheap little cigarette that was extending into the upper regions its bluish streamlet, but was rather related to the host's depressed condition of spirit. Nikolai Apollonovich was expecting that at any second now his uneasy visitor would break off his chatter which he had evidently started with a sole purpose in view – that of tormenting him with expectation – yes: he would break off his chatter and remind him of how he, Nikolai Apollonovich, had once given, through the mediation of a strange stranger – as it were, to put it more precisely . . .

In a word, he had once given an obligation, dreadful for himself, to execute which he was compelled not only by honour; Nikolai Apollonovich had really only given the dreadful promise out of despair; what had prompted him to it was a failure in his life; later that failure had gradually been erased. It might have seemed that the dreadful promise would lose its validity of itself: but the dreadful promise remained: it remained, though only because it had not been retracted: Nikolai Apollonovich, to tell the truth, had thoroughly forgotten about it; but it, the promise, continued to live in the collective consciousness of a certain rash and hasty circle, at the same time as the sense of life's bitterness under the influence of the failure had been erased; Nikolai Apollonovich himself would undoubtedly have classed his promise among promises of a humorous nature.

The appearance of the *raznochinets* with the small black moustache, for the first time after these last two months, filled Nikolai Apollonovich's soul with complete terror. Nikolai Apollonovich quite distinctly remembered an exceedingly sad circumstance. Nikolai Apollonovich quite distinctly remembered all the most minor details of the situation in which he had given his promise and suddenly found those details murderous to himself.

But why ... – was it not so much that he had given a dreadful promise but rather that he had given the dreadful promise to a frivolous party?

The answer to this question was exceedingly simple: Nikolai Apollonovich, in studying the methodology of social phenomena, had doomed the world to fire and the sword.

And so now he turned pale, turned grey and at last turned green; his face even suddenly somehow began to turn dark blue; this latter tinge was probably caused by the atmosphere in the room, which was tobaccofied to the extreme.

The stranger stood up, stretched, squinted tenderly at the little bundle and suddenly gave a childish smile.

'Look, Nikolai Apollonovich' – Nikolai Apollonovich started in fright – '... I haven't really come to see you for tobacco, about tobacco, I mean ... this stuff about tobacco is quite incidental ...'

'I understand.'

'Tobacco is as tobacco does: but I haven't really come to see you about tobacco, but about business ...'

'How pleasant.'

'And even not about business: the whole nub of the matter lies in a service – and you may, of course, refuse me this service ...'

'Oh come, how pleasant ...'

Nikolai Apollonovich turned even bluer; he sat plucking at a button on the sofa; and without managing to pluck the button off, began to pluck horsehair out of the sofa.

'It's extremely awkward for me, but remembering ...'

Nikolai Apollonovich started: the stranger's shrill, high falsetto rent the air; this falsetto was preceded by a second's silence; but that second seemed like an hour to him then, an hour did it seem. And now, hearing the shrill falsetto pronouncing the word 'remembering', Nikolai Apollonovich nearly shrieked out loud:

'My proposal? . . .'

But he at once took himself in hand; and he merely observed:

'Very well, I am at your service,' – and as he did so he thought that it was this politeness that had ruined him . . .

'Remembering your sympathy, I have come . . .'

'Anything I can do,' Nikolai Apollonovich shrieked and as he did so thought that he was a thorough numbskull . . .

'A small, oh, a very small service . . .' (Nikolai Apollonovich listened with keen attention):

'I'm sorry . . . could you let me have an ashtray . . .'

. . . .

Arguments in the Street Became More Frequent

The days were foggy, strange: over the north of Russia poisonous October walked with frozen tread; and in the south he spread muggy mists. Poisonous October blew a golden sylvine whisper, and humbly that whisper lay down on the earth, – and humbly a rustling aspen crimson lay down on the earth, in order to twine and chase at the feet of the passing pedestrian, and to whisper, weaving from the leaves the yellow-red alluvial deposits of words. That sweet peeping of the blue tit, which in September bathes in a leafy wave, had not bathed in a leafy wave for a long time: and the blue tit itself now hopped lonely in a black mesh of branches, which like the mumbling of a toothless old man all autumn sends its whistle out of woodlands, leafless groves, front gardens and parks.

The days were foggy, strange; an icy hurricane was already approaching in shreds of pewter and dark blue cloud; but everyone believed in the spring: the spring was what the newspapers wrote about, the spring was what the civil servants of the fourth class[18] argued; the spring was what a certain government minister, popular at the time, pointed to; the scent, nay, even the violets of early May themselves were what the effusions of a certain Petersburg *coursiste* breathed.

The ploughmen had long ago ceased to claw their eroding lands; the ploughmen left their harrows and wooden ploughs for a while;

the ploughmen gathered under the cottages in their wretched little groups for the joint discussion of newspaper reports; talked and argued, in order suddenly in a unanimous throng to rush towards the *barin*'s colonnaded house, reflected in the torrents of the Volga, the Kama or even the Dnieper; through all the long nights above Russia shone the bloody glow of estates on fire, resolving itself by day into the blackness of smoky columns. But then in the deciduous brushwood thicket one could see a hidden detachment of shaggy-headed Cossacks aiming the muzzles of their rifles, as the shrieking alarm sounded; thereupon the Cossack detachment darted out on their shaggy horses: dark blue, bearded men, brandishing whips, rushed whooping for a long, long time here and there across the autumn meadows.

Thus it was in the villages.

But thus it was in the towns also. In workshops, print shops, barbers' shops, dairies, little taverns, the same loquacious character hung about; with his black shaggy hat pulled down over his eyes and forehead, a hat that had evidently been acquired on the fields of bloodstained Manchuria;[19] and with a Browning that had been borrowed from somewhere stuck in his side pocket, the loquacious character repeatedly shoved into the hands of the first person he encountered a badly typeset leaflet.

Everyone was waiting for something, afraid of something, hoping for something; at the slightest noise they poured quickly on to the street, gathered into a crowd and again dispersed; in Arkhangelsk that was how the Lapps, the Karelians and the Finns acted; in Nizhne-Kolymsk – the Tungus; on the Dnieper – both Yids and *khokhols*. In Petersburg, in Moscow everyone acted like that: in the intermediate, higher and lower institutes of learning: waited, were afraid, hoped; at the slightest rustle poured quickly on to the street; gathered into a crowd and again dispersed.

Arguments in the street became more frequent: with yardkeepers, caretakers; arguments in the streets with shabby non-commissioned police officers; the yardkeeper, the policeman and especially the district superintendent were most insolently picked on by: the worker, the sixth-form pupil, the artisan Ivan Ivanovich Ivanov and his spouse Ivanikha, even the shopkeeper – the merchant of the First Guild Puzanov, from whom in better and recently past days the superintendent had 'obtained' at times sturgeon, at times salmon, now unpressed caviare; but now in place of salmon, sturgeon and caviare against the district superintendent together with other 'riff-raff' rose the merchant of the First Guild, his worthiness, Puzanov, a person not unknown, who had many times visited the governor's house, for after all, – a fishery and then a steamship line on the Volga; after all, an 'opportunity' like this had kept the superintendent quiet. Grey himself, in his grey little coat he now walked like an imperceptible shadow, deferentially tucking up his sword and keeping his eyes down: and at his back were wordy comments, reprimands, laughter and even indecent abuse; while to all this the district militia officer said: 'You won't be able to win the trust of the population, go into retirement.' But he went on trying to win their trust: whether by rebelling against the caprice of the government, or by entering into a special agreement with the inhabitants of the transit prison.

Thus in those days was the district superintendent dragging out his life in Kemi: similarly did he drag it out in Petersburg, Moscow, Orenburg, Tashkent, Solvychevodsk, in a word, in those towns (provincial, district, downgraded) that go to make up the Russian Empire.

Petersburg is surrounded by a ring of many-chimneyed factories.

A many-thousand human swarm makes its way to them in the morning; and the suburbs seethe; and swarm with people. All the factories were at that time in fearful agitation, and the worker-representatives of the crowds had all to a man turned into loquacious characters; among them the Browning circulated; and one or two other things as well. There in those days the usual swarms were growing exceedingly and fusing one with another into a many-headed, many-voiced, enormous blackness; and then the factory inspector reached for the telephone receiver: whenever he reached for the telephone receiver, that meant: a hail of stones would fly from the crowd at the window-panes.

The agitation that embraced Petersburg in a ring seemed to penetrate even into the very centres of Petersburg, began to grip first the islands, then rushed across the Liteyny and Nikolayevsky Bridges; and from there went surging on to Nevsky Prospect: and although on Nevsky Prospect there was always the same circulation of the human myriapod, the constitution of the myriapod was changing in a striking manner; the observer's experienced gaze had already long noted the appearance of the black shaggy hat, pulled down over the eyes, brought here from the fields of bloodstained Manchuria: then the loquacious character had begun to step along Nevsky Prospect, and suddenly the percentage of passing top hats had fallen; the loquacious character displayed here his true quality: he bustled with his shoulders, the fingers of his chilled and frozen hands stuffed into his sleeves; there also appeared on Nevsky the restless cries of the anti-government urchins who rushed at full tilt from the station to the Admiralty waving little journals, red in colour.

In all the rest there were no changes: only once – crowds inundated the Nevsky in the company of clergy:[20] they bore upon their arms a certain professor's coffin, moving towards the station: but before them went a sea of green; bloodstained satin ribbons fluttered.

The days were foggy, strange: poisonous October walked with frozen tread; the frozen dust rushed about the city in brown whirlwinds; and humbly the golden whisper of leaves lay down on the paths of the Summer Garden, and humbly at one's feet a rustling crimson laid itself down, in order to twine and chase at the feet of the passing pedestrian, and to whisper, weaving from the leaves the yellow-red alluvial deposits of words: that sweet peeping of the blue tit, which all August bathed in the leafy wave, had not bathed in the leafy wave for a long time, and the blue tit of the Summer Garden itself now hopped lonely in a black mesh of branches, along the bronze fencing and over the roof of Peter's little house.[21]

Such were the days. And the nights – have you ever gone out at night, penetrated into the god-forsaken suburban vacant lots, in order to listen to the nagging, angry note on 'oo'? Ooo-ooo-ooo: thus did space resound; the sound – was it a sound? If it was a sound, it was indubitably a sound from some other world; this sound attained a rare strength and clarity: 'ooo-ooo-ooo' resounded low in the fields of suburban Moscow, Petersburg, Saratov: but no factory siren blew, there was no wind; and the dogs were silent.

Have you heard this October song of the year 1905? This song did not exist earlier; this song will not exist again: ever.

He Calls for Me, My Delvig Dear

As he walked up the red staircase of the Institution, his hand resting on the cold marble of the banister, Apollon Apollonovich Ableukhov caught the toe of his shoe on the broadcloth and – stumbled; involuntarily his step became slower; consequently: it was perfectly natural that his eyes (without any preconceived bias) should linger on the enormous portrait of the minister, who was directing before him a sad and compassionate gaze.

Along Apollon Apollonovich's backbone gooseflesh ran: the Institution was poorly heated. To Apollon Apollonovich this white room seemed like a plain.

He feared spatial expanses.

He feared them more than zigzags, than broken lines and sectors; country landscape simply scared him: beyond the wastes of snow and ice there, beyond the jagged line of the forests the blizzard raised an intersectedness of aerial currents; there, by a stupid chance, he had very nearly frozen to death.

This had been some fifty years ago.

At this hour of his lonely freezing it had seemed as though someone's cold fingers, heartlessly stuck into his chest, had stiffly stroked his heart: the icy hand had drawn him on; following the icy hand he had climbed the steps of his career, ever keeping before his eyes that same fateful, improbable expanse; there, from there – the icy hand had beckoned; and measurelessness flew: the Russian Empire.

Apollon Apollonovich Ableukhov sat tight behind the city wall for many years, hating with all his soul the lonely rural district distances, the smoke of the hamlets and the jackdaw that sat upon the scarecrow; only once did he dare to cross those distances by express train, travelling on an official errand from Petersburg to Tokyo.

About his stay in Tokyo Apollon Apollonovich said nothing to anyone. Yes – apropos of the portrait of the minister . . . He would say to the minister:

'Russia is an icy plain, over which wolves have roamed for many hundreds of years . . .'

The minister would look at him with a velvety gaze that caressed the soul, smoothing with a white hand his grey, sleek moustache; and say nothing, and sigh. The minister accepted the large number of departments under his direction as an agonizing, sacrificial, crucifying cross; upon the completion of his service he had intended to . . .

But he died.

Now he was resting in his coffin; Apollon Apollonovich Ableukhov was now completely alone – into the immeasurable spaces the ages fled away; ahead – an icy hand revealed: immeasurabilities.

Immeasurabilities flew towards him.

Rus, Rus! He saw – you, you!

It was you who raised a howl with winds, with blizzards, with snow, with rain, with black ice – you raised a howl with millions of living, conjuring voices! At that moment it seemed to the senator as though a certain voice in the expanses were summoning him from a lonely grave mound; a lonely cross did not sway there; no lamp winked at the snowy whirlwinds; only the hungry wolves, gathering into packs, pitifully echoed the winds.

Beyond doubt, with the passage of the years there had developed in the senator a fear of space.

The illness had grown more acute: since the time of that tragic death; true, the image of the departed friend visited him at nights, stroking him with a velvety gaze in the long nights, stroking with a white hand his grey, sleek moustache, because the image of his departed friend was forever united in his consciousness now with a fragment of verse:

> And he is not – and Rus he has abandoned,
> The land he raised . . .

In Apollon Apollonovich's consciousness that fragment arose whenever he, Apollon Apollonovich Ableukhov, crossed the reception room.

After the quoted fragment of verse there would arise another fragment of verse:

And it seems my turn has come,
He calls for me, my Delvig dear,
Companion of my lively youth,
Companion of my mournful youth,
Companion of our youthful songs,
Our feasts and pure intentions' way.
Thither, to the crowd of familiar shades
A genius gone from our midst for aye.

The series of verse fragments was angrily interrupted:

And o'er the earth new thunderclouds have gathered
And the hurricane them . . .

As he remembered the fragments, Apollon Apollonovich became particularly frosty; and with particular precision did he run out to present his fingers to the petitioners.

Meanwhile the Conversation Had a Sequel

Meanwhile Nikolai Apollonovich's conversation with the stranger had a sequel.

'I have been instructed,' said the stranger, accepting an ashtray from Nikolai Apollonovich, 'yes: I have been instructed to give you this little bundle here for safekeeping.'

'Is that all!' cried Nikolai Apollonovich, not yet daring to believe that the appearance of the stranger, which had troubled him so much, in no way concerned *that dreadful* proposal and was merely connected with a most inoffensive little bundle; and in a transport of distracted joy he was already on the point of smothering the little bundle in kisses; and his face covered with grimaces, manifesting a stormy life; he swiftly rose and moved towards the little bundle; but then for some reason the stranger also rose, and for some reason he suddenly rushed between the bundle and Nikolai Apollonovich; and when the hand of the senator's dear son stretched out towards the notorious bundle, the stranger's hand unceremoniously grabbed Nikolai Apollonovich's fingers:

'Be more careful, for God's sake . . .'

Nikolai Apollonovich, drunk with joy, muttered some incoherent apology and again distractedly stretched out his hand towards the object: and for a second time the stranger prevented him from taking the object, stretching out his hand in entreaty:

'No: I earnestly ask you to be more careful, Nikolai Apollonovich, more careful . . .'

'Aa . . . yes, yes . . .' This time too Nikolai Apollonovich took nothing in: but no sooner had he caught hold of the bundle by the edge of the towel, than this time the stranger shouted into his ear in a voice of perfect anger . . .

'Nikolai Apollonovich, I say to you a third time: be more careful . . .'

This time Nikolai Apollonovich was surprised:

'It's literature, I expect? . . .'

'Well, no . . .'

. . . .

Just then a distinct metallic sound rang out: something clicked; in the silence there was the thin squeak of a trapped mouse; at the same moment the soft stool was overturned and the stranger's footsteps began to thud into the corner:

'Nikolai Apollonovich, Nikolai Apollonovich,' his frightened voice rang out, 'Nikolai Apollonovich – a mouse, a mouse . . . Tell your servant quickly . . . to, to . . . clear it away: I find it . . . I cannot . . .'

Nikolai Apollonovich, putting down the little bundle, marvelled at the stranger's consternation:

'Are you afraid of mice? . . .'

'Quick, quick, take it away . . .'

As he leapt out of his room and pressed the bell button, Nikolai Apollonovich presented, it must be admitted, a most absurd sight; but most absurd of all was the fact that in his hand he held . . . an anxiously struggling mouse; the mouse was, it was true, running around inside a wire trap, but Nikolai Apollonovich had absent-mindedly inclined his notable face right down to the trap and was now with the greatest attention examining his grey female captive, running a long, sleek, yellowish fingernail along the metal wire.

'A mouse,' – he raised his eyes to the lackey; and the lackey deferentially repeated after him:

'A mouse, sir . . . Indeed it is, sir . . .'

'Look: it's running, running . . .'

'It's running, sir . . .'

'It's afraid, too . . .'

'Of course it is, sir . . .'

From the open door of the reception room the stranger now peeped out, gave a frightened look and again concealed himself:

'No – I can't . . .'

'Is his honour frightened, sir? . . . It's all right: a mouse is one of God's creatures . . . Of course, sir . . . It too is . . .'

For a few moments both servant and *barin* were preoccupied with contemplating the female captive: at last the venerable servant took the trap into his hands.

'A mouse . . .' Nikolai Apollonovich repeated in a satisfied voice and with a smile returned to the guest who awaited him. Nikolai Apollonovich had a peculiarly soft spot for mice.

. . . .

At last, Nikolai Apollonovich took the bundle into his work room: somehow he was struck in passing only by the bundle's heavy weight; but on this he did not reflect; as he went into the study, he tripped on a multicoloured Arabian rug, having caught his foot in a soft crease; then something in the bundle clinked with a metal sound, and at this clinking the stranger with the small black moustache leapt up; behind Nikolai Apollonovich's back the stranger's hand described that same zigzag-shaped line that had recently frightened the senator so badly.

But nothing happened: the stranger saw only that on a massive armchair in the next room a red domino and a small black satin mask were luxuriantly spread; the stranger fixed his eyes in astonishment upon this small black mask (it shocked him, to tell the truth), while Nikolai Apollonovich opened his writing desk and, having cleared sufficient space, carefully put the little bundle inside; the stranger with the small black moustache, continuing to examine the domino, began meanwhile animatedly to express a certain thoroughly threadbare thought of his:

'You know . . . Loneliness is killing me. I have completely lost the art of conversation these last months. Don't you notice that I get my words mixed up, Nikolai Apollonovich?'

Nikolai Apollonovich, offering the stranger his Bokharan back, only muttered absent-mindedly through clenched teeth:

'Well, that happens to everyone, you know.'

Nikolai Apollonovich was at this moment carefully covering the little bundle with a cabinet-size photograph of a brunette; as he covered the bundle with the brunette, Nikolai Apollonovich fell into reflection, not taking his eyes from the photograph; and the froglike expression passed over his faded lips for a moment.

Meanwhile, into his back, the stranger's words went on resounding.

'Every sentence of mine gets mixed up. I want to say one word, and instead of it I say the wrong one entirely: I keep going around and about . . . Or I suddenly forget, well, what the most ordinary object is called; and, when I do remember it, I doubt whether that is really its name. I say over and over again: lamp, lamp, lamp; and then I suddenly fancy that there is no such word as "lamp". And sometimes there is no one to ask; and if there was, then to ask simply anyone would be shameful, you know: people would take one for a madman.'

'Oh, come . . .'

Incidentally, concerning the bundle: if Nikolai Apollonovich had taken a somewhat more attentive attitude towards his visitor's injunction to be more careful with the bundle, he would probably have realized that the bundle which was in his opinion most inoffensive was not as inoffensive as he thought, but he, I repeat, was concerned with the portrait; concerned so much, that the thread of the stranger's words got lost inside his head. And now, having caught the words, he barely understood them. While into his back the pompous falsetto still drummed:

'It is difficult to live as one excluded, Nikolai Apollonovich, like myself, in a Torricellian vacuum . . .'[22]

'Torricellian?' Nikolai Apollonovich said in surprise, without turning his back, having taken nothing in.

'That is correct – Torricellian, and this, please observe, is for the benefit of the community; the community, society – and what, permit me to ask, kind of society do I see? The society of a *certain* person who is unknown to you, the society of my house's yard-keeper, Matvei Morzhov,[23] and the society of grey woodlice: brrr

... there are woodlice in the attic where I live ... Eh? How do you like that, Nikolai Apollonovich?'

'Yes, you know ...'

'The public cause! Well, for me it long ago turned into a private cause, one that does not permit me to see other people: why, the public cause has excluded me from the list of the living.'

The stranger with the small black moustache had evidently quite by chance landed upon his favourite topic: and, having quite by chance landed upon his favourite topic, the stranger with the black moustache forgot about the purpose of his visit, forgot, doubtless, his rather wet little bundle, even forgot the number of extinguished cigarettes that were fetidly amassing: like all people who are forcibly constrained to silence and are talkative by nature, he sometimes experienced an inexpressible need to tell someone, no matter whom, the sum total of his thoughts: a friend, an enemy, a yardkeeper, a policeman, a child, even ... a hairdresser's dummy exhibited in a window. Sometimes at night the stranger talked to himself. In the setting of the luxurious, multicoloured reception room this need to talk suddenly awakened invincibly, like some bout of hard drinking after a month-long abstinence from vodka.

'I'm not joking: what joke is there; why, in this joke I have spent more than two years; it is all right for you to joke, you who are included in all kinds of society; but my society is the society of bedbugs and woodlice. I am I. Do you hear me?'

'Of course I hear you.'

Nikolai Apollonovich really was now listening.

'I am I: but they try to tell me that I am not I, but some kind of "we". But I ask you – why do they do this? And now my memory has broken down: a bad sign, a bad sign, pointing to the beginning of some brain disorder' – the stranger with the small black moustache began to pace from corner to corner – 'you know, the loneliness is killing me. And sometimes one even gets angry: the public cause, social equality, while I ...'

Here the stranger suddenly broke off his discourse, because Nikolai Apollonovich, closing the desk, now turned to the stranger and, having seen that this latter was already pacing about his little study, making a mess with ash on the desk, on the red satin domino; and, having seen all this, Nikolai Apollonovich, in consequence of some reason that passed all understanding, turned a dark red colour and rushed to clear the domino away; by doing so he merely assisted a change in the field of attention within the stranger's brain.

'What a beautiful domino, Nikolai Apollonovich.'

Nikolai Apollonovich rushed towards the domino as though he intended to cover it with his multicoloured robe but was too late: the stranger had touched the brightly rustling silk with his hand:

'Beautiful silk . . . I expect it cost a great deal: I expect you go to masked balls, Nikolai Apollonovich . . .'

But Nikolai Apollonovich turned an even deeper red:

'Yes, now and again . . .'

He almost tore the domino free and went to put it away in a cupboard, as though he had been caught in the enactment of some crime; like a caught thief, he hurriedly put the domino away; like a caught thief, he ran back for the little mask; having hidden everything, he now calmed down, breathing heavily and looking suspiciously at the stranger; but the stranger, it must be confessed, had already forgotten the domino and had now returned to his favourite topic, all the time continuing to pace about and make a mess with ash.

'Ha, ha, ha!' the stranger jabbered, quickly lighting a cigarette as he moved about. 'You are surprised that I can still be an agent of movements that are not without notoriety, liberating for some and highly inconvenient for others, well, even for your dad? I myself am surprised; it's all nonsense, that I've been acting until recently according to a strictly worked-out plan: it's, I mean, listen: I act according to my own discretion; but what do you suggest I do, every time my discretion merely makes a fresh rut in their activity; to tell you the truth, it is not I who am in the Party, but the Party that is in me . . . Does that surprise you?'

'Yes, I must confess it does: it surprises me; and I must confess that I would never act together with you.' Nikolai Apollonovich was beginning to listen to the things the stranger was saying more closely, things that were becoming ever more rounded, ever more resonant.

'And yet nevertheless you did take my little bundle from me: so we are acting in concert, aren't we?'

'But that doesn't count; what kind of action is there there . . .'

'Well, of course, of course,' the stranger interrupted him, 'I was joking.' And he fell silent, gave Nikolai Apollonovich an affectionate look and this time said quite openly:

'You know, I have long wanted to see you: to have a heart-to-heart talk; I see so few people. I wanted to tell you about myself. You see, I'm elusive not only for the movement's opponents, but also for its insufficient well-wishers. So to speak, the quintessence of the revolution, yet here is the strange thing: you all know about the methodology of social phenomena, you immerse yourselves in diagrams, statistics, you probably even know Marx in his entirety; yet I – don't go thinking I haven't read anything: I'm well-read, very, only that's not what I'm talking about, not the figures of statistics.'

'So in what are you well-read, then? . . . No, permit me, permit me: in my little cupboard I have some cognac – would you like some?'

'I've no objection . . .'

Nikolai Apollonovich reached into the little cupboard: soon before the guest appeared a small cut-glass decanter and two small cut-glass glasses.

Nikolai Apollonovich treated his guests to cognac while he was talking to them.

As he poured cognac for his guest with the greatest of absent-mindedness (like all Ableukhovs, he was absent-minded), Nikolai Apollonovich kept thinking that now would be a most convenient opportunity to refuse the proposal of *that day*; but when he tried to express his thought in words, he grew embarrassed: out of cowardice he did not want to manifest cowardice in the stranger's presence: and besides: he did not want, in his joy, to burden himself with a ticklish conversation, when he might make the refusal by letter.

'I'm reading Conan Doyle just now, for relaxation,' the stranger jabbered, '– don't get angry – that's a joke, of course. Though, as a matter of fact, let it not be a joke; after all, if I am to be perfectly frank, the scope of my reading will all seem equally barbarous to you: I'm reading the history of gnosticism, Gregory of Nyssa,[24] Ephraem Syrus[25] and the Apocalypse.[26] That is my privilege, you know; one way or the other, I am a colonel in the movement who has been transferred from the field of action (for meritorious services) to staff headquarters. Yes, yes, yes – I'm a colonel. For long service, of course; while now you, Nikolai Apollonovich, with your methodology and your intellect – are an NCO; in the first place, you are an NCO because you are a theoretician; and among your generals, where theory is concerned, things are not going very well; I mean, admit it – they're not going very well; and they, your generals, are for all the world like bishops, but bishops from among the monkhood; and a young little academist[27] who has studied Harnack[28] but has bypassed the school of experience and has never spent time with a schemonach[29] is for a bishop merely an irritating ecclesiastical appendage; that is what you are with all your theories – an appendage; believe me, an irritating one!'

'Why, in your words I hear a touch of Narodnaya Volya.'[30]

'Well, so what of it? It's the Narodnovoltsy who have the power, after all, not the Marxists. But forgive me, I've wandered . . . what was I talking about? Yes, about long service and the books I read. So you see, it's like this: the originality of my intellectual food proceeds from the same eccentricity; I'm just as much of a revolutionary braggart as any other fire-eating braggart with a St George's medal;[31] all is forgiven an old braggart and ace swordsman.'

The stranger reflected, poured a glass: drank it – poured another.

'And in any case, why shouldn't I find my own, personal, independent way; after all, I seem to live a private sort of life – within four yellow walls; my fame is growing, society repeats my Party nickname, while the circle of people who are in any kind of human relation to me is, believe me, equivalent to zero; people first learned of me in those glorious days when I got settled into forty-five degrees of frost . . .'

'I say, were you exiled?'

'Yes, to the Yakutsk region.'[32]

An awkward silence ensued. The stranger with the small black moustache looked out of the window at the expanse of the Neva; a pale grey dampness hung there: there was the end of the earth and there was the end of infinity; there, through the greyness and dampness, poisonous October was already whispering something, beating tears and rain against the panes; and the rainy tears on the panes overtook one another, in order to twine into streams and draw the hooked signs of words; in the chimneys a sweet squeaking of wind could be heard, while a network of black chimneys, from far, far away, sent its smoke under the sky. And the smoke fell in tails above the dark-coloured waters. The stranger with the small black moustache lightly touched his glass with his lips, looked at the yellow liquid: his hands trembled.

Nikolai Apollonovich, now listening attentively, said with a kind of . . . almost malice:

'Well, and you haven't said a word to the crowds about your dreams for the time being, I hope? . . .'

'Naturally, I'm keeping quiet for the time being.'

'Well, that means you're lying; I'm sorry, but the point of the matter is not in words: you are all the same lying and lying once and for all.'

The stranger gave him a look of amazement and continued, irrelevantly enough:

'For the time being I am spending all my time reading and thinking: and all this exclusively for myself alone: that is why I am reading Gregory of Nyssa.'

Silence ensued. Downing another glass, from behind the cloud of tobacco smoke the stranger emerged as the victor; he had of course been smoking all the while. The silence was broken by Nikolai Apollonovich.

'Well, and what about after your return from the Yakutsk region?'

'I successfully escaped from the Yakutsk region; I was brought out in a pickled cabbage barrel;[33] and now I am what I am: an underground activist; only don't go thinking that I acted in the name of social utopias or in the name of your railway mentality: your categories remind me of rails, and your life is a carriage that flies on the rails: at that time I was a desperate Nietzschean. We're all Nietzscheans: I mean, you too – an engineer of your railway line, the creator of a scheme – you too are a Nietzschean; only you will never admit it. Well, so it's like this: for us Nietzscheans the masses who are (as you would say) inclined to agitation and stirred by social instincts, turn into an executive apparatus (another of your engineers' expressions), in which people (even people such as you) are the keyboard on which the fingers of the pianist (take note: the expression is my own) fly freely, overcoming difficulty for difficulty; and while some ditherer in the stalls beneath the concert platform listens to the divine sounds of Beethoven, for the artist and for Beethoven the important thing is not the sounds, but some kind of septachord. You know what a septachord is, don't you? We are all like that.'

'The sportsmen of the revolution, in other words.'

'Well, is a sportsman not an artist? I am a sportsman out of a pure love for art: and so I am an artist. It is good to model from the unformed clay of society a bust that will be remarkable for all eternity.'

'But wait, wait – you are falling into a contradiction: a septachord, that is a formula, a term, while a bust, surely that is something living? A technique – and an inspiration through art? Technique I understand perfectly.'

An awkward silence ensued again: with irritation Nikolai Apollonovich plucked a horsehair from the multicoloured fabric of his couch: he did not consider it necessary to enter into a theoretical argument; he was used to arguing in a regular fashion, not rushing from topic to topic.

'Everything in the world is built upon contrasts: and my usefulness to society has led me into melancholy, icy expanses; for the time being I have been mentioned and then well and truly forgotten, as being there – alone, in emptiness: and to the degree that I have withdrawn into emptiness, rising above the rank and file, even above the NCOs' (the stranger grinned without malice and tweaked his small moustache) '– all the Party prejudices, all the categories, as you would say, have gradually fallen away from me: you know, I only have one category from the Yakutsk region. And do you know what it is?'

'What is it?'

'The category of ice . . .'

'And what is that, then?'

Whether as a result of his thoughts or of the liquor he had drunk, Aleksandr Ivanovich's face really did take on a strange expression: both the colour and even the size of his face changed strikingly (there are faces that change in a trice); now he looked decidedly as though he had had a drop or two.

'The category of ice is the icy expanses of the Yakutsk province; I carry them around in my heart, you know, they are what marks me out from everyone; I carry ice around with me; yes, yes, yes: ice marks me out; marks me out, in the first place, as a man outside the law, living on a forged passport; in the second place, in this ice there has matured within me for the first time the special sense that even when I am out visiting I am abandoned to immensity . . .'

The stranger with the small black moustache stole imperceptibly over to the window; there, on the other side of the panes, a platoon of grenadiers was passing in the greenish fog: strapping lads and all in grey greatcoats. Swinging their left arms, they passed: row upon row went past, their bayonets showing black through the fog.

Nikolai Apollonovich felt a strange chill: once again he had an unpleasant sensation: his Party's promise had not yet been taken back; as he listened to the stranger now, Nikolai Apollonovich got the wind up: like Apollon Apollonovich, Nikolai Apollonovich did not like spaces; even more was he horrified by the icy spaces that so manifestly wafted towards him from Aleksandr Ivanovich's words.

As for Aleksandr Ivanovich, over there, by the window, he smiled . . .

'The article of the revolution is not necessary to me: it's an article for you, the theoreticians, the publicists, the philosophers.'

At this point, as he looked out of the window, he impetuously broke off his discourse; jumping down from the window-sill, he began to stare intently at the foggy slush; what had happened was this: out of the foggy slush a carriage had rolled up; Aleksandr Ivanovich saw both the carriage door flying open and Apollon Apollonovich Ableukhov, in a grey coat and a tall black top hat with a stony face that was reminiscent of a paperweight, quickly jumping out of the carriage, casting a momentary and frightened glance at the mirror-like reflections of the panes; quickly he rushed to the entrance porch, unbuttoning a black kid glove as he went. Aleksandr Ivanovich, now in his turn frightened of something, suddenly brought his hand to his eyes as though he wanted to shield himself from a certain troublesome thought. A constrained whisper tore itself from his breast.

'He . . .'

'What is it? . . .'

Nikolai Apollonovich now also came over to the window.

'It's nothing in particular: your dad has just driven up in a carriage.'

The Walls Were Snow, Not Walls!

Apollon Apollonovich did not like his spacious flat; the furniture there shone so tiresomely, so eternally: and when the covers were put on, the furniture in its white covers stood before the gaze like snowy hills; resonantly, distinctly the parquets here returned the senator's tread.

Resonantly, distinctly thus did the hall return the senator's tread, a hall more like a corridor of the grandest dimensions. From a ceiling covered in white garlands, from a moulded circle of fruit there hung a chandelier with fragments of rock crystal, draped with a muslin cover; as though it were transparent, the chandelier swung and trembled regularly like a crystal tear.

While the parquetry, like a mirror, shone with little squares.

The walls were snow, not walls; these walls were everywhere lined with high-legged chairs; their high white legs were covered in gold riffles; from everywhere among the chairs, upholstered in pale yellow plush, rose columns of white alabaster; and on all the white columns towered an alabaster Archimedes. Not one single Archimedes, but different Archimedes, for their common name was the Ancient Greek statesman. Coldly from the walls did an icy mirror flash; but some solicitous hand had hung circular frames along the walls; below the glass a pale-toned painting stood out; the pale-toned painting imitated the frescoes of Pompeii.

Apollon Apollonovich glanced in passing at the Pompeian frescoes and remembered whose solicitous hand had hung them along the walls; the solicitous hand belonged to Anna Petrovna: Apollon Apollonovich pursed his lips with distaste and went into his study; in his study Apollon Apollonovich was in the habit of locking himself in; an unaccountable sadness was evoked by the spaces of the suite of rooms; out of them someone eternally familiar and strange seemed for ever to be running; Apollon Apollonovich would have been very glad to move out of his enormous suite of rooms into one more modest; after all, his subordinates lived in more modest little flats; while he, Apollon Apollonovich, must for ever renounce that captivating narrowness: the exaltedness of his position compelled one to this; thus was Apollon Apollonovich compelled to idly languish in the cold flat on the embankment; he often recollected the former resident of these shining rooms: Anna Petrovna. It was already two years since Anna Petrovna had left him for an Italian artist.

The Person

With the appearance of the senator, the stranger began to grow nervous; his hitherto smooth discourse was interrupted: the alcohol was probably having its effect; generally speaking, Aleksandr Ivanovich's health excited serious apprehension; his conversations with himself and with others produced in him an almost culpable state of mind, were painfully reflected in his spinal vertebral column; there appeared in him an almost gloomy loathing in relation to the conversation that agitated him; this loathing he later transferred to himself; on the face of it these innocent conversations enervated him dreadfully, but most unpleasant of all was the fact that the more he spoke, the more there developed in him a desire to talk even more: to the point of hoarseness, of an astringent sensation in the throat; now he could not stop, exhausting himself more and more; sometimes he would talk to the point where afterwards he experienced genuine attacks of persecution mania: emerging in words, they continued in dreams: at times his unusually ominous dreams grew more frequent: dream followed dream; sometimes three nightmares a night; in these dreams he was always surrounded by some sort of ugly faces (for some reason most often Tartars, Japanese or Orientals in general); these ugly faces invariably left the same nasty impression; with their nasty eyes they kept winking at him; but what was most astonishing of all was that at this time he invariably remembered a most senseless word, seemingly a cabbalistic one, but in actual fact the devil knows what: *enfranshish*; with the help of this word he struggled in dreams with the crowds of spirits that surrounded him. Furthermore: even when he was awake there appeared on the dark yellow wallpaper of his abode a certain fateful face; and then to cap it all, from time to time all kinds of rubbish would begin to appear to him: and it appeared to him in the whiteness of day, if the autumnal Petersburg day is really white, and not yellow-green with murky saffron reflections; and then Aleksandr Ivanovich experienced the same thing that the senator had experienced yesterday, having met his, Aleksandr Ivanovich's, gaze. The same fateful phenomena began in him with attacks of deathly anguish, caused, in all probability, by prolonged sitting still: and then Aleksandr Ivanovich would begin to run frightenedly out into the green-yellow fog (in spite of the risk of being shadowed); as he ran through the streets of Petersburg, he called in at little taverns. Thus did alcohol, too, appear on the scene. After the alcohol a shameful feeling also instantly appeared: for the leg, no, sorry, for the stocking of the leg of a certain ingenuous *coursiste*, which had nothing whatever to do with her herself; there began apparently quite innocent little jokes, giggles, smiles. It would all end with the wild and nightmarish *enfranshish* dream.

All this Aleksandr Ivanovich remembered, and he hunched his shoulders convulsively: it was as though with the senator's arrival the same thing had once again arisen within his soul; some kind of irrelevant thought would not give him any peace; sometimes, by chance, he would go over to the door and listen to the boom of distant footsteps that barely reached him; that was probably the senator pacing about his study.

In order to interrupt his thoughts, Aleksandr Ivanovich again began to pour out those thoughts into a rather lacklustre discourse:

'Here you are, Nikolai Apollonovich, listening to my chatter: yet here, too: in all these discourses of mine, for example in the assertion of my personality, an indisposition has once again mixed itself. Here I am talking to you, arguing with you – but it's not you I'm arguing with, but myself, only myself. You see, my interlocutor means precisely nothing to me: I am able to talk to the walls, to the posts, to complete idiots. I don't listen to other people's thoughts: that's to say, I only hear what affects me, and mine. I struggle, Nikolai Apollonovich: solitude attacks me: for hours, days, weeks I sit in my garret and smoke. Then it begins to seem to me that *everything's all wrong*. Do you know that state?'

'I can't picture it clearly. I have heard that it's caused by one's heart. The sight of space, when there's nothing all around ... That's more comprehensible to me.'

'Well, but not to me: so here you sit and say, why am I who I am: and apparently I am not who I am ... and you know, the table stands before me. The devil knows what it is: both a table and not a table. And then you say to yourself: the devil knows what life has done to me. And I want I to become I ... But here are *we*, in Russian *my*. In general I despise all words that have *y* in them, in the very sound *y* there is some kind of Tartar abomination, Mongolianism, perhaps, the East. Listen to it: *y*. Not a single cultured language has *y* in it: it's something obtuse, cynical, slimy.'

Here the stranger with the small black moustache remembered the face of a certain person who irritated him; it too reminded him of the letter *y*.

Without being able to do much about it, Nikolai Apollonovich entered into conversation with Aleksandr Ivanovich.

'You keep talking about the greatness of personality: but tell me, is there no control over you; are you not attached?'

'Are you referring to *a certain person*, Nikolai Apollonovich?'

'I'm referring to precisely no one: I just ...'

'Yes – you are right: *a certain person* appeared soon after my escape from the icy wastes: he appeared in Helsingfors.'[34]

'Who was this person – a person of authority in your party?'

'The highest: it's around him that the course of events takes place: most important events: do you know the *person*?'

'No, I don't.'

'Well then, look: you said just now that you're not in the Party at all, but that the Party is in you; so what is the result of that; it means that you yourself are in *a certain person*.'

'Oh, well, he sees me as his centre.'

'And what about burdens?'

The stranger started.

'Yes, yes, yes: a thousand times yes: *a certain person* places the most terrible *burdens* on me; the burdens keep locking me up in the same cold: the cold of the Yakutsk province.'

'So,' Nikolai Apollonovich quipped, 'the physical plain of a not so remote province has turned into a metaphysical plain of the soul.'

'Yes, my soul, it's like outer space; and from there, from outer space, I look at everything.'

'Listen, and do you have there . . .'

'Outer space,' Aleksandr Ivanovich interrupted him, 'at times plagues me, desperately plagues me. Do you know what I call that space?

'I call that space my abode on Vasily Island: four perpendicular walls covered with wallpaper of a darkish yellow hue; when I sit within those walls, no one comes to visit me: the house's yardkeeper, Matvei Morzhov, comes; and also within those precincts *the person* comes.'

'But how did you end up there?'

'Oh – *the person . . .*'

'Again the person?'

'Always him: he has turned into, so to speak, the guardian of my damp threshold; if he wants me to, I can stay there for weeks without going out, in the interests of security; after all, my appearance on the streets always presents a danger.'

'So that is where you cast your shadow on Russian life from – the shadow of the Elusive One.'

'Yes, from four yellow walls.'

'But listen: where is your freedom, where does it come from?' Nikolai Apollonovich laughed, as though taking revenge for the words that had just been spoken. 'Your freedom comes from not much more than twelve cigarettes smoked one after the other. Listen, why, *the person* has caught you. How much do you pay for the lodgings?'

'Twelve roubles, no, sorry – twelve fifty.'

'And here you devote yourself to the contemplation of outer space?'

'Yes, here: and here everything is all wrong – objects are not objects: here I have reached the conviction that the window is not a window; the window is a slit on to immensity.'

'Here you probably arrived at the notion that those at the top of the movement know what is inaccessible to those at the bottom, for the top,' Nikolai Apollonovich continued his mockery. 'What is the top?'

But Aleksandr Ivanovich replied calmly:

'The top of the movement is a universal, fathomless void.'

'Then what is all the rest for?'

Aleksandr Ivanovich grew animated.

'Oh, it's in the name of illness . . .'

'How do you mean, illness?'

'Oh, that same illness that so exhausts me: the strange name of that illness is as yet unknown to me, but I know the symptoms very well: unaccountable depression, hallucinations, fears, vodka, smoking; the vodka gives me a frequent and dull pain in my head; and lastly, a peculiar feeling in my vertebrae: it torments me in the mornings. And do you think that I am the only one who is ill? It would seem not: you too, Nikolai Apollonovich – you too – are also ill. Almost everyone is ill. Ach, stop it, please; I know, I know it all in advance, what you're going to say, yet none the less: ha-ha-ha! – nearly all the ideological Party workers – they too are ill with the same illness; it's just that its features are emphasized in me in more relief. You know: years and years ago, whenever I met a Party comrade I used to like to study him, if you know what I mean; there would be a meeting lasting many hours, business matters, smoke, conversations and all of them about such noble and exalted things, and my comrade would get excited, and then, you know, that comrade would invite me to a restaurant.'

'Well, and what followed from that?'

'Well, vodka, of course; and so on; glass after glass; and I would look; after a glass of vodka, round that interlocutor's lips a little smirk would appear (a kind of smirk, Nikolai Apollonovich, that I can't describe to you), and then I knew: one couldn't rely on my ideological interlocutor; one could trust neither his words nor his actions: that interlocutor of mine was ill with lack of will, with neurasthenia; and nothing, believe me, would guarantee him against softening of the brain; such an interlocutor is capable not only of failing to keep a promise in a difficult hour; he is also capable of quite plainly and simply stealing, and betraying, and raping a little girl. Even his presence in the Party is a provocation, a provocation, a dreadful provocation. From that time on there has been revealed to me the meaning, you know, of those little wrinkles around the lips, of those weaknesses, little chuckles, little grimaces; and no matter where I have turned my eyes, everywhere, everywhere I am greeted by nothing but cerebral disorder, a general, secret, elusively developed provocation, a little chuckler underneath the public cause that is *of a kind* – of a kind, Nikolai Apollonovich, that I don't seem to be able to describe to you at all. But I am able to detect it unerringly; I have detected it in you, too.'

'And you don't have it?'

'I have it, too: I have long ceased to trust any public cause.'

'So you're a *provocateur*, then. Don't be offended: I'm talking about a purely ideological provocation.'

'Me. Yes, yes, yes. I am a *provocateur*. But all my provocation is in the name of a single great idea that is mysteriously leading somewhere; or again, not an idea, but a spirit.'

'What kind of spirit?'

'If one is to talk of a spirit, then I cannot define it with the help of words: I can call it a general thirst for death; and I grow intoxicated by it with ecstasy, with bliss, with horror.'

'About the time that you began, in your own words, to grow intoxicated by the spirit of death, that little wrinkle probably appeared in you.'

'It did.'

'And you began to smoke and drink.'

'Yes, yes, yes: and peculiar lustful feelings appeared, too: you know, I have never been in love with a woman: I've been in love – how should I say it: with individual parts of the female body, with items of toilette, with stockings, for example. But men have fallen in love with me.'

'Well, and did that *certain person* appear precisely at that time?'

'How I hate him. I mean, you know – yes, I'm sure you know not by your will but by the will of the fate that has exalted itself above me – the fate of the Elusive One – my identity, that of Aleksandr Ivanovich, has turned into an appendage of my own shadow. The shadow of the Elusive One is known; I – Aleksandr Ivanovich Dudkin – am unknown to anyone at all; and no one wants to know me, either. And after all, the person who starved, froze and in general experienced something was not the Elusive One, but Dudkin. Aleksandr Ivanovich Dudkin was, for example, distinguished by an extreme sensitivity; while the Elusive One was both cold and cruel. Aleksandr Ivanovich Dudkin was from nature distinguished by a vividly expressed sociability and was not averse to enjoying life. While the Elusive One has to be ascetically silent. In a word, even today Dudkin's elusive shadow makes its triumphant procession: in the brains of youth, of course; why, I myself have been under the influence of the *person* – but look, just look at how I've ended up!'

'Yes, you know . . .'

And both again fell silent.

'And finally, Nikolai Apollonovich, a strange nervous indisposition also crept up on me: under the influence of that indisposition I came to an unexpected conclusion: I, Nikolai Apollonovich, realized completely that out of the cold of my *outer space* I was aflame with a secret hatred not of the government at all, but of – *a certain person*; after all, that person, who had turned me, Dudkin, into the shadow of Dudkin, had expelled me from the three-dimensional world, having spread me, so to speak, on the wall of my garret (my favourite posture during insomnia, you know, is to stand up against the wall and spread myself, stretch my arms in both directions). And there in my spread position against the wall (I stand like that for hours, Nikolai Apollonovich) one night I came to my second conclusion; this conclusion was somehow strangely connected with a certain phenomenon that may be understood if one takes into account my developing illness.'

Aleksandr Ivanovich deemed it appropriate to remain silent about the phenomenon.

The phenomenon consisted of a strange hallucination: from time to time on the brownish-yellow wallpaper of his abode a spectral face would appear; at times the features of this face formed into a Semite; more often, however, Mongolian features showed through in this face: while the whole face was swathed in an unpleasant, saffron-yellow sheen. Now a Semite, now a Mongol fixed upon Aleksandr Ivanovich a gaze full of hatred. Aleksandr Ivanovich would then light a cigarette; and through the bluish clouds of tobacco smoke the Semite or Mongol would move his yellow lips, and it was as though within Aleksandr Ivanovich the same word kept echoing:

'Helsingfors, Helsingfors.'

Aleksandr Ivanovich had been in Helsingfors after his escape from places not so very remote: with Helsingfors he had no particular connections: there he had merely met *a certain person*.

So why Helsingfors in particular?

Aleksandr Ivanovich continued to drink cognac. The alcohol worked with systematic gradualness; after vodka (wine was beyond his means) there followed a uniform effect: an undular line of thoughts became a zigzag one; its zigzags intersected; if he went on drinking, the line of thoughts would disintegrate into a series of fragmentary arabesques, brilliant for those who thought it; but only brilliant for him alone at that moment alone; he had only to sober up a little for the salt of brilliance to vanish off somewhere; and the brilliant thoughts seemed simply a muddle, for at those moments thought indubitably ran ahead of both tongue and brain, beginning to revolve with frantic speed.

Aleksandr Ivanovich's excitement transmitted itself to Ableukhov: the bluish streams of tobacco smoke and twelve crushed cigarette ends positively irritated him; it was as though some invisible third person suddenly stood before them, raised aloft from the smoke and this little pile of ash here; this third person, having emerged, now exercised dominion over all.

'Wait: perhaps I shall come out with you; I seem to have a splitting headache: out there, in the fresh air, we can continue our conversation without hindrance. Wait a moment. I'll just change.'

'That is an excellent idea.'

A sharp knock at the door broke off the conversation; before Nikolai Apollonovich had conceived the design of ascertaining who had knocked there, like one distracted, the half-drunk Aleksandr Ivanovich quickly threw open the door; there, from the door opening was thrust, almost flung, at the stranger a bald cranium with ears of enlarged dimensions; the cranium and Aleksandr Ivanovich's head very nearly banged together; Aleksandr Ivanovich recoiled in bewilderment and looked at Nikolai Apollonovich, and, having looked at him, saw nothing but a . . . hairdresser's dummy: a pale, waxen beau with an unpleasant, timid smile on a mouth that was stretched to the ears.

And again he cast a glance at the door, but in the wide open doorway stood Apollon Apollonovich with ... a most enormous watermelon under his arm ...

'Indeed, sir, indeed, sir ...'

'I think I'm intruding ...'

'You know what, Kolenka, I've brought you this little melon – here ...'

According to the tradition of the house in this autumn season Apollon Apollonovich, as he returned home, sometimes bought an Astrakhan watermelon, of which both he and Nikolai Apollonovich were fond.

For a moment all three were silent; each of them at that moment experienced a most candid, purely animal fear.

'This, Papa, is a friend of mine from university ... Aleksandr Ivanovich Dudkin ...'

'Indeed, sir ... Very pleasant, sir ...'

Apollon Apollonovich presented two of his fingers: *those eyes* were not staring dreadfully – was it the same face that had looked at him in the street – Apollon Apollonovich saw before him only a timid man who was obviously dejected by need.

Aleksandr Ivanovich seized the senator's fingers with ardour; that *other, fateful* thing had flown away somewhere: Aleksandr Ivanovich saw before him only a pathetic old man.

Nikolai Apollonovich looked at them both with that unpleasant smile; but he too calmed down; the timid young man presented his hand to the weary skeleton.

But the hearts of all three were pounding; the eyes of all three avoided one another. Nikolai Apollonovich ran off to get ready: *she* had wandered under the windows there: that meant she was depressed; but today there awaited her – what awaited her? ...

His thought was interrupted: from the cupboard Nikolai Apollonovich pulled out his *domino* and put it on over his frock coat; he pinned up its red, satin skirts with pins; on top of all the rest he put on his Nikolayevka.

Apollon Apollonovich, meanwhile, entered into conversation with the stranger; the disorder in his son's room, the cigarettes, the cognac – all this had left in his soul an unpleasant and bitter aftertaste; only Aleksandr Ivanovich's replies brought him any calm: the replies were incoherent. Aleksandr Ivanovich kept flushing and his replies were not to the point. Before him he saw only kindly wrinkles; on those kindly wrinkles eyes looked: the eyes of a hunted man; and the rumbling voice was shouting something with a crack of hysteria; Aleksandr Ivanovich listened only to the last words, and caught at the very most a series of jerky exclamations:

'You know . . . even when he was a schoolboy at the gymnasium, Kolenka knew all those birds . . . He used to read Kaigorodov . . .'[35]

'He had an inquiring mind . . .

'But now he's not the same: he's given it all up . . .

'And he doesn't go to the university . . .'

Thus did the old man of sixty-eight jerkily shout at Aleksandr Ivanovich; something that resembled sympathy stirred in the heart of the Elusive One . . .

Into the room now came Nikolai Apollonovich.

'Where are you going?'

'Why, Papa, I'm off on business . . .'

'You are . . . so to speak . . . With Aleksandr . . . with Aleksandr . . .'

'With Aleksandr Ivanovich . . .'

'Indeed, sir . . . With Aleksandr Ivanovich, then . . .'

But to himself Apollon Apollonovich thought: 'What of it, perhaps it's for the best: and perhaps *the eyes* were only something I dreamed . . .' And at the same time Apollon Apollonovich also reflected that poverty was not a sin. Only why had they had to drink cognac (Apollon Apollonovich entertained a revulsion towards alcohol)?

'Yes: we're off on business . . .'

Apollon Apollonovich began to search for a suitable word:

'Perhaps . . . you'd like to dine . . . And Aleksandr Ivanovich would like to dine with us . . .'

Aleksandr Ivanovich looked at his watch:

'But in any case . . . I don't wish to get in your way . . .'

. . . .

'Goodbye, Papa . . .'

'My respects, sir . . .'

. . . .

When they opened the door and walked along the booming corridor, little Apollon Apollonovich appeared there, following them – in the semi-twilight of the corridor.

Yes, as they walked along in the semi-twilight of the corridor, Apollon Apollonovich stood there; craning his neck in pursuit of that couple, he was staring with curiosity.

All the same, all the same . . . Yesterday the eyes had looked:[36] in them there were both hatred and fear; and those eyes had been real: they belonged to *him*, the *raznochinets*. And the zigzag was – most unpleasant, or had this not happened – never happened?

'Aleksandr Ivanovich Dudkin . . . A student at the university.'

Apollon Apollonovich began to stalk off after them.

. . . .

In the sumptuous vestibule Nikolai Apollonovich stopped before the old lackey, trying to catch one of his own thoughts that had run away.

'Ye-ee . . . es . . .'

'Very good, sir!'

'E – er . . . The mouse!'

Nikolai Apollonovich continued helplessly to rub his forehead, trying to remember what it was he was supposed to express with the aid of the verbal symbol, mouse: this often happened to him, especially after he had been reading very serious treatises that consisted solely of unimaginable words: after he had been reading those treatises every object, even more than that – every name of an object seemed to him inconceivable, and vice versa: everything conceivable proved to be completely insubstantial, without object. And apropos of this Nikolai Apollonovich pronounced a second time, with an injured look:

'The mouse . . .'

'Precisely so, sir!'

'Where is it? Listen, what have you done with the mouse?'

'With the one that was here earlier? Let it out on to the embankment . . .'

'Really?'

'For goodness' sake, *barin*: the way we always do.'

Nikolai Apollonovich was distinguished by an unusual tenderness for these small creatures.

Their minds set at rest on the subject of the mouse's fate, Nikolai Apollonovich and Aleksandr Ivanovich set off on their way.

As a matter of fact, both set off on their way because both thought someone was looking at them from the balustrade of the staircase both searchingly and sadly.

. . . .

He Appeared, He Appeared

A certain gloomy building[37] towered up on a certain gloomy street. It was just getting dark; the street lamps had begun to shine palely, lighting up the entrance porch; the fourth storeys were still crimson with the sunset.

It was to here that from every end of Petersburg individuals made their way; their complement was of a dual nature; their complement was, in the first place, enlisted from the working-class, shaggy-headed individual – in hats that had been brought from the bloodstained fields of Manchuria; in the second place, that complement was enlisted from protesters in general: the protester walked abundantly on long legs; he was pale and fragile; sometimes he fed on *phytin*,[38] sometimes he also fed on cream; today he was walking with a most enormous gnarled stick; if my protester were to be placed in one pan of the scales, and his gnarled stick to be placed in the other, then the said implement would without doubt outweigh the protester; it was not quite clear who was following whom; whether the cudgel was capering in front of the protester, or whether he himself was walking along behind the cudgel; but most probable of all was that the cudgel hopped all on its own from Nevsky, Pushkin, the Vyborg Side, even from Izmailovskaya Rota; the protester was dragged after it; and he was panting, he could barely keep up; and the pert boy who was rushing about at the hour when the evening supplement of the newspaper came out – that pert boy could have toppled the protester, had the protester not been a worker, but only what he was – a protester.

This protester who was what he was had begun, not without purpose, to stroll about of late: around Petersburg, Saratov,

Tsarevokokshaisk, Kineshma; not every day did he stroll thus ...
What happened was that one went out in the evening for a
walk: quiet and harmonious was the sunset; and so harmoniously
did a young lady laugh in the street; with the young lady my
individual laughed softly and harmoniously – without any cudgel:
chaffed, smoked; with a most good-natured air chatted with the
yardkeeper, with a most good-natured air chatted with constable
Brykachev.

'Well now, Brykachev, I dare say you're fed up standing here?'

'Of course, *barin*: the work isn't easy.'

'Just wait: soon it will change.'

'God grant that it will be to something good, sir; you can't go
against the evil spirit, as you yourself know.'

'No, indeed, one can't ...'

The individual was not a bad sort; and constable Brykachev was
not a bad sort either: and they both laughed; and a five-copeck piece
flew into Brykachev's fist.

The following day what happened again was that one went out
for a walk – and what? Quiet and harmonious was the sunset; there
was still the same contentment in nature; the theatres and the
circuses were all in action; the urban water supply was also in good
working order; and – yet no: everything was all wrong.

Cutting across a public garden, a street, a square, shifting dolefully
from one foot to the other in front of the monument to a great
man, yesterday's good-natured individual began to walk with his
enormous cudgel; sternly, silently, solemnly, so to speak, with
emphasis, the individual advances his feet in galoshes and lacing
boots with turned-up flaps; sternly, silently, solemnly the individual
strikes his cudgel on the pavement; with constable Brykachev not a
word; and constable Brykachev does not say a word, either, but just
stares into space, with determination.

'Move along now, gentleman, move along, don't block the
thoroughfare.'

And one looks: somewhere superintendent Podbrizhny is
circulating.

My protester's eye fairly jumps: this way and that way; have any
other protesters like himself gathered in a little group in front of the
monument to the great man? Have they gathered on the square in

front of the transit prison? But the monument to the great man is surrounded by police; while on the square there is no one.

He walks, he walks, my individual, sighs with commiseration; and returns to his quarters; and his mother gives him tea with cream to drink. – You may as well know: that day the newspapers had criticized something: something – some: measure – of prevention, so to speak: whatever it was; if they criticized a measure – the individual would begin to ferment.

The following day there is no measure: and the individual is not on the streets either; and my individual is content, and my constable Brykachev is content; and superintendent Podbrizhny is content. The monument to the great man is not surrounded by police.

Did my protesting individual appear on this nice October day? He appeared, he appeared! In the street the shaggy Manchurian hats also appeared; both those individuals and those hats dissolved in the crowd; but this way and that way the crowd wandered aimlessly; while the individuals and the Manchurian hats made their way in one direction – to the gloomy building with the crimson summit; and outside the gloomy building that was crimson with sunset the crowd was exclusively made up of individuals and hats; a young lady from an educational establishment was also involved in it all.

But now they were barging, and barging at the entrance-porch doors – how they barged, how they barged! And how could it be otherwise? A working man has no time to spend on propriety: and there was a bad smell; while the crush began on the pavement.

Along the corner, near the pavement, good-naturedly embarrassed, a small detachment of police stamped their feet up and down (it was cold); while the officer in charge was even more embarrassed; grey himself, in a little grey coat, he was shouting like an unnoticed shadow, deferentially tucking up his sabre and keeping his eyes down; while to his back he received verbal comments, reprimands, laughter and even: indecent abuse – from the artisan Ivan Ivanovich Ivanov, from his spouse, Ivanikha, from his worthiness the merchant of the First Guild Puzanov (fishery and steamship company on the Volga) who had been passing here and had risen up together with the rest. The grey little officer in charge was shouting ever more timidly:

'Move along, gentlemen, move along!'

But the dimmer he grew, the more insistently did the many-legged horses snort there behind the fence: from behind the teeth made of logs – no, no – a shaggy head rose; and if one were to peep over the fence, one would be able to see that it was only some kind of folk who had been driven in from the steppes who had whips in their fists and rifles behind their backs and who were angry about something, angry: impatiently, angrily, silently those ragged fellows danced on their saddles; and their shaggy little horses – they also danced.

It was a detachment of Orenburg Cossacks.

Inside the gloomy building there was a saffron-yellow darkness; here everything was lit by candles; it was impossible to see anything except bodies, bodies and bodies: bent, half-bent, barely bent and not bent at all: those bodies were sitting round, standing round everything that could be sat and stood round; they occupied an amphitheatre of seats that soared aloft; the rostrum was not visible, nor was the voice that bequeathed from the rostrum:

'Ooo-ooo-ooo.' There was a hooting in space and through this 'ooo' one heard from time to time:

'Revolution ... Evolution ... Proletariat ... Strike ...' And then again: 'Strike ...' And again: 'Strike.'

'Strike ...' – a voice blurted out; the hooting grew even louder: between two loudly uttered *strikes* there just barely stole out: 'Social democracy.' And again disappeared into the bass-voiced, continuous, dense ooo-ooo ...

Obviously what was being said was that in this place and that place and this place there already was a strike; that in this place and that place and this place a strike was being prepared, and so they ought to strike – here and here: to strike right in this very place; and – not to budge!

Escape

Aleksandr Ivanovich was returning home along the empty prospects that ran parallel to the Neva; the light of a court carriage went flying past him; from beneath the vault of the Winter Canal the

Neva was revealed to him; there, on the small, curved bridge, he observed the nightly shadow.

Aleksandr Ivanovich was returning to his wretched abode in order to sit in solitude amidst the brown stains and to follow the life of the woodlice in the dampish cracks in the walls. His morning trip outside after the night sooner resembled an escape from the creeping woodlice; Aleksandr Ivanovich's repeated observations had long ago led him to the thought that the tranquillity of his night quite simply depended on the tranquillity of the day he had spent: only what he had experienced in the streets, in the little restaurants, in the tearooms had he brought home with him of late.

So with what was he returning today?

His experiences trailed after him like a flying, power-laden tail that was invisible to the eye; Aleksandr Ivanovich experienced these experiences in reverse order, letting his conscious retreat into the tail (that is, behind his back): at those moments it always seemed to him that his back had opened and that from that back, as from a door, some giant's body was preparing to hurl itself into the abyss: this giant's body was the experience of that day's twenty-four hours; the experiences began to smoke like a tail.

Aleksandr Ivanovich was thinking: he had only to return home and the events of that day's twenty-four hours would start to break down the door; he would none the less try to trap them in the garret door, ripping the tail from the back; and the tail would break in all the same.

Behind him Aleksandr Ivanovich left the bridge a-glitter with diamonds.

Further on, beyond the bridge, against the background of a nocturnal St Isaac's, before him the perennial rock rose out of the green darkness: extending a heavy and green-covered hand the perennial Horseman[39] raised aloft above the Neva his bronze-laurel crown; above a grenadier who had fallen asleep under his shaggy hat the horse had flung out its two front hooves in bewilderment; while below, under its hooves, the shaggy grenadier's hat that belonged to the drowsing old man slowly swayed. As it fell from the hat, the metal badge struck his bayonet.

A vacillating semi-shadow covered the Horseman's face; and the metal of his face was divided by an ambiguous expression; the palm of a hand cut into the turquoise air.

Since that fraught time when the metal Horseman had come tearing to the bank of the Neva, since that time fraught with days when he had thrown his steed on to the grey Finnish granite[40] – Russia was divided in two; divided in two were the very destinies of the fatherland; divided in two, suffering and weeping, until the last hour, is Russia.

Russia, you are like a steed! Into the darkness, into the emptiness your two front hooves have raced; and firmly in the granite soil have struck root – your two back ones.

Do you too want to detach yourself from the stone that holds you, as some of your reckless sons have detached themselves from the soil – do you too want to detach yourself from the stone that holds you and hang in the air without bridle, in order later to go plunging down into the watery chaoses? Or do you want, perhaps, to rush, tearing the mists to shreds, through the air, in order together with your sons to disappear in the clouds? Or, having reared up on your hind legs, Russia, have you fallen into reflection for long years before the menacing fate that threw you here – in the midst of this gloomy North, where even the very sunset is a matter of many hours, where time itself lunges in turn now into frosty night, now into diurnal radiance? Or will you, frightened by the leap, once again lower your hooves[41] in order, snorting, to carry the great Horseman into the depths of the flat expanses out of the illusory lands?

But it will not be! . . .

Once it has soared up on its hind legs, measuring the air with its eyes, the bronze steed will not lower its hooves: a leap over history – there will be; great will be the turmoil; the earth will be cleaved; the very mountains will come crashing down because of the great *shaking of the earth*,[42] and our native plains will be made everywhere humped because of the *shaking of the earth*. Nizhny, Vladimir and Uglich[43] will end up on humps.

But Petersburg will sink.

In those days all the peoples of the earth will come rushing from their places; there will be a great strife – a strife without precedent in the world: yellow hordes of Asiatics, having moved from their long-occupied places, will turn the fields of Europe crimson with oceans of blood; there will be, there will be – a Tsushima![44] There will be, there will be – a new Kalka![45]

Kulikovo Field,[46] I wait for you!

On that day the final Sun will shine above my native land. If, Sun, you do not rise, then, oh, Sun, the shores of Europe will sink beneath the heavy Mongol heel, and above these shores the foam will curl; the creatures born of earth will once more sink to the bottom of the oceans – into the primordial, the long-forgotten chaoses . . .

Arise, oh, Sun!

. . . .

A turquoise breach rushed across the sky; while towards it through the storm clouds flew a stain of burning phosphorus, suddenly changed there into a solid, brightly shining moon; for an instant everything flared: the waters, the chimneys, the granites, the silvery flutings, the two goddesses above the arch, the roof of the four-storeyed house; the cupola of St Isaac's looked bathed in light; they flared – the Horseman's brow, the bronze-laurel crown; the lights of the islands died; while an ambiguous vessel in the middle of the Neva turned into an ordinary fishing schooner; from the captain's bridge a bright point of light shone sparklingly; perhaps it was the glow from the pipe of the blue-nosed bosun, wearing a Dutch hat with earflaps, or the bright lantern of a sailor on watch. Like a gentle soot, from the Bronze Horseman flew a gentle semishadow; and the shaggy-headed grenadier was drawn more blackly, together with the Horseman, on the paving slabs.

For an instant human fortunes were clearly illumined to Aleksandr Ivanovich: one could see what was going to happen, one could perceive what would never happen: thus all became clear; fate seemed to brighten; but he was afraid to look into his own fate; stood before fate shaken, agitated, experiencing anguish.

And – the moon cut into a cloud . . .

Again ragged arms of cloud went furiously racing; the misty strands of some kind of witches' tresses kept racing; and ambiguously among them gleamed the burning stain of phosphorus . . .

At this point resounded – a deafening, inhuman roar: its enormous headlamp unendurably gleaming, a motor car raced past, puffing kerosene – from beneath the arch towards the river. Aleksandr Ivanovich studied how the yellow, Mongol mugs[47] cut across the square; the unexpected nature of it made him fall; in front of him fell his wet hat. Behind his back there then arose a mumbling that resembled a ritual lamentation.

'Lord Jesus Christ! Save us and have mercy on us!'

Aleksandr Ivanovich turned round and realized that near him the old Nikolayevsky grenadier had begun to whisper.

'Merciful Lord, what is that?'

'A motor car: some eminent Japanese visitors . . .'

Of the motor car there was not a trace.

The spectral outline of a lackey's cocked hat and the wing of an overcoat stretched into the wind raced from mist to mist with the two lights of a carriage.

Styopka[48]

Near Petersburg, from Kolpino the high road winds: this place – there is no gloomier place! As you ride on the train towards Petersburg of a morning, you have woken up – you look: outside the windows of the carriage all is dead; not a single soul, not a single village; as though the human race had died out, and the very earth were a corpse.

Here on the surface, which consists of a tangle of frozen bushes, a black cloud presses itself against the earth from afar; the horizon there is leaden; gloomy estates creep away under the sky . . .

Many-chimneyed, many-smoke-columned Kolpino!

From Kolpino to Petersburg the high road winds: winds like a grey ribbon; its broken metal is bordered by a line of telegraph poles. There a factory-hand was plodding along with a little bundle on a stick; he had been working in a gunpowder factory and had been given the sack for some reason; and was going on foot to Petersburg; around him the yellow reeds bristled; and the wayside stones lay dead; the barriers flew up and were lowered again, the striped milestones alternated in turn, the telegraph wire jingled without end or beginning. The factory-hand was the son of a decayed shopkeeper; his name was Styopka; he had only worked at the suburban factory for about a month; and had left the factory: before him squatted Petersburg.

Many-storeyed heaps already squatted behind the factories; the factories themselves squatted behind the chimneys – over there, there, and also – there; there was not a single cloudlet in the sky, but from those places the horizon looked as though it had been smeared with soot, and a population of one and a half million choked there on the soot.

Over there, there, and also – there: noxious cinders smeared everything; and on the cinders chimneys bristled; here a chimney rose up high; barely squatted – there; further off – a row of emaciated chimneys towered up, becoming in the end simply fine hairs; in the distance dozens of fine hairs could be counted; above the soot-blackened opening of one nearby chimney, threatening the sky with an injection, a lightning conductor stuck up.

All this my Styopka saw; and to all this my Styopka paid – zero attention; sat on a pile of broken road-metal, with his boots off; bound up his feet again, chewed the pulp of a loaf. And then: dragged himself off towards the poisonous place, towards the stain of soot: towards Petersburg itself.

Towards the evening of that day the door of a yardkeeper's lodge opened: the door squealed, and the door bolt rattled: in the middle of the yardkeeper's lodge was the yardkeeper. It was Matvei Morzhov, he was immersed in reading the newspaper, and, of course, it was the *Stock Exchange Gazette*; meanwhile the buxom yardkeeper's wife (her ear always ached), who had piled up heaps of plump pillows on the table, was busying herself with the extermination of bedbugs with the help of Russian turpentine; and there was a harsh and astringent smell in the yardkeeper's lodge.

At that moment, squealing, the door of the yardkeeper's lodge opened and the block rattled; while on the threshold of the doorway Styopka stood uncertainly (the Vasily Island yardkeeper, Matvei Morzhov, was the only other person from his village in the whole of Petersburg; and of course Styopka came to see him).

Towards evening a vodka bottle appeared on the table; pickled cucumbers appeared, Bessmertny[49] the shoemaker appeared with a guitar. Styopka refused the vodka; those who drank were Morzhov and Bessmertny the shoemaker.

'Will you look at that, now . . . A fellow, a fellow from my own village has something to report,' smirked Morzhov.

'It's all because they ain't got the right ideas,' shrugged Bessmertny the shoemaker; touched a string with his finger; there was a sound: bam, bam.

'And how's the priest of Tselebeyevo?'[50]

'A real fairy tale: he's drunk all the time.'

'And the schoolmarm?'

'Oh, the schoolmarm's all right: they say she's going to marry Frol the hunchback.'

'Will you listen to that . . . the things, the things a fellow, a fellow from my own village has to tell,' said Matvei Morzhov, with emotion; and taking a cucumber in two fingers, he took a bite of that cucumber.

'It's all because they ain't got the right ideas,' shrugged Bessmertny the shoemaker: touched a string with his finger; there was a sound: bam, bam. And Styopka talked; always about the same thing: how strange people[51] had turned up in their village, that it had turned out, about all the rest, that those strange people had proclaimed that a child would be born, that there would, that was to say, be an 'amansapation', a universal 'amansapation'; and it had also turned out that this was going to happen soon, they said; but concerning the fact that he, Styopka, had himself attended the prayers of these very strange people, he said not a word; and he also talked about a visiting *barin*,[52] and all the rest of it taken together: what the *barin* was like, about all the rest: had fled to the village from his, the *barin*'s, fiancée; and so on; the *barin* had himself gone to join the strange people, but had not been able to resist their wisdom (even though he was a *barin*); you know, they were writing about him, saying he'd gone into hiding – about all the rest; and also: into the bargain, he robbed a merchant's wife; so it turned out all together that the birth of the child, the 'amansapation' and the rest of it were going to happen soon. Morzhov the yardkeeper was extremely astonished at all this buffoonery, while Bessmertny the shoemaker was not astonished: he blew on his vodka.

'It's all because they ain't got the right ideas – that's why there's the thefts, and the *barin*, and the granddaughter, and the universal emancipation; that's why there are the strange people; they ain't got no ideas: and neither does anyone else.'

He touched a string with his finger, and – 'bam', 'bam'.

But Styopka made not a sound in response to this: said nothing of the fact that he had received communiqués from those people even at the Kolpino factory; and so on, about it all: what and how. Most silent of all was he about the fact that at the Kolpino factory he had struck up an acquaintance with a *circle*, that they had had meetings near Petersburg itself; and all the rest of it. That ever since last year some of the gentry themselves, if one was to believe those people, had been attending the meetings – to excess: and – all together . . . Of all this Styopka said not a word to Bessmertny; but sang a little song:

> Tilimbru-tilishee –
> Sweet-smelling sweet pea;
> Cockerel with a crest
> By the windows pecked he.
> Child-timbru, my little child –
> Darling little Annie,
> Don't you touch the cockerel now,
> Here for you's some money.

But in response to this song Bessmertny the shoemaker merely shrugged; with all his five fingers he began to strum on the guitar: 'Tilimbru, ti-lim-bru: pam-pam-pam-pam.'

And sang:

> Never will I see you –
> Never will I see you –
> A bottle of ammonia
> In my jacket I've got.
> The ammonia from the bottle
> Down my dried-up throat I'll shove,
> In convulsions I'll fall on the pavement –
> I won't see my darling dove!

And with his five fingers on the guitar: tilimbru, tilimbru: pam-pam-pam . . . In response to which Styopka was not found wanting: he amazed everyone:

Above temptations and above misfortune
An angel stood with golden trumpet –
O Light, O Light,
Immortal Light!
Light us O immortal Light –
Before you we are as children:
You are
In Heaven!

The young *barin* who lived in garret accommodation and who had looked in at the yardkeeper's lodge listened with great attention; he questioned Styopka about the very strange people, asking him how they proclaimed the coming of the Light, and when this would come to pass; but even more did he ask them about that visiting *barin*, about Daryalsky – about all of it. The *barin* was a thin sort of fellow: obviously ill; and from time to time the *barin* emptied a glass, so that Styopka said some more edifying things to him, such as:

'*Barin*, you're ill; and so tobacco and vodka will soon make you kaput; I myself, sinful as it is, used to drink: but now I've taken the pledge. It was tobacco and vodka that started it all; and I know who it is makes people into drunkards: it's the Japs!'

'And how do you know?'

'About vodka? From Count Lev Nikolayevich Tolstoy – have you had occasion to read his booklet "The First Distiller"[53] – it says so right there; and that's what those people near Petersburg say, too.'

'And how do you know that it's the Japs?'

'That's just the way the Japs are: everyone knows about the Japs ... If you'll be so good as to remember that hurricane that passed over Moscow, they also said it was the souls of the slain; that means they must have passed over Moscow from the next world, and so they must have died without repenting. And this also means that there will be a revolt in Moscow.'

'And what will happen to Petersburg?'

'Just what's happening now: the Chinamen are building some sort of idol-worshippers' temple!'[54]

Then the *barin* took Styopka home with him, to his garret: the *barin*'s accommodation was not good; well, and the *barin* found it creepy on his own: so he took Styopka home with him; they passed the night there.

He took him home with him, sat him down in front of him, produced a tattered piece of writing from a suitcase; and read the piece of writing to Styopka: 'Your political convictions are as clear to me as the palm of my hand: all the same, it's the work of the devil, all the same, it's possession by a terrible power; you don't believe me, yet I really do know: I know that soon you will find out, as many will soon find out ... I too have been torn from the impure claws.

'A great day is approaching: there remains a decade until the beginning of the end: remember it, write it down, and pass it on to posterity; of all years, 1954 will be the most significant. This will affect Russia, for Russia is the cradle of the Church of Philadelphia;[55] Our Lord Jesus Christ himself blessed this church. I realize now why Solovyov spoke of the cult of Sophia.[56] Do you remember that? In connection with the fact that the Nizhny Novgorod female sectarians[57] ... And so on ... and so on ...'

Styopka sniffed, while the *barin* read the piece of writing: read it for a long time.

'So that's it – well, well, well. And what *barin* wrote this?'

'Oh, he lives abroad, a political exile.'

'Well, well.'

. . . .

'And what will happen, Styopka?'

'What I heard was that first of all there will be killings, and after that universal discontent; and after that all kinds of diseases – pestilence, famine, and also, the cleverest people say, all kinds of agitations: the Chinamen will rise up against one another; the Mohammedans will also get very agitated, only it won't work out.'

'Well, and what after that?'

'Well, all the rest of it will happen at the end of 1912;[58] except that in 1913 ... But wait! There's a certain prophecy, *barin*: to the effect that we must listen ... a sword will be raised against us ... and the victor's crown will go to the Japs: and then again there will be the birth of the new child. And then again, the Prussian emperor

... But wait. Here's a prophecy for you, *barin*: we must build Noah's Ark!'

'But how?'

'All right, *barin*, we shall see: you must talk to me, and I to you about this – in a whisper.'

'But what are we whispering about?'

'Still the same thing, the same: Christ's second coming.'

'Enough of this: it's all nonsense.'

. . . .

'Even so, come, Lord Jesus!'[59]

END OF THE SECOND CHAPTER

CHAPTER THE THIRD

in which it is described how Nikolai Apollonovich Ableukhov
puts his foot in it with his venture

Though he's an ordinary sort of fellow,
No second-class Don Juan he,
No demon, nor a gypsy even.
But simply dweller of the capital,
Of kind that everywhere we find a host,
Neither in face nor intellect
Much different from the average most.[1]

                                        A. Pushkin

A Holiday[2]

In a certain important place there occurred a phenomenon important in the extreme; this phenomenon occurred, that is to say, it
happened.

In connection with this incident, in the above-mentioned place
there appeared, with extremely serious faces, in embroidered uniform jackets, some persons of extreme and extraordinary powers;
they, so to speak, turned out to be there.

This was a day of extraordinary events. It was, of course, sunny.
From its very earliest hours the sun scintillated in the sky; and
everything that could scintillate, did scintillate: Petersburg roofs,
Petersburg spires, Petersburg domes.

Somewhere out there a shot was fired.[3]

If you had found time to cast a glance at that important place,
you would have seen only lacquer, only lustre; the glitter on the
mirror-like windows; well, and of course – also the glitter beyond
the mirror-like windows; the glitter on the columns; the glitter on
the parquetry; the glitter by the entrance porch, too; in a word,
lacquer, lustre and glitter!

That was why since an early hour at the various ends of the

capital of the Russian Empire all the ranks, from the third class to the first class inclusive,[4] silver-haired elders with perfumed whiskers and bald spots shining like lacquer, had been energetically putting on starched linen as though it were some knightly armour; and thus, in white, they took from cupboards their red lacquered boxes, reminiscent of ladies' diamond-cases; a yellow, old man's fingernail would press the spring, and this would make, with a click, the red lacquered lid fly open with pleasant resilience, exquisitely to reveal upon a bed of soft velvet its dazzling star; just then the same grey valet would bring into the room a coat-hanger on which one could see, first: a dazzlingly white pair of trousers; second: a uniform jacket of black lustre with a gilded breast; to these white trousers stooped a bald spot that burned like lacquer, and the grey-haired little old man, without groaning, donned on top of the white, white pair of trousers the uniform jacket of brilliant black lustre with gilded chest, on to which the silver of his grey hair aromatically fell; obliquely then did he wind around himself a bright red satin sash, if he was a cavalier of St Anne;[5] but if he was a cavalier of a higher order, then his sparkling chest was wound in a blue sash. After this festive ceremony the corresponding star was placed on the golden chest, the sword was fastened, from a specially shaped cardboard box a three-cornered hat with a plume was taken, and the grey-haired cavalier of the order – all a-glitter and a-tremble – set off in a black lacquered carriage to a place where all was a-glitter and a-tremble; to an extremely important place where already rows of extremely important persons with extremely important faces were standing. This glittering file, lined up by the rod of the chief master of ceremonies, constituted the central axle of our wheel of state.

This was a day of extraordinary events; and it was bound, of course, to shine forth; it – shone forth, of course.

From the very earliest morning all darkness vanished and there was a light whiter than electric light, the light of day; in this light scintillated all that could scintillate: Petersburg roofs, Petersburg spires, Petersburg cupolas.

At noon a cannon shot thundered.

On an extremely sunny morning, from beneath dazzlingly white sheets that suddenly flew off the bed in the dazzling little bedroom, a figure flitted out – small, all in white; that figure was somehow reminiscent of a circus rider. The impetuous figure, according to a custom hallowed by grey antiquity, proceeded to strengthen its body with Swedish gymnastics, stretching its arms and legs apart and bringing them together again, and then squatting down on its heels a dozen (and more) times. After this useful exercise the figure sprinkled its bald cranium and hands with eau-de-Cologne (triple strength, from the Petersburg Chemical Laboratory).

Then, after he had washed his cranium, hands, chin, ears and neck in cold water from the tap, and after he had satiated his organism with coffee specially brought to the room, Apollon Apollonovich Ableukhov, like the other little old men of exalted rank, confidently buttoned himself up in starched linen, pushing two striking ears and a bald spot that shone like lacquer through the opening of an armour-like shirt. After that, going out into the dressing room, Apollon Apollonovich Ableukhov took from the little cupboard (like the other little old men) his red lacquered boxes, under the lid of which, on their soft velvet bed, lay all his rare, valuable decorations. As to the others (less than the others), to him, too, was brought the lustre-pouring uniform jacket with the gilded breast; the white cloth trousers were brought, a pair of white gloves, the specially shaped cardboard box, the black scabbard of the sword, from the hilt of which hung a silver fringe; under the pressure of a yellow fingernail all ten red lacquered lids flew open and there were extracted: the White Eagle,[6] and corresponding star, and a blue sash; finally, diamond insignia were extracted; all these things settled upon the embroidered chest. Apollon Apollonovich stood before the mirror, white and gold (all — a-glitter and a-tremble!), pressing the sword to his hip with his left hand, and with his right pressing to his chest the plumed three-cornered hat and the pair of white gloves. In this trembling aspect Apollon Apollonovich ran along the corridor.

But in the drawing-room the senator for some reason paused in embarrassment; the extreme pallor of his son's face and his son's dishevelled look had evidently struck the senator.

On this day Nikolai Apollonovich rose earlier than he needed to; incidentally, Nikolai Apollonovich had not slept at all the night before: late in the evening a *likhach*[7] had flown up to the entrance porch of the yellow house; Nikolai Apollonovich, distractedly, had leapt from the carriage and proceeded to ring the doorbell with all his might; and when the door had been opened by the lackey in grey with gold braid, then Nikolai Apollonovich, without taking off his overcoat, somehow managing to get entangled in its skirts, ran up the staircase and then through a series of empty rooms; and behind him the door clicked shut. Soon some sort of shadows began to move to and fro outside the yellow house. Nikolai Apollonovich kept pacing about his room; at two o'clock in the morning footsteps could still be heard in there, and they could still be heard at half-past two, at three, at four.

Unwashed and sleepy-eyed, Nikolai Apollonovich sat morosely by the fireplace in his multicoloured robe. Apollon Apollonovich, radiance a-tremble, stopped involuntarily, reflected in the glitter of the parquets and mirrors; he stood against the background of a pier-glass, surrounded by a family of fat-cheeked cupids, who were thrusting their flames into golden garlands; and Apollon Apollonovich's hand drummed out something on the incrustation of the little table. Nikolai Apollonovich, suddenly waking up, leapt to his feet, turned round and involuntarily screwed up his eyes: and was dazzled by the white and golden little old man.

The white and golden little old man was his father; but at that moment Nikolai Apollonovich experienced no rush of kindred feeling at all; he was experiencing something quite the reverse – perhaps the same thing he had experienced in his office; in his office Nikolai Apollonovich performed acts of terrorism on himself – number one on number two: the socialist on the nobleman; and the corpse on the man in love; in his office Nikolai Apollonovich cursed his mortal self and, to the degree that he was the image and likeness of his father, he cursed his father. It was clear that his likeness to a god was bound to hate his father; but perhaps his mortal self loved his father all the same? Nikolai Apollonovich could scarcely bring himself to admit this to himself. Love? . . . I do not know if that word is apposite here. Nikolai Apollonovich knew his father as it were sympathetically, knew him down to the finest convolutions, the imperceptible tremors of inexpressible sensations; more than that; in sympathetic terms he was absolutely his father's equal; most of all he was surprised at the fact that from a psychic point of view he did not know where the senator's spirit ended within him and where, from a psychic point of view, it began, the spirit of him that was the wearer of those sparkling diamond insignia that flashed on the gleaming leaves of his embroidered chest. In the twinkling of an eye he did not so much imagine himself as actually experience himself in that sumptuous uniform jacket; whatever he would feel as he contemplated an unshaven sloven like himself in a multicoloured Bokhara robe would seem to him a violation of good form. Nikolai Apollonovich realized that he would feel disgust, that in his own way his parent would be right to feel disgust, and that his parent was feeling that disgust right now – here. He also realized that a mixture of animosity and shame now compelled him to spring up quickly like this before the white and golden little old man:

'Good morning, Papa!'

But the senator, continuing sympathetically in his son and perhaps instinctively experiencing something not entirely alien to him either (as it were, the voice of doubts that once existed within him, too – in the days of his professorship), in his turn imagined himself in a state of conscious undress, contemplating his careerist upstart of a son dressed entirely in white and gold – before his parent's undress – timidly blinked his little eyes and with a kind of impossibly exaggerated *naïveté*, cheerfully and very familiarly replied:

'My respects, sir!'

It is probable that the wearer of the diamond insignia was completely unaware of his true ending as he continued in the psyche of his son. In both of them, logic was developed decidedly to the detriment of the psyche. Their psyche appeared to them as a chaos from which only surprises were born; but when both came into psychic contact with each other, they resembled two dark air vents turned face-to-face into a complete abyss; and from abyss to abyss flowed a most unpleasant little draught; both felt that little draught here as they stood before each other; and the thoughts of both mingled, so that the son could probably continue the thought of the father.

Both lowered their eyes.

Least of all could their ineffable closeness resemble love; Nikolai Apollonovich's consciousness was, at any rate, unfamiliar with such love. Nikolai Apollonovich experienced their ineffable closeness as a shameful physiological act; at that moment he would have approached the discharge of any closeness as a natural discharge of the organism: these discharges were to be neither loved nor detested: they were to be disdained.

On his face appeared a helpless froglike expression.

'Are you in full dress today?'

Fingers were thrust into fingers; and the fingers jerked back. Apollon Apollonovich evidently wanted to express something, probably, to give a verbal explanation of the reasons for his appearing in this formal attire; and he also wanted to ask a question about the reason for his son's unnatural pallor, or at least inquire why his son had appeared at such an unusual hour. But somehow the words got stuck in his throat, and Apollon Apollonovich merely had a fit of coughing. At that moment the lackey appeared and said that the carriage was ready and waiting. Apollon Apollonovich, pleased about something, gratefully nodded to the lackey and began to hurry.

'Yes, sir, yes, sir; very good, sir.'

Apollon Apollonovich, a-glitter and a-tremble, flew past his son; soon his footsteps ceased to resound.

Nikolai Apollonovich followed his parent with his eyes: again on his face a smile appeared; abyss turned away from abyss; the draught ceased to blow.

Nikolai Apollonovich Ableukhov remembered Apollon Apollonovich Ableukhov's recent official circular, which was quite out of accordance with Nikolai Apollonovich's plans; and Nikolai Apollonovich came to the decisive conclusion that his parent, Apollon Apollonovich, was quite simply and plainly a downright scoundrel . . .

Soon the little old man was climbing the trembling staircase that was entirely carpeted in bright red cloth; on the bright red cloth, bending, his small legs began with unnatural swiftness to form angles, which swiftly calmed Nikolai Apollonovich's spirit: he loved symmetry in all things.

Soon many little old men such as himself approached him: side-whiskers, beards, bald spots, chins, gold-chested and adorned with decorations, guiding the movement of our wheel of state; and there, by the balustrade of the staircase, stood a gold-chested little group who were discussing in a murmuring bass the fateful rotation of the wheel over the potholes in the road, until the chief master of ceremonies, passing by with his rod, asked them all to form up in a line.

But immediately after the extraordinary levee, circumambulation and graciously uttered words, the little old men once again swarmed together – in the hall, in the vestibule, by the columns of the balustrade. For some reason one sparkling swarm suddenly marked itself out, and from its centre came a restless but restrained sound of talking; from there, from the centre, it was as if a velvet bumble-bee of enormous dimensions had begun to drone; he was shorter than all the others in stature, and when the gold-chested little old men surrounded him he could not be seen at all. And when Count Doublevé, of *bogatyr*-like[8] stature, with a blue sash over his shoulder, passing a hand through his grey hair, approached the group of little old men with a kind of easy familiarity and screwed up his eyes, he saw that this droning centre was Apollon Apollonovich. At once Apollon Apollonovich broke off his discourse, and with a cordiality that was not excessively lively, but was cordiality none the less, extended his hand to that fateful hand which had just signed the terms of a certain extraordinary treaty; the treaty had however been signed in . . . America. Count Doublevé somehow managed to stoop gently down to the bare cranium that came up to his shoulder, and a hissed witticism crept adroitly into an ear of pale green tints; this witticism did not, as a matter of fact, call forth a smile; the surrounding gold-chested little old men did not smile at the joke either; and the group melted away of its own accord. Together with the dignitary of *bogatyr*-like appearance, Apollon Apollonovich, too, descended the staircase; before Apollon Apollonovich Count Doublevé walked in a bent position; above them descended the sparkling little old men, below them the hook-nosed ambassador of a distant state, a little old man with red lips, Oriental; between them – small, white and gold and straight as a rod – Apollon Apollonovich descended against a fiery background of the cloth that covered the staircase.

. . . .

At this hour a large-scale military review was taking place on the wide Field of Mars; a *carré* of the Imperial Guard stood there.

From afar, through the crowd, behind the steel bristle of the bayonets of the Preobrazhentsy, the Semyonovtsy, the Izmailovtsy, the grenadiers, one could see ranks of white-horsed detachments; a solid gold ray-reflecting mirror seemed to advance slowly to a point from a point; the multicoloured insignia of the squadrons began to flutter in the air; silver bands both melodically wept and summoned from there; one could see there a row of squadrons – Cuirassiers and Horse Guards; one could also see each squadron itself – Cuirassier, Horse Guard – one could see the *galopade* of the riders in the row of squadrons – Cuirassiers, Horse Guards – fair-haired, enormous and covered in armour, in white, smooth, tight-fitting kidskin trousers, and gold and sparkling coats of mail, and radiant helmets, some crowned with a silver dove, some with a two-headed eagle; the riders of the row of squadrons pranced; the rows of the squadron pranced. And, crowned by a metal dove, on his horse before them danced the pale-moustached Baron Ommergau; and likewise crowned by a dove haughtily pranced Count Aven – Cuirassiers, Horse Guards! And out of the dust like a bloody cloud, plumes lowered, Hussars swept past on their grey chargers; their pelisses showed scarlet, their fur capes showed white in the wind behind them; the earth thundered, and sabres clanged upwards: and above the rumbling, above the dust, a stream of bright silver suddenly flowed. The red cloud of Hussars flew past somewhere to the side, and the parade ground was emptied. And again, there, in space, azure riders now emerged, giving up both to the distances and to the sun the silver of their armour: that must be a division of Gendarmes of the Guard; from afar a bugle voiced their complaint about the crowd: but they were suddenly hidden from view by brown dust; a drum rattled; infantrymen marched past.

To a Mass Meeting

After the dank early October slush, the Petersburg roofs, the Petersburg spires, and the Petersburg domes were at last dazzlingly bathed one day in frosty October sunshine.

That day Angel Peri was left alone; her husband was not at home; he was in charge of provisions – somewhere out there; the uncombed angel fluttered in her pink *kimono* between the vases of chrysanthemums and Mount Fujiyama; the skirts of the *kimono* flapped like satin wings, while the owner of that *kimono*, the aforementioned angel, kept biting, under the hypnosis of one and the same idea, now her handkerchief and now the end of her black tress of hair. Nikolai Apollonovich remained, of course, a scoundrel of scoundrels, but that newspaper contributor Neintelpfain – he too! – was also a brute. The angel's feelings were dishevelled in the extreme.

In order to bring at least some order to her dishevelled feelings, Angel Peri put her feet up on a quilted settee and opened her book: Henri Besançon, *Man and His Bodies*. The angel had already opened this book many times, but ... but: the book kept falling from her hands; Angel Peri's little eyes kept closing impetuously, and in her tiny nose a stormy life would awake: her nose whistled and snuffled.

No, today she would not fall asleep: Baroness R.R. had already inquired one day about the book; and having learned that the book had been read, one day slyly asked: 'What can you tell me, *ma chère?*' But *ma chère* said nothing; and Baroness R.R. shook her finger at her: not in vain, after all, did the inscription in the book begin with the words: 'My devachanic friend',[9] and end: 'Baroness R.R. – a mortal shell, but with a Buddhic spark.'

But – wait, wait: what are 'devachanic friend', 'shell' and 'Buddhic spark'? Well, Henri Besançon will explain that. And this time Sofya Petrovna immerses herself in Henri Besançon; but no sooner does she stick her little nose into Henri Besançon, distinctly detecting in its pages the odour of the baroness herself (the baroness perfumed herself with opoponax),[10] than the doorbell rang and in like a storm flew the *coursiste* Varvara Yevgrafovna: Angel Peri did not have time to hide the precious book properly; and the angel was caught redhanded.

'What's that?' Varvara Yevgrafovna cried sternly, applied her pince-nez to her nose, and bent over the book ...

'What's this you've got? Who gave you it?'

'Baroness R.R. ....'

'Why, of course . . . But what is it?'

'Henri Besançon . . .'

'You mean Annie Besant . . . *Man and His Bodies*? . . . What nonsense is this? . . . And have you read Karl Marx's *Manifesto*?'

The little blue eyes blinked timidly, while the crimson lips pouted resentfully.

'The bourgeoisie, sensing its end, has seized upon mysticism: we shall leave the sky to the sparrows and from the kingdom of necessity create the kingdom of freedom.'[11]

And Varvara Yevgrafovna triumphantly looked the angel over with a peremptory glance through her pince-nez: and Angel Peri's little eyes began to blink more helplessly; this angel respected Varvara Yevgrafovna and Baroness R.R. equally. And now she had to choose between them. Fortunately, however, Varvara Yevgrafovna did not make a scene; crossing her legs, she wiped her pince-nez.

'It's about this . . . You will, of course, be going to the Tsukatovs' ball . . .'

'Yes, I will,' the angel replied, guiltily.

'It's about this: according to the rumours that have reached me, our mutual acquaintance Ableukhov will also be going to this ball.'

The angel flushed crimson.

'Well, then: please give him this letter.' Varvara Yevgrafovna thrust a letter into the angel's hands.

'Give it to him; and that's all there is to it: you'll give it to him?'

'I . . . will . . .'

'Very well then, and I've no time to idle away with you here: I'm going to a mass meeting . . .'

'Varvara Yevgrafovna, be a dear and take me along with you.'

'But won't you be afraid? We may get beaten up . . .'

'No, take me, take me – be a darling dear.'

'Oh well then, all right: let's go. Only you're going to change; and the rest of it, powder yourself . . . So be quick about it . . .'

'Oh, instantly: in a flash!'

. . . .

'O Lord, quick, quick . . . My corset, Mavrushka! . . . My black woollen dress, yes, that one: and shoes – those ones, any ones. Oh, but no: the high-heeled ones.' And the skirts rustled in falling: the pink *kimono* flew across the table on to the bed . . . Mavrushka got into a muddle: Mavrushka knocked a chair over . . .

'No, not like that, but tighter: even tighter . . . those are not hands you have – they're stumps . . . Where are the garters – eh, eh? How many times have I told you?' And the corset crackled its bone; while her trembling hands could still on no account pile up at the nape of her neck the black nights of her tresses . . .

Sofya Petrovna Likhutina, an ivory hairpin in her teeth, began to squint: she was squinting at a letter; and the letter bore the clear inscription: *To Nikolai Apollonovich Ableukhov.*

That she would meet 'him' tomorrow at the Tsukatovs' ball, talk to him, give him this letter – that was both frightening and painful: there was something fateful here – no, one must not think of it, must not think of it!

A disobedient black lock sprang out from the nape of her neck.

Yes, a letter. The letter was clearly marked: *To Nikolai Apollonovich Ableukhov.* Only the strange thing was that this handwriting was the handwriting of Lippanchenko . . . What nonsense!

Now, in a black woollen dress that fastened at the back, she fluttered forth from the bedroom:

'Well, let's go, let's go, then . . . By the way, that letter . . . Who is it from? . . .'

'?'

'Oh well, never mind, never mind: I'm ready.'

Why was she in such a hurry to be off to the mass meeting? In order, *en route*, to try to find out what was going on, to ask questions, to try to get what she wanted?

And ask what questions?

Outside the entrance porch they collided with the *khokhol*-Little Russian Lippanchenko:

'Well, well, well: where are you going?'

Sofya Petrovna waved in vexation both a plush velvet hand and a muff:

'I'm going to a mass meeting, a mass meeting.'

But the crafty *khokhol* was not to be put off so easily:

'Splendid: I'll come with you.'

Varvara Yevgrafovna flared up, stopped: and stared fixedly at the *khokhol.*

'I think I know you: you rent a room ... from the Manpon woman.'

Here the shameless, crafty *khokhol* was thrown into the most violent embarrassment: he suddenly began to puff and pant, to back away, raised his hat a little and fell behind.

'Tell me, who is that unpleasant individual?'

'Lippanchenko.'

'Well, that's quite untrue: his name isn't Lippanchenko, it's Mavrokordato, a Greek from Odessa; he visits the room through the wall from me: I wouldn't advise you to receive him in your home.'

But Sofya Petrovna was not listening. Mavrokordato, Lippanchenko – it was all the same ... The letter, now, the letter ...

Noble, Slender, Pale . . .

They were walking along the Moika.

To their left the last gold and the last crimson of the garden trembled in the leaves; and, approaching more closely, one could have seen the blue tit as well; while from the garden on to the stones obediently stretched a rustling thread, in order to twine and chase at the feet of the passing pedestrian and to whisper, weaving from the leaves yellow and red alluvial deposits of words.

'Ooo-ooo-ooo . . .' – thus did space resound.

'Do you hear?'

'What is it?'

. . . .

'Ooo-ooo.'

. . . .

'I don't hear anything.'

But that sound was heard softly in towns, woodlands and fields, in the suburban expanses of Moscow, Petersburg, Saratov. Have you heard this October song of the year nineteen hundred and five? This song did not exist earlier; this song will not exist ...

'It must be a factory siren: there's a strike at a factory somewhere.'

But no factory siren was sounding, there was no wind; and the dog was silent.

To the right, below their feet, was the blue of the Moika canal, while behind it above the water rose the reddish line of the embankment's stones, crowned by trellised iron lace: that same bright building of the Alexandrine era rested on its five stone columns; and the entrance showed gloomy between the columns; above the second storey still passed the same stripe of ornamental stucco: ring upon ring – the same stucco rings.

Between the canal and the building, drawn by its own private horses, an overcoat flew past, concealing in its beaver fur the freezing tip of a haughty nose; and a bright yellow cap-band swayed, and the pink cushion of the driver's hat flickered ever so slightly. Drawing even with Likhutina, high above his bald spot flew the bright yellow cap-band of one of Her Majesty's Cuirassiers: it was Baron Ommau-Ommergau.

Ahead, where the canal curved, rose the red walls of the church, tapering to a high tower and a green steeple; while more to the left, above a ledge of houses and stone, the dazzling cupola of St Isaac's rose sternly in a glassy turquoise.

Here too was the embankment: depth, a greenish blue. There far away, far away, almost further than was proper, the islands fell and cowered: the buildings also cowered; at any moment the depths might come washing, surging over them, the greenish blue. And above this greenish blue an unmerciful sunset sent here and there its radiant crimson blow: and the Troitsky Bridge shone crimson; and so did the Palace.

Suddenly under this depth and greenish blue a clear silhouette appeared against the crimson background of the sunset: in the wind a grey Nikolayevka beat its wings; and a waxen face with protruding lips nonchalantly threw itself back: in the bluish expanses of the Neva its eyes constantly looked for something, could not find it, flew past above her modest little fur hat; did not see the hat: did not see anything – either her, or Varvara Yevgrafovna: saw only the depth, and the greenish blue; rose and fell – there fell the eyes, on the other side of the Neva, where the banks cowered and the buildings of the islands showed crimson. While ahead, snuffling, ran a dark, striped bulldog, carrying a small silver whip in its teeth.

Drawing level, he came to his senses, screwed up his eyes slightly, touched his cap-band slightly with his hand; said nothing – and walked off there: there only the buildings showed crimson.

With completely squinting eyes, hiding her little face in her muff (she was now redder than a peony), Sofya Petrovna helplessly nodded her little head somewhere to the side: not to him, but to the bulldog. While Varvara Yevgrafovna fairly stared, breathed heavily, fastened her eyes.

'Ableukhov?'

'Yes . . . apparently.'

And, hearing an affirmative reply (she was short-sighted), Varvara Yevgrafovna began to whisper to herself excitedly:

> Noble, slender, pale,
> Hair like flax has he;
> Rich in thought, in feeling poor
> N.A.A. – who can he be?[12]

There, there he was:

> Famous revolutionary,
> Though aristocrat.
> But better than his shameful folks
> A hundred times, mark that.

There he was, the regenerator of the rotten order, to whom she (soon, soon!) was going to propose a citizens' marriage upon the accomplishment of the mission that had been appointed to him, upon which there would follow a universal, world-wide explosion: here she choked (Varvara Yevgrafovna was in the habit of swallowing her saliva too loudly).

'What is it?'

'Nothing: a lofty motif came into my head.'

But Sofya Petrovna was not listening any more: unexpectedly to herself, she turned and saw that there, there on the front square of the palace in the light purple thrust of the Neva's last rays, somehow strangely turned towards her, stooping, and hiding his face in his collar, which caused his student's peaked cap to slip down, stood

Nikolai Apollonovich; it seemed to her that he was smiling in a most unpleasant manner and in any case cut a rather ridiculous figure: wrapped tightly in his overcoat, he looked both round-shouldered and somehow lacking arms, with the wing of the overcoat dancing most preposterously in the wind; and, seeing all that, she swiftly turned her little head.

Long yet did he stand, bent, smiling in an unpleasant manner and in any case cutting the rather ridiculous figure of a man without arms, the wing of his overcoat dancing so preposterously in the wind against the crimson stain of the sunset's wedge. But in any case he was not looking at her: was it indeed possible for him, with his awkwardness, to study retreating figures; he was laughing to himself and staring far, far away, almost further than was proper – there, where the island buildings sank, where they barely glimmered through the mist in the crimson smoke.

While she – she wanted to cry; she wanted her husband, Sergei Sergeich Likhutin, to go up to that scoundrel, suddenly strike him in the face with a cypress fist and say, apropos of this, his honour-able, officer's word.

The unmerciful sunset sent blow upon blow from the very horizon itself; higher rose the immensity of the rosy ripples; yet higher the small white clouds (now rosy) like fine impressions of broken mother-of-pearl were disappearing in a turquoise all; that turquoise all poured evenly between the splinters of rosy mother-of-pearl: soon the mother-of-pearl, drowning in the heights, as if retreating into an oceanic depth – would extinguish in the turquoise the most delicate reflections: the dark blue, the bluish-green depth would surge everywhere: over houses, granite and water.

And there would be no sunset.

Comte–Comte–Comte!

The lackey served the soup. Before the senator's plate, as a prelimi-nary, he placed the pepper-pot from the cruet-stand.

Apollon Apollonovich appeared out of the doorway in his small grey jacket; just as quickly did he sit down; and the lackey removed the lid from the smoking tureen.

The left-hand door opened; swiftly through the left-hand door sprang Nikolai Apollonovich, wearing a student's uniform jacket buttoned up to the neck; the jacket had a very high collar (from the time of Emperor Alexander I).

Both raised their eyes to each other; and both were embarrassed (they were always embarrassed).

Apollon Apollonovich flung his gaze from object to object; Nikolai Apollonovich felt his daily confusion: his two completely unnecessary arms hung down on both sides of his waist; and in an access of fruitless obsequiousness, running up to his parent he began to wring his slender fingers (finger against finger).

A daily spectacle awaited the senator: his unnaturally polite son overcame, with unnatural swiftness, at a skip and a run, the expanse of distance from the door – all the way to the dinner table. Apollon Apollonovich impetuously rose (anyone would have said – leapt up) before his son.

Nikolai Apollonovich tripped against the table leg.

Apollon Apollonovich proffered to Nikolai Apollonovich his pudgy lips; to these pudgy lips Nikolai Apollonovich pressed two lips; the lips touched one another; and two fingers shook the customarily sweating hand.

'Good evening, Papa!'

'My respects, sir . . .'

Apollon Apollonovich sat down. Apollon Apollonovich caught hold of the pepper-pot. It was Apollon Apollonovich's custom to over-pepper his soup.

'From the university? . . .'

'No, I've been out for a walk . . .'

And a froglike expression fleeted across the grinning mouth of the courteous offspring, whose face we have had time to examine taken in isolation from all the grimaces, smiles or gestures of courtesy that were the bane of Nikolai Apollonovich's life, if only because of the *Grecian mask* there remained not a trace; these smiles, grimaces, or simply gestures of courtesy streamed in a kind of constant cascade before the fluttering gaze of the absent-minded papa; and his hand, as it brought the spoon to his mouth, clearly trembled, splashing soup.

'Have you come from the Institution, Papa?'

'No, from the minister . . .'

. . . .

We saw in the foregoing that when he sat in his office Apollon Apollonovich came to the conviction that his son was an arrant rogue: thus daily did the sixty-eight-year-old papa commit upon his own blood and his own flesh a certain act which, though comprehensible, was none the less an act of terrorism.

But those were abstract, office conclusions, which were not taken out into the corridor, nor (even more so) into the dining-room.

'Would you like some pepper, Kolenka?'

'I'd like some salt, Papa . . .'

Apollon Apollonovich, looking at his son, or rather fluttering around the grimacing young philosopher with fleeting eyes, according to the tradition of this hour gave himself up to a rush of, so to speak, paternality, avoiding the office in his thoughts.

'Well, I like pepper: pepper makes everything tastier . . .'

Nikolai Apollonovich, lowering his eyes to his plate, banished the tiresome associations from his memory: the Neva sunset and the inexpressible quality of the rosy ripples, the most delicate reflections of mother-of-pearl, the bluish-green depth; and against the background of most delicate mother-of-pearl . . .

'Indeed, sir! . . .

'Indeed, sir! . . .

'Very good, sir . . .'

Apollon Apollonovich was engaging his son (or rather – himself) in conversation.

The silence over the table grew heavier.

This silence during the eating of the soup did not trouble Apollon Apollonovich in the slightest (old people are not troubled by silence, while nervous youth is) . . . As he searched for a topic of conversation, Nikolai Apollonovich experienced genuine torment over his now cold plate of soup.

And unexpectedly to himself he burst out:

'I say . . . I . . .'

'I say, what?'

'No . . . Just . . . nothing . . .'

Over the table silence weighed.

Nikolai Apollonovich again, unexpectedly to himself, burst out (this was true fidgetiness, now!)

'I say . . . I . . .'

But what was this 'I say I'? He had not yet thought up a sequel to the words that leapt out; and there was no idea to accompany the 'I say . . . I . . .'. And Nikolai Apollonovich stumbled . . .

'I shall have to think up something to go with "I say I",' he thought. And could think of nothing.

Meanwhile Apollon Apollonovich, disturbed a second time by his son's preposterous verbal confusion, suddenly hurled up his gaze questioningly, sternly and capriciously, indignant at the 'mumbling' . . .

'I'm sorry: what did you say?'

While in the head of his dear offspring senseless words frantically began to revolve:

'Perception . . .

'Apperception . . .'[13]

'Pepper is not pepper, but a term: terminology . . .

'Logia, logic . . .'

And suddenly out whirled:

'I say . . . I . . . read in Cohen's *Theorie der Erfahrung* . . .'[14]

And stumbled again.

'Well, and what sort of book is that, Kolenka?'

In addressing his son, Apollon Apollonovich involuntarily observed the traditions of childhood; and in intercourse with this *arrant rogue* addressed the arrant rogue as 'Kolenka', 'dear offspring', 'my friend' and even – 'my good fellow' . . .

'Cohen, the most important representative of European Kantianism.'

'I'm sorry – Kantianism?'

'Kantianism, Papa.'

'Kan-ti-an-ism?'

'Precisely . . .'

'But wasn't Kant refuted by Comte?[15] Is it Comte you mean?'

'Not Comte, Papa – Kant! . . .'

'But Kant is not scientific . . .'

'It's Comte who's not scientific . . .'

. . . .

'I don't know, I don't know, my friend: in our time we saw it differently . . .'

. . . .

Apollon Apollonovich, now tired and for some reason unhappy, slowly rubbed his eyes with small, cold fists, repeating absent-mindedly:

'Comte . . .

'Comte . . .

'Comte . . .'

Lustre, lacquer, glitter and some kind of red sparks began to rush about in his eyes (Apollon Apollonovich always saw before his eyes, so to speak, two different types of space: the space that is ours and also the space of some spinning network of lines, which turned gold at nights).

Apollon Apollonovich reasoned that his brain was once again suffering violent rushes of blood caused by the intense haemorrhoidal condition he had been in all the previous week; his cranium leaned against the dark side of his armchair, into a dark depth; his dark blue eyes stared questioningly:

'Comte . . . Yes: Kant . . .'

He thought for a moment and hurled his eyes up at his son:

'Well, and what sort of book is that, Kolenka?'

. . . .

It was with instinctive cunning that Nikolai Apollonovich had begun to talk about Cohen; a conversation about Cohen was a most neutral conversation; with this conversation *other conversations* were got out of the way; and any kind of explanatory scene was postponed (from day to day – from month to month). And moreover: the habit of holding edifying conversations had been preserved in Nikolai Apollonovich's soul from the days of his childhood: from the days of childhood Apollon Apollonovich had encouraged conversations of this kind in his son: thus formerly upon Nikolai Apollonovich's return from the gymnasium had son explained to papa with visible ardour the details of cohorts, testudos and *turres*; along with other details of the Gallic War; with satisfaction then did Apollon Apollonovich attend to his son, indulgently encouraging the interests of the gymnasium. And in later years Apollon Apollonovich would even put his hand on Kolenka's shoulder.

'You ought to read Mill's *Logic*,[16] Kolenka: you know, it's a useful book . . . Two volumes . . . In my time I read it from cover to cover . . .'

And Nikolai Apollonovich, who had only just swallowed Sigwart's *Logic*,[17] none the less took to entering the dining-room for tea with a most enormous tome in his hand. Apollon Apollonovich would, as if casually, ask him with affection:

'What's that you're reading, Kolenka?'

'Mill's *Logic*, Papa.'

'Indeed, sir, indeed, sir . . . Very good, sir!'

. . . .

Even now, divided to the end, they unconsciously returned to old memories: their dinners frequently concluded with an edifying conversation . . .

At one time Apollon Apollonovich had been a professor of the philosophy of law:[18] during that time he had read much and to the end. All that had vanished without a trace: faced with the elegant pirouettes of congeneric logic, Apollon Apollonovich felt a futile heaviness. Apollon Apollonovich was unable to answer the arguments of his dear offspring.

He did, however, reflect: 'One must give Kolenka credit: his mental apparatus is distinctly developed.'

At the same time Nikolai Apollonovich felt with satisfaction that his parent was an uncommonly conscientious listener.

Even a semblance of friendship would arise between them by dessert: they were sometimes reluctant to break off the dinner-time conversation, as if they were both afraid of one another; as though each of them were privately and sternly signing a death sentence on the other.

Both stood up: both began to walk about the enfilade of rooms; white Archimedes rose into the shadow: there, there; and also there; the enfilade of rooms lay black; from afar, from the drawing-room, came the reddish flashes of a fermentation of light; from afar, from the drawing-room, a glint of fire began to crackle.

Thus once upon a time had they wandered about the empty enfilade of rooms – the little boy and the . . . still tender father; the still tender father would pat the fair-haired little boy on the shoulder; afterwards the tender father would lead the little boy over to the window and raise his finger to the stars:

'The stars are far away, Kolenka: it takes a pencil of rays more than two years to travel from the nearest star to the earth . . . that's how it is, my boy!' And then one day the tender father wrote his son a little poem:

> Silly little simpleton
> Kolenka is dancing:
> He has put his dunce-cap on –
> On his horse he's prancing.

Thus once had the contours of the little tables emerged from the shadows, the rays of the embankment lights flown through from the window-pane: the incrustations of the little tables were beginning to shine. Had the father really come to the conclusion that the blood of his blood was the blood of a scoundrel? Did the son really laugh at old age?

> Silly little simpleton
> Kolenka is dancing:
> He has put his dunce-cap on –
> On his horse he's prancing.

Had this happened? Perhaps it had not . . . anywhere, ever?

Both now sat on the satin drawing-room couch, in order aimlessly to drawl insignificant words: they looked intently and expectantly into each other's eyes, and the red flame from the hearth breathed warmth on to them both; shaven, grey and old, Apollon Apollonovich stood out, ears and jacket, against the twinkling flame: it was with just such a face as this that he had been depicted against a background of burning Russia on the cover of a little street journal. Extending a dead hand and not looking his son in the eye, Apollon Apollonovich asked in a failing voice:

'My friend, does that that . . . mm . . . that, er . . . visit you often?'

'Who, Papa?'

'Oh that fellow, what's his name . . . the young man . . .'

'A young man?'

'Yes – with a small black moustache.'

Nikolai Apollonovich bared his teeth in a grin, and suddenly began to wring his sweaty hands . . .

'You mean the fellow you found in my study today?'

'Why yes – the very same . . .'

'Aleksandr Ivanovich Dudkin! . . . No . . . You don't say so . . .'

And having said 'You don't say so', Nikolai Apollonovich reflected:

'Well, why did I say "You don't say so"?'

And, having reflected, added:

'He just comes to visit me.'

. . . .

'If . . . if . . . this is an indiscreet question, then . . . I suppose . . .'

'What, Papa? . . .'

'He came to you on . . . university business?'

. . . .

'Though actually . . . if my question is, so to speak, out of place . . .'

'Why out of place?'

'He's not a bad sort . . . a pleasant young man: poor, as one can see . . .'

. . . .

'Is he a student?'

'Yes, he is.'

'At the university?'

'Yes, that's right . . .'

'Not the technical institute? . . .'

'No, Papa . . .'

Apollon Apollonovich knew that his son was lying; Apollon Apollonovich looked at his watch; Apollon Apollonovich got up, indecisively. Nikolai Apollonovich was tormentingly aware of his arms, and Apollon Apollonovich's eyes began to roam in confusion:

'Yes, that's right . . . There are many special branches of knowledge in the world: every specialism is profound — you are right. You know, Kolenka, I'm tired.'

Apollon Apollonovich was trying to ask his son, who was rubbing his hands, about something . . . He stood for a bit, looked for a bit, and . . . did not ask, but lowered his eyes: for a moment Nikolai Apollonovich felt shame.

Mechanically Apollon Apollonovich extended his pudgy lips to his dear offspring: and his hand shook . . . two fingers.

'Good night, Papa!'

'My respects, sir!'

Somewhere to the side a mouse began to shuffle, to rustle, and suddenly squeaked.

. . . .

Soon the door of the senator's study opened: holding a candle, Apollon Apollonovich ran into a certain room that had no comparison, in order to devote himself to . . . reading the newspaper.

. . . .

Nikolai Apollonovich went over to the window.

Some kind of phosphorescent stain was racing both mistily and furiously across the sky; the distances of the Neva were misted over by a phosphorescent sheen, and this made the soundlessly flying surfaces begin to gleam green, giving off now there, now here a spark of gold; here and there on the water a tiny red light would flare up and, having blinked, retreat into the phosphorescently extended murk. Beyond the Neva, showing dark, the massive buildings of the islands rose, casting into the mists their palely shining eyes — infinitely, soundlessly, tormentingly: and they seemed to be weeping. Higher up, ragged arms furiously extended some kind of vague outlines; swarm upon swarm they rose above the Neva's waves; while from the sky the phosphorescent stain hurled itself upon them. Only in one place that had not been touched by chaos — there, where by day the Troitsky Bridge was thrown across — enormous clusters of diamonds showed misty above a glittering swarm of annulated, luminous serpents; both twining and untwining, the serpents sped from there in a sparkling file; and then, diving down, rose to the surface like strings of stars.

Nikolai Apollonovich was lost in contemplation of the strings.

. . . .

The embankment was empty. From time to time the black shadow of a policeman passed, looming black against the light mist and dissolving again; they loomed black and disappeared in the mist, the buildings on the other side of the Neva; and the spire of the Peter and Paul Fortress loomed black and again retreated into the mist.

Some kind of female shadow had long now loomed black against the mist: standing by the railings, it did not retreat into the mist but stared straight at the windows of a yellow house. Nikolai Apollonovich smiled a most unpleasant smile: applying his pince-nez to his nose, he studied the shadow; Nikolai Apollonovich's eyes bulged with amorous cruelty, as he stared and stared at that shadow; joy distorted his features.

No, no: it was not she; but she too, like that shadow, kept walking and walking round the yellow house; and he saw her; everything in his soul was troubled. She loved him, without doubt; but a fateful and terrible vengeance awaited her.

The black, fortuitous shadow had already dissolved in the mist.

. . . .

In the depths of the dark corridor a metal bolt rattled, in the depths of the dark corridor light flickered: holding a candle, Apollon Apollonovich was returning from a certain place that had no comparison: his grey, mouse-coloured dressing-gown, his grey, shaven cheeks and the enormous contours of his completely dead ears were sculpted from afar in the dancing lamps. Apollon Apollonovich Ableukhov walked to the door of his study in order to sink back into complete darkness; and the place of his passage yawned gloomily, from the open door.

. . . .

Nikolai Apollonovich thought: 'It's time.'

Nikolai Apollonovich knew that the mass meeting today would last until late at night, that *she* was going to the meeting (the guarantee of this was the fact that Varvara Yevgrafovna was *accompanying* her: Varvara Yevgrafovna took everyone to the meetings). Nikolai Apollonovich reflected that more than two hours had already passed since he met them, on the way to the *gloomy building*; and now he thought: '*It's time . . .*'

The Mass Meeting

In the spacious vestibule of the gloomy building there was a desperate crush.

The crush carried Angel Peri, swaying her back and forth between someone's back and chest, and she made desperate efforts to stretch out her hands to Varvara Yevgrafovna: but Varvara Yevgrafovna, who could not hear, was somewhere over there, flailing, struggling, pushing; and then she suddenly vanished in the crush; along with her vanished the chance to question her about the letter. What need had she of the letter! In her eyes the stains of the sunset still shone crimson; and there, there: somehow strangely turned towards her on the front square of the palace in the light crimson glow of the last rays of the Neva, stooping, hiding his face in his collar, stood Nikolai Apollonovich with a most unpleasant smile. No! In any case he cut a rather ridiculous figure: looked round-shouldered and somehow lacking arms with that wing of his overcoat that was so preposterously dancing in the wind; she felt like crying from deep offence, as though he had struck her painfully with a small silver whip, that same silver whip which the dark, striped bulldog carried in its teeth, snorting; she wanted her husband, Sergei Sergeich Likhutin, to go up to that scoundrel and suddenly strike him in the face with a cypress fist and say, apropos of this, his officer's word; in her eyes the small clouds of the Neva still fleeted like fine impressions of broken mother-of-pearl, between which evenly poured the turquoise all.

But in the crush the most delicate reflections died, from all sides chests, backs and faces came surging, a black darkness into a foggy yellowish murk.

And the individuals kept barging and barging, the shaggy hats and the young ladies: body barged into body; nose flattened against back; the small head of a pretty female gymnasium pupil squeezed against one's chest, while at one's feet a second-form boy cheeped;

under pressure from behind, an outrageously extended nose was pierced by a hat-pin, and there too a chest was threatened with puncture by the perforatingly sharp angle of an elbow; there was nowhere to take one's coat off; steam hung in the air, illumined by candles (as it proved later, the electricity suddenly broke down – the electric power station had evidently begun to get up to mischief: soon it would get up to mischief for a long time).

And everyone barged, everyone struggled: of course, Sofya Petrovna got stuck for a long time at the foot of the staircase, but Varvara Yevgrafovna fought her way out, of course, and was now pushing, struggling and beating somewhere high up at the top of the staircase; some kind of highly respectable Jew in a lambskin hat, with spectacles and very grey hair had fought his way out together with her: swinging round to face backwards, in utter horror he pulled his own coat by the skirts; and could not pull it free; failing to do so, he started to shout:

'A fine public; not a public, but a *schweinerei*! A R-russian *schweinerei*! . . .'

'Vell, and what are you up to, vy are you in our R-r-assia?' was heard from somewhere below.

This was a Bundist-socialist[19] Jew arguing with a Jew who was not a Bundist, but was a socialist.

In the hall body sat upon body, body pressed against body; and the bodies swayed; they were agitated and shouted to one another that in this place and that place and that place there was a strike, that in this place and that place and that place a strike was in preparation, that people were going to strike – in this place, in this place and this place: were going to strike right here, in this very place: and – not to budge!

First a party worker from the intelligentsia spoke about this, and then a student repeated the same thing after him; after the student a *coursiste*; after the *coursiste* a class-conscious proletarian, but when a non-class-conscious proletarian tried to repeat the same thing, a representative of the lumpen proletariat began to trumpet to the whole hall, as out of a barrel, in such a great, thick voice that everyone started:

'Com . . . rradds! . . . I'm a poor man – a prrroletarian, com . . . rrraddds! . . .'

Thunderous applause.

'Yes, com . . . rradds! . . . And that means that this is government . . . tyranny . . . yes! yes! I'm a poor man, and I say: strr-ike, com-rradds!'

Thunderous applause (True! True! Stop him speaking! It's an outrage, ladies and gentlemen! He's drunk!).

'No, I'm not drunk, com-rradds! . . . And that means that this bourgeoisie . . . how can you work, work . . . One single word; grab his legs and into the water with him; that's to say . . . strike!'

(Blow of fist on table: thunderous applause).

But the chairman stopped the worker from speaking any more.

The best speaker of all was the respected collaborator on a certain respected newspaper, Neintelpfain: he spoke, and at once vanished. Some kind of little boy made an attempt to proclaim a boycott from the top of the four steps of the rostrum: but the little boy was laughed down; was it worth bothering with nonsense like this when there were strikes in this place and that place and that place, when there was a strike right here – and not to budge? And the little boy, almost weeping, came down from the top of the four steps of the rostrum; and then a sixty-five-year-old female *zemstvo* official mounted those steps and told the assembly:

> Sow the useful, the good, the eternal,
> Sow, and the Russian people will give you a heartfelt
> Thank you![20]

But the sowers laughed. Then someone suddenly proposed the destruction of everyone and everything: he was a mystical anar-chist.[21] Sofya Petrovna did not hear the anarchist, but was pressed back, and it was a strange thing: Varvara Yevgrafovna had explained to Sofya Petrovna more than once that at mass meetings the useful and the good were sown, which deserved a hearty *thank you* on her part. But oh no, oh no! They all laughed wildly at the old female official of sixty-five who told them the same thing (about sowing); for then why had the seed not sprouted in her little heart? What had grown, obscurely, were some kind of nettles; and her little head ached dreadfully; whether because she had seen him before, whether because she had such a tiny forehead, or whether because some kind of possessed individuals were staring at her from all sides, individuals who had gone on strike in this place and that place, and had now come to go on strike here, to stare at her out of the yellow, foggy murk, to bare their teeth in loud laughter. And this chaos awoke within her an anger that was incomprehensible even to herself; after all, she was a lady, and one ought not to arouse chaos in ladies; this chaos concealed all kinds of cruelties, crimes, falls; in every lady at that time a criminal lurked; something criminal had long lurked within her.

Now she was approaching the corner together with an officer who was walking with her, whom people regarded with a smile, whispering condescendingly to one other, and who suddenly took offence at the boycott that had been declared by the little boy, and offended, quickly walked away – she was approaching the corner, and as she did so a detachment of Cossacks flew out in front of her at full gallop from the gateway of the house next door on their unkempt horses; blue bearded men in tall, shaggy Astrakhan hats and with rifles at the ready, real ragamuffins, dancing brazenly, mutely, impatiently in their saddles – there, to the building. Seeing this, some sort of worker came running towards the officer from the corner, stretched out his hand to him and began to say, panting:

'Mr Officer, Mr Officer!'

'Sorry, I've no small change . . .'

'Oh, that's not what I want: what's going to happen there now? . . . What's going to happen? . . . Those defenceless young ladies there – the *coursistes* . . .'

The officer grew embarrassed, turned red, for some reason touched his cap in salute:

'I don't know, to tell you the truth . . . That's not why I'm here . . . I'm only just back from Manchuria; look – here's my St George's medal . . .'

And something had already happened over there.

Tatam: Tam, Tam![22]

It was now late.

Sofya Petrovna was returning home quietly, hiding her little nose in her downy muff; at her back, Troitsky Bridge stretched infinitely over to the islands, withdrawing into those silent places; and shadows stretched across the bridge; on the great iron bridge, above the damp, damp railings, above the greenish water that seethed with bacilli, there came behind her in the gusts of Neva wind – bowler, cane, coat, ears, moustache and nose.

Suddenly her eyes stopped, dilated, blinked, crossed: under the damp, damp railings, bow-legged, sat a dark, tiger-like beast, snuffling and slavering on a small silver whip it had in its teeth; the dark, tiger-like beast turned its snub-nosed muzzle away from her; and when she cast a glance at the averted muzzle, she saw: that same waxen face, making its lips protrude above the damp railings, above the greenish water that seethed with bacilli, stretched forth there out of the overcoat; with his lips protruding, he seemed to be thinking some magical thought, one which had echoed within her, too, these past few days, because these past few days the words of a certain homely romance had so tormentingly sung themselves to her:

> Gazing at the rays of purple sunset
> You stood upon the bank of the Neva.[23]

And lo and behold: there he was, standing on the bank of the Neva, somehow dully staring into the green, or rather, no – letting his gaze fly away to where the banks cowered, where the buildings of the islands squatted submissively and from where above the white walls of the fortress hopelessly and coldly the sharp, unmerciful, cold spire of Peter and Paul stretched tormentingly towards the sky.

All of her stretched out to him – what use were words, what use were reflections! But again – again he had not noticed her; his lips protruding, his eyes glassily dilated, he looked quite simply like an armless freak; and again without arms into the wind flew the wings of his overcoat above the railings of the bridge.

But when she moved away, Nikolai Apollonovich slowly turned round to face her and went mincing off at a fair pace, stumbling and tripping on the long skirts of his coat; but at the corner of the bridge a *likhach* was waiting: and the *likhach* flew off; and when the *likhach* caught up with Sofya Petrovna Likhutina, Nikolai

Apollonovich, leaning out and squeezing the bulldog's collar in his hands, turned, round-shouldered, to the small, dark figure who had stuck her little nose so forlornly into her muff; looked, and smiled; but the *likhach* flew past.

Suddenly the first snow began to fall; and with such lively little diamonds did it sparkle in the circle of light from the street lamp as it danced; the light circle just barely illumined now a side of the palace, and the small canal, and the small stone bridge; into the depths ran the canal; all was deserted: a solitary *likhach* was whistling on the corner, waiting for someone; a grey Nikolayevka lay carelessly tossed on the carriage.

Sofya Petrovna Likhutina stood on the arch of the small bridge and looked dreamily – into the depths, into the small canal that lapped in its shroud of vapour; Sofya Petrovna Likhutina had stopped at this spot before; had stopped with him here, once upon a time; and sighed about Liza, arguing earnestly about the horrors of *The Queen of Spades*[24] – about the divine, charming, wonderful harmonies of a certain opera, and had then sung in a low voice, conducting with her finger:

'Tatam: tam, tam! . . . Tatatam: tam, tam, tam!'

Now again she stood here; her lips opened, and a small finger was raised:

'Tatam, tam, tam! . . . Tatatam: tam, tam!'

But she heard the sound of running footsteps, looked – and did not even utter a scream: suddenly a red domino almost perplexedly thrust itself from round the side of the palace, rushed hither and thither, as though it were searching for something, and, seeing a woman's shadow on the arch of the small bridge, threw itself towards it; in its jerky running it stumbled on the stones, stretching forward its mask with narrow slits for the eyes; and behind the mask a stream of icy Neva wind began to play in a thick fan of lace, black of course; and as the mask ran towards the small bridge, Sofya Petrovna Likhutina, without even having time to reflect that the domino was a joker, that some tasteless prankster (and we know who it was) had quite simply decided to play a joke on her, that behind the velvet mask and the black lace beard there quite simply hid a human face; there it was now, staring at her vigilantly through the oblong slits. Sofya Petrovna thought (she had, after all, such a tiny little forehead) that some sort of hole had formed in this world, and from there, from the hole, and not from this world at all, the buffoon had rushed at her: as to who this buffoon was, she would probably not have been able to answer.

But when the black lace beard, stumbling, flew on to the small bridge, the buffoon's satin blades flew aloft with a rustling in a gust of the Neva's wind and, gleaming red, fell over there, beyond the railings – into the dark-coloured night; the all too familiar trouser straps were revealed, and the fearsome buffoon became a buffoon who was merely pathetic; at that moment a galosh slipped on a salience in the stone: the pathetic buffoon came crashing down on the stone at full tilt; and above him now there resounded not even laughter at all: simply a loud guffaw.

'You wretched little frog, you freak – you red buffoon . . .'

A swift female foot rewarded the buffoon angrily with kicks.

Some kind of bearded men now came running along the canal; and a police whistle sounded from afar; the buffoon leapt to his feet; the buffoon rushed to the *likhach*, and from afar one could see something red helplessly floundering about in the carriage, trying to pull a Nikolayevka about its shoulders as it flew. Sofya Petrovna began to cry, and fled from this accursed place.

Soon, in pursuit of the *likhach*, a snub-nosed bulldog ran out from behind the Winter Canal, barking; its short legs flickered in the air, and behind them, behind the short legs, on rubber tyres, in pursuit, sprawling, two agents of the secret police were already hurtling.

Shadows

Shadow was talking to shadow:

'My dear, dear fellow, you have left out one rather important fact which I have learned with the help of my own methods.'

'What is it?'

'You haven't made a sound about the red domino.'

'And do you know, then?'

'Not only do I know: I followed him all the way to his lodgings.'

'Well, and who is the red domino?'

'Nikolai Apollonovich.'

'Hm! Yes, yes: but the incident has not yet come to a head.'

'Don't try to wriggle out of it: you've simply let it drop.'

'?!?'

'Yes, yes: you've let it drop . . . And yet you reproached me with the counterfeiter, reproached me with a fifty-copeck piece – remember? While I said nothing about the fact that you have artificial hair.'

'Not artificial – dyed . . .'

'It comes to the same thing.'

'How is your cold?'

'Better, thank you.'

. . . .

'I haven't dropped it.'

'Evidence?'

'Why do you say that: I'm not short of evidence.'

. . . .

'Evidence?'

'You will just have to believe me.'

'Evidence!!!'

But sardonic laughter was heard in reply.

'Evidence? You need evidence? The evidence is the Petersburg "Diary of Events". Have you read the "Diary" these last few days?'

'I will confess: I haven't.'

'But I mean, it's your duty to know what Petersburg is talking about. If you were to look in the "Diary" you would realize that news about the domino preceded his appearance near the Winter Canal.'

'Hm-hm.'

'You see, you see, you see: but now you say something. Ask me who wrote all this in the "Diary".'

'Well, who was it?'

'Neintelpfain, my collaborator.'

. . . .

'I will confess that I didn't expect you to pull off a stunt like that.'

'And yet you attack me, shower me with caustic remarks: but I've told you a hundred times that I'm a collaborator in the cause, that this undertaking has been set like the mechanism of a clock. You're still in blissful ignorance, and all along my Neintelpfain has been making a sensation.'

'Hm-hm-hm: speak louder – I can't hear you.'

. . . .

'I hope you will give your agents instructions that they're to leave Nikolai Apollonovich in perfect peace, otherwise: otherwise – I can't vouch for success in what lies ahead.'

'I will confess that I've already told the newspapers about this recent incident.'

'Oh my God, why, you must be a complete . . .'

'What?'

'A complete . . . idealist: this time, as always, you have interfered in my sphere of authority . . . I hope to God that at least his father doesn't find out!'

A Mad Dog Yelped

We left Sofya Petrovna Likhutina in a difficult situation; we left her on the Petersburg pavement that cold night, when police whistles began to sound from somewhere in the distance, and all around some kind of dark contours ran. Then she herself, outraged, ran in the opposite direction; into her soft muff she poured tears of outrage; she would never be able to reconcile herself to the dreadful occurrence that had shamed her for ever. It would have been better if Nikolai Apollonovich had outraged her in some other way, if he had struck her, if he had even thrown himself off the small bridge in his red domino – all the rest of her life she would have remembered him with a terrible shiver, remembered until her dying day. Sofya Petrovna Likhutina did not consider the Winter Canal as just any prosaic place where one might allow oneself to do what he had just allowed himself; not for nothing, after all, had she sighed

repeatedly over the strains of *The Queen of Spades*; there was something similar to Liza in this situation of hers (what the similarity
was, she could not have said exactly); and it went without saying
that she had dreamt of seeing Nikolai Apollonovich here as Hermann. And Hermann? . . . Hermann had behaved like a wretched
little pickpocket thief: he had, in the first place, thrust his mask at
her with ridiculous cowardice from round the side of the palace; in
the second place, having flapped his domino in front of her with
ridiculous haste, he had sprawled on the small bridge; and then
from under the folds of satin the trouser straps had prosaically
appeared (those trouser straps had finally driven her to fury); to
crown all these monstrosities, which had nothing to do with Hermann, this Hermann had been running away from a Petersburg
policeman; Hermann had not remained where he was and torn the
mask off with a heroic, tragic gesture; he had not said audaciously
in a hollow, dying voice in front of everyone: 'I love you'; and
Hermann had not then shot himself. No, Hermann's shameful
behaviour had turned the very thought of the domino into a
pretentious harlequinade; and above all, she had been injured by
this shameful behaviour; well, what kind of Liza could she be, if
there was no Hermann! So, vengeance on him, vengeance on him!

Sofya Petrovna Likhutina flew into the small flat like a storm. In
the illumined hallway hung an officer's coat and a peaked cap: that
meant that her husband was now back, and without taking her coat
off, Sofya Petrovna Likhutina flew into her husband's room; throwing the door wide open with a prosaically coarse gesture – she flew
inside: with her streaming boa, her soft muff, her burning, burning
little face, which was somehow unattractively swollen: flew inside –
and stopped.

Sergei Sergeyevich Likhutin was evidently getting ready for bed;
his double-breasted jacket hung rather modestly on the coat-rack,
while he himself, in a dazzlingly white shirt cross-girdled with
braces, knelt, as if broken, like a dying silhouette; before him an
icon gleamed and an icon-lamp sputtered. Sergei Sergeyevich's face
was outlined lustrelessly in the half-light from the blue lamp, with a
pointed little beard of exactly the same colour and a hand, also of
the same colour, raised to his forehead; hand, face, beard and white
chest were carved from some kind of hard, fragrant wood; Sergei

Sergeyevich's lips were barely moving; and Sergei Sergeyevich's forehead barely nodded towards the small blue flame, and barely did his clenched, bluish fingers move as they pressed against his forehead – in order to make the sign of the cross.

Sergei Sergeyevich Likhutin first placed his bluish fingers on his chest and on both shoulders, bowed, and only then, rather reluctantly, turned round. Sergei Sergeyevich Likhutin was not alarmed, was not embarrassed; getting up off his knees, he assiduously began to brush away the specks of dust that clung to them. After these slow actions, he asked coolly:

'What's the matter, Sonyushka?'

Sofya Petrovna was irritated and somehow even offended by her husband's cool composure, just as she was offended by that blue flame over there in the corner. Abruptly she fell on to a chair and, covering her face with her muff, sobbed aloud to the whole room.

Then Sergei Sergeyevich's whole face grew kinder, softened; his thin lips relaxed, a wrinkle cut across his brow, giving his face a look of compassion. But Sergei Sergeyevich had only a vague idea of how he ought to act in this ticklish situation – whether to give free rein to female tears, and then put up with a scene and reproaches of coldness, or on the other hand go down on his knees before Sofya Petrovna, respectfully lift her little head from the muff with a gentle hand, and with that hand wipe away her tears, embrace her in brotherly fashion and cover her little face with kisses; but Sergei Sergeyevich was afraid of seeing a grimace of contempt and boredom; and Sergei Sergeyevich chose the middle way: he simply patted Sofya Petrovna on her trembling shoulder:

'Now, now, Sonya . . . Now that's enough . . . Enough, my little child! Baby, baby!'

'Stop it, stop it! . . .'

'What is it? What's wrong? Tell me! . . . Let us discuss it coolly and rationally.'

'No: stop it, stop it! . . . Coolly and rationally . . . stop it! One can see . . . aaah . . . you have . . . cold fish-blood.'

Sergei Sergeyevich stepped back from his wife in offence, stood undecidedly, and then sank into a nearby armchair.

'Aaah . . . To leave your life like that! . . . So you can be in charge of provisions somewhere out there! . . . To go away! . . . To know nothing! . . .'

'You're wrong, Sonyushka, if you think I don't know anything at all . . . Look . . .'

'Oh, please stop it! . . .'

. . . .

'Look, my dear: ever since . . . I moved into this room . . . In a word, I have my self-respect: and you must understand that I don't want to hamper your freedom . . . What is more, I cannot hamper you: I understand you; and I know very well that it's not easy for you, my dear . . . I have hopes, Sonyushka: perhaps some day once again . . . Well, but I won't, I won't insist! But you must understand me, too: my distance, my cool rationality, are not the result of coldness at all . . . Well, but I don't insist, I won't insist . . .'

. . . .

'Perhaps you'd like to see Nikolai Apollonovich Ableukhov? Perhaps something has happened between you? Then tell me everything: tell it without hiding anything; we shall discuss your position together.'

'Don't dare speak of him to me! . . . He is a scoundrel, a scoundrel! . . . Another husband would have shot him long ago . . . But you? . . . No, stop it!'

And incoherently, in agitation, having dropped her little head to her breast, Sofya Petrovna told everything as it was.

Sergei Sergeyevich Likhutin was a simple man. And simple men are struck by the inexplicable absurdity of an action even more than by low-down behaviour, by murder or a bloody manifestation of brutality. A man is capable of understanding human treachery, crime, even human disgrace; after all, to understand something means almost to find a justification for it; but how is one to explain to oneself, for example, the action of a socially accepted and, it would appear, thoroughly honourable man, if to this socially accepted and thoroughly honourable man there suddenly comes a completely absurd fantasy: to get down on all fours on the threshold of a certain fashionable drawing-room flapping the skirts of his tailcoat? That would be, if I may say so, a complete abomination! The incomprehensibility, the futility of that abomination cannot be justified, in the same way that blasphemy, sacrilege and any sort of futile mockery cannot be justified! No, rather let a thoroughly honourable man squander the state's money with impunity, as long as he never gets down on all fours, because after an action like that everything is defiled.

Angrily, vividly, distinctly, Sergei Sergeyevich Likhutin pictured to himself the buffoon-like aspect of the satin domino in the unlit entrance porch, and . . . Sergei Sergeyevich began to blush, blushed a bright carrot colour: the blood rushed to his head. He and Nikolai Apollonovich had, after all, played together as children; Sergei Sergeyevich had subsequently been surprised at Nikolai Apollonovich's philosophical abilities; Sergei Sergeyevich had nobly permitted Nikolai Apollonovich, as an honourable man of good society, to come between himself and his wife and . . . Sergei Sergeyevich Likhutin angrily, vividly, distinctly pictured to himself the buffoon-like grimaces of the red domino in the unlit entrance porch. He got up and began to pace agitatedly about the tiny little room, compressing his fingers to a fist and furiously raising his compressed fingers each time he made a sharp turn; when Sergei Sergeyevich lost his temper (he had only ever lost his temper two or three times – no more), this gesture always appeared; Sofya Petrovna sensed very well what the gesture meant; she was a little frightened of it; she was always a little frightened, not of the gesture, but of the silence that made the gesture manifest.

'What are you . . . doing?'

'Nothing . . . It's all right . . .'

And Sergei Sergeyevich Likhutin continued to pace about the tiny little room, his fingers compressed to a fist.

The red domino! . . . A vileness, a vileness and a vileness! And it had been standing there, outside the entrance door – what?! . . .

Nikolai Apollonovich's behaviour had shocked the second lieutenant in the extreme. He now experienced a mixture of revulsion and horror; in a word, he experienced that sense of aversion that commonly seizes us when we observe complete idiots performing their bodily functions directly beneath them, or when we observe a black, furry-legged insect – a spider, say . . . Bewilderment, outrage and fear turned simply into fury. To have disregarded his urgent letter, to have insulted his officer's honour with a clownish escapade, to have insulted his dear wife with some spider-like grimace! . . . And Sergei Sergeyevich Likhutin gave himself his honourable officer's word – at all costs he would crush the spider, crush it; and, having taken this decision, he continued to pace and pace, red as a crayfish, compressing his fingers to a fist and jerking his muscular arm up each time he made a turn; he now struck fear into Sofya Petrovna, too: also red, with her half-open, pouting lips and her cheeks from which the glistening tears had not been wiped, she was closely observing her husband from there, from that armchair.

'What are you doing?'

But Sergei Sergeyevich now replied in a hard voice; in that voice there sounded at one and the same time menace, sternness and suppressed fury.

'Nothing . . . It's all right.'

To tell the truth, at this moment Sergei Sergeyevich was experiencing something approaching revulsion at his beloved wife, too; as though she too had shared in the clownish shame of the red mask which had wriggled about – there, at the entrance door.

'Go to your room: sleep . . . leave all this to me.'

And Sofya Petrovna Likhutina, who had long ago stopped crying, rose without demur and quietly went to her room.

Remaining alone, Sergei Sergeyevich Likhutin continued to pace, with a cough now and then; drily this came from him, most unpleasantly, distinctly, now 'cahuh-cahuh', and 'cahuh-cahuh'. Sometimes a wooden fist, as if carved from hard, fragrant wood, was raised above the little table; and it seemed that at any moment the table would fly into pieces with a deafening crack.

But the fist would unclench itself.

At last, Sergei Sergeyevich Likhutin began quickly to undress; he undressed, covered himself with a flannelette blanket, and – the blanket slipped off; Sergei Sergeyevich Likhutin lowered his legs to the floor, stared fixedly at some point with an unseeing gaze and, unexpectedly to himself, began to whisper in the very loudest of whispers:

'Aah! How do you like this? I shall shoot you like a dog . . .'

Then from the other side of the wall a little voice was heard, loud and tearful.

'What is it, what are you doing?'

. . . .

'Nothing . . . it's all right . . .'

Sergei Sergeyevich dived back under his blanket again and covered his head with it, in order to sigh, to whisper, to offer entreaties, to issue threats to someone, for something . . .

. . . .

Sofya Petrovna did not summon Mavrushka. She quickly threw off her fur coat, hat and dress; and all in white, stepping forth from a fountain of objects which she contrived to scatter around her during those three or four minutes, she threw herself on the bed; and sat now with her feet tucked up and her black-haired, angry little face with its protruding lips, above which a small moustache was clearly visible, dropped into her hands, and around her was a fountain of objects; thus was it always. All Mavrushka ever did was to clear up after her mistress; Sofya Petrovna had only to remember some item of her toilet, and the item was not to hand; and then into the air flew blouses, handkerchiefs, dresses, hairpins and hatpins, anyhow and anywhere; from Sofya Petrovna's little hand began to shoot a coloured waterfall of various objects. This evening Sofya Petrovna did not call Mavrushka; that meant that a fountain of objects was in progress.

Sofya Petrovna found herself involuntarily listening to Sergei Sergeyevich's restless pacing behind the partition; and she also listened to the nightly strains of the grand piano above her head: there someone played over and over again the same antique tune of a polka-mazurka, to the strains of which her mother, laughing, had danced with her when she had been but a mite of two years old. And to the strains of this polka-mazurka, strains that were so antique and so innocent of everything, Sofya Petrovna's anger began to subside, being replaced by weariness, complete apathy and the merest hint of irritation with regard to her husband, in whom she, Sofya Petrovna, had in her own opinion aroused jealousy towards *the other man*. But as soon as jealousy was, in her opinion, aroused in her husband, Sergei Sergeyevich, then her husband, Sergei Sergeyevich, became distinctly disagreeable to her; she experienced a feeling of awkwardness, as though some alien hand had stretched out to the cherished little box in which she kept her letters and which was locked up in the drawer over there. On the contrary: just as Nikolai Apollonovich's smile had at first struck her with aversion, and then from the sense of aversion she had derived a sweet mixture of rapture and horror at that same smile, so in the shamefulness of Nikolai Apollonovich's behaviour there, on the small bridge, she suddenly discovered a sweet source of revenge: she regretted that when he had fallen before her in that pathetic guise of a buffoon, she had not stamped on him and kicked him with her little feet; she suddenly felt she wanted to torment and torture him, while she did not feel she wanted to torment her husband, Sergei Sergeyevich; neither torment him nor kiss him. And Sofya Petrovna suddenly discovered that her husband had nothing whatever to do with this fateful occurrence that had taken place between them; this occurrence was supposed to remain a secret between her and *him*; but now she herself had told her husband everything. Her husband's connection not only with her but also with *the other man*, with Nikolai Apollonovich, had become above all offensive to her: after all, from this incident Sergei Sergeyevich would, of course, draw completely false conclusions; above all, he would of course be unable to comprehend anything of it at all: neither the fateful, sweet-and-sinister sensation, nor the change of costume; and Sofya Petrovna found herself involuntarily listening to the antique strains of the polka-mazurka and the restless, disagreeable pacing on the other side of the partition; from the excessiveness of her black, unfastened tresses she frightenedly stretched her pearly little face with its dark blue, somehow dulled eyes, clumsily bending that little face down against her barely trembling knees.

At that moment her gaze fell on the dressing-table mirror; below the dressing-table mirror Sofya Petrovna saw the letter she was supposed to give to *him* at the ball (she had forgotten about the letter altogether). At that first moment she decided to send the letter back with the messenger, send it back to Varvara Yevgrafovna. How dare they force letters to him on her! And she would have sent it back if her husband had not interfered in it all first (if only he would go to bed!). But now, under the influence of her protest against any kind of interference in *their* personal affairs, she took a simple view of the matter, too simple a view: of course, she had a perfect right to tear open the envelope and read any secrets there might be in it (how dare he have secrets!) In a flash, Sofya Petrovna was over by the table; but just as she touched the alien letter, behind the partition a furious whispering arose; the bed creaked.

'What are you doing?'

From behind the partition she received the reply:

'Nothing . . . it's all right.'

The bed began to squeal plaintively; all grew quiet. With trembling hand, Sofya Petrovna tore open the envelope . . . and as she read, her swollen little eyes grew large; their dullness brightened, and was replaced by a dazzling glitter, the paleness of her little face first took on the tints of pinkish apple-blossom petals, then became as rosy as a rose; and when she had finished reading the letter, her face was simply crimson.

Nikolai Apollonovich was now entirely in her clutches; her whole being trembled with horror at him and at the impossibility of inflicting upon him a terrible, irreparable blow during the two months of suffering she had endured; and that blow he would now receive from these little hands. He had wanted to frighten her with his buffoonish masquerade; but he had not even been able to execute the buffoonish masquerade in proper fashion and, taken by surprise, he had committed many outrages; well, now let him be blotted from her memory, and let him be Hermann! Yes, yes, yes: she herself would inflict the cruel blow simply by giving him the letter with its dreadful contents. For an instant she was seized by a sense of giddiness as she contemplated the path she had condemned herself to; but it was too late to hold her ground, to leave the path: had she not herself summoned the red domino? Well, and if he had summoned before her the image of a fearsome domino, let all the rest of it be accomplished: let the bloody domino's path be a bloody one!

The door squeaked: Sofya Petrovna barely had time to crumple the opened letter in her hand, when in the doorway of the bedroom stood her husband, Sergei Sergeyevich Likhutin; he was all in white: in a white nightshirt and white drawers. The appearance of a complete outsider, and in such an indecent aspect, drove her to fury:

'You might at least get dressed . . .'

Sergei Sergeich Likhutin was thoroughly covered in confusion, and quickly left the room, only to reappear a moment later; this time he was, at least, wearing a dressing-gown; Sofya Petrovna had already managed to hide the letter. With an unpleasant, dry firmness that was unusual for him, Sergei Sergeich addressed her simply:

'*Sophie* . . . I want you to promise me something: I earnestly request you not to go to the soirée at the Tsukatovs' tomorrow.'

Silence.

'I hope you will give me that promise; common sense should prompt you: spare me the need for explanations.'

Silence.

'I should like you yourself to admit the impossibility of your going to the ball after what has just taken place.'

Silence.

'At any rate, I have given my honourable officer's word that you will not be at the ball.'

Silence.

'Otherwise I should quite simply have to forbid you from going.'

'All the same, I am going to the ball . . .'

'No, you are not!'

Sofya Petrovna was shocked by the threatening, wooden voice in which Sergei Sergeyevich pronounced this phrase.

'Yes, I am.'

A painful silence ensued, during which all that was heard was a kind of gurgling in Sergei Sergeyevich's chest, which made him clutch nervously at his throat and shake his head twice, as though he were making an effort to ward off the inevitability of some dreadful occurrence; suppressing within with an incredible effort an explosion that was almost about to burst forth, Sergei Sergeich Likhutin quietly sat down, as straight as a rod:

'Look: it was not I who pressed you for details. You yourself called me as a witness of what has just happened.'

Sergei Sergeyevich could not utter the words *red domino*: the thought of what had just taken place made him instinctively experience a kind of abyss of depravity into which his wife had slid down an inclined plane; what was depraved about it, apart from the wild absurdity of the whole incident, Sergei Sergeyevich could not for the life of him tell: but he sensed that it was so, and that this was no ordinary everyday romance, that it involved not merely an unfaithfulness, a fall. No, no, no: over all this hung a whiff of Satanic excesses that poisoned the soul for ever, like prussic acid; he had smelt the sweetish smell of bitter almonds quite clearly when he had come in, and had experienced a most violent attack of suffocation; and he had known, known for certain: if Sofya Petrovna, his wife, were to be at the Tsukatovs' tomorrow, if she were to meet there that loathsome domino – everything would go to rack and ruin: the honour of his wife, and his own, officer's honour.

'Look. After what you have told me, don't you understand that it is out of the question for you to meet him there; that it would be a vile, vile thing to do; and that in fact I have given my word that you will not be there. Have pity then, *Sophie*, on yourself, and me, and . . . him, because otherwise . . . I . . . do not know . . . I cannot guarantee . . .

But Sofya Petrovna was growing more and more indignant at the brazen interference of this officer who was totally alien to her, an officer, what was more, who had dared to appear in the bedroom in a most indecent aspect with his absurd interference; picking up some dress that was lying on the floor (she had suddenly noticed that she was *déshabillée*), and covering herself with it, she retreated into a dark corner; and from there, from the dark, shadowy corner, she suddenly shook her head decisively:

'Perhaps I might not have gone, but now, after this interference of yours, I shall go, I shall go, I shall go!'

'No: that shall not be!!!'

What was this? It seemed to her that a deafening shot rang out in the room; at the same time an inhuman howl also rang out: a thin, hoarse falsetto shouted something incoherent; a man made of cypress wood leapt to his feet, and the armchair toppled and slammed against the floor, while the blow of a fist smashed the cheap little table in two; then the door slammed; and all was deathly quiet.

The strains of the polka-mazurka from upstairs broke off; above her head, feet began to stamp; voices began to babble; at last, someone in the flat above, indignant at the noise, began to beat on the floor with a scrubbing brush, thereby evidently wishing to express from up there his enlightened protest.

Sofya Petrovna Likhutina shrank inwardly and began to sob insultedly from the dark little corner; it was the first time in her life that she had had to face such fury, because before her just then had stood ... not a human being, even, not a wild beast. Here before her there had just yelped – a mad dog.

The Senator's Second Space

Apollon Apollonovich's bedroom was simple and small: four grey, mutually perpendicular walls and a single slit of a window with a small white lace curtain; the sheets, the towels and pillowslips on the high-plumped pillows were distinguished by the same whiteness; before the senator went to sleep the valet sprayed the sheet with an atomizer.

Apollon Apollonovich would only permit the use of triple-strength eau-de-Cologne from the Petersburg Chemical Laboratory.

Then: the valet placed a glass of lemon water on the bedside table and hurriedly withdrew. Apollon Apollonovich always undressed himself.

In a most precise manner he threw off his robe; in a most precise manner he threw off his little jacket and his miniature trousers, remaining in his knitted, tightly fitting drawers and singlet; and, thus attired in his underwear, before he went to sleep Apollon Apollonovich strengthened his body with gymnastics.

He would spread his arms and legs; then move them apart and turn his waist this way and that, squatting down twelve times and more, in order then, in conclusion, to pass on to an even more useful exercise: lying down on his back, to strengthen his stomach muscles, Apollon Apollonovich would set about working his legs.

Apollon Apollonovich had recourse to these most useful exercises especially frequently on days when he suffered from haemorrhoids.

After these most useful exercises Apollon Apollonovich pulled the blanket over him in order to devote himself to peaceful rest and to embark upon a journey, for sleep (let us add for our part) is a journey.

This evening, Apollon Apollonovich did the same thing. His head wrapped in the blanket (with the exception of the tip of his nose), he was now hanging from his bed above a timeless void.

But here we shall be interrupted and asked: 'What do you mean — above a void? What about the walls, and the floor? And ... so on? ...'

We shall reply.

Apollon Apollonovich always saw *two* spaces: one that was material (the walls of rooms and the walls of carriages), and another which was not exactly spiritual (it, too, was material) ... well, how may one put it: above Senator Ableukhov's head Senator Ableukhov's eyes saw strange currents: highlights, gleams, misty, opalescent dancing spots emerging from whirling centres, clouding in twilight the limits of material space; space swarmed in space, and this latter, overshadowing all the rest, disappeared in its turn in an immensity of vacillating, swaying perspectives, which consisted ... well, as it were, of Christmas tree tinsel, of little stars, sparks, lights.

Before he went to sleep, Apollon Apollonovich usually closed his eyes and opened them again; and lo and behold: little lights, misty spots, threads and stars, like some bright scum on a bubbling, immensely vast darkness, unexpectedly (for only a quarter of a second) and suddenly formed into a clear picture: of a cross, a polyhedron, a swan, a pyramid filled with light. And then it all flew apart.

Apollon Apollonovich had a strange secret: a world of figures, contours, shimmerings, strange physical sensations — in a word: a *universe* of strange manifestations. This *universe* always appeared before he fell asleep; and appeared in such a way that Apollon Apollonovich, going to sleep, remembered at that instant all the earlier inarticulacies, rustlings, crystallographic figures, the golden, chrysanthemum-like stars racing through the darkness on rays that resembled myriapods (sometimes a star like that would bathe the senator's head in golden boiling water: gooseflesh would run across his cranium): in a word, he remembered all that he had seen the previous day before going to sleep, so as not to remember it again in the morning.

Sometimes (not always) before the very last moment of daytime consciousness, Apollon Apollonovich, as he went to sleep, would notice that all the threads, all the stars, forming a bubbling vortex, made a corridor that ran away into immeasurable distance and (what was most surprising) he would feel that this corridor began from his head, i.e. it, the corridor, was an infinite extension of his own head, the crown of which suddenly opened – an extension into immeasurable distance; thus the old senator, before going to sleep, received the most strange impression that he was looking not with his eyes, but with the very centre of his head, i.e. he, Apollon Apollonovich, was not Apollon Apollonovich but *something* that had lodged in his brain and was looking out of there, out of his brain; when the crown of his head opened up this something was able both freely and simply to run along the corridor *until a point where it plunged into the abyss* that was revealed there, far away down the corridor.

This was the senator's *second space* – the land of the senator's nightly journeys; and of this, enough . . .

With his head wrapped in the blanket, he was now hanging from his bed above a timeless void, the lacquered floor fell away from the legs of the bed and the bed stood, so to speak, on the unknown – but then a strange, distant clatter reached the senator's ears, like the clatter of small and swiftly beating hooves:

'Tra-ta-ta . . . Tra-ta-ta . . .'

And the clatter was coming nearer.

A strange, a very strange, an exceedingly strange circumstance: the senator thrust out an ear to the moon; and – yes: it was highly probable that in the hall of mirrors someone was knocking.

Apollon Apollonovich thrust out his head.

The golden, bubbling vortex suddenly flew apart in all directions above the senator's head; the chrysanthemum-like star that was a myriapod moved towards the crown of that head, swiftly disappearing from the senator's field of vision; and, as always, the tiles of the parquet floor instantly flew up from beyond the abyss towards the legs of the iron bed; at this point Apollon Apollonovich, small and pale, reminiscent of a plucked chicken, suddenly rested his two yellow heels on the rug.

The clatter continued: Apollon Apollonovich leapt up and ran out into the corridor.

The rooms were lit by the moon.

Clad in nothing but his singlet and holding a lighted candle, Apollon Apollonovich journeyed forth into the rooms. Straining after his alarmed master was the little bulldog who turned out to be here, indulgently wagging his little docked tail, jingling his collar and snuffling through his smacked-in muzzle.

Like a flat wooden lid, the hairy chest heaved with painful crepitations, and the pale green tinted ear listened to the clatter. The senator's gaze happened to fall on a pier-glass: but strangely did the pier-glass reflect the senator: arms, legs, hips and chest were swathed in dark blue satin: that satin threw off a metallic gleam in all directions from itself: Apollon Apollonovich turned out to be clad in blue armour; Apollon Apollonovich turned out to be a little knight and from his hand extended not a candle but some kind of luminous phenomenon which shone with the spangles of a sabre blade.

Apollon Apollonovich screwed up his courage and rushed to the hall; the clatter was coming from there:

'Tra-ta-ta . . . Tra-ta-ta . . .'

And he snarled at the clatter:

'On the basis of which article of the Code of Laws?'[25]

As he shouted this, he saw that the indifferent little bulldog was peacefully and sleepily snuffling there beside him. But – what effrontery! – from the hall someone shouted in reply:

'On the basis of an emergency regulation!'

Indignant at the brazen reply, the little blue knight waved the luminous phenomenon which he held clutched in his hand and rushed into the hall.

But the luminous phenomenon was melting in his little fist: it streamed between his fingers like air and lay at his feet like a little ray. And the clatter – Apollon Apollonovich now saw – was the clicking of the tongue of some kind of wretched Mongol: there some kind of fat Mongol with a physiognomy which Apollon Apollonovich had seen during his time in Tokyo (Apollon Apollonovich had once been sent to Tokyo) – there some kind of fat Mongol was appropriating for himself the physiognomy of Nikolai

Apollonovich – *appropriating*, I say, because this was not Nikolai Apollonovich, but simply a Mongol, as seen in Tokyo; none the less his physiognomy was the physiognomy of Nikolai Apollonovich. This Apollon Apollonovich was unwilling to grasp; with his little fists he rubbed his astonished eyes (and again he did not feel his hands, as he did not feel his face); two intangible points simply rubbed against each other – the space of the hands probed the space of the face). And the Mongol (Nikolai Apollonovich) was approaching with a mercenary end in view.

Here the senator shouted a second time:

'On the basis of what regulation?

'And of what paragraph?'

And space replied:

'There are neither paragraphs nor regulations now!'

. . . .

And unknowing, unfeeling, suddenly bereft of ponderability, suddenly bereft of the very sensation of his body, turned merely into vision and hearing, Apollon Apollonovich imagined that he had lifted up the space of his eyes (he could not say positively by touch that his eyes were lifted up, for he had thrown off the sense of corporeality), and, having lifted up his eyes in the direction of the site of the crown of his head, he saw that there was no crown, for in the place where the brain is compressed by strong, heavy bones, where there is no sight, no vision – Apollon Apollonovich saw inside Apollon Apollonovich a round, gaping breach into a dark blue distance (in place of the crown); the gaping breach – a dark blue circle – was surrounded by a wheel of flying sparks, highlights, gleams; at that fateful moment when according to his calculations the Mongol (only imprinted on his consciousness, but no longer visible) was creeping up on his helpless body (in that body the dark blue circle was a way out of the body) – at that very moment, with a roaring and a whistling like the sound of the wind in a chimney, something began to suck Apollon Apollonovich's consciousness from beneath the vortex of flashing lights (through the dark blue breach in the crown of his head) out into stellar infinity.

Here a scandal took place (at that moment Apollon Apollonovich's consciousness noted that something similar had already happened: where and when, he could not recall) – here something scandalous occurred: the wind whistled Apollon Apollonovich's consciousness out of Apollon Apollonovich.

Apollon Apollonovich flew out through the circular breach into the blueness, into the darkness, like a gold-plumed star; and, having flown sufficiently high above his head (which seemed to him like the planet Earth), the gold-plumed star, like a rocket, soundlessly disintegrated into sparks.

For a moment there was nothing: there was pretemporal darkness; and in the darkness a consciousness swarmed – not some other consciousness, a universal one, for example, but a perfectly ordinary consciousness: the consciousness of Apollon Apollonovich.

This consciousness now turned back, emitting from itself only two sensations: the sensations fell like arms; and this is what the sensations sensed: they sensed some kind of form (recalling the form of a bathtub), filled to the brim with sticky and stinking filth; the sensations, like arms, began to splash about *in the bathtub*; Apollon Apollonovich could only compare what the *bathtub* was filled with to the dungy water in which a repulsive behemoth splashed about (this he had seen several times in the waters of the zoological gardens of enlightened Europe). In a moment the sensations had stuck to the vessel which, as we have said, was full to the brim with abomination; Apollon Apollonovich's consciousness tried to tear itself away, into space, but the sensations were dragging something heavy behind that consciousness.

The consciousness opened its eyes, and the consciousness saw the very thing it inhabited: it saw a little yellow old man who resembled a plucked chicken; the old man was sitting on the bed; he was resting his bare heels against the rug.

A moment: and the consciousness turned out to be this very same little yellow old man, for this little yellow old man was listening from the bed to a strange, distant clatter, like the clatter of swiftly beating hooves:

'Tra-ta-ta . . . Tra-ta-ta . . .'

Apollon Apollonovich realized that the whole of his journey along the corridor, through the hall, and through his head – had been a dream.

And hardly had he thought this than he woke up: it was a double dream.

Apollon Apollonovich was not sitting on the bed, but Apollon Apollonovich was lying with his head wrapped in the blanket (except for the tip of his nose): the clatter in the hall turned out to be a door banging.

That was probably Nikolai Apollonovich returning home: Nikolai Apollonovich returned late at night.

'Indeed, sir . . .

'Indeed, sir . . .

'Very good, sir . . .'

Only there was something wrong with his back: a fear of being touched on the backbone . . . Was he developing *tabes dorsalis*?[26]

END OF THE THIRD CHAPTER

CHAPTER THE FOURTH

in which the line of the narrative is broken

Grant God that I may not go mad . . .[1]

A. Pushkin

The Summer Garden

Prosaically, solitarily this way and that ran the paths of the Summer Garden; cutting across these expanses, the gloomy pedestrian quickened his pace from time to time, and then finally disappeared in an endless emptiness: the Field of Mars cannot be crossed in five minutes.

The Summer Garden was sunk in gloom.

The summer statues were each hidden under boards; the grey boards looked like coffins stood on end; and the coffins stood on either side of the paths; in these coffins light nymphs and satyrs had taken shelter, so that the tooth of time should not gnaw them away with snow, rain and frost, because time sharpens its iron tooth on everything; and the iron tooth will uniformly gnaw away both body and soul, even the very stones.

Since olden times this garden had been growing emptier, greyer, smaller; the grotto had subsided into ruins, the fountains had ceased to splash, the summer gallery had collapsed and the waterfall dried up; the garden had grown smaller and cowered behind the iron railings, those same iron railings that overseas visitors from the English lands, in wigs and green caftans, came here to admire; and they puffed their smoke-clogged pipes.

Peter himself had planted this garden, watering with his own watering-can the rare trees, the fragrant herbs and mints; from Solikamsk the tsar had ordered cedars, from Danzig – barberries, and from Sweden apple trees; he had built fountains everywhere, and the shattered spray of the mirrors, like a delicate spider's web, had let through glimpses here of the red camisoles of the loftiest personages, their curling ringlets, their black moorish faces and the crinolines of the ladies; leaning on the faceted handle of a black and gold stick, here a grey cavalier was leading his lady to the pool; while in the green, seething waters the black muzzle of a seal emerged, sniffing, from the very bottom; the lady uttered a gasp, and the grey cavalier smiled playfully and stretched out his stick to the black monster.

In those days the Summer Garden extended further, taking space from the Field of Mars for the avenues that were so dear to the tsar's heart and were planted on both sides with yew and meadow-sweet (the garden too had evidently been gnawed by the merciless tooth of time); enormous shells from the Indian seas raised their rosy trumpets from the porous stones of the stern grotto; and a personage, taking off his plumed hat, inquisitively put his ear to the opening of the rosy trumpet; and from it came a chaotic roar; at this time other personages were drinking fruit punch in front of this mysterious grotto.

And in later times, beneath the figured pose of a statue by Irelli,[2] which stretched its fingers into the closing day, there came the sound of laughter, whispers and sighs, and the large round jewels of the sovereign's maids of honour gleamed. That happened in the spring, on Whit Monday; the evening atmosphere grew thicker; suddenly it was shaken by a mighty, organ-like voice that flew out from under a grove of sweetly drowsing elms: and from there light suddenly expanded – diverting, green; there, in the green lights, bright red musicians of the hunt, stretching forth their horns, melodically filled the environs with sound, shaking the zephyrs and cruelly disturbing the deeply wounded soul: the languorous lament of those upraised horns – have you not heard it?

All that was, and now it is no more; now gloomily ran the paths of the Summer Garden; a black, frenzied flock wheeled above the roof of Peter's little house; unendurable was its hubbub and the heavy flapping of its tattered wings; the black, frenzied flock suddenly swooped down on the branches.

Nikolai Apollonovich, perfumed and clean-shaven, was making his way along a frozen path, muffled up in his overcoat: his head had fallen into its fur, and his eyes had a strange light in them; no sooner had he resolved to immerse himself in work today than a messenger had brought him a note; the unknown handwriting summoned him to a rendezvous in the Summer Garden. And it was signed 'S'. Who could the mysterious 'S' be? Well, of course, the 'S' stood for Sofya (she had evidently altered her handwriting). Nikolai Apollonovich, perfumed and clean-shaven, made his way along the frozen path.

Nikolai Apollonovich had an agitated air; of recent days he had lost sleep and appetite; for about a week now a fine dust had settled without hindrance on a page of Kantian commentaries; while in his soul there was a novel current of emotion; this sweet, disturbing current he had felt within himself in past times, too ... to be sure, rather dully and remotely. But ever since the day he had called forth nameless tremors in Angel Peri by his conduct, nameless tremors had revealed themselves within him, too: as though he had summoned dully throbbing forces out of his mysterious depths, as though within him the bag of Aeolus had burst, and the sons of far-off gusts had drawn him with whistling whips through the air to some strange lands. Did this condition really only augur the return, merely, of sensual excitements? Perhaps it was love? But love was something he denied.

Already he was looking around him anxiously, searching on the paths for the familiar outline in its little black fur coat and black muff; but there was – no one; not far away some kind of frump lay sprawled on a bench. Suddenly the frump got up from the bench, marked time for a moment, and then came towards him.

'Don't you ... recognize me?'

'Oh, hello!'

'I think you still haven't recognized me! But I'm Solovyova.'

'Why, for goodness' sake, you are Varvara Yevgrafovna!'

'Well, let's sit down here, on the bench . . .'

Nikolai Apollonovich sat down painfully beside her: after all, he had been summoned to a rendezvous in precisely this little avenue; and now here was this unfortunate circumstance! Nikolai Apollonovich began to think of a way of getting this frump off his hands as soon as possible; still searching for the familiar outline, he looked around him to right and to left; but of the familiar outline there was still no sign.

At his feet the dry path was beginning to throw its yellow-brown and worm-eaten leaves; there, somehow lustrelessly, rising straight up against a steel horizon, was a dark-tinged mesh of criss-crossed branches; at times the dark-tinged mesh began to drone; at times the dark-tinged mesh began to sway.

'Did you get my note?'

'What note?'

'The one signed "S".'

'Oh, so it was *you* who sent me it?'

'Well, yes, it was . . .'

'But what did the "S" stand for?'

'What do you mean? Why, my name is Solovyova.'

Everything came crashing down, and he had thought, and he had thought . . .! The nameless tremors suddenly sank to the bottom. 'What can I do for you?'

'I . . . I wanted to ask you, I wondered if you had received a little poem signed *A Flaming Soul*?'

'No, I haven't.'

'How can it be? Do the police open and inspect my letters? Oh, how vexing! Without that fragment of poetry I must confess it is hard to explain all this to you. I wanted to ask you something about the meaning of life . . .'

. . . .

'I'm sorry, Varvara Yevgrafovna, I haven't time.'

'How can it be? How can it be?'

'Goodbye! Please excuse me – we shall arrange a more convenient time for this conversation. Shan't we?'

Varvara Yevgrafovna tugged him indecisively by the fur edge of his overcoat; he decisively stood up; she did likewise; but even more decisively did he extend to her his perfumed fingers, touching her red hand with the edge of his rounded fingernails. At that moment she was unable to think of anything that would detain him; and then he fled from her in complete vexation, wrapping himself up haughtily and aggrievedly, and hiding his face in the fur of his Nikolayevka. The leaves moved off sluggishly, surrounding the skirts of the overcoat with dry, yellowish circles; but the circles grew narrower, curling more restlessly in spirals; the golden spiral, whispering something, danced ever more briskly. A vortex of leaves began to swirl impetuously, wound itself round and round and fled, without spinning, somewhere to the side, somewhere to the side; a red palmate leaf barely moved, flew up and spread itself. There, somehow lustrelessly, rising straight up against a steel horizon, was a dark-tinged mesh of criss-crossed branches; into that mesh he walked; and when he walked into that mesh, a frenzied flock of crows flew up and began to circle above the roof of Peter's little house; the dark-tinged mesh began to sway; the dark-tinged mesh began to drone; and some timidly mournful sounds flew down; and they all fused into one sound – the sound of an organ-like voice. And the evening atmosphere grew thicker; again it seemed to the soul as if there were no present; as if this evening thickness would be lit from behind those trees by a green, luminous cascade; and there, amidst all the fiery light, bright-red huntsmen, stretching forth their horns, would again melodically draw waves of organ music from the zephyrs.

Madame Farnois

And indeed, it was somewhat late when Angel Peri deigned to open her innocent little eyes from the pillows that day; but the eyes had stuck together; and the little head was quite manifestly developing a dull and hollow ache; Angel Peri managed to remain in a state of somnolence for a long time yet; beneath her curls some kind of inarticulacies, anxieties, half-hints kept swarming: her first complete thought was a thought about the soirée: something was going to happen! But when she tried to develop this thought, her little eyes stuck together properly and again moved off into some kind of inarticulacies, anxieties, half-hints; and from these indistinct phenomena there again rose only: Pompadour, Pompadour, Pompadour – and why Pompadour? But her soul radiantly illumined that word: the costume in the spirit of Madame Pompadour – azure, with flowerlets, Valenciennes lace, silvery slippers, pompons! She had had such a long argument with her dressmaker the other day about the costume in the style of Madame Pompadour; Madame Farnois had on no account been willing to cede to her on the matter of *blonde lace*; had kept saying: 'And why do you want *blonde lace*?' But how could she do without *blonde lace*? In the opinion of Madame Farnois, *blonde lace* must look so, be included on such-and-such occasions; and in Sofya Petrovna's opinion, *blonde lace* must not look like that at all. At first Madame Farnois said to her: 'With my taste, and your taste – how can it fail to be in the style of Madame Pompadour?' But Sofya Petrovna had been unwilling to cede, and Madame Farnois offendedly proposed to take the material back from her. 'Take it to Maison Tricotons:³ There, madame, they won't contradict you . . .' But to give it to Maison Tricotons: fi, fi, fi! And the *blonde lace* was abandoned, as were the other controversial points of the Madame Pompadour style: the light *chapeau Bergère* for the hands, for example, though a panniered skirt could on no account be dispensed with.

Thus did they reach an agreement.

As she immersed herself in thoughts about Madame Farnois, Pompadour and Maison Tricotons, Angel Peri felt tormentingly that again everything was all wrong, that something had happened that would make both Madame Farnois and Maison Tricotons vanish into thin air; but taking advantage of her state of semi-sleep, she was consciously unwilling to try to catch the elusive impression of the real events of the day before; at last she remembered – only two words: *domino* and *letter*; and she leapt out of bed, wringing her hands in aimless languor; there had been some third word, and with it she had fallen asleep last night.

But Angel Peri could not remember the third word; the third word might have been some quite unprepossessing sounds: husband, officer, *second lieutenant*.

As far as the first two words were concerned, Angel Peri firmly resolved not to think about them until the evening; while the third, unprepossessing word did not merit attention. But it was precisely this unprepossessing word that she ran up against; for no sooner, no sooner had she fluttered through to the drawing-room from her stuffy little bedroom and dashed, with perfect innocence, into her husband's room, in the supposition that her husband, the officer, the second lieutenant Likhutin, had as always gone off to take charge of provisions, than suddenly: to her very great surprise that second lieutenant's room proved to be locked and inaccessible to her: second lieutenant Likhutin, in spite of all his habits, in spite of the cramped quarters, the loss of comfort, common sense and honest decency – had evidently ensconced himself in there.

Only now did she remember yesterday's outrageous scene; and with pouting lips slammed the bedroom door (he had locked himself in, and so would she). But, having locked herself in, she saw the broken dressing table.

'*Barynya*, will you have coffee in your room?'

'No, I don't want any . . .'

. . . .

'*Barin*, will you have coffee in your room?'

'No, I don't want any.'

. . . .

'*Barin*, the coffee is cold.'

Silence.

'*Barynya*, someone is here, *barynya*!'

'From Madame Farnois?'

'No, from the laundress!'

Silence.

. . . .

In an hour there are sixty minutes; while a minute entirely consists of seconds; the seconds ran away, forming minutes; heavy, the minutes began to throng; and the hours dragged themselves along.

Silence.

In the middle of the day Her Majesty's Yellow Cuirassier Baron Ommergau rang at the door with a two-pound bonbonnière of chocolates from Krafft's.[4] The two-pound bonbonnière was not refused admittance; but he was.

At about two o'clock in the afternoon His Majesty's Blue Cuirassier Count Aven rang at the door with a bonbonnière from Ballet's;[5] the bonbonnière was received, but he was refused admittance.

A Leib Hussar in a tall fur hat was also refused; the Hussar shook his plumed hat and stood with a double bunch of brilliant lemon-coloured chrysanthemums; he called after Aven, shortly after four o'clock.

Verhefden also came flying with a box for the Mariinsky Theatre. Only Lippanchenko did not call: of Lippanchenko there was no sign.

At last, late in the evening, towards ten o'clock, a girl appeared from Madame Farnois with an enormous cardboard box; she was received at once; but as she was being received and there was tittering in the hallway apropos of this, the door of the bedroom clicked, and from there a tearful little face pushed inquisitively forth; an angry, hurried cry was heard:

'Bring it quickly.'

But at the same time the lock of the study door also gave a click; from the study a shaggy head pushed forth: looked and disappeared. Was this really the second lieutenant?

Petersburg Slipped away into the Night

Who does not remember the evening before the memorable night? Who does not remember that day's melancholy flight to rest?

Above the Neva an enormous and crimson sun ran behind the factory chimneys: the Petersburg buildings were covered by the finest puff of smoke and seemed to begin to melt, turning into the lightest, smoky amethyst lace; and from the window-panes a golden, flaming reflection cut through everywhere; and from the tall spires the radiance flashed like rubies. All the usual weights − both indentations and projections − were slipping away into a burning ardour: both the entrance porches with their caryatids and the cornices of the brick balconies.

The rust-red palace[6] began to run violently with blood; this old palace had been built by Rastrelli; like a soft blue wall this old palace had stood then in a white flock of columns; with admiration the late Empress Yelizaveta Petrovna[7] once used to open a window from there on to the distances of the Neva. In the reign of Emperor Aleksandr Pavlovich[8] this old palace was repainted pale yellow; in the reign of Emperor Aleksandr Nikolayevich[9] the palace was repainted a second time: from that time it became rust-red, running with blood towards sunset.

On that memorable evening all was aflame, even the palace was aflame; while all the rest, that did not enter the flame, darkened sluggishly; as did the row of lines and walls when there, in the fading lilac sky, in the little mother-of-pearl-like clouds, some kind of sparkling lamps kept languorously flaring up; as did, sluggishly, some sort of the very lightest of flames.

You would have said that the past was glowing there, sunset-red.

A short plump lady, all in black, who had paid off her cab driver down there by the bridge, had for a long time now been wandering to and fro beneath the windows of a yellow house; her hand trembled rather strangely; and in her trembling hand there barely trembled a tiny reticule, not in the Petersburg fashion. The plump lady was of considerable years and looked as though she suffered from shortness of breath; now and then her plump fingers plucked at her chin, which jutted imposingly from under her collar and was peppered here and there with small grey hairs. Standing opposite the yellow house, she was trying with trembling fingers to open the little reticule: the little reticule would not obey; at last the little reticule opened, and with a haste that was inappropriate to her years the lady took out a small, lace-patterned handkerchief, turned towards the Neva and began to cry. As she did so, her face was illumined by the sunset, and the small moustache above her lips was clearly visible; placing her hand on the stone, she looked with a childlike and quite unseeing gaze at the foggy, many-chimneyed distance and the watery depths.

At last, the lady hurried in agitation towards the entrance porch of the yellow house and rang the doorbell.

The door flew open; a little old man with gold braid on his lapels thrust his bald patch out of the opening at the sunset; the unendurable radiance from the other side of the Neva made him screw up his watery eyes.

'What do you want? . . .'

The lady of considerable years began to grow excited: something between tender emotion and carefully concealed shyness lit up her features.

'Dmitrich? . . . Don't you recognize me?'

Here the lackey's bald patch began to tremble and it fell into the tiny reticule (which was in the lady's hand):

'Little mother, *barynya* mine! . . . Anna Petrovna!'

'Yes, Semyonych, it's me . . .'

'But how on earth? Where have you come from?'

The tender emotion which might have been carefully concealed shyness once again sounded in the pleasant contralto.

'From Spain. Well, I wanted to see how you were managing here without me.'

'*Barynya* of ours, our own . . . Please come in, ma'am! . . .'

Anna Petrovna ascended the staircase: the staircase was still covered by the same velvety carpet. On the walls gleamed the same ornamental display of weapons: under the *barynya*'s watchful eye a Lithuanian brass helmet had once been hung here, and there a Templar's sword, rusted through everywhere; and today they gleamed just the same: from here, a Lithuanian brass helmet; from there, the cross-shaped hilts of completely rusted swords.

'Only there's no one here, ma'am; neither the young *barin* nor Apollon Apollonovich.'

Above the balustrade the pedestal of white alabaster still stood as before, and, as before, the same Niobe raised to heaven her alabaster eyes; this *before* again clustered round (though three years had gone by, and in those years so much had been experienced). Anna Petrovna remembered the Italian cavalier, and again felt within herself that carefully concealed shyness.

'Would you like some chocolate, or coffee, ma'am? Would you like a samovar?'

Anna Petrovna barely managed to turn her back on the past (here all was the same as before).

'So how have you been without me these past years?'

'Oh, all right, ma'am . . . Only if I may be so bold as to say so, ma'am, when you're not here there isn't any order. But otherwise there haven't been any consequences: it's just been as it was before . . . Have you heard about the *barin*, Apollon Apollonovich?'

'Yes, I have . . .'

'Yes, ma'am, all the marks of distinction . . . the tsar's favours . . . What do you expect: the *barin*'s an important man!'

'Has the *barin* aged?'

'The *barin*'s being appointed to a post: a senior one: – the *barin*'s just the same as a minister: that's the sort of *barin* he is . . .'

It suddenly seemed to Anna Petrovna that the lackey was viewing her with a slightly reproachful look; but this was only how it seemed: he had merely frowned because of the unendurable radiance from the other side of the Neva, as he opened the door to the reception room.

'Well, and Kolenka?'

'Kolenka, ma'am, Nikolai Apollonovich, rather, is such a clever one, if I may permit myself to observe it, ma'am! His honour is good at learning; and he's good at anything he puts his mind to . . . What a handsome fellow he's become . . .'

'Well, what do you expect? He was always like his father . . .'

As she said it, she lowered her eyes and turned the little reticule over in her fingers.

As before, the walls were set with high-legged chairs; from all sides between the chairs, which were upholstered in pale yellow plush, rose cold, white columns; and from each white column a stern male figure of cold alabaster looked reproachfully down at her. And with sheer hostility did the ancient, greenish glass, beneath which Anna Petrovna had had a decisive conversation with the senator, flash at her from the walls: and there – a pale-toned painting – Pompeian frescoes; the senator had brought those frescoes into her life when she had been his fiancée: thirty years had passed since that time.

Anna Petrovna was enveloped by the same drawing-room hospitality: she was enveloped by lacquers and lustres; she felt a pang in her breast as before; her throat constricted with the old enmity; Apollon Apollonovich might perhaps forgive her; but she would not forgive him: in the lacquered house the storms of life passed noiselessly, but the storms of life passed here disastrously.

Thus did a rush of dark thoughts drive her to the hostile banks; distractedly she leaned against the window – and saw the rosy little clouds racing above the waves of the Neva; the ragged little clouds were escaping from the funnels of small, receding steamers that threw from their sterns a stripe of gleaming sapphires to the banks: as it licked the stone pier, the stripe was thrown back and interlaced with the stripe that came to meet it, scattering its sapphires into a single, serpentine gold thread. Higher up, the lightest of flames turned to ashes in the clouds; the ash was strewn generously: all the openings in the sky were filled with ash; then everything changed insidiously with a single-coloured lightness; and for an instant it appeared as though the grey row of lines, spires and walls, with a barely descending shadowy darkness that fell on the masses of the stone walls – as though this grey row were the finest lace.

'Will you be staying with us, *barynya*?'

'I? . . . I'm in a hotel.'

. . . .

In this melting greyness there suddenly dimly emerged a large number of dots, looking in astonishment: lights, lights, tiny lights filled with intensity and rushed out of the darkness in pursuit of the rust-red blotches, as cascades fell from above: blue, dark violet and black.

Petersburg slipped away into the night.

Their Dancing Shoes Tapped

The doorbell rang and rang.

Some sort of angel-like creatures came through from the hallway into the ballroom, dressed in blue, white, and pink gowns, silvery, sparkling; they fluttered gauze, fans and silks, exuding all around a beneficial atmosphere of violets, lily of the valley, lilies and tuberoses; their marble-white shoulders, dusted lightly with powder, would within an hour or two be flushed crimson and covered in perspiration; but now, before the dancing, their little faces, their shoulders and their thin, exposed arms seemed even paler and thinner than on ordinary days; all the more considerably did the charm of these creatures somehow restrainedly flare into sparks in their eyes, while the creatures, sheer angelets, formed both rustling and coloured swarms of fluttering muslin; their white fans coiled and uncoiled, causing a light breeze; their dancing shoes tapped.

The doorbell rang and rang.

Cheerfully into the ballroom from the hallway came some kind of firm-chested genii in tight-fitting tailcoats, uniform jackets and pelisses – law students, hussars, high-school students and people who were nothing in particular – with moustaches and without them – all without beards; they exuded all around a kind of reliable joy and reserve. Unobtrusively they penetrated the circle of brilliant gauze and seemed to the young ladies more malleable than wax; and one had only to take one look, and there, here a light, downy fan was already beginning to beat against the chest of a mustachioed genius like a butterfly's wing that had settled trustfully on that chest, and the firm-chested hussar would shyly begin to exchange his frivolous hints with the young ladies; with precisely the same caution do we incline our face to a gentle moth that has happened to settle on our finger. And on the red background of the hussar's gold-textured attire, as against the magnificent rising of a fabulous sun, the slightly rosy profile stood out clearly and simply; the accumulating whirlwind of the waltz would soon turn the slightly rosy profile of the innocent angel into the profile of a fiery demon.

The Tsukatovs were not, strictly speaking, giving a ball: it was at most only a children's party in which grown-ups wanted to take part; to be sure, there was a rumour that maskers would be coming to the party; the prospect of their appearance surprised Lyubov' Alekseyevna, it had to be said; after all, it was not Christmas; but such, evidently, were the traditions of her charming husband that for the sake of dancing and children's laughter he was prepared to break all the statutes of the calendar; her charming husband, the possessor of two silver side-whiskers, was even to this day called Coco. In this dancing household he was, it goes without saying, Nikolai Petrovich, the household's head and the father of two pretty daughters of eighteen and fifteen respectively.

These charming fair-haired creatures were dressed in gauzy gowns and silver dancing shoes. Ever since eight o'clock they had been waving their feathery fans at their father, at the housekeeper, at the chambermaid, and even ... at the venerable *zemstvo* official[10] of mastodon-like proportions (a relative of Coco's) who was staying in the house. At last the long-awaited timid ring was heard; the door of the brightly lit ballroom flew open; and tightly clad in his tailcoat, a ballroom pianist, resembling a black, long-legged bird, rubbing his hands, very nearly tripped over a passing waiter (who had been summoned to this glittering house on the occasion of the ball); in the waiter's hands a cardboard sheet completely covered with cotillion trinkets began to rattle, began to tremble: medals, ribbons and little bells. The modest ballroom pianist spread out a row of sheet music, raised and lowered the wing of the grand piano, carefully blew the dust off the keys and, without visible purpose, he pressed a pedal with his gleaming shoe, putting one in mind of a conscientious engine driver testing the boilers of his locomotive before the train left the station. Having convinced himself that the instrument was working properly, the modest ballroom pianist gathered up the tails of his coat, sat down on the low piano stool, flung back his whole body, let his fingers fall on the keys, for a moment froze – and a thunderous chord shook the walls: as though a whistle had been sounded, summoning to a long journey.

And now amidst these raptures, as though he were his own man, not anyone else's, Nikolai Petrovich Tsukatov began to turn round and round with supple movements and, spreading wide the silvery lace of his side-whiskers with his fingers, his bald patch and smoothly shaven chin gleaming, rushed from couple to couple, dropping an innocent joke to a blue-clad young man, firmly poking two fingers at a firm-chested moustache-wearer, saying loudly into the ear of a more respectable man: 'Oh, let them enjoy themselves: they tell me I have danced my life away; but you know, this innocent enjoyment saved me in my time from many of the sins of youth: from wine, women and cards.' And amidst these raptures, as though he were not his own man, but someone else's, somehow idly, biting the thick felt of his little yellow beard, the *zemstvo* official clumsily stamped, trod on the ladies' trains, loitered lonely amidst the couples, and then went off to his room.

He Was Dancing to a Close

As usual, from time to time drawing-room visitors made their way through the ballroom – indulgently they advanced into the ballroom along the walls; insolent fans splashed their fronts, they were lashed by beaded skirts, their faces were dusted clean by a hot wind of hurtling couples; but they made their way noiselessly along the walls.

A rather fat man whose face was unpleasantly pitted with smallpox scars was the first to traverse this hall; the lapels of his frock-coat stuck out impossibly, because he had pulled his frock-coat tight over his belly, which was of respectable proportions; he was the editor of a conservative newspaper, the liberal son of a priest.[11] In the drawing-room he kissed the plump hand of Lyubov' Alekseyevna, a lady of forty-five with a puffy face that fell on to her corset-supported bosom in a double chin. If one looked out of the ballroom through the two intermediate rooms, one could observe from afar his standing sojourn in the drawing-room. There in the distance burned the azure globe of an electric chandelier; there in the shimmering azure light, rather heavily, stood the editor of the conservative newspaper on his elephant legs, showing mistily through suspended flocks of bluish tobacco smoke.

And as soon as Lyubov' Alekseyevna asked him some innocent question, the enormously fat editor turned it into a question of great significance:

'No need to tell me – no, madam! Well, you see, they think like that because they're all idiots. I can undertake to prove it with exactitude.'

'But after all, my dear man, Coco . . .'

'It's all a Jewish Freemason swindle, madam: the organization, the centralization . . .'

'All the same, there are very nice well-bred people among them and people who are, moreover, from our social circle,' the hostess interjected timidly.

'Yes, but our social circle doesn't know where sedition gets its power.'

'And in your opinion?'

'The power of sedition is in Charleston . . .'[12]

'Why in Charleston?'

'Because that is where the head of all sedition lives.'

'Who is this head?'

'The antipope . . .' the editor bellowed.

'And what is the antipope?'

'Ah well, one can see you haven't read anything.'

'Oh, how interesting all this is: tell me, please.'

Thus did Lyubov' Alekseyevna exclaim with surprise, inviting the pockmarked editor to sink into a soft armchair; and as he sank, he said:

'Yes, yes, my good friends!'

From afar, from the drawing-room, through the two intermediate rooms they could see the glittering and shimmering that were coming out of the open door of the ballroom. There resounded a thunderous:

'*Rrreculez!* . . .'

'*Balancez, vos dames!* . . .'

And again.

'*Rrreculez!* . . .'

Nikolai Petrovich Tsukatov had danced his life away; now Nikolai Petrovich was dancing his life to a close; doing so lightly, inoffensively, without vulgarity; not a single small cloud darkened his soul; his soul was pure and innocent, like this bald patch that burned like the sun or like this smoothly shaven chin between side-whiskers, like the moon looking out through the clouds.

Everything went dancingly for him.

He had begun to dance when he was a small boy; had danced better than any of the others; and he had been invited to people's homes as an experienced dancer; towards the end of his course at the high school acquaintances had danced into his life; towards the end of his days at the Law Faculty a circle of influential patrons had danced itself of its own accord out of an enormous circle of acquaintances; and Nikolai Petrovich Tsukatov set about dancing a career in the civil service. By that time he had danced away an estate; having danced away the estate, with frivolous simple-heartedness he started going to balls; and from those balls brought to himself with remarkable ease his companion in life, Lyubov' Alekseyevna: this completely accidental companion turned out to have an enormous dowry: and ever since then Nikolai Petrovich had danced in his own home; children were danced out; then the children's education was danced out – it was all danced easily, unpretentiously, joyfully.

Now he was dancing himself to a close.

The Ball

What is a drawing-room during a merry waltz? It is merely an appendage to the ballroom and a refuge for mammas. But the cunning Lyubov' Alekseyevna, taking advantage of her husband's good nature (he had not a single enemy) and her enormous dowry, taking advantage, further, of the fact that their house was profoundly indifferent to everything – everything, that is, apart from dancing, of course – and was therefore a neutral meeting place – taking advantage of all this, the cunning Lyubov' Alekseyevna, leaving it to her husband to direct the dancing, conceived a desire to direct the meetings of the most varied persons; here meetings took place between: a *zemstvo* official and a civil service official; a publicist and the director of a government department; a demagogue and a Judophobe. This house had been visited, and even lunched in, by Apollon Apollonovich.

And while Nikolai Petrovich wove the *contredanse* into unexpected figures, in the indifferently cordial drawing-room more than one conjuncture was woven and unwoven.

People danced here, too, in their own way.

This evening, as usual, drawing-room visitors made their way through the ballroom from time to time; the second to do so was a man of truly antediluvian appearance with a sugar-sweet face that was absent-minded to an atrocious degree, with a crease in his frock-coat that had ridden up on his down-covered back, making his unpretentious black half-belt protrude indecently between the tails; he was a professor of statistics; from his chin hung a ragged yellowish beard, and on to his shoulders fell, like thick felt, a mane that had never seen a comb. One was struck by his lower lip, which looked as though it were falling away from his mouth.

The fact was that in view of mounting events there was in preparation something akin to a *rapprochement* between one of the groups of supporters of, so to speak, if not radical, at any rate thoroughly humane reforms, and the truly patriotic hearts – a *rapprochement* that was not fundamental but rather conditional, temporarily brought about by the rumbling of the avalanche of mass meetings that was descending on everyone. The supporters of, so to speak, gradual but at any rate thoroughly humane reforms, shaken by the thunder of this terrible avalanche, suddenly in fear began to draw closer to the supporters of the existing norms, but did not make the first move; the liberal professor[13] had taken it upon himself, in the name of the common weal, to be the first to step across a threshold which was, so to speak, a fateful one for him.

One should not forget that he was respected by the whole of society, and that the latest protest petition had been signed by him; at the latest banquet his goblet had been raised to greet the spring.

But, as he entered the brightly lit ballroom, the professor lost his composure: the bright lights and shimmerings evidently dazzled him; his lower lip fell away from his mouth in surprise; in a most good-natured manner he contemplated the exultant ballroom, jibbed, faltered, took his unfolded handkerchief out of his pocket in order to remove from his moustache the moisture he had brought in from the street, and blinked at the couples who had fallen quiet for a moment between two figures of the quadrille.

Now he was approaching the drawing-room, and the shimmering light of the azure electric chandelier.

The editor's voice stopped him on the threshold:

'Do you understand now, madam, the connection between the war with Japan and the Jews who threaten us with a Mongol invasion and with sedition? The antics of our Jews and the emergence of the Boxers in China[14] have a most clear and obvious connection.'

'I understand, now I understand!'

This was Lyubov' Alekseyevna exclaiming. But the professor stopped in alarm: he, at any rate, remained to the marrow of his bones a liberal and a supporter, so to speak, of thoroughly humane reforms; this was the first time he had been to this house, and he had expected to find Apollon Apollonovich here; of him, however, there was apparently no sign: there was only the editor of a conservative newspaper, that same editor who had just, to express it humanely, thrown at the twenty-five years' enlightened activity of the gatherer of statistical facts a coagulation of the most indecent filth. And the professor suddenly began to puff and pant, to blink angrily at the editor, began to snort into his ragged beard in a rather ambiguous way, picking up the moisture that hung from his moustache with his bright red lower lip.

But the hostess's double chin turned first to the professor, then to the editor of the conservative newspaper and, pointing each of them out to the other with her lorgnette, she introduced them to each other, which caused them both to be taken slightly aback, and then each thrust his cold fingers into the hand of the other, pudgy, sweaty ones into pudgy dry ones, liberal-humane ones into ones that were not humane at all.

The professor grew even more embarrassed; he bowed slightly, snorted ambiguously, sat down in an armchair, sank into it, and began to fidget restlessly there. As for the newspaper editor, he continued, as though nothing had happened, his conversation with the hostess that had been interrupted. Ableukhov could have come to the rescue, but . . . Ableukhov was not there.

Was all this really required of the professor because of a witty conjuncture, a protest petition he had just signed and a goblet that had flown to greet the spring at a banquet?

But the fat man continued:

'Do you understand, madam, the activity of these Jews and Masons?'

'I understand, now I understand.'

The liberally grunting and lip-chewing professor could hold out no longer; turning to the hostess, he commented:

'Allow me, too, madam, to interject a modest remark of my own – a scientific remark: the information being given here has a perfectly clear source of origin.'

But the fat man suddenly interrupted him.

While over there, over there . . .

Over there the ballroom pianist suddenly and elegantly broke off his musical dance with a thunderous stab in the bass with one hand, while with his other hand he turned a page of music with an expert movement in the twinkling of an eye, and with his hand suspended in the air, his fingers spread expressively between the keyboard and the music, he turned the whole of his body somehow expectantly towards the host, flashing the enamel of his dazzlingly white teeth.

And then, to greet the ballroom pianist's gesture, Nikolai Petrovich Tsukatov suddenly thrust his smoothly shaven chin out of his raging side-whiskers, making to the ballroom pianist a sign of encouragement and approval; and then with head inclined, as if he were butting space, he somehow hurriedly threw himself in front of the couples at the highlights on the parquetry, twisting the end of one greying side-whisker in two fingers. And after him an angel-like creature flew helplessly, stretching her heliotrope scarf in space. Nikolai Petrovich Tsukatov, having derived inspiration from his dancing flight of fantasy, flew like lightning to the ballroom pianist and roared, like a lion, to the whole ballroom:

'*Pas-de-quatre, s'il vous plait!*'

And after him the angel-like creature helplessly flew.

Meanwhile servants appeared, running promptly into the corridor. For some reason tables, stools and chairs were carried out from somewhere and then carried in again; a pile of fresh sandwiches was brought in on a porcelain dish. There was also a chiming of forks. A stack of fragile plates was brought in.

Couple after couple poured into the brightly lit corridor. Jokes were scattered and laughter was scattered in a single, unbroken roar, and in a single unbroken rumbling chairs were moved about.

Puffs of cigarette smoke rose in the corridor, in the smoking room; puffs of cigarette smoke rose in the vestibule. Here, pulling a glove from his fingers and thrusting his hand in his pocket, a young cadet fanned his cheeks with a darkened glove; embracing, two young girls were telling each other some sacred secrets which had, perhaps, only just come into being; brunette talked to blonde, and the little blonde was snorting and biting her delicate little handkerchief.

If one stood in the corridor one could also see a corner of the dining-room, which was packed full with guests; and into there open sandwiches, bowls laden with fruit, bottles of wine, bottles of tart, nose-tingling fizzy drinks were being carried.

Now in the impossibly brightly-lit room only the ballroom pianist remained, gathering his music; thoroughly wiping his hot fingers, carefully passing a soft rag over the keyboard of the grand piano and putting the music into piles, this modest ballroom pianist, in whose presence the servants opened all the vents in the windows one by one, moved off indecisively through the lacquered corridor, resembling a black, long-legged bird. With pleasure he too was thinking of tea and sandwiches.

Through the doors that led into the drawing-room, out of the semi-darkness sailed a lady of forty-five with a fleshy chin that fell on to her corset-supported bosom. And looked through her lorgnette.

While into the ballroom after her sailed a rather fat man whose face was unpleasantly pitted with smallpox scars, and whose belly of respectable proportions was pulled in tight by a crease in his frock-coat.

Somewhere over there, at a distance, the professor of statistics, who until now had been sitting as at daggers drawn, was also plodding along; now he bumped into the *zemstvo* official, who was standing bored by the passageway, suddenly recognized that official, smiled cordially, and even began to pluck a button on his frock-coat with two fingers, as though he were grasping at a cast sheet-anchor; and now there resounded:

'According to statistical information . . . The annual consumption of salt by the average Dutchman . . .'

And again there resounded:

'The annual consumption of salt by the normal Spaniard . . .'

'According to statistical information . . .'

As Though Someone Were Complaining

They were waiting for the maskers. And still the maskers were not there. It had evidently only been a rumour. Yet they went on waiting for the maskers all the same.

And then the tinkling of the doorbell was heard: it was a timid sound; as though someone who had not been invited were giving a reminder of himself, asking to be let in out of the damp, cruel fog and the slush of the streets; but no one answered him. And then again the little bell began to ring, more loudly.

As though someone were complaining.

At that moment, panting, a girl of ten years ran out of the two intermediate rooms and saw the ballroom, which had just been full, glittering with an absence of people. There, by the entrance to the hallway, a door banged inquiringly, while the door's faceted and diamond-spawning handle began to sway slightly; and when a void had sufficiently appeared between the walls and the door, a small black mask thrust itself cautiously out of the void as far as its nose, and two pale sparks gleamed in the slits of the eyes.

Then the ten-year-old child saw between the wall and the door the small black mask and from the slits two hostile eyes fixed on her; now the whole masker pushed his way in, and a black beard made of gently curling lace was revealed; after the beard in the doorway, rustling, a satin cape sluggishly appeared, and the child, who had at first raised her fingers to her eyes in alarm, now joyfully smiled, began to clap her hands, and with a cry of: 'Here are the maskers, they've come!' she hurriedly ran back into the depths of the enfilade of rooms – to where, amidst the suspended flocks of bluish tobacco smoke, the misty professor on his elephant legs showed through.

The bright blood-red domino, stepping abruptly over the threshold, drew his satin cape over the lacquered tiles of the parquet floor; and just barely was it registered on the tiles of the parquet floor, like a floating crimson ripple of its own reflections; running crimson through the ballroom, as if an unsteady pool of blood were running from parquet to parquet; while towards it heavy feet began to tread, and enormous boots began to squeak from the distance towards the domino.

The *zemstvo* official, who had now become firmly established in the ballroom, stopped in perplexity, clutching with one hand at a tuft of his beard; meanwhile the lonely domino seemed to be imploring him not to drive him out of this house back into the Petersburg slush, imploring him not to drive him out of this house back into the cruel and dense fog. The *zemstvo* official evidently wanted to make a joke, because he hemmed and hawed; but when he tried to express his joke in words, that joke assumed a rather incoherent form:

'Mm . . . Yes, yes . . .'

The domino was advancing towards him, imploring with the whole of his body, advancing towards him with a red, rustling outstretched arm and the transparent lace lifted ever so slightly from his head that hung down from its stooping shoulders.

'Tell me, please, are you a masker?'

Silence.

'Mm . . . Yes, yes . . .'

But the masker implored; he threw forward the whole of his outstretched body – in the void, over the lacquered surfaces, the highlights, above the pool of his own reflections; rushing, lonely, about the ballroom.

'There's a fine thing . . .'

And again he threw himself forward, and again the red reflections slipped forward.

Now the *zemstvo* official, puffing and panting, began to retreat.

Suddenly he waved his arm; and he turned; quickly he began, God knows why, to return whence he had come, where the azure electric light shone, where in the azure electric light the professor of statistics stood with his pulled-up frock-coat, showing mistily through the flocks of tobacco smoke; but the *zemstvo* official was nearly knocked off his feet by an onrushing swarm of young ladies: their ribbons fluttered, party forfeits fluttered in the air and knees rustled.

This twittering swarm had come running out to look at the masker who had dropped by; but the twittering swarm stopped at the door, and its merry exclamations suddenly seemed to become a barely breathing rustle; at last this rustle grew silent; heavy was the silence. Suddenly behind the young ladies' backs an insolent young cadet declaimed:

> Who art thou, art thou, guest forbidding,
> Fateful domino?
> Look now – swathed in cape of crimson
> He doth come and go.[15]

And on the lacquers, on the lights and above the ripple of his own reflections the domino seemed to run dolefully to the side, and the wind from the open window whistled on the bright satin in an icy blast; poor domino: as if he had been exposed in the act of some offence – he kept leaning forward his outstretched silhouette; his red-rustling arm stretched forward, as though imploring them all not to drive him out of this house back into the Petersburg slush, imploring them not to drive him out of this house back into the cruel and damp fog.

And the young cadet faltered.

'Tell us, domino: are you the one who rushes about the prospects of Petersburg?'

'Ladies and gentlemen, have you read today's "Diary of Events"?'
'What if we have?'
'Oh, the red domino has been seen again . . .'
'Ladies and gentlemen, that is foolishness.'

The lonely domino continued to say nothing.

Suddenly one of the young ladies at the front, the one who, with head inclined, had narrowed her eyes severely at the unexpected guest – began to whisper something expressively to her female friend.

'Foolishness . . .'

'No, no: I don't feel quite myself . . .'

'I suppose the cat has got the dear domino's tongue: but he is a domino . . .'

'There isn't really anything we can do with him . . .'

'But he *is* a domino!'

The lonely domino continued to say nothing.

'Would you like some tea and sandwiches?'

'What about this, would you like this?'

Having thus exclaimed, the young cadet, turning round, threw at the domino, over the motley-coloured heads of the young ladies, a rustling stream of confetti.[16] In the air the arc of a paper streamer unwound for an instant; and when the end of it struck the masker with a dry crack, the arc of paper, coiling, lost momentum and sank to the floor; and to this amusing joke the domino made no reaction, merely stretched out his arms, imploring them not to drive him out of this house into the Petersburg street, imploring them not to drive him out of this house into the cruel and thick fog.

'Ladies and gentlemen, let us go back inside . . .'

And the swarm of young ladies ran away.

Only the one who had been standing closer than anyone else to the domino tarried for a moment; she measured the domino with a compassionate gaze; for some reason she sighed, then turned and went; and again turned round, and again said to herself:

'All the same . . . It's . . . it's somehow not right.'

A Dried-up Little Figure

This was, of course, still him: Nikolai Apollonovich. He had come there today to say – to say what?

He had himself forgotten; forgotten his own thoughts; and forgotten his hopes; had revelled in his own predestined role: a godlike, impassive creature had flown off somewhere; there remained a naked passion, and the passion had become a poison. The feverish poison penetrated his brain, pouring invisibly out of his eyes like a fiery cloud, entwining him in clinging, blood-red satin: it was as if he now looked at everything with a charred countenance out of the fires that baked his body, and the charred countenance turned into a black mask, while the fires that baked his body turned into red silk. He had now truly become a buffoon, an outrageous and red one (as she had once called him). Revengefully did this buffoon now violate some truth – was it his own, or hers? – perfidiously and keenly; yet again: did he love or hate?

It was as though he had been casting a spell on her all these last days, stretching cold hands out of the windows of the yellow house, stretching cold hands from the granite into the fog of the Neva. He wanted to seize, while loving, the mental image he had summoned up, he wanted, while taking revenge on her, to strangle the silhouette that fluttered somewhere; that was why all these days cold hands had stretched out of space into space, that was why all these days some kind of unearthly confessions had whispered out of space into her ears, some kind of whistling invocations of disaster and some kind of wheezing passions; that was why incoherent whistlings sounded in her ears, while the crimson of the leaves chased beneath her feet the rustling alluvial deposits of words.

That was why he had just come to that house: but she, the traitress, was not there; and in a corner he reflected. In the fog it was as if he saw the surprised, venerable *zemstvo* official; as if somewhere in the distance, in the labyrinth of mirrors, before him the figures of the laughing young ladies floated past like unsteady blobs; and when out of this labyrinth from the cold, greenish surface the distant echoes of questions with a paper serpent of confetti assailed him, he was surprised in the way that people marvel in dreams: was surprised at the emergence into the bright world before him of a reflection that was not real; but at the same time as he looked on them all as vacillating reflections that raced about in a dream, those reflections evidently took him for an apparition from the other world; and as an apparition from the other world, he drove them all away.

Then once again distant echoes drifted to him, and he turned slowly: both vaguely and dimly – somewhere over there, somewhere over there – a dried-up little figure, without hair, without whiskers, without eyebrows, quickly traversed the ballroom. Nikolai Apollonovich could with difficulty make out the details of the little figure that had flown into the ballroom – the strain to his vision through the slits of the mask gave him a pain in his eyes (apart from everything else, he suffered from short-sightedness), and only the contours of the greenish ears stood out – somewhere over there, somewhere over there. There was in all this something familiar, something near and alive, and Nikolai Apollonovich jerkily, in oblivion, rushed over to the little figure in order to see it at close quarters; but the little figure jerked back, seemed even to clutch at its heart, ran away, and was now looking at him. Great was Nikolai Apollonovich's amazement: right there before him stood a kindred face; it seemed to him covered in wrinkles that had eaten away at cheeks, forehead, chin and nose; from a distance one might have taken that face for the face of a Skopets, more young than old; but close to this was a feeble, sickly old man, conspicuous by his barely noticeable side-whiskers; in a word – under his nose Nikolai Apollonovich saw his father. Apollon Apollonovich, fingering the rings of his watch chain, fixed his eyes in poorly concealed fear at the satin domino who had so unexpectedly assailed him. In these blue eyes flickered something like a surmise; Nikolai Apollonovich felt an unpleasant shiver, for it was uncanny to look brazenly from behind the mask at that impassive gaze before which at ordinary times he lowered his eyes with incomprehensible diffidence; yes, it was uncanny now in that gaze to read fear, and a kind of helpless, sickly senility; and the surmise, quickly flickering past, was read as the answer to a riddle: Nikolai Apollonovich thought he had been recognized. This was not the case: Apollon Apollonovich simply thought that some clumsy prankster was terrorizing him, the courtier, with the symbolic colour of his brilliant cape.

All the same, he began to feel his own pulse. Nikolai Apollonovich had on several occasions recently noticed this gesture of the senatorial fingers, which was made in stealth (the senator's heart was evidently growing tired of functioning). Seeing this same gesture now, he felt something that resembled pity; and involuntarily he stretched his red-rustling arms to his father; as if he were imploring his father not to run away from him gasping in a bout of palpitations of the heart, as if he were imploring his father to forgive him for all his past sins. But Apollon Apollonovich had continued to feel his pulse with his trembling fingers and was now running away in the throes of palpitations – somewhere over there, somewhere over there . . .

Suddenly the doorbell rang: the whole room was filled with maskers; a black row of Capuchins burst in, the black Capuchins quickly formed a chain around their red confrère and began to dance some kind of dance around him; their satin skirts fluttered and coiled; the tops of their hoods flew up and fell uproariously back again; but on the chest of each a skull and crossbones was embroidered; and the skulls danced in time.

Then the red domino, defending himself, ran out of the ball-room; the black flock of Capuchins chased after him with loud laughter; thus did they fly along the wide corridor and into the dining-room; all who sat at the table began to bang their plates in welcome.

'Capuchins, maskers, clowns.'

Flocks of mother-of-pearl pink and heliotrope young ladies leapt up from their seats, and so did hussars, law students, students. Nikolai Petrovich Tsukatov jumped up on the spot with a goblet of Rhine wine, bellowing out his thunderous *vivat* in honour of the strange company.

And then someone observed:

'Ladies and gentlemen, this is too much . . .'

But he was hauled off to dance.

In the ballroom the pianist, arching his spine, had begun to set his fluffed-up quiff of hair dancing over his fingers that raced over the keys, pouring out runs; the treble danced all over the place and the bass sluggishly ground into motion.

And looking with an innocent smile at a black Capuchin who whirled his satin cape with an especially brazen movement, an angel-like creature in a little violet skirt suddenly leaned over the opening of his hood (a mask stared her in the face); and with her hand the creature seized hold of the hump of a striped clown, one of whose legs (it was blue) flew into the air, while the other (it was red) bent down to the parquetry; but the creature was not afraid;

she gathered up her hem, and from thence thrust forth a little silvery dancing shoe.

And off they went – one, two, three . . .

And after them went the Spanish lasses, the monks and the devils; the harlequins, the pelisses, the fans, the exposed backs, the scarves of silver laminae; above them all, swaying, danced a lanky palm tree.

Only over there, solitary, leaning against the window-sill, between the lowered greenish curtains, Apollon Apollonovich gasped in a paroxysm of his heart trouble, the extent of which not a single person knew.

Pompadour

Angel Peri stood in front of the dim oval mirror that was ever so slightly deflected: everything disappeared down into there and grew dim down there: the ceiling, the walls and the floor; and she herself disappeared down there, into the depth, the greenish dimness; and there, there – out of the fountain of objects and the muslin–lace foam there was now emerging a beautiful woman with luxuriantly fluffed hair and a beauty-spot on her cheek: Madame Pompadour!

Her hair, which curled in ringlets and was only just held together by a ribbon, was grey as snow, and the powder-puff was frozen above the powder-box in such slender little fingers; her tautly drawn-in, pale azure waist bent just so slightly to the left with a black mask in her hand; from her tightly cut corsage, like living pearls, breathing, her breasts showed mistily, while from her tight, rustling sleeves Valenciennes lace surged quietly in airy folds; and everywhere, everywhere around her *décolletage*, below the *décolletage*, surged that lace; beneath her corsage the flounces of the panniered skirt, which looked as though it had risen above the languorous breathing of zephyrs, rocked and played, and it shone with a garland of silver grasses in the form of airy festoons; below that were those same little dancing shoes; and on each of the little shoes a pompon showed silver. But it was strange: in this attire she seemed suddenly older and less attractive; instead of small rosy lips, she had indecently red ones that pouted, and they spoiled her little face, those too-heavy lips; and when she looked askance, for a moment there was something witch-like about Madame Pompadour: at that moment she hid the letter in the slit of her corsage.

At this same moment Mavrushka came running into the room holding a staff of light-coloured wood with a gold handle, from which ribbons fluttered: but when Madame Pompadour stretched out her little hand in order to take this staff, what proved to be in her hand was a note from her husband; it said: 'If you go out this evening, you will never return to my house again. Sergei Sergeyevich Likhutin.'

That note related not to her, Madame Pompadour, of course, but to Sofya Petrovna Likhutina, and Madame Pompadour smiled at the note contemptuously; she looked fixedly at the mirror, at the depth, the greenish dimness: there far, far away a gentle ripple seemed to rush; suddenly out of that depth and greenish dimness some sort of waxen face seemed to thrust itself into the crimson light of the vermilion lampshade; and she turned round.

Behind her shoulders motionlessly stood her husband, the officer; but again she laughed contemptuously, and raising her panniered skirt slightly by the festoons, she floated smoothly away from him in curtsies; a quietly flowing zephyr carried her away from him, and her crinoline rustled, swaying like a bell in the zephyr's sweet currents; and when she was in the doorway, she turned to face him, and with her hand, on which a satin mask dangled, she thumbed her nose at the officer, smiling slyly as she did so; then outside the door a peal of laughter resounded and the innocent exclamation:

'Mavrushka, my coat!'

Then Sergei Sergeich Likhutin, second lieutenant in His Majesty's Gregorian Regiment, white as death, completely calm, ironically smiling, skipped along after the graceful mask and then, with a click of his spurs, stood deferentially with the fur coat in his hand; with even greater deference did he throw the coat about her shoulders, opened wide the door and courteously pointed outside – into the dark-coloured dark; and when, rustling, she passed into that darkness, turning up her little face at such a humble service, the humble servant, with a click of his spurs, made her another low bow. The dark-coloured darkness surged over her – surged from all sides: it flooded her rustling outlines; for a long time something went on rustling and rustling, out there on the steps of the staircase. The outer door banged shut; then Sergei Sergeich Likhutin, still with the same abrupt gestures, began to walk about everywhere and everywhere put out the electric lights.

A Fateful Event

The ballroom pianist elegantly broke off his musical dance with a thunderous stab in the bass, while with his other hand he turned a page of music with an expert movement; but at that moment Nikolai Petrovich Tsukatov suddenly thrust his smoothly shaven chin out of his raging side-whiskers, swiftly rushing out in front of the couples over the highlights of the parquetry, impetuously drawing after him a helpless creature:

'*Pas-de-quatre, s'il vous plaît! . . .*'

'Come with me,' said some kind of Madame Pompadour to Nikolai Apollonovich importunately, and Nikolai Apollonovich, who had not recognized Madame Pompadour, reluctantly gave her his hand; and, glancing with a barely visible smile at her red cavalier, with a peculiarly fierce movement of her upturned mask, Madame Pompadour stretched her hand forward and helplessly placed it on the domino's hand; while with her other hand, with its quivering fan and covering of kid glove, Madame Pompadour gathered up her hem of azure mists, and from it, with a rustle, a silvery dancing shoe was thrust the merest way.

And off they went, off they went.

One, two, three – and the gesture of a foot beneath a backward-flexed waist.

'Do you recognize me?'

'No.'

'Are you still looking for someone?'

One, two, three – and again a flexing, and again a little shoe was thrust forth.

'I have a letter for you.'

And behind the first couple – the domino and the marquise – came harlequins, Spanish girls, young ladies as pale as mother-of-pearl, law students, hussars and helpless muslin creatures; fans, bare shoulders, silvery backs and scarves.

Suddenly one of the red domino's hands seized hold of her slender, azure waist, and his other hand, taking her hand, felt a letter in it: at that same moment the dark green, black and cloth-covered arms of all the couples, and the red arms of the hussars seized all the slender waists of the heliotrope, *gris-de-perle*, rustling female partners, in order again, again and again to whirl in some turns of the waltz.

Flying out in front of them all, the grey-haired host bellowed at the couples:

'*A vos places!*'

And after him flew a helpless adolescent.

Apollon Apollonovich

Apollon Apollonovich had recovered from his palpitations; Apollon Apollonovich looked into the depths of the enfilade of rooms; hidden in the dark curtains, he stood unnoticed by anyone; he was trying to get away from the curtains in such a way that his appearance in the drawing-room would not betray the strange behaviour of a government official. Apollon Apollonovich tried to conceal the paroxysm of his heart trouble from everyone; but it would have been even more unpleasant for him to admit that this evening's attack had been caused by the appearance before him of the red domino: the colour red was, of course, an emblem of the chaos that was leading Russia to ruin; but he did not want to admit that the domino's preposterous desire to frighten him had any political tinge.

And Apollon Apollonovich was ashamed of his fear.

Recovering from the paroxysm, he cast glances around the ballroom. All that he saw there struck his gaze with garish gaudiness; the images that fleeted there had a kind of repulsive touch that shocked him personally: he saw a monster with a double-eagled head; somewhere over there, somewhere over there – quickly the ballroom was traversed by the dried-up little figure of a knight and the flashing blade of a sword, in the image and likeness of some luminous phenomenon; he ran dimly and unclearly, without hair, without moustache, the contours of his greenish ears standing out and glittering diamond insignia dangling on his chest; and when out of the maskers and Capuchins a one-horned creature flung itself at the little knight, with its horn it broke off the knight's luminous phenomenon; in the distance something clinked and fell to the floor in the likeness of a beam of moonlight; strangely, this image awoke in Apollon Apollonovich's consciousness some recently forgotten incident he had encountered, and he felt his backbone; for a moment Apollon Apollonovich thought he had *tabes dorsalis*. With revulsion he turned away from the gaudy ballroom; and passed into the drawing-room.

Here, when he appeared, everyone rose from their seats; courteously towards him came Lyubov' Alekseyevna; and the professor of statistics, who had risen from his place, mumbled:

'We have once had occasion to meet: very happy to see you; I have some business with you, Apollon Apollonovich.'

To which Apollon Apollonovich, kissing the hostess's hand, rather drily remarked:

'Well, you know, I see callers at the Institution.'

With this reply he cut off the possibility of a certain liberal party coming to meet the government. The conjuncture was upset; and the professor had no option but to abandon that glittering house, and in future to sign without hindrance all the expressions of protest, in future to raise without hindrance his goblet at all the liberal banquets.

Getting ready to leave, he approached the hostess, on whom the editor was continuing to practise his eloquence.

'You think that Russia's ruin is being prepared for us in the hope of social equality. Somehow I doubt it. They quite simply want to sacrifice us to the devil.'

'Oh, but how?' the hostess exclaimed in surprise.

'Very simply, madam: you are only surprised because you have read nothing about this question . . .'

'But wait, wait!' the professor said, once again interjecting a remark. 'You are basing yourself on the fabrications of Taxil[17] . . .'

'Taxil?' interrupted the hostess, suddenly taking out a small, exquisite writing pad and starting to write it down:

'Taxil, you say? . . .'

'They are preparing to sacrifice us to Satan, because the higher levels of Jewish Freemasonry belong to a certain cult, called Palladism[18] . . . This cult . . .'

'Palladism?' the hostess interrupted, again starting to write something in her notebook.

'Pa-lla- . . . What was it, again?'

'Palladism.'

From somewhere the housekeeper was heard giving an anxious sigh, and then a tray was brought, on which stood a faceted decanter, filled to the top with cooling fruit punch, and was placed in the room between the drawing-room and the ballroom. And standing in the drawing-room, one could observe again and again and again how, from the melodic system of the surf of sound that beat against the walls, and from the ripple of the muslin-and-lace couples who swayed to and fro in the waltz, now one, now another young girl, covered in gleams of light, her little face flushed and the transparent yellow of her tresses dishevelled on her back, broke loose, broke loose and ran through, laughing, to the next room, the high heels of her white silk dancing shoes tapping, and quickly poured from the decanter the acidulous ruby liquid: thick, iced fruit punch. And gulped it down avidly.

And the hostess distractedly abandoned her interlocutor.

'But tell me . . .'

Putting her miniature lorgnette to her eyes, she saw that there in the next room a law student in a rustling little silk uniform jacket with the waist pulled in too tight, had fluttered out of the ballroom to the flushed young girl who was drinking fruit punch and, rolling his r's in the French manner in a thunderous little bass, the law student was jokingly pulling the glass of ruby fruit punch out of the young girl's hand and shyly taking a cold sip from it. And Lyubov' Alekseyevna, breaking off the editor's ferocious discourse, stood up, rustling, and sailed through to the semi-dark room in order to sternly observe:

'What are you doing here – you must dance, dance.'

And then the happy couple returned to the ballroom that seethed with gleams of light; the law student embraced with a snow-white glove the young girl's waist that was as slender as a wasp; the young girl threw herself back on this snow-white glove; both suddenly began to fly intoxicatingly, moving their legs with extreme swiftness, cutting through the flying dresses, shawls and fans that wove sparkling patterns around them; at last, they themselves became a kind of radiant sparks. Over there the ballroom pianist, arching his spine in bizarre fashion, leaned over his flying fingers on the keys somehow stealthily, in order to pour out some rather garish sounds in the treble: they too ran off in pursuit of one another; then the pianist, leaning back wearily, with a squeak of the piano stool ran his fingers over some thick bass notes . . .

. . . .

'Taxil made up a complete fable about the Masons,' rang the caustic voice of the professor. 'Unfortunately many people believed that fable; but later Taxil renounced the fable in decisive fashion; he publicly confessed that his sensational statements to the pope were merely his own plain mockery at the obscurantism and evil will of the Vatican. But for that Taxil was anathemaed in a papal encyclical . . .'

Here someone new came in – a bustling, taciturn-like gentleman with an enormous wart near his nose – and suddenly began to nod and smile to the senator, rubbing his fingers together; and with ambiguous meekness he led the senator off to a corner:

'You see . . . Apollon Apollonovich . . . the director of Department X has proposed . . . how should one put it . . . Well, to ask you a certain ticklish question.'

More than this it was hard to make out: one could hear the little gentleman whispering something in the pale ear with ambiguous meekness, and then Apollon Apollonovich flung himself at him with a kind of pathetic fear.

'Speak to the point . . . My son?'

'That's precisely it, precisely it: that is the delicate question.'

'My son has relations with . . .?'

More than this one could not make out; all one could hear was:

'Nonsense . . .

'It's all utter nonsense . . .'

'To be sure, it's a pity that this inappropriate joke should have assumed such an inappropriate character that the press . . .

'And you know: I will confess that we have given the Petersburg police instructions to follow your son . . .

'Only for his own good, naturally . . .'

And again there was a whispering. And the senator asked:

'A domino, you say?'

'Yes – the very same one.'

With these words the bustling little gentleman pointed to the next room, where somewhere the bustling domino, moving jerkily about, was trailing his satin cape over the lacquered tiles of the parquetry.

A Scandal

Sofya Petrovna Likhutina, when she had handed over the letter, slipped away from her cavalier and sank helplessly on to a soft stool; her arms and legs refused to work.

What had she done?

She saw the red domino running past her into a corner of the empty intermediate room; and there, unnoticed, the domino tore the paper of the envelope; a note began to whisper in brightly rustling hands. The red domino, in his efforts to see the small, minute handwriting of the note better, involuntarily pushed the mask up on to his forehead, making the black lace of his beard reveal through two luxuriant folds the domino's pale face, as if they were two flaps of a black silk cap; from the trembling flaps that face was thrust, waxen, frozen, with protruding lips, and his hand trembled, and the note trembled in his fingers; and a cold sweat appeared on his forehead.

The red domino did not see Madame Pompadour now, who was watching him from the corner; he was now entirely absorbed in reading; he began to fidget, threw open the satin skirts of his long garment, revealing his ordinary apparel – a dark green frock-coat; Nikolai Apollonovich pulled out his gold pince-nez and, putting it to his eyes, inclined his face towards the little note.

Nikolai Apollonovich jerked right back; his eyes fixed on her with horror; but he did not see her: his lips apparently whispered things that were quite inarticulate – and Sofya Petrovna wanted to rush to him from her corner, because she could no longer endure these widened eyes that were fixed on her. At this point people came into the room; the red domino nervously hid the note in his trembling fingers, withdrawing them into the folds of his garment; but the red domino forgot to lower his mask. Thus he stood, with the mask raised on his forehead, his mouth half open and his eyes unseeing.

Even faster than before did the young girl come rushing into the room again after the waltz in order to cool off; she almost knocked down the *zemstvo* official, who was for some reason dozing solitarily near the entrance, stopped in front of a pier-glass, set straight a ribbon that had settled in her hair and, putting one foot on a chair, tied her snow-white dancing shoe; she began a suspicious whispering with her female friend, who was also a young girl, hearing the torrent of sounds, the discordant rustling shuffling, the hoarse cries from the drawing-room, the laughter, the peremptory shouts of the master of ceremonies, hearing the barely audible jingling of cavaliers' spurs.

Suddenly she saw the domino with his unlowered mask; and, having seen him, exclaimed:

'So that's who you are! Hello, Nikolai Apollonovich, hello: who could ever have recognized you?'

Sofya Petrovna Likhutina saw Nikolai Apollonovich smile long-sufferingly, dart away somehow strangely, and rush off back to the ballroom.

There stood two rows of dancers, floating away into the delicately blinded gaze in transfusions of mother-of-pearl pink, *gris-de-perle*, heliotrope, bluish and white velvets and silks: on the silks, on the velvets lay shawls, scarves, veils, fans and beads, on the shoulders lay heavy lace made of silver laminae; at the slightest movement there a scaly spine flashed; everywhere now one could see flushed arms, fingers uncontrollably playing with the laminae of fans, coarsening blotches in the white velvet, rising and falling *décolletages* and cheeks that were quite crimson, in a haze of coiffures disturbed by dancing.

There stood two rows of dancing couples, floating away into the gaze in black, greenish and bright red hussar cloth, gold collars that cut into chins, padded uniformed chests and padded shoulders, snow-white openings of frock-coat waistcoats that cracked when pressed, and the lustre of frock-coats the colour of ravens' wings.

Nikolai Apollonovich impetuously flew past the maskers and the cavaliers, moving jerkily on his trembling legs; and his blood-red satin cape trailed after him over the lacquered tiles of the parquetry, only barely registering itself on the tiles of the parquetry like a flying, crimson ripple of its own reflections; crimson, that ripple, like an unsteady red lightning, licked the parquetry in front of the monstrous runner.

This flight of the red domino with the mask raised on to his forehead, beneath which the face of Nikolai Apollonovich protruded in front, caused a real scandal; the merry couples rushed from the spot; one young lady had a fit of hysterics; while two maskers suddenly revealed their bewildered faces in fright; and when, having recognized the fleeing Ableukhov, Leib Hussar Shporyshev grabbed him by the sleeve with the words: 'Nikolai Apollonovich, Nikolai Apollonovich, for God's sake tell us what's the matter with you.' Nikolai Apollonovich, like a wild beast brought to bay, grinned pathetically with a mad countenance, making an effort to laugh, but did not succeed in smiling; Nikolai Apollonovich, tearing his sleeve loose, disappeared through the doorway.

An indescribable confusion ran through the ballroom; the young ladies and cavaliers busily told one another their impressions; everyone was alarmed; the maskers who had, only just now, been mysteriously fleeting about, all these dark blue little knights, harlequins and Spanish girls, had lost their sense of intrigue; from behind the mask of a two-headed monster that ran up to Shporyshev came a disturbed and familiar voice:

'For God's sake explain what all this means!'

And Leib Hussar Shporyshev recognized Verhefden's voice.

This commotion in the ballroom was instinctively transmitted through the two intermediate rooms and into the drawing-room; and there, there, where the azure globe of the electric chandelier burned, where in the shimmering azure light the drawing-room visitors somehow heavily stood, showing mistily through the suspended flocks of bluish tobacco smoke – these visitors looked with alarm in there – to the ballroom. Among this group the dried-up little figure of the senator stood out, his pale face, as if made of papier mâché, the lips firmly pressed together, his two small side-whiskers and the contours of his greenish ears: precisely thus had he been depicted on the front page of some wretched little street journal.

In the ballroom raged a contagion of surmise, excitement and rumour apropos of the strange, highly strange, exceedingly strange behaviour of the senator's son; there it was said, in the first place, that this behaviour had been caused by some drama; in the second place, the rumour was started that Nikolai Apollonovich, who had visited the Tsukatovs' house in secret, was the red domino who was creating a sensation in the press. The meaning of it all was discussed. It was said that the senator knew nothing of it; from afar, from the ballroom, heads nodded towards the drawing-room, where the little figure of the senator now stood and from where his dried-up face protruded indistinctly amidst the suspended flocks of bluish tobacco smoke.

Well, But What If?

We left Sofya Petrovna Likhutina alone at the ball; now we shall return to her again.

Sofya Petrovna Likhutina had stopped in the middle of the ballroom.

Before her for the first time her terrible vengeance[19] had appeared: the crumpled little envelope had now passed into his hands, and Sofya Petrovna Likhutina scarcely understood what she had done; Sofya Petrovna did not understand what she had read yesterday in the crumpled envelope. But now the contents of the dreadful note appeared clearly before her: Nikolai Apollonovich's letter invited him to throw some sort of bomb with a clock mechanism, a bomb which apparently lay in his writing desk; to judge by the hints, the letter proposed that he throw this bomb at *the senator* (everyone called Apollon Apollonovich *the senator*).

Sofya Petrovna stood bewilderedly amidst the maskers with her pale azure waist barely flexed, wondering what it all meant. It was, of course, some wicked, base joke; but she had so much wanted to frighten him with this joke: after all, he was ... a base coward.

Well, but what if . . . what if what was in the letter were true? What if . . . if Nikolai Apollonovich really did keep objects of such dreadful content in his writing desk? And if people heard about it? And now he would be arrested? . . . Sofya Petrovna stood bewilderedly amidst the maskers with her pale azure waist, pulling at her curls, which were silvery-grey with powder and luxuriantly ringleted.

And then she began to spin round uneasily among the maskers; and then the Valenciennes lace she was wearing began to flutter; while the panniered skirt below her corsage, which looked as though it had risen beneath the breathing of languorous zephyrs, swayed its flounces and gleamed like a garland of silver grasses in the form of light festoons. Around her, voices, fusing together in a whisper, grumbled ceaselessly, constantly, tiresomely like a fateful spindle. A little flock of grey-browed matrons, rustling their satin skirts, was preparing to leave *this kind of* merry ball; this one, stretching out her neck, was summoning her daughter, who was dressed as a *paysanne*, from the midst of a swarm of clowns; another, putting her miniature lorgnette to her eyes, was growing uneasy. And above everything hung a disturbing atmosphere of scandal. The ballroom pianist stopped churning up the air with sounds; he put his elbow on the lid of the grand piano; waited to be asked to play for more dancing; but no such requests came.

The cadets, the little high-school students, the law students – they all dived into the waves of clowns and, having dived, disappeared; and were no longer there; from all sides came lamentations, rustlings, whisperings.

'No, did you see, did you see? Do you understand?'

'Don't say it – it's dreadful . . .'

'I have always said it, I have always said it, *ma chère*: he has raised a scoundrel. Even *tante Lise* said it; Mimi said it; *Nicolas* said it.'

'Poor Anna Petrovna: I understand her! . . .'

'Yes, and I too understand: we all do.'

'Here he is, here he is.'

'What dreadful ears he has . . .'

'He's to be made a minister . . .'

'He'll ruin the country . . .'

'He ought to be told . . .'

'But look: the *Bat* is looking at us; as though he senses that we're talking about him . . . And the Tsukatovs are hanging around him – it's simply shameful to look . . .'

'They don't dare to tell him why we're leaving . . . They say that Madame Tsukatova is from a family of priests.'

Suddenly the hissing of an ancient dragon was heard from the agitated little flock of grey-browed matrons:

'Look! He's off: he's not a high official, but a chicken.'

. . . .

Well, but what if . . . if Nikolai Apollonovich really was keeping a bomb in his desk? After all, someone might find out about it; why, he might bump into the desk (he was absent-minded). Perhaps he did his studies in the evening at his desk, with an open book. Sofya Petrovna clearly imagined the sclerotic Ableukhov forehead with small bluish veins bent over the work desk (in the desk, a bomb). A bomb was something round that must not be touched. And Sofya Petrovna shuddered. For a moment she clearly imagined Nikolai Apollonovich rubbing his hands over the tea tray; on the desk the red horn of the gramophone threw passionate Italian arias into their ears; well, why should they quarrel? And why the preposterous delivery of the letter, the domino and all the rest . . .

An extremely fat man (a Spaniard from Granada) adhered to Sofya Petrovna; she stepped to the side, and the fat man (a Spaniard from Granada) did likewise; for a single moment he was squeezed against her in the crowd, and she fancied that his hands began to rustle over her skirt.

'You are not a *barynya*: you are a *dushkanchik*.'

'Lippanchenko!' And she struck him with her fan.

'Lippanchenko! Now explain to me . . .'

But Lippanchenko interrupted her:

'You should know better, madam; do not play at being naïve.'

And Lippanchenko, adhering to her skirt, squeezed right up close against her: and she began to flounder, striving to tear herself free of him; but the crowd pressed them even closer; what was he doing, this Lippanchenko? Ah, why he was indecent.

'Lippanchenko, you're not allowed to do that.'

But he laughed greasily:

'But I saw you delivering . . .'

'You mustn't say a word about that.'

But he laughed greasily:

'Very well, very well! And now come with me into this wonderful night . . .'

'Lippanchenko! You're an insolent fellow . . .'

She tore herself free of Lippanchenko.

Clicking his castanets in pursuit of her did the Spaniard from Granada go, performing some kind of passionate Spanish *pas*.

Well, but what if the letter was not a joke: what if . . . if he were doomed. No, no, no! Such horrors do not exist; and neither do the kind of wild beasts that could force an insane son to raise his hand against his father. All that was simply the jokes of his companions. She was stupid – all that had happened was that she had obviously been frightened by the joke of his friends. And as for him, as for him: he too had been frightened by the joke of his friends; why, he was just a little coward: had run away from her there, too (there, by the Winter Canal); she did not consider the Winter Canal as any old prosaic spot from which one could run at the whistle of a policeman . . .

He had not behaved like Hermann: had slipped, fallen, showing the straps of his trousers from beneath the silk. And now: he had not laughed at the naïve joke of his revolutionary friends, and he had not recognized her as the one who had delivered the letter: had run through the ballroom, holding his mask in his hands and exposing his face to the laughter of cavaliers and ladies. No, let Sergei Sergeich Likhutin teach the insolent coward a lesson! Let Sergei Sergeich Likhutin challenge the coward to a duel . . .

The second lieutenant! . . . Sergei Sergeich Likhutin! . . . second lieutenant Likhutin had, ever since yesterday evening, been behaving in a most indecent manner: had been snorting something into his moustache and clenching his fist; had the temerity to come into her bedroom with an explanation in nothing but his long johns; and had then had the effrontery to pace about on the other side of the wall until it was morning.

Dimly she pictured yesterday's mad shouts, bloodshot eyes and fist falling on the table: had Sergei Sergeich gone insane? He had long been an object of suspicion to her: the silence of all these three last months was suspicious; these times when he went running off to work were suspicious. Oh, she was lonely, the poor thing: now she needed his firm support; she wanted her husband, second lieutenant Likhutin, to hug her like a child and carry her in his arms . . .

Instead of that the Spaniard from Granada again leapt up and whispered in her ear:

'Eh, eh, eh? Won't you come riding? . . .'

Where was Sergei Sergeich now, why was he not at her side; she somehow felt afraid of going back as before to her little flat on the Moika, where, like a wild beast in its lair, her rebellious husband lay feverishly abed.

And she stamped her little heels:

'I'll show him!'

And again:

'I'll teach him a lesson!'

And the Spaniard from Granada flew away from her in confusion.

Sofya Petrovna shuddered as she remembered the grimace with which Sergei Sergeich had handed her cloak, pointing to the exit. How he had stood behind her shoulders there! How contemptuously she had laughed then and, raising her panniered skirt slightly by its festoons, had sailed smoothly away from him amidst curtsies (why had she not curtsied to Nikolai Apollonovich when she had given him the letter – curtsies had been coming to her)! How she had spoken in the doorway, how she had thumbed her nose at the officer, with a sly smile! Yet the only thing was: she was afraid to return home.

And she stamped her little heels in vexation.

'I'll show him!'

And again:

'I'll teach him a lesson!'

Yet still she was afraid to go back.

She was even more afraid of staying here; nearly everyone had now dispersed: the young people and the maskers had dispersed; with a bewildered air the good-natured host was going up now to this person, now to another with a little anecdote; finally he cast a forlorn glance round the emptying ballroom, cast a forlorn glance at the crowd of buffoons and harlequins, openly advising them with his gaze to spare the glittering room any further jollity.

But the harlequins, swarming together into a gaudy little flock, were behaving in a most indecent fashion. One brazen fellow stepped forth from their midst, began to dance and sing:

> The von Sulitzes have gone,
> Ableukhov too we lack . . .
> The prospects, harbour and the streets
> are full of rumours black! . . .
> Filled to the top with treachery,
> the senator you praise . . .
> But there's no law of emergency,
> No law at all these days!
> He is a patriotic dog –
> with medals tight he's packed;
> But anyone can now commit
> A terroristic act.

Nikolai Petrovich Tsukatov perceived in the twinkling of an eye how the decency of his merry house was violated by the venomous little poem. Nikolai Petrovich Tsukatov flushed deeply, looked at the cheeky harlequin in a most good-natured manner, turned his back and walked away from the door.

The White Domino

Now it was time to leave. Most of the guests had already dispersed: Sofya Petrovna Likhutina was loitering solitarily about the emptying rooms; only the Spaniard from Granada clicked in response to her agitation his resonant castanets. There in the empty enfilade she unexpectedly saw a solitary, white domino; the white domino seemed to emerge at once from nowhere, and – now, look:

> someone sad and tall, whom she thought she had
> seen a large number of times, quite recently, today
> – someone sad and tall, entirely swathed in white
> satin, was coming towards her through the empty-
> ing rooms; from behind the slits of his mask the
> bright light of his eyes was looking at her; it

seemed to her that the light had begun to stream so sadly from his forehead, from his stiffening fingers . . .

Sofya Petrovna trustingly called out to the domino's dear possessor:

'Sergei Sergeyevich! . . . Oh, Sergei Sergeyevich! . . .'

Yes, there could be no doubt: it was Sergei Sergeich Likhutin; he had repented of yesterday's scandal; he had come for her – to take her away.

Sofya Petrovna again called out to the domino's dear possessor – sad and tall:

'It is you, isn't it? . . . It's you?'

But the tall, sad domino shook his head, put a finger to his lips and told her to be silent.

Trustingly she held out her hand to the white domino: how the satin gleamed, how cool the satin was! And her azure little hand began to rustle, having touched this white arm, and hung helplessly on it (the arm of the domino's possessor proved to be hard as wood); for a moment above her little head a radiant mask inclined, displaying from beneath the white lace a handful of beard, like a sheaf of ripe grain.[20]

Never had she seen Sergei Sergeyevich in this dazzling guise before; and she whispered:

'Have you forgiven me?'

From behind the mask a sigh responded to her.

'Shall we make it up now?'

But the tall, sad figure slowly shook its head.

'Is it . . . you, Sergei Sergeyevich?'

But the tall, sad figure slowly shook its head.

Now they were going through into the vestibule: the inexpressible surrounded them, the inexpressible stood all around. Sofya Petrovna Likhutina, taking off her little black mask, buried her face in her caressing furs, but the tall, sad figure, who had put on his coat, did not take off his mask. With amazement Sofya Petrovna looked at the tall, sad figure: was surprised that he had not been handed an officer's jacket; instead of that jacket he put on a torn little coat, from which his elongated hands peeped somehow strangely, reminding her of lilies. With the whole of herself she rushed towards him amidst the astonished lackeys, who were watching the spectacle; the inexpressible surrounded them, the inexpressible stood all around.

But the tall, sad figure in the lighted doorway slowly shook its head and told her to be silent.

Since evening the sky had become a continuous, dirty slush; since nightfall the continuous, dirty slush had descended to earth; fog had descended to earth, becoming for a time a blackish gloom, through which the reddish blotches of the streetlights horribly emerged. Sofya Petrovna Likhutina saw how above a reddish blotch, hunched, the caryatid of the entrance porch fell, and how it hung; how in the blotch a piece of the little house next door with bay windows and small carved wooden sculptures protruded. The tall outline of her unknown companion loomed before her. And she whispered to him imploringly:

'I'd like a cab!'

The tall outline of her unknown companion with the flaxen-white beard, who had lowered his red-stained little peaked cap on to his mask, waved his arm into the fog:

'Cab!'

Sofya Petrovna Likhutina understood everything now: the sad outline had a beautiful, caressing voice –

– a voice she had heard a large number of times, had heard quite recently, last night: yes, last night in a dream; but she had forgotten it, as she had forgotten altogether the dream of the night that had passed – . . .

He had a beautiful, caressing voice, but . . . – there could be no doubt, his voice was not Sergei Sergeyevich's. And yet she hoped, and yet she wished that this (so she wished) beautiful and caressing but alien person was her husband. But her husband had not come for her, had not led her out of hell: a stranger had led her out of hell.

Who could he be?

The unknown outline raised its voice several times: its voice grew stronger, stronger and stronger, and it seemed that behind the mask, too, someone was growing stronger, immensely huge. The silence merely threw itself upon the voice; on the other side of someone else's gate a dog responded. A street ran off that way.

'Well then, who are you?'

'You all deny me: I look after you all. You deny me, and then you call on me . . .'

At this point Sofya Petrovna Likhutina realized for an instant what was standing before her: tears constricted her throat; she wanted to fall at these slender feet and suddenly entwine the unknown figure's slender knees in her arms, but at that moment a carriage began prosaically to clatter and a sleepy, round-shouldered Vanka[21] moved forward into the street lamp's bright light. The wondrous outline helped her into the carriage, but when she stretched forth her trembling arms to it beseechingly from the carriage, the outline slowly put a finger to its lips and told her to be silent.

But the carriage had already moved off: if only it had stopped and, oh, if only it had turned back – turned back to that bright place where for an instant before her the tall, sad figure had stood and where he was no longer, since from there now only the yellow eye of the street lamp gleamed on the flagstones.

She Forgot What Had Happened

Sofya Petrovna forgot what had happened. Her future sank away into the blackish night. The irremediable came crawling towards her; the irremediable embraced her; and at this point receded: house, flat and husband. And she did not know where the cab driver was taking her. Into the blackish-grey night behind her a piece of the recent past fell away: the masked ball, the harlequins; and even (imagine!) – even the tall, sad figure. She did not know where the cab driver was taking her away from.

After the piece of the recent past, the whole of that day fell away, too: the scrape she had got into with her husband and the scrapes she had got into with Madame Farnois on account of 'Maison Tricotons'. Scarcely had she moved on, seeking a support for her consciousness, than she wanted to summon up the impressions of yesterday, – and yesterday also fell away, like a piece of an enormous road that was paved with granite; it fell away and struck against some utterly dark bottom. And somewhere the impact resounded, shattering the stones.

Before her fleeted the love of this unhappy summer; and the love of the unhappy summer, like everything else, fell away from her memory; and again an impact resounded, shattering the stones. Having fleeted past, they sank away: her springtime conversations with *Nicolas* Ableukhov; having fleeted past, they sank away: the years of her marriage, her wedding: some kind of void tore them off and devoured them, piece by piece. And she could hear the blow of the metal, shattering the stones. Her whole life fleeted past, and her whole life sank away, as though her life had never been, and as though she herself were a soul that had not been born into life. Some kind of void began directly behind her back (for everything was falling into it, striking against some bottom); the void extended into the ages, and in the ages all one could hear was impact upon impact; those were the pieces of her lives falling as they plunged towards some bottom. As though some metal horse, clopping resonantly on the stone, were trampling the past behind her back; as though there behind her back, clopping resonantly on the stone, a metal horseman was pursuing her.

And when she turned round, she was presented with a spectacle: the outline of the Mighty Horseman ... There – two equine nostrils penetrated the fog, flaming, like a white-hot column.

Bronze-wreathed Death was overtaking her.

At this point Sofya Petrovna came to her senses: overtaking the carriage, an orderly flew past, holding a torch into the fog. For an instant his heavy bronze helmet flashed by; and after him, rumbling, flaming, a fire brigade went hurtling into the fog.

'What's that over there – a fire?' Sofya Petrovna asked, turning to the cab driver.

'It seems to be: they were saying the islands are on fire.'

The cab driver announced this to her out of the fog: the carriage stood outside her entrance porch on the Moika.

Sofya Petrovna remembered everything: everything came floating out before her with a horribly prosaic quality; as though this hell, these dancing maskers and the Horseman had not existed. Now the maskers seemed to her mere pranksters, who were probably acquaintances who visited *their* house, too; and the tall, sad figure – he was probably one of the *comrades* (she thanked him for seeing her to her cab). Only now Sofya Petrovna bit her plump little lip in vexation:

how could she have made a mistake and mixed up an acquaintance with her husband? And whispered into his ears confessions about some quite nonsensical guilt? Why, now the unknown acquaintance (and she thanked him for seeing her to her cab) would tell everyone utter rubbish, saying she was afraid of her husband. And gossip would start going round the town ... Oh, Sergei Sergeich Likhutin: soon you will recompense me for this unnecessary disgrace!

She struck the entrance-porch door with her little foot in indignation; in indignation the entrance-porch door banged behind her lowered little head. Darkness engulfed her, for a moment the inexpressible seized hold of her (thus it is, probably, in the first instant after death); but Sofya Petrovna Likhutina was not thinking about death at all: on the contrary – she was thinking about something very simple. She was thinking about how in a moment she was going to tell Mavrushka to get the samovar ready for her; while the samovar was being got ready she would nag and lecture her husband (she was, after all, able to nag for more than four hours at a stretch); and when Mavrushka brought her the samovar, she and her husband would have a reconciliation.

Now Sofya Petrovna Likhutina rang the doorbell. The loud ringing informed the nocturnal flat of her return. In a moment or two she would hear Mavrushka's hurried step near the vestibule. But the hurried step was not heard. Sofya Petrovna felt offended, and rang again.

Mavrushka was evidently asleep: she had only to go out of the house, and that silly woman fell on her bed ... But her husband, Sergei Sergeich, was a fine one, too: he had, of course, been waiting for her with impatience for more than hour or two; and, of course, he had heard the doorbell, and had, of course, realized that the maid had fallen asleep. And – he didn't budge! Oh! Tell me, if you please! He was still offended!

Well, then let him do without tea and reconciliation! ...

Sofya Petrovna began to ring the doorbell again: the doorbell tinkled – again and again ... No one, nothing! And she lowered her little head right down to the keyhole; and when she lowered her little head right down to the keyhole, then on the other side of the keyhole, just an inch or so away from her ear, she plainly heard: someone jerkily, heavily and noisily breathing through their nose, and the striking of a match. In the name of the Lord Jesus Christ, who could be breathing like that in there? And Sofya Petrovna stepped back from the door in amazement, having stretched forth her little head.

Was it Mavrushka? No, it was not Mavrushka ... Was it Sergei Sergeich Likhutin? Yes, it was he. But why was he so silent in there, why did he not open the door, why had he put his head to the keyhole, breathing so jerkily?

In anticipation of something unpleasant, Sofya Petrovna began to hammer desperately at the prickly felt of the door. In anticipation of something unpleasant Sofya Petrovna exclaimed:

'Open up, I say!'

But whoever it was went on standing behind the door, saying nothing and breathing so frightenedly, so horribly jerkily.

'Sergei Sergeich! That's enough of this ...'

Silence.

'Is that you? What's wrong with you in there?'

Tap, tap, tap – whoever it was stepped away from the door.

'But what is this? Oh, Lord: I'm afraid, I'm afraid ... Open up, dear!'

Something began to howl loudly behind the door and then ran as fast as its legs would carry it into the rooms at the back, first with a scuffling and then with a moving of chairs; it seemed to her that a lamp tinkled loudly in the drawing-room; from somewhere in the distance a table thundered as it was moved. Then all was quiet for a moment.

And then there was a horrific rumbling, as though the ceiling had fallen in and as though slaked lime were showering down from above; in this rumbling Sofya Petrovna Likhutina was struck by one sound only: the muffled falling from somewhere above of a heavy human body.

The Alarm

Apollon Apollonovich Ableukhov, to put it trivially, could not stand any kind of social visits that took him out of the house; as far as he was concerned, the only sensible visit was to the Institution or to take a report to the minister. Thus had the director of the Ministry of Justice once jestingly observed to him.

Apollon Apollonovich Ableukhov, to put it candidly, could not stand direct conversations that involved looking the other person in the face: conversation by means of the telephonic wire got rid of the inconvenience. From Apollon Apollonovich's desk telephone wires ran to every department. Apollon Apollonovich listened to the hooting of the telephone with satisfaction.

Only once had some prankster, in response to Apollon Apollonovich's query as to which department he was from, struck the palm of his hand on the telephone mouthpiece with all his might, from which Apollon Apollonovich received the impression that someone had given him a slap on the cheek.

In Apollon Apollonovich's opinion, every exchange of words had a manifest purpose that was as straight as a line. Everything else he categorized as tea-drinking and the smoking of cigarette ends: Apollon Apollonovich unflinchingly called all cigarettes cigarette ends: and his assumption was that Russians were good-for-nothing tea-drinkers, drunkards and nicotine addicts (he had several times proposed a tax increase on products of the latter substance); it was because of this that by the age of forty-five the Russian, in Apollon Apollonovich's opinion, gave himself away by his indecent paunch and his blood-red nose; Apollon Apollonovich rushed like a bull at anything red (even a nose).

Apollon Apollonovich was himself the owner of a deathly-grey little nose and a slender little waist – you would have sworn it was the waist of a young girl of sixteen – and was proud of it.

None the less, Apollon Apollonovich had a peculiarly deft explanation for the visits of guests: *jours fixes* were for most of them a place where they could drink tea and smoke cigarette ends together, as long as the visitor did not plan to acquire a post in an idle department and would therefore attempt to ingratiate himself in the house he was visiting, and as long as he did not plan to procure his son a post in that department, or to marry that son to the daughter of the head of that department (there was one such idle department). With that department Apollon Apollonovich waged a dogged struggle.

Apollon Apollonovich had gone to the Tsukatovs' with one

single end in view: to strike a blow at the department. The department had begun to flirt with a certain party which, though doubtless a moderate one, was suspicious not for its rejection of order but for its wish to very slightly change that order. Apollon Apollonovich despised compromises, despised the party's representatives and, above all, the department. He wanted to show the department's representative and the party's representative what his future conduct was going to be like with regard to the department in the lofty post that had only just been offered him.

That was why Apollon Apollonovich with displeasure considered himself obliged to spend an evening at the Tsukatovs', where he had under his nose a most unpleasant object of contemplation: the convulsions of dancing legs and the blood-red, unpleasantly rustling folds of harlequin costumes; he had seen these red rags somewhere before: yes, on the square in front of the Kazan Cathedral; there these red rags had been called banners.

These red rags now, at a simple little soirée and in the presence of the head of the aforesaid Institution struck him as an inappropriate, unworthy and downright disgraceful practical joke; while the convulsions of the dancing legs put him in mind of a certain regrettable (though unavoidable) measure for the prevention of state crimes.

With hostility Apollon Apollonovich looked askance at his hospitable hosts, and became disagreeable.

For him, the dancing of the red clowns turned into dancing of a different, bloody sort; this dancing, like all dancing, as a matter of fact, began in the street; this dancing, like all dancing, continued beneath the crossbeam of two not unfamiliar pillars. Apollon Apollonovich thought: if one permits this apparently innocent dancing here, it will of course continue in the street; and the dancing will, of course, end – there, there.

Apollon Apollonovich had, as a matter of fact, danced in his youth: the polka-mazurka, probably, and, perhaps, the lancers.

One circumstance made the high-ranking personage's melancholy mood doubly worse: that absurd domino was disagreeable to him in the extreme, having given him a serious attack of pectoral angina (whether it really was pectoral angina, Apollon Apollonovich was doubtful; and it was a strange thing: the true nature of angina was decidedly known to all who had to turn, even a little, the wheels of such imposing mechanisms as, for example, the Institution). So there it was: the absurd domino, a ridiculous buffoon, had met him in the most insolent manner upon his appearance in the ballroom; upon his entrance to the ballroom the absurd domino (a ridiculous buffoon) had come running up to him with grimaces.

Apollon Apollonovich vainly tried to remember where he had seen the grimaces: and could not remember.

With undisguised boredom, with barely mastered revulsion Apollon Apollonovich had sat solemnly in state, like a stick, erect, with a tiny porcelain cup in his most miniature hands; perpendicularly on the multicoloured Bokhara rug rested his thin little legs with their sinewy calves, forming lower parts which below his kneecaps made ninety-degree angles with the upper parts; perpendicularly to his chest his thin hands stretched out towards the little porcelain cup of tea. Apollon Apollonovich Ableukhov, a person of the first class, looked like the small figure of the Egyptian that was depicted on the rug – angular, broad-shouldered, defying all the laws of anatomy (for Apollon Apollonovich had no muscles: Apollon Apollonovich consisted of bones, sinews and veins).

It was with this angularity, which seemed as though elevated by him to a habit, that Apollon Apollonovich, the Egyptian, was expounding a most wise system of prohibitions to the professor of statistical information who had come to this soirée – the leader of a newly-formed party, a party of *moderate* governmental change, though *change none the less*; and with the same dry angularity, which seemed as though elevated by him to a habit, was doctorially expounding a system of the wisest counsels to the editor of the conservative newspaper, who was the son of a liberal priest.

With neither of them did Apollon Apollonovich, a personage of the first class, have anything in common: they both had fat, so to speak, bellies (from intemperance in the matter of tea); they were both, incidentally, red-nosed (from immoderate consumption of alcoholic beverages). One of them was, in addition, the son of a priest, and where the sons of priests were concerned, Apollon Apollonovich Ableukhov had an understandable weakness, one that he had, moreover, inherited from his forefathers: that of not being able to endure them. When Apollon Apollonovich conversed in the course of his duties with country, town and consistorial priests,

priests' sons and grandsons, he quite plainly sensed a bad smell from their feet; after all, one could not help noticing that country priests, town priests . . . even consistorial priests with their sons and grandsons, quite plainly, had dirty, unwashed necks and yellow fingernails.

Suddenly Apollon Apollonovich grew decidedly flustered between the two pot-bellied frock-coats that belonged to the priest's son and the moderate traitor, as though his sense of smell had quite plainly detected a bad odour from their feet; but the eminent man of state's agitation did not in the slightest proceed from an irritation of his olfactory centres; his agitation proceeded from a sudden shock to his sensitive aural membrane: just then the ballroom pianist again let his fingers fall on the grand piano, and Apollon Apollonovich's auditory apparatus heard all the consonances and melodic passages through a mesh of harmonic dissonances, like the aimless scraping of at least a dozen fingernails over glass.

Apollon Apollonovich Ableukhov turned right round; and there he saw the convulsions of the ugly legs that belonged to this company of state criminals: no, sorry: of dancing young people; among this devilish dancing his attention was still struck by the domino, who had unfolded his bloody satin in the dance.

Apollon Apollonovich vainly tried to remember where he had seen all these gestures. And could not remember.

And when a sugary and mangy-looking little gentleman flew up to him deferentially, Apollon Apollonovich grew animated in the extreme, tracing with his hand a triangle of greeting in space.

The fact was that the mangy little gentleman, despised by everyone, was, so to speak, a necessary figure: well, of course, it went without saying: a figure of a transitional age, whose existence Apollon Apollonovich in principle censured, whose existence within the bounds of legality was, of course, deplorable, but . . . what could one do? He was necessary, convenient and . . . in any case, since the figure existed, one had to reconcile oneself to him. The good thing about the mangy little gentleman, if one were to take account of the difficulty of his situation, was that the mangy little gentleman, knowing his own worth, assumed no airs of any kind; did not dress himself up in the ballyhoo of idly uttered phrases, like that professor; did not bang his fist on the table in a most indecent manner, like that editor. The sugary little gentleman, in his own quiet way, silently served various departments, while remaining attached to one department. Apollon Apollonovich could not help valuing the little gentleman, for he made no attempt to be on an equal footing with civil servants or with people who were simply members of society – in a word, the mangy little gentleman was an out-and-out lackey. What was so strange about that? Apollon Apollonovich was extremely considerate to lackeys: no lackey who had served in the Ableukhov household had yet had cause for complaint.

And with emphasized politeness, Apollon Apollonovich immersed himself in a detailed conversation with the little figure.

The fact that he brought away from this conversation struck him like thunder: the blood-red, unpleasant domino, the ridiculous buffoon, about whom he had just been reflecting, in the wake of the little gentleman's words, turned out to be ... No, no (Apollon Apollonovich made a grimace as though he had seen a lemon being sliced, and the blade that did the slicing being oxidized in the juice) – no, no: the domino turned out to be his *own* son! ...

But was he really his *own* son? His *own* son might, after all, turn out quite simply to be Anna Petrovna's son, thanks to the predominance, so to speak, in his veins of his mother's blood; and in his mother's blood – in Anna Petrovna's blood – there was according to the most precisely conducted inquiries ... priests' blood (Apollon Apollonovich had made these inquiries after his wife's escape)! It was probable that her priests' blood had *befouled* the immaculate Ableukhov family, having given her eminent husband a son who was simply *foul*. Only a *foul* son – a real mongrel – could have got up to *such ventures* (there had been nothing like it in the Ableukhov family since the time that the Kirghiz–Kaisak, Ab-Lai, had migrated to Russia – since the time of Anna Ioannovna).

The senator had been struck most of all by the fact that the foul domino who was leaping about over there (Nikolai Apollonovich) had, according to what the little gentleman had reported, a past so foul that the Jewish press was writing about these foul habits; here Apollon Apollonovich decidedly regretted that during all these recent days he had not found time to run through the 'Diary of Events' – in a certain place that had no comparison he had only had time to acquaint himself with the leading articles that came from the pens of moderate state criminals (as for the leading articles by immoderate state criminals, Apollon Apollonovich did not read them).

Apollon Apollonovich altered the position of his body: quickly he got up and was about to run through to the next room in order to investigate the domino, but from there, from the room, a clean-shaven little high-school student, dressed in a tight-fitting frock-coat and trousers, came flying up to him at top speed; and absent-mindedly Apollon Apollonovich very nearly gave him his hand to shake; on closer inspection the clean-shaven little high-school student turned out to be Senator Ableukhov: in his running dive Apollon Apollonovich had very nearly bumped into a mirror, having confused the arrangement of the rooms.

Apollon Apollonovich altered the position of his body, turning his back to the mirror; and – there, there: in the room between the drawing-room and the ballroom, Apollon Apollonovich again saw the foul domino (the mongrel), absorbed in the reading of some (probably foul) note (probably of pornographic content). And Apollon Apollonovich did not have sufficient courage to catch his son in the act.

Apollon Apollonovich several times altered the position of the aggregate of sinews, skin and bones that he called his body, and looked like a small Egyptian. With immoderate nervousness he rubbed his little hands and approached the card tables over and over again, having suddenly discovered an extreme politeness, an extreme curiosity with regard to diverse objects; of the statistician Apollon Apollonovich inquired irrelevantly about the potholes in the roads of the Ukhtomsk district of the province of Ploshchegorsk; while of the *zemstvo* official from the province of Ploshchegorsk he inquired about the consumption of pepper on the island of Newfoundland. The professor of statistics, touched by the attention of the eminent man of state, but not at all conversant with the pothole question in the province of Ploshchegorsk, promised to send the person of the first class a certain reputable guide to the geographical peculiarities of the entire planet Earth. While the *zemstvo* official, who was uninformed about the pepper question, hypocritically observed that pepper was consumed by the Newfoundlanders in enormous quantities, which was an invariable fact in all countries that had a constitution.

Soon to Apollon Apollonovich's ears some kind of bashfully arisen whispers, rustlings and crooked chuckles came drifting; Apollon Apollonovich plainly noticed that the convulsion of the dancing legs had suddenly ceased: for a single moment his agitated spirit was calmed. But then his head began to work again with dreadful clarity; the fateful premonition he had had all these uneasily passing hours was confirmed: his son, Nikolai Apollonovich, was a most dreadful scoundrel, because only a most dreadful scoundrel could behave in such a repulsive manner: for several days to wear a red domino, for several days to go around with a mask on, for several days to excite the Jewish press.

Apollon Apollonovich realized with decided clarity that for as long as the officers, young ladies, ladies and final-year students of the teaching and educational institutions were dancing there in the ballroom, his son, Nikolai Apollonovich, was dancing towards . . . But Apollon Apollonovich could not form any clear idea of *what precisely* Nikolai Apollonovich was dancing his way towards: Nikolai Apollonovich was, like it or not, his son, and not simply some . . . person of the male gender, begotten by Anna Petrovna, perhaps, the devil knew where; Nikolai Apollonovich had, after all, the ears of all the Ableukhovs – ears of incredible dimensions, and protruding, moreover.

This thought about ears softened Apollon Apollonovich's anger somewhat: Apollon Apollonovich put off his intention of driving his son out of the house, making no more precise inquiry into the reasons that had made his son wear a domino. But at any rate Apollon Apollonovich had now been deprived of his post, he would have to renounce the post; he could not accept the post until he had washed away the disgraceful stains in his son's conduct (who was, whether one liked it or not, an Ableukhov), which drew down shame upon the house.

With this deplorable thought and with crooked lips (as though he had sucked dry a pale yellow lemon), Apollon Apollonovich took his leave of them all and swiftly ran out of the drawing-room, accompanied by his hosts. And when, as he flew through the ballroom, he looked round in the most utter horror in the direction of the walls, finding the expanse of the illumined ballroom excessively huge, he saw plainly: a little flock of grey-browed matrons whispering venomously to one another.

To Apollon Apollonovich's ears floated only one word: 'Chicken.'

Apollon Apollonovich hated the sight of the headless, plucked chickens that were sold in the shops.

For better or worse, Apollon Apollonovich swiftly ran through the ballroom. In his utter *naïveté*, he did not know, after all, that in the whispering ballroom there was not now a single soul for whom the identity of the red domino who had recently danced here would have been a secret: yet no one said a word about the fact that his son, Nikolai Apollonovich, had a quarter of an hour earlier rushed into indecent flight through the ballroom, where now he himself was running with such manifest haste.

The Letter

Nikolai Apollonovich, shocked by the letter, ran past the merry *contredanse* a quarter of an hour before the senator. How he had left the house, he could not remember at all. He came to his senses in utter prostration in front of the Tsukatovs' entrance porch; continued to stand there in a continuous dark dream, in the continuous dark slush, mechanically counting the number of waiting carriages, mechanically following the movement of someone tall and sad who was keeping order there: it was the district police inspector.

Suddenly the tall, sad man strolled past under Nikolai Apollonovich's nose: Nikolai Apollonovich was suddenly burned by his blue gaze; the police inspector, waxing angry at the student in an overcoat, shook his flaxen beard: glared and walked on.

Quite naturally Nikolai Apollonovich also moved off, in the continuous dark dream, in the continuous dark slush, through which the rust-coloured blotch of a street lamp stubbornly stared: out of the fog, over the spike of the lamp, the caryatid of the entrance porch fell upon the blotch from above with a deathly hue, and inside the blotch a small piece of the house next door stood out;

the little house was black, one-storeyed, with bay windows and small carved wooden sculptures.

But no sooner had Nikolai Apollonovich moved off than he noted with indifference that his feet were completely absent: some sort of soft parts began to squelch incoherently in a puddle; vainly did he try to control those parts: the soft parts would not obey him; they had every appearance of the outline of feet, but he could not feel any feet (there were no feet). Nikolai Apollonovich lowered himself involuntarily on to the front step of the little house; and sat there for a moment, wrapped up in his overcoat.

This was natural in his position (his entire conduct was completely natural); just as naturally did he throw open his greatcoat, exposing the red blotch of his domino cape; just as naturally did he begin to rummage in his pockets, pull out a small, crumpled envelope, and read the contents of the note over and over again, trying to detect in it the trace of a straightforward joke, or a trace of mockery. But he could detect no traces of either the one or the other . . .

'Remembering your proposal of the summer, we hasten to inform you, comrade, that it is now your turn to act; and so you are immediately encharged with carrying out of the deed against . . .' – here Nikolai Apollonovich could read no further, because his father's name stood there – and then: 'The material you need, in the form of a bomb with a clock mechanism, has been suitably delivered in a bundle. Please hurry: time does not wait; it is desirable that the whole venture be carried out in the next few days . . .' This was followed by a slogan: both slogan and handwriting were familiar to Nikolai Apollonovich in equal degree. This had been written by the Unknown One: he had several times received notes from this Unknown One.

There could be no doubt.

Nikolai Apollonovich's arms and legs sagged; Nikolai Apollonovich's lower lip fell away from the upper one.

Right from the fateful moment when some lady or other had handed him the crumpled little envelope, Nikolai Apollonovich had kept trying to catch at plain coincidences, at completely irrelevant, idle thoughts that like flocks of frenzied crows, frightened by a shot, rise from a tree with many boughs and begin to circle – this way and that, this way and that, until the next shot; thus did completely idle thoughts circle in his head, such as, for example: concerning the number of books that would fit on a shelf of his bookcase; concerning the patterns of the flounces on the petticoat of some female person he had formerly loved, when that person used to go out of the room, raising her skirt just a little (that this person was Sofya Petrovna he somehow did not remember).

Nikolai Apollonovich kept trying not to think, not to understand: to think, to *understand* – could there be any understanding of *this*; *this* had *come, overwhelmed, roared*; if one thought about it, one would simply throw oneself through a hole in the ice . . . What could one think? There was no point in thinking here . . . because *this* . . . *this* . . . Well, what was *this?* . . .

No, here no one was capable of thinking.

In the first moment after he had read the note through, something in his soul bellowed piteously: bellowed as piteously as a meek ox bellows under the butcher's knife. In that first moment he found his father with his gaze; and his father looked merely so-so, so-so: looked small, old – looked like a little chicken with no feathers; he felt sick with horror; in his soul something again bellowed piteously: so submissively and piteously.

At this point he had gone rushing off.

And now Nikolai Apollonovich kept trying to catch at externals: that caryatid in the entrance porch; there was nothing particularly remarkable about it: it was a caryatid . . . And yet – no, no! There was something wrong about the caryatid – he had never seen anything like it; it was hanging over a flame. And that little house there: there was nothing particularly remarkable about it – it was a small, black house.

No, no, no!

There was more to the little house than met the eye, as there was more to everything else, too: everything within him had been dislocated, torn; he himself was torn; and from somewhere (he knew not from where) he had never yet been, he was watching!

Here were his feet – there was nothing particularly remarkable about his feet . . . But no, no! They were not feet – they were completely soft and unfamiliar parts, dangling there idly.

But Nikolai Apollonovich's attempt to catch at irrelevant thoughts and trivia was suddenly broken off when the entrance-porch door of that tall house where he had just been behaving like a madman began noisily to fly open, and from it group after group came pouring out; there in the fog carriages moved off, and so did the lights of the lamps at their sides. With an effort, Nikolai Apollonovich moved away from the front step of the small black house, Nikolai Apollonovich turned off into an empty back alley.

The back alley was as empty as everything else: as the spaces up aloft there; as empty as the human soul. For a moment Nikolai Apollonovich tried to remember about transcendental objects, about the fact that the events of this transitory world do not encroach in the slightest on the immortality of its centre and that even the thinking brain is only a phenomenon of consciousness; that for as long as he, Nikolai Apollonovich, acted in this world, he was not he; and he was a transitory shell; his true contemplative spirit was none the less capable of lighting his way for him: of lighting his way for him even *with this*; of illuminating even . . . this . . . But all around *this* rose: rose in the form of fences; and at his feet he noticed: some kind of gateway and a puddle.

And the light did not shine.[22]

Nikolai Apollonovich's consciousness endeavoured vainly to shine; it did not shine; however horrible the darkness was, the darkness remained. Looking round in fear, pathetically he somehow managed to creep over to the blotch of light from the street lamp; beneath the blotch babbled the rivulet of a pavement gutter, and over the blotch an orange peel sped by. Nikolai Apollonovich again applied himself to the note. The flocks of thoughts flew away from the centre of his consciousness like flocks of frenzied birds frightened by a storm, but there was no centre of consciousness, either: a murky hole gaped there, before which Nikolai Apollonovich stood bewildered, as before a murky well. But where and when had he stood in similar fashion? Nikolai Apollonovich made an effort to remember; and could not remember. And again applied himself to the note: the flocks of thoughts plunged, swift as birds, into that empty hole; and now some kind of wretched, flaccid little thoughts swarmed there.

'Remembering your proposal of the summer,' Nikolai Apollonovich read again, and tried to find something he could take exception to. And could not find anything.

'Remembering your proposal of the summer' . . . There had indeed been a proposal, but he had forgotten about it: he had once remembered about it, and then these events of the only just bygone past had come rushing in, the domino had come rushing in; Nikolai Apollonovich glanced at the recent past in consternation, and found it simply uninteresting; there had been some lady or other with a pretty little face; though, as a matter of fact, nothing particularly remarkable: a lady, a lady and a lady! . . .

The flocks of thoughts flew away from the centre of consciousness a second time; but there was no centre of consciousness; before his eyes was the gateway, while in his soul there was an empty hole; Nikolai Apollonovich began to reflect over the empty hole. Where and when had he stood in similar fashion? Nikolai Apollonovich made an effort to remember; and – remembered: he had stood in similar fashion in the gusts of Neva wind, leaning over the railings of the bridge, and had looked at the bacillus-infected water (why, it had all come from that night: the dreadful proposal, the domino, and now . . .) Now: Nikolai Apollonovich stood, stooping low and continuing to read the note of dreadful content (all this had happened once: had happened a great many times).

'We hasten to inform you that it is now your turn to act,' read Nikolai Apollonovich. And turned round: behind his back there was the sound of footsteps; some kind of restless shadow loomed ambiguously in the gusts of the back alley. Over his shoulder Nikolai Apollonovich saw: a bowler hat, a walking stick, a coat, a small beard and a nose.

Nikolai Apollonovich went towards the passer-by, peering expectantly; and saw a bowler hat, a walking stick, a coat, a small beard and a nose; all these things walked past, paying no attention (all one could hear was footsteps and a heart beating fit to burst); to *all these things* Nikolai Apollonovich turned round and looked away into the grimy fog – to where they were swiftly walking: the bowler hat, the walking stick and the ears; for a long time he continued to stand leaning over (this too had happened before once), with his mouth wide open in a most unpleasant fashion and presenting at any rate a rather absurd figure (he was wearing a Nikolayevka) with a wing of the coat dancing so preposterously in the wind . . . Could anyone as short-sighted as he really see anything at all apart from the edge of the fence?

And he returned to his reading.

'The material you require, in the form of a bomb with a clock mechanism, has been suitably delivered in a bundle . . .' Nikolai took exception to this sentence: no, it had not been delivered, it had not! And, having taken exception, he experienced something akin to hope that all this was a practical joke . . . A bomb? . . . He had no bomb? . . . No, no, – yes!!

. . . .

In a bundle?!

. . . .

Now it all came back to him: the conversation, the bundle, the suspicious visitor, the bleak September day, and all the rest. Nikolai Apollonovich distinctly remembered how he had taken the little bundle, how he had shoved it into the writing desk (the little bundle had been wet).

Only now was Nikolai Apollonovich able to realize the utter horror of his position. What was he to do, what was he to do? And for the first time he was seized by an inexpressible fear: he felt a sharp stabbing in his heart: the edge of the gateway began to revolve before him; and the darkness comprehended him, as it had just embraced him; his 'I' turned out to be merely a black receptacle, if not a cramped storeroom, immersed in absolute darkness; and here, in the darkness, in the place where his heart was, a spark flared . . . with frenzied swiftness it turned into a crimson sphere: the sphere expanded, expanded, expanded; and the sphere burst: everything burst . . . Nikolai Apollonovich came to his senses: some mangy little gentleman or other with a wart beside his nose (wait: he fancied he had just seen the little gentleman; he fancied he had seen the little gentleman at the ball; he fancied that the little gentleman had been standing in front of *the other, old one* in the drawing-room there, rubbing his little hands) – the mangy little gentleman with the wart beside his nose stopped two paces from him in front of an old fence – to attend to a natural need; but, as he stood in front of the old fence, he turned his face towards Ableukhov, made a sort of clicking sound with his lips and grinned very slightly:

'I expect you've been to the ball?'

'Yes, I have . . .'

Nikolai Apollonovich had been caught unawares; and anyway, what was so special about it: attending a ball was not yet a crime.

'I already know . . .'

'What's that? But how do you know?'

'Well, under your overcoat there's a, how should I put it: well, a piece of domino showing.'

'Well, yes, it is a domino . . .'

'And it was showing yesterday as well . . .'

'What do you mean, yesterday?'

'Beside the Winter Canal . . .'

'My good sir, you forget yourself . . .'

'Oh, come on: you're the domino.'

'I beg your pardon?'

'Yes – the very one.'

'I do not understand you: and in any case it is odd to go up to an unknown person . . .'

'Oh, you're not at all unknown: you're Nikolai Apollonovich Ableukhov: and you're also the *Red Domino* they're writing about in the newspapers . . .'

Nikolai Apollonovich was whiter than a sheet:

'Listen,' he said, stretching out his hand to the sugary little gentleman. 'Listen . . .'

But the little gentleman would not stop:

'I know your father, Apollon Apollonovich, too: I've just had the honour of chatting to him.'

'Oh, believe me,' Nikolai Apollonovich began to writhe in agitation, 'those are all filthy rumours . . .'

But, having attended to his natural need, the little gentleman slowly moved away from the fence, did up his coat, stuck his hand in his pocket familiarly and gave a meaningful wink:

'Where are you going?'

'To Vasily Island,' Nikolai Apollonovich blurted out.

'I'm going there too: so we're fellow-travellers, then.'

'Actually, I'm going to the Embankment . . .'

. . . .

'You evidently don't know where you ought to go,' the mangy little gentleman grinned, 'and so – let's drop in at a nice little restaurant.'

Back alley ran off into back alley: back alleys brought them out to the street again. Ordinary inhabitants ran about the street in the form of small black restless shadows.

Fellow-Travellers

Apollon Apollonovich Ableukhov, in a grey coat and tall black top hat, with a face that recalled a grey chamois leather, slightly encrusted with green, leapt out through the open entrance-porch door in fright, and ran down the front steps at a staccato pace, suddenly finding himself on the wet and slippery entrance that was shrouded in damp fog.

Someone called out his name, and in response to this deferential call the black outline of a carriage moved into the circle of the street lamp out of the reddish murk, presenting its coat of arms: a unicorn goring a knight; just as Apollon Apollonovich Ableukhov, having bent his foot at an angle in order to support it on the footboard of the carriage, was depicting an Egyptian silhouette in the dampish fog, just as he was about to jump into the carriage and fly off with it into that dampish fog, the door of the entrance porch was thrown wide open behind him; the mangy little gentleman, who had just a few moments ago revealed to Apollon Apollonovich the honest but deplorable truth, appeared in the street; moving his bowler hat down on to his nose, the little gentleman trotted away to the left.

Apollon Apollonovich then lowered his angularly raised foot, touched the front of his top hat with a glove and gave the dumbstruck driver a dry command: to go home without him. Then Apollon Apollonovich performed an incredible action; such an action had been unknown in the history of his life for about the last fifteen years: Apollon Apollonovich, blinking bewilderedly and pressing his hand to his heart in order to moderate his shortness of breath, ran in pursuit of the little gentleman's back that was slipping away into the fog; but please take note of one essential fact:

the lower extremities of the eminent man of state were minute in the extreme; if you take note of this essential fact, you will, of course, understand that Apollon Apollonovich, to assist himself, began to wave his little hand about as he ran.

I communicate this precious small detail of the behaviour of a person of the first class, recently deceased, solely for the attention of the numerous collectors of material for his forthcoming biography which, it appears, has recently been written about in the newspapers.

Well, so this is how it was.

Apollon Apollonovich Ableukhov performed two most incredible deviations from the code of his measured life; in the first place: he did not avail himself of the services of a carriage (if one takes his spatial illness into account, this may be called a genuine feat); in the second place: in a most literal and non-metaphoric sense he rushed through the dark night along the most deserted of streets. And when the wind knocked his tall top hat from his head, when Apollon Apollonovich Ableukhov squatted down over a puddle in order to extract the top hat from it, he began to shout after the back that was running off somewhere in a cracked voice:

'Mm . . . Listen! . . .'

But the back paid no heed (actually, it was not a back, but a pair of ears running on top of a back).

'Stop, I say . . . Pavel Pavlovich!'

The back that flickered there stopped, turned its head there and, recognizing the senator, ran towards him (it was not the back that ran towards him, but the owner of the back – the gentleman with the wart). The gentleman with the wart, having seen the senator squatting over the puddle in order to extract his top hat, was extremely amazed and proceeded to fish the floating top hat out of the puddle.

'Your excellency! . . . Apollon Apollonovich! How on earth did you get here? . . . Here you are, sir, please be so good as to take it, sir.' (With these words the mangy little gentleman handed the eminent man of state his very tall top hat, which had first been given a preliminary wipe by the sleeve of the little gentleman's coat).

'Your excellency, what about your carriage? . . .'

But Apollon Apollonovich, putting on his top hat, broke off his effusions.

'The night air does me good . . .'

Both set off in the same direction: as they went, the little gentleman tried to fall in with the senator's pace, something that was truly impossible (Apollon Apollonovich's little steps could have been studied under the lens of a microscope).

Apollon Apollonovich raised his eyes to his fellow-traveller: blinked and said – said with evident confusion:

'I . . . knowest-thou – er, you, sir,' (this time, too, Apollon Apollonovich made a mistake in the ending of a word) . . .

'Yes, sir?' the little gentleman said, pricking up his ears.

'I, you know . . . would like to have your most precise address, Pavel Pavlovich.'

'Pavel Yakovlevich! . . .' the fellow-traveller timidly corrected him.

'I'm sorry, Pavel Yakovlevich: you know, I have a poor memory for names . . .'

'It doesn't matter, sir, for heaven's sake: it doesn't matter sir.'

The mangy little gentleman thought slyly: 'He's still thinking about his son . . . He also wants to know . . . but he's too ashamed to ask . . .'

'Well, then, Pavel Yakovlevich, sir: give me your address.'

Apollon Apollonovich Ableukhov, unfastening his coat, fished out his notebook that was bound in the hide of a dead rhinoceros; both men stood beneath the street lamp.

'My address,' the little gentleman said in a sudden fit of agitation, 'is a changeable address: most often I'm on Vasily Island. Well, here it is: Eighteenth Line, House 17. Care of the master shoemaker, Bessmertny. I rent two rooms from him. They're rented to District Clerk Voronkov . . .'

'Indeed, sir, indeed, sir, indeed, sir, I shall be coming to see you in a day or two . . .'

Suddenly Apollon Apollonovich raised the arcs of his eyebrows: wonderment was displayed on his features:

'But why,' he began, 'why . . .'

'Why is my last name Voronkov, when I'm really called Morkovin?'

'Precisely . . .'

'Well, you see, Apollon Apollonovich, it's because I live there on a false passport.'

Apollon Apollonovich's face displayed squeamishness (after all, he denied the existence of such figures even in principle).

'And my real lodgings are on the Nevsky . . .'

Apollon Apollonovich thought: 'What can one do about it: the existence of such figures in a time of transition and within the bounds of strict legality is a sad necessity; and yet all the same, a necessity.'

'At the present time, your excellency, I am, as you see, engaged mainly in investigative work: these are exceedingly important times.'

'Yes, you are right,' Apollon Apollonovich agreed.

'A crime whose importance affects the whole state is in preparation . . . Oh, be careful: there's a puddle here . . . This crime . . .'

'Indeed, sir . . .'

'Very soon we shall be able to reveal . . . There's a dry place here, sir; permit me to take your hand.'

Apollon Apollonovich was walking across an enormous square: within him awoke his fear of such wide spatial expanses, and he involuntarily pressed up close against the little gentleman.

'Indeed, sir, indeed, sir: very good, sir . . .'

Apollon Apollonovich tried to keep his spirits up in this enormous spatial expanse, yet lost his composure all the same; Mr Morkovin's icy hand suddenly touched him, took him by the hand, led him past some puddles: and he followed, followed, and followed the icy hand; and the spatial expanses flew towards him. Yet Apollon Apollonovich hung his head: the thought of the fate that was threatening Russia overcame for a moment all his personal fears: his fear about his son and his fear of crossing such an enormous square; Apollon Apollonovich cast a glance at the selfless guardian of the existing order: Mr Morkovin led him to the pavement all the same.

'A terrorist act is in preparation?'

'The very same, sir . . .'

'And its victim? . . .'

'A certain high official is to fall . . .'

Gooseflesh ran down Apollon Apollonovich's spine: the other day Apollon Apollonovich had received a threatening letter; in the letter he had been informed that in the event he were to accept the senior position, a bomb would be thrown at him; Apollon Apollonovich had contempt for all anonymous letters; and he had torn up the letter; and accepted the position.

'Forgive me for asking, please, but if it is not a secret: who are they going to make their target now?'

Here something truly strange occurred: all the objects around suddenly seemed to cower down, grew noticeably damper and looked nearer than they ought to have done; while Mr Morkovin also seemed to cower down, also looked nearer than he ought to have done: looked ancient and somehow familiar; a little ironic smile wandered over his lips as, bowing his head to the senator, he declared in a tiny whisper:

'What do you mean, who? It's you, your excellency, you!'

Apollon Apollonovich looked: there was the caryatid of the entrance porch; there was nothing particularly remarkable about it: it was a caryatid. And yet – no, no! There was something wrong about the caryatid – he had never seen anything like it in all his life: it was hanging in the fog. There was the side of the house; there was nothing particularly remarkable about the side: it was a side like other sides – made of stone. And yet – no, no: just as there was more to everything than met the eye: everything within him had been dislocated, torn loose; he had been torn loose from himself and was muttering senselessly into the midnight darkness:

'What's that? . . . No, wait, wait! . . .'

Apollon Apollonovich Ableukhov was still on no account able to realistically imagine that this glove-clad hand that was twisting a button on another man's coat, that these legs here, and this weary, utterly weary (believe me!) heart could, under the influence of the expansion of gases within some bomb out there, suddenly, in the twinkling of an eye, be turned . . . into . . .

'What I mean is, what?'

'Just as I say, Apollon Apollonovich, sir – it's all quite simple . . .'

That *it* was so simple, Apollon Apollonovich could not believe: at first he gave a kind of provocative snort into his grey little side-whiskers (– his side-whiskers would go, too!), thrust out his lips (his lips would not exist then), and then acquired a pinched look, lowered his head right down and stared mindlessly at the dirty rivulet of the pavement gutter babbling at his feet. All around there was a babbling of wet blotches, a rustling, a whispering: the autumnal season's old woman's whisper came to his ears.

Under the street lamp Apollon Apollonovich stood, rocking his ashen-grey countenance slightly from side to side, opened his eyes in astonishment, rolled them, turning up the whites (a carriage thundered, but it seemed as though something terrible and heavy were thundering there: like blows of metal shattering life).

Mr Morkovin had evidently begun to feel really sorry for this aged outline that seemed to be settling into the mud before him. He added:

'Don't be afraid, your excellency, for the strictest precautions have been taken; and we won't allow it: there is no direct danger either today or tomorrow . . . In a week's time you'll know all there is to know . . . Just wait a little . . .'

As he observed the piteously trembling blotch-like face that resembled that of a corpse, illumined by the pale sheen of the street lamp's flame, Mr Morkovin found himself thinking: 'How he has aged; why, he's just a ruin . . .' But, with a barely perceptible groaning, Apollon Apollonovich turned his beardless countenance towards Mr Morkovin and suddenly gave a sad smile that made enormous wrinkly pouches form under his eyes.

A moment later, however, Apollon Apollonovich completely recovered himself, looked younger, whiter: firmly he shook Morkovin's hand and walked, as straight as a stick, into the grimy autumn fog, calling to mind the profile of the mummy of Pharaoh Rameses II.

The night was black, dark blue and lilac, shading into the reddish blotches of the street lamps as into the fiery blotches of a fiery rash. Gateways, walls, fences, courtyards and entrance porches loomed – and from them issued every imaginable kind of babbling and every imaginable kind of sigh; the many dissonant sighs in the side-lane of fleeing windy gusts, somewhere over there, behind the houses, the walls, the fences and gateways, combined into consonant sighs; while the fleeting babbling of the rivulets, somewhere over there, behind the houses, the walls, the fences and gateways, all united into one fleeting babble; all the babblings became a sighing; and all the sighs began to babble there.

Ugh! How damp, how dank it was, how dark blue and lilac the night was as it moved painfully into the bright red rash of the street lamps, and how from this dark blue lilac murk Apollon Apollonovich ran out under the circles of the street lamps and again ran off from a red circle into the lilac murk!

The Madman

We left Sergei Sergeyevich Likhutin at that fateful moment in his life when, white as death, completely calm, with an ironic smile on his firmly compressed lips he rushed at top speed out to the room at the front (to the vestibule, in other words) after his disobedient wife and then, with a click of his spurs, stood deferentially in front of the door with her fur coat in his hands; and when Sofya Petrovna Likhutina rustled provocatively past the nose of the angry second lieutenant, Sergei Sergeyevich Likhutin, as we saw, began still with the same too rapid gestures to walk about everywhere and everywhere put out the electric lights.

But why did he reveal his unusual state of mind by this strange action? What, pray, could be the connection between *all this filth* and the electric lights? There was just as little sense here as there was in the connection between the tall and angular, sad figure of the second lieutenant in his dark green uniform, with his too rapid gestures and the provocative, flaxen little beard on his face that had suddenly grown younger and looked as though it had been carved from fragrant cypress wood. There was no connection: except perhaps – the mirrors: in the light they reflected – a tall, angular man with a little face that had suddenly grown younger: the tall, angular reflection with the little face that had suddenly grown younger, going right up to the surface of the mirror, took hold of itself by the white, slender neck – oh, oh, oh! There was no connection and never had been any between the light and the gestures.

'Click, click, click,' went the switches, nevertheless, plunging the tall, angular man with the too-rapid gestures into darkness. Perhaps this was not second lieutenant Likhutin?

No, put yourself in his dreadful position: being reflected so foully in the mirrors, all because some domino had delivered an insult to his honourable home, all because, in accordance with his officer's word of honour, he was now obliged not to allow his wife over the threshold. No, enter into his dreadful position: it was second lieutenant Likhutin, of that there could be no doubt – him in person.

'Click, click, click,' went the switch in the next room, now. The switch in the third room clicked likewise. This sound alarmed Mavrushka; and when she came shuffling through from the kitchen into the rooms, she was engulfed in thick, total darkness.

And she muttered:

'What's all this, then?'

But out of the darkness came a dry, slightly muffled cough:

'Get out of here . . .'

'How can I, *barin* . . .'

Someone whistled to her from the corner in a commanding, indignant whisper:

'Get out of here . . .'

'How can I, *barin*: why, I must tidy up for the *barynya* . . .'

'Get out of the rooms altogether.'

. . . .

'And then, you yourself know, the beds have not been made . . .'

. . . .

'Out, out, out! . . .'

. . . .

And no sooner had she left the room and gone into the kitchen, than the *barin* came through to her in the kitchen:

'I want you to get right out of the house altogether . . .'

'But how can I, *barin* . . .?'

'Get out, get out as quickly as you can . . .'

'But where am I to go?'

'You know best: I don't want you to set foot . . .'

'*Barin*! . . .'

'In this house until tomorrow . . .'

'But *barin*! . . .'

'Out, out, out . . .'

He threw her fur coat into her hands, and – pushed her out through the door: Mavrushka began to cry; she was dreadfully a-feared: it was easy seeing the *barin* wasn't himself: she ought to have gone to the yardkeeper and the police station, but instead, silly woman, she went to the house of a female friend.

Oh, Mavrushka . . .

. . . .

How dreadful is the lot of an ordinary, completely normal man: his life is decided by a vocabulary of easily understandable words, by the use of extremely unambiguous actions; those actions draw him into a boundless distance, like a wretched little vessel that is rigged with words and gestures that are completely expressible; but if the wretched little vessel happens to run aground on the under-water rock of life's incoherence, then the wretched little vessel, having run aground on the rock, falls to pieces, and the simple, straightforward swimmer drowns in the space of a moment . . . Ladies and gentlemen, the slightest bump from life is enough to deprive ordinary people of their reason; no, madmen do not know such risks of harm to the brain: their brains are probably woven from some very light, ethereal substance. For the simple, straightforward brain all that those brains penetrate is altogether impenetrable: all that the simple, straightforward brain can do is be broken to pieces; and it is broken to pieces.

Ever since the previous evening Sergei Sergeich Likhutin had been experiencing a most acute cerebral pain, as though he had struck his forehead against an iron wall while running at full tilt; and as he stood before the wall, he saw that the wall was not a wall, that it was penetrable and that there, on the other side of the wall, was a light invisible to him, and some kind of laws of absurdity, like out there, on the other side of the walls of the little flat, where there was both light and the movement of cabs . . . Here Sergei Sergeich Likhutin uttered a heavy groan and shook his head, experiencing the most acute cerebral workings that were unknown even to him. Over the wall crept reflections: some little steamer must be passing along the Moika, leaving intensely bright stripes on the waters.

Sergei Sergeich Likhutin groaned again and again; again and again did he shake his head: his thoughts had got finally confused, as had everything else. He had begun his reflections with an analysis of his unfaithful wife, and ended by catching himself thinking some sort of senseless rubbish: perhaps the hard surface was impenetrable to him alone, and the mirrored reflections of the rooms were really the rooms themselves; in those real rooms lived the family of some visiting officer; the mirrors ought to be covered up: it was uncomfortable to have to study with curious gazes the behaviour of a married officer and his young wife; one could find all sorts of rubbish there; and Sergei Sergeich Likhutin began to catch himself thinking this rubbish; and found that he himself was occupying himself with rubbish, becoming distracted from important, really important thoughts (it was just as well that Sergei Sergeich Likhutin had switched off the electric lights; the mirrors would have distracted him dreadfully, and just now he needed all the exertion of his will in order to detect some train of thought within himself).

So that was why, after his wife left, second lieutenant Likhutin had begun to walk about everywhere and everywhere put out the electric lights.

What was he to do now? Yesterday evening *it* had – *begun*: come *creeping*, *hissing*: what was *it* – why had *it begun*? Apart from the fact of Nikolai Apollonovich Ableukhov's disguise, there was decidedly nothing to get hold of here. The second lieutenant's head was the head of an ordinary man: this head refused to serve in this delicate question, and the blood rushed to his head: a wet towel on his temples would be a good thing now; and Sergei Sergeich Likhutin put a wet towel on his temples: put it on them, and then tore it off again. Something, at any rate, had happened; and at any rate he, Likhutin, had got involved in it; and, having got involved, he had become united with it; here *it* was: knocking, playing, beating, twitching his temporal veins.

A man of the most simple straightforwardness, he had smashed against a wall: while there, into the depths on the other side of the mirror, he could not penetrate: all he could do was, out loud, in his wife's presence, give his honourable word as an officer that he would not voluntarily readmit his wife to the premises, if that wife were to go to the ball without him.

What was he to do? What was he to do?

Sergei Sergeich Likhutin grew agitated and struck another match: the reddish-brown flambeaux illumined the face of a madman; anxiously now did it press up close against the clock: two hours had already passed since Sofya Petrovna had left; two hours, that was a hundred and twenty minutes; having counted the number of minutes that had elapsed, Sergei Sergeich began to count the seconds, too:

'Sixty times a hundred and twenty? Two times six are twelve; and carry one in your mind . . .'

Sergei Sergeich Likhutin clutched his head:

'One in your mind; my mind − yes: my mind was smashed against the mirror . . . The mirrors ought to be taken out! Twelve, carry one in your mind − yes: one little piece of glass . . . No, one lived second . . .'

His thoughts had grown confused: Sergei Sergeich Likhutin was pacing about in complete darkness: tap-tap-tap went Sergei Sergeich's footsteps; and Sergei Sergeich went on counting:

'Two times six are twelve; and carry one in your mind: one time six is six; plus − one unit; an abstract unit is not a little piece of glass. And then two zeroes: and that makes seven thousand two hundred massive seconds.'

And, having triumphed over this most complex cerebral work, Sergei Sergeich Likhutin, rather inappropriately, displayed his triumph. Suddenly he remembered: his face grew dark:

'Seven thousand two hundred massive seconds since she ran off: two hundred thousand seconds − no, it's all finished!'

On the expiration of seven thousand seconds, the two hundred and first second had, it appeared, opened in time the beginning of the fulfilment of his officer's word: he had lived through the seven thousand two hundred seconds as though they had been seven thousand years; from the creation of the world until the present time not much more had elapsed, after all. And it seemed to Sergei Sergeich that ever since the creation of the world he had been imprisoned in this darkness with a most acute headache: by spontaneous thinking, the brain's autonomy in spite of his self-tormenting personality. And Sergei Sergeich Likhutin feverishly began to fuss about in a corner; for a moment he fell quiet; began to cross himself; hurriedly from some little box or other he threw out a rope (it looked like a snake), uncoiled it, and made a noose with it: the noose refused to tighten. And Sergei Sergeich Likhutin, in despair now, ran into his little study; the rope went trailing after him.

But what was Sergei Sergeich Likhutin doing? Was he keeping his officer's word? No, good heavens, no. All he did was for some reason take soap out of a soap dish, squat down and soap the piece of rope in front of a small basin placed on the floor. And as soon as he had soaped the piece of rope, all his actions assumed a downright fantastic tinge; indeed one could have said: never in his life had he done such original things.

Well, judge for yourself!

For some reason he got up on to a table (having first taken the cloth off it); and lifted a Viennese chair from the floor and put it on the table; clambering up on the chair, he carefully took down a lamp; carefully put it down at his feet; then instead of the lamp Sergei Sergeich Likhutin affixed to the hook the rope, slippery with soap; crossed himself and froze; and slowly, holding his noose, raised it above his head with the look of a man who has resolved to wind a snake around his neck.

But a certain brilliant idea had dawned on Sergei Sergeich: he must shave his hairy neck; and, what was more: he must calculate the number of thirds and fourths: twice multiply by the number sixty – seven thousand two hundred.

With this brilliant idea, Sergei Sergeich Likhutin strode into his little study; there by the light of a candle-end he began to shave his hairy neck (Sergei Sergeich had sensitive skin, and this sensitive skin became covered with pimples when he shaved). Having shaved his chin and neck, Sergei Sergeich suddenly cut off one of his moustaches with the razor: he must shave off the other one too because – how would it be otherwise? When they broke down the door there and came in, they would see him with only one moustache, and moreover . . . in such a position; no, one must never begin an undertaking without having shaved properly.

And Sergei Sergeich Likhutin shaved himself clean: and, having shaved, he looked like a most complete idiot.

Well, now there was no point in lingering: it was all finished – his face had a quality of complete shavenness. But just at that moment the doorbell rang in the vestibule; and Sergei Sergeich threw down the soapy razor in annoyance, spattering all his fingers with little hairs, and looked at the clock with regret (how many hours had flown by?) – what was he to do, what was he to do? For one moment Sergei Sergeich thought of postponing his undertaking; he had not known that he would be caught in the act; of the fact that there was no time to lose he was reminded by the doorbell, which rang for a second time; and he jumped up on to the table in order to take the noose down from the hook; but the rope would not obey, slipping in his soapy fingers; Sergei Sergeich Likhutin got down again in the most rapid fashion and began to creep stealthily into the vestibule; and while he was creeping stealthily into the vestibule, he noticed: the blue-black gloom that had suffused the room all night like ink was beginning to melt away; slowly the inky gloom was turning grey, becoming a grey gloom: and in the greying gloom objects were delineated; a chair placed upon the table, a lamp on the floor; and above all this – a wet noose.

In the vestibule Sergei Sergeich Likhutin put his head to the door; he froze; but agitation must have induced such a degree of forgetfulness in Sergei Sergeich that it was inconceivable for him to undertake any action of any kind: why, Sergei Sergeich Likhutin had not noticed at all that he was breathing heavily; and when on the other side of the door he heard his wife's anxious cries, he began to shout at the top of his voice from fright; having shouted, he saw that all was lost and rushed to put his original plan into practice; swiftly jumped up on the table, stuck out his freshly-shaven neck; and quickly began to tighten the rope around his freshly-shaven neck that was covered in pimples, first for some reason putting two fingers between the rope and his neck.

After this he for some reason shouted:

'Word and deed!'[23]

He pushed the table away with one foot; and the table rolled away from Sergei Sergeich on brass casters (this was the sound that Sofya Petrovna Likhutina had heard – there, on the other side of the door).

What Next?

In a moment . . . –

Sergei Sergeich Likhutin's legs began to jerk convulsively in the darkness; as they did so he distinctly saw the reflections of the street lamps on the air vent of the stove; he distinctly also heard a knocking and a scratching at the front door; something pressed two fingers with force against his chin, and he was unable to tear them away; it further seemed to him that he was choking; above him now there was a sound of cracking (that must be the veins in his head bursting), and slaked lime was flying all around; and Sergei Sergeich Likhutin went crashing down (straight towards death); and at once Sergei Sergeich Likhutin rose up from this death, having received a good, healthy kick in the next existence; at this point he saw that he had regained his senses; and when he regained his senses, he realized that he had not risen up from the dead, but had sat down on some kind of flat material object; he was sitting by himself on the floor, experiencing pain in his spine and his fingers which had somehow got through between the rope and his throat, and were now jammed there; Sergei Sergeich Likhutin began to pull at the rope around his neck; and the noose widened.

At this point he realized that he had very nearly hanged himself: had not succeeded in hanging himself – by a very small margin. And he sighed with relief.

Suddenly the inky gloom turned grey; and became a grey gloom: at first greyish; and then – only just perceptibly grey; Sergei Sergeich Likhutin saw quite plainly that he was sitting absurdly surrounded by walls, that the walls were quite plainly hung with grey Japanese landscapes, imperceptibly fusing with the surrounding night; the ceiling, which at night had plainly been adorned by the reddish-brown lace of the street lamp, had now begun to lose its lace; the lace of the street lamp had long run out, was becoming dim blotches that stared in astonishment at the greyish morning.

But let us return to the unhappy second lieutenant.

A few words must be said in Sergei Sergeich's justification; Sergei Sergeich's sigh of relief escaped from him unconsciously, in the way that the movements of people who wilfully drown themselves are unconscious at the moment before their immersion in the cold, green depths. Sergei Sergeich Likhutin (do not smile!) had quite seriously intended to settle all his accounts with the earth, and he would without any doubt at all have realized this intention, had not the ceiling been rotten (for this one must blame the builder of the house); so that the sigh of relief did not in any way concern Sergei Sergeich's personality, but rather his fleshly, animal and impersonal shell. However this may have been, this shell was squatting down and listening to everything (to a thousand rustlings); while Sergei Sergeich's spirit was displaying the most complete sang-froid.

In the twinkling of an eye all his thoughts became clear; in the twinkling of an eye a dilemma arose before his consciousness: what was he to do now, what was he to do? His revolvers were hidden away somewhere; it would take too long to find them ... The razor? With the razor – ugh! And involuntarily everything in him winced; to begin an attempt with the razor after the first attempt he had just made ... No: the most natural thing was to stretch out here on the floor, leaving the future to fate; yes, but in that natural instance Sofya Petrovna (she had undoubtedly heard the crash) would instantly rush, if she had not already rushed, to the yard-keeper; the police would be telephoned, a crowd would gather; under pressure from her, the front door would be broken down, and *they* would burst in here; and, having burst in, would see him, second lieutenant Likhutin, with his face unusually shaven (Sergei Sergeich had not suspected that he would look such an idiot without his moustache) and with a rope around his neck, squatting there amidst pieces of plaster.

No, no, no! Never would the second lieutenant come to that: the honour of his uniform was dearer to him than the word he had given his wife. There remained only one thing: to open the door in shame, attain a reconciliation with his wife, Sofya Petrovna, as soon as possible, and give her a plausible explanation for the mess and the plaster.

Quickly he threw the rope under the sofa and in a most ignominious fashion ran to the front door, on the other side of which nothing was now audible.

With the same involuntary breathing, he opened the front door, standing indecisively on the threshold; he was seized by a burning shame (he had not succeeded in hanging himself!); and the raging storm died away within his soul; as though, having torn loose from the hook he had broken off within himself all that had just raged there: his anger at his wife, his anger in connection with Nikolai Apollonovich's outrageous behaviour. After all, he himself had now committed an outrage that was unprecedented and could not be compared with anything that had gone before: had wanted to hang himself – and instead of that had torn the hook out of the ceiling.

In a moment . . . –

No one came running into the room: even so, there was someone standing out there (he could see); at last, Sofya Petrovna Likhutina rushed in; rushed in and burst into sobs:

'But what is this? What is this? Why is it dark in here?'

And Sergei Sergeich lowered his eyes in embarrassment.

'What was all that noise and racket?'

Embarrassed, Sergei Sergeich squeezed her cold little fingers in the darkness.

'Why are your hands all covered in soap? . . . Sergei Sergeyevich, dear, what does this mean?'

'You see, Sonyushka . . .'

But she interrupted him:

'Why are you hoarse? . . .'

'You see, Sonyushka . . . I . . . stood in front of the open ventilator window too long (it was a careless thing to do, of course) . . . Well, and so I got hoarse . . . But that's not the point . . .'

He faltered.

'No, don't, don't,' Sergei Sergeich Likhutin almost shouted, tugging away his wife's hand, which was about to turn on the electric light, 'not here, not right now – let's go into that room.'

And he dragged her by force into the little study.

In the little study the objects could already be discerned quite plainly; and for a moment it seemed as if the grey row made up of the lines of the chairs and the walls with the imperceptibly recumbent planes of shadows and an infinity of some kind of shaving prerequisites was only an airy lace, a cobweb; and through this extremely fine cobweb the dawn sky was emerging shamefacedly and tenderly in the window. Sergei Sergeich's face stood out indistinctly; but when Sofya Petrovna bent right down to his face, she saw before her . . . No, it was beyond description: she saw before her the completely blue face of an unknown idiot; and the eyes of this face were guiltily lowered.

'What have you done? Have you shaved? Why, you're simply some kind of fool! . . .'

'You see, Sonyushka,' his frightened whisper sounded hoarsely in her ears, 'there's a certain circumstance here . . .'

But she was not listening to her husband, and rushed off in unaccountable anguish to examine the rooms. After her from the little study came tearful and hoarsely resonant cries:

'You'll find things in a mess everywhere . . .

'You see, my dear, I was trying to mend the ceiling . . .

'The ceiling had cracked over there . . .

'I had to . . .'

But Sofya Petrovna Likhutina was not listening at all: she stood in alarm before a pile of pieces of plaster that had fallen on the carpet, and, showing black in their midst, a hook that had come crashing to the floor; the table, on top of which a chair lay capsized, had been violently pushed aside; from beneath the soft couch on which Sofya Petrovna had so recently read Henri Besançon – from beneath the soft couch protruded a grey noose. Sofya Petrovna trembled, went numb and hunched her shoulders.

There outside the windows splashed the lightest of flames, and suddenly everything was illuminated, as a roseate ripple of cloudlets entered the flames like a mesh of mother-of-pearl; and now in the breaks of that mesh showed the merest hint of light blue: a soft tenderness showed light blue everywhere; everything was filled with a trembling timidity; everything was filled with the astonished question: 'But how can it be? How can it be? Am I not shining?' There on the windows, on the spires the greatest trembling was observed; there on the tall spires a gleam showed tall, ruby red. Over her soul the lightest of voices suddenly passed: and in a flash of illumination she saw a pale pink, pale carpet-coloured wedge made by a ray from the rising sun fall from the window on the grey noose. Her heart was filled with a sudden trembling and the astonished question: 'But how can it be? How can it be? How could I have forgotten?'

At this point Sofya Petrovna Likhutina bent down to the floor and stretched out her hand towards the rope, on which the most delicate roseate lace was glowing; Sofya Petrovna Likhutina kissed the rope and quietly began to weep: a shape from her far-off childhood, now once again returned (a shape not forgotten entirely – where had she seen it: somewhere recently, today?): this shape began to rise above her, rose and now stood behind her back. And when she turned round and looked behind her, she saw: behind her stood her husband, Sergei Sergeyevich Likhutin, lanky, sad and clean-shaven: his meek, blue gaze was raised towards her:

'Oh, forgive me Sonyushka!'

For some reason she fell at his feet, embracing them and weeping:

'Poor, poor man: my beloved! . . .'

What they whispered between themselves, only God knows: it all remained between them; one could see: his dry hand raised above her into the glow of the dawn:

'God will forgive . . . God will forgive . . .'

The shaven head burst out laughing so happily: for who could not now laugh, when such light, light flames were laughing in the sky?

A ragged, roseate cloudlet stretched along the Moika: this was a cloudlet from the funnel of a small passing steamboat; from its stern gleamed a green stripe of cold that struck against the bank, suffusing it with amber, giving – here, there – a suggestion of golden sparks, giving – here, there – a suggestion of diamonds; as it flew away from the bank, the stripe broke against a stripe that beat towards it, making both stripes begin to shine like a swarm of ringed snakes. Into this swarm moved a boat; and all the snakes were cut into strings of diamonds; the strings were immediately entwined into a silver-tracing tinsel, in order then to rock like stars on the watery surface. But the momentary agitation of the waters was calmed; the waters became smooth, and all the stars on them were extinguished. Now again the shining water-green surfaces moved between the stone banks. A green-black sculpture rose towards the sky; strangely from the bank rose a green, white-columned building, like a living piece of the Renaissance.

The Ordinary Man

Into the far-off distance, this way and that, stretched alleys and streetlets, streets, simply, prospects; now out of the darkness emerged the lofty-summited side of a house, made of brick, composed of nothing but burdens, now out of the darkness a wall gaped with an entrance porch above which two stone Egyptians raised the stone projection of the balcony aloft in their hands. Past the lofty-summited house, past its brick side, past all the million-pood colossi – out of darkness into darkness – in the Petersburg fog Apollon Apollonovich walked, walked, walked, overcoming all the burdens: before him was delineated a grey, somewhat rotten little fence.

At this point from somewhere at the side a low door flew open and remained open; white steam came belching out, there was a sound of swearing, the pathetic tinkling of a balalaika and a voice. Apollon Apollonovich found himself listening to the voice, as he surveyed the dead gateways, a street lamp chattering in the wind, and a latrine.

The voice sang:

> In spirit to Thee, Father,
> Heavenward in thought we flee
> And for our food sincerely
> We give our thanks to Thee.

Thus sang the voice.

The door banged shut. In the ordinary man in the street Apollon Apollonovich suspected something petty, something that flew past behind the glass of carriage windows (after all, the distance between the nearest wall and the carriage door was calculated by Apollon Apollonovich in many millions of versts). And now before him all the spatial expanses were displaced: the life of the ordinary man in the street had suddenly surrounded him with gateways and walls, and the ordinary man himself appeared before him as a voice.

And the voice sang:

In spirit to Thee, Father,
Heavenward in thought we flee
And for our food sincerely
We give our thanks to Thee.

Was this what the ordinary man in the street was like? Apollon Apollonovich began to feel an interest in the ordinary man, and there was a moment when he almost knocked at the first door he came to, in order to find the ordinary man; here he remembered that the ordinary man was preparing to punish him with a shameful death: his top hat slipped down on one side, and his emaciated shoulders sagged flaccidly over his chest: –

– yes, yes, yes – they had blown him to pieces: not him, Apollon Apollonovich, but someone else, his best friend, sent by fate only once; for a moment Apollon Apollonovich remembered that grey moustache, the green depth of the eyes that had been fixed on him as the two of them had bent over a geographical map of the Empire, and their young old age had flamed with dreams (this had been exactly a day before) ... But *they* had blown to pieces even his best friend, the *first among the first* ... It is said to last a second; and then – as if nothing had ever been ... But what of it? Every man of state is a hero, but – brr-brr ... –

Apollon Apollonovich Ableukhov adjusted his top hat and straightened his shoulders as he walked out into the damp-rotten and unpleasant fog, the damp-rotten life of the ordinary man, into these meshes of walls, gateways, fences, that were filled with slime and were subsiding wretchedly and flaccidly, in a word – into one continuous squalid, rotten, empty and general latrine. And it seemed to him now that he was hated by this stupid wall and this rotten fence; Apollon Apollonovich knew by experience that *they* hated him (day and night he went covered by the fog of *their* spite). Who were *they*? An insignificant little band, stinking like everything else? Apollon Apollonovich's cerebral play erected his misty planes before his gaze; but all the planes were blown to pieces; Russia's gigantic map appeared before him, who was so small: could *these* really be enemies: enemies – the gigantic totality of the races that inhabited these spaces: *a hundred million.* No, more . . .

'From Finland's icy cliffs to fiery Colchis . . .'[24]

What? They hated him? . . . No: Russia stretched, that was all. And him? . . . Him they were going to . . . were going to . . . No: brr-brr . . . An idle cerebral game. Better to quote Pushkin:

> It's time, my friend, it's time . . . For peace the heart is asking.
> Day runs after day. And every day that's passing
> Takes with it particles of life. Together you and I
> Intend to live some more. Look yonder – and we die.[25]

Who was it he intended to live together with? His son? His son was a most dreadful scoundrel. With the ordinary man in the street? The ordinary man in the street was going to . . . Apollon Apollonovich remembered that he had once intended to spend his life with Anna Petrovna, on his retirement from government service to move to Finland, but then, then: Anna Petrovna had gone away – yes, sir, gone away! . . .

'She went away, you know: there's nothing to be done about it . . .'

Apollon Apollonovich realized that he had no companion in life (until that moment he had somehow not found time to remember this) and that death in the line of duty would at least be an adornment to the life he had lived. He began to feel somehow childlike and sad and quiet – so quiet that it was almost comfortable. Around him all that was audible was the rustling of a streaming puddle, like someone's plea – always about the same thing, about the same thing – about what had not been, but what could have been.

Slowly the black-grey gloom that all night had suffocated everything and everyone was beginning to melt away. Slowly the black-grey gloom turned greyer and became a grey gloom: greyish at first;

then only just perceptibly grey; while the walls of the houses, which had been illumined at night by the street lamps, began to fuse palely with the departing night. And it seemed that the reddish-brown street lamps, which only just now had been casting reddish-brown light around them, suddenly began to run low; and ran out completely by degrees. The feverishly burning flambeaux disappeared on the walls. At last, the street lamps became dim points that stared in astonishment into the greyish mist; and for a moment it seemed as though the grey row of lines, spires and walls with the imperceptibly lying planes of shadows, with the infinitude of window openings – was not a colossus of stones, but an airily risen lace that consisted of patterns of a most delicate craft, and through these patterns the dawn sky bashfully peeped.

Towards Apollon Apollonovich rushed a poorly dressed young adolescent; a girl of about fifteen, bound with a kerchief; while behind her in the fog moved the outline of a man: bowler hat, walking stick, a coat, ears, moustache and nose; the outline had obviously accosted the adolescent with the most villainous propositions; Apollon Apollonovich considered himself a knight; unexpectedly to himself, he removed his top hat:

'Dear lady, may I be so bold as to offer you my arm as far as your home: at this late hour it is not without risk for young persons of your sex to appear in the street.'

The poorly dressed adolescent quite distinctly saw some kind of small black figure there raising a top hat before her; a shaven, dead head crept out from a collar for a moment and then crept back inside again.

They walked in deep silence; everything seemed closer than it ought to: wet and old, receding into the ages; Apollon Apollonovich had seen all this before from a distance. And now – here it was: gateways, little houses, walls and, pressed fearfully against his arm, this adolescent for whom he, Apollon Apollonovich, was not a villain, not a senator: just a kind old man she did not know.

They walked to a small green house with a crooked gate and a rotted gateway; at the little front entrance the senator raised his top hat and said farewell to the adolescent; and when the door slammed shut behind her, the old man's mouth twisted mournfully; the dead lips began to chew on total emptiness; just then from somewhere in the distance came something that sounded like the singing of a violin bow: the singing of a Petersburg chanticleer, announcing something unknown and waking someone unknown.

Somewhere to the side splashed the lightest of flames, and suddenly everything was illuminated, as a roseate ripple of cloudlets entered the flames like a mesh of mother-of-pearl; and in the breaks of that mesh a little blue scrap now showed blue. The row of lines and walls grew heavier and more clearly outlined; some kind of heavy weights emerged – both indentations and projections; entrance porches emerged, caryatids and the cornices of brick balconies; but in the windows, on the spires, a shimmering was more and more noticeable; from the windows, too, the ruby red gleam of the spires began to come.

The lightest of lace turned into morning Petersburg: Petersburg decked itself out lightly and whimsically, there stood the sand-coloured houses with their five storeys; there stood the dark-blue houses, there the grey ones; the reddish-brown palace began to glow like dawn.

END OF THE FOURTH CHAPTER

CHAPTER THE FIFTH

in which the story is told of the little gentleman with the wart
near his nose and of the sardine tin with dreadful contents

> When morning and its star doth gleam,
> And it will play, the brilliant day,
> Then I, perhaps, will yet descend
> Beneath the tomb's mysterious canopy.[1]
>
> A. Pushkin

The Little Gentleman

Nikolai Apollonovich was silent all the way.

Nikolai Apollonovich turned round and stared straight into the
face of the little gentleman who was running after him.

'Excuse me: with whom . . .'

The Petersburg slush rustled in melting streams; over there a
carriage flew past into the fog with the light of the street
lamps . . .

'With whom do I have the honour . . .?'

All the way he had heard the tiresome squelching of the galoshes
that were running after him and had felt running over his back the
small and inflamed eyes of that little bowler hat that had tagged
along after him ever since he had left the gateway – back there, in
the little alley.

'Pavel Yakovlevich Morkovin . . .'

And lo: Nikolai Apollonovich turned round and stared straight
into the little gentleman's face; the face said nothing: bowler hat,
walking-stick, coat, little beard and nose.

After that he fell into oblivion, turning away towards the wall,
along which the shadowy little bowler hat ran all the way, slightly
tilted to one side; the sight of this bowler hat filled him with
revulsion; the Petersburg dampness began to crawl under his skin;

the Petersburg slush rustled in melting streams; the ice-covered ground, the sleety drizzle soaked his coat.

The bowler hat on the wall now expanded its shadow, now diminished; again the distinctive voice was heard behind Ableukhov's back:

'I bet it pleases you to assume this tone of indifference out of sheer coquetry . . .'

All this had happened somewhere before.

'Listen,' Nikolai Apollonovich tried to say to the bowler hat. 'I will confess I am surprised; I will confess I . . .'

Then over there the first bright apple flared; there – a second one; there – a third; and a line of electric apples delineated the Nevsky Prospect, where the walls of the stone buildings are suffused by a fiery murk all the Petersburg night long and where the bright little restaurants display into the complete confusion of that night their brilliant blood-red signs, beneath which feathered ladies dart about, hiding the carmine of their painted lips in boas – among top hats, cap-bands, bowler hats, Russian shirts, overcoats – in the dim dregs of light that reveal from beyond the poor Finnish marshes above many-versted Russia the wide-open, white-hot jaws of Gehenna.

Nikolai Apollonovich followed, kept following the running of the black, shadowy bowler hat along the walls, the age-old dark shadow; Nikolai Apollonovich knew: the circumstances of his encounter with the enigmatic Pavel Yakovlevich would not permit him to break off that encounter right there and then – by the little fence – with any real dignity for himself: he must with the greatest of caution ascertain what this Pavel Yakovlevich really knew about him, what had really been said between him and his father; that was why he had been slow in taking his leave.

Here the Neva opened out: the stone curve of the Winter Canal showed beneath itself a tearful spaciousness, and from there rushed onslaughts of wet wind; on the other side of the Neva rose the outlines of islands and houses; and sadly cast their amber eyes into the fog; and it seemed that they wept.

'So you're really not averse to, as it's called, coming to an understanding with me?' the same mangy little voice importuned behind his back.

Here was the square; the same grey rock towered up on the square; the same horse flung out its hoof; but it was a strange thing: a shadow covered the Bronze Horseman. And it seemed that the Horseman was not there; there in the distance, on the Neva, stood some kind of fishing schooner; and a tiny light gleamed on board the schooner.

'It's time I was off home . . .'

'Oh, come on: you can't go home now!'

And they walked across the bridge.

Ahead of them walked a couple: a seaman of forty-five, dressed in black leather; he had a fur hat with earflaps, his cheeks were bluish and he had a bright reddish-brown beard with streaks of grey in it; his neighbour, quite simply a kind of giant in enormous boots, with a dark green wool felt hat, strode along – dark-browed, dark-haired, with a small nose and a small moustache. Both reminded one of something; and both walked through the open door of a little restaurant under a diamond sign.

Under the letters of the diamond sign Pavel Yakovlevich Morko-vin grabbed Ableukhov by the wing of his Nikolayevka with incomprehensible insolence:

'This way, Nikolai Apollonovich, into the restaurant: here – that's it – this way, sir! . . .'

'But wait a moment . . .'

Here Pavel Yakovlevich, keeping his hand on the wing of the overcoat, proceeded to yawn: he bent, stooped, and then stretched, bringing his open oral cavity right up to Nikolai Apollonovich, like some cannibal preparing to swallow Ableukhov: swallow him without fail.

This fit of yawning passed to Ableukhov; the latter's lips began to twist:

'Aaa – a: aaaa . . .'

Ableukhov tried to tear himself free:

'No, it's time I was going, it really is.'

But the mysterious gentleman, having received the gift of the word, interrupted in a disrespectful manner:

'Oh, I know you: are you bored?'

And without letting him speak, interrupted him again:

'Well, I'm bored, too: and what's more, you can add, I've got a cold: all these past few days I've been trying to cure it with a tallow candle . . .'

Nikolai Apollonovich was about to interject something, but his mouth was torn apart in a yawn:

'Aaa: aaa – aaa! . . .'

'Well, well – you see how bored you are!'

'I just feel sleepy . . .'

'Well, let us assume you are, yet all the same (please try to put yourself in my position): this is a rare occasion, a most r-r-are occasion . . .'

There was nothing for it: Nikolai Apollonovich shrugged his shoulders the merest bit and with a barely perceptible disgust opened the restaurant door . . . Coat-hangers sagging with blackness: with bowler hats, sticks, coats.

'A rare occasion, a most r-rare occasion,' Morkovin said, snapping his fingers. 'I tell you this straight: a young man of such exceptional talents as yourself? . . . Let him go? . . . Leave him in peace?! . . .'

A thickish, white vapour containing some sort of pancake smell, mixed with the wetness from the street; with an icy burning sensation a numbered tag fell into the palm of a hand.

'Hee-hee-hee,' said Pavel Yakovlevich, letting himself go – he had taken off his coat and was rubbing his hands. 'It's interesting for me to get to know a young philosopher: don't you think so?'

The Petersburg street was beginning now, in the restaurant premises, to bake with a pungent fever, crawling over the body like dozens of tiny, red-legged ants:

'You see, everyone knows me . . . Aleksandr Ivanovich, your father, Butishchenko, Shishiganov, Peppóvich . . .'

After these words that had been spoken, Nikolai Apollonovich felt the most lively curiosity, aroused by three circumstances; in the first place: the stranger – for the umpteenth time! – had stressed his acquaintance with his father (that signified something); in the second place: the stranger had made a slip in speaking about Aleksandr Ivanovich and had mentioned this name and patronymic alongside his father's name; lastly, the stranger had mentioned a number of surnames (Butishchenko, Shishiganov, Peppóvich) that sounded so strangely familiar . . .

'She's an interesting one, sir,' Pavel Yakovlevich said to

Ableukhov with a nudge, referring to a bright-lipped prostitute in a light orange dress with a Turkish cigarette in her teeth . . . 'What's your attitude to women? . . . Perhaps you ought to . . .'

'?'

'Oh well, I won't go on about it: I can see you're a modest fellow . . . And anyway there isn't time . . . We've got one or two things to . . .'

While all around was heard:

'Who did you say?'

'Who? . . . Ivan! . . .'

'Ivan Ivanych! . . .'

'Ivan Ivanych Ivanov . . .'

'So then I said: Ivvan-Ivanch? . . . Eh? . . . Ivvan-Ivanch? . . . What are you up to, then, Ivvan-Ivanch? Ai, ai, ai! . . .'

'And Ivan Ivanych . . .'

'That's all rubbish.'

'No, it's not rubbish . . . Ask Ivan Ivanych: there he is over there, in the billiards room . . . Ei, ei!'

'Ivvan! . . .'

'Ivan Ivanych!'

'Ivvan Ivvanych Ivanov . . .'

'And what a swine you are, Ivan Ivanych!'

Somewhere all hell was let loose; from in there a machine, like a dozen clamorous horns, throwing ear-splitting sounds into nowhere – suddenly bellowed: below the machine the merchant, Ivan Ivanych Ivanov, brandishing a green bottle, had risen into a dancing position with a lady in a tattered blouse; the grime of her dirty cheeks burned there; from beneath her reddish-brown hair, from beneath the crimson feathers that had fallen on to her forehead, pressing a handkerchief to her lips so as not to hiccup out loud, the goggle-eyed lady was laughing; and as she laughed her breasts began to bounce; Ivan Ivanych Ivanov gave a neighing laugh; the drunken audience thundered all around.

Nikolai Apollonovich stared in amazement: how could he have ended up in such a filthy place and in such filthy company at the very moment when . . .

'Ha-ha-ha-ha-ha-ha,' roared the same little drunken group, as Ivan Ivanych Ivanov seized his lady by the hair and bent her down to the floor, tearing out an enormous crimson feather; the lady wept, expecting blows; but they managed to tear the merchant away from her in time. Embitteredly, tormentedly inside the wild machine, roaring and beating tambourines, the terrible times of old, like a volcanic eruption of subterranean violence rushing at us out of the depths, grew in volume, spread and wept into the restaurant hall out of golden pipes:

'Aa-ba-a-ate un-re-est of the paa-aassions . . .'[2]
'Fall asle-e-eep thou ho-ope-less he-e-art . . .'

. . . .

'Ha-ha-ha-ha-ha-ha! . . .'

A Glass of Vodka!

There are the dirty rooms of an old, infernal drinking-house; there are its walls; these walls have been painted by a painter's hand: the foam of the Finnish breakers, from where – out of the distances, penetrating the dank and greenish fog, the tarred rigging of a vessel was once more flying towards Petersburg on great, shadowy sails.

'You must admit, now . . . Hey, two glasses of vodka! – you must admit . . .' Pavel Yakovlevich Morkovin was shouting – he was white, white: bloated – utterly swollen, run to fat; yet his white, yellowish little face seemed thin, even though it had grown obese, run to fat: here, like a bag; there, like a nipple; here, like a little white wart . . .

'I bet I present a riddle to you, over which your mental apparatus is working vainly at this moment . . .'

There, there was a table: at the table a seaman of forty-five, dressed in black leather (and apparently a Dutchman), leaning his bluish face over his glass.

'Do you want picon essence in it? . . .'

The Dutchman's blood-red lips – for the umpteenth time – drew in the Allasch[3] that burned like a flame . . .

'So you'll have picon essence, then?'

And beside the Dutchman a ponderous colossus, who was as if made of stone, sat down heavily at the table.

'Yes, with picon essence.'

Black-browed, black-haired, the colossus laughed ambiguously in Nikolai Apollonovich's direction.

'Well, young man?' came the stranger's small tenor above his ear just then.

'What?'

'What have you got to say about my behaviour out in the street?'

And it seemed that the colossus now struck his fist on the table – the crash of splitting boards, the chime of shattered glasses filled the restaurant.

'What has anyone got to say about your behaviour in the street? Ach, why do you go on about the street? I must say I really don't know.'

Here the colossus produced a pipe from the heavy folds of his caftan, stuck it between his strong lips, and a heavy cloud of stinking baccy began to smoke above the table.

'Shall we have another glass?'

'Yes, let's have another . . .'

. . . .

Before him gleamed the astringent poison; and wishing to calm himself, he fished on to his plate some kind of limp leaves or other; and stood there with the full glass in his hand, while Pavel Yakovlevich poked anxiously about, trying to get hold of a slippery saffron milkcap mushroom with his fork; and, having got hold of the slippery mushroom, Pavel Yakovlevich turned round (specks of dust hung on his moustache).

'Don't you think it was strange *back there*?'

Thus had he stood once before (for all this had happened – before) . . . But the glasses clinked resonantly together; that was how the glasses had clinked . . . – where had they clinked?

'Where?'

Nikolai Apollonovich made an effort to remember. Nikolai Apollonovich, alas, could not remember.

'Oh, *back there* – by the fence . . . No, landlord, I don't want the sardines: they're floating in yellow slime.'

Pavel Yakovlevich made Ableukhov an elucidatory gesture.

'When I found you *back there*: you were standing over a puddle and reading a note: well, I thought, a rare occasion, a most r-rare occasion . . .'

Tables stood all around; at the tables some kind of mongrel breed was carousing; and it thronged, thronged here, this breed: neither human beings nor shadows – striking one with their thievish little tricks and manners; they were all inhabitants of the islands, and the inhabitants of the islands are a strange, mongrel breed: neither human beings nor shadows. Pavel Yakovlevich Morkovin was also from an island: he smiled and giggled, striking one with his thievish little tricks and manners.

'You know, Pavel Yakovlevich, I must admit I expect an explanation from you . . .'

'Of my behaviour?'

'Yes!'

'I will explain it . . .'

Again the astringent poison gleamed: he was getting drunk – everything spun round; the little drinking house shone more transparently; the Dutchman looked more bluish, and the colossus more enormous; its shadow was broken on the walls and seemed as if crowned with some kind of wreath,

Pavel Yakovlevich was growing shinier and shinier – floating in fat, running to fat: here like a bag; here like a nipple; here like a little white wart; this puffy face evoked in his memory the tip of a floating, pig-fat tallow candle.

'Shall we have a third?'

'Yes, a third . . .'

. . . .

'Well, so what have you got to say about our conversation in the gateway?'

'About the domino?'

'Well, of course! . . .'

'All I've got to say is what I've already said . . .'

'You can be perfectly frank with me.'

Nikolai Apollonovich wanted to turn away from Mr Morkovin's reeking lips in disgust, but held himself in check; and when he received a smacking kiss on the lips, he involuntarily cast his gaze, full of torment, at the ceiling, sweeping with one hand a lock of his thinning hair away from his high forehead, while his lips stretched in an unnatural smile and, strainedly twitching, began to tremble (in the same unnatural manner as the legs of tormented frogs twitch when those legs are touched by the ends of electrical wires).

'Well now: that's better; don't give any thought to it: never mind about the domino. I simply thought of the domino in order to get to know you . . .'

'Excuse me, you've spilled sardine oil on yourself,' Nikolai Apollonovich said, interrupting him, and thinking to himself: 'He's still playing a crafty game, trying to search me out: I must be careful . . .' We have forgotten to note: Nikolai Apollonovich had removed his domino cape in the hallway of the restaurant.

'I think you'll agree: it's a wild idea that you're the domino . . . Hee-hee-hee: where do people get such ideas from, eh? Do you hear me? Hey, Pavlusha, old chap, I tell myself, this is quite simply a curious flash that came to you – by the fence, too, while you were performing, so to speak, a necessary human function . . . The domino! . . . As simple as that, just a pretext for getting to know you, you dear man, because you are very, very, very famous: for your intellectual qualities.'

They moved away from the vodka counter, picking their way between the tables. And again from in there the machine, like a dozen clamorous horns, throwing ear-splitting sounds into nowhere – suddenly bellowed; flocks of little bells began to jangle, shattering against one's ears; from a separate office came someone's brazen boasting.

'Waiter: a clean tablecloth . . .'

'And vodka . . .'

'Well, so there it is, sir: we've finished with the domino. And now, dear fellow, about another little point that connects us . . .'

. . . .

'You said something about a point that connects us . . . What point is that?'.

They put their elbows on the table. Nikolai Apollonovich experienced a sensation of drunkenness (from tiredness, probably); all the colours, all the sounds, all the smells struck more outrageously against his white-hot brain.

'Yes, yes, yes: a most curious, a most interesting little point . . . Splendid: I shall have kidneys in madeira, and will you . . . also have kidneys?'

'What is this point?'

'Waiter, two portions of kidneys . . . You were pleased to ask about the most curious little point? Well, so there it is, sir – I will admit: the ties that have bound us are sacred ties . . .'

'?'

'They are ties of kinship.'

'?'

'Blood ties . . .'

Just then the kidneys were served.

'Oh, do not suppose that those ties . . . Salt, pepper, mustard! – were connected with the shedding of blood:[4] but why are you trembling, my little pigeon? Why, I say, you're blushing, you're on fire, like a young maiden! Would you like some mustard? Here's the pepper.'

Nikolai Apollonovich, like Apollon Apollonovich, overpeppered his soup; but he remained with the pepper-pot hanging in the air.

'What did you say?'

'I said to you: here's the pepper . . .'

'About blood . . .'

'Eh? About ties? By blood ties I mean ties of kinship.' Here the little table ran about the hall (the vodka was having its effect); the little table expanded without sense or measure; while Pavel Yakovlevich flew away together with the edge of the table, tied a dirty napkin under his chin, fussed about in the napkin and looked like a corpse maggot.

'All the same, you must forgive me, I must not have understood you at all: tell me – what do you mean by our kinship?'

'Well, you see, Nikolai Apollonovich, I am your brother.'

'My brother?'

Nikolai Apollonovich even got up from the table, but his face leaned over the table towards the little gentleman; with nervously quivering nostrils his face now looked white and pink beneath a thatch of hair that had risen on end; his hair was a sort of lustreless colour.

'Illegitimate, of course, for I, whatever you may say, am the fruit of an unhappy love affair your father had ... with the house seamstress ...'[5]

Nikolai Apollonovich sat down again; his dark blue and, moreover, darkened eyes, and the lightest fragrance of White Rose perfume, and his thin fingers that were tearing at the tablecloth expressed the languor of death: the Ableukhovs had always valued the purity of their blood; he too valued that blood; – how could it be, how could it be: his father, then, must have had ...

'Your papa must have had an interesting little r-romance in his youth ...'

Nikolai Apollonovich suddenly thought that Morkovin was going to continue his sentence with the words: 'which ended with my appearance' (what rubbish, what a crazy idea!)

'Which ended with my appearance in the world.'

Madness!

This had happened once before somewhere.

'And so on this occasion of our kindred meeting let us both have another drink.'

Embitteredly, tormentedly inside the wild machine, roaring and beating tambourines, the terrible times of old, like a cry rushing at us out of the depths, grew in volume, spread and wept into the restaurant hall out of golden pipes.

. . . .

'You were going to say that my father ...'

'Our *mutual* father.'

'Very well then, our *mutual* father,' said Nikolai Apollonovich, shrugging his shoulders.

'Ah-ha-a: your shoulder! How it shrugged!' Pavel Yakovlevich interrupted him. 'It shrugged – do you know why?'

'Why?'

'Because for you, Nikolai Apollonovich, kinship with a fellow like me, is, whatever you may say, offensive ... And then, you know, you've grown brave.'

'Grown brave? Why should I be cowardly?'

'Ha-ha-ha!' laughed Pavel Yakovlevich, not listening to him. 'You've grown brave because in your opinion ... Have some more kidneys ...'

'Most grateful, I'm sure . . .'

'My excellent curiosity and our conversation by the fence have been explained . . . And some sauce . . . You must forgive me, please, my little pigeon, for applying to you the psychological method of, so to speak, torture – by waiting, of course; I am probing you, my dear fellow, from this side, from that side: I'll run this way and that; I'll lie in ambush. And then I'll jump out . . .'

Nikolai Apollonovich screwed up his eyes, and from his dark, very long eyelashes his eyes gleamed blue with a wild and astringent determination not to ask for mercy, as his fingers drummed on the table.

'The same thing is true of what I said about our kinship with each other; that too was probing: to see how you'd react . . . And now I must at one and the same time please you and vex you, sir . . . No, you must forgive me – I always act in a manner like this when I make a new acquaintance: it remains for me to observe to you that we are brothers, but . . . by different fathers.'

'? . . .'

'I was of course joking about Apollon Apollonovich: there was no little romance with a seamstress; none at all – heh-heh-heh-heh – no romance at all . . . An exceptionally moral man in our immoral time . . .'

'Then why are we – brothers?'

'By conviction.'

'How can you know what my convictions are?'

'You're a died-in-the-wool terrorist, Nikolai Apollonovich.'

(Everything, everything, everything in Nikolai Apollonovich had fused into a continuous state of languor; everything, everything, everything had fused into a single torture).

'I also am a confirmed terrorist: be so good as to notice that I had a hidden purpose in throwing you some surnames that are not entirely unknown: Butishchenko, Shishiganov and Peppóvich . . . Do you remember, I mentioned them earlier? There was a subtle hint there, one might say, if you like . . . Aleksandr Ivanovich Dudkin, the Elusive One! . . . Eh? Eh? . . . You understand, you understand? But don't get upset: you do understand, for you're a man who's read a bit, one of our theoreticians, a most clever rogue: ah, my scoundrel, let me kiss you . . .'

'Ha-ha-ha,' Nikolai Apollonovich laughed, throwing himself against the back of his wretched chair, 'ha-ha-ha-ha-ha . . .'

'Ee-hee-hee,' Pavel Yakovlevich chimed in, 'ee-hee-hee . . .'

'Ha-ha-ha,' Nikolai Apollonovich continued to roar.

'Ee-hee-hee,' Morkovin giggled in concert.

The colossus at the next table turned angrily towards them and stared closely.

'What do you want?'

Nikolai Apollonovich lost his temper.

'You'd better watch out.'

'Well, I'll tell you this,' Nikolai Apollonovich said with complete earnestness, making it look as though he had mastered a frenzied bout of laughter (he had been laughing forcedly) – 'you are mistaken, because my attitude towards terrorism is a negative one; and, quite apart from anything else: tell me what you base your conclusion on?'

'For heaven's sake, Nikolai Apollonovich! Why, I know all about you: about the little bundle, about Aleksandr Ivanych Dudkin and about Sofya Petrovna . . .'

. . . .

'I know it all from personal curiosity and also: as part of my duties in government service . . .'

'Ah, so you're in government service?'

'Yes: in the secret police.'

'The secret police?'

'Come, my dear fellow, why do you clutch at your chest with an expression as though you had a most dangerous and secret document there . . . A glass of vodka! . . .'

I Annihilate Irrevocably

For an instant both froze; from behind the edge of the table Pavel Yakovlevich Morkovin, an official of the secret police, grew, stretched, stood erect with a finger raised aloft; then the sharp tip of this hooked finger reached across the table and caught hold of one of Nikolai Apollonovich's buttons; then, with an altogether guilty smile, Nikolai Apollonovich fished out of his side pocket a small bound book which turned out to be a notebook.

'Ah, ah, ah! Please be so good as to let me see that notebook ... for inspection ...' Nikolai Apollonovich did not offer any resistance: he was still sitting with the same guilty smile; his torture had passed all limits; the ecstasies of the tormented and the inspiration of the sacrificial role had disappeared; present instead were: humbleness, obedience (the remains of shattered pride); one way remained open to him: the way of blind insensibility. There was nothing for it: he handed the notebook to the police spy for inspection like a slandered hypocrite (the shameless deceiver!)

Then from behind the edge of the table Pavel Yakovlevich, bending over the notebook, thrust forward his head, which looked as though it were attached not to his neck, but to his two hands; for a single moment he became quite simply a monster: at that moment Nikolai Apollonovich saw: a foul head, blinking little eyes, with hair that looked like doghair groomed with a comb, snapping in a repulsive laugh, with yellow folds of skin, ran above the table on ten twitching fingers, looking like an enormous insect: a ten-legged spider, rustling over the paper with its feet.

But it was all a comedy ...

Pavel Yakovlevich evidently wanted to frighten Ableukhov with the pretence of this investigation (a charming little joke!); still snapping with laughter, he threw the notebook back to Ableukhov across the table.

'But why, for goodness' sake: such obedience ... After all, it's not as if I were going to interrogate you ... Don't be afraid, my little pigeon: I've been appointed to keep an eye on the secret police by the Party ... and there was no need for you to be so alarmed, Nikolai Apollonovich: I do assure you, no need at all ...'

'Are you making fun?'

'Not a bit of it! ... Were I a real policeman, you would have already been arrested, because your gesture, you know, was worthy of attention; first you clutched at your chest with a frightened expression on your face, as though you had a document there ... If you ever meet a police spy in future, do not repeat that gesture; that gesture gave you away ... Agreed?'

'Possibly ...'

'And then, permit me to observe – you made another slip: you took out an innocent notebook when no one had yet asked you to do so; took it out in order to distract attention from some other thing; but you did not achieve your purpose; you did not distract attention, you attracted it; made me go on thinking that you had some document in your pocket . . . Ach, how light-minded you are . . . I mean, look at this page of the notebook you gave me; you unwittingly revealed a little love secret to me: here, look, admire your handiwork . . .'

The animal howls of the machine could be heard: the screaming of a giant bull having its throat cut in a slaughter-house: the tambourines were bursting, bursting, bursting.

. . . .

'Listen!'

Nikolai Apollonovich uttered this *listen* with genuine fury.

'What is this torture for? If you are really what you pretend to be – waiter, the bill! – then your behaviour, and all your little grimaces are unworthy.'

They both got up.

In the white clouds of stench that belched from the kitchen stood Nikolai Apollonovich – pale, white and in a state of rabid fury, his red mouth torn open without any laughter, in the aura of the flaxen and lustreless thatch of his very fair hair: like a wild animal with its teeth bared, brought to bay by hounds, he turned round contemptuously to face Morkovin, having thrown the waiter a fifty-copeck piece.

The machine had fallen silent now; for a long time the neighbouring tables had been emptying, and the mongrel breed had dispersed about the Lines of the island; suddenly the white electricity went out in all the rooms; the reddish light of a candle penetrated the deathly void; and the walls melted away in the darkness; only there, where a candle stood and the edge of a paint-daubed wall was visible, white foam beat, hissing, into the hall. And from there, out of the distance, on his shadowy sails, the Flying Dutchman flew towards Petersburg (Nikolai Apollonovich's head was, to be sure, spinning after the seven glasses he had drunk); from the table rose the forty-five-year-old seaman (was it the Dutchman?); for a moment his eyes flashed with greenish spark; but he vanished in the darkness.

As for Mr Morkovin, straightening his little frock-coat, he looked at Nikolai Apollonovich with a kind of reflective tenderness (the latter's state of mind had evidently seized him, too); melancholically, he sighed; and lowered his eyes; for about a minute they did not utter a single word.

At last Pavel Yakovlevich spoke without haste.

'That's enough: I find it as hard as you do . . .

'Why try to conceal it, comrade? . . .

'I didn't come here to play jokes . . .

'Isn't there something we have to settle? . . .'

. . . .

'?'

. . . .

'Why, yes, yes: we must come to an agreement about the day when you will fulfil your promise . . . Indeed, Nikolai Apollonovich, you are a strange fellow, of a kind rarely encountered; could you really have supposed for a moment that I was idly loafing about the streets after you, and at last with difficulty found a pretext for conversation . . .'

And then, sternly gazing into Ableukhov's eyes, he added with dignity: 'Nikolai Apollonovich, the Party expects an immediate answer . . .'

Nikolai Apollonovich was quietly going down the stairs; the end of the staircase receded into darkness; and at the bottom – by the door – stood: *them*; who *they* were was a question to which he could not have given any positive, precise answer: a black outline and some kind of green, ultra-green darkness that seemed to be glowing dimly like phosphorus (it was the falling ray of a street lamp outside); and *they* were waiting for him.

And as he approached that door, on both sides of him he felt the vigilant stare of an observer: and one of them was that same giant who had been drinking Allasch at the table next to him: illuminated by the ray of the outside street lamp, he stood there by the door like a bronze-headed colossus; as Ableukhov entered the ray, for a moment a metallic face stared at him, glowing like phosphorus; and a green arm, weighing many hundreds of poods, threatened him.

'Who is that?'

'Someone who annihilates us irrevocably.'

'A police spy?'

'Never . . .'

The door of the restaurant slammed.

The tall, many-headed street lamps, tormented by the winds, shimmered with strange lights, expanding into the long Petersburg night; the black, black pedestrians flowed forth from the darkness; once again the bowler hat ran beside him along the wall.

'Well, and if I refuse the assignment?'

'I will arrest you . . .'

'You? Arrest me?'

'Do not forget that I . . .'

'That you're a conspirator?'

'I am an employee of the secret police; as an employee of the secret police I will arrest you . . .'

The wind of the Neva was whistling in the telegraph wires and lamenting in the gateways; icy shreds of clouds half torn to tatters were visible; and it seemed that in a moment or two from the most ragged clouds bands of busy rain would break loose – to chirr, lisp and beat over the stone paving with drops, curling their cold bubbles on the gurgling puddles.

'What would the Party say to you?'

'The Party would support me: using my position in the secret police, I would take revenge on you for the Party . . .'

'Well, and what if I were to denounce you to the authorities?'

'Try it . . .'

Then, from the most ragged cloud, bands of busy rain began to fall – to chirr, lisp and beat over the stone paving with drops, curling their cold bubbles on the gurgling puddles.

'No, Nikolai Apollonovich, I beg you – let us put joking to one side: because I am very, very serious; and I must observe: your doubt and indecisiveness mortify me; you should have weighed up all the chances beforehand . . . You could have said no (for goodness' sake, you've had two months). You did not bother to do that at the right time; you have one path; and you must choose what lies ahead of you – either arrest, suicide or murder. I hope that now you understand me? . . . Good-bye . . .'

The little bowler hat went trotting off in the direction of the Seventeenth Line, while the overcoat set off towards the bridge.

Petersburg, Petersburg!

Falling like fog, you have pursued me, too, with idle cerebral play: you are a cruel-hearted tormentor: but you are an unquiet ghost: for years you have attacked me; I too ran through your dreadful prospects, in order to take a flying leap on to this gleaming bridge . . .

Oh, great bridge, shining with electricity! Oh, green waters, seething with bacilli! I remember a certain fateful moment; over your damp railings I too leant on a September night: a moment – and my body would have flown into the mists.

On the great cast-iron bridge Nikolai Apollonovich turned round; behind him he saw nothing, no one: above the damp, damp railings, above the greenish water that seethed with bacilli he was whiningly seized by nothing but the cold Neva wind; here, on this very spot, two and a half months before, Nikolai Apollonovich had given his terrible promise; that same waxen face, its lips protruding, had stretched forward out of a grey overcoat above the damp railings; above the Neva he stood, staring dully at the greenness – or rather: letting his gaze fly over to where the banks cowered; and then rather quickly began to mince away, tripping clumsily over the skirts of his overcoat.

Some kind of phosphorescent stain, both misty and frenzied, rushed across the sky; the Neva distances became misted by a phosphorescent sheen; and this made the soundlessly flying surfaces begin to gleam greenly, reflecting now here, now there a spark of gold. On the other side of the Neva now rose the massive buildings of the islands, casting into the fog eyes that had begun to burn. Higher up, some kind of obscure outlines frenziedly stretched out ragged hands; swarm upon swarm they ascended.

The embankment was empty.

From time to time the black shadow of a policeman walked past; the square was empty; on the right the Senate and the Synod raised their storeys. The rock, too, loomed: with a kind of particular curiosity Nikolai Apollonovich goggled at the massive outline of the Horseman. Earlier, when he had passed here with Pavel Yakov-levich, it had seemed to Ableukhov that the Horseman was not there (the shadow had concealed him); but now a rippling semi-shadow covered the Horseman's face; and the metal of his face smiled ambiguously.

Suddenly the storm clouds were torn apart, and the clouds began to smoke like a green puff of melted bronze beneath the moon . . . For a moment everything flared up: waters, roofs, granite; the Horseman's face, the bronze laurel wreath flared; many thousands' worth of metal hung down from the lustreless green shoulders of the bronze-headed colossus; the cast face and the wreath that was green with time and the many hundred-pood-weighted arm that was imperiously extended straight in Nikolai Apollonovich's direction began to gleam phosphorescently; in the bronze hollows of the eyes bronze thoughts showed greenly; and it seemed: that the arm was about to move (the heavy folds of the cloak would ring against the elbow), the metal hooves would fall on the rock with a loud crash, and a voice that would shatter the granite would resound over all Petersburg:

'Yes, yes, yes . . .'

'It is I . . .

'I annihilate irrevocably.'

For an instant everything was suddenly bathed in light for Nikolai Apollonovich; yes – now he understood what sort of a colossus it was that had sat there at the table in the Vasily Island drinking house (had he too been visited by the vision?); as he had walked to that door, this very face had appeared coming towards him out of the corner, illumined by the street lamp; and now this green arm threatened him. For an instant everything became clear to Ableukhov: his fate was bathed in light: yes – he must; and yes – he was doomed.

But the storm clouds cut into the moon; the strands of witches' tresses flew over the sky.

Roaring with laughter, Nikolai Apollonovich fled from the Bronze Horseman:

'Yes, yes, yes . . .

'I know, I know . . .

'I am lost irrevocably . . .'

In the empty street a shaft of light: it was a court carriage carrying bright red lamps that looked like bloodshot eyes; the ghostly outline of a lackey's three-cornered hat and the outline of the wings of his overcoat flew with the light out of fog into fog.

Griffins

And the prospects stretched – over there, over there: the prospects stretched; the gloomy pedestrian did not hurry his step: the gloomy pedestrian looked painfully around him: these infinities of buildings! The gloomy pedestrian was Nikolai Apollonovich.

. . . Without losing a moment, he must at once undertake – but what was he to undertake? After all, was it not he, was it not he who had so lavishly sown the seeds of the theory concerning the absurdity of all forms of pity? Had he not, in front of that silent little group, once expressed his opinions – always about one and the same thing: about his suppressed revulsion for the *barin*, for the *barin*'s old ears, for all his Tartardom and aristocratic haughtiness, including . . . including that birdlike, outstretched neck . . . with a subcutaneous vein.

At last he hired some tardy Vanka and his cab: past him the four-storeyed buildings moved and flew.

The Admiralty presented its eight-columned flank: turned pink and vanished; from the other side, across the Neva, between white borders of plaster the walls of an old building threw their bright carrot colour; a black-and-white sentry booth stood as it always did, on the left; an old Pavlovsk grenadier was striding back and forth in a grey overcoat there; he had his sharp sparkling bayonet thrown over his shoulder.

Evenly, slowly, listlessly, Vanka trotted past the Pavlovsk grenadier: evenly, slowly, listlessly, Nikolai Apollonovich, too, bumped past the Pavlovsk grenadier. The bright morning, ablaze with the sparks of the Neva, had turned all the water over there into an abyss of pure gold; and into the abyss the funnel of a small whistling steamboat disappeared at full tilt; he saw that the dried-up little figure on the pavement was quickening his tardy pace, somehow bobbing along over the paving-stones – that dried-up little figure who . . . in whom . . . whom he recognized: it was Apollon Apollonovich. Nikolai Apollonovich wanted to detain the cab driver in order to give the little figure enough time to move away, in order to . . . it was already too late: the old, shaven head turned towards the cab driver, gave a shake, and turned away. Nikolai Apollonovich, so as not to be recognized, turned his back towards the tardy pedestrian: he hid his nose in his beaver; all that could be seen was a collar and a peaked cap; already the yellow block of a house had risen before him into the fog.

Apollon Apollonovich Ableukhov, having seen the adolescent girl to her home, was now hurrying towards the doorway of the yellow house; past him, too, the Admiralty had just moved its eight-columned flank; the black-and-white striped booth was on the left where it usually was; now he was walking along the embankment, contemplating there, on the Neva, the abyss of pure gold into which the funnel of a small whistling steamboat had just flown at full tilt.

At this point Apollon Apollonovich Ableukhov heard behind his back the thunder of the carriage; turned his old, shaven head towards the carriage; and when the cab drew level with the senator, the senator saw: there, writhing on the seat – an old-looking and misshapen young man, wrapped up in his overcoat in a most unpleasant manner; and when this young man looked at the senator, his nose hidden in his overcoat (all that could be seen were his eyes and peaked cap), the senator's head jerked away towards the wall so swiftly that his top hat struck against the stone fruit of the black house ledge (Apollon Apollonovich Ableukhov methodically re-adjusted his top hat), and for a moment Apollon Apollonovich Ableukhov stared into the watery depths: into the emerald-red abyss.

Here it seemed to him that the eyes of the unpleasant young man, having caught sight of him, began in the twinkling of an eye to dilate, dilate, dilate: in the twinkling of an eye they unpleasantly dilated and stopped in a gaze full of horror. In horror did Apollon Apollonovich stop before the horror: this gaze pursued Apollon Apollonovich more and more often; this was the gaze with which his subordinates looked at him, this was the gaze with which the passing mongrel breed looked at him: and the student, and the shaggy Manchurian hat; yes, yes, yes: they looked with *that same* gaze and dilated with *that same* glitter; while already the cab, overtaking him, was bouncing tiresomely over the stones; and the number on the number-plate fleeted by: 1905; and in utter fright, Apollon Apollonovich stared into the crimson, many-chimneyed distance; and Vasily Island stared tormentingly, offensively, brazenly at the senator.

Nikolai Apollonovich jumped out of the carriage, tripping clumsily on the skirts of his overcoat, looking old and bad-tempered, ran as quickly as he could to the entrance porch of the yellow house, waddling like a duck and flapping the wings of his overcoat in the air against the backdrop of the bright crimson dawn; Ableukhov stood by the porch; Ableukhov rang; and, as many times before (and precisely so it was today) the voice of the nightwatchman, Nikolaich, rushed at him from somewhere in the distance:

'Good day to you, Nikolai Apollonovich, sir! . . . Very grateful to you sir . . . A little on the late side, sir!'

And, as many times before, precisely so today, a fifteen-copeck piece fell into the hand of Nikolaich, the nightwatchman.

Nikolai Apollonovich tugged violently at the bell-pull: oh, if only Semyonych in there would open the door quickly, for otherwise – that dried-up little figure would appear out of the fog (why was he not in a carriage?); and on either side of the massive house steps he saw the gaping jaws of a griffin, rosy with the dawn, and holding in its claws the rings for the flagpoles on which were hoisted the red white and blue flag that flapped its tricoloured cloth above the Neva on certain days of the calendar; above the griffins the Ableukhov coat of arms, too, was sculpted in the stone; this coat of arms portrayed a long-plumed knight amidst rococo scrolls, gored by a unicorn; a wild thought, like a fish darting for a moment to the surface of the waters, passed through Nikolai Apollonovich's head: Apollon Apollonovich, who spent his life beyond the threshold of that branded door, was the knight who was being gored; and this thought was followed by another, which darted altogether obscurely, without rising to the surface (thus from afar does a fish show dimly): the old family coat of arms referred to all the Ableukhovs; he too, Nikolai Apollonovich, was being gored – but gored by whom?

The whole of that mental *galimatias* went fleeting through his soul in one tenth of a second: and now there, now there, on the pavement – in the fog – he saw that dried-up little figure hurrying up to the house: that dried-up little figure was approaching swiftly, – that dried-up little figure, in whom ... whom ... who from a distance presented, he thought, the aspect of a puny, prematurely born infant: with a deeply yellow face that was emaciated and haemorrhoidal, Apollon Apollonovich Ableukhov, his parent, looked like death in a top hat; Nikolai Apollonovich – sometimes crazy thoughts occur to one – imagined the little figure of Apollon Apollonovich in the moment of fulfilling conjugal relations with his mother, Anna Petrovna: and Nikolai Apollonovich felt with new intensity a familiar sense of nausea (after all, in one of those moments he had been conceived).

He was seized by indignation: no, let it happen, what was going to happen!

Meanwhile the little figure was drawing closer. Nikolai Apollonovich perceived to his shame that the access of his fury, artificially warmed, was decidedly fading: he was seized by the familiar sense of confusion, and ...

And an unpleasant spectacle presented itself to Apollon Apollonovich's gaze: Nikolai Apollonovich, looking old and somehow very bad-tempered, with a deeply yellow face, with eyelids red and inflamed, with lip protruding – Nikolai Apollonovich leapt swiftly down the front steps and, waddling like a duck, ran guiltily towards his parent, with a blinking, evasive gaze, and a perfumed hand stretched forth from under the fur of his overcoat:

'Good morning, Papa ...'

Silence.

'I wasn't expecting to meet you – I've been at the Tsukatovs.'

Apollon Apollonovich thought that this apparently shy young man was – a scoundrelly young man; but Apollon Apollonovich Ableukhov was embarrassed by this thought, especially in the presence of his son; and, having become embarrassed, Apollon Apollonovich Ableukhov shyly muttered:

'I see, sir, I see: good morning, Kolenka ... Well, fancy meeting you here ... Eh? Yes, yes, yes ...'

And as many times before, precisely so today, at this point the voice of Nikolaich the nightwatchman rang out:

'Good day to you, your excellency, sir!'

On the front entrance, on both sides of the door, the griffins opened wide their beaklike jaws; the long-plumed stone knight in rococo scrolls and with chest torn asunder was being gored by a unicorn: the more dazzlingly and ethereally the rosy-fingered portents of day flew away across the sky, the more distinctly did all the projections of the buildings loom heavy; the more crimson, more purple was the jaw-gaping griffin.

The doors burst open; the Ableukhovs were embraced by the familiar smell of their chambers; the lackey's vein-covered fingers were thrust through the opening of the door: grey-haired Semyonych, the sleep still in his eyes, in a hurriedly thrown-on jacket seized by the collar in a seventy year-old hand, screwed up his eyes in the unendurable Neva glitter as he let the masters in.

The Ableukhovs flew through the opening of the door almost side by side.

Red as Fire

They both knew that a talk was imminent; this talk had been maturing throughout long years of silence; Apollon Apollonovich, handing his top hat, coat and gloves to the lackey, got somehow entangled with his galoshes; the poor, poor senator: how could he have known that Nikolai Apollonovich had *that same* errand with him? In equal measure, Nikolai Apollonovich could not have guessed that the whole story of the red domino was known to his parent in its entirety. Both at that moment were breathing in the smells of the familiar chambers; on to the vein-covered hand of the lackey fell a sumptuous beaver, shining silver; the overcoat fell down somehow sleepily – but now Nikolai Apollonovich stood before his father's eyes in his domino cape. At the sight of this domino, through Apollon Apollonovich's mind, some lines long ago committed to memory began to whirl:

Colours of a fiery hue
On my palm I throw,
That amidst the light's abyss
Red as fire he'll show.[6]

With a hand just as covered in veins as Semyonych's (only properly washed), he felt his side-whiskers:

'Er ... er ... A red domino? ... Tell me what it's about, please! ...'

'I was at a fancy-dress ball ...'

'Indeed ... Kolenka ... Indeed, sir ...'

Apollon Apollonovich stood before Kolenka with a kind of bitter irony, half mumbling, half chewing his lips; wretchedly, with irony, the skin on his forehead gathered into tiny wrinkles; wretchedly did it tauten on his skull. An imminent accounting could be sensed: one could sense that the fruit that had grown on the tree of their lives had now ripened; in a moment or two it would fall: it fell, and ... – suddenly:

Apollon Apollonovich dropped a pencil (by the steps of the velvet staircase); Nikolai Apollonovich, following ancient habit, deferentially rushed to pick it up; Apollon Apollonovich, in his turn, rushed to forestall his son's complaisance, but stumbled, falling to his heels and touching the stairs with his hands; quickly his bald head flew downwards and forwards; ending up unexpectedly under the fingers of his son, who had stretched out his hands: Nikolai Apollonovich saw before him for an instant his father's yellow, vein-covered neck, which looked like a crayfish's tail (an artery throbbed at one side); Nikolai Apollonovich failed to control his clumsy movements, and unexpectedly touched the neck; the neck's warm pulsation frightened him, and he jerked his hand away, but jerked it away too late: under the touch of his cold hand (which was always slightly sweaty) Apollon Apollonovich turned and saw – *that same* gaze; the senator's head jerked momentarily in a tic, the skin gathered wretchedly in wrinkles above his skull and his ears twitched slightly. In his domino Nikolai Apollonovich looked as though he were entirely covered in flame; and the senator, like an over-agile Japanese who had studied the techniques of ju-jitsu, threw himself to one side, and suddenly straightened up on his crunching knees – up, up and to the side . . .

All this lasted but a moment. Nikolai Apollonovich silently picked up the pencil and handed it to the senator.

'Here, Papa!'

A pure trifle, knocking them together, had given birth within them both to an explosion of the most heterogeneous thoughts and feelings; Apollon Apollonovich was completely discomfited by the outrageousness of what had just happened: of his alarm in response to the deference of the insignificant service his son had performed for him (this man in red was after all his son: the flesh of his flesh: and to be afraid of one's own flesh and blood was shameful – of what was he frightened?); none the less the outrageous thing had happened: he had squatted on his heels *under* his son and had physically experienced *that same* gaze on himself. Together with discomfiture Apollon Apollonovich felt annoyance: he reassumed a dignified manner, bent his waist coquettishly and proudly compressed his lips into a ring, taking the retrieved pencil into his hands.

'Thank you, Kolenka . . . I'm very grateful to you . . . And I wish you a pleasant sleep . . .'

At that same moment the son found his father's gratitude equally discomfiting; Nikolai Apollonovich felt the blood rush to his cheeks; and when he thought he was turning pink he was already crimson. Apollon Apollonovich gave his son a stealthy glance; and perceiving that his son was crimson in the face, he himself began to turn pink; in order to conceal the pinkness, he flew with great rapidity up the staircase, flew in order to take his rest at once in his little bedroom, wrapped in a most delicate sheet.

Nikolai Apollonovich found himself alone on the stairs of the velvet staircase, immersed in deep and persistent thought: but the lackey's voice broke the train of his thoughts.

'Good heavens! . . . My mind went blank, sir! . . . I can't remember a thing! *Barin*, my dear *barin*: you see, something has happened! . . .'

'What's happened?'

'Oh, something that I just *can't* . . . How can I tell you – I do not dare . . .'

On that step of the grey, velvet-carpeted staircase (trodden by the feet of ministers), Nikolai Apollonovich waited; while from the window, on that very spot where his parent had stumbled, a fine mesh of purple stains fell at his feet; this fine mesh of purple stains for some reason reminded him of blood (blood was showing purple on the old armaments, too). A familiar, hateful sense of nausea, though not of the earlier (and dreadful) dimensions, rose from his stomach: was he suffering from indigestion?

'Something really *has* happened! Yes – well, here it is, then, sir: our *barynya* . . .

'Our *barynya*, Anna Petrovna, sir . . .

'She's here, sir!!'

· · · · · · · ·

At that moment Nikolai Apollonovich began to gape with nausea: and the enormous opening of his mouth expanded at the dawn: he stood there, red as a torch.

The lackey's ancient lips stretched forth beneath a blond cap of the most sumptuous and delicate hair:

'She's here, sir!'

'Who is here?'

'Anna Petrovna, sir . . .'

'And who might she be? . . .'

'Who, sir . . . Your maternal parent . . . Why, *barin*, little dove, you are just like a stranger: it's your mother . . .'

'?'

'She's come back to Petersburg from Shpain . . .'

· · · · · · · ·

'She has sent a letter by messenger, sir: she's staying at a hotel . . . Because – you yourself know why . . . She's in such a situation, that . . .'

'?'

'His eminent excellency Apollon Apollonovich had just been pleased to go out, when a messenger arrived with a letter, sir ... Well, I put the letter on the table and gave the messenger twenty copecks ...

'I would reckon that not an hour had passed when – gracious Lord: she herself suddenly appeared, sir! ... She obviously knew for certain that there was nobody home, sir ...'

. . . .

Before him gleamed the battle mace: the stain of fallen air showed so strangely purple; the stain of fallen air showed tormentingly purple: a purple column stretched from wall to window; specks of dust danced in the column and looked red. Nikolai Apollonovich thought that man, too, was only a column of smoking blood.

. . . .

'The doorbell rang ... So of course I went and opened the door ... I saw: a *barynya*. I didn't know, a respectable *barynya*; only very plainly dressed; and all – in black ... I said to her: "How can I oblige you, madam?" And she said to me: "Mitry Semyonych, don't you recognize me?" And I fell on her dear hand: "Little mother," I said, "Anna Petrovna ..."'

. . . .

The first scoundrel who came along had only to prod a man quite simply with a blade for his white, hairless skin to be sliced open (in the manner in which a jellied piglet with horseradish sauce is sliced), and the blood that throbbed at his temples to pour out in a stinking puddle ...

. . . .

'And Anna Petrovna – God grant her health, sir – looked: looked, her ladyship did, at me ... She looked at me and said in tears: "I want to see how you've managed here without me ..." And from her reticule – a reticule, it was, of foreign fashion – she took out her hanky, sir ...

'I had the strictest orders not to let anyone in, if you will be pleased to know ... Well, but I let our *barynya* in ... And she ...'

The little old man's eyes bulged; he remained with his mouth wide open and probably thought that the masters in the lacquered house had long ago gone mad: instead of displaying any surprise, regret or joy, Nikolai Apollonovich flew up the staircase, flapping his bright red satin whimsically into space like the tail of a lawless comet.[7]

. . . .

He, Nikolai Apollonovich . . . Or was it not he? No, it was he – he: he thought he had told them that day that he hated the repellent old man; that the repellent old man, the wearer of diamond insignia, was quite simply an inveterate swindler . . . Or had he said all that to himself?

No – to them, to them!

The reason that Nikolai Apollonovich had flown up the staircase, not letting Semyonych finish, was that he had clearly imagined: a certain foul act perpetrated by one scoundrel on another; suddenly he imagined the scoundrel; the gleaming scissors snipping in this scoundrel's fingers as this scoundrel clumsily rushed to sever the bony old codger's sleepy artery; the bony old codger's forehead gathered into wrinkles; the bony old man's neck was warm and its pulse was throbbing and it was . . . somehow crayfish-like; the scoundrel snipped the scissors about the bony old codger's artery, and the stinking, sticky blood poured on to his fingers and the scissors, while the old codger – beardless, wrinkled, bald – at this point wept sobbing aloud and stared straight into his, Nikolai Apollonovich's, eyes with a beseeching expression, squatting down and trying to press with a shaking finger that opening in his neck, from which with barely audible whistlings the red streams reeled, reeled and reeled . . .

So vividly did this image appear before him that it was as if it had just happened (after all, when the old man had fallen on to his hands he might in the twinkling of an eye have torn down the battle mace, taken a swing with it, and . . .) So vividly did this image appear before him that he felt frightened.

For this reason it was that Nikolai Apollonovich had rushed into flight through the rooms, past lacquer and sheen, his heels clattering, and running the risk of summoning the senator from his far-off bedchamber.

A Bad Omen

If to their excellencies, eminences, gracious sirs and citizens I were to put the question: what is the lodging of our imperial high officials, then, probably, these persons of venerable rank would reply to me directly in that affirmative sense that the lodging of our high officials is, in the first instance, space, by which we all mean a totality of rooms; these rooms consist: of a single room that is called a *salle*, or a hall, either of which please note – will do equally well: they consist, further, of a room for the reception of multivarious guests; and so on, so on, and so on (the remainder here is trivia).

Apollon Apollonovich Ableukhov was a Real Privy Councillor; Apollon Apollonovich was a person of the first class (which is, again – the same thing), and finally: Apollon Apollonovich Ableukhov was a high official of the Empire; all of this we have seen from the first lines of our book. So there it was: as a high official, even as a functionary of the Empire, he could not but take up his residence in spatial expanses that possessed three dimensions; and he took up his residence in spatial expanses: in cubic spaces that consisted, please note: of a hall (or – a *salle*) and so on, so on, and so on, things we have managed to observe from a cursory inspection (the remainder is trivia); among these trivia was his study, as were – being not particularly remarkable – his rooms.

These not particularly remarkable rooms were now illumined by the sun; and now the incrustation of the tables was firing into the air, and the mirrors were now merrily gleaming: and all the mirrors began to laugh, because the first mirror, which looked into the hall from the drawing-room, now reflected the white, as if flour-covered, countenance of a Petrushka, the Petrushka of the puppet-booth, bright red as blood, who had taken a running dive out of the hall (one heard the stamp of his footsteps); at once mirror threw reflection to mirror; and in all the mirrors the Petrushka of the puppet-booth was reflected: it was Nikolai Apollonovich, who had flown headlong into the drawing-room and now stood there as though rooted to the spot, letting his eyes run from mirror to cold mirror, because he saw: the first mirror, the one that looked into the hall from the drawing-room, reflected a certain little object to Nikolai Apollonovich: a skeleton in a buttoned-up frock-coat, possessing a skull from which to right and to left a naked ear and a small side-whisker curled; but between side-whiskers and ears the sharpened little nose looked larger than it ought to have done; above the sharpened little nose two dark eyesockets were lifted in reproach . . .

Nikolai Apollonovich realized that Apollon Apollonovich was waiting for his son here.

Instead of his son, Apollon Apollonovich saw in the mirrors quite simply a red puppet from a booth; and seeing the booth puppet, Apollon Apollonovich froze; the booth puppet had stopped in the middle of the hall so strangely and bewilderedly . . .

Then, unexpectedly to himself, Apollon Apollonovich closed the doors to the hall; retreat was cut off. That which he had begun must be finished quickly. Apollon Apollonovich regarded the talk about the strange behaviour of his son as a painful surgical act. Like a surgeon darting up to the operating table on which scalpels, saws and drills are laid out, Apollon Apollonovich, rubbing yellow fingers, walked right up to *Nicolas*, stopped, and, seeking the eyes that were avoiding him, unwittingly fished out his spectacle-case, twirled it between his fingers, put it away again, coughed rather restrainedly, was silent for a moment, and then said:

'I'll tell you what it is: the domino.'

At the same time he thought that this apparently shy young man, grinning from ear to ear and avoiding looking him straight in the eye with *that same* gaze – this shy young man and insolent Petersburg domino, about which the Jewish press had been writing, were one and the same person; that he, Apollon Apollonovich, a person of the first class and a pillar of gentle society – he had sired him; at that same moment Nikolai Apollonovich rather embarrassedly observed:

'Yes, well . . . a lot of people were wearing masks . . . And so I also went along in a . . . little costume . . .'

At that same moment Nikolai Apollonovich thought that this two-arshin little body of his father's, constituting in circumference no more than twelve and a half vershoks,[8] was the centre and circumference of some immortal centre: in there, after all, was the seat of the 'I'; and any board at all that broke at the wrong moment was capable of crushing that centre: crushing it for good; perhaps under the influence of this perceived idea, Apollon Apollonovich ran as quickly as he could towards that distant table, and drummed two fingers on it, as Nikolai Apollonovich, advancing on him, guiltily laughed:

'It was fun, you know . . . We danced, you know . . .'

But to himself he thought: skin, bones and blood, with not a single muscle; yes, but this obstacle – skin, bones and blood – must, by a command of fate, be blown to pieces; if that were to be avoided today, it would come surging back again tomorrow evening, and tomorrow night it would . . .

Here Apollon Apollonovich, catching *that same* gaze glowering at him in the gleaming mirror, turned on his heels and caught the end of the sentence.

'Then, you know, we played *petit-jeu*.'[9]

Staring intently at his son, Apollon Apollonovich made no reply; and *that same* gaze gloweringly fixed itself on the parquetry of the floor . . . Apollon Apollonovich remembered: why, this strange Petrushka had been a small body; once upon a time he had carried that small body with fatherly tenderness in his arms; the fair-curled little boy, putting on a little dunce-cap made of paper, would climb up on his neck. His voice out of tune and cracking, Apollon Apollonovich had sung hoarsely:

> Silly little simpleton
> Kolenka is dancing:
> He has put his dunce-cap on –
> On his horse he's prancing.

Afterwards he had carried the child up to this very mirror; in the mirror both old man and young man were reflected; he would show the boy the reflections, saying:

'Look, little son: there are strangers there.'

Sometimes Kolenka would cry, and later he would scream at nights. And now? And now? Apollon Apollonovich saw not a 'little body' but a body: alien, large . . . Was it alien?

Apollon Apollonovich began to circulate about the drawing-room, both back and forth:

'You see, Kolenka . . .'

Apollon Apollonovich lowered himself into a deep armchair.

'Kolenka, I must . . . That is, not I, but – I hope – *we* must . . . must have an accounting: do you have sufficient time at your disposal now? The question, and it is a disturbing one, concerns the fact that . . .' Apollon Apollonovich stumbled in mid-sentence, again ran over to the mirror (at that moment the chimes of the clock struck), and out of the mirror at Nikolai Apollonovich looked death in a frock-coat, lifting a gaze of reproach, drumming its fingers; and the mirror cracked with loud laughter: across it like lightning a crooked needle flew with a gentle crunching sound; and froze there for ever in a silvery zigzag.

Apollon Apollonovich had cast his gaze at the mirror, and the mirror had cracked; superstitious people would have said:

'A bad omen, a bad omen . . .'

And of course, they would have been right: a talk was imminent.

Nikolai Apollonovich was obviously trying to postpone the accounting for as long as possible; but since last night the accounting was superfluous: everything would now account for itself in any case. Nikolai Apollonovich regretted that he had not made a dash for it out of the drawing-room in time (how many hours already had the agony been stretching, stretching: and under his heart something was swelling, swelling); he experienced a strange voluptuous pleasure in his horror: and could not tear himself away from his father.

'Yes, Papa: I must admit that I have been expecting us to have some sort of an accounting.'

'Ah . . . you've been expecting it?'

'Yes, I have.'

'Are you free?'

'Yes, I am free.'

He could not tear himself away from his father: before him . . . But here I must make a brief digression.

Oh, worthy reader: we have presented the exterior of the wearer of diamond insignia in exaggerated, excessively sharp outlines, but without any kind of humour; we have presented the exterior of the wearer of diamond insignia merely as it would appear to any passing observer – and not at all as it would doubtless have revealed itself to itself and to us: we, after all, have taken its measure; we have penetrated a soul shaken to the very limits and into furious whirlwinds of consciousness; it will, then, do no harm to remind the reader of the aspect of that exterior in its most general outlines, because we know: as is the visible aspect, so also is the essence within. Here it is sufficient merely to note that if this essence were to appear before us, if all these whirlwinds of consciousness were to rush past us, tearing the frontal bones apart, and if we were able to coldly open up the blue sinewy swellings, then . . . But – silence. In a word, in a word: the passing gaze would perceive here, in this very spot, the skeleton of an old gorilla covered by a frock-coat . . .

'Yes, I am free . . .'

'In that case, Kolenka, go to your room: you must gather your thoughts first. If you find in yourself something that it would do no harm for us to discuss, come to see me in my study.'

'Very well, Papa . . .'

'Yes, and by the way: please take off those puppet-booth rags . . . To be quite frank, I don't like all that one little bit! . . .'

'?'

'No, I don't like it one little bit! I don't like it in the extreme!!'

Apollon Apollonovich let his hand drop; two yellow bones drummed distinctly on the card table.

'Actually,' said Nikolai Apollonovich, getting confused, 'actually, I ought to be . . .'

But the door slammed: Apollon Apollonovich had circulated into his little study.

By the Card Table

Nikolai Apollonovich remained where he was, by the card table: his gaze began to run over the leaves of the bronze incrustation, the boxes and shelves that jutted out of the walls. Yes, it was here that he had played; here for long hours he had sat – in this armchair here, on the pale satin azure of whose seat little garlands twined; and just as before, the copy of David's painting *Distribution des aigles par Napoléon Premier*. The painting depicted the great emperor wearing a wreath and a purple mantle, stretching out his hand to the assembly of marshals.

What would he say to his father? Would he again, painfully, lie? Lie, when lying was now useless? Lie, when his present position made any lying impossible? Lie . . . Nikolai Apollonovich remembered how he had lied in the years of his distant childhood.

Here was the grand piano, a period piece, yellow: it touched the parquetry with the little wheels of its narrow legs. Once upon a time his mother, Anna Petrovna, had sat here, once the old sounds of Beethoven had shaken the walls here: time-honoured antiquity, exploding and complaining, had risen in the youthful heart with the same languor as did the pale moon that rose, entirely red, and then higher above the city bore its pale yellow sadness . . .

So it was time to go to an accounting, was it – and what was he to account for?

At that moment the sun looked in through the windows, the bright sun cast there from on high its sword-like rays: the golden, thousand-armed Titan of old furiously hung a curtain over the void, illumining spires and roofs and streams and stones and pressing its divine sclerotic forehead against the window-pane; the golden, thousand-armed Titan mutely complained about its loneliness out there: 'Come here, to me – to the good old sun!'

But the sun seemed to him like a most enormous thousand-legged tarantula, attacking the earth with insane passion . . .

And involuntarily Nikolai Apollonovich screwed up his eyes, because everything flared: the lampshade flared; the lamp glass was scattered with amethysts; sparks flashed on the wing of a golden cupid (below the mirror's surface a cupid thrust its heavy flame into the roses of a wreath); the surface of the mirrors flared up – yes: a mirror had cracked.

Superstitious people would have said:

'A bad omen, a bad omen . . .'

Just then, amidst all the gold and brilliance, a dim outline rose behind Ableukhov's back; over all this, as mute as a sunbeam, ran a distinct muttering:

'And what are . . . we . . .'

Nikolai Apollonovich raised his countenance . . .

'What are we . . . to do about the *barynya*?'

And caught sight of Semyonych.

He had completely forgotten about his mother's return; and she, his mother, had returned; with her had returned the old days – with their ceremoniousness and scenes, with his childhood and his twelve governesses, each of whom was a nightmare personified.

'Yes . . . I really don't know . . .'

Before him Semyonych worriedly chewed his old lips.

'Ought I to inform the master?'

'Does Papa not know?'

'I haven't dared . . .'

'Then go and tell him . . .'

'Yes, I'll go . . . I'll tell him . . .'

And Semyonych went into the corridor.

The old days had returned: no, the old days would not return; if the old days did return, they would look different. And the old days looked at him – horribly!

All, all, all of it: this gleaming of sunlight, the walls, the body, the soul – it would all collapse into ruins; all, all would collapse, collapse; and there would be: blind delirium, bottomlessness, bomb.

A bomb is a swift expansion of gases . . . The roundness of the expansion of the gases evoked in him a certain absurdity he had forgotten, and a sigh helplessly escaped from his lungs into the air.

In his childhood Kolenka had suffered from delirium; at nights a small elastic ball would sometimes begin to bounce in front of him, made perhaps of rubber, perhaps of the matter of very strange worlds; the elastic ball, as it touched the floor, made a quiet, lacquered sound on the floor: pépp-peppép; and again: pépp-peppép. Suddenly the ball, swelling up horribly, would assume the perfect semblance of a sphere-shaped fat gentleman; and the fat gentleman, having become an agonizing sphere, kept getting bigger and bigger and bigger and threatened to fall on top of him and burst.

And as he grew distended, becoming an agonizing sphere that was about to burst, he bounced, turned crimson, flew closer, making a quiet, lacquered sound on the floor:

'Pépp . . .'

'Péppovich . . .'

'Pépp . . .'

And he would burst into pieces.

And Nikolenka, altogether in delirium, would proceed to shriek idle, nonsensical things – always about one and the same: that he too was becoming round, that he too was a round zero; everything in him was being zeroed – ze-eroed – ze-e-e-r . . .

And his governess, Karolina Karlovna,[10] in her white night shift, with devilish curl-papers in her hair, which had assumed a tinge of the horrible thing that had just happened to him – a Baltic German woman who had leapt from her feather bed at the sound of his shrieks – Karolina Karlovna looked at him angrily out of the yellow circle of the candle, and the circle – got bigger and bigger and bigger. And Karolina Karlovna would repeat many times:

'Calm down, little Kolenka: it is growth . . .'

She did not look, but turned into a *karlitsa*, a dwarf; and it was not growth, but distension: distended, bulged, burst: –

Pépp Péppovich Pépp . . .

'What, am I delirious?'

Nikolai Apollonovich put his cold fingers to his forehead: there was going to be – blind delirium, bottomlessness, bomb.

And in the window, through the window – from far, far away, where the banks cowered down, where the cold buildings of the islands squatted in obedience, gleaming mutely, sharply, tormentingly, mercilessly, the spire of Peter and Paul poked into the high sky.

Along the corridor passed Semyonych's steps. There was no point in delaying: his parent, Apollon Apollonovich, was waiting for him.

Packets of Pencils

The senator's study was exceedingly unpretentious; in the centre, of course, towered the writing desk; but this was not the main thing; incomparably more important here was the following: bookcases ran along the walls; on the right, cases numbers one, three and five; on the left, numbers two, four and six; their shelves bent under books that were arranged according to plan; in the centre of the desk lay a textbook on 'Planimetry'.

Before retiring for the night, Apollon Apollonovich usually spent time turning the pages of this little book in order to calm the recalcitrant life within his head for sleep, in the contemplation of most blissful outlines: parallelepipeds, parallelograms, cones, cubes and pyramids.

Apollon Apollonovich lowered himself into the black armchair; the chair's leather-upholstered back would have tempted anyone to lean back in it, all the more so on such a sleepless, trying morning. Apollon Apollonovich Ableukhov was stiffly prim with himself; and on this trying morning he sat completely erect at the writing desk, waiting for his good-for-nothing son to appear. As he waited for his son, he pulled out a little drawer; there under the letter r he took out a small diary, marked 'Observations'; and there, in the 'Observations', he began to write down his thoughts, which had been schooled by experience. The quill squeaked: 'A man of state is distinguished by humanism . . . A man of state . . .'

An observation began with a fair copy; but as he made his fair copy he was interrupted; a frightened sigh was heard behind his back; Apollon Apollonovich permitted himself a powerful application of pressure, turned (the quill had broken), and saw Semyonych.

'*Barin*, your excellency . . . I make so bold as to inform you (it slipped my memory earlier) . . .'

'What is it?'

'Well, it's – e-e-er . . . How to tell you, I don't know . . .'

'Ah – indeed, sir, indeed, sir . . .'

Apollon Apollonovich's whole torso was cut out, presenting to the eye of the outward observer a most absolute combination of lines: grey, white and black; and resembled an etching.

'Well, you see, sir: our *barynya*, sir – I make so bold as to inform you – Anna Petrovna, sir . . .'

Apollon Apollonovich suddenly turned angrily towards the lackey his enormous ear . . .

'What is it? Eh-h? . . . Speak louder, I can't hear.'

The trembling Semyonych bent right down to the pale green ear that was staring at him expectantly:

'The *barynya* . . . Anna Petrovna, sir . . . Has come back . . .'

'? . . .'

'From Shpain . . . to Petersburg . . .'

. . . .

'Indeed, sir, indeed, sir; very good, sir . . .'

. . . .

'She's sent a letter by messenger, sir . . .

'She's staying at a hotel . . .

'No sooner had it pleased your excellency to go out, sir, than a messenger came, sir, with a letter, sir . . .

'Well, I put the letter on the table, and gave the messenger – twenty copecks . . .

'Not an hour had passed, when suddenly: I heard this – ring at the door . . .'

. . . .

Apollon Apollonovich, arm placed upon arm, sat in absolute impassivity, without movement; he seemed to be sitting without thought: indifferently his gaze fell on the spines of the books; from the spine of one book gleamed the imposing inscription: *Code of Russian Law: Volume One*. And next to it: *Volume Two*. On the desk lay packets of documents, an inkwell gleamed golden, one noticed pens and quills; on the desk stood a heavy paperweight in the form of a small pedestal on which a silver muzhik (a loyal one) was raising a communal winebowl in a toast of health. Apollon Apollonovich, his arms folded, sat facing the pens and the packets of documents without a movement, without a quiver . . .

. . . .

'I opened the door, your excellency: . . . I saw: a *barynya* I didn't know, a respectable *barynya* . . .

'I said to her: "How can I oblige you?" And she said to me: "Mitry Semyonych . . ."

'And I fell on her dear hand: "Little mother," I said, "Anna Petrovna . . ."

'She looked, and she was in tears . . .

'She said: "I wanted to see how you've managed without me . . ."'

. . . .

Apollon Apollonovich made no reply, but again pulled out a drawer, extracted a dozen pencils (very, very cheap ones), took a couple of them in his fingers – and the pencil stems snapped in the senator's fingers. Apollon Apollonovich sometimes expressed his mental torment by this method: the breaking of packets of pencils, which were kept for this eventuality in a drawer marked with the letter b.

'Very well . . . You may go . . .'

. . . .

But, as he snapped his packets of pencils, he still managed to preserve a look of indifference: and no one, no one would have said that the stiff, prim *barin*, not long before this moment, out of breath and very nearly weeping, had escorted the cook's daughter through the slush; no one, no one would have said that the enormous protuberance of his forehead had so recently concealed a desire to sweep away the rebellious crowds, which girded the earth as by a chain, with an iron prospect.

And when Semyonych went away, Apollon Apollonovich, throwing the fragments of pencil into the wastepaper basket, leaned his head right back against the back of the black armchair: the little old face grew younger; quickly he began to straighten his necktie; quickly he leapt up and began to scuttle about, circulating from corner to corner: small in stature and somehow overactive, Apollon Apollonovich would have reminded anyone of his son: even more did he resemble a photographic snapshot of Nikolai Apollonovich that had been taken in 1904.

Just then, crash upon crash resounded from some distant chamber – or plain ordinary rooms; starting from somewhere in the distance, the crashes came nearer; as though someone were coming there, metallic, terrible; and then there was a crash that shattered everything. Apollon Apollonovich involuntarily stopped in his tracks, and was about to run to the door, to lock his study, but . . . reflected, and remained where he was, because the crash that had shattered everything turned out to be the sound of a banging door (the sound came from the drawing-room); ineffably and tormentingly, someone came towards the door with loud coughing and an unnatural shuffling of slippers: the terrible days of old, like a cry advancing on us from out of the depths, suddenly lodged themselves in his memory with the sounds of the ancient song to whose strains Apollon Apollonovich had first fallen in love with Anna Petrovna:

'Aa-ba-a-ate un-re-est of the paa-aassions . . .'

'Fall asle-e-eep . . . thou ho-ope-less he-e-art . . .'

But why, and what did it mean?

The door opened: on its threshold stood Nikolai Apollonovich, in uniform, even wearing a sword (thus had he been dressed at the ball, only now he had removed his domino cape), but in slippers and a brightly coloured Tartar skullcap.

'Here I am, Papa . . .'

The bald head turned towards its son; as he searched for the appropriate phrase, he began to snap his fingers:

'Look, Kolenka.' Instead of talking about the domino (was this any time for dominoes?) he began to talk about another circumstance: the circumstance that had just compelled him to have recourse to the tied-up packet of pencils.

'Look, Kolenka: until now I have not shared with you a piece of news that you have doubtless heard, *mon ami* . . . Your mother, Anna Petrovna, has returned . . .'

Nikolai Apollonovich gave a sigh of relief and thought: 'So that's it,' but pretended to be disturbed:

'Of course, of course: I – know . . .'

Indeed: now for the first time Nikolai Apollonovich clearly realized that his mother had returned; but, having realized this, he set about his old custom: the contemplation of the sunken chest, the neck, the ears, the fingers and the chin of the old man who ran before him . . . Those little hands, that little neck (there was something crayfish-like about it)! The frightened, embarrassed look and the quite maidenly bashfulness with which the old man . . .

'Anna Petrovna, *mon ami*, has committed an action that . . . that . . . I find, so to speak, hard . . . hard, Kolenka, to class-i-fy with sufficient composure . . .'

Something in the corner began to rustle: there a mouse had begun to tremble and hide – and it gave a squeak.

'In a word, this action is, I hope, known to you; I have refrained from discussing this action with you until now – as you will have noticed – out of regard for your natural feelings . . .'

Natural feelings! These feelings were by any standards unnatural . . .

'For your natural feelings . . .'

'Yes, thank you, Papa: I understand you . . .'

'Of course,' – Apollon Apollonovich thrust two fingers into his waistcoat pocket and again began to scuttle to and fro in a diagonal (from corner to corner). 'Of course: your mother's return to Petersburg is an unexpected event for you.'

(Apollon Apollonovich let his gaze rest on his son, raising himself slightly on tiptoe.)

'A completely . . .'

'Unexpected event for all of us . . .'

'Who could have thought that Mamma would return . . .'

'That is what I say, too: who could have thought it?' – Apollon Apollonovich threw up his hands in bewilderment, shrugged his shoulders and exchanged bows with the floor – 'that Anna Petrovna would return . . .' And went scuttling off again: 'This completely unexpected event may end, as you have every reason to suppose, in a change' (Apollon Apollonovich raised his finger meaningfully, thundering to the whole room in a bass voice, as though he were delivering an important speech to the whole room) 'in our domestic status quo, or else' (he turned) 'everything will remain as it was before.'

'Yes, that is what I suppose . . .'

'In the first case – you are welcome!'

Apollon Apollonovich bowed to the door.

'In the second case' – Apollon Apollonovich began to blink bewilderedly – 'you will see her, of course, but I . . . I . . . I . . .'

And Apollon Apollonovich raised his eyes to his son; his eyes were melancholy: the eyes of a trembling doe brought to bay.

'Truly, Kolenka, I do not know: but I think . . . As a matter of fact, this is so hard to explain to you, when one takes into account the naturalness of the feeling that . . .'

The gaze with which the senator turned towards him began to make Nikolai Apollonovich tremble, and it was a strange thing: he felt a sudden rush – can you imagine of what? Of love? Yes, of love for this old despot who was doomed to be blown to pieces.

Under the influence of this emotion he darted towards his father:

another moment, and he would have fallen to his knees before him, in order to confess and to beg for mercy; but at the sight of his son's movement towards him, the old man again compressed his lips, ran away to the side and began to wave his little hands in fastidious disgust:

'No, no, no! Please stop it! . . . Yes, sir, I know what you want . . . You have heard me, now please try to leave me in peace.'

Two fingers drummed commandingly on the desk; the hand was raised and pointed to the door:

'You, dear sir, are trying to lead me by the nose; you, dear sir, are no son of mine; you are the most dreadful scoundrel.'

All this Apollon Apollonovich did not say, but shouted; these words burst out unexpectedly. Nikolai Apollonovich did not remember how he leapt out into the corridor with his old sense of nausea and flow of repulsive thoughts: those fingers, that neck and those two protruding ears would become blood-red slush.

Pépp Péppovich Pépp

Nikolai Apollonovich very nearly struck his forehead against the door of his room; and then the electric light clicked on (why? the sun, the sun was looking in the windows there!); overturning a chair as he went, he rushed over to the desk:

'Ai, ai, ai . . . Where is the key?'

'?'

'¡'

'Ah! . . .

'Right, here it is, sir! . . .

'Very good, sir . . .'

Like Apollon Apollonovich, Nikolai Apollonovich was in the habit of talking to himself.

And – yes: he was in a hurry . . . He pulled out the drawer, but the drawer would not obey; he threw packets of tied-up letters out of the drawer on to the desk; there proved to be a large cabinet photograph under the packets; his gaze fleeted over the photograph; and from there a charming little lady cast her answering gaze: she looked with a teasing smile – the cabinet photograph flew to one side; under the photograph lay the little bundle; with affected indifference he weighed it in his hand: there was something rather heavy in it; he rapidly put it down.

Nikolai Apollonovich quickly began to undo the knots of the napkin, pulling at an embroidered end that depicted a pheasant; the short – and rather overactive – Nikolai Apollonovich now resembled the senator: even more did he resemble a photographic snapshot that had been taken of the senator in 1860.

But why was he fussing so? Calm, oh, he must be more calm! Even so, his trembling fingers could not undo the knot; and in any case there was no point in undoing it: all was now clear. Nevertheless, he untied the little bundle; his amazement knew no bounds.

'A bonbonnière . . .

'Ah! . . .

'A ribbon! . . .

'How do you like that?'

Like Apollon Apollonovich, Nikolai Apollonovich was in the habit of talking to himself.

But when he tore off the ribbon, his hopes were crushed (he had had some sort of hope), because inside it – inside the bonbonnière, under the pink ribbon – instead of sweet confectioneries from Ballet's there was a plain ordinary tin; the lid of the tin burned his finger with a most unpleasant chill.

At this point, in passing, he noticed a timing mechanism that was affixed to the side: one had to turn a small metal key to make a sharp black arrow point to the scheduled time. Nikolai Apollonovich dully felt a certainty rise up in his consciousness, one that must inevitably prove his wretchedness and weakness: he felt that he would never be able to turn that key, for there was no means of stopping the mechanism once it had been set in motion. And in order to cut off all further retreat right there and then, Nikolai Apollonovich at once embraced the small metal key between his fingers; whether it was because his fingers trembled, or because Nikolai Apollonovich feeling dizzy, had plunged into the very abyss that he had wanted to avoid with all his heart and soul – the key slowly turned to one o'clock, then to two o'clock, and Nikolai Apollonovich . . . made an involuntary *entrechat*: flew off somewhere to the side; having flown off somewhere to the side, he squinted back at the desk again: the little tin box continued to lie on the desk; it was a sardine tin, with oily sardines (he had once eaten too many sardines and had never touched them since); a sardine tin, like any other sardine tin: shiny, with rounded corners . . .

No – no – no!

Not a sardine tin, but a sardine tin with dreadful contents!

The metal key had already turned to two o'clock, and the peculiar life that lay, inaccessible to the mind, within the sardine tin, had already flared into action; and although the sardine tin was still the same, it was not the same; in there were certainly crawling: the hour and minute hands; the bustling second hand was racing around the perimeter until the moment (that moment was now not far away) – until the moment, until the moment when . . .

> – the sardine tin's dreadful contents would suddenly swell up outrageously; would rush and expand without measure; and then, and then the sardine tin would fly into pieces . . .
>> – streams of the dreadful contents would rather nimbly spread in circles, tearing the desk to pieces with a crash: something would burst inside him, smack, and his body would also be torn to pieces; together with the splinters, together with the gas that sprayed in all directions it would be splattered like loathsome blood-red slush on the cold stones of the walls . . . –
> – it would all take place in a hundredth of a second: in a hundredth of a second the walls would collapse, and the dreadful contents, growing bigger, bigger and bigger, would trail down the dim sky with splinters, blood and stone.

Into the dim sky shaggy puffs of smoke would swiftly unfurl, letting down their tails on to the Neva.

What had he done, what had he done?

For the little box still stood on the table; now that he had turned the key, he must at once take that little box and put it in a suitable place (for example – in the small white bedroom, under the pillow);

or at once crush it under his heel. But to hide it in a suitable place, under his father's plumped-up pillow, so that the old, bald head, wearied by what had just taken place, would fall on the bomb with a bump – no, no, no: of that he was not capable; that was treachery.

Crush it under his heel?

But at this thought he experienced something that made his ears positively twitch: he felt such a vast sense of nausea (from the seven glasses of vodka he had drunk) that it was as if he had swallowed the bomb, like a pill; and now something distended in the pit of his stomach: it was perhaps made of rubber, perhaps of the matter of very strange worlds . . .

Never would he crush it, never.

It remained to throw it into the Neva, but there was time for that: he only had to turn the small key twenty times more; and *meanwhile* it was all postponed; now that he had turned the key, he must immediately extend that *meanwhile*; but he lingered, sinking into the armchair in complete helplessness; the nausea, coupled with a strange weakness and drowsiness, overwhelmed him dreadfully; and the weakened idea freeing itself from his body, kept drawing for Nikolai Apollonovich some kind of wretched, idle, helpless arabesques . . . immersing itself in drowsiness.

. . . .

Nikolai Apollonovich was an enlightened man; Nikolai Apollonovich had not devoted the best years of his life to philosophy in vain; his prejudices had long ago fallen away from him, and Nikolai Apollonovich found soothsaying and all kinds of miracles foreign to him; soothsaying and miracles were a cause of obscurantism (why was he thinking about irrelevant matters, when he ought to be *thinking about this* . . . *What* was he to think about? Nikolai Apollonovich made an effort to rise out of his drowsiness; and was unable to do so) . . . were a cause of obscurantism . . . all kinds of miracles . . . the concept of the source of perfection; for the philosopher, the source of perfection was Thought; God, in a manner of speaking, or Perfect Law . . . And the law-makers of the great religions expressed their laws in figurative form; Nikolai Apollonovich, in a manner of speaking, respected the law-makers of the great religions, without, of course, believing in their divine essence.

Yes: why was he thinking about religion? Was there any time to think ... After all, it had happened: so quickly ... What had happened? ... Nikolai Apollonovich's final attempt to rise out of his drowsiness was not crowned with success; he remembered nothing; everything seemed peaceful ... to the point of ordinariness, and his weakened thought, freeing itself from his body, kept senselessly drawing some kind of wretched, idle, helpless arabesques.

Nikolai Apollonovich particularly respected the Buddha, in the belief that Buddhism had superseded all other religions in both the psychological and the theoretical regard; in the psychological regard, teaching a love even for animals; and in the theoretical: having developed its logic through the loving agency of Tibetan lamas. Yes: Nikolai Apollonovich remembered that he had once read the logic of Dharmakirti with a commentary by Dharmottara[11] ...

This was in the first place.

In the second place: in the second place (let us observe for our own part), Nikolai Apollonovich Ableukhov was a man of instinct (not Nikolai Apollonovich number one, but Nikolai Apollonovich number two); from time to time, between the two doors of the entrance porch, he (like Apollon Apollonovich) was assailed by a certain strange, very strange, exceedingly strange condition: as though everything that lay beyond the door was not what it was, but something else: just what, Nikolai Apollonovich could not have said. Imagine merely that beyond the door there was nothing, and that if one were to fling the door wide open, then the door would open on an empty, cosmic immensity, into which all that was left was for one to ... throw oneself headfirst, in order to fly, fly and fly – and having flown somewhere, perceive that the immensity was the sky and the stars – the same sky and stars that we see above us, and in seeing do not see. It remained for one to fly there, past strangely immobile, now untwinkling stars and crimson planetary spheres – in absolute zero, in an atmosphere of two hundred and seventy-three degrees of cold. That was what Nikolai Apollonovich experienced now.

A strange, very strange condition of semi-sleep.

The Last Judgement

Such was the condition in which he sat facing the sardine tin: seeing, but not seeing; hearing, but not hearing; as though, at that lifeless moment when this weary body crashed into the armchair's black embrace, this spirit crashed straight from the parquet tiles of the floor into some kind of lifeless sea, an absolute zero degrees; and seeing, did not see; no, saw. When his weary head inclined soundlessly on to the table (and the sardine tin), looking at him through the open door to the corridor was the strange, bottomless thing that Nikolai Apollonovich had tried to throw off, passing to an everyday task: a remote astral journey, or sleep (which, we shall observe, is the same thing); and the open door continued to yawn amidst the everyday, opening in the everyday its un-everyday depth: cosmic immensity.

To Nikolai Apollonovich it seemed that from the door, standing in immensity, someone was looking at him, that some head was thrust through from out there (one had only to look at it and it vanished): the head of some *god* (Nikolai Apollonovich would have classified this head as the head of a wooden idol of the kind that one encounters even today among the peoples of the north-east who have inhabited the dim tundras of Russia from time immemorial). After all, it was precisely gods such as these to which, perhaps, in ancient times his Kirghiz–Kaisak ancestors had prayed; those Kirghiz–Kaisak ancestors had, according to legend, had dealings with the Tibetan lamas; they swarmed pretty massively in the blood of the Ab-Lai-Ukhovs. Was that not the reason why Nikolai Apollonovich had experienced a tenderness towards Buddhism? Here heredity was at work; heredity flowed into his consciousness; in his sclerotic veins heredity throbbed in millions of yellow blood corpuscles. And now, when the open door showed Ableukhov immensity, he treated this highly strange circumstance with due indifference (after all, this had already happened): and lowered his head into his hands.

Another moment – and he would have calmly embarked upon his usual astral journey, unfurling from his mortal shell a misty, cosmic tail, permeating through the walls into the limitless, but the dream was interrupted: ineffably, tormentingly, silently, someone was coming towards the door, churning up winds of non-existence: the terrible old days, like the advancing howl of a moving taxi, suddenly gathered strength in the sounds of an old song.

Nikolai Apollonovich sooner guessed than recognized that song:

'Aa-ba-a-ate . . . un-re-est of the paa-aassions . . .'

And not long before, the machine had roared:

'Fall asle-e-eep . . . thou ho-ope– . . .'

'Aaah' came a roar from the doorway: the horn of a gramophone? the horn of a taxi? No: in the doorway stood an ancient, ancient head.

Nikolai Apollonovich leapt to his feet.

An ancient, ancient head: Confucius or Buddha? No, the person who was looking in through the door was probably his great-great-grandfather, Ab-Lai.

The brightly-coloured, iridescent silk robe muttered and whispered; for some reason Nikolai Apollonovich was reminded of his own Bokharan robe, which had iridescent peacock feathers on it . . . The brightly-coloured, iridescent silk robe, on which small, sharp-beaked, golden, winged dragons crawled over a misty, smoky-sapphire field (and into it); the five-tiered, pyramid-shaped head-dress with golden brims looked like a mitre; above the man's head a many-rayed aureole both shone and crackled: a wondrous sight, and one familiar to us all! In the centre of this aureole a wrinkled countenance parted its lips in a *Chronic* aspect,[12] the hallowed Mongol came into the brightly coloured room; and the breezes of millennia wafted in behind him.

For an initial moment Nikolai Apollonovich Ableukhov thought that Chronos had come to pay him a visit in the guise of his Mongol ancestor, Ab-Lai (that was what was concealed in him!); his gaze began to move restlessly: in the hands of the Stranger he sought the blade of the traditional scythe; but there was no scythe in his hands: in one yellowish hand, as fragrant as the first lily, there was only an oriental saucer with a small, sweet-smelling heap of pink Chinese apples: paradise apples.

Paradise was something that Nikolai Apollonovich rejected: paradise, or the garden (which, as he had seen, was the same thing) was incompatible in Nikolai Apollonovich's mind with the ideal of the higher good (let us not forget that Nikolai Apollonovich was a Kantian; more than that: a Cohenite); in this sense he was a Nirvanic person.

By Nirvana he meant – Nothing.

And Nikolai Apollonovich remembered: he – the old Turanian[13] – had been reincarnated a great number of times; had been incarnated today, too: in the blood and the flesh of a pillar of the nobility of the Russian Empire, in order to fulfil a certain ancient, secret purpose: to shake loose all the foundations; in the tainted Aryan blood the Ancient Dragon was to flare up and devour everything in flame; the ancient Orient was showering our time with a hail of invisible bombs. Nikolai Apollonovich – an old Turanian bomb – was now bursting with ecstasy, having seen his native land; on Nikolai Apollonovich's face there now appeared a forgotten, Mongolian expression; now he looked like a mandarin of the Middle Empire, enveloped in a frock-coat for his arrival in the West (after all, he was here with a single and most secret mission).

'Indeed, sir . . .

'Indeed, sir . . .

'Indeed, sir . . .

'Very good, sir!'

It was a strange thing: how he suddenly reminded him of his father!

Thus the ancient Turanian, choking with ecstasy, enveloped for a time in a mortal Aryan shell, rushed towards the stack of old exercise books in which the theses of a system of metaphysics he had devised were sketched; both in embarrassment and in joy did he grasp at the exercise books: all the exercise books formed themselves before him into one enormous cause – the cause to which his entire life was devoted (they had come to resemble the sum total of Apollon Apollonovich's deeds). The cause to which his life was devoted turned out to be not simply a cause of life: the continuous, enormous, Mongol cause could be glimpsed everywhere in the notes under all the headings and all the paragraphs: a great mission that had been entrusted to him before his birth: the mission of a destroyer.

This visitor, the hallowed Turanian, stood motionless: the darkness of his eyes, which were as dense as night, expanded; while his hands – his hands: rhythmically, melodically, smoothly they rose into the limitless heights; and his garments swished; their sound was like the trembling of passing wings; the smoky field of the background cleared, deepened and became a piece of distant sky, gazing through the torn air of this little study: that dark-sapphire crevice – how had it come to be in this bookcase-lined room? Into it flew the small dragons that were embroidered on the iridescent robe (indeed, the robe had become a crevice); in its depths small stars gleamed . . . And the olden days infused with the sky and the stars: and from there washed an indigo air, infused with stars.

Nikolai Apollonovich rushed towards the visitor – Turanian to Turanian (subordinate to superior) with a pile of exercise books in his hand:

'Paragraph One: Kant (proof that he, too, was a Turanian).

'Paragraph Two: value, conceived as no one and nothing.

'Paragraph Three: social relations based on value.

'Paragraph Four: the destruction of the Aryan world by a system of values.

'Conclusion: the ancient Mongol cause.'

But the Turanian replied:

'The task has not been understood: instead of Kant, it ought to be: The Prospect.

'Instead of value it should be numeration: by houses, floors and rooms, for time everlasting.

'Instead of a new order: the circulation of the citizens of The Prospect – regular, and in a straight line.

'Not Europe's destruction, but its unalterability . . .

'That is what the Mongol cause is . . .'

. . . .

To Nikolai Apollonovich it seemed that he was condemned; and the bundle of exercise books in his hands disintegrated into a small pile of ash; while the wrinkled countenance, horribly familiar, leaned right up against him: at this point he looked at an ear, and understood, understood everything: the old Turanian, who had once instructed him in all the precepts of wisdom, was Apollon

Apollonovich; it was against him that, having misunderstood science, he had raised his hand.

It was the Last Judgement.

. . . .

'But how can this be? But who is this?'
'Who is it? Your father . . .'
'But who is my father?'
'Saturn . . .'[14]
'But how is this possible?'
'Nothing is impossible! . . .'

. . . .

The Last Judgement commenced.

Here indeed were some kind of dreams from the past; here indeed the planetary cycles rushed in a wave of billions of years: there was no Earth, no Venus, no Mars, only three nebulous rays revolving around the Sun; a fourth had just burst, and enormous Jupiter was preparing to become a world; only ancient Saturn was raising, from its fiery centre, black waves of aeons: nebulae raced; and now with Saturn, his parent, Nikolai Apollonovich was thrown into immensity; and only distances flowed all around.

At the end of the Fourth Kingdom he was on the earth, the sword of Saturn hung suspended like an unfinished thunderstorm; the continent of Atlantis collapsed; Nikolai Apollonovich, an Atlantean, was a depraved monster (the earth would not support him – had sunk beneath the waves); after that he was in China: Apollon Apollonovich, the *bogdykhan*,[15] ordered Nikolai Apollonovich to slaughter many thousands (the order was carried out); and in comparatively recent times, when thousands of Tamerlane's horsemen descended on Rus, Nikolai Apollonovich had come galloping into this Rus on his swift horse of the steppes; after that was incarnated in the blood of a Russian nobleman; and resumed his old habits: and just as he had formerly slaughtered thousands there, now today did he want to tear and destroy: to throw a bomb at his father: to throw the bomb in the most swiftly passing interval of time. But his father was – Saturn, the circle of time made one turn, and closed; the Kingdom of Saturn returned (here his heart burst with sweetness).

The flow of time ceased to exist: for thousands of millions of years matter had ripened in the spirit; but he conceived a thirst to tear apart time itself; and now all was being destroyed.

'Father!'

'You wanted to blow me to pieces; and so all is being destroyed.'

'Not you, but . . .'

'Too late: birds, animals, people, history, the world – everything is tumbling down, collapsing on to Saturn . . .'

Everything was falling on to Saturn; the atmosphere outside the windows was growing darker, blacker, everything had reverted to its ancient, incandescent state, expanding without limit, bodies ceased to be bodies; everything was whirling backwards – whirling horribly.

'*Cela . . . tourne . . .*' Nikolai Apollonovich began to roar in the most complete horror, having now finally lost his body, but without having noticed it . . .

'No . . . *Sa . . . tourne . . .*'

· · · · · · · ·

Having lost his body, he none the less felt his body: a certain invisible centre, which had previously been both consciousness and 'I', turned out to possess a semblance of that previous, incinerated past; the premisses of Nikolai Apollonovich's logic were wrapped in bones; the syllogisms around these bones were suddenly wrapped in tough sinews; while the contents of logical activity were covered by both flesh and skin; thus Nikolai Apollonovich's 'I' again displayed a corporeal image, even though it was not a body; and in this *non-body* (the exploded 'I') an alien 'I' was revealed: this 'I' had come racing from Saturn and had returned to Saturn.

He sat facing his father (as he had been sitting earlier) – without a body, but in a body (there was a strange thing!): outside the windows of his study, in the most utter darkness, a loud muttering could be heard: 'tourne – tourne – tourne'.

The chronology of the years was running backwards.

'And what sort of chronology do we have anyway?'

But Saturn, Apollon Apollonovich, bursting into loud laughter, replied:

'None, Kolenka, none: our chronology, my dear boy, is zero . . .'

The dreadful contents of Nikolai Apollonovich's soul whirled restlessly (in the place where his heart ought to be), like a humming top: swelled up and expanded; and it seemed: the dreadful contents of his soul – a round zero – were turning into an agonizing sphere; it seemed: here was the logic – his bones would be blown to pieces.

It was the Last Judgement.

'Ai, ai, ai: what then is "I am"?'

'I am? Zero . . .'

'Well, and zero?'

'That, Kolenka, is a bomb . . .'

Nikolai Apollonovich realized that he was only a bomb; and he burst with a bang: from the place where Nikolai Apollonovich's likeness had just emerged from the armchair and where now some kind of wretched broken shell (like an eggshell) was visible, a lightning-bearing zigzag rushed, falling into the black waves of aeons . . .

· · · · · · · ·

At this point Nikolai Apollonovich woke up from his dream; with a tremble he realized that his head was resting on the sardine tin.

And leapt to his feet: a terrible dream . . . But what was it? He could not remember the dream; the nightmares of his childhood had returned: Pépp Péppovich Pépp, who swelled up from a little ball into a mighty colossus, had evidently decided to lie quiet for the time being – in the sardine tin; his old childish hallucinations were returning, because –

> – Pépp Péppovich Pépp, the little ball with dreadful contents, is quite simply a Party bomb: there it inaudibly chatters with its hands and second hand; Pépp Péppovich Pépp will grow bigger and bigger and bigger. And Pépp Péppovich Pépp is going to burst: everything is going to burst . . .

'What, am I delirious?'

In his head again with horrifying swiftness began to whirl: but what was he to do? There was quarter of an hour left: should he give the key another turn?

He had already turned the small key twenty times; and twenty times something had hoarsely croaked in there, inside the little tin: for a short time his old hallucinations had gone away, so that morning could be morning, and afternoon could be afternoon, evening could be evening; at the end of the coming night, however, no movement of a key would be able to postpone anything: something would happen that would make the walls collapse, and the purple-illumined heavens blow into pieces, mingling with splattered blood into a single dim, primordial darkness.

END OF THE FIFTH CHAPTER

CHAPTER THE SIXTH

in which the events of a rather grey little day are related

Behind him always the Bronze Horseman came
Galloping with heavy clatter.[1]

A. Pushkin

Once again the Thread of His Existence Was Found

It was a dim Petersburg morning.

Now let us return to Aleksandr Ivanovich; Aleksandr Ivanovich had woken up; Aleksandr Ivanovich half opened his stuck-together eyes: the events of the night fled – into the subconscious world; his nerves had come unstrung; the night for him was an event of gigantic proportions.

The transitional state between waking and sleep was throwing him somewhere: as though he were jumping out of the window from the fifth floor; his sensations were opening a howling breach for him in this world; he was flying into this breach, shooting through into a teeming world of which it is insufficient to say that within it substances similar to furies launched attacks: the very fabric of the world appeared to him as a fabric of furies.

Only when it was very nearly morning did Aleksandr Ivanovich begin to master this world; and then he landed in bliss; the awakening flung him rapidly down from there; he felt sorry about something, and as he did so his whole body both ached and throbbed.

In the first moment after his awakening he noticed that he was shaking with a most intense ague; all night he had tossed about: something must have happened . . . Only, what was it?

His delirious running through the misty prospects, or up and down the steps of a mysterious staircase, had lasted all the long night; or, more correctly, fever had done the running: through his veins; his memory was telling him something, but his memory was slipping away; and he was unable to connect anything with his memory.

It was all – fever.

Frightened in earnest now (in his loneliness Aleksandr Ivanovich was afraid of illnesses), he thought that it would do him no harm to stay at home.

With this thought he began to drift off into oblivion; and, as he did so, he thought:

'I ought to take some quinine.'

He fell asleep.

And waking up, added:

'And strong tea . . .'

And reflecting again, to this he added:

'With dried raspberries . . .'

He thought about the fact that he had passed all these recent days with a thoughtlessness that was impermissible in his situation; this thoughtlessness seemed all the more shameful to him because days of enormous and heavy import were approaching.

In spite of himself, he sighed.

'And I ought also to – strictly stay off the vodka . . . Not read the Revelations . . . Not go down and see the yardkeeper . . . And also those talks I've been having with Styopka who lives at the yardkeeper's: I shouldn't talk to Styopka . . .'

At first these thoughts of raspberry tea, vodka, Styopka and the Revelations of St John calmed him, reducing the events of the night to the most utter nonsense.

But, having washed in icy cold water from the tap with the help of a wretched scrap of soap and a yellow soapy slush, Aleksandr Ivanovich again felt an onrush of nonsense.

He cast his gaze around his twenty-five rouble room (an attic lodging).

What a miserable abode it was!

The principal adornment of the miserable abode was the bed; the bed consisted of four cracked boards, put together any old how on a wooden trestle; conspicuous on the cracked surface of this trestle were nasty dried, dark red spots, which had probably been made by bedbugs, since Aleksandr Ivanovich had been stubbornly struggling with these dark red spots for many months with the aid of insect powder.[2]

The trestle was covered by a thin little mattress stuffed with bast; on top of the mattress, over one single dirty sheet, Aleksandr Ivanovich had carefully thrown a small knitted blanket which could hardly have been called striped: the meagre hints here of some blue and red stripes that had once existed were covered by deposits of grey, which had, however, appeared in all probability not as a result of dirt, but of many years of active use; with this gift from someone (his mother, perhaps) Aleksandr Ivanovich was still somehow loath to part; he was, perhaps, loath to part with it because of an absence of means (it had even been with him to the Yakutsk region and back).

In addition to the bed ... yes: here I must say: above the bed hung a small icon depicting Serafim of Sarov's[3] thousand nights of prayer amidst the pine trees, on a stone (here I must say – Aleksandr Ivanovich wore a small silver cross under his shirt).

In addition to the bed one could observe a small, smoothly planed table that was deprived of all ornament: tables precisely such as this figure in the aspect of stands for wash-bowls – in cheap country dachas; tables precisely such as this are sold everywhere at markets on Sundays; this table served Aleksandr Ivanovich in his abode at once as a writing desk and as a bedside table; while the wash-bowl was altogether absent; in performing his toilet Aleksandr Ivanovich took advantage of the services of a water tap, a sink and a sardine tin that contained a scrap of Kazan soap floating in its own slime; there was also a clothes-rack: with trousers; the tip of a worn-down shoe gazed out from under the bed with its perforated toe (Aleksandr Ivanovich had dreamed that this perforated shoe was a living creature: a domestic creature, perhaps, like a dog or a cat; it shuffled around independently, creeping about the room and rustling in the corners; when Aleksandr Ivanovich was about to feed it a piece of white bread he had chewed in his mouth, the shuffling creature had bitten him on the finger with its perforated opening, and then he had woken up).

There was also a brown suitcase that had long ago altered its original shape, and contained objects of the most dreadful contents.

All the furnishings of the room, if such it may be called, faded into the background before the colour of the wallpaper, unpleasant and brazen, neither quite dark yellow nor quite dark brown, showing enormous stains of damp: in the evenings a woodlouse crawled now over this stain, now over another. All the furnishings of the room were shrouded in bands of tobacco smoke. One had to smoke for at least twelve hours non-stop in order to turn the colourless atmosphere into a dark grey, dark blue one.

Aleksandr Ivanovich Dudkin surveyed his abode, and was again (as had previously happened) seized by a yearning to get out of the smoke-steeped room – away: yearned for the street, for the grimy fog, in order to adhere, to be glued, to be fused with shoulders, with backs, with greenish faces on a Petersburg prospect and to show his solid, enormous, grey face and shoulder.

Swarms of the October mists were greenly clinging to the window of his room; Aleksandr Ivanovich Dudkin felt an uncontainable desire to be permeated by the fog, to permeate his thoughts in it in order to drown in it the nonsense that chattered in his brain, to extinguish it by flashes of delirium that emerged in fiery spheres (the spheres later burst), extinguish it by means of a gymnastics of striding legs; he had to stride – to stride again, again and again; from prospect to prospect, from street to street; to stride until his brain grew completely numb, until he flopped down at the table of an eating-house and scorched himself inside with vodka. Only in this aimless wandering through the streets and crooked lanes – under the street lamps, the fences, the chimneys – can the thoughts that oppress the soul be extinguished.

As he put on his wretched little coat, Aleksandr Ivanovich felt his ague; and with melancholy he thought:

'Oh, now I could do with some quinine!'

But where would he get quinine . . .

And, as he went down the staircase, he again thought with melancholy:

'Oh, now I could do with some strong tea with dried raspberries! . . .'

The Staircase

The staircase!

Threatening, shadowy, damp – it had pitilessly echoed his shuffling step: threatening, shadowy, damp! That had been last night.

Here Aleksandr Ivanovich Dudkin for the first time remembered that he really had passed this way yesterday: it had *happened*. But what had happened?

What?

Yes: from every door – a disastrous silence was expanding at him; it enlarged without measure and kept forming some kind of rustlings; and without measure, without cease the unknown cretin there swallowed his own spittle with viscous distinctness (that had not been in a dream, either); there were terrible, unfamiliar sounds, all woven from the hollow groanings of the ages; from above, through the narrow windows, one could see – and he did see it – how the gloom there from time to time swept past, whipped up into ragged outlines, and how everything was illumined, when a pale, dim turquoise spread itself at his feet without a single sound, in order to lie untrembling and dead.

There – to there: there the moon was gazing.

But the swarms kept rushing: swarm after swarm – shaggy-maned, transparent and smoky, thunder-bringing – all the swarms hurled themselves at the moon: the pale, dim turquoise grew dark; from all sides shadow burst out, shadow kept covering everything.

Here for the first time Aleksandr Ivanovich Dudkin remembered how yesterday he had run up this staircase, exerting his last fading energies and without any hope (what hope?) of overcoming – what, precisely? While some kind of black outline (was this really real?) kept running for all it was worth – at his heels, on his track.

And was annihilating him irrevocably.

. . . .

The staircase!

On a grey weekday it is peaceful, everyday; down at the bottom a hollow banging reverberates: that is someone chopping cabbage – the tenant in flat number four has set up in the cabbage trade for the winter; on an ordinary day this is what it looks like – railings, doors, stairs; on the railings: a cat-smelling, half-torn, worn-through carpet – from flat number four; a floor-polisher with a swollen cheek was beating it with a carpet-beater; and some blonde hussy or other, sneezing into her apron from the dust, as she comes out of the door; between the floor-polisher and the hussy, of their own accord, words emerge:

'Oh!'

'Give us a hand, then, dearie . . .'

'Stepanida Markovna . . . What else have you brought out here . . .'

'All right, all right . . .'

'And what sort of . . .'

'Now it's "brought out here", and in there it's "having your tea" . . .'

'And what sort of – I say – work is it . . .'

'At the meeting you wouldn't loaf about: the work would go swimmingly . . .'

'Don't you say bad things about the meeting. You'll be grateful to them later on!'

'Then give this feather mattress a beating, oh, you – knight in armour!'

. . . .

The doors!

That one, there; and that one there . . . The oilcloth has been ripped off that one; the horsehair bulges shaggily out of the holes; while on this door a card has been fixed with a pin; and on it is written 'Zakatalkin' . . . Who Zakatalkin is, what his first name, what his patronymic, what profession he practises – I leave it to the curious to judge: 'Zakatalkin' – and that is all.

From behind the door the bow of a violin diligently saws out a familiar little tune. And a voice is heard:

'To the beloved fatherland . . .'

I suppose Zakatalkin is a violinist employed in service: a violinist from the little orchestra of some restaurant.

That is all that can be noticed from an observation of the doors . . . Yes – one more thing: in former years a tub was placed near the door, which gave off a rancid smell: for filling with water from the water cart: with the installation of water the water carts have gone out of use in the cities.

The stairs?

They are strewn with cucumber rinds, splashes of street dirt and eggshells . . .

And, Tearing Himself Free, Broke into a Run

Aleksandr Ivanovich Dudkin cast his gaze about the staircase, the floor-polisher and the hussy, who was trudging out of the doorway with another feather mattress; and − it was a strange thing: the everyday simplicity of this staircase did not dispel what had been experienced here the night before; and now, in broad daylight, amidst the stairs, the eggshells, the floor-polisher and the cat, which was devouring a chicken entrail on the window sill, to Aleksandr Ivanovich returned the sense of fear he had once experienced before: all that had happened to him during the past night really happened; and tonight what had really happened would return: he would return at night: the staircase would be shadowing and threatening; some kind of black outline would again dog his heels behind the door with the card that read 'Zakatalkin' there would again be the cretin's swallowing of spittle (perhaps − of spittle, but perhaps − of blood) . . .

And the familiar, impossible words would resound with utter distinctness:

'Yes, yes, yes . . . It is I . . . I annihilate irrevocably . . .'

Where had he heard that?

. . . .

Out of here! To the street! . . .

He must start striding again, keep striding, striding away: until his strength was completely exhausted, until his brain was completely numb and then flop down at the table of an eating-house, so that he should not dream of murky phantoms; and then resume his old activity: trudging through Petersburg, losing himself in the damp reeds, in the hanging mists of the seashore, to turn his back on everything in torpor and to regain consciousness amidst the damp lights of the Petersburg suburbs.

Aleksandr Ivanovich Dudkin was about to go trotting off down the many-staired stone staircase; but suddenly stopped; he had noticed that some strange fellow in a black Italian cloak and a similarly fantastically turned-down hat, striding three steps at a time, was hurtling towards him, his head bowed low, and desperately twirling a heavy cane in his hand.

His back was bent.

This strange fellow in the black Italian cloak flew at Aleksandr Ivanovich hurry-scurry; he very nearly poked him in the chest with his head; and when his head jerked back, Aleksandr Ivanovich Dudkin saw, right in front of his nose, the deathly pale and perspiring forehead of – imagine! – Nikolai Apollonovich: a forehead with a throbbing, swollen vein; only by this characteristic sign (the leaping vein) did Aleksandr Ivanovich recognize Ableukhov: not by his wildly squinting eyes, nor by his strange, foreign attire.

'Hello: I've – come to see you.'

Nikolai Apollonovich rapped out these words at great speed; and – what do you suppose? Did he rap them out in a threatening whisper? Oh, and how he was puffing and panting. Without even offering his hand, he swiftly pronounced – in a threatening whisper:

'I must observe to you, Aleksandr Ivanovich, that I *cannot do it*.'

'?'

'You do, of course, realize that I *cannot do it*: I *cannot*, and I *do not want* to do it; in a word – I *will not do it*.'

'!'

'This is a refusal: an irreversible refusal. You may communicate it to the proper quarters. And I ask you to leave me in peace . . .'

As Nikolai Apollonovich said this, his face displayed confusion, even, almost, alarm.

Nikolai Apollonovich turned; and, twirling his heavy cane, Nikolai Apollonovich rushed back down the stairs, as though he were rushing into flight.

'But wait, but wait,' Aleksandr Ivanovich Dudkin cried, hurrying after him and feeling beneath his feet the tremor of the staircase as it flew past.

'Nikolai Apollonovich?'

By the exit he caught Ableukhov by the sleeve, but the latter tore himself away. Nikolai Apollonovich turned towards Aleksandr Ivanovich; with a barely trembling hand Nikolai Apollonovich held on to the brim of his dashingly cocked hat; and, trying not appear afraid, blurted out in a semi-whisper:

'This is, so to speak . . . vile . . . Do you hear?'

He quickened his pace across the little courtyard.

Aleksandr Ivanovich snatched at the door for a moment; Aleksandr Ivanovich felt the most intense anxiety: an insult – for nothing, about nothing; for a second he hung back, wondering what he should do now; involuntarily he began to twitch; with an unconscious movement he exposed his most delicate neck; and then in two leaps caught up with the fugitive.

He seized hold of the black edge of the Italian cloak that was flying away from him; at this point, the cloak's owner began desperately to tear himself away; for an instant they began to wallow about among the stacked firewood and in the struggle something fell ringing on the asphalt. With raised cane, Nikolai Apollonovich jerkily, panting with anger, began to shout out loudly some impermissible and, above all, offensive nonsense of his own: offensive to Aleksandr Ivanovich.

'Is this what you call revolutionary action, Party work? Surrounding me with detectives . . . Dogging my heels everywhere I go . . . When you yourself have lost faith in everything . . . Read the Book of Revelation . . . While at the same time you shadow me . . . My dear sir, you . . . you . . . you . . .'

At last, tearing himself free, Nikolai Apollonovich Ableukhov broke into a run: they flew along the street.

The Street

The street!

How it has changed: how it, too, has been changed by these grim days!

Over there – those cast-iron bars of the fence of some little garden; the crimson leaves of the maples beat into the wind there, striking against the bars; but the crimson leaves have already blown away; and only the branches – dry skeletons – have stood out black there, grinding together.

It was September: the sky was light blue and cloudless; but now all that has changed: ever since morning, the sky has begun to fill with a flood of heavy tin: September is no more.

They were flying along the street.

'But wait, Nikolai Apollonovich,' the excited and greatly offended Dudkin kept on, 'you must agree that we can't possibly part now until we've had an explanation . . .'

'There's nothing more to talk about,' Nikolai Apollonovich snapped curtly from under his dashingly cocked hat.

'Explain yourself more clearly,' Aleksandr Ivanovich insisted in his turn.

Offence and anxious astonishment were displayed on his twitching features; the astonishment was, we shall say for our own part, on this occasion unfeigned, so unfeigned, indeed, that Nikolai Apollonovich Ableukhov could not but notice its unfeigned quality in spite of the distraction of his wrath.

He turned round and without his previous vehemence, but with a kind of tearful malice, began impetuously to jabber:

'No, no, no! . . . What more do we have to explain? . . . And do not dare to argue with me . . . I myself have a right to demand greater accountability . . . After all, it is I who am suffering, not you, not your comrade . . .'

'What? . . . But what do you mean?'

'To give me the bundle . . .'

'Well?'

'Without any warning, explanation or request . . .' Aleksandr Ivanovich flushed deeply all over.

'And then to disappear into thin air . . . To threaten me with the police through some middleman . . .'

At this undeserved accusation, Aleksandr Ivanovich nervously twitched towards Ableukhov:

'Stop: what police?'

'Yes, the police . . .'

'What police do you mean? . . . What abomination is this? . . . Which one of us is crazy?'

But Nikolai Apollonovich, whose tearful malice had again mounted into fury, whispered hoarsely in his ear:

'Oh, what I'd like to do to you,' his hoarse cry sounded (his mouth with its bared teeth seemed to smile: biting, it hurled itself at

Aleksandr Ivanovich's ear) . . . 'What I'd like to do to you is to . . . this very moment – in this very place: what I'd like to do to you is to . . . in broad daylight as an example to this public here, Aleksandr Ivanovich, my dearest fellow . . .' (he grew confused) . . .

Over there, there . . .

In that carved little window of that glossy little house on a summer evening into the sunset that same wretched little old woman kept chewing her lips ('What I'd like to do to you is to . . .' came drifting across to Aleksandr Ivanovich from somewhere far away); from August the little window had been closed and the old woman had disappeared; in September a brocade coffin had been carried outside; behind the coffin went a little group: a gentleman in a worn coat and a peaked cap with a cockade; with him – seven fair-haired little boys.

The coffin was nailed up.

('Yes, sir, Aleksandr Ivanovich, yes, sir,' came drifting across to Aleksandr Ivanovich from somewhere).

After that, peaked caps went darting into the house, and feet went shuffling up and down the staircase; it was said that behind those walls missiles were being manufactured; Aleksandr Ivanovich knew that the missile in question had been brought first to him in his garret – from that little house.

And at this he gave an involuntary shudder.

How strange: rudely returned to reality (he was a strange man: he thought about the little house at the very same time as Nikolai Apollonovich was hurling his phrases at him . . .) – well, it was like this: of the delirious ravings of the senator's dear son about the police, and about his decisive, irreversible refusal, Aleksandr Ivanovich understood only one thing:

'Listen,' he said. 'The little that I understand about what you are saying is – is just this: the whole question is in the little bundle . . .'

'I'm talking about *it*, of course: you gave *it* to me with your own hands for safe keeping.'

'It's strange . . .'

It was strange: the conversation was taking place *outside that very same little house* where the bomb had come from: while the bomb, becoming a mental bomb, was describing a true circle, so that this talk about the bomb had arisen in the place where the bomb had arisen.

'But please be more calm, Nikolai Apollonovich: I must confess I find your agitation incomprehensible ... Here you are, insulting me: what is it that you consider so blameworthy in that action of mine?'

'How do you mean?'

'Well, what's so ignoble about the Party' – these words he pronounced in a whisper – 'having asked you keep the bundle until the time? When you yourself agreed to it? And – that's all there is to it ... So that if you find it disagreeable to look after the little bundle at your place, it won't cost me anything to pop in and collect it ...'

'Oh, please drop that look of innocence; if it were only a matter of the bundle ...'

'Shh! Quiet: someone might hear us ...'

'If it were only the bundle, then ... I would understand you ... But that isn't the point; don't pretend you don't know anything about it ...'

'Then what is the point?'

'The coercion.'

'There's been no coercion ...'

'That you're subjecting me to an investigation by the organization ...'

'I repeat, there's been no coercion: you willingly agreed; and as for the investigation, then I ...'

'Yes, that was then – in the summer ...'

'What do you mean, in the summer?'

'In principle I agreed, or, more correctly, offered, and ... perhaps ... I did give a promise, supposing that there could be no compulsion here, just as there is no compulsion in the Party; but if you do use compulsion, then you are quite simply a little bunch of suspect intriguers ... Well, so what, then? ... I gave a promise, but I never thought that my promise could not be retracted ...'

'Wait ...'

'Don't interrupt me; I didn't know that they would interpret my offer in *that* way: that they would twist it like *that* ... And would propose that I do *that* ...'

'No, wait: I'm going to interrupt you all the same . . . You're talking about some promise? Please be more precise . . .'

At this point Aleksandr Ivanovich dimly remembered something (my goodness, how he had forgotten it all!)

'Yes, so it's *that* promise you mean? . . .'

He remembered how one day in the little eating-house the *person* had told him (the thought of this *person* made him experience an unpleasant something-or-the-other) – the *person*, Nikolai Stepanych Lippanchenko, in other words – well, so there it was: had told him that Nikolai Apollonovich – fie! . . . He did not want to remember! . . . and he quickly added:

'No, you see, I'm *not talking about that*, that's *not the point*.'

'How do you mean, *not the point*? The whole nub of the matter lies in my promise: in a promise that was interpreted irreversibly and *ignobly*.'

'Quiet, quiet, Nikolai Apollonovich, what in your opinion is ignoble here? Where is the ignoble action?'

'What do you mean?'

'Yes, yes, yes: where? The Party asked you to look after the bundle . . . That is all . . .'

'That's all, in your opinion?'

'Yes . . .'

'If it were a matter of the bundle, then I would understand you: but I'm sorry . . .' And he waved his arm.

'There's no point in us talking: don't you see that the whole of our conversation keeps treading around the same old subject: we're on a hiding to nothing, that's all . . .'

'Yes, I've noticed . . . Yet all the same: you keep on talking about some coercion or other, and now I've just remembered: I did hear rumours – back then, in the summer . . .'

'Well?'

'Rumours about an act of violence that you had proposed to us: and so it appears that this plan originated not with us, but with you!'

Aleksandr Ivanovich remembered (the *person* had told him everything that day in the little eating-house as he poured the liqueur): Nikolai Apollonovich Ableukhov had at that time proposed to them through some middleman that he do away with his father with his own hands; he remembered that the *person* had spoken that day with repugnant calm, adding, however, that the Party had one option left: to refuse the offer; the plan's unusual nature, the unnatural aspect of the choice of victim and the touch of cynicism, bordering on infamy – all this provoked in Aleksandr Ivanovich's sensitive heart an attack of violent loathing (Aleksandr Ivanovich had been drunk at the time; and so his entire conversation with Lippanchenko seemed later on like the mere play of an intoxicated brain, and not a sober reality); all this he remembered now:

'And I must confess . . .'

'To demand of me,' Ableukhov interrupted, 'that I . . . that I should . . . with my own hands . . .'

'Just so . . .'

'It is loathsome!'

'Yes – it's loathsome; and, so to speak, Nikolai Apollonovich, I never believed it at the time . . . If I had believed it, you would have fallen then . . . in the esteem of the Party . . .'

'So you too consider it a vile thing?'

'I'm sorry: yes I do . . .'

'There you are, you see! You yourself call *it* a vile thing; and yet you yourself must have put your hand to that *vile thing*?'

Something suddenly began to make Dudkin grow agitated: his most delicate neck twitched:

'Wait . . .'

And, clutching with a trembling hand at the buttons of the Italian cloak, he fairly drilled his eyes into some point that lay elsewhere:

'Don't get carried away: here we are reproaching each other, yet we both agree . . .' – with astonishment he transferred his eyes to Ableukhov's eyes – 'on the right name for this action . . . It is a vile thing, is it not?'

Nikolai Apollonovich gave a shudder.

They were silent for a moment . . .

'You see, we both agree . . .'

Nikolai Apollonovich, taking his handkerchief from his pocket, stopped and wiped his face.

'That surprises me . . .'

'And me . . .'

In bewilderment they looked each other in the eye. Aleksandr Ivanovich (he had now forgotten that he was shaken by fever) again stretched out his hand and touched a finger on the edge of the Italian cloak:

'In order to untie the whole of this knot, answer me this: this promise to . . . with your own hands (and so on) . . . This promise did not originate with you? . . .'

'No! No!'

'And so that means that you are not implicated in *such* a murder, not even in thought – I ask because the thought is sometimes expressed by chance in unconscious gestures, intonations, looks – even: in the trembling of lips . . .'

'No, no . . . that is . . .' Nikolai Apollonovich caught himself, caught himself up right there and then for catching himself out loud in the expression of some suspicious train of thought he had had; and, having caught himself up out loud, blushed; and – began to explain:

'That is, I have not loved my father . . . And I think I said so several times . . . But would I ever . . .? Never?'

'Very well, I believe you.'

At this point Nikolai Apollonovich, as ill luck would have it, blushed to the roots of his hair; and, having blushed, began to try to explain himself again, but Aleksandr Ivanovich decisively shook his head, not wishing to touch on a small, delicate nuance of incommunicable thought that had flashed to them both at the same time.

'Oh, don't . . . I believe you . . . That's not what I mean – I mean something else: look, I want you to tell me . . . Tell me now candidly: am I, perhaps, implicated?'

Nikolai Apollonovich looked at his naïve interlocutor with astonishment: looked, blushed, and with extreme passion, with a forced conviction that was necessary to him now in order to conceal some thought – he shouted:

'Yes, I think you are . . . You helped *him* . . .'

'Who?'

'The Unknown One . . .'

'?'

'And it was the *Unknown One* who demanded . . .'

'!'

'The enaction of a vile deed . . .'

'Where?'

'In a revolting note he wrote . . .'

'I know of no such person . . .'

'The Unknown One,' Nikolai Apollonovich insisted bewilderedly, 'is a comrade of yours in the Party . . . Why are you so surprised? What surprises you so much?'

. . . .

'I do assure you: we don't have any *Unknown One* in the Party . . .'

. . . .

Now it was Nikolai Apollonovich's turn to be surprised:

'What? There isn't any Unknown One in the Party? . . .'

'But please be more quiet . . . No . . .'

'I've been getting notes for three months now . . .'

'Who from?'

'Him . . .'

They both fell silent.

They had both begun to breathe heavily, and both fixed eyes on questioningly raised eyes; and to the degree that one bewilderedly lowered his head, in fear and horror, so did a shadow of faint hope gleam in the eyes of the other.

. . . .

'Nikolai Apollonovich' – an infinite sense of indignation, which had overcome his fear, spread over Aleksandr Ivanovich's pale cheekbones in two crimson spots – 'Nikolai Apollonovich!'

'Well?' the other said, gripping his arm.

But Aleksandr Ivanovich was still unable to recover his breath; at last he raised his eyes, and – well, there it was: something melancholy, the kind of thing that happens in dreams – something inexpressible, something that could be understood by anyone with no need of words, now suddenly wafted from his forehead, from his stiffening fingers.

'Well, well – stop tormenting me!'

But Aleksandr Ivanovich Dudkin, putting a finger to his lips, continued to shake his head and say nothing: something inexpressible, but able to be understood in dreams, flowed invisibly from him – from his forehead, from his stiffening fingers.

At last with effort he said:

'I assure you – I give you my word of honour: I have nothing to do with this murky episode . . .'

At first Nikolai Apollonovich did not believe him.

'What did you say? Say it again now, don't be silent: you must understand my position . . .'

'I have nothing to do with it . . .'

'Well, and so what does that mean?'

'I don't know . . .' And he added abruptly: 'No, no, no: it's a lie, it's a delirium, an abracadabra, a gibe . . .'

'How would I know? . . .'

Nikolai Apollonovich looked at Aleksandr Ivanovich with unseeing eyes; and then into the depths of the street: how the street had changed!

'How would I know? . . . That doesn't make me feel any better . . . I didn't sleep last night.'

The top of a carriage rushed swiftly into the depths of the street: how the street had changed – how these grim days had changed it!

The wind from the shore blew in gusts: the last leaves were scattered; there would be no more leaves until May; how many would there be in May? These fallen leaves were indeed the last leaves. Aleksandr Ivanovich knew it all by heart: there would be, there would be days full of blood and horror: and then everything would collapse; oh, whirl, oh, blow, last days that cannot be compared with anything that went before!

Oh, whirl, oh blow through the air, you – last leaves! Again an idle thought . . .

The Hand of Succour

'So *he* was at the ball?'

'Yes, *he* was . . .'

'He was talking with your father . . .'

'That's right: he also mentioned you . . .'

'He met you in a side-lane afterwards? . . .'
'And took me to a little restaurant.'
'And his name was? . . .'
'Morkovin . . .'
'Abracadabra!'

. . . .

When Aleksandr Ivanovich Dudkin, tearing himself away from the contemplation of the twining leaves, at last turned to reality, he realized that Nikolai Apollonovich, running ahead, was jabbering away with a liveliness uncharacteristic of him, to a point that was even extreme; he was gesticulating; with his profile inclined low, his mouth split apart by an unpleasant grin, he looked like a tragic, antique mask which did not combine with the swift agility of a lizard into one consonant whole: in a word, he looked like a grasshopper with a frozen face.

From time to time Aleksandr Ivanovich merely interjected comments:

'And did *he* talk about the secret police?'

'Yes, he tried to intimidate me with the secret police, too . . .'

'Asserting that such intimidation is in the plan of the Party and approved by the Party? . . .'

'Well, yes, he did . . .' Nikolai Apollonovich said with a certain irritation and, blushing, tried to inquire:

'But you yourself, I remember, said that day that the Party prejudices . . .'

'What did I say?' Dudkin flared up, sternly.

'I remember you said that the Party prejudices of the lower echelons were not shared by the upper echelons, which you serve . . .'

'Rubbish!' – and here Dudkin's whole torso twitched: and in agitation he kept increasing his pace.

Nikolai Apollonovich in his turn seized him by the arms with a shadow of faint hope, replying to the questions like a schoolboy, and smiling unnaturally. At last, snatching the moment again, he continued his effusions about the events of the night before: about the ball, about the mask, about the flight through the ballroom, about the sitting on the front step of the small black house, about the gateway, the note; and finally – about the filthy little eating-house.

It was genuine delirium.

The abracadabra had jumbled everything up; they had all long ago lost their minds, unless, that was, *that which annihilates irrevocably* existed in reality.

. . . .

From the street towards them rolled thick, black human masses: many-thousand swarms of bowler hats rose up like waves. From the street towards them rolled: lacquered top hats, they rose out of the waves like the funnels of steamships; from the street into their faces foamed: an ostrich feather; a pancake-shaped cap smiled with its cap-band; and the cap-bands were: blue, yellow, red.

From every side popped out the most importunate nose.

Noses flowed past in large numbers: the aquiline nose and the cockerel nose; the duck-like nose, the hen's nose; and so on, and so on . . .; the nose was turned to one side; or the nose was not at all turned: greenish, green, pale, white and red.

All this rolled towards them from the street: senselessly, hurriedly, abundantly.

Nikolai Apollonovich, pleading, and barely able to keep up with Dudkin, still seemed to be afraid to put into shape before him his fundamental question, which had arisen out of the discovery that the author of the dreadful note could not be the bearer of a Party directive; in this consisted now his principal thought: a thought of the most enormous importance – because of its practical conse-quences; this thought had now got stuck inside his head (their roles were changed: now it was Aleksandr Ivanovich, not Nikolai Apollon-ovich, who was desperately pushing away the bowler hats that were surrounding them).

'And so, that means, you suppose – and so, that means, in all this a mistake has crept in?'

Having made this timid approach to his thought, Nikolai Apollon-ovich felt handfuls of goose-pimples spreading over his body: well, but what if he were to present himself – he reflected – and – overcame his fear.

'The note, you mean?' said Aleksandr Ivanovich, raising his eyes suddenly; and tore himself away from a morose contemplation of the flowing abundance: of bowler hats, heads and moustaches.

'Well, of course: to call it a mistake is to put it too mildly . . . It's not a mistake, but a loathsome piece of charlatanry that has become involved in all this; the absurdity has been maintained in its completeness – with a deliberate aim: to arbitrarily interfere in the relation between people who are closely bound to each other, to confuse them; and in the Party's chaos wreck the Party's revolutionary action.'

'Well, help me, then . . .'

'An impermissible mockery,' Dudkin said, interrupting him, 'has been perpetrated – one made of gossip and phantoms.'

'But I implore you, please tell me what I ought to do . . .'

'And a betrayal has been perpetrated on everything: there is a whiff of something menacing, ominous here . . .'

'I don't know . . . I'm confused . . . I . . . didn't sleep last night . . .'

'And all of it is a phantom.'

Now Aleksandr Ivanovich Dudkin stretched out his hand to Ableukhov in a rush of sympathy; and here, in passing, noticed: Nikolai Apollonovich was significantly shorter than him (Nikolai Apollonovich was not distinguished by his stature).

'Now, now, please gather your composure . . .'

'Oh Lord! It's easy for you to say: *composure* – I didn't sleep last night . . . I don't know what to do now . . .'

'Sit and wait.'

'Will you come to see me?'

'I tell you – sit and wait: I will undertake to help you.'

He spoke with such confidence and conviction, inspiration, almost, that Ableukhov calmed down for a moment; but, to tell the truth, in his rush of fellow-feeling, Aleksandr Ivanovich had overestimated the degree of help he could provide . . . Indeed: how could he be of help? He was solitary, cut off from social intercourse; the conspiracy had blocked access to the very body of the Party for him; for Aleksandr Ivanovich had never been a member of the Committee, even though he had boasted to Ableukhov about the headquarters; if he were able to help, then he could only help by means of Lippanchenko; he could tell Lippanchenko, act through

Lippanchenko. Above all he would have to get hold of Lippanchenko. Before he did anything else he must calm this man who had been shaken to the depths of his soul, as quickly as possible.

And he calmed him:

'I am certain that I will be able to untangle the knots of this loathsome plot: and today, without delay, I shall make the proper inquiries, and . . .'

And – faltered: only Lippanchenko would be able to give him the proper information; there was no one else . . . What if he were not in Petersburg?

'And . . .?'

'And will give you an answer tomorrow.'

'Thank you, thank you, thank you.' And Nikolai Apollonovich rushed to shake his hand; at this Aleksandr Ivanovich was in spite of himself embarrassed (everything depended on where the *person* was and what information he had at his disposal).

'Oh, please don't: your case touches us all personally . . .'

But Nikolai Apollonovich, who until that moment had been in a state of the utmost horror, was only able to respond to each word of support either completely apathetically or – ecstatically.

And Nikolai Apollonovich responded ecstatically.

Meanwhile Nikolai Apollonovich had once again flown into the thought that was preoccupying Aleksandr Ivanovich; a certain little fact had struck him: Nikolai Apollonovich both vowed and swore that the dreadful commission proceeded from an unknown, anonymous person; the anonymous person had already written to Ableukhov several times; and it was clear: that unknown anonymous person was actually an *agent provocateur*.

What was more . . .

From Ableukhov's confused words one could nevertheless draw a conclusion; his special relations with the Party were at work here, and it was from those special relations that the whole sordid business was growing; Aleksandr Ivanovich made an effort to clarify yet one or two other things; and made the effort in vain: his thought fell like rain into the abundance that was flowing towards them – of moustaches, beards, chins.

Nevsky Prospect

Beards, moustaches, chins: that abundance was made of the upper extremities of human bodies.

Shoulders, shoulders, shoulders flowed past; all the shoulders formed a thick mass, as black as coal; all the shoulders formed a highly viscous and slowly flowing mass, and Aleksandr Ivanovich's shoulder adhered momentarily to the mass; so to speak, it stuck to it; and Aleksandr Ivanovich Dudkin followed his capricious shoulder, in keeping with the law of the body's indivisible wholeness; thus was he thrown on to Nevsky Prospect; there he sank into the blackly flowing mass like a grain of roe.

What is a grain of roe? It is both a world and an object of consumption; as an object of consumption the grain of roe does not have sufficient wholeness; such wholeness is represented by caviare: the sum total of grains of roe; the consumer is not aware of grains of roe; but he is aware of caviare, that is, of the mass of grains of roe that are spread on the sandwich that is served to him. Thus, in similar fashion, are the bodies of the individuals who fly along the paving of the Nevsky Prospect transformed into the organ of a common body, into grains of roe: the pavements of the Nevsky are the surface of a sandwich. The same thing happened to the body of Dudkin, who flew along here; the same thing happened to his stubborn thought: it instantly stuck to an alien thought, inaccessible to the mind, the thought of an enormous, many-legged creature that was running along the Nevsky.

They left the pavement; here many legs were running; and silently they stared in wonderment at the many legs of the dark, moving human mass: that mass, incidentally, did not flow, but crept: crept and shuffled – crept and shuffled on flowing legs; the mass was glued together from many thousands of little members; each little member was a body: the bodies moved on legs.

There were no people on Nevsky Prospect; but a creeping, wailing myriapod was there; into a single damp space multivarious voices were poured – a multivariety of words; articulate phrases broke there one against the other, and horribly there did the words fly apart like the shards of bottles that were empty and had all been broken in one single place: all of them, jumbled up together, again wove into a sentence that flew into infinity without end or beginning; this sentence seemed meaningless and woven from fantasies: the ceaseless flow of the sentence that was formed from meaninglessness hung above the Nevsky like black soot; above the expanse stood the black smoke of fantasies.

And with these fantasies, swelling out from time to time, the Neva roared and struggled between its massive walls of granite.

The creeping myriapod is horrible. Here, along the Nevsky, it has been moving for centuries. And higher up, above the Nevsky — there the seasons move: the springs, the autumns, the winters. The sequence there is variable; and here — the sequence of springs, summers, winters is unchanging; this sequence of springs, summers and winters is the same. And the periods of the seasons have, as is well known, their limits; and — period follows period; summer follows spring; autumn follows summer and moves into winter; and in the spring everything thaws. The human myriapod has no such limits; and nothing replaces it; its links change, but it remains entirely the same; somewhere out there, beyond the railway station, its head turns; its tail thrusts into Morskaya; and along the Nevsky shuffle the arthropodal links — without a head, without a tail, without consciousness, without thought; the myriapod creeps as it has crept; it will creep as it has crept.

Just like a scolopendra!

And the frightened metal horse rose up long ago over there on the corner of Anichkov Bridge;[4] and the metal groom has hung on it: will the groom saddle the horse, or will the horse injure the groom? This competition will last for years, and — beyond them, beyond!

And beyond them, beyond: ones, twos, threes and couple after couple — they blow their noses, cough, shuffle, laughing and maliciously gossiping, and they pour into the damp expanse with multivarious voices a multivariety of words that have been torn loose from the sense that gave them birth: bowler hats, feathers, service caps; service caps, cockades, feathers; tricorne, top hat, service cap; umbrella, shawl, feather.

Dionysus

But someone was talking to him!

Aleksandr Ivanovich Dudkin dragged his thought away from the moving tide of abundance; its flowing streams of nonsense polluted pretty well everything; after bathing in the mental collective, his thought also became nonsense; with difficulty he directed it towards the words that chattered into his ear: these words were Nikolai Apollonovich's; Nikolai Apollonovich had long been beating his ear with words; but the passing words, flying into his ears like splinters, shattered the sense of the phrases; that was why Aleksandr Ivanovich found it hard to understand what was being repeated over and over again into his eardrum; into his eardrum idly, long-windedly, tormentingly, the drumsticks beat out a fine tattoo: Nikolai Apollonovich, tearing himself out of the thick mass, went jabbering on without cease, swiftly.

'Do you understand,' Nikolai Apollonovich kept saying, 'do you understand me, Aleksandr Ivanovich . . .'

'Oh, yes, I understand . . .'

And Aleksandr Ivanovich tried to extract with his ear the phrases that were addressed to him: this was not so easy, because the passing words shattered against his ears like a hail of stones:

'Yes, I understand you . . .'

'There, inside the tin,' Nikolai Apollonovich kept saying, 'life must be stirring: the clock inside it has been ticking strangely . . .'

At this point Aleksandr Ivanovich thought:

'What tin, what tin is he talking about? And what has any tin got to do with me?'

But when he had listened more carefully to what the senator's son was repeating, he realized that it was the bomb he was talking about.

'Life must have stirred inside it when I set it in motion; it was all right, it was dead . . . I turned the key; even, yes: began to sob, I assure you, like a drunken body, half awake, when it's shaken out of slumber . . .'

'So you set it in motion?'

'Yes, it started ticking . . .'

'The hand?'

'For twenty-four hours.'

'Why did you do that?'

'I put it, the tin, on the desk and looked at it, looked and looked; my fingers reached out for it of their own accord; and – it just happened: my fingers somehow turned the key of their own accord . . .'

'What have you done?! Throw it into the river immediately!?!' – Aleksandr Ivanovich cried, throwing up his hands in unfeigned alarm; his neck twitched.

'Do you understand, it made a face at me? . . .'

'The tin?'

'As a matter of fact, I was seized by a very large number of constantly changing sensations as I stood over it: a very large number . . . Simply the devil knows what . . . I must confess I have never experienced anything like it in all my life . . . I was overcome by revulsion – and so much so that revulsion made me burst . . . All kinds of rubbish came crawling, and, I repeat – a terrible revulsion at *it*, the incredible, the incomprehensible: at the very shape of the tin, at the thought that sardines had, perhaps, once floated in it (I cannot stand the sight of them); a revulsion at it rose as at some enormous, hard insect that was chattering in my ears its incomprehensible insect chatter; do you understand – it had the effrontery to babble something at me? . . . Eh? . . .'

'Hmm . . .'

'A revulsion, as at an enormous insect whose shell gives off a savour of nauseating tin; there was something part-insect, part-unplated metal dish about it . . . Can you imagine – I was bursting, nauseated . . . I mean, it was as if I had . . . swallowed it . . .'

'Swallowed it? Ugh, how ghastly . . .'

'Simply the devil knows what – I swallowed it; do you understand what that means? Became a bomb walking on two legs with a repulsive ticking in my belly.'

'Quiet, Nikolai Apollonovich – quiet: someone may hear us here!'

'They won't understand any of it: it's impossible to understand it . . . This is what you have to do: keep it in your desk, stand and listen to its ticking . . . In a word, you have to experience it all for yourself, in sensations . . .'

'But you know,' Aleksandr Ivanovich said, getting interested in what he was saying now – 'I do understand you: the ticking . . . You hear the sound differently; if you only listen closely to the sound, you will hear in it – something that's the same, and yet different . . . I once tried to frighten a neurasthenic; began to tap my finger on the table, with a hidden meaning, you know – in time to the conversation; well, so then he looked at me, turned pale, fell silent and when he asked: "Why are you doing that?" I replied to him: "For no reason," and went on tapping the table. Can you imagine – he had a fit: he was so offended that he wouldn't return my greeting when I met him in the street . . . I understand that . . .'

'No, no, no; it's impossible to understand it . . . There was something that rose up, came back to my memory – some kind of delirious fantasies that were unfamiliar and yet familiar . . .'

'You remembered your childhood – didn't you?'

'It was as though a bandage had been removed from all my sensations . . . There was a stirring above my head – you know? My hair stood on end: I understand what that means; only it wasn't that – not my hair, because one stands with one's head exposed. *To have one's hair stand on end* – I understood that expression last night; and it wasn't my hair; it was my whole body, standing, like hair – *on end*: it was bristling with little hairs; and my legs and my arms and my chest – they were all as if made of invisible fur that was being tickled with straw; or like this, too: as if one were getting into a cold bath of Narzan mineral water and there were little bubbles of carbon dioxide on one's skin – tickling, pulsating, racing – faster and faster, so that if one froze, the throbbing, pulsating and tickling would turn into some kind of powerful feeling, as though one were being torn to pieces, as though the limbs of one's body were being pulled apart in contrary directions: as though in the front one's heart was being torn out, while in the rear, in the rear, from one's back, like a long branch from a wattle fence, one's backbone was being torn out; as if one were being pulled up by one's hair and down by one's feet into the bowels of the earth . . . One moved – and everything froze, as though . . .'

'In a word, Nikolai Apollonovich, you were like Dionysus being torn to pieces ... But, joking apart: now you are speaking quite a different language; I do not recognize you ... You are not speaking in Kantian terms any longer ... I haven't heard this language from you before ...'

'But I just told you: it's as though a bandage had fallen – from all my sensations ... Not in Kantian terms – that's true, what you said ... Kant is out of it completely! ... There everything is different ...'

'There, Nikolai Apollonovich, logic has been introduced into the blood, or rather, the sensations of the brain in the blood or – dead stagnation; and so now you have received a real shock from life, and the blood has rushed to your brain; that is why in your words one can hear the pulsation of real blood ...'

'You know, when I stand above *it*, and – tell me, please: it seems to me – yes, but what was I talking about?'

'It "seems" to you, you said,' Aleksandr Ivanovich confirmed ...

'It seems to me – that I swell up all over, that I've been swelling up for a long time: perhaps for hundreds of years; and that I'm walking around, without noticing – like a swollen monster ... It really is dreadful.'

'It all comes from your sensations ...'

'But tell me, I'm ... not ...'

Aleksandr Ivanovich smiled sympathetically:

'On the contrary, you've grown thinner: your cheeks are drawn and you have circles under your eyes.'

'I stood there, over *it* ... But it wasn't "me" standing there – not me, not me, but ... some, so to speak, giant with the most enormous idiot's head and a sinciput that had not grown together; and at the same time – my body was pulsating; on absolutely every part of my skin I felt little needles: they were stabbing and pricking me; and I plainly felt the pricking – at a distance of at least a quarter of an arshin from my body, outside my body! ... Eh? ... Just think about it! Then a second, and a third: a huge number of jabs in a completely physical sensation – outside, beside my body ... While the jabs, the throbbings, the pulsations – you understand! – outlined my own contours – beyond the limits of my body, outside my skin: my skin was inside my sensations. Was that it? Or had I been turned inside out, with my skin facing inwards, or had my brain jumped out?'

'You were simply beside yourself . . .'

'It's all very well for you to say "beside yourself"; everyone says "beside yourself"; that expression is just an allegory, supported not by physical sensations, but at best merely by emotion. But I felt *beside myself* in a completely physical, physiological sense, and not at all in an emotional one . . . Of course, in addition, I was also *beside* myself in your sense: that is, I was shocked. But the main thing wasn't that, but the fact that the sensations of my organs flowed around me, suddenly expanded, dilated and exploded into space: I exploded, like a bo –'

'Sh-hh!'

'Into pieces! . . .'

'Someone might hear . . .'

'But who was it standing there, experiencing – me, or someone else? It happened to me, inside me, outside me . . . You see what verbiage results? . . .'

'Remember, earlier, when I visited you, with the little bundle, I asked you why *I* was *I*. You didn't understand me at all at the time . . .'

'But now I understand it all: but it's dreadful, really dreadful . . .'

'No, it isn't dreadful – it's the genuine experience of Dionysus: not verbal, not literary, of course . . . The experience of the dying Dionysus . . .'

'Simply the devil knows what!'

'Now calm down, Nikolai Apollonovich, you're dreadfully tired; and no wonder: to go through so much in the course of a single night . . . It would knock anyone off his feet.' Aleksandr Ivanovich put his hand on Nikolai Apollonovich's shoulder; the shoulder was at the level of his chest; and that shoulder was trembling; Aleksandr Ivanovich now experienced quite plainly and simply a need to get away from Nikolai Apollonovich, who was trembling nervously before him, in order to give himself a clear and calm account of what had happened.

'But I am calm, completely calm; you know, I wouldn't mind having a drink now; a bit of courage and uplift . . . I mean, can you tell me for certain that the commission is an illusion?'

Aleksandr Ivanovich could do nothing of the kind; none the less, with unusual fervency, Aleksandr Ivanovich merely snapped out:

'I guarantee it . . .'

A Revelation

At last he managed to get away.

Now he must start striding; keep striding, and again striding – until his brain was completely stupefied, in order to collapse at a table in the eating-house – to reflect, and drink vodka.

Aleksandr Ivanovich remembered: the letter, the letter! He was supposed to have delivered the letter himself – on the instructions of *a certain person*: delivered it to Ableukhov.

How he had forgotten it all! He had taken the letter with him when he had set off then for Ableukhov's – with the little bundle; he had forgotten to deliver the letter; had delivered it soon after to Varvara Yevgrafovna, who had told him that she was going to meet Ableukhov. That letter might have proved to be the fateful one.

But no, and no!

It was not that one; *that* one, the *fateful* one had, according to Ableukhov, been delivered at the ball; and – by some kind of masker . . . The masker, the ball and – Varvara Yevgrafovna Solovyova.

No, and no!

Aleksandr Ivanovich calmed down: so *that* letter was certainly not *this* one, the one that had been delivered by Solovyova and sent to him by Lippanchenko; so he, Aleksandr Ivanovich Dudkin, was not implicated in this matter; but – and this was the main thing: the dreadful commission could not have proceeded from the *person*; this was the principal trump card in his hands: a trump card that vanquished his delirium and all his delirious suspicions (those suspicions had rushed through his head when he had promised, vouched for the Party – for Lippanchenko, because Lippanchenko was his organ of communication with the Party); had he not had this trump card in his hands, if, that was to say, the letter had come from the Party, from Lippanchenko, then the *person*, Lippanchenko, would have been a suspicious person, and he, Aleksandr Ivanovich Dudkin, would have been associated with a suspicious personality.

And the delirious dreams would have arisen.

Hardly had he put all this together and was already preparing to cut across the flood of carriages in order to jump into a horse-car that was speeding towards him (there were, after all, no trams yet), than a voice hailed him:

'Aleksandr Ivanovich, wait . . . Wait a moment . . .'

He turned round and saw that Nikolai Apollonovich, whom he had left an instant before, was running after him, panting, through the crowd – trembling and sweaty all over; with a feverish light in his eyes he was waving his stick over the heads of the astonished passers-by . . .

'Wait a moment . . .'

Oh, good Lord!

'Wait: I can't just let you go like that, Aleksandr Ivanovich . . . Look, there's something else I want to tell you . . .' He took him by the arm and guided him to the nearest shop window.

'Something else has been revealed to me . . . Was it a revelation I had perhaps – there, as I stood over the little tin? . . .'

'Listen, Nikolai Apollonovich, I have to go now; and I have to go in connection with a matter that involves you . . .'

'Yes, yes, yes: I won't take a moment . . . Just a second, a third . . .'

'Well – all right then: I am listening . . .'

Now Nikolai Apollonovich displayed in his appearance something that was quite simply inspiration; in his joy he had evidently forgotten that not everything had been untangled for him yet, and that – above all: *the tin was still ticking, tirelessly traversing the twenty-four hours.*

'It was as though I had a revelation that I was growing; I was growing, if you know what I mean, into immeasurability, traversing space; I assure you that this was real: and all the objects were growing with me; the room, and the view over the Neva, and the spire of Peter and Paul; they were all swelling up, growing; and then the growing stopped (there was simply no more room left for growth anywhere, into anything); but in this fact, that it was ending, in the end, in the conclusion – there, it seemed to me, was some kind of another beginning for me: a post-terminal one, perhaps . . . Somehow it seemed extremely preposterous, unpleasant and deranged, – deranged – that was the principal thing; deranged, perhaps, because I didn't possess an organ that would have been able to make sense of this meaning, which was, so to speak, post-terminal; instead of my sense organs I had a "zero" sense; and I perceived something that was not zero, and not one, but less than one. The whole absurdity was, perhaps, only that the sensation was a sensation of *zero minus something* – five, for example.'

'Listen,' Aleksandr Ivanovich interrupted, 'I had rather you told me this: did you receive the letter through Varvara Yevgrafovna Solovyova? You did, didn't you? . . .'

'The letter . . .'

'Not the *little note* . . . the letter that came through Varvara Yevgrafovna . . .'

'Oh, you mean the one about that poem with the inscription "A Fiery Soul"?'

'Well, I don't know anything about that: in a word, the letter that came through Varvara Yevgrafovna . . .'

'Yes, I got it, I got it . . . No – as I was saying, this *zero minus something* . . . What was that?'

Oh, Lord: still about the same thing! . . .

'You ought to read the Apocalypse . . .'

'I have heard from you before the reproach that I am unfamiliar with the Apocalypse; but now I shall read it – I shall read it without fail; now that you have finally put my mind at rest about . . . *all this*, I feel an interest awakening within me in the circle of your reading; you know, I shall settle down at home, drink bromide and read the Apocalypse; I'm most enormously interested: something has remained from the night: everything is what it is – yet different . . . For example, look, here: the shop window . . . And in the shop window there are reflections: there is a gentleman in a bowler hat walking past – look – off he goes . . . It's you and I, do you see? And yet it's – somehow strange . . .'

'Yes, it is somehow strange,' said Aleksandr Ivanovich, nodding his head in confirmation: Lord, but this fellow seemed to be a specialist in the field of 'somehow strange'.

'Or then again: objects . . . The devil only knows what they really are: they're what they are – and yet different . . . I perceived that from the tin: the tin was a tin; and yet – no, no: it wasn't a tin, but a . . .'

'Shh!'

'A tin with dreadful contents!'

'Well, you'd do best to throw the tin into the Neva; and everything will come right again; everything will return to its place . . .'

'No, it won't, it won't, it won't . . .'

He sadly dodged the rushing couples; sadly he sighed, because he knew: it would not come right again, it would not, would not – not ever, ever!

Aleksandr Ivanovich was astonished at the flood of garrulity that had gushed from Ableukhov's lips; to be quite honest, he did not know what to do with such garrulity: whether to try to calm him down, to support him, or, on the contrary – to break off the conversation (Ableukhov's presence was simply weighing him down).

'Nikolai Apollonovich, it's just your sensations that appear strange to you; it's just that you've been sitting too long with Kant in an unaired room; you've been struck by a tornado – and you've started to notice things about yourself: you have listened carefully to the tornado; and you have heard yourself in it . . . Your states of mind have been described in a variety of forms; they are the subject of observations, of study . . .'

'But where, where?'

'In fiction, in poetry, in the *psychiatries*, in occult resarch.'

Aleksandr Ivanovich could not help smiling at the scandalous (from his point of view) illiteracy of this intellectually developed scholastic and, having smiled, continued seriously:

'A psychiatrist . . .'

'?'

'Would call . . .'

'Yes, yes, yes . . .'

'All that . . .'

'That *everything is what it is, and yet different*?'

'Well, call it that if you will – for him the more usual term is: pseudo-hallucination . . .'

'?'

'That is, a kind of symbolic sensation that does not correspond to the stimulus of a sensation.'

'Well, so what: saying that is equivalent to saying nothing! . . .'

'Yes, you're right . . .'

'No, it doesn't satisfy me . . .'

'Of course: a modernist would call this sensation the sensation of the abyss — that is to say, he would look for an image that corresponds to a symbolic sensation that is not normally experienced.'

'So there's an allegory here.'

'Don't confuse allegory with symbol; an allegory is a symbol that has become current usage; for example, the normal meaning of your "beside oneself"; while a symbol is your appeal to what you have experienced there — near the tin; an invitation to experience artificially something that you experienced *for real* . . . But a more suitable term would be a different one: the pulsation of the elemental body. That is precisely how you experienced yourself; under the influence of a shock the elemental body within you gave a perfectly real shudder, for a moment became separated, unstuck from your physical body, and then you experienced all the things that you experienced there: trite verbal combinations like *bezdna* (abyss) — *bez dna* (without a bottom) or *vne . . . sebya* (beside (outside) . . . oneself) acquired depth, became a vital truth for you, a symbol; according to the doctrine of certain schools of mysticism, the experiences of one's elemental body turn verbal meanings and allegories into real meanings, into symbols; and it's because the works of the mystics abound in these symbols that now, after what you have experienced, I advise you to read those mystics . . .'

'I told you that I will: and — I will . . .'

'And as for what happened to you, I can only add one thing: sensations of that kind will be your first experience beyond the grave, as Plato describes it, adducing in evidence the assertions of the Bacchantes . . . There are schools of experience where these sensations are deliberately provoked — do you not believe me? . . . There are: I can tell you that with certainty, because the only friend I have — and he is a close friend — is there, in those schools; the schools of experience transform your nightmare by means of hard work into a harmonious accord, studying its rhythms, movements and pulsations, and introducing all the sobriety of consciousness into the sensation of expansion, for example ... But why are we standing here? We've talked for far too long ... What you need to do is go home now and ... throw the tin into the river; and stay at home, stay at home: don't set foot anywhere (you are probably being followed); so stay at home, read the Apocalypse, drink bromide: you're dreadfully exhausted ... Though perhaps you're better off without bromide: bromide dulls the consciousness; people who abuse bromide become incapable of doing anything ... Well, and now I rush away, and – on a matter that concerns you.'

Having pressed Ableukhov's hand, Aleksandr Ivanovich suddenly slipped away from him into the black stream of bowler hats, turned from that stream and shouted once more from there:

'And throw the tin in the river!'

His shoulder adhered to the other shoulders; he was swiftly carried off by the headless myriapod.

Nikolai Apollonovich gave a shudder: life was bubbling in the little tin; the timing mechanism was working even now; he must go home quickly, quickly; in a moment he would hire a cab; when he got home, he would put the tin in his side pocket; and – into the Neva with it!

Nikolai Apollonovich again began to feel that he was expanding; at the same time, he felt: it was drizzling.

The Caryatid

There, opposite, the crossroads showed black; and there was the street; the caryatid of the entrance porch hung there stonily.

The *Institution* towered up from there; the *Institution*, where the person who dominated everything was Apollon Apollonovich Ableukhov.

There is a limit to the autumn; to winter, too, there is a limit: the very periods of time themselves flow by in cyclic fashion. And above these cycles hung the bearded caryatid of the entrance porch; giddily its stone hoof is crushed into the wall; it looks as though it might break loose in its entirety and spill into the street as stone.

And yet – it does not break away.

What it sees above it is, like life, mutable, inexplicable, inarticulate: clouds float there; a white, mackerel sky twines in inexplicability; or it drizzles; drizzles, as now: as it did yesterday, and the day before yesterday.

What it sees beneath its feet is, like itself, immutable: immutable is the flow of the human myriapod along the illumined paving; or: as now – in the gloomy dampness; the deathly pale rustling of moving legs; and the faces, eternally green; no, from them one cannot tell that events are already rumbling.

Observing the passage of the bowler hats, you would never say that events were rumbling, for example, in the little town of Ak-Tyuk, where a workman at the railway station who had had an argument with a railway policeman, appropriated a credit bill[5] from the policeman, introducing it into his stomach with the aid of his oral orifice, for which reason the railway doctor introduced an emetic into that stomach; observing the passage of the bowler hats, no one would say that already in the theatre at Kutais the audience had exclaimed: 'Citizens! . . .' No one would have said that a police superintendent in Tiflis had uncovered the manufacture of bombs, that the library in Odessa had been closed and that in ten of Russia's universities mass meetings had been held, attended by many thousands of people – on the same day, at the same time; no one would have said that at that very same time thousands of staunch Bundists came flocking to a gathering, that the workers of Perm had shown themselves obstinate and that at that very same time, surrounded by Cossacks, the Reval iron foundry began to unfurl its red flags.

Observing the passage of the bowler hats, no one would have said that 'the new life' was welling up, that Potapenko[6] was finishing the play that bore that same title, that the strike on the Moscow-Kazan railway had already begun; panes of glass had been smashed at the stations, warehouses had been broken into, work had been stopped on the Kursk, Windau, Nizhny Novgorod and Murom railways; and tens of thousands of coaches and wagons, stunned, came to a standstill in the multivarious expanses; communication froze dead. Observing the passage of the bowler hats, no one would have said that in Petersburg events were already rumbling, that the typesetters from almost every printing works had elected delegates and gathered in swarms; and – factories were on strike: the shipyards, the Aleksandrovsky Factory, and others; that the suburbs of Petersburg were teeming with Manchurian hats; observing the passage of the bowler hats, no one would have said that the passers-by were *those* people, and not *those* people; that they did not simply stride along, but strode, concealing an unease within themselves, feeling that their heads were the heads of idiots, with sinciputs that had not grown together, cut by sabres, smashed by plain old wooden stakes; if they had put their ears to the ground, they would have heard someone's kindly rustling: the rustling of incessant revolver fire – from Arkhangelsk to Kolkhida and from Libava to Blagoveshchensk.

But the circulation was not broken: monotonous, sluggish, deathly, the bowler hats still flowed beneath the feet of the caryatid.

. . . .

The grey caryatid leaned over and looked beneath its feet: at the same crowd; there was no limit to the contempt in the old stone of its eyes; there was no limit to its satiety; and no limit to its despair.

And oh, if only it had the strength!

Its muscular arms would straighten on elbows that flew up above its stone head; and its chiselled sinciput would jerk frenziedly; its mouth would tear open in a thunderous roar, in a protracted, desperate roar; you would say: 'That is the roar of a hurricane' (thus did the black thousands of peaked caps of the city thugs roar in the pogroms); as from the whistle of a locomotive, steam would pour over the street; the cornice of the balcony itself would leap up above the street, broken away from the wall; and disintegrate into heavy, loudly rumbling stones (very soon afterwards the windows of the *zemstvo* councils and the provincial *zemstvo* assemblies were smashed with stones); this old statue would break off into the street in a hail of stone, describing a swift and blinding arc in the darkening air; and, growing bloody with the splinters, it would settle on top of the frightened bowler hats that were passing here – deathly, monotonous, sluggish . . .

. . . .

On this rather grey little Petersburg day a heavy, sumptuous door flew open; a clean-shaven lackey in grey with gold braid on his lapels rushed out from the vestibule to give directions to the coachman; the horses hurled themselves to the entrance porch and pulled up the lacquered carriage; the clean-shaven lackey in grey looked stupid and drew himself straight to attention, as Apollon Apollonovich Ableukhov, somewhat stooped, bent, unshaven, with a painfully swollen face and a drooping lip touched the edge of his top hat (the colour of a raven's wing) with his gloves (the colour of a raven's wing).

Apollon Apollonovich Ableukhov cast a momentary glance filled with indifference at the erect lackey, at the carriage, the coachman, the great black bridge, the indifferent expanses of the Neva, where the misty, many-chimneyed distances were so wanly outlined, and where ashen rose the indistinct Vasily Island with its striking tens of thousands.

The erect lackey slammed the carriage door, on which an old aristocratic coat of arms was depicted: a unicorn goring a knight; the carriage swiftly flew into the grimy fog – past the lustrelessly looming blackish cathedral, St Isaac's, past the equestrian monument to the Emperor Nicholas – to the Nevsky, where a crowd was swarming, where, breaking loose from the wooden pole, tearing the air with their crests, where they fluttered and snatched, flew the gently whistling blades of a red calico banner; the black outline of the carriage, the silhouette of the lackey's three-cornered hat and the wings of his overcoat flying in the wind suddenly cut into the thick, shaggy mass, where Manchurian hats, cap bands, and service caps, swarming together, broke against the panes of the carriage in a distinct singing.

The carriage came to a standstill in the crowd.

Down, Tom!

'*Mais j'espère . . .*'

'You hope?'

'*Mais j'espère que oui . . .*' the voice of a foreigner jangled from behind the door.

Aleksandr Ivanovich's footsteps tapped against the boards of the little terrace with deliberate firmness; Aleksandr Ivanovich did not like eavesdropping. The door that led into the apartment was half open.

It was getting dark: it was getting dark blue.

No one heard his footsteps. Aleksandr Ivanovich Dudkin decided not to eavesdrop; and so he stepped across the threshold of the doorway.

In the room there was a heavy fragrance; a mixture of perfumery and some kind of astringent sourness: that of medicaments.

Zoya Zakharovna Fleisch was paying compliments as always. She was endeavouring to make some visiting foreigner sit down; the foreigner was declining the invitation.

It was getting dark; it was getting dark blue.

'Oh, how glad I am to see you . . . Very, very glad to see you: wipe your feet, take your coat off . . .'

But no answering gladness followed; Aleksandr Ivanovich shook Zoya's hand.

'I hope you have received a fine impression of Russia . . . Don't you think . . .' she said, addressing the wiry foreigner. 'Such unprecedented enthusiasm?'

And the Frenchman jangled drily:

'*Mais j'espère . . .*'

Zoya Zakharovna Fleisch, rubbing her puffy fingers, turned her kindly, somewhat bewildered gaze now on the Frenchman, now on Aleksandr Ivanovich; she had bulging eyes: they were coming out of their sockets. Zoya Zakharovna looked about forty; Zoya Zakharovna was a large-headed brunette; her stout cheeks were enamelled; from her cheeks powder flaked.

'But he's not here yet . . . Is it *him* you need to see?' she asked Aleksandr Ivanovich, quite unexpectedly; in this fleeting question there was a hidden anxiety; hostility was perhaps concealed in it; and perhaps, hatred; but the anxiety, hostility and hatred were sweetly covered over: by her smile and her gaze; thus in sticky-sweet candies that are offered for sale is all the repulsive filth of the unventilated confectioners' kitchens concealed.

'Well, all the same, I'll wait for *him*.'

Aleksandr Ivanovich bowed to the Frenchman; he reached out for a pear (there was a bowl of Duchesse pears on the table); at this point Zoya Zakharovna Fleisch moved the bowl away from

Aleksandr Ivanovich: Aleksandr Ivanovich was so fond of pears.

Pears were as pears might be, but they were not the most important thing right now.

The most important thing was the voice: the voice that began to sing from somewhere; the voice was completely cracked, impossibly loud and sweet; and moreover: the voice had an impermissible accent. At the dawn of the twentieth century it was not done to sing like that: it was simply shameless: people in Europe do not sing that way. Aleksandr Ivanovich fancied that the singer was a burning, voluptuous-tempered man with dark hair; he quite certainly had dark hair; he had one of those sunken chests that sagged between his shoulders, and the eyes of a regular cockroach; perhaps he was consumptive; and, probably, from the south: an Odessan or even a Bulgarian from Varna (that was better, perhaps); his linen was not quite tidy; he was some kind of populist propagandist, and he hated the countryside. As he formed his ideas about the song's invisible performer, Aleksandr Ivanovich reached out for a second pear.

Meanwhile Zoya Zakharovna Fleisch would not let the Frenchman leave her side for a moment:

'Yes, yes, yes: we are experiencing events of historic importance ... Everywhere cheerfulness and youth ... The historians of the future will write ... Don't you believe me? Come to the mass meetings ... Listen to the ardent outpourings of emotion, take a look – everywhere there is rapture.'

But the Frenchman did not wish to sustain the conversation.

'*Pardon, madame, monsieur viendra-t-il bientôt?*'

In order not to be a witness of this unpleasant conversation, which was somehow demeaning to his sense of national feeling, Aleksandr Ivanovich went right up to the window, very nearly stumbling over a shaggy St Bernard that was gnawing a bone on the floor.

The windows of the little dacha looked out to sea: it was getting dark, it was getting dark blue.

The eye of a lighthouse turned; the light began to blink: 'one-two-three' – and went out; the dark cloak of a distant passer-by flapped in the wind out there; even further away the crests of waves curled; the lights of the shore were scattered like luminous grain;

the many-eyed seashore bristled with reeds; from far away a siren began to wail.

What a wind!

'Here is an ashtray for you . . .'

The ashtray was lowered under Aleksandr Ivanovich's nose: but Aleksandr Ivanovich was a touchy man, and he stubbed out his cigarette-end in the flower vase: did so from a spirit of protest.

'Who's that singing?'

Zoya Zakharovna made a gesture, from which it was plain that Aleksandr Ivanovich was lagging behind; impermissibly lagging behind.

'What? Don't you know? . . . No, of course you don't . . . Well, then I may as well tell you: it's Shishnarfiev . . . That's what comes of being a lone wolf . . . Shishnarfiev – he has made himself at home with us all . . .'

'I've heard his name somewhere . . .'

'Shishnarfiev is wonderfully artistic . . .'

Zoya Zakharovna pronounced this phrase with a determined look – with a look as if to say that he, Aleksandr Ivanovich, had placed a most inappropriate question mark over the owner of the name, who was well known to everyone for his artistic nature and had made friends with them all. But Aleksandr Ivanovich did not intend to dispute the talents of this selfsame gentleman.

All he asked was:

'Is he an Armenian? A Bulgarian? A Georgian?'

'No, no . . .'

'A Croat? A Persian?'

'He's a Persian from Shemakha,[7] and he very nearly lost his life in the slaughter in Isfahan . . .'

'And is he a . . . Young Persian?'[8]

'Of course . . . Didn't you know . . . You ought to be ashamed . . .'

A look of regret, of condescension towards him, and – Zoya Zakharovna Fleisch turned to the Frenchman.

Aleksandr Ivanovich, naturally, did not listen to their conversation: he listened to the hopelessly cracked tenor; the Young Persian activist was singing a passionate gypsy romance and casting a gloomy shadow on one's thoughts. Incidentally: Aleksandr

Ivanovich reflected on the fact that the features of Zoya Fleisch's face had in all fairness been taken from the faces of the most diverse beauties: the nose – from one, the mouth – from another, the ears – from yet another beautiful woman.

Taken together, however, they produced a decidedly irritating effect. And Zoya Zakharovna appeared to be sewn together from many beautiful women, while herself being far from beautiful – and that was no understatement! But her most essential feature was her adherence to the category of what are called burning oriental brunettes.

Zoya Zakharovna's bombastic chatter flew across none the less and overtook Aleksandr Ivanovich:

'Are you here about money?'

Silence.

'Money from abroad is needed . . .'

An impatient movement of the elbow.

'Your editor had better not come here after the rout of the T.T. organization . . .'

But the Frenchman said not a word.

'Because documents were found . . .'

If Aleksandr Ivanovich had been able to think about the matter, the news of the rout of the T.T. might (this we shall say) have knocked him off his feet; but he listened – to the Young Persian activist exuberantly singing a romance. Meanwhile the Frenchman, fairly driven out of his mind by Zoya Fleisch's importuning of him, said by way of rebuff:

'*Je serai bien triste d'avoir manqué l'occasion de parler à monsieur.*'

'It's all the same: speak to me, instead . . .'

'*Excusez, dans certains cas je préfère parler personellement . . .*'

A shrub flailed in the window.

Between the branches of the shrub one could see the waves foaming, and a sailing vessel rocking to and fro, vesperal and dark blue; in a thin layer it cut the darkness with its sharp-winged sails; on the surface of the sail the bluish night slowly grew denser.

The sail seemed to be being obliterated altogether.

Just then a cab drove up to the little garden; the body of a heavy fat man, who was manifestly suffering from shortness of breath, unhurriedly tumbled out of the carriage; burdened by half a dozen packages oscillating on strings, an awkward hand seemed slowly to fuss over a leather purse; from under an arm a bag fell clumsily over a puddle; tearing the paper that held them as they flew, winter apples rolled in the mud.

The gentleman began to fuss over the puddle, picking up the apples; his coat fell open; he was apparently groaning; closing the gate, he again very nearly spilled his purchases.

The gentleman approached the small dacha along the yellow garden path between two rows of shrubs that were bent in the wind; the same familiar, oppressive atmosphere was spread around; covered by a hat with earflaps, the man's sinister head seemed suddenly to settle on his chest; the small eyes set deep in their sockets did not on this occasion move about at all (as they moved about before any fixed gaze); the small, deepset eyes stared wearily at the window-panes.

Aleksandr Ivanovich managed to detect in those little eyes (just imagine!) some kind of peculiar joy of their own, one mixed with weariness and sadness – a purely animal joy: at warming oneself, sleeping properly and having a good supper after having endured so many travails. Thus the bloodthirsty beast: returning to its lair, the bloodthirsty beast seems meek and domesticated, displaying the good nature of which it, too, is capable; in friendly fashion this beast then sniffs at its mate; and licks its whimpering cubs.

Is this the *person?*

Yes: this is the *person*: and the *person* is on this occasion not terrifying; his aspect is prosaic; but this is the person.

. . . .

'Here he is!'

'*Enfin* . . .'

'Lippanchenko! . . .'

'Hello . . .'

The yellow dog, the St Bernard, hurled itself through the room with a joyful roar and, jumping up, fell with its paws straight on the *person*'s chest.

'Down, Tom! . . .'

As he desperately defended his purchases from the shaggy St Bernard, the *person* did not even have time to spot his uninvited guests; his broad, flat, square face was stamped with a mixture of humour and helpless fury; all that slipped out was a childish remark:

'He's slobbering again.'

And, turning helplessly away from Tom, the person exclaimed:

'Zoya Zakharovna, free me from him . . .'

But the dog's broad tongue disrespectfully licked the tip of the *person*'s nose; at this, the *person* emitted a piercing cry – a helpless cry (while yet at the same time – imagine! – smiling) . . .

'Now then, Tomka!'

But having seen that there were guests, and that the guests were waiting, chuckling impatiently at this idyll of domestic life, the *person* stopped laughing and snapped without the slightest courtesy:

'Very well, very well! I shall be with you in a moment . . .'

And as he did so his drooping lip twitched touchily; on the lip was written:

'There is no peace even here . . .'

The person rushed into a corner; there he stamped about – in the corner: he had still not taken off his galoshes, which were new and somewhat tight-fitting; for a long time still he continued to stand in the corner, delaying in taking off his coat and rummaging about in one of its tightly stuffed pockets (as though a twelve-chambered Browning were concealed in it); at last his hand came out of the pocket – holding a child's doll, a cork-tumbler.

He threw this doll on the table.

'And this is for Akulina's Manka . . .'

At this the guests, to be quite honest, opened their mouths wide.

After this, rubbing his cold hands, he turned to the Frenchman with timid suspicion:

'Please . . . this way . . . This way . . .'

And – hurled at Dudkin:

'You'll have to wait . . .'

Frontal Bones

'Zoya Zakharovna . . .'

'Hah?'

'Shishnarfiev – I understand: he's a Young Persian activist, a fiery artistic nature; but tell me – what is the Frenchman doing here?'

'Much knowledge makes a man old,' she replied in un-Russian manner, and her immoderate breasts began to move under her tightly stretched bodice; an atomizer hissed in her hand.

In the room a heavy fragrance was smelt: a mixture of a perfumery and an artificially prepared tooth (whoever has sat in the premises of dentists will certainly be familiar with that smell – not an agreeable one).

At this point, Zoya Zakharovna moved towards Aleksandr Ivanovich.

'So you're still living . . . like a hermit . . .'

Aleksandr Ivanovich's lips pursed themselves somehow crookedly:

'Your lover did his best to bring that about long ago . . .'

'?'

'If I'm not a hermit, it doesn't matter: someone else will be a hermit . . .'

The turn the conversation had taken was plainly not to Zoya Zakharovna's liking, and the atomizer began to hiss nervously in her hands once again; Aleksandr Ivanovich smiled an unpleasant smile, and – recovered himself.

'And I must say that distraction does not suit me.'

Zoya Zakharovna accepted this new current of thought; and she hastened to be witty:

'Is that why you're so distracted: spilling ash on my tablecloth?'

'I'm sorry . . .'

'It's all right: here is an ashtray for you . . .'

Aleksandr Ivanovich reached out for another pear; and, having made this movement, Aleksandr Ivanovich said to himself in vexation:

'What a skinflint she is . . .'

He had seen that the bowl of Duchesse pears (he was very fond of Duchesse pears) – the bowl of Duchesse pears was not there.

'What is it? Here's your ashtray . . .'

'I know: I was looking for a Duchesse pear . . .'

Zoya Zakharovna did not offer the Duchesse pears.

The doors into the distant room were not closed at all: he looked through the half-open door with insatiable avidity; there two seated outlines were visible. The little Frenchman was babbling on; he seemed to be jangling; while the person boomed tonelessly, interrupting the little Frenchman; as he talked he kept snatching up writing materials – now this, now that; and scratching the nape of his neck with an angular gesture of his hand; the things that the Frenchman was telling him were evidently agitating the *person* in earnest; Aleksandr Ivanovich detected a gesture that was quite simply one of self-defence.

'Boom-boom-boom . . .'

That was what it sounded like in there.

While Tom the St Bernard had placed his slobbering muzzle on the person's checked knee; and the person was distractedly stroking the dog's coat. At this point Aleksandr Ivanovich's observations were interrupted: they were interrupted by Zoya Zakharovna.

'Why have you stopped coming to see us?'

He distractedly looked at her grinning mouth: looked and commented:

'Oh, I just have: after all, you yourself said – I'm a hermit . . .'

The gold of a dental filling gleamed in reply:

'Don't turn your back on us.'

'But I'm not, not in the slightest . . .'

'You're just offended with him . . .'

'There you go again . . .' Aleksandr Ivanovich attempted, by way of a retort, and broke off his justifications: they sounded – unconvincing.

'You're simply offended at him. Everyone is offended at him. And now *Lippanchenko* has got involved . . . This *Lippanchenko*! . . . It's spoiling his reputation . . . But try to understand: *Lippanchenko* is a necessary role he has assumed . . . Without *Lippanchenko* he would have been arrested long ago . . . With *Lippanchenko* he covers us all . . . But everyone believes in *Lippanchenko* . . .'

Some people have an unfortunate characteristic: a bad smell from their mouths . . . Aleksandr Ivanovich turned away.

'Everyone is offended at him . . . But tell me' – Zoya Zakharovna snatched at the atomizer – 'where will you find a worker like that?

... Eh? Where will you find him? ... Who, tell me, would agree to be *Lippanchenko*, renouncing all his natural sentiments, to be *Lippanchenko* – to the end ...'

Aleksandr Ivanovich thought that the person was perhaps too much *Lippanchenko*: but did not want to raise any objection.

'I assure you ...'

But she interrupted:

'Aren't you ashamed to abandon him *like this*, to conceal things like this, to lie in hiding; I mean, Kolechka is in torment; to break all his old, intimate ties from the past ...'

Aleksandr Ivanovich remembered with amazement that 'Kolechka' was the *person*: for how many months had he, to be quite honest, not remembered this?

'Well, so what if he drinks and makes a boor of himself; and – well – has his bit of fun ... After all, it's true: better men have ruined themselves with drink, indulged in lust and debauchery ... And from personal inclination. But Kolechka does it merely as a blind – as *Lippanchenko*: it's for security, accountability, before the police, for the sake of the common cause that he's ruining himself so.'

Aleksandr Ivanovich, in spite of himself, smiled ironically, but caught a mistrustful, angry look that was directed at him:

'What ...'

And hurried to reply:

'No ... I didn't mean ... anything ...'

'You see, there is a most terrible sacrifice here ... You would not believe how much threatens him; Nikolai is destroying himself with forced frequent drinking bouts, the binges that are obligatory in his position ...'

Aleksandr Ivanovich knew that Zoya Zakharovna suspected him of making too frequent visits to little restaurants with Lippanchenko, of training Lippanchenko ... in many things ...

'You see, it may end badly ...'

Well, life, too; it might end badly here: he, Aleksandr Ivanovich, was slowly going out of his mind. Nikolai Apollonovich had been weighed down by difficult circumstances; something not right had been introduced into their souls; it was something that involved neither the police, nor tyranny, nor danger, but some kind of psychical rottenness; without being cleansed, could one really proceed with the great national cause? He remembered: 'In fear of God and in faith proceed.'⁹ But they had proceeded without any fear. And had they had any faith? And proceeding thus, they had transgressed some kind of psychical law: they had become criminals, not in that sense, of course . . . but – in another.

They had all transgressed.

'Remember Helsingfors and the boating excursions . . .' – here Zoya Zakharovna's voice rang with a genuine sadness. 'And afterwards: those rumours . . .'

'What rumours?'

He was interested, he gave a start.

'Rumours about Kolechka! . . . Do you think he doesn't suspect, isn't tormented, doesn't cry out at night?' (Aleksandr Ivanovich noted down in his memory that – *he cries out at night*) 'How they talk about him after all that. And – there is no gratitude, no consciousness that the man has sacrificed everything . . . He knows it all: says nothing, grieves . . . That is why he is gloomy . . . He's not able to act against his conscience. He always looks unpleasant' – tears very nearly rang in Zoya Zakharovna's voice – 'he looks unpleasant . . . with that . . . unfortunate external appearance. Believe me – he is a child, a child . . .'

'A child?'

'Do you find that surprising?'

'No,' he faltered, 'only, you know, I find it somehow strange to hear that, try as I may, I somehow can't get my picture of Nikolai Stepanovich to come together . . .'

'A real child! Look: the doll – the cork-tumbler' – with her hand she pointed at the doll, with a flash of her bracelet – 'You will go away: you will say unpleasant things to him, while he – he! . . .'

'?'

'He will put the cook's daughter on his knee and play at dolls with her . . . You see? And they will reproach him for perfidy . . . Lord, he plays at soldiers! . . .'

'Does he now?'

'Tin ones: he buys Persians, orders boxfuls of them from Nuremberg . . . Only – it is a secret . . . That is what he is like! . . . But,' – her eyebrows moved sharply together – 'but . . . in his childlike quick temper he is capable of anything.'

From her words, Aleksandr Ivanovich was becoming more and more convinced that the *person* was compromised in earnest; and he, to be quite honest, had not known that; these hints at *something* he now took into consideration as he let his gaze slip away to where they sat . . .

Steeply on to that chest the narrow-browed head now appeared to be falling; deeply hidden in the eye sockets were the searching, gimlet-like little eyes, that flitted from object to object; the lip was twitching and sucking in air. There were many things in that face: the face stood before Dudkin with an unmasterable revulsion, forming itself into that same *strange whole* that his memory carried away to the garret, in order there at night to pace, to boom – to bore, gimlet-like, to suck, to flit to and fro and to force from itself unutterable thoughts that did not exist anywhere.

Now he was closely studying the oppressive features that were by their very nature heavily constructed.

That frontal bone . . . –

That frontal bone jutted out with one stubborn effort: to understand: whatever happened, at whatever cost – to understand, or . . . be blown to pieces. Neither intellect, nor fury, nor treachery did the frontal bone manifest, but only an effort – without thought, without feeling: to understand . . . And frontal bones could not understand; the forehead was sorrowful: small and narrow, covered in transverse wrinkles; it seemed to be weeping.

Those searching, gimlet-boring little eyes . . .

Those searching, gimlet-boring little eyes (if one had raised their lids!)[10] – they too would have become . . . ordinary . . . little eyes.

They too were sad.

And the lip that was sucking the air was reminiscent – well, yes, truly it was – of an eighteen-month-old nursing infant (only there was no teat); if one had put a real teat in his mouth, it would not have been surprising if the lip had kept sucking; but without a teat this movement would have imparted to his face a most unpleasant little tinge.

Just think of it, too: playing at soldiers!

So a close analysis of the monstrous head revealed only one thing: the head was the head of a premature child; someone's puny little brain had been covered before its time with fatty and bony growths; and at the same time as the frontal bone protruded excessively on the outside with superciliary arcs (take a look at the skull of a gorilla), at that same time, perhaps, an unpleasant process was taking place called, in popular parlance, the softening of the brain.

The combination of inner sickliness and rhinoceros-like obstinacy – perhaps it was that this combination within Apollon Apollonovich had formed a chimera, and the chimera had grown – at nights: on a piece of dark yellow wallpaper it grinned like a real Mongol.

Thus he thought; but in his ears he began to hear, over and over again:

'A cork-tumbler . . . cries out at night . . . Orders them from Nuremberg in boxfuls . . . A real child . . .'

And added, on his own part:

'Knocks in heads with his forehead . . . Practises vampirism . . . Indulges in debauchery . . . And – drags people to their ruin . . .'

And again he began to hear, over and over again:

'A child . . .'

But heard it only in his ears: Zoya Zakharovna had already gone out of the room.

Not Good . . .

It was a strange thing!

Until now, the behaviour of a *certain person* in relation to Aleksandr Ivanovich had from time immemorial merely borne the character of one continuous string of obligations, and importunate ones at that; for many months, on many occasions, in many different ways, the person had been tracing his ornamental pattern of flattery around Aleksandr Ivanovich; Aleksandr Ivanovich had wanted to believe in that flattery.

And he had believed in it.

He viewed the *person* with repugnance; he felt a physiological revulsion towards him; more than that: Aleksandr Ivanovich Dudkin had been avoiding the *person* all these recent days, when he had been experiencing an agonizing crisis of loss of faith in everything. But the *person* had overtaken him everywhere; he had often mockingly thrown the *person* all too open challenges; the *person* had accepted these challenges stoically – with cynical laughter, and if he had asked the *person* what was the reason for that laughter, the *person* would have replied:

'It concerns you.'

But he knew that the *person* was guffawing at their common cause.

He kept telling the *person* that the programme of their Party was unsound, abstract, blind; and the *person* agreed; but he knew that the *person* took part in the elaboration of the programme; if he had inquired as to whether provocation had got mixed up in the programme, the *person* would have replied:

'No, no: daring . . .'

In the end he tried to shock *him* with his mystical *credo*, with the assertion that the People and the Revolution were not categories of reason, but divine Hypostases of the universe; the *person* had nothing against mysticism: listened with attention; and – even tried to understand.

But could not understand.

Except – except: the *person* stood before him; received all his protests and all his extreme conclusions in submissive silence; patted him on the shoulder and dragged him off to a little inn; there, at a table, they sipped cognac; sometimes, to the accompaniment of the tambourines of the machine, the *person* would say to him:

'So what? What am I: nothing . . . I am only a submarine; but you are our battleship, and a great ship must sail . . .'

None the less, the *person* had chased him off to the garret: and, having chased him off to the garret, had hidden him there; the battleship had lain in the dockyard without a crew, without guns; all these recent days Aleksandr Ivanovich's sailing had been confined to sailing from inn to inn; one could even say that during these weeks of protest the *person* had turned Aleksandr Ivanovich into a drunkard.

Hospitably had the *person* greeted him; of all the conversations they had had, one indubitable impression had remained: had Aleksandr Ivanovich suddenly needed serious assistance, the *person* would have been bound to give him that assistance; all that went without saying, of course; but Aleksandr Ivanovich was afraid of receiving good turns or assistance for himself.

Only today an opportunity had presented itself.

He had given Ableukhov his word that he would disentangle it all; and that he was doing: with the help of the *person*, of course. A fateful confusion of circumstances had simply thrown Ableukhov into some kind of abracadabra; he would describe the abracadabra to the *person*, and the *person* would then, he believed, be able to disentangle it all.

His appearance here had been provoked merely by the promise he had given to Ableukhov; and now – here it was, take it or leave it . . .

The *person*'s tone towards him had changed, in an offensive manner; he had noticed that from the *person*'s first appearance at the little dacha; the *person*'s tone towards him had become unrecognizable – unpleasant, offensive, stiff (with such a tone do the heads of institutions greet petitioners, with such a tone does the editor of a newspaper greet a newspaper reporter, a gatherer of information about fires and thefts; and thus does a guardian speak to a candidate in place of a teacher in . . . Solvychegodsk, in Sarepta . . .)

Here it was – take it or leave it . . .

Yes: after his conversation with the Frenchman (the Frenchman had now withdrawn), the *person*, contrary to the whole manner in which he had been behaving towards Aleksandr Ivanovich, had not come out of the study but continued to sit – there, at the writing desk; and – the effect was an offensive one: as though he, Aleksandr Ivanovich, were not there at all; as though he were not an acquaintance, but – the devil knows what! – an unknown petitioner, with time at his disposal. Aleksandr Ivanovich Dudkin was none the less the Elusive One; his Party nickname had made a noise in Russia and abroad; and, above all: he was by origin a hereditary nobleman, while the *person*, the *person* – hm-hm: he considered that by appearing in the *person*'s quarters he was doing the *person* an honour.

It was getting dark: it was getting dark blue.

And in the darkening all, in the semi-gloom of the little study, the *person*'s jacket showed repulsively yellow; his square head was completely bowed down against the table (above his back only a dyed quiff was visible), presenting the broad, muscular back and a neck that was doubtless unwashed; the back somehow bulged as it presented itself to the gaze; and presented itself wrongly: not

decently, but . . . somehow . . . mockingly. And from here it seemed
to him that from in there, stoopingly bent, out of the semi-twilight
of the little study, a shoulder and a back were bursting with
insolence; and he mentally undressed them; fatty skin appeared, that
could be sliced with the same ease as the skin of sucking-pig with
horseradish sauce; a cockroach was crawling by (there were evidently
large numbers of them here); he felt revolted: he – spat.

Suddenly a fatty fold of neck bulged out between the back and
the nape of the neck in a faceless smile: as though a monster had
settled down in the armchair there; and the neck looked like a face;
as though what had settled down in the armchair was a monster
with a noseless, eyeless mug; and the fold of neck looked like a
toothlessly ripped-open mouth.

There, on bandy legs, a clumsy monster had fallen back unnaturally – in the semi-twilight of the room.

Ugh, what filth!

Aleksandr Ivanovich jerked his shoulder away and put his back
to the back; he began to pluck his small moustache with an
independent air; he would have liked to have looked offended, but
looked merely independent; he plucked his small moustache with
an air that said that he was one thing, and the back was another.
He would have liked to have gone out, slamming the door; but it
was impossible to go out: Nikolai Apollonovich's peace of mind
depended on this conversation; and so: to go out, slamming the
door, was out of the question; and so he was still dependent on the
person.

Aleksandr Ivanovich, we have said, put his back to the back; but
the back with the fold of neck was none the less a magnetic back;
and he turned round to face it: he could not help doing so . . . At
this point, the *person*, in his turn, turned sharply in his chair: the
inclined, narrow-browed head stared steadily, resembling a wild
boar, ready to sink its tusk into any pursuer whatever; turned, and
again turned away. The gesture that accompanied this turn cried
eloquently aloud – with sheer desire to inflict an insult. But the
gesture expressed not only this. The *person* must have noticed
something in the gaze that was fixed on it, because the gaze of the
small, blinking eyes said caustically:

'Ah, ah, ah . . . So that's the game, my good chap, is it?'

Aleksandr Ivanovich clenched his fist in his pocket. And again turned away.

The hours were ticking. Aleksandr Ivanovich grunted twice, so that his impatience would touch the *person*'s hearing (he must both stand up for himself and not insult the *person* too much; were he to insult the *person*, after all, Nikolai Apollonovich might suffer because of it) . . . But Aleksandr Ivanovich's grunting came out sounding like the timid spasm of a preparatory form pupil before the teacher. What had happened to him? Where had this timidity come from? He was not in the slightest afraid of the *person*: he was afraid of the hallucination that emerged back there, on the wallpaper – but as for the *person* . . .

The *person* went on writing.

Aleksandr Ivanovich grunted again. And again. This time the *person* responded.

'You'll have to wait . . .'

What kind of a tone was that? What kind of dryness was that?

At last the *person* sat up slightly, and turned round; a heavy hand described a gesture of invitation in the air:

'Now then, what can I do for you . . .'

Aleksandr Ivanovich seemed completely at a loss; his anger, which had passed all bounds, was expressed in a fidgety forgetting of commonly used words:

'You see . . . I've . . . come . . .'

'?'

'As you know, or rather . . . What the devil! . . .' And suddenly he snapped out briefly:

'There's some business . . .'

But the *person*, having thrown himself back in his armchair (he was on the point of mercilessly strangling the *person* in that armchair), drummed a nibbled finger on the table with an annihilating look; and – hollowly boomed:

'I must warn you . . . I have no time today to listen to wordy explanations. And so . . .'

What was this?

'So I would ask you, my dearest fellow, to express yourself as briefly and precisely as possible . . .'

And pressing his chin into his Adam's apple, the *person* stared out of the windows; and from there space, empty with light, threw rustling handfuls of its falling leaves.

'But tell me, since when have you had this . . . tone,' burst from Aleksandr Ivanovich not merely with irony, but even with a kind of bewilderment.

But the *person* interrupted him again; interrupted him in a most unpleasant manner:

'Well, sir?'

And crossed his arms on his chest.

'My business . . .' and he faltered . . .

'Well, sir . . .'

'Has become very important . . .'

But the *person* interrupted a third time:

'We shall discuss its degree of importance later.'

And screwed up his little eyes.

Aleksandr Ivanovich Dudkin, inexplicably bewildered, blushed and felt that he could no longer force out a sentence. Aleksandr Ivanovich said nothing.

The *person* said nothing.

The falling leaves beat at the windows: the red leaves, knocking against the panes as they floated down, exchanged whispered secrets; there the branches — dry skeletons — formed a misty, blackish mesh; the wind was blowing in the street: the blackish mesh was beginning to sway; the blackish mesh was beginning to drone. Incoherently, helplessly, getting mixed up in his expressions, Aleksandr Ivanovich gave an account of the Ableukhov incident. But in the degree to which he became inspired by the story, overcoming the potholes in the structure of his discourse, the drier and more stern did the person become: the more impassively did his forehead protrude and then relax its wrinkles; the puffy little lips ceased sucking; and at the point in the story where Morkovin, the *agent provocateur*, appeared, the person jerked up his eyebrows and twitched his nose: as though until that point he had been trying to act on the narrator's conscience, as though after that point the narrator had become totally without conscience, so that all the limits of the tolerance of which the *person* was capable were from that point on transgressed; and his patience finally snapped:

'Eh? . . . You see? . . . And you said? . . .'

Aleksandr Ivanovich started.

'Say what?'

'Nothing: continue.'

Aleksandr Ivanovich screamed in complete despair:

'But I've said it all! What more can I add?'

And, pressing his chin into his Adam's apple, the person looked down, reddened, sighed, fixed a reproachful gaze on Aleksandr Ivanovich with eyes that were unblinking now (it was a sad gaze); and – whispered barely audibly:

'Not good . . . Not good, not good at all . . . I wonder you are not ashamed! . . .'

In the adjacent room Zoya Zakharovna appeared with a lamp; the maid, Malanya, was laying the table: and glasses were being set out; Mr Shishnarfiev appeared in the dining-room; his little tenor scattered like small glass beads, but all those beads were crushed by . . . the accent of a Young Persian; Shishnarfiev himself was concealed from view by a flower vase; all this Aleksandr Ivanovich noticed from afar, and – as if through a dream.

Aleksandr Ivanovich felt a tremor in his heart; and – horror; at the words 'I wonder you are not ashamed' he had felt his cheeks blush bright crimson; a manifest threat lurked banefully in the words of his fearsome interlocutor; Aleksandr Ivanovich began to squirm involuntarily in his seat, as he remembered something that he had not done and was not his fault at all.

It was strange: he did not dare to ask again what the hidden threat was in the *person*'s tone, and what he meant when he had used the word 'ashamed' in connection with him. None the less, he swallowed this 'ashamed'.

'But what am I to tell Ableukhov about this *provocateur*'s letter?'

Here the frontal bones approached his forehead.

'What do you mean – *provocateur*'s? It wasn't a *provocateur*'s letter at all . . . I must cool you down. The letter to Ableukhov was written by myself.'

This tirade was pronounced with a dignity that had mastered anger, reproach and offence; that had mastered itself, and now condescended to . . . a disparaging meekness.

'What? The letter was written by you?'

'And came – through you: do you remember? . . . Or have you forgotten?'

The *person* pronounced the words 'have you forgotten' with an air that seemed to indicate that Aleksandr Ivanovich was perfectly well aware of all this, but was for some reason pretending not to be; in general, the *person* gave him plainly to understand that now he was going to play with his dissembling like a cat with a mouse . . .

'Remember: I gave this letter to you back there – at the little inn . . .'

'But I assure you that I gave it not to Ableukhov but to Varvara Yevgrafovna . . .'

'That will do, Aleksandr Ivanovich, that will do, old chap: you don't need to try to pull the wool over the eyes of your own people: the letter found its addressee . . . And the rest is subterfuge . . .'

'And are you the author of the letter?'

Aleksandr Ivanovich's heart was trembling and beating so hard that it seemed it might fall out; like a bull, it began to roar; and – rushed forward.

But the *person* tapped a finger meaningfully on the table, replacing his air of indifference with a granite-like firmness; the *person* shouted:

'What do you find so surprising? That I should have written the letter to Ableukhov? . . .'

'Of course . . .'

'Forgive me, but I would say that your amazement borders on open dissembling . . .'

From behind the vase, over there, Shishnarfiev's black profile thrust itself forward; Zoya Zakharovna began to whisper to the profile, but the profile merely nodded its head; and then stared at Aleksandr Ivanovich. But Aleksandr Ivanovich saw nothing. He only exclaimed, rushing over to the *person*:

'Either I have gone mad, or – you have!'

The person winked at him:

'Well?'

While his air said:

'Ah, ah, ah, my good chap: I saw you watching us earlier . . . Do you think you can fool me? . . .'

Something happened: cheerfully, even somehow merrily, even with a kind of half-baked ardour, the *person* clicked his tongue, as though he wanted to exclaim:

'But my good chap, the baseness really is with you – only with you; not with me.'

But all he said was:

'Eh? . . . Eh? . . .'

Then, making it look as though he had with difficulty suppressed his sardonic laughter, the *person* sternly, imposingly, condescendingly placed his heavy hand on Aleksandr Ivanovich's shoulder. Reflected, and added:

'Not good . . . Not good, not good at all.'

And that same strange, oppressive and familiar state of mind seized hold of Aleksandr Ivanovich: a sense of doom before a piece of dark yellow wallpaper on which – in a moment – something fateful would appear. At this point Aleksandr Ivanovich felt the ineffable sense of guilt behind him; he looked, and it was as if a cloud were hanging over him, smoking around him from where the *person* was sitting, and smoking out of the *person*.

But the *person* was staring at him with his narrow-browed head; sitting there, and repeating:

'Not good . . .'

A painful silence ensued.

'Actually, of course, I am still waiting for the proper evidence; one cannot proceed without evidence . . . But actually: the accusation is a serious one; the accusation, I shall tell you plainly, is so serious that . . .' – here the person sighed.

'But what evidence?'

'I do not want to judge you personally for the time being . . . We in the Party act, as you know, on the basis of facts . . . And the facts, the facts . . .'

'But what facts?'

'Facts about you are being gathered . . .'

That was all he needed!

Getting up from the armchair, the *person* cut off the tip of a Havana cigar and began ambiguously to hum a little tune; now he was imperviously enclosed in his fragrance; strode into the dining-room, and amiably gripped Shishnarfiev by the shoulder.

Shouted in the direction of the kitchen, from where there was such a tasty smell of roast meat.

'I'm dying for a bite to eat . . .'

Surveyed the table and observed:

'I'd like a liqueur . . .'

Then he strode back into the little study.

. . . .

'Your visits to the yardkeeper's lodge . . . Your friendship with the house police, with the yardkeeper . . . And finally: your drinking bouts with the police clerk Voronkov . . .'

And in response to a questioning, bewildered gaze – a gaze full of horror – Lippanchenko, the *person*, that is, continued a caustic, many-meaninged whisper, placing his hand on Aleksandr Ivanovich's shoulder.

'As if you yourself didn't know! Looking surprised like that! You mean you know who Voronkov is?'

'Voronkov? Voronkov?! . . . Wait . . . what about it . . . What's going on here? . . .'

But the *person*, Lippanchenko, roared with laughter, holding his sides:

'You don't know? . . .'

'I won't assert that: I know . . .'

'Splendid! . . .'

'Voronkov is a clerk from the police station: he visits the house of yardkeeper Matvei Morzhov . . .'

'You are pleased to keep a rendezvous with a police investigator, you are pleased to go drinking with a police investigator, like I do not know what, like the latest little sleuth . . .'

'Wait! . . .'

'Not a word, not a word,' said the *person*, beginning to wave his hand as he saw that Aleksandr Ivanovich, who was frightened now in good earnest, was trying to say something.

'I repeat: the fact of your obvious part in a provocation has not yet been established, but . . . I warn you – I warn you out of friendship: Aleksandr Ivanovich, my dear fellow, you have been doing something wrong . . .'

'I?'

'Step back: it is not too late . . .'

For a moment Aleksandr Ivanovich had a plain impression that the words 'step back, it is not too late' were a kind of condition set by *a certain person*: he was not to insist on an explanation of the incident with Nikolai Apollonovich; something else seemed to be there, too – the *person* (he remembered) had himself received a very bad name here; something of the kind was happening here – that was plain: Zoya Zakharovna Fleisch's hints just now – at what else besides?

But no sooner had Aleksandr Ivanovich reflected and, having reflected, plucked up his courage somewhat, than the familiar, malevolent expression – the expression of *that same* hallucination – passed fleetingly over the fat man's face; and the frontal bones were tensed in a single violent act of stubbornness – to break his will: whatever happened, at whatever cost – to break it, or . . . explode into pieces.

And the frontal bones broke it.

Aleksandr Ivanovich, sleepily and in a state of depression, somehow drooped, and the *person*, in revenge for the moment of resistance to his will that had just taken place, once again advanced; the square head inclined low.

The little eyes – the little eyes were trying to say:

'Ah, ah, ah, my good chap . . . So that's your game?'

And the mouth sprayed spittle:

'Don't pretend to be such a simpleton . . .'

'I'm not pretending . . .'

'All Petersburg knows it . . .'

'Knows what?'

'About the exposure of T . . . T . . .'

'What?'

'Yes, yes . . .'

If the *person* had deliberately wanted to distract Aleksandr Ivanovich's thought from anything that would enable him to discover the true motives of the *person*'s behaviour, he had completely succeeded, because the news of the exposure of T . . . T . . . shook the feeble Aleksandr Ivanovich as if by thunder.

'Oh Lord Jesus Christ! . . .'

'Jesus Christ!' the person mocked. 'You knew about it before any of us . . . Until the experts give their testimony, let us assume that it is so . . . Only: do not redouble the suspicion you attract to yourself: and not a word about Ableukhov.'

Aleksandr Ivanovich must at that moment have had an extremely idiotic air, because the person continued to roar with laughter and teased him with the black grin of his wide open mouth: with the same grin does a beast's bloody carcass with flayed hide stare at us from a butcher's shop.

'Don't pretend, my dear fellow, that you know nothing about Ableukhov's role in all this; or that you know nothing about the reasons that forced me to punish Ableukhov by means of the commission I gave him; that you know nothing about how that mangy little worm played his role: the role, observe, has been played skilfully; and my little calculation was correct – my calculation that he would be sentimental, dithering, like you' – the *person* had softened: with the admission that Aleksandr Ivanovich, too, suffered from dithering he generously removed the accusation he had a moment earlier made against Aleksandr Ivanovich; that was no doubt why at the word 'dithering' something fell from Aleksandr Ivanovich's soul; he was already vaguely, vaguely trying to persuade himself that he had been wrong with regard to the *person*.

'Yes, my calculation was correct: it would appear that the noble son hates his father, is preparing to bump him off, while at the same time he pokes about among us with little talks and other balderdash; he's collecting pieces of paper, and when his collection of them is complete, he is going to present it to his dear papa . . . Yet you are all somehow inexplicably drawn to this loathsome creature . . .'

'But Nikolai Stepanych, he was – weeping . . .'

'So what, did his tears surprise you . . . Why, you are a strange fellow: tears are the usual condition of an educated investigator; why, when the educated investigator bursts into tears he thinks that he is doing so sincerely: and he possibly even regrets that he is an investigator; only those educated tears don't make us feel any easier in the slightest . . . You too, Aleksandr Ivanovich, you also weep . . . But by that I don't at all mean to infer that you are guilty' (this was not true: the person had only just now repeatedly mentioned the subject of guilt; and for a moment this *not true* filled Aleksandr Ivanovich with horror; subconsciously in his soul, like lightning, one thing had flashed: 'A bargain is being struck: I am being asked to believe a repulsive slander, or, more precisely, since I don't believe it, I'm being asked to go along with it at the price of having the slander removed from myself . . .' All this flashed beyond the threshold of his consciousness, because the terrible truth had been locked up beyond that threshold above his eyes by the frontal bones of the *person* and the oppressive atmosphere of the storm and the glitter of the little eyes with their 'aha, my good chap' . . . And he thought that he was starting to believe that slander).

'I am sure that you, Aleksandr Ivanych, are clean, but as for. Ableukhov: right here in this drawer I have a dossier for safe-keeping: later on I shall submit it to the judgement of the Party.' Here the *person* began desperately to stamp about the little study – from corner to corner – clumsily beating his hand against his starched chest. But in his tone one could hear an unfeigned vexation, a desperation – quite simply, a kind of nobility (the bargain had evidently been struck successfully).

'Later on, believe me, I shall be understood: but now the situation makes it necessary for the contagion to be torn out swiftly by the roots . . . Yes . . . I am acting like a dictator, by my will alone . . . But – believe me – I regret it: I regretted signing his sentence, but . . . dozens are perishing . . . because of your . . . senator's dear son . . . Remember, you yourself once nearly perished (Aleksandr Ivanovich thought that he had already perished) . . . Had I not . . . Remember the Yakutsk region! . . . Yet you intercede for him, condole with him . . . Weep, then, weep! There is something to weep about: dozens are perishing!!! . . .'

Here the *person* rolled his swift little eyes and walked out of the study.

It had got dark: there was blackness.

. . . .

Darkness had fallen; and it had risen between all the objects in the room; tables, cupboards, armchairs – everything had receded into profound darkness; Aleksandr Ivanovich went on sitting in the darkness – all on his own; the darkness entered his soul: he – wept.

Aleksandr Ivanovich remembered all the nuances of the *person*'s discourse and considered that all those nuances had been sincere ones; the *person* had probably not been lying; and the suspicions, the hatred – all that could be explained by Aleksandr Ivanovich's morbid condition: some chance midnight nightmare, in which the principal role was played by the *person*, might by chance become connected with some chance ambiguous remark of the *person*'s; and the food for a mental illness on a basis of alcoholism was ready; while the hallucination of the Mongol and the meaningless whisper of 'Enfranshish' that he had heard in the night – all that had done the rest. Well, what was the Mongol on the wall? Delirium. And that nefarious word.

'Enfranshish, enfranshish . . .' – what was it?

An abracadabra, an association of sounds – no more.

True, he had harboured uncharitable feelings towards the *certain person* previously, too; but this was also true: he was obligated to the *person*; – the *person* had got him out of trouble; his revulsion and horror were not justified by anything except . . . delirium: *the stain on the wallpaper*.

Oh, then he was ill, he was ill . . .

Darkness was falling: had fallen, was all around; with a kind of serious menace emerged – table, armchair, cupboard; the darkness entered his soul – he wept: Nikolai Apollonovich's moral profile now arose for the first time in its true light. How could he not have understood it?

He remembered his first meeting with him (Nikolai Apollonovich had given a little talk at the home of some mutual acquaintances in which all values were overthrown): the impression was not a pleasant one; and – further: Nikolai Apollonovich had, to tell the truth, displayed an especial curiosity about all the Party's secrets; with the absent-minded air of an awkward degenerate, he had poked his nose into everything: after all, that absent-mindedness could be affected. Aleksandr Ivanovich thought for a bit: an *agent provocateur* of superior type could of course easily possess an outward appearance like that of Ableukhov – that sadly reflective air (avoiding the gaze of the person he was talking to) and the froglike expression of those pursed lips; Aleksandr Ivanovich was slowly becoming convinced: Nikolai Apollonovich had behaved strangely throughout this whole business: and dozens were perishing . . .

To the degree in which he became persuaded of Ableukhov's involvement in the matter concerning the exposure of T.T., so did the terror-laden, oppressive feeling that had gripped him during his conversation with the *person* die away; something light, almost carefree entered his soul. Aleksandr Ivanovich had for some reason long had an especial hatred of the senator: Apollon Apollonovich inspired him with an especial revulsion, similar to the revulsion inspired in us by a phalanx, or even a tarantula; on the other hand, at times he liked Nikolai Apollonovich; but now the senator's son had united for him with the senator in a single spasm of revulsion and in a desire to root out, exterminate this tarantula-like breed.

'O, filth! . . . Dozens are perishing . . . O, filth . . .'

Better even the woodlice, the piece of dark yellow wallpaper, better even the *person*: in the *person* there was at least the grandeur of hatred; with the *person* one could at any rate unite in the desire to exterminate spiders:

'O, filth! . . .'

Across the room from him the table was already gleaming hospitably; on the table 'savouries' had been laid out: sausage, *sig* and cold veal cutlets; from afar came the contented humming of the *person*, who had at last grown tired, and Shishnarfiev's voice; this latter was taking his leave; at last he left.

Soon the *person* came barging into the room, walked up to Aleksandr Ivanovich, and placed a heavy hand on his shoulders:

'Right, then! It's better if we don't quarrel, Aleksandr Ivanovich; if our own people are at odds with one another . . . then how will we ever . . .'

. . . .

'Well, let's go and have something to eat . . . Eat with us . . . Only let us not hear a word of all this over supper . . . It's all so depressing . . . And there's no reason for Zoya Zakharovna to know about it, either: she's tired of me . . . And I'm pretty tired, too . . . We're all pretty tired . . . And it's all just − nerves . . . You and I are nervous people . . . Well − to supper, to supper . . .'

The table gleamed hospitably.

The Sad and Melancholy One Again

Aleksandr Ivanovich rang the doorbell a great number of times.

Aleksandr Ivanovich rang the doorbell outside the gate of his forbidding house; the yardkeeper did not open up for him; when he rang, the only reply from the other side of the gate was the barking of a dog; in the distance a midnight cockerel raised its lonely voice at midnight; and – died away. The Eighteenth Line stretched away – over there: into the depths, into the emptiness.

Emptiness.

Aleksandr Ivanovich experienced something that resembled satisfaction, indeed: his arrival within these lamentable walls was being delayed; all night within these lamentable walls there were rustlings, crashes and squeals.

Eventually – and this was the main thing: he would have to surmount twelve cold steps: and, turning, count their familiar number once again.

Aleksandr Ivanovich always did this four times.

In all: ninety-six echoing stone steps; further: he had to stand in front of the felt-covered door; he had with fear to put the half-rusted key in the lock. It was too risky to light a match in this pitch darkness; the light of a match might suddenly illumine the most diverse rubbish; like a mouse; and something else besides . . .

Thus did Aleksandr Ivanovich reflect.

That was why he always lingered before the gate of his forbidding house.

And – look there, now . . . –

> – Someone sad and tall, whom Aleksandr Ivanovich had several times seen down by the Neva, again appeared in the depths of the Eighteenth Line. This time he quietly stepped into the bright circle of the street lamp; but it looked as though the bright golden light had begun to stream from his brow, from his stiffening fingers . . .
>
> – Thus did the unknown friend appear on this occasion too.

Aleksandr Ivanovich remembered how one day the charming

inhabitant of the Eighteenth Line had been hailed by a little old woman who was passing in a straw hat and bonnet with lilac ribbons.

Misha, she had called him then.

Aleksandr Ivanovich shuddered every time the sad, tall figure, as he walked past, turned on him an inexpressible, all-seeing gaze; and as he did so, his sunken cheeks gleamed white in the same way. After these encounters on the Neva, Aleksandr Ivanovich saw without seeing, and heard without hearing.

'If only he would stop! . . .

'Oh, if only! . . .

'And, oh, if only he would hear me out! . . .'

But the sad, tall figure, without looking, without stopping, had already walked past.

The sound of his footsteps receded distinctly: this distinct sound proceeded from the fact that the feet of this passer-by were not shod, like those of the others, in galoshes. Aleksandr Ivanovich turned round and tried to say something to him softly; he wanted softly to call out to this unknown Misha . . .

But that place to which Misha had already irrevocably gone – that place stood empty now in a bright, shimmering circle; and there was nothing, no one, except wind and slush.

And from there blinked the fiery yellow tongue of a street lamp.

. . . .

None the less, he rang the doorbell again. A Petersburg cockerel answered the bell again: the dampish sea wind whistled through the chinks; the wind moaned in the gateway and on the other side of the street struck with all its might against an iron sign that said 'Cheap Public Dining-Room'; and the iron fell with a crash into the darkness.

Matvei Morzhov

At last the gate began to creak.

The bearded yardkeeper, Matvei Morzhov, Aleksandr Ivanovich's friend of long standing, admitted him over the house's threshold: retreat was cut off; and the gate closed.

'Why so late?'

'I had business . . .'

'Is his honour still out looking for a job?'

'Yes, that's right, I am . . .'

'Of course you are: there aren't any jobs now . . . Except maybe, if there's a vacancy at the police station . . .'

'But they won't have me at the police station, Matvei . . .'

'Of course: why should you go to the police station . . .'

'So you see?'

'And there aren't any jobs now . . .'

The bearded yardkeeper, Matvei Morzhov, sometimes sent his plump wife, who suffered permanently from an illness of the ear, to Aleksandr Ivanovich, now with a piece of pie, now with an invitation to visit; thus, they drank together on holidays, in the yardkeeper's lodge: as a man who had gone underground, it was proper for Aleksandr Ivanovich to maintain the closest friendship with the house police.

And besides.

It was simply a good opportunity to come down from his cold garret without danger (as we have seen, Aleksandr Ivanovich hated his garret, and used to stay in it for weeks on end without going out, when to do so seemed risky).

Sometimes to their company were added: Voronkov the police clerk and Bessmertny the shoemaker. And of late Styopka had been spending all his time in the yardkeeper's lodge: Styopka was out of work.

Aleksandr Ivanovich, finding himself in the little courtyard, distinctly heard the same old song floating to his ears from the yardkeeper's lodge:

> Some girls
> Don't like a clerk, –
> But I'd love one
> Any day . . .
> Eddicated
> People
> Know
> Just what to say . . .[11]

. . . .

'Got visitors again?'

Matvei Morzhov scratched the nape of his neck with ferocious reflectiveness:

'We're having a bit of fun . . .'

Aleksandr Ivanovich smiled:

'That's the clerk from the police station, isn't it? . . .'

'Who do you mean . . . Yes, that's him . . .'

Suddenly Aleksandr Ivanovich remembered that the name of Voronkov the clerk had been pressingly mentioned – back there, by the *person*; how did the *person* know Voronkov the clerk, and about Voronkov the clerk, and about their meetings? At the time, he was surprised, and had forgotten to ask.

> Mamma buy me
> For a dress
> Some silk
> That's grey;
> Now I shall
> Respect
> Vasyutka
> Son of Aleksei! . . .
>
> . . . .

Morzhov the yardkeeper, perceiving that Aleksandr Ivanovich was undecided about something, snuffled with his nose, and gloomily snapped out:

'Well, then . . . Into the lodge . . . Come on in . . .'

And Aleksandr Ivanovich would have gone: in the yardkeeper's lodge it was warm and crowded and intoxicating; while in his garret it was lonely and cold. And yet – no, no: Voronkov the police clerk was there; the *person* had spoken ambiguously about Voronkov the police clerk; and – the devil knew what he was! But the main thing was: that to go into the lodge would have been a decided act of cowardice; would have been to run away from his own walls.

With a sigh, Aleksandr Ivanovich replied:

'No, Matvei: it's time I went to bed . . .'

'Of course: as you think best! . . .'

But how they were singing in there:

> Mamma buy me
> For a dress
> Some silk
> That's blue:
> Now it is
> Vasilyev's son
> To whom I'll be true!

'Or wouldn't you like a drink of vodka?'

And simply with a kind of despair, simply with a kind of fury he shouted out:

'No, no, no!'

And hurled himself into flight towards the silvery cords of firewood.

Then Matvei Morzhov, walking away, threw open the door of the lodge for a moment: white vapour, a pencil of rays, a hubbub of voices, and a smell of warmed-up dirt that had been brought in from the street on boots came out from there in a sharp rush for an instant; and then – bang: the door slammed shut behind Matvei Morzhov.

Retreat was cut off a second time.

Again the moon lit up the distinct outlines of the little square courtyard and the silvery cords of aspen wood, between which Aleksandr Ivanovich flitted as he steered a course towards the black entrance porch. At his back, words came floating across to him from the yardkeeper's lodge; that was probably Bessmertny the shoemaker singing.

> The rails of the long railway line! . . .
> The embankment! . . . The signal's hand!
> As the train into washed-away clay
> Flew plunging from sleepers to land.
> A scene of shattered rail coaches!
> A scene of unfortunate folk! . . .

The rest was not audible.

Aleksandr Ivanovich stopped: yes, yes, yes: it was starting; he had not yet managed to shut himself up in his dark yellow cube, yet already: it was starting, emerging – his inevitable, nightly torture. And this time it had started outside the rear entrance door.

. . . .

The same thing was still going on: *they* were keeping an eye on Aleksandr Ivanovich . . . It had started like this: once, as he returned home, he had seen a man whom he did not know coming down the staircase, and the man had said to him:

'You are connected with Him . . .'

Who the man coming down the staircase was, and who *He* (with a capital letter) was, Who connected people to Himself, Aleksandr Ivanovich had not waited to find out, and had instead rushed up the staircase away from the stranger. The stranger had not pursued him.

And – it had *happened* to Dudkin a second time: he had encountered in the street a man in a peaked cap pulled deep down over his eyes, and with a face so dreadful (inexpressibly dreadful) that a lady whom he did not know and who happened to be passing at the time had seized Aleksandr Ivanovich by the coat-sleeve in alarm:

'Did you see? That is horrible, why, it is horrible . . . That does not happen! . . . Oh, what is it? . . .'

Meanwhile, the man had passed by.

But in the evening, on the third-floor landing, Aleksandr Ivanovich had been seized by some kind of arms and shoved against the railings, in a manifest attempt to push him – there, down there . . . Aleksandr Ivanovich had defended himself, struck a match, and . . . there was no one on the staircase: footsteps neither descending nor ascending. It was deserted.

Finally at night of late Aleksandr Ivanovich had heard inhuman shrieking . . . from the staircase: how someone shrieked! . . . Shrieked, and then cried out no more.

But the tenants did not hear the shrieking.

Only once had he heard that shrieking – there, by the Bronze Horseman: that was exactly what the shrieking sounded like. But that had been a motor car, lit up by reflectors. Only once had Stepan, who was out of work, and sometimes whiled away the nights with him, heard . . . the shrieking. But in response to all Aleksandr Ivanovich's pestering, all he would say, morosely, was:

'That's *them* looking for you . . .'

As to who *they* were, about that Styopka kept mum. And said not

another word. Only this Styopka began to avoid Aleksandr
Ivanovich's company, and came to see him less frequently; and as
for spending the night – not on your life . . . And neither to the
yardkeeper, nor to Voronkov the police clerk, nor to the shoemaker did Styopka say a word. And neither did Aleksandr
Ivanovich . . .

But to be forcibly dragooned *into all this*, and not to be able to
tell anyone about it!

'That's *them* looking for you . . .'

Who were *they*, and why were *they* looking? . . .

. . . .

There, right now, for example.

Aleksandr Ivanovich involuntarily cast his gaze aloft: to a small
window on the fifth, attic floor; and there was light in the window:
one could see some kind of angular shadow restlessly slouching
about in the window. In an instant he felt about in his pocket for
the key to his room: he had the key with him. Then who was up
there in his locked room?

Was it perhaps a search? Oh, if only that were all it were: he
would fly to the search, like the happiest of men; even if they were
to arrest him and put him in . . . the Peter and Paul Fortress, they
would at least be human beings – *not them*.

'That's *them* looking for you . . .'

Aleksandr Ivanovich drew a deep breath and vowed to himself in
advance not to be excessively frightened, because the events in
which he might now be involved were simply an idle, cerebral
game.

Aleksandr Ivanovich went in through the back entrance.

A Lifeless Ray Was Falling through the Window

Yes, yes, yes: there *they* stood; that was how *they* had stood at the
time of his last nocturnal return. And *they* were waiting for him.
Who *they* were, it was positively impossible to say: two outlines. A
lifeless ray was falling through the window from the third floor; it
lay whitishly on the grey steps.

And in the most total darkness the whitish blotches lay there so horribly calmly – dauntlessly.

It was into this particular whitish blotch that the railings of the staircase ran; and next to the railings *they* stood: two outlines; they let Aleksandr Ivanovich through, standing to the right and the left of him; this was how they had let Aleksandr Ivanovich through on that occasion, too; had said nothing, had not moved a muscle, had not flinched; all he felt was someone's evil eye, screwed up, but not blinking, trained on him out of the darkness.

Should he approach *them*, whisper in their ears the incantation that had arisen in his memory out of a dream?

'Enfranshish, enfranshish! . . .'

It was hard – to enter this whitish blotch under their fixed gaze: to be lit up by the moon, feeling on both sides the keen stare of an observer; and again – what was it, to feel the observers of the back staircase behind one's back, ready for anything at any second; it was hard, was it not, to refrain from quickening one's step and to cough indifferently?

For Aleksandr Ivanovich had only to rush suddenly, as swift as lightning, up the steps of the staircase, and the observers would rush up after him.

Here the whitish blotches became grey blotches and then began harmoniously to melt; and melted away altogether in the total darkness (a black cloud had evidently covered the moon).

Aleksandr Ivanovich calmly entered the place that had previously been white, and could no longer see the eyes, from which he concluded that his eyes too could not be seen (poor fellow, he consoled himself with the vain thought that he would be able to slip upstairs to his garret unseen). Aleksandr Ivanovich did not quicken his step, and even – began to tweak his small moustache; and . . .

. . . Aleksandr Ivanovich could not endure it any longer.

He flew like an arrow up to the second-floor landing (oh, what an indiscretion!). And, having flown up to the landing, he permitted himself something that definitely lowered him in the opinion of the outline standing there.

Leaning over the railings, he hurled down a bewildered, frightened glance, having first thrown down a lighted match: the iron struts of the railings flared; and amidst this yellow glimmering Aleksandr Ivanovich plainly discerned silhouettes.

Great was his amazement!

One of the silhouettes was quite simply the Tartar, Makhmudka, who lived in the basement; in the yellow shimmer of the dying match as it fell past, Makhmudka was leaning towards a little gentleman of ordinary appearance; the little gentleman of ordinary appearance was wearing a bowler hat, but had the features of an Oriental; and the hook-nosed, Oriental man was trying to ask Makhmudka something, and Makhmudka was shaking his head.

After that, the match went out: nothing could be discerned.

But the burning match had betrayed Aleksandr Ivanovich's presence to the hook-nosed Oriental; feet began quickly to shuffle upstairs; and now, right above Aleksandr Ivanovich's ear, a glib voice rang out, but . . . imagine, without an accent.

'Excuse me, are you Andrei Andreich Gorelsky?'

'No, I'm Aleksandr Ivanovich Dudkin . . .'

'Yes, according to your false passport . . .'

Aleksandr Ivanovich started: he was indeed living on a false passport, but his name, patronymic and surname were: Aleksandr Alekseyevich Pogorelsky, not Andrei Andreich Gorelsky.

Aleksandr Ivanovich started, but . . . decided that attempts at concealment would serve no purpose:

'I am he, but what is your business? . . .'

'Excuse me, please: on the first occasion I came to see you at such an inopportune time . . .'

'That's all right . . .'

'This unlit back staircase: your flat turned out to be locked . . . And there is someone in there . . . I preferred to wait for you at the entrance . . . And then this back staircase . . .'

'But who is waiting for me there? . . .'

'I do not know: the voice of some man of the common people answered me from within . . .'

Styopka! . . . Thank God: it was Styopka!

'But what is your business? . . .'

'Forgive me, I have heard so much about you: you and I have mutual friends . . . Nikolai Stepanych Lippanchenko, at whose home I am received like a son . . . I have long, long wanted to make

your acquaintance ... I have heard that you are a night-owl ...
And so I took the liberty ... Actually, I live in Helsingfors and am
here on a visit, though my home is in the south ...'

Aleksandr Ivanovich quickly realized that his guest was lying;
and lying, moreover, in a most insolent fashion, for the *same* story
had been repeated once before (where and when – that he could not
remember at the moment: perhaps it had all happened in a dream
that had instantly been forgotten; and now it had arisen once again).

No, no, no: there was something altogether fishy here; but he
must not let on; and Aleksandr Ivanovich replied into the total
darkness:

'With whom do I have the honour of speaking?'

'My name is Shishnarfne, I am a Persian subject ... You and I
have already met ...'

'Shishnarfiev? ...

'No, Shishnarfne: they added the v ending to my name – for the
sake of *russisme*, perhaps ... You and I were together today – back
there, at Lippanchenko's; two hours I sat, waiting for you to finish
your business conversation, and then I couldn't wait for you any
longer ... Zoya Zakharovna did not warn me in time that you
would be there. I have long been seeking a meeting with you ... *I
have been looking for you for a long time ...*'

This last sentence, like the transformation of Shishnarfiev into
Shishnarfne, again dreamily reminded him of something: it was
something nasty, depressing, worrying.

'You and I have met before?'

'Yes ... don't you remember? In Helsingfors ...'

Aleksandr Ivanovich dimly remembered something; unexpectedly
to himself he lit another match and brought this match right up to
Shishnarfiev's – or rather, Shishnarfne's – nose; for a moment the
walls flared with a yellow reflection, the struts of the railings
glimmered; and out of the darkness before his very face suddenly
formed the face of the Persian subject; Aleksandr Ivanovich clearly
remembered now having seen this face in a Helsingfors coffee
house;[12] but the face had for some reason not lowered its suspicious
eyes from Aleksandr Ivanovich on that occasion, too.

'Do you remember?'

Aleksandr Ivanovich remembered more, more: namely: it had

been in Helsingfors that all the symptoms of the illness that menaced him had begun; it was precisely in Helsingfors that the whole of that idle cerebral game of his, a game that seemed as if inspired by someone else, had begun.

He recalled that at that period he had had occasion to develop a paradoxical theory about the necessity of destroying culture, because the period of obsolete humanism was over and cultural history now stood before us like weathered marl; a period of healthy brutishness was beginning, pushing forth out of the depths of the people (the hooliganism, the violence of the Apachés),[13] from the heights of the aristocracy (the revolt of the arts against established forms, the love of primitive culture, exoticism) and from the bourgeoisie itself (the Oriental ladies' fashions, the cakewalk – a Negro dance; and – so on); at this time Aleksandr Ivanovich was preaching the burning of libraries, universities, and museums; he also preached summoning the Mongols (later on he took fright at the Mongols). All the phenomena of contemporary reality were divided by him into two categories; the symptoms of an already obsolete culture and the signs of a healthy barbarism, compelled for the moment to hide under a mask of refinement (the phenomenon of Nietzsche and Ibsen) and under this mask to infect the heart with a chaos that was already secretly crying out in people's souls.

Aleksandr Ivanovich invited them to remove their masks and openly exist with chaos.

He recalled that he had preached this that day in the Helsingfors coffee house; and when someone asked him how he would view Satanism, he had replied:

'Christianity is obsolete: in Satanism there is a crude fetish worship, that is, a healthy barbarism . . .'

And that day – he remembered – by his side, at a table, Shishnarfne had sat, never taking his eyes off him.

The preaching of barbarism had ended in an unexpected fashion (in Helsingfors, that same day): had ended in a complete nightmare; Aleksandr Ivanovich had seen (half in a dream, half in a state of falling asleep) himself being whirled through what might most simply be called interplanetary space (but which was not that): whirled in order to perform an act that was quite commonplace *there*, but was from our point of view none the less infamous; this had indubitably been in a dream (between ourselves – what is a dream?), but a hideous dream that had had its effect in bringing the preaching to an end; the unpleasant thing about it all was that Aleksandr Ivanych could not remember whether he had performed the *act* or not; Aleksandr Ivanych subsequently considered this dream to have been the beginning of his illness, but – even so: he did not like to remember it.

This was the reason why back then he had begun to read the Book of Revelation on the sly.

And now, here on the staircase, the mention of Helsingfors had a dreadful effect. Helsingfors rose before him. He found himself thinking:

'That is why I have been hearing over and again these past few weeks, without any meaning: "Hel-sin-fors, Hel-sin-fors . . ."'

And Shishnarfne continued:

'Do you remember?'

The matter had taken a repulsive turn: he must rush into flight immediately – up the stone flights of stairs; he must take advantage of the darkness; otherwise a phosphorescent light would cast whitish blotches through the windows. But Aleksandr Ivanovich lingered in the most total horror; for some reason he had been shocked by his commonplace visitor's surname:

'Shishnarfne, Shishnarfne . . . I know it from somewhere . . .'

And Shishnarfne continued:

'So will you permit me to come in? . . . I must confess I have grown tired, waiting for you . . . I hope you will excuse me this midnight visit of mine . . .'

And in a fit of involuntary terror, Aleksandr Ivanovich shrieked out:

'You are welcome . . .'

But thought:

'Styopka there will get me out of it.'

. . . .

Aleksandr Ivanovich ran up the staircase. After him ran Shishnarfne; the infinite series of steps did not seem to be taking them to the fifth floor: the end of the staircase was not in sight; and it was impossible to run back down again: at his shoulders ran Shishnarfne, while before him from his little room came a stream of light.

Aleksandr Ivanovich thought:

'How could Styopka have dropped in to see me: after all, I have the key on me, don't I?'

But, feeling about in his pocket, he realized that the key was not there: instead of the door key he had the key to his old suitcase.

Petersburg

Aleksandr Ivanovich flew, not himself, into his wretched room and saw that Stepan was sprawled on the dirty trestle of the bed over a guttering candle; his shaggy head was sunk low before an open book with Church Slavonic lettering.

Stepan was reading the Prayer Book.

Aleksandr Ivanovich remembered Styopka's promise: to bring the Prayer Book with him (he was interested in a prayer it contained – St Basil the Great's prayer, the admonitory one, to devils).[14] And he caught at Styopka.

'It's you, Styopka: oh, I'm glad!'

'Here, *barin*, I've brought you the Pr –' – but after a look at the visitor who had entered, Styopka added – 'what you asked for . . .'

'Thank you . . .'

'While I was waiting for you, I got absorbed in reading . . .' (again a look in the direction of the visitor) '. . . It's time I went . . .'

Aleksandr Ivanovich caught at Styopka with his hand:

'Don't go away, stay for a bit ... This *barin* is Mr Shishnarfiev . . .'

But from the door a metallic voice rapped out hoarsely:

'Not Shishnarfiev, but . . . Shish-nar-fne . . .'

And what made *him* insist on the absence of the v ending? *He* was visible outside the door; *he* took off his little bowler hat; did not throw off his little coat and surveyed the room with a questioning gaze:

'It's not very nice in your room . . . A bit damp . . . and cold . . .'

The candle was burning down: the wrapping paper flared, and suddenly the walls began to dance in a watery red light.

. . . .

'No, *barin*, let me go: it's time I went' – Styopka began to fuss at this point, squinting in hostile fashion at Aleksandr Ivanovich and not looking at the guest at all – 'let me go – until another time.'

He took the Prayer Book with him.

Under Stepan's fixed gaze Aleksandr Ivanovich lowered his eyes; the fixed gaze, it seemed to him, was a condemning gaze. And what was he going to do with Stepan now? He wanted to say something to Stepan; he had hurt Stepan; Stepan would not forgive; and, it seemed to him, Stepan was now thinking:

'No, *barin*, if *folk like that* have taken to coming to visit you, there is nothing to be done; and the Prayer Book is no use . . . *Folk like that* don't come to see everyone; and those to whom *they* come are birds of the same feather . . .'

That meant, that meant, if Stepan thought he was – the visitor: was indeed suspicious . . . And then, how would he manage, he, alone – without Styopka:

'Stepan, please stay.'

But Stepan waved him away, not without a shade of revulsion: as though he were afraid that *this fellow* might come bothering him, too:

'It's *you* he's come to see: not me . . .'

And in his soul reverberated:

'It's *you* they're looking for . . .'

The door banged shut behind Stepan. Aleksandr Ivanovich was about to shout after him to tell him to leave the Prayer Book, but . . . was too ashamed. Suddenly he would utter the little words, 'Prayer Book', so compromising for a free-thinker; but – Aleksandr Ivanovich had vowed to himself in advance: not to be excessively frightened, because the events that he might be involved in after Stepan left would be an auditory and visual hallucination. The flames, blood-red torches, having done their dance, were dying on the walls; the paper had burned up: the little flame of the candle was dying; everything was a deathly green colour . . .

. . . .

With a gesture of his hand he invited the visitor to sit down on the blanket-covered trestle at the little table; he himself stood in the doorway, so that if necessary he would be able to get out to the staircase and lock the visitor in, while he went racing off down all ninety-six steps as fast as his legs would carry him.

The visitor, leaning on the window-sill, lit a cigarette and jabbered; his black contour was delineated against the shining green spaces beyond the window (there the moon was racing through the clouds) . . .

'I see that I have come to visit you at the wrong time . . . that I am evidently troubling you . . .'

'It's all right, very glad to see you,' Aleksandr Ivanovich Dudkin said, trying unconvincingly to reassure his guest, but himself in need of reassurance, and warily feeling with a hand behind his back to see if the door was locked or unlocked.

'But . . . I have so much wanted to see you, have looked for you everywhere, and when we did not manage to meet at Zoya Zakharovna Fleisch's, I asked her to give me your address; and from her, from Zoya Zakharovna, I came straight to you: to wait for you . . . All the more, since I am leaving tomorrow at first light.'

'Leaving?' Aleksandr Ivanovich asked, echo-like, because it seemed to him: the visitor's words had divided into two inside him: and while his outer ear had heard 'I am leaving at first light', some other kind of ear had distinctly heard:

'I am leaving in the daytime, but will come back at twilight . . .'

But he did not persist, continuing to hear the words beating at his ears, resounding, but not responding.

'Yes, I am leaving for Finland, for Sweden . . . That is where I live; though actually, my home is in Shemakha; but I live in Finland: I confess that the climate of Petersburg is harmful to *me*, too . . .'

This 'to *me*, too' echoed, divided in his consciousness. The Petersburg climate was harmful to everyone; the visitor could have easily managed without emphasizing 'to *me*, too'.

'Yes,' Aleksandr Ivanovich replied mechanically, 'Petersburg stands on a swamp . . .'

At this the black contour on a background of green spaces beyond the window (there the moon was racing through the clouds) darted away, and – went off to write complete balderdash.

'Yes, yes, yes . . . For the Russian Empire Petersburg is a most characteristic little dot . . . Take the geographical map . . . But concerning the fact that our capital city, abundantly adorned with monuments, also belongs to the land of the world beyond the grave . . .'

'Oh, oh, oh!' thought Aleksandr Ivanovich: 'I must keep my ears pricked up, so that I'll be able to run away in time . . .'

But he retorted:

'You say our capital city . . . But it isn't yours: *your* capital city is not Petersburg but Teheran . . . For you, an Oriental, the climatic conditions of *our* capital . . .'

'I'm a cosmopolitan: why, I have been in both Paris and London . . . Yes – what was I saying: that *our* capital city,' the black contour went on, 'belongs to the land of the world beyond the grave – it is not done to speak of this for some reason when compiling geographical maps, guidebooks and directories; the venerable Mr Baedeker keeps eloquently silent about it; the modest provincial who is not informed of this in time gets into a fix at the Nikolayevsky or even the Varshavsky Station; he reckons in terms of Petersburg's visible administration: he has no shadow passport.'

'What do you mean?'

'Well, quite simply: when I set off for the land of the Papuans, I know that in the land of the Papuans a Papuan awaits me: Karl Baedeker warns me in advance about this sad phenomenon of nature; but how would it be if on the way to Kirsanov I were to encounter the camp of a swarthy Papuan horde, something that will, as a matter of fact, soon happen in France, for France is arming the black hordes on the quiet and will introduce them into Europe – you will see: actually, that ought to serve your purpose – your theory of the brutalization and overthrow of culture: do you remember? . . . In the Helsingfors coffee house I listened to you with sympathy.'

Aleksandr Ivanovich was growing more and more out of sorts: he was shaken by fever; it was especially loathsome to hear a reference to a theory he had abandoned; after his dreadful Helsingfors dream, he had manifestly realized the connection between that theory and Satanism; he had rejected all that, as an illness; and now, when he was ill again, the black contour was returning it all to him with interest, in a revolting fashion.

There, in the moonlit little cupboard of a room, against the background of the window, the black contour was becoming ever thinner, more aerial, lighter; he looked like a sheet of dark, black paper, motionlessly stuck in the window frame; his resonant voice, outside him, resounded of itself in the midst of the square room: but most surprising of all was the fact that the very centre of the voice was moving in a most noticeable fashion – from the window – in Aleksandr Ivanovich's direction; it was an independent, invisible centre, from which earsplitting sounds grew louder and louder:

'And so, what was I saying? Yes ... about the Papuan: the Papuan is, so to speak, an earthborn creature; the biology of the Papuan, though it is even somewhat primitive – is not alien to you, Aleksandr Ivanovich. In the end you will come to terms with the Papuan; well, even if it's with the help of the spirituous liquor to which you have been rendering tribute all these recent days and which has created a most favourable atmosphere for our meeting; and moreover: in Papua, too, there exist some sort of institutes of legal foundation which have, perhaps, been approved by the Papuan parliament ...'

It passed through Aleksandr Ivanovich's mind that the visitor's behaviour was not proper at all, because the sound of the visitor's voice was separated from the visitor in a most indecent manner; and indeed the visitor himself, who had frozen motionless on the windowsill – or did his eyes deceive him? – had plainly become a layer of soot on the moonlit pane, while his voice, becoming ever more resonant and acquiring the timbre of a gramophone screeching, resounded right above Aleksandr Ivanovich's ear.

'A shadow is not even a Papuan; the biology of shadows has not yet been studied; and so I tell you this – never come to terms with a shadow: you will not understand its demands; in Petersburg it will enter into you through the bacilli of all kinds of diseases that are swallowed in the very water that comes through the taps ...'

'And in vodka,' Aleksandr Ivanovich interjected, and found himself thinking: 'Why did I say that? Or have I bitten on fever? Have I been answering myself, echoing myself?' He at once decided to dissociate himself once and for all from this balderdash; if he did not at once decompose this balderdash with his mind, then his mind would itself decompose in the balderdash.

'No, sir: in vodka you will only introduce me into your mind . . . Not in vodka but in water do you swallow the bacilli, and I am not a bacillus; and – look here: since you do not have a proper passport, you are subject to all kinds of consequences: why, ever since the very first days of your sojourn in Petersburg your stomach has not been digesting properly; you have been threatened by cholerine . . . thereupon follow incidents from which neither petitions nor complaints to the Petersburg police will deliver you; your stomach does not digest properly? . . . But – what about Dr Inozemtsev's drops?[15] You are dispirited by depression, hallucinations, gloominess – all consequences of cholerine – then go to the Farce Theatre . . . Give yourself a bit of entertainment . . . Now tell me, Aleksandr Ivanovich, for friendship's sake – you do suffer from hallucinations, don't you?'

'Why, he is simply mocking me,' thought Aleksandr Ivanovich.

'You suffer from hallucinations – it is not the constable but the psychiatrist who will tell me about them . . . In a word, your complaints, addressed to the visible world, will remain without result, like all complaints: after all, one must admit that we do not live in a visible world . . . The tragedy of our situation is that we are, like it or not, in an invisible world; in a word, complaints to the visible world will remain without result; and therefore it remains to you to make a respectful petition to the world of shadows.'

'But is there such a thing?' Aleksandr Ivanovich shrieked with defiance, preparing to leap out of the cupboard of a room and lock the visitor in, a visitor who was becoming ever more subtle: into this room came a thickset young man who possessed three dimensions; as he leaned against the window he became simply a contour (and, in addition: two-dimensional); moreover: he became a thin layer of black soot, like the one that falls out of a lamp if the lamp is badly trimmed; and now this black window soot, forming a human contour, grey all over, was smouldering to ash that gleamed in the moonlight; and already the ash had smouldered away: the contour was entirely covered in green blotches – openings into the spaces of

the moon; in a word: there was no contour. The fact of it was plain
– here the decomposition of matter itself was taking place; that
matter had turned, all of it, without residue, into a substance of
sound that jabbered deafeningly – only where? To Aleksandr
Ivanovich it seemed that it was jabbering inside himself.

'You, Mr Shishnarfne,' said Aleksandr Ivanovich, addressing
space (for after all, Shishnarfne was no longer there), 'are perhaps
an issuer of passports for the world beyond?'

'Original,' jabbered Aleksandr Ivanovich, replying to himself –
or more correctly, something jabbered out of Aleksandr Ivanovich
... 'Petersburg possesses not three dimensions, but four; the
fourth is subject to obscurity and is not marked on maps at all,
except as a dot, for a dot is the place where the plane of this
existence touches against the spherical surface of the immense
astral cosmos; so any dot of Petersburg space is capable in the
twinkling of an eye of throwing up an inhabitant of that dimension, from which a wall is no salvation; so you see, a moment ago
I was there – in the dots that are on the window-sill, and now I
have appeared . . .'

'Where?' Aleksandr Ivanovich wanted to exclaim, but could not,
because his throat exclaimed:

'I have appeared . . . out of a dot in your larynx . . .'

Aleksandr Ivanovich looked around him in bewilderment as his
throat, automatically, ceasing to obey him, hurled out
deafeningly:

'One needs a passport here . . . As a matter of fact, you are
registered with us there: all you have to do now is to complete a
final passport application; this passport is made out inside you; you
will sign it inside yourself by means of some extravagant little
action, for example . . . Oh yes, the little action will come to you:
you will perform it yourself; that kind of signing is acknowledged
among us as the best kind . . .'

Had my panic-stricken hero been able to take a look at himself
from the side at that moment, he would have been horrified: in the
greenish, moonlit little cupboard of a room he would have seen
himself clutching at his stomach and bawling with effort into the
absolute emptiness in front of him; his head was thrown right back,
and the enormous opening of his yelling mouth would have seemed

to him a black abyss of non-existence; but Aleksandr Ivanovich could not jump out of himself: and he did not see himself; the voice that was thunderously booming out of him seemed to him like an alien automaton.

'But when was I registered with you there?' lurched through his brain (the balderdash had vanquished his mind).

'Oh, then: after the act,' his mouth deafeningly ripped itself apart; and, having ripped itself apart, closed.

At this point before Aleksandr Ivanovich a veil was suddenly rent: he remembered everything clearly ... That dream in Helsingfors, when *they* had whirled him through some kind of ... yes ... spaces that were connected with our spaces in their mathematical point of contact, so that while remaining fixed to space he had none the less truly been able to sail off into spaces – well, and so: when *they* had whirled him through different spaces ...

He had done *it*.

By doing it he had united himself with *them*, and Lippanchenko was merely an image that alluded to this; he had done *it*; and *with it* strength had entered him; racing from organ to organ and seeking the soul in the body, this strength was gradually taking hold of him entirely (he had become a drunkard, sensual passion had begun to play naughty tricks, et cetera).

And while *it* was happening to him, he had thought that *they* were looking for him; but *they* were inside him.

And while he thought this, out of him came roarings that were like the roarings of motor-car horns:

'Our spaces are not like yours; there everything flows backwards ... And there Ivanov is some kind of Japanese, for that name, read backwards, is Japanese: Vonavi.'

'So your name, too, has to be read back to front,' lurched through his brain.

And he grasped it: 'Shishnarfne, Shish-nar-fne ...' That was a familiar word, which he had uttered as he had performed the *act*; only that drowsily familiar word had to be turned back to front.

And in a fit of involuntary terror, he made an effort to shriek out:

'Enfranshish.'

And from the depths of himself, starting near his heart, but really through the apparatus of his larynx came the reply:

'You summoned me . . . Well – here I am . . .'

Now *Enfranshish*[16] itself had come for his soul.

· · · · · · · ·

With a monkey-like hop Aleksandr Ivanovich leapt out of his own room: the key turned in the lock; he was stupid – he ought to have jumped out of his body, not his room; perhaps the room was his body, and he was merely a shadow? That must be the case, because from the other side of the locked door menacingly boomed the voice that had just boomed out of his own throat:

'Yes, yes, yes . . . It is I . . . I annihilate irrevocably . . .'

· · · · · · · ·

Suddenly the moon lit up the steps of the staircase: in the most total darkness emerged, barely perceptible, grey, whitish, pale and then also phosphorescently burning blotches.

The Loft

By a chance piece of negligence, the loft was not locked; and Dudkin rushed inside.

He banged the door shut behind him.

It is strange at night in a loft; its floor is strewn with earth; you walk smoothly over a soft surface; suddenly: a thick beam flies under your feet and lands you on all fours. Brightly the moon's transverse rays stretch like white rafters: you walk through them.

Suddenly . . . –

A transverse beam confers a wallop on your nose with all its might; you risk being left for ever with a broken nose.

The motionless white blotches – of long underwear, towels and sheets . . . A puff of wind flutters by – and the white blotches stretch: long underwear, towels and sheets.

Everything is deserted.

Aleksandr Ivanovich somehow ended up in the loft all at once; and, having ended up in the loft, was surprised that the loft was unlocked; the house laundress, completely immersed in thoughts of her intended, probably had left the door open after her. When Aleksandr Ivanovich slipped through this door he felt reassured, kept quiet: sighed with relief; behind him there were neither running footsteps, nor the gramophone screeching of the abracadabra; nor even a banging door.

But through the broken panes of the window a song could be heard from far away:

> Mamma buy me for a dress
> Some silk that's blue . . .

The dully banging door resolved itself into the beating of his heart; and the shadow that was falling downstairs merely into a shadow over the moon; the rest was a hallucination; he must undergo a cure – that was all.

Aleksandr Ivanovich listened closely. And – what could he hear? What he could hear you already know: the quite distinct sound of a cracking rafter; and – a dense silence: that is – a mesh woven of nothing but rustlings; among them, firstly – in the corner there were shushes and hushes; secondly – a tension of the atmosphere caused by the inaudible impact of footsteps; and – the sound of some kind of idiot swallowing his saliva.

In a word – just ordinary, domestic sounds: and there was no reason to be afraid of them.

At this point Aleksandr Ivanovich regained control of himself; and he could have returned: in his room – he knew this now for certain – there was no one, nothing (the attack of illness had passed). But all the same he did not feel like leaving the loft: carefully, amidst the long underwear, towels and sheets, he walked over to the window with its autumn cobwebs and stuck his head through the splinters of glass: what he saw now breathed towards him with reassurance and peace-instilling sadness.

Beneath his feet he saw clearly – and with distinct and dazzling simplicity: the well-marked square of the courtyard, that from here looked toylike, the silvery cords of ash wood, from which he had so recently looked up in unfeigned alarm at the windows of his room; but also, and this was the main thing: in the yardkeeper's lodge they were still making merry; a hoarse little song was coming from the lodge; the door block rattled; and two small figures appeared; one of them burst out bawling:

> I see, O Lord, my own unrighteousness:
> Falsehood has deceived me to my face,
> Falsehood has blinded my eyes . . .
> I was sorry to lose my white body,
> I was sorry to lose my coloured raiment,
> Sweet victuals,
> Intoxicating drink –
> I, Pontius, feared the archpriests,
> I, Pilate, went in dread of the Pharisees.
> Washed my hands – washed away my conscience!
> An innocent did I consign to crucifixion . . .

This was sung by: Voronkov the police station clerk and Bessmertny the basement shoemaker. Aleksandr Ivanovich thought: 'Should I go down and join them?' And would have gone down . . . had it not been for – the staircase.

The staircase frightened him.

The sky had cleared. The turquoise island roof that was somewhere there, below him, to the side – the turquoise island roof whimsically traced its silvery scales, and then those silvery scales merged entirely with the living tremor of the Neva's waters.

And the Neva seethed.

And cried there despairingly in the whistle of a small, late-passing steamboat, of which all that could be seen was the receding eye of a red lantern. Further away, on the other side of the Neva, stretched the Embankment; above the boxes of yellow, grey and brown houses, above the columns of grey and brown-red palaces, rococo and baroque, rose the dark walls of an enormous temple made by hand of man, its golden dome stuck sharply up into the world of the moon – from stone walls black-grey, cylindrical and slightly raised in form, surrounded by a colonnade: St Isaac's . . .

And, scarcely visible, the golden Admiralty soared into the sky like an arrow.

The voice sang:

> Have mercy, Lord!
> Forgive, Christ! . . .

To the tsar my rank I will return – I pine for my soul,
Will sell my house – give to the poor,
dismiss my wife – seek out God . . .
Have mercy, Lord!
Forgive, Christ!

. . . .

Probably at one o'clock in the morning – there, on the square, the little old grenadier was snoring, supporting himself on his bayonet; his shaggy cap rested against the bayonet, and the grenadier's shadow lay motionless on the patterned interweavings of the railings.

The entire square was deserted.

At this midnight hour the metal hooves fell and clanged on the rock; the horse snorted through its nostrils into the white-hot fog; the Horseman's bronze outline now detached itself from the horse's croup, and a jingling spur impatiently grazed the horse's flank, to make the horse fly down from the rock.

And the horse flew down from the rock.

Over the stones raced a *heavily resonant** clatter – across the bridge: to the Islands. The Bronze Horseman flew on into the fog; in his eyes was a greenish depth; the muscles of his metal hands straightened, tautened; and the bronze sinciput darted; the horse's hooves fell on the cobblestones, on the swift and blinding arcs; the horse's mouth split apart in a deafening neighing, reminiscent of the whistlings of a locomotive; the thick steam from its nostrils splashed the street with luminous boiling water; horses that were coming the other way snorted and shied in horror; and passers-by, in horror, closed their eyes.

Line after Line flew past: as did a piece of the left bank – with quays, steamer funnels and a dirty heap of sacks stuffed with hemp; as did vacant lots, barges, fences, tarpaulins and numerous small houses. While from the seashore, from the outskirts of the city, a side gleamed out of the fog: the side of a turbulent little drinking-house.

The very oldest Dutchman, clad in black leather, leaned forward, away from the mildewed threshold – into a cold pandemonium (the

* Pushkin.

moon had fled behind a cloud); and a lantern quivered in his fingers under his bluish face in its black leather hood: evidently, from there the Dutchman's sensitive ear had heard the horse's heavy clattering and locomotive-like neighing, because the Dutchman had abandoned the other seamen like himself, whose glasses chimed from morning to morning.

He evidently knew that here the furious, drunken feast would drag on all the way until the dim morning; he evidently knew that when the clock struck long after midnight, the sturdy Guest would come flying to the hollow chiming of the glasses: to knock back the fiery Allasch; to shake more than one hawser-rubbed hand, which from the captain's bridge would turn the heavy steamship wheel outside the very forts of Kronstadt; and in pursuit of the foam-seething stern that had not replied to the signal, a cannon's iron muzzle would cast its roar.

But the vessel would not be overtaken: it would enter the cloud that had settled over the sea; would fuse with it, would move with it – into the clear blue of the hours before dawn.

All this the very oldest Dutchman knew, clad in black leather and craning forward into the fog from the mildewy steps: now he could discern the outline of the flying Horseman . . . The clattering could already be heard over there; and – the nostrils snorted, penetrating the fog, as they flamed, like a luminous white-hot pillar.

. . . .

Aleksandr Ivanovich walked away from the window, reassured, pacified, shivering (a cold breeze was blowing at him through the glass splinters); while towards him the white blotches began to sway – long underwear, towels and sheets; the breeze fluttered by . . .

And the blotches moved.

Timidly he opened the loft door; he had decided to go back to his little cupboard-like room.

How Could It Have Happened . . .

Illumined, covered in phosphorescent blotches, he was now sitting on the dirty bed, resting from his attacks of terror; the visitor had just been – here; and here – a dirty woodlouse was crawling: the visitor had gone. These attacks of terror! During the night there had been three, four, five of them; the hallucination had been followed by a clearing of his consciousness.

He sat inside the clearing like the moon that was shining far away – in front of fleeing clouds; and like the moon, his consciousness shone, illumining his soul as the moon illumines the labyrinths of the prospects. Far in front and behind, his consciousness lit up the cosmic ages and the cosmic expanses.

In those expanses there was no soul: neither person nor shadow.

And – the expanses were deserted.

Amidst his four mutually perpendicular walls he seemed to himself a prisoner captured in expanses, if, that was, a captured prisoner did not sense freedom more than anyone else, and if this narrow little interval between walls was not equal in volume to the whole of outer space.

Outer space was deserted! His deserted room! ... Outer space was the final attainment to which wealth could aspire ... Monotonous outer space! ... His room had always been characterized by monotony ... A beggar's abode would seem excessively luxurious compared to the wretched furnishings of outer space. If he really had moved away from the world, the world's luxurious splendour would seem wretched compared to these dark yellow walls ...

· · · · · · · ·

Aleksandr Ivanovich, resting from the attacks of delirium, began to dream of how he had risen high above the world's sensual mirage.

A mocking voice retorted:

'The vodka?'

'The smoking?'

'The lustful feelings?'

So was he really raised above the world's mirage?

His head sagged; that was where the illnesses and the terrors and the persecution came from – from insomnia, cigarettes, and the abuse of spirituous liquors.

He felt a most violent stab of pain in a diseased molar tooth; he clutched at his cheek with his hand.

His attack of acute insanity was illuminated for him in a new way; now he knew the truth of acute insanity; insanity itself, in essence, stood before him like a report by his diseased organs of sense – to his self-conscious 'I'; while Shishnarfne, the Persian subject, symbolized an anagram; it was not, in essence, he who was trying to overtake, pursue and track down his 'I' – no, the overtaking and attacking was being done by the organs of his body, which had grown heavier; and, as it fled away from them, his 'I' was becoming a 'not-I', because through the organs of sense – not from the organs of sense – his 'I' was returning to itself; the alcohol, the smoking, the insomnia were gnawing at his body's feeble constitution; the constitution of our bodies is closely connected to space; and when he had begun to disintegrate, all the spaces had cracked; now bacilli had begun to crawl into the cracks in his sensations, while in the spaces that enclosed his body spectres had begun to hover ... So: who was Shishnarfne? With his reverse – the abracadabra-like dream, Enfranshish; but that dream was undoubtedly caused by the vodka. The intoxication, Enfranshish, Shishnarfne were only stages of alcohol.

'I'd do better not to smoke, not to drink: then my organs of sense will serve me again!'

He – gave a shudder.

Today he had been guilty of betrayal. How had he failed to realize that? For he had undoubtedly been guilty of betrayal: out of fear, he had let Nikolai Apollonovich fall into Lippanchenko's hands: he distinctly remembered the outrageous buying and selling. He, without believing, had believed, and in this there was treachery. Lippanchenko was even more of a traitor; that Lippanchenko was betraying them, Aleksandr Ivanovich knew; but had hidden his knowledge from himself (Lippanchenko had an inexplicable power over his soul); in this was the root of the illness: in this terrible knowledge that Lippanchenko was a traitor; the alcohol, the smoking, the depravity were only consequences; the hallucinations must only be the final links in the chain that Lippanchenko had deliberately begun to forge for him. Why? Because Lippanchenko knew that he *knew*; and precisely by virtue of this knowledge Lippanchenko would not let go.

Lippanchenko had enslaved his will; the enslavement of his will had come about because the dreadful suspicion would have given everything away; because he kept wanting to dispel the dreadful suspicion; he drove the dreadful suspicion away by constantly keeping company with Lippanchenko; and, suspecting his suspicion, Lippanchenko would not let him move one step out of his sight; thus each had become bound to the other; he poured mysticism into Lippanchenko; and the latter poured alcohol into him.

Aleksandr Ivanovich now clearly remembered the scene in Lippanchenko's study; the brazen cynic, the scoundrel had outmanoeuvred him on this occasion, too; he remembered Lippanchenko's fatty and loathsome neck with its fatty, loathsome fold; as though the fold had been insolently laughing in there, until Lippanchenko turned round, caught his gaze on his neck; catching that gaze, Lippanchenko had understood everything.

That was why he had started trying to frighten him: had stunned him with an attack and mixed up all the cards; insulted him to death with suspicion and then offered him a sole way out: to pretend that he believed in Ableukhov's treachery.

And he, the Elusive One, had believed in it.

Aleksandr Ivanovich leapt to his feet; and in helpless fury he shook his fists; the deed was done; had been achieved!

That was what the nightmare had been about.

. . . .

Aleksandr Ivanovich had now quite clearly translated the inexpressible nightmare into the language of his feelings; the staircase, the little room, the loft were Aleksandr Ivanovich's abominably neglected body; the rushing inhabitant of those mournful spaces, whom *they* were attacking, who was running away from *them*, was his self-conscious 'I', which was ponderously dragging away from itself the organs that had fallen off; while Enfranshish was a foreign substance that had entered the abode of his spirit, his body – with vodka; developing like a bacillus, Enfranshish raced from organ to organ; it was it that was causing all the sensations of persecution, so that later, striking at the brain, it could cause a severe irritation within it.

. . . .

He remembered his first meeting with Lippanchenko; the impression had not been a pleasant one; Nikolai Stepanovich had, to tell the truth, displayed curiosity concerning the human weaknesses of the people who entered into association with him; an *agent provocateur* of superior type could easily possess that clumsy outward appearance, that pair of senselessly blinking eyes.

He had probably looked like a simpleton.

'Filth . . . O, filth!'

And to the degree that he became absorbed in Lippanchenko, in the contemplation of the parts of his body, his ways, his habits, so before him there grew – not a man, but a tarantula.

And at that point something made of steel entered his soul:

'Yes, I know what I shall do.'

A brilliant idea dawned on him: it would all so simply come to an end: how had this not occurred to him earlier; his mission was clearly delineated.

Aleksandr Ivanovich burst into loud laughter:

'The filth thought he could outmanoeuvre me.'

And again he felt a violent stab of pain in the molar tooth: Aleksandr Ivanovich, torn away from his reverie, clutched at his cheek; the room – universal space – again looked like a wretched room; consciousness was fading (like the light of the moon in the clouds); fever was making him shiver with anxiety and terrors, and the minutes were slowly being fulfilled; one cigarette was being smoked after the other – to the paper, to the wadding . . .

When suddenly . . . –

The Guest

Aleksandr Ivanovich Dudkin heard a strange thundering noise; the strange noise thundered downstairs; and was then repeated (he had begun to repeat himself) on the staircase; crash after crash resounded amidst intervals of silence. As though someone were overturning a heavy, many-pood weight of metal on the stone with all his might; and the blows of the metal, shattering the stone, resounded higher and higher, closer and closer. Aleksandr Ivanovich realized that some kind of rough intruder was smashing the staircase to pieces downstairs. He listened closely to ascertain whether someone would open a door on the staircase and put an end to the nocturnal vagrant's disgraceful behaviour . . .

And crash thundered upon crash; step after step was being shattered to pieces down there; and stone showered down beneath the blows of the heavy tread: to the dark yellow garret, from landing to landing, some fearsome being made of metal was stubbornly coming upstairs; from step to step many thousand poods were falling now with a shaking din; the steps were crumbling; and – now: with a shaking din the landing flew away from the door.

The door split apart and burst: there was a swift cracking sound – and it flew off its hinges; dim, melancholy emanations spilled from there in cloudy green billows; there the moon's expanses began – at the shattered door, at the landing, so that the garret room itself was revealed in its ineffability, while in the centre of the threshold, from walls that let through expanses the colour of vitriol – inclining a crowned, green-coloured head, stretching forth a heavy green-coloured arm, stood an enormous body, burning with phosphorus.

It was the Bronze Guest.

The lustreless metal cloak hung down heavily – from shoulders that were shot with brilliance and from armour that was like fish-scales; cast-metal lip melted and trembled ambiguously, because once again now Yevgeny's fate[17] was being repeated; thus did the past century repeat itself – now, at the very moment when beyond the threshold of a wretched entrance the walls of an old building were falling apart in vitriol-coloured expanses; in precisely similar fashion was Aleksandr Ivanovich's past dismantled; he exclaimed:

'I remembered . . . I've been waiting for you . . .'

The bronze-headed giant had been racing through periods of time right up to this moment, completing an iron-forged circle; quarter-centuries had flowed by; and Nicholas had ascended the throne; and the Alexanders had ascended the throne; while Aleksandr Ivanych, a shadow, had tirelessly been traversing that same circle, all the periods of time, fleeting through the days, the years, the minutes, through the damp Petersburg prospects, fleeting – in his dreams, awake, fleeting . . . tormentingly; and in pursuit of him, and in pursuit of everyone – the blows of metal had crashed, shattering lives: the blows of metal had crashed – in vacant lots, in towns; they had crashed – on entrance porches, landings, the steps of midnight staircases.

The periods of time had crashed; I have heard that crashing. Have you heard it?

Apollon Apollonovich Ableukhov is a blow of crashing stone; Petersburg is the blow of a stone; the caryatid of the entrance porch that is going to break loose over there is that same blow; the pursuits are inevitable; and so are the blows; you will not find sanctuary in a garret; the garret has been prepared by Lippanchenko; and the garret is a trap; one must break out of it, break out of it with blows . . . on Lippanchenko!

Then everything will take a different turn; under the blow of the metal that shattered stones, Lippanchenko will fly into pieces, the garret will come crashing down and Petersburg will be destroyed; the caryatid will be destroyed under the blow of the metal; and the blow to Lippanchenko will make Ableukhov's bare head split in two.

Everything, everything, everything was illumined now, when after ten decades the Bronze Guest himself came on a visit and said to him resonantly:

'Greetings, dear offspring!'

Only three steps: the cracks of three beams splitting under the feet of the enormous guest; with his metal rear the emperor cast in bronze resonantly clanged against a chair; his green elbow fell with all the heaviness of bronze on the cheap little table from under the fold of his cloak, with bell-like, booming sounds; and with slow absent-mindedness, the emperor removed his bronze laurels from his head; and the bronze laurel crown fell, with a crash, from his brow.

And, jangling and clanking, a hand weighing many hundreds of poods took from the folds of the camisole a small, red-glowing pipe, and, indicating the pipe with his eyes, winked at it:

'Petro Primo Catharina Secunda . . .'[18]

Stuck it into his strong lips, and the green smoke of unsoldered bronze began to rise beneath the moon.

Aleksandr Ivanych, Yevgeny, now understood for the first time that he had fled for a century in vain, that behind him the blows had crashed without any anger – in villages, towns, entrance porches, staircases; he had been pardoned from time immemorial, and all that had been, combined with all that was coming towards him – was only a series of ghostly passages through trials and torments before the trump of the Archangel.

And – he fell at the feet of the Guest:

'Master!'

In the Guest's bronze eye sockets shone a bronze melancholy; on to his shoulder amicably fell a hand that shattered stones and broke collar-bones, glowing red-hot.

'It's all right: die, be patient a little while . . .'

The metal Guest, glowing beneath the moon with a thousand-degree fever, now sat before him burning, red-purple; now, annealed, he turned a dazzling white and flowed towards the inclining Aleksandr Ivanovich in an incinerating flood; in complete delirium Aleksandr Ivanovich trembled in an embrace of many poods: the Bronze Horseman flowed with metals into his veins.

Scissors

'*Barin*: are you asleep?'

Aleksandr Ivanovich Dudkin had for a long time now felt someone pulling at him.

'Er, *barin*! . . .'

At last he opened his eyes and forced himself into the gloomy day.

'But *barin*!'

A head bent down.

'What is it?'

All that Aleksandr Ivanovich could work out at this stage was that he was stretched out on the trestle.

'The police?'

The corner of the hot pillow jutted out before his eye.

'There aren't any police . . .'

A dark red blotch was crawling away over the pillow – brr: and – through his consciousness fleeted:

'That's a bedbug.'

He tried to raise himself on one elbow, but fell into oblivion again.

'Oh Lord, do wake up . . .'

He raised himself on his elbow:

'Is that you, Styopka?'

He saw a spurt of moving steam; the steam came from a teapot: on his table he saw a teapot and a cup.

'Oh, how splendid: tea.'

'What's splendid about it: you're burning, *barin* . . .'

Aleksandr Ivanych noticed with astonishment that he still had all his clothes on; not even his wretched little overcoat had been removed.

'How did you get here?'

'I dropped in to see you: an awful lot of factories are on strike; the police were chasing me . . . I dropped in to see you, with the Prayer Book, that is . . .'

'Why yes, I remember, I have the Prayer Book.'

'What do you mean, *barin*: you must have dreamed it . . .'

'But we saw each other yesterday, didn't we . . .'

'We haven't seen each other for two days.'

'But I thought: it seemed to me . . .'

What had he thought?

'I dropped in to see you today; I saw you lying and groaning; you were tossing about, burning – all aflame.'

'But I've recovered, Styopka.'

'Funny kind of recovery! . . . Here, I've boiled you up some tea; I've brought bread; a hot *kalatch*; drink up and you'll feel better. It's not good for you to lie about like that . . .'

Metallic boiling water had flowed through his veins in the night (that he remembered).

'Yes – yes: I had quite a substantial fever in the night, my dear fellow . . .'

'And no wonder . . .'

'A fever of a hundred degrees . . .'

'You'll stew yourself away with all that alcohol.'

'Stew in my own boiling water, eh? Ha-ha-ha . . .'

'Why not? They were talking about an alcoholic fellow who had puffs of smoke coming out of his mouth . . . And he stewed himself away . . .'

Aleksandr Ivanovich smiled an unpleasant smile.

'You've drunk yourself to the little devils . . .'

'There were little devils, there were . . . That is why I asked for the Prayer Book: so I could read them a lecture.'

'You'll drink yourself to the Green Dragon, too . . .'

Aleksandr Ivanovich gave another crooked smile:

'Well, and all Russia, my friend . . .'

'What?'

'Is from the Green Dragon . . .'

And he thought to himself:

'Oh, what's got into me? . . .'

'That's not true at all: Russia is Christ's . . .'

'You're raving . . .'

'You're raving yourself: you'll drink yourself to *her*, to *the one herself* . . .'

Aleksandr Ivanovich leapt up in fear.

'To whom?'

'You'll drink yourself to the *white . . . woman . . .*'

That delirium tremens was sneaking up on him, there was no doubt.

'Oh! I know: I'd like you to go down to the chemist's . . . And buy me some quinine: the hydrochloric kind . . .'

'Oh, all right, then . . .'

'And remember: not the sulphate; the sulphate is pure indulgence . . .'

'It's not quinine you want, *barin* . . .'

'Away now – off you go! . . .'

Stepan went out of the door, and Aleksandr Ivanovich shouted after him:

'And Styopushka, get some dried raspberries, too: I want some raspberry jam in my tea.'

And he thought to himself:

'Raspberries are a splendid sudorific,' – and with nimble, somehow flowing gestures, he ran over to the water tap; but hardly had he washed himself than inside him everything flared up again, confusing reality with delirium.

Yes. As he had been talking to Styopka, he had had a constant impression that something was waiting for him outside the door: something primordially familiar. There, outside the door? And he leapt to open it; but outside the door there was only the landing; and the railings of the staircase hung over the abyss; now Aleksandr Ivanovich stood over the abyss, leaning against the railings, clicking a completely dry tongue and shivering with ague. There was some taste, some sensation of copper: both in his mouth and on the tip of his tongue.

'*It* is probably waiting in the courtyard . . .'

But in the courtyard there was no one, nothing.

In vain did he run about the secluded corners (between the cubes of stacked firewood); the asphalt gleamed silver; the aspen logs gleamed silver; there was no one, nothing.

'But where is *it*?'

Styopka was running by there with his purchases; but he scuffled round behind the firewood away from Styopka, because it had dawned on him:

'*It* is in a metal place . . .'

What was that place, and why was *it* a metallic *it*? About all such matters Aleksandr Ivanovich's whirling consciousness responded very vaguely. Vainly did he endeavour to remember: there remained no memory at all of the consciousness that had dwelt in him; there remained but one recollection: some other consciousness really had been here; that other consciousness had very elegantly unfolded pictures before him; in that world, not at all similar to ours, *it* dwelt . . .

It would appear again.

With awakening, every other consciousness was transformed into a mathematical dot, not a real one; and so, therefore, *it* was compressed by day as a small part of a mathematic dot; but a dot has no parts; and so: *it* did not exist.

There remained a memory of the absence of a memory and of a matter that must be executed, that would tolerate no procrastination; there remained a memory – of what?

Of a metal place . . .

Something had dawned on him: and with light, springy steps he ran to the crossing of two streets; at the crossing of the two streets (he knew this) an iridescent gleam came sprinkling out of a shop window . . . Only where was the little shop? And – where was the crossroads?

Objects shone there.

'Are there metal things there?'

A remarkable predilection!

Why had such a predilection manifested itself in Aleksandr Ivanovich? Indeed: on the corner of the crossroads metal things shone; this was a cheap little shop that sold all kinds of goods: knives, forks, scissors.

He entered the little shop.

From behind a dirty desk a sleepy mug (probably the owner of these drills, blades, and saws) dragged itself towards the counter that had begun to shine with steel; the narrow-browed head fell somehow steeply on to the chest; in the eye sockets, behind spectacles, hid small, reddish-brown eyes:

'I'd like, I'd like . . .'

And not knowing what to take, Aleksandr Ivanovich caught hold of the notched edge of a small saw; it flashed and squealed: 'squee-squee-squee'. Meanwhile the shopowner surveyed his customer from under his brows; it was not surprising that he looked from under his brows: Aleksandr Ivanovich had leapt down from his garret quite by chance; as he had lain in his little overcoat on the bed, so had he leapt outside: and his little coat was crumpled and smeared with dirt; but above all: he had put no hat on; his shock-haired, uncombed head and excessively glittering eyes would have frightened anyone.

That was why the shopowner was surveying him from under his brows, wrinkling his forehead, raising features that were oppressive and by their very nature heavily constructed; with unmasterable revulsion the face stared at Dudkin.

But this face, trying to control itself, boomed plaintively:

'Is it a saw you want?'

While the inquisitively drilling little eyes said ferociously:

'Ah, ha, ha! . . . A man with the DT''s: so that's what it's all about . . .'

This only appeared to be so.

'No, you know, a saw – it wouldn't be very easy for me, with a saw . . . I'd like, you know, one of those sharpened Finnish knives.'

But the person snapped coarsely:

'Sorry: I've no Finnish knives.'

The drilling little eyes seemed to be saying decisively:

'If I let you have a knife, there's no saying what you'll . . . get up to . . .'

Had their eyelids been raised, the inquisitively drilling little eyes would have become plain, ordinary little eyes; all the same, the resemblance struck Aleksandr Ivanovich: imagine – the resemblance to Lippanchenko. Here the figure for some reason turned its back; and threw at the visitor a gaze that would have felled a bull.

'Well, it's all the same: scissors will do . . .'

As he said this, he thought: why this fury, this resemblance to Lippanchenko? But was at once reassured: what sort of resemblance was there, really?

Lippanchenko was clean shaven, while this fat fellow had a curly beard.

But at the thought of *a certain person*, Aleksandr Ivanovich now remembered: absolutely everything – absolutely everything! He remembered with complete clarity, why it had dawned on him, this idea of running down to a little shop that sold such items. What he was planning to do was really quite simple: snip – and that was it.

He began to shake over the scissors:

'Don't wrap them up – no, no . . . I live quite near here . . . Give them to me as they are: I'll take them as they are . . .'

So saying, into his pocket he put the miniature scissors, of the kind that is probably used by dandies to cut their nails in the mornings, and – rushed off.

Astonished, frightened, suspicious, the square, narrow-browed head, with its protruding frontal bone, stared after him (from behind the gleaming counter); that frontal bone protruded with one single, intense, stubborn effort: to understand what had happened: to understand, come what may, to understand, at whatever cost; to understand, or . . . explode into pieces.

And the frontal bone could not understand; the forehead was pathetic: narrow, covered in diametrical wrinkles; it seemed to be weeping.

END OF THE SIXTH CHAPTER

CHAPTER THE SEVENTH

or: the events of a rather grey little day continue still

Weary am I, friend: the heart asks peace.
The days fly after days . . .[1]

A. Pushkin

Immeasurabilities

We left Nikolai Apollonovich at that moment when Aleksandr Ivanovich Dudkin, astonished at the flood of garrulity that suddenly burst from Ableukhov's mouth, shook his hand and nimbly darted into the black flood of bowler hats, while Nikolai Apollonovich felt himself expanding again.

We left Nikolai Apollonovich at that moment when the heavy confluence of his circumstances was suddenly and unexpectedly resolved into well-being.

Until that moment massifs of delirium and monstrous shadows had been piling up; menacing Gaurisankars[2] of events had piled up and come crashing down again – within a space of twenty-four hours: the wait in the Summer Garden and the disturbing cawing of the jackdaws; the dressing in red silk; the ball – or rather: the people flying through the halls in fright, flying in the harlequinade – the striped, the belled, the harlequins, the fiery-legged buffoons, the yellow hunchbacked Pierrot and the deathly pale clown who frightened the young ladies; some kind of blue masker, who had danced with curtseys, and had given him a little note with a curtsey; and – his shameful flight from the ballroom nearly all the way to the latrine – by the gateway, where the mangy little gentleman had caught him; and at last – Pepp Peppovich Pepp, or rather: the sardine tin with dreadful contents, which was . . . still . . . ticking.

The sardine tin with dreadful contents, capable of turning everything around it into a sheer mass of bloody slush.

We left Nikolai Apollonovich outside the shop window; but we abandoned him; between the senator's son and ourselves steady drops began to fall; a mesh of drizzle accumulated; in that mesh all the customary weights, projections and ledges, caryatids, entrance porches, cornices of brick balconies lost their distinctness of outline, growing sluggishly dim and only just barely discernible.

Umbrellas were being opened.

Nikolai Apollonovich stood outside the window and thought there was no name for the grievous outrage – no: the outrage that had been going on for a day and a night, or rather, twenty-four hours, or – eighty thousand six hundred pocket-ticking seconds: eighty thousand moments, or rather, that many points in time; but no sooner had a moment advanced and on it advanced – second, moment, point – than it somehow, smartly spreading in circles, turned slowly into a cosmic, swelling sphere; this sphere was bursting; his heel was slipping away into universal voids: the time-traveller was hurtling, he knew not where and into what, plunging down, perhaps, into universal space, to . . . a new instant; thus did the day and night stretch, the eighty thousand pocket-ticking seconds, each of them – was bursting: his heel was slipping into immeasurabilities.

No, there was no name for the grievous outrage!

It was better not to think. And – somewhere thoughts were being thought; perhaps – in his swelling heart some sort of thoughts were hammering, thoughts that had never arisen in his brain and were yet arising in his heart; his heart was thinking; his brain was feeling.

All of its own accord a most clever plan arose, worked out in tiny detail; and a plan that was – comparatively – risk-free, but . . . base, yes . . . base!

The only thing was, who had thought it out? Was it possible, was it possible that Nikolai Apollonovich could have thought up this plan?

The matter stood like this: –

all these past hours prickly fragments of thoughts had swum before his eyes, in a play of fiery, coloured flashes and starlike sparks, like the merry tinsel on a Christmas tree: ceaselessly they fell into a single place illumined by consciousness – out of darkness into darkness; now the little figure of a buffoon made faces, and now a lemon-yellow Petrushka rushed past at a gallop – out of darkness into darkness – through the place illumined by consciousness; while consciousness shone dispassionately on all the swarming images; and when they were welded together, consciousness inscribed on them a shattering, inhuman meaning; then Nikolai Apollonovich very nearly spat with revulsion:

'An ideological cause?

'There was no ideological cause . . .

'There is a base terror and a base animal instinct: to save one's own skin . . .

'Yes, yes yes . . .

'I am an out-and-out scoundrel . . .'

But we have already seen that it was to precisely such a conviction that his venerable papa was gradually coming.

. . . .

But had *all this* (what, we shall see in what follows) taken place consciously in his will, in his alertly beating heart and inflamed brain? No, no, no!

But there were still these swarms of thoughts that thought themselves; it was not he who thought the thoughts, but . . . the thoughts that thought themselves . . . Who was the author of the thoughts? All morning he was unable to answer this question, but . . . something was being thought, being sketched, rising up; it was emerging above the *sardine tin* – precisely there: all this had probably crawled out of the *sardine tin*, when he had awoken from the dream that was now forgotten, and had seen that he was resting his head on the sardine tin – had crawled out of the *sardine tin*; then he had hidden the *sardine tin* – he did not remember where, but . . . he thought it had been . . . in the desk; then he had leapt out of the accursed house in good time, while everyone there was still asleep; and he had whirled about the streets, running from coffee house to coffee house.

It was not his head that was thinking, but . . . *the sardine tin*.

But in the streets *it* still continued to rise, forming, sketching, tracing; if his head was thinking, then his head – it too! – had also turned into the sardine tin with dreadful contents, which was . . . still . . . ticking, or else it was not he that controlled his thoughts, but the thunderously resonant prospect (on the prospect all personal thoughts turn into an impersonal jumble); but if the jumble was thinking, then he did not prevent the jumble from pouring in through his ears.

That was why the thoughts were being thought.

Something grey and soft was stirring beneath the bones of his head: soft, and, above all, grey, like ... the prospect, like a flagstone of the pavement, like the foggy felt that pressed ceaselessly in from the seashore.

At last – the plan, thought out, prepared in every aspect (we shall speak of this in what follows), appeared in his field of consciousness – at a most unsuitable moment, when Nikolai Apollonovich, who had dashed, God knows why, into the vestibule of the university (where the chapel is), was leaning casually against one of the four massive columns, chatting with a passing lecturer who bent forward to him and, spraying him with spittle, hurriedly proceeded to inform him of the contents of a German article, when – yes: within his soul something suddenly burst (as a doll inflated with hydrogen bursts into flabby pieces of the celluloid from which balloons are made): he – with a start, reeling back, tearing himself free – ran, himself not knowing where, because – for this very reason: just then it was revealed to him:

– the author of the plan was himself ...

He was an out-and-out scoundrel! ...

When he realized this, he rushed to Vasily Island, to the Eighteenth Line; a shabby cab driver took him there; and from the carriage, straight into the cab driver's back, a jerky, indignant whisper was heard:

'Eh? ... Tell me, please? ... A sham ... an impostor ... a murderer ... Simply – to save his own skin ...'

He probably gave vent to his indignation loudly, because the cab driver turned round to him in annoyance:

'What is it, sir?'

'Nothing ... It doesn't matter ...'

And the cab driver thought:

'The *barin*'s a queer fish, so he is ...'

Nikolai Apollonovich, like Apollon Apollonovich, was in the habit of talking to himself.

The winds repeated:

'Father-murderer! . . .'

'Impostor! . . .'

Not his own man, Nikolai Apollonovich leapt from the carriage; cutting across the small asphalt courtyard, and the cords of aspen wood, he flew in to the back staircase, in order to rush up the stairs and – he knew not why; probably, out of sheer curiosity: to look in the eye the culprit of the event, the one who had brought him the bundle, because the 'refusal' he had devised was – of course – a mere pretext: he could dispense with throwing the 'refusal' in his face (and thereby gain time).

At this point he collided with Aleksandr Ivanovich: the rest we have seen.

. . . .

There was no name for the grievous outrage!

Yes – but his heart, warmed by all that had happened to him, slowly began to melt: the icy heart-shaped lump became a heart; before it had beaten meaninglessly; now it beat with a meaning; and feelings beat within him; those feelings had quivered unexpectedly; and now these concussions shook and overturned his entire soul.

That colossus of a house had just amassed above the street in piles of brick balconies; having run across the roadway, he could have felt its stone flank with his hand; but when it began to drizzle, its stone flank began to float in the fog.

As everything was floating now.

It began to drizzle – and the colossus of coupled stones had now become uncoupled; now it was lifting – from beneath the rain into the rain – a lace of weightless contours and only barely defined lines – simply a kind of rococo: the rococo was receding into nothing.

A wet glitter began to gleam on the shop windows, the house windows, the chimneys: the first trickle began to gush from a drainpipe; from another drainpipe steady drops began to drip; the pallid pavements dissolved in tiny specks: their dry, deathly pallor sluggishly turned brown; a tyre flying past snorted mud.

And on and on it went . . .

In the misty-wafting wetness, covered by the umbrellas of the passers-by, Nikolai Apollonovich disappeared; the prospects were floating in mists; the colossi of the buildings seemed to be being squeezed out of space into some other space: vaguely from there did their patterns loom there made from a jumble – of caryatids, steeples, walls. His head began to spin; he leaned against the shop window; something within him had burst, blown to pieces; and – a piece of his childhood arose.

· · · · · · · ·

He was with the old lady, with Nokkert,³ – his governess – on her trembling knees, he saw, his head was resting; the old lady was reading under the lamp:

> Wer reitet so spät durch Nacht und Wind?
> Es ist der Vater mit seinem Kind . . .

Suddenly – outside the windows the gusts of the storm hurled themselves about; and there the darkness was in riot, and the noise was in riot: the pursuit of the child was probably taking place out there; on the wall the governess's shadow was trembling.

And again . . . –

Apollon Apollonovich – small, grey, old – is teaching Kolenka the French *contredanse*; he advances smoothly and, as he counts off the steps, claps out the time with his hands: promenades to the right, to the left; promenades – both forward and back; in lieu of music he snaps out – in a quick patter, loudly:

> Who gallops, who rushes beneath the cold gloom:
> A horseman out late, with him his young son . . .

And then he raises to Kolenka his hairless brows:

'My dear fellow, hm hm, how do you like the first figure of the quadrille?'

All the rest was 'cold gloom', because the pursuit reached its mark: the son was torn away from the father:

> In his arms the child lay dead . . .

After this moment, all his past life proved to be a play of the mist. The piece of his childhood was hidden.

· · · · · · · ·

The wet glitter gleamed on shop windows, on windows, on

chimneys; the brown wetness of the pavement was like polish; a tyre snorted mud. In the misty-wafting wetness, covered by the umbrellas of the passers-by, Nikolai Apollonovich disappeared; the colossi of the houses seemed to be being squeezed out of space into space; their patterns began to loom there, made of jumbled lines – of caryatids, steeples, walls.

The Cranes

Nikolai Apollonovich wanted to return to his motherland, the nursery, because he had realized: he was a small child.

Everything, everything must be shaken off, forgotten, *everything, everything* must be learned again, as it is learned in childhood; his old, forgotten motherland – he could hear it now. And – above everything suddenly rang out the voice of his lonely and yet beloved childhood, a voice that had not sounded for a long time; and had sounded – now.

The sound of that voice?

It is as indistinct as the call of the cranes above the city; the cranes flying high up there – in the city's rumble the city-dwellers cannot hear them; but they fly, fly past above the city – the cranes! . . . Somewhere, on Nevsky Prospect, let us suppose, in the quiver of the flying carriages and the uproar of the newspaper-sellers, where above it all perhaps only the throat of the motor car rises – among those metal throats, at a pre-vesperal, vernal hour, on the paving the dweller of the woodless plains, who has landed in the city by chance, will arise as though rooted to the spot; he will stop – lean his shaggy, bearded head to one side, and stop you.

'Shhh! . . .'

'What is it?'

And he, the dweller of the woodless plains, who has landed in the city by chance, will to your amazement shake his head and smile a cunning, cunning smile:

'Can't you hear them?'

'? . . .'

'Listen . . .'

'What? What is it?'

And he will sigh:

'There . . . the cranes . . . are calling.'

You also listen.

At first you will hear nothing; and then, from somewhere up above, in the spaces you will hear: a familiar, forgotten sound – a strange sound . . .

There the cranes are calling.

You both raise your heads. A third, a fifth, a tenth person raises his head.

At first the universal spaces dazzle you all; nothing, apart from air . . . And yet – no: there is something apart from air . . ., because amidst all that blue there clearly emerges – something that is none the less familiar: northwards . . . fly . . . the cranes!

Around you there is an entire ring of inquisitive people; they all have their heads raised, and the pavement is blocked; a policeman makes his way through; and yet – no: he cannot restrain his curiosity; has stopped, thrown back his head; he is looking.

And a murmur:

'The cranes! . . .'

'They're coming back again . . .'

'Dear creatures . . .'

Above the accursed Petersburg roofs, above the boarded roadway, above the crowd – that pre-vernal image, that familiar voice!

. . . .

So also – the voice of childhood!

It is not audible; yet it – exists; from time to time the calling of the cranes above the Petersburg roofs – will be heard! Thus the voice of childhood.

It was something of this kind that Nikolai Apollonovich heard now.

As though someone sad, whom Nikolai Apollonovich had never seen before, had outlined around his soul a solid, penetrating circle and had entered his soul; the bright light of his eyes began to transpierce his soul. Nikolai Apollonovich gave a start; something rang out, that had been compressed within his soul; now it receded lightly into immensity; yes, here was immensity, saying dauntlessly:

'You all persecute me! . . .'

'What? What? What?' Nikolai Apollonovich said, trying to make out that voice; and the immensity said dauntlessly:

'I look after you all . . .'

Thus did it speak.

Nikolai Apollonovich cast his eyes over space in astonishment, as though he expected to see before him the owner of the singing voice; but what he saw was something else; namely: he saw a dense, floating mass – of bowler hats, moustaches, chins; walked further – simply the misty prospect; and in it floated his gaze, as everything floated now.

The misty prospect seemed familiar and kindly; ai-ai-ai – how sad the misty prospect seemed; and the flood of bowler hats with its faces? All these faces that were passing here – passed reflective, unutterably sad.

But the voice's owner was not there.

. . . .

Only who was that there? There, on that side? Outside that colossus of a house, over there? And – under a pile of balconies?

Yes, someone was standing there.

Just like him, Nikolai Apollonovich; and standing, like him, outside a shop window – under an open umbrella . . . And not conspicuous: he might possibly be looking at something . . . so it might seem; impossible to make out his face. And what was so special about him? On this side stood Nikolai Apollonovich, not particularly remarkable, for his own satisfaction . . . Well, and the other man, too, was not conspicuous: like Nikolai Apollonovich, like all the other people who were passing – just a casual passer-by; and he too was sad and kindly (as everyone was kindly now); looked about him with an independent air: as if to say, so what, there's nothing special about me: I've got a few whiskers on my face, too! . . . No – he was clean-shaven . . . The outline of his little overcoat recalled, but . . . what? Was he nodding? . . .

Simply wearing some sort of little peaked cap.

And where had it happened before?

Should he approach him, the kindly owner of the peaked cap? After all, it was a public prospect; well, truly! There was room for everyone on this public prospect . . . Simply, in an unconspicuous manner –

approach: look at the objects that were there . . . behind glass on the other side of the shop window. For everyone had a right . . .

Stand independently there beside him, and when an opportunity arose cast a fleeting glance, a glance that was dissembling – apparently absent-minded, but in fact attentive, –

– at him!

Make sure: as if to say: what is this?

No, no, no! . . . Touch the doubtless ossifying fingers, and weep with stupid happiness! . . .

Fall down prostrate on the paving!

'I am sick, deaf, heavy laden . . . Give me rest, Master, give me shelter . . .'

And hear in reply:

'Arise . . .

'Go . . .

'Sin no more . . .'

. . . .

No, of course there would be no reply.

But of course – the sad figure would not reply, because there could be no replies for the present; the reply would come later – in an hour, in one year, or five, or perhaps even more – in a hundred, in a thousand years; but a reply there would be! But now the sad, tall figure, never seen in dreams, but absolutely no more than a stranger, but a stranger with a hidden purpose, and, so to speak, a mysterious stranger – the sad, tall figure would simply look at him and put a finger to his lips. Without looking, without stopping, he would walk there through the slush . . .

And in the slush disappear . . .

. . . .

But a day would come.

All this would alter in the twinkling of an eye. And all the passing strangers – those who had passed before one another (in a backstreet somewhere) at a moment of mortal danger, those who spoke of that inexpressible moment with an inexpressible look and then withdrew into immensity – they would all, all meet!

No one would take the joy of that meeting away from them.

I'm Going My Own Way . . . I'm Not Getting
in Anyone's Way . . .

'What am I doing,' thought Nikolai Apollonovich. 'This is no time to be day-dreaming . . .'

There was no time to be lost now . . . Time was passing, and the sardine tin was ticking away; he must go straight to the desk; carefully wrap the whole thing up in paper, put it in his pocket, and into the Neva with it . . .

And now he moved his eyes away from that colossus of a house where the stranger was standing under a pile of brick balconies with an open umbrella, because again the ill-famed mass of torsos had begun to flow on its many legs – the mass of human bodies that had been rushing here for springs, summers, winters: of ceaseless bodies.

And lost his resolve, looked again.

The stranger was still there; he was evidently waiting, as Nikolai Apollonovich had been waiting, for the rain to stop; suddenly he moved off, suddenly fell into the human current – into those couples and those foursomes; his three-cornered hat, gleaming with lustre, covered him; his umbrella stuck up helplessly.

'I ought to turn away, and go my own way! And so, really, ought he, the stranger!'

But no sooner had he thought this than (he noticed) from beneath his gleaming three-cornered hat and out of the shoulders of the people who were rushing past, the small peaked cap again began to show itself; risking ending up under a cab, he ran across the roadway; he was absurdly stretching forth the umbrella, which was being torn away by the wind.

Well, how was he to turn away now? How could he go his own way?

'What's he up to?' thought Nikolai Apollonovich, and was, unexpectedly to himself, astonished:

'Oh, so that's what he looks like, is it?'

The stranger had undoubtedly lost by being close to; being in the distance was more advantageous; he appeared more mysterious; more melancholy; his movements were more sluggish.

'Heh! . . . But for pity's sake: he looks like an idiot, doesn't he? Ai, that little peaked cap! Do you see that cap? He keeps running on those crane's legs; his little coat is fluttering, his umbrella is torn; and one of his galoshes doesn't fit . . .'

'Phoo!' a self-respecting citizen would have expressed himself inarticulately at this point and kept on walking, his lips pressed shut offendedly, with an independent air: a self-respecting citizen would have certainly felt something – something of the following kind:

'Oh, let him be! . . . I'm going my own way . . . I'm not getting in anyone's way . . . I can give way when the occasion arises. But do you think I'm going to . . .? No, no, no: I have my own way to go . . .'

Nikolai Apollonovich, it must be admitted, did not feel himself to be a self-respecting citizen in any way (after all, what kind of respect could there be now?); but the stranger probably did, in spite of his little coat, his wretched little umbrella and the galosh that was falling off his foot.

As though he were saying:

'Well, see here: I am just a chance passer-by, but a passer-by who respects himself . . . And I won't let anyone get in my way . . . I won't give way to anyone . . .'

Now Nikolai Apollonovich felt hostility; and, having already prepared himself to step aside, changed his tactics: did not step aside; thus they nearly collided, nose to nose; Nikolai Apollonovich – astounded; the stranger – without any astonishment; it was remarkable: a large, numb hand (with goose-pimples) was raised to the cap; while a hoarse and wooden tattoo decisively rapped out:

'Ni-ko-lai A-pol-lo-no-vich!! . . .'

Only now did Nikolai Apollonovich begin to notice that the individual who had so swiftly flown up (he was an artisan, perhaps) had bandaged up his throat; he probably had a boil on his throat (as is well known, a boil, impeding one's freedom of movement, may appear in a most inconvenient fashion on one's Adam's apple, on one's backbone (between the shoulder-blades) – may appear . . . in an indescribable place! . . .)

But a more detailed reflection on the properties of insidious boils was broken off:

'You don't seem to recognize me?'

(Ai, ai, ai!) . . .

'With whom do I have the honour,' Nikolai Apollonovich began, pressing his lips together offendedly, but, on taking a closer look at the stranger, suddenly staggered back, threw off his hat and exclaimed with a wholly contorted mouth:

'No . . . is it you? . . . But what put you here? . . .'

He had probably intended to exclaim: 'What brought you here . . .'

Of course: it was hard to perceive that the chance passer-by, who looked like a beggar, was Sergei Sergeich, because, for one thing, Likhutin was dressed in civilian clothes, and they sat on him like a saddle on a cow; and, for another: Sergei Sergeich Likhutin was – ai, ai, ai! – clean-shaven: that was what it was! Instead of a small, twining blond beard, what protruded was a kind of pimply, awkward void; and – where had his little moustache gone? This place that was free of hair (between his lips and his nose) had turned a familiar physiognomy into an unfamiliar physiognomy – quite simply, into a sort of unpleasant void.

The absence of the customary Likhutin beard and the customary Likhutin moustache gave the second lieutenant the shocking appearance of an idiot:

'No . . . Or perhaps my eyes deceive me, but . . . it seems to me, Sergei Sergeyevich, that . . . you . . .'

'Quite correct: I am in civvies . . .'

'No, it's not that, Sergei Sergeich . . . not that . . . That is not what astounds me . . . No, what astounds me is . . .'

'What?'

'You have somehow been entirely transformed, Sergei Sergeich . . . You must please excuse me . . .'

'That is a trivial matter, sir . . .'

'Oh, of course, of course . . . I didn't mean anything by it . . . I just meant that you've shaved . . .'

'Hey, what is this?' Likhutin said, taking offence now. 'What is this about "you've shaved"? Why shouldn't I? Yes, I've shaved . . . I couldn't sleep last night . . . Why shouldn't I have shaved? . . .'

In the second lieutenant's voice Nikolai Apollonovich was struck by what was quite simply a kind of fury, some kind of overpowering fraughtness that was quite out of keeping with being shaved.

'Yes, I've shaved . . .'

'Of course, of course . . .'

'Well, what of it?' said Likhutin, refusing to calm down. 'I'm leaving the service . . .'

'You're leaving it? . . . Why? . . .'

'For private reasons, which concern me personally . . . Those trivial details do not concern you, Nikolai Apollonovich . . . Our private matters do not concern you.'

Now second lieutenant Likhutin began to draw closer.

'As a matter of fact, there are matters which . . .'

Nikolai Apollonovich, pushing into passers-by with his back, began plainly to retreat:

'There are matters, Sergei Sergeich? . . .'

'Matters which, sir . . .'

Nikolai Apollonovich caught the plainly ominous note in the second lieutenant's hoarse voice; and it seemed to him that the latter was for some reason distinctly preparing to seize his arms.

'Have you got a cold?' he said, abruptly changing the subject, and jumped down off the pavement; in explanation of his comment he touched his own neck, alluding to the bandage round Likhutin's neck, to some sort of cold in the throat — some quinsy or — influenza.

But Sergei Sergeyevich turned red, and swiftly jumped down off the pavement, continuing his advance in order to . . . to . . . Several passers-by stopped and looked:

'Ni-ko-lai Apollo-novich! . . .'

'?'

'I really haven't come running after you in order to talk to you about your neck, the devil take it . . .'

A third, a fifth, a tenth person stopped, doubtless supposing that some pilferer had been caught.

'It has nothing to do with the matter . . .'

Ableukhov's attention grew acute; to himself he whispered:

'Eh? . . . What has nothing to do with what matter?' And, evading Likhutin, he again found himself on the damp pavement.

'What is the matter, then? . . .'

Where was his memory?

The matter he had to discuss with the second lieutenant was no joke. Yes – the domino! The devil take it, the domino! Nikolai Apollonovich had completely forgotten about the *domino*; now he merely remembered:

'There is a matter, there is . . .'

Sofya Petrovna Likhutina had without doubt gone and talked to everyone about the incident in the unlit entrance porch; she had also talked about the incident beside the Winter Canal.

It was to this matter that Likhutin was proceeding now.

'*This* is all I needed . . . Oh, the devil take it: how inconvenient it is! . . . How very inconvenient! . . .'

And suddenly everything was overcast.

The swarms of bowler hats grew dark; vengefully the top hats began to gleam; from all sides the nose of the ordinary man in the street began once more to hop: noses flowed by in great numbers: aquiline, cockerel-like, hen-like, greenish, grey; and – a nose with a wart on it: absurd, hurried, enormous.

Nikolai Apollonovich, avoiding Likhutin's gaze, surveyed all this and fixed his eyes on the shop window.

Meanwhile Sergei Sergeich Likhutin, seizing Ableukhov's arm and, now pressing it, now quite simply squeezing it, gathering around him a crowd of inquisitive gawpers – implacably, indefatigably snapped out in a wooden falsetto: – why, here was the beating of drumsticks! –

'I . . . I . . . I . . . have the honour to inform you that since this morning I . . . I . . . I . . .'

'?'

'I have been on your trail . . . And I have been, have been everywhere – to your lodgings, incidentally . . . I was let into your room . . . I sat there . . . Left a note . . .'

'Oh, what a pit . . .'

'None the less,' the second lieutenant interrupted (why, here was the beating of drumsticks), 'having a matter to settle with you: an urgent discussion of business . . .'

'Now it's beginning,' dashed through Ableukhov's brain, and he saw his reflection in the large shop window amidst gloves, umbrellas and similar articles.

Meanwhile a cold, whistling pandemonium had broken out along the Nevsky, swooping, rattling and whispering with small, staccato, steady drops against the umbrellas, the sternly bent backs, drenching the hair, drenching the frozen, stringy hands of artisans, students, and workers; meanwhile a cold, whistling pandemonium had broken out along the Nevsky, pouring a poisonous, mocking, metallic highlight on to the street signs, twisting billions of wet grains of dust into funnels, forming tornadoes, driving and driving them through the streets, shattering them against stones; and further, driving the bat's wing of the clouds out of Petersburg through the vacant lots; and already a cold, whistling pandemonium had broken out above the vacant lots; with a mettlesome, buccaneer whistling it caroused through the expanses – of Samara, Tambov, Saratov – in gullies, sands, thistles, wormwood, tearing the straw from the roofs, tearing down the high-topped haystacks and spreading its sticky rot across the threshing-floors; a heavy, granular sheaf is born from it; the native, spring-water well is blocked up by it; woodlice will appear; and through a series of wet villages typhus goes raging.

The wing of the clouds has been torn; the rain has stopped; the wetness has dried up ...

The Conversation Had a Sequel

Meanwhile the conversation had a sequel:

'I have a matter to discuss with you ... What I mean is – a conversation that will brook no delay; I've asked everywhere how we might meet: by the way, I went and asked about you at the home of ... what is her name again? ... Our mutual acquaintance, Varvara Yevgrafovna ...'

'Solovyova?'

'That's it ... I had a very painful conversation with Varvara Yevgrafovna – concerning you ... Do you understand me? ... So much the worse ... But what was I ... Yes – this Solovyova, Varvara Yevgrafovna (by the way, I locked her in) gave me an address: the address of a friend of yours ... Dudkin? ... Well, it doesn't matter ... Of course, I went to that address, and before I got as far as Mr – Dudkin, is it? – met you in the courtyard ... You

were running away from there . . . Yes, sir . . . And what is more –
not alone, but with a person I did not know . . . No, don't: *nomina
sunt odiosa* . . . You looked agitated, and Mr . . .? *Nomina sunt odiosa* –
also looked agitated . . . I did not venture to interrupt your conversation with Mr . . . Excuse me – perhaps you retain that gentleman's
surname in your memory . . .'

'Sergei Sergeyevich, I . . .'

'Wait, sir! . . . I did not venture to interrupt your conversation,
of course, although . . . to tell you the truth, I had only managed to
catch you with great difficulty . . . Well, then: I followed you; at a
certain distance, of course, so as not to be a witness of the
conversation: I do not like to stick my nose in, Nikolai Apollonovich
. . . But about that we can talk later . . .'

Here Likhutin fell into reflection, and for some reason he turned
round and looked into the distance of the Nevsky.

'I followed you . . . Right to this place . . . The two of you were
talking about something . . . I walked behind you, and I must admit
that I felt annoyed . . . Listen,' he said, breaking off his narration,
which was like a typographical composition, haphazardly scattered,
gathered together and haphazardly read – 'Don't you hear?'

'No . . .'

'Shh! . . . Listen . . .'

'What is it?'

'A sort of musical note – an "oo" . . . There . . . there . . . it's
started to hoot . . .'

Nikolai Apollonovich turned his head; it was strange – carriages
were hurriedly flying past – and all in the same direction; the
pedestrians quickened their step (every moment or so they were
given a shove); some were turning back; they collided with those
who were coming towards them; equilibrium was completely destroyed; he looked round and did not listen to Likhutin.

'After that you were left alone, and you leaned against the
shop window; then it started to rain . . . I also leaned against the
shop window, on the other side . . . You kept staring at me,
Nikolai Apollonovich, but you pretended you hadn't noticed me
at all . . .'

'I didn't recognize you . . .'

'And I bowed to you . . .'

'It's as I thought,' Nikolai Apollonovich continued to reflect in annoyance, 'he's pursuing me . . . He's going to . . .'

What was he going to do to him?

About two and a half months ago, Nikolai Apollonovich had received a short letter from Sergei Sergeich, in which Sergei Sergeich Likhutin had in a persuasive tone requested him not to disturb the peace of his ardently beloved spouse – this was after the *bridge*; some of the phrases in the letter were underlined three times; from them emanated something very, very serious – it was a rather unpleasant verbal blast, without hints, but straight to the point . . . And in an answering letter, Nikolai Apollonovich had promised . . .

He had given his promise, and – broken it.

What was this?

Blocking the pavement, the passers-by had stopped; the very broad prospect was empty of carriages; neither the busy clacking of the tires, nor the clip-clop of the horses' hooves could be heard: the carriages flew past, forming there, in the distance – a black, motionless heap, forming here – a bare, boarded void against which the pandemonium again threw in cascades its swarms of crackling drops.

'Look there, do you see?'

'Oh, how strange, how strange?'

It was as if for a moment the enormous round, flat slabs of granite had been exposed, over which for millennia the white foam of a waterfall had rushed; but from there, from the distances of the prospect, from the most complete emptiness and purity, between the two rows of deserted pavement, over which a thousand-voiced buzzing that increased in loudness was approaching (like the buzz of a swarm of bumble-bees) – from there a smart cab came rushing; half-standing in it, a beardless, tattered *barin* was flexed without a hat, clutching a tall and heavy flagstaff in his hand: and, tearing themselves away from the wooden staff like crests in the air, lightly-whistling blades of red calico cloth fluttered and tore – into the cold, the enormous void; it was strange to see the red, flying banner coming down the empty prospect; and when the carriage had passed, all the bowler hats, the tricornes, the top hats, the cap-bands, the feathers, the service caps began to hoot, to shuffle, to jostle their elbows and suddenly surged off the pavement into the middle of the prospect; from the ragged clouds the pale disc of the sun poured down for a moment with a straw-coloured tint – on the houses, on the mirror-like panes, on the bowler hats, on the cap-bands. The pandemonium had rushed past. The rain had stopped.

The crowd swept both Ableukhov and Likhutin off the pavement; separated by a pair of elbows, they ran where all were running; taking advantage of the crush, Nikolai Apollonovich had the inten-tion of slipping away from the untimely conversation and throwing himself into the first carriage that stood there in the distance and, without losing any precious time, driving away in the direction of home: for the bomb was there . . . in the writing desk . . . ticking away! Until it was in the Neva he would have no peace!

The running people jostled him with their elbows; small black figures were pouring out of the shops, the courtyards, the barbers' shops, the intersecting prospects; and into the shops, the courtyards, the lateral prospects the small black figures ran hurriedly back again; they wailed, roared, stamped: in a word, there was panic; from afar – above the heads there, blood seemed to gush; seething red crests unwound from the black soot, like throbbing lights and like deer's antlers.

And, oh, how untimely!

From behind two or three shoulders, on a level with him, the hateful little peaked cap looked out and two vigilant eyes were anxiously fixed on him: even in the commotion, second lieutenant Likhutin did not lose sight of him, doing his utmost to break through to Ableukhov, who had broken through the crowd away from him: while all Ableukhov wanted to do was sigh with relief.

'Don't lose sight of me . . . Nikolai Apollonovich; though actu-ally, it doesn't matter . . . I won't leave you alone.'

'It's as I thought,' Ableukhov was now finally convinced, 'he's pursuing me: he'll never let me go . . .'

And he began to break his way through to the carriage.

While behind them, from the distances of the prospect, above the heads and the rumble of voices the banners came licking like flowing tongues and like flowing radiances; and suddenly everything – the flames and the banners – stopped and froze: the sound of singing came clearly thundering out.

At last Nikolai Apollonovich broke through to the carriage; but no sooner did he try to raise his foot into it, in order to make the driver break further through the crowd, than he felt himself again seized by the second lieutenant's hand, thrust forward over some-one else's shoulder; at this point he stood still, as though rooted to the spot, and, simulating indifference, he said with a forced smile:

'A demonstration! . . .'

'It doesn't matter: I have a matter to discuss with you.'

'I . . . you see . . . I . . . also agree with you completely . . . We have something to talk about . . .'

Suddenly, from somewhere in the distance, a scattered crackling of gunfire came flying past; and from the distance, torn into pieces, the same radiances that had risen in the soot above the heads of the crowd began to rush this way and that; the red whirlpools of the banners began to wave about there, and swiftly scattered on the solitarily protruding crests.

'In that case, Sergei Sergeich, let us do our talking in a coffee house . . . Why don't we go to a coffee house . . .'

'What do you mean, a coffee house . . .' Likhutin said, indignantly. 'I am not accustomed to having business conversations in such places . . .'

'Sergei Sergeyevich? But where, then? . . .'

'Well, I'm thinking, too . . . Since you've got into the carriage, let us go to my flat . . .'

These words were said in a tone that was manifestly dissembling: here Nikolai Apollonovich bit his lips very nearly until the blood came:

'At his home, at his home . . . How can it be – at his home? That means I'll have to closet myself with the second lieutenant eye to eye, give an account of my inappropriate escapades with Sofya Petrovna; perhaps I will have to explain to her indignant husband in her presence why I did not keep my word . . . It's plain to see: it's a trap . . .'

'But, Sergei Sergeyevich, I think that for several reasons which I am sure you will understand, I wouldn't feel comfortable at your flat . . .'

'Oh, come now!'

To be fair to Nikolai Apollonovich, he did not list any more reasons; he obediently said: 'I am ready.' And he behaved calmly; his lower jaw trembled slightly – that was all.

'As an enlightened, humane man, Sergei Sergeyevich, you will understand me . . . In a word, in a word . . . it's in connection with Sofya Petrovna.'

Suddenly, growing confused, he broke off.

They sat down in the carriage. And – it was high time: there, where the banners had just been rushing about and from where dry bursts of crackling gunfire had come, there was now not a single banner; but from there surged such a crowd, pressing against those who were running ahead, that the carriages that had swarmed into clusters and were standing here, flew into the depths of the Nevsky – in the opposite direction, where now the circulation had been re-established, where along the street grey-clad police inspectors ran, and gendarmes danced on horses.

Off they went.

Nikolai Apollonovich saw that the human myriapod was flowing here, as though nothing had happened; as it had flowed here for centuries; the seasons ran there, higher; to them a term was fixed; but the human myriapod had no such term; it would crawl as it crawled; and it crawled as it crawled: ones, twos, fours; and couple after couple: bowler hats, feathers, service caps; service caps, service caps, feathers; tricorne, top hat, service cap; shawl, umbrella, feather.

Now it all disappeared: they turned off the prospect; above the stone buildings in the sky towards them rushed ragged clouds with a hanging band of rain; Nikolai Apollonovich bent completely under the burden of the unexpected weight that had fallen; a ragged cloud crept up; and when the grey, bluish band covered them – the busy drops began to beat, to rattle, to whisper, spinning their cold bubbles on the gurgling puddles; Nikolai Apollonovich sat bent in the carriage, his face wrapped in his Italian cloak; for a moment he forgot where he was going; a troubled feeling remained: he was going – under duress.

The heavy confluence of circumstances now once again came weighing down.

The heavy confluence of circumstances – can one thus describe the pyramid of events that had piled up during these recent days, like massif upon massif? A pyramid of massifs that shattered the soul, and precisely – a pyramid! . . .

In a pyramid there is something that exceeds all the notions of man; the pyramid is a delirium of geometry, that is, a delirium that cannot be measured by anything; the pyramid is a satellite of the planet, created by man; it is both yellow and dead, like the moon.

The pyramid is a delirium that is measured by figures.

There is a horror compounded of figures – the horror of thirty signs laid end to end, where the sign is, of course, a zero; thirty zeros with a unit are a horror; cross out the unit, and the thirty zeros will collapse.

There will be – zero.

There is no horror in a unit, either; in itself the unit is a nonentity; namely – a unit! . . . But a unit plus thirty zeros will form itself into the monstrosity of a quintillion: a quintillion – oh, oh, oh! – hangs on a little thin black stick; the unit of a quintillion repeats itself more than a billion billion times, repeated more than a billion times.

Through immeasurabilities it drags itself.

Thus does man drag himself through universal space from time everlasting to time everlasting.

Yes, –

like a human unit, or rather, like that thin little stick, Nikolai Apollonovich had lived in space until now, accomplishing a run from time everlasting –

> – in the costume of Adam, Nikolai Apollonovich was a little stick; ashamed of his thinness, he had never been to a Russian bathhouse with anyone –

– since time everlasting!

And now on the shoulders of this little stick the monstrosity of a quintillion had fallen, that is to say: more than a billion billions, repeated more than a billion times; an unpresentable *something* had taken a gigantic *nothing* into itself: and the gigantic *nothing* had been swelling in presentable fashion since time everlasting –

> – thus does a stomach swell, thanks to the development of gases, from which all the Ableukhovs had suffered –

– since time everlasting!

An unpresentable *something* had taken a gigantic nothing into itself; the gigantic, empty, zero had made the *something* swell up to the point of horror. Quite simply some Gaurisankars distended themselves; while he, Nikolai Apollonovich, was exploding like a bomb.

Eh? A bomb? A sardine tin?

In the twinkling of an eye, everything raced past that had raced past since morning: his plan flew through his head.

What was it?

The Plan

Yes, yes, yes! . . .

To bring in the sardine tin by stealth: to put it under his father's pillow; or – no: to put it under the mattress in a corresponding place. And – his expectation would not deceive him: precision was guaranteed by the clock mechanism.

He would say to him:

'Good night, Papa!'

In reply:

'Good night, Kolenka! . . .'

To give him a squelching kiss on the lips, to go to his room.

To undress impatiently – he must undress without fail! To lock the door with a click, and pull the blanket over his head.

To be an ostrich.

But in the warm, feather bed begin to shiver, to breathe jerkily – from the jolts of his beating heart; to feel miserable, afraid, to try to hear: the bang there would be in there . . . the crash there would be in there – from behind the flock of stone walls; to wait for the bang, the crash that would blow the silence to pieces, blow the bed, the table and the wall to pieces; having blown to pieces, perhaps . . . having blown to pieces, perhaps . . .

To feel miserable, afraid, to try to hear . . . And then hear the familiar flopping of slippers towards . . . the place that had no comparison.

From his light French reading to turn – simply to cotton wool, with which to stop up his ears; to put his head under the pillow. To be finally convinced: nothing would help any more! Instantly throwing off the blanket, to stick out his perspiration-covered head – and in an abyss of fear dig a new abyss.

To wait and wait.

Now there was only half an hour left; there already was the greenish lightening of dawn; the room turned blue, turned grey; the flame of the candle grew smaller; and now there were only fifteen minutes left; now the candle was going out; eternities were sluggishly flowing by, not minutes, but precisely – eternities; then a match would strike: five minutes had passed . . . To reassure oneself that *all that* would not be soon, but only after ten sluggish revolutions of time, and be shakingly deceived, because –

> – an unrepeatable, never yet heard, attracting sound
> would all the same . . . –

> – crash!! . . .

> . . . .

Then: –

quickly putting his bare legs into long johns (no, why long johns: better to be as he was, without long johns!) – or even in his undershirt, his face twisted and white –

> – yes, yes, yes! –

> – to jump out of his warm
> bed and go pattering through with bare feet into a
> space that was full of mystery: into the black
> corridor; to race and race – like an arrow: towards
> the unrepeatable sound, bumping into servants and
> taking into his chest a peculiar smell: a mixture of
> smoke, burning and gas with . . . *something else*, that
> was more horrible than burning, gas or smoke.

As a matter of fact, though, there would probably be no smell.

To run into the room that was full of smoke and very cold; choking with a loud cough, to leap back out again in order to quickly thrust himself again through the black hole in the wall that had formed after the sound (a lighted candelabra would somehow be dancing in his hand).

There: beyond the hole . . . –

in place of the devastated bedroom, a rust-red flame would illumine

... would illumine a mere trifle: clouds of smoke belching from all sides.

And would also illumine ... no! ... A veil must be thrown over that scene – a veil of smoke, of smoke! That was all there was: smoke and more smoke!

All the same ...

To push in under that veil if only for a moment, and – ai, ai! The completely red half of a wall: that redness was flowing; the walls must be wet; and they must be sticky, sticky ... All this would be his first impression of the room; and probably his last. Pell mell, between two impressions would impress itself: plaster, splinters of shattered parquetry and torn shreds of scorched rugs; those shreds would be smouldering. No, one had better not, but ... a shin-bone?

Why had it survived intact, and not the other parts?

All that would happen in a trice; while in a trice, behind his back: an idiotic rumble of voices, the uneven patter of feet in the depths of the corridor, the desperate wail – imagine! – of the scullery maid; and – the sound of the telephone being used (someone was probably calling the police) ...

To drop the candelabra ... Squatting down, to shiver beside the hole in the October wind that was blowing through the hole (all the window-panes had been smashed by the noise); and – to shiver, to pull his nightshirt around him, until a compassionate lackey –

> – perhaps, the valet, the very man on whom soon afterwards it would be easiest to unload the blame (shadows would fall on him of their own accord) –
>
> – until the compassionate lackey dragged him into the adjacent room and forcibly poured cold water into his mouth ...

But, getting up from the floor, to see: –
beneath his feet *that same* dark-red stickiness that had splashed here after the loud noise; it had splashed out of the hole with a shred of

torn-off skin . . . (from which part of the body?). To lift his gaze —
and see above him, sticking to the wall . . .

Brr! . . . Then suddenly to faint.

. . . .

To play out the comedy to the end.

Only twenty-four hours later, before the tightly nailed-up coffin
(for there was nothing to bury) — before the coffin to rap out an
Acathistus,[4] leaning over a candle in a uniform jacket with a close-
fitting waist.

Only two days later, his freshly-shaven, marble, godlike countenance tucked away in the fur of his Nikolayevka, to pass to the
hearse, outside in the street, with the air of an innocent angel; and
to clutch his service cap in white kid-gloved fingers, proceed
sorrowfully to the cemetery in the company of that whole exalted
retinue . . . behind a heap of flowers (behind the coffin). Gold-
chested, white-trousered little old men would drag that heap of
flowers up the staircase in their trembling hands — with swords and
ribbons.

The heap would be dragged by eight little bald old men!

. . . .

And — yes, yes!

To give evidence at the inquest, but of a kind that . . . would all
the same cast a shadow . . . on whomever it might be (not intention-
ally, of course) . . .; and a shadow must be cast — a shadow on
whomever it might be; if not — the shadow would fall on him . . .
How could it be otherwise?

The shadow would be cast.

. . . .

> Silly little simpleton
> Kolenka is dancing:
> He has put his dunce-cap on —
> On his horse he's prancing.

. . . .

And it became clear to him: that very moment when Nikolai Apollonovich was heroically dooming himself to be the executioner of a death penalty – a death penalty *in the name of an idea* (so he thought), that moment, and nothing else, was the creator of such a plan, and not the grey prospect along which he had rushed all morning; action in the name of an idea was combined, however agitated he had been, with infernally cold-blooded dissembling and, perhaps, with slander: the slander of the most innocent persons (most convenient of all was the valet: after all, he received visits from his nephew, who was a pupil at a vocational school, and, it seemed, not a member of the Party, but . . . all the same . . .)

There was none the less calculation in his cold-bloodedness. A lie had been added to parricide, and so had cowardice; but, above all, so had – baseness.

. . . .

> Noble, slender, pale,
> Hair like flax has he;
> Rich in thought, in feeling poor
> N.A.A. – who can he be?

. . . .

He was a scoundrel . . .

. . . .

All that had happened during these past two days was facts, where the fact was a monster: a heap of facts, or rather, a pack of monsters; before these two days there had been no facts; and no monsters had pursued him. Nikolai Apollonovich had slept, read, eaten: had even lusted: after Sofya Petrovna; in a word: it had all flowed within bounds.

But – but! . . .

He had not eaten as others do, had not loved as others do; not as others do, had he experienced lust: his dreams had been heavy and obtuse; while his food had seemed to lack savour, the lust he had felt after the scene on the bridge had assumed a most absurd tinge – of mockery with the help of the *domino*; and besides: he hated his father. There was something that was dragging itself behind him, that cast a peculiar light on the working of all his functions (why did he keep shuddering, why did his arms dangle like lashes? And his smile had become – froglike); this *something* was not a fact, but a fact remained; this fact consisted of *something*.

What was the *something*?

A promise to the Party? He had not taken his promise back; and although he was not thinking . . . others were probably thinking (we know what Lippanchenko was thinking); and thus there it was: he ate in a strange way and slept in a strange way, lusted and hated in a strange way, too . . . His small figure also seemed strange – in the street; with the wing of his Nikolayevka flapping in the wind, and as if he were round-shouldered . . .

And so, it was the promise that had emerged by the bridge – there, there: in a gust of Neva wind, when over his shoulder he had caught sight of a bowler hat, a cane, a moustache (the inhabitants of Petersburg are distinguished by – hm-hm – qualities! . . .)

And beside, his standing by the bridge was merely a consequence of his having been driven to the bridge; and it was lust that had driven him; he had experienced the most passionate feelings *somehow in the wrong way*, he had burst into flame *in the wrong way, not in a good way*, coldly.

It must be the cold that was at the root of it all.

The cold had fallen while he was still only a child, when he, Kolenka, had been called, not Kolenka, but – his father's spawn! He had felt ashamed. Later on, the meaning of the word 'spawn' had been revealed to him in its entirety (through the observation of shameful goings-on in the life of domestic animals), and, he remembered – Kolenka had cried: he had transferred the shame of his engendering on to the culprit of his shame: his father.

For hours on end he had stood in front of the mirror, watching his ears grow: they grew.

Only then did Kolenka understand that all living things in the world are 'spawn', that there are no human beings, because they are 'engenderings'; that is, an unpleasant sum total of blood, skin and flesh – unpleasant because the skin sweats, and flesh goes rotten in the warmth; while blood gives off a smell that is not that of May violets.

Thus his psychic warmth was identified with boundless stretches of ice, with the Antarctic; while he – a Pirie, a Nansen, an Amundsen

– went round and round in the ice; or his warmth became a bloody slush (man, as is well known, is slush sewn up in skin).

So the soul did not exist.

He hated his own, native flesh; and lusted for that of others. Thus from very earliest childhood he had nurtured within him the larvae of monsters: and when they matured, they crawled out within twenty-four hours and stood around – like facts with horrible contents. Nikolai Apollonovich had been eaten alive; had flowed into monsters.

In a word, he himself had become the monsters.

'Little frog!'

'Freak!'

'Red buffoon!'

Indeed: in his presence they had joked about blood, called him 'spawn'; and he had begun to joke about his own blood – a 'buffoon', the 'buffoon' was not a mask, the mask was 'Nikolai Apollonovich' ...

The blood in him had prematurely decomposed.

It had prematurely decomposed: that was evidently why he aroused revulsion; that was why his little figure seemed strange in the street.

This decrepit earthen vessel must be blown to pieces: and it was being blown to pieces ...

The Institution

The Institution ...

Someone instituted it; since that time it has existed; while before that time there was nothing but the days of yore. Thus does the 'Archive' inform us.

The Institution.

Someone instituted it, before it existed there was darkness, someone moved above the darkness; there was darkness and there was light – circular number one, at the foot of the circular of the last five years was the signature: 'Apollon Ableukhov'; in the year 1905 Apollon Apollonovich Ableukhov was the soul of circulars.

The light shines in darkness. Darkness has not embraced it.

. . . .

The Institution . . .

And – the torso of a goat-footed caryatid. Since the time when a carriage drawn by a pair of lathered black horses flew up to its front steps, since the time when a court lackey in a tricorne hat donned obliquely on his head and a winged greatcoat opened wide for the first time the lacquered, embossed flank and, with a click, the door threw aside its coat of arms adorned with crown (a unicorn goring a knight); since the time when out of the funereal cushions of the carriage a parchment-faced statue placed its shoe on the entrance-porch granite; since the time when, for the first time, returning bows, a hand invested in the leather of a glove touched the brim of a top hat: – since that time the Institution that cast over Russia its mighty power had weighed down with a power even mightier.

Section marks[5] that had been buried in dust arose.

I am struck by the very outline of a section mark: on to the paper fall two coupled hooks, – reams of paper are destroyed; the section mark is a devourer of papers, that is, a paper phylloxera; the section mark bites into the tyranny of the obscure abyss like a tick, – and truly: there is something mystical in it: it is the thirteenth sign of the zodiac.

Above an enormous portion of Russia a headless frock-coat was multiplying like a section mark; and a section mark swollen like a senator's head was rising – above starched neck-linen; through the white-columned, unheated halls and upon the stairs of red cloth a headless circulation passed, and that circulation was directed by Apollon Apollonovich.

Apollon Apollonovich is the most popular government official in Russia with the exception of . . . Konshin[6] (whose unfailing signature you bear on credit bills).

And so: –

The Institution exists. In it is Apollon Apollonovich: more correctly, was, because he is dead . . . –

> – I recently visited the grave: above a heavy black marble slab rises a black marble eight-pointed cross; beneath the cross is a distinct haut-relief that carves out an enormous head that bores into you loweringly with the emptiness of its

eyes; a demonic, Mephistophelean mouth! At the bottom – the modest inscription: 'Apollon Apollonovich Ableukhov – Senator' . . . The year of his birth, the year of his death . . . A god-forsaken grave! . . . –

– Apollon Apollonovich exists: he exists in the director's office: he is in it every day, except for the days when he has haemorrhoids.

There exist, moreover, in the Institution offices . . . of reflection.

And there exist simply rooms; mostly – halls; desks in each hall. At the desks there are clerks; at each desk there are a pair of them; before each: a quill and ink and a respectable pile of papers; the clerk scratches across the paper, turns over the leaves, rustles a leaf and makes his quill squeal (I think that the sinister plant 'heather', *veresk*, derives from 'squealing', *vereshchanie*); like the adversarial autumn wind, which the winds work up – through forests, through ravines; like the rustle of sand – in vacant lots, in the expanses of the salt-marshes – of Orenburg, Samara, Saratov; –

– the same rustling persisted above the grave: the sad rustling of the birches; their catkins, their young leaves were falling on the black marble, eight-pointed cross, and – peace to his ashes! –

In a word: the Institution exists.

· · · · · · · · · ·

It is not lovely Proserpina rushing away through the land to the kingdom of Pluto, where the Cocytus boils with white foam; each day it is the senator, abducted by Charon, rushing away to Tartarus on tangled, lathered, black-maned steeds; above the gates of melancholy Tartarus hangs Pluto's bearded caryatid. The waves of Phlegethon splash: papers.

· · · · · · · · ·

In his director's office, Apollon Apollonovich Ableukhov sits each day with a tensed vein at his temple, one leg crossed on the other, and a vein-covered hand – at the lapel of his frock-coat; the logs crackle in the fireplace, the sixty-eight-year-old man breathes the bacillus of the section mark, that is to say, the coupling of hooks; and this breathing spreads all over the enormous expanse of

Russia; every day a tenth of our motherland is covered by the bat's wing of the clouds. Apollon Apollonovich Ableukhov, struck by a happy thought, one leg crossed on the other, a hand at the lapel of his frock-coat, then inflates his cheeks like a bladder; then he seems to blow (such is his habit); little blasts of chill air blow through the unheated rooms; tornado-like funnels of multivarious papers begin to wind about; from Petersburg a wind begins, somewhere on the outskirts a hurricane breaks out.

Apollon Apollonovich sits in his study . . . and blows.

And the backs of the clerks bend; and the leaves of paper rustle; thus do the winds race – about the stern, pine-covered summits . . . Then he draws in his cheeks; and everything – rustles: a dry flock of papers, like a fateful fall of leaves, gathers speed from Petersburg . . . to the Sea of Okhotsk.

The cold pandemonium spreads – over fields, over forests, over villages, in order to hoot, to attack, to roar with laughter, in order to sting with hail, rain and black ice the paws and hands – of birds, animals, wayfarers, to overturn on him the striped posts of the toll-bars – to leap out from the canal on to the high road like a striped milestone, to lord it like a grinning cipher, to uncover the homelessness and endlessness of the road and to stretch out gloomy nets from streaming darkness . . .

North, familiar north! . . .

Apollon Apollonovich Ableukhov – a man of the city and a fully well-bred gentleman: sits in his office while his shadow, piercing through the stone of the wall . . . pounces on passers-by in the fields: with a mettlesome, buccaneer whistling it carouses through the expanses – of Samara, Tambov, Saratov – in gullies and in yellow sands, thistles, wormwood, or in the wild *tatarnik*, exposing the sandy bald patches, tearing the high-topped haystacks, fans a suspicious flame in the barn; the red village cockerel is born from it; the native, spring-water well is blocked up by it; woodlice will appear; when it falls on the crops with harmful dews the crops grow thin; the cattle rots . . .

Multiplies the number of ravines and digs them.

Wags would probably say: not Apollon Apollonovich, but . . . Akvilon Apollonovich.

. . . .

The multiplication of the quantity of paper that has flown before a clerk within the space of a day, blown out of the doors of the Institution, the multiplication of that paper by the paper of the rushing clerks forms a production, or rather a manufacture of paper that must be carried out not in carts, but by Furies.

At the foot of each paper is the signature: Apollon Ableukhov.

That paper rushes along the railway branches from the railway centre: Saint Petersburg; and – to the principal town of the province; having fluttered his flock about the corresponding centres, Apollon Apollonovich creates in those centres new breeding grounds of paper production.

Normally a paper with (X's) signature circulates as far as the offices of the provincial administration; the paper is received by all the civil servants (they are councillors, I think): the Chichibabins, the Sverchkovs, the Shestkovs, the Teterkos, the Ivanchi-Ivan-chevskys; from the principal town of the province Ivanchi-Ivanchev-sky correspondingly sends papers to the towns of: Mukhoyedinsk, Likhov, Gladov, Morovetrinsk and Pupinsk (all district towns); Kozlorodov, the assessor, also receives the paper.

The whole picture changes.

Kozlorodov, the assessor, having received the paper, ought at once himself to get into a britzka, a cabriolet or a jolting droshky, in order to go dancing over the potholes – through fields, through forests, through villages, through mire, – and slowly get bogged down in clay or brown sand, submitting himself to the assault of striped, raised milestones and striped toll-bars (in the wilderness Apollon Apollonovich assaults the wayfarers); but instead of this, Kozlorodov simply stuffs Ivanchi-Ivanchevsky's inquiry into his side pocket.

And just goes off to his club.

Apollon Apollonovich is lonely: and so already he is reproducing himself a thousandfold in the milestones; and he will not get there on his own; neither will Ivanchi-Ivanchevsky get there. There are thousands of Kozlorodovs; behind them stands the ordinary man in the street, of whom Ableukhov is afraid.

That is why Apollon Apollonovich smashes only the boundary marks of his horizon: and of their places are deprived – the Ivanchevskys, the Teterkos, the Sverchkovs.

Kozlorodov is permanent.

Existing beyond reach – beyond the ravines, beyond the potholes, beyond the forests – he goes out and plays vint[7] in Pupinsk.

It is also good that he is playing vint *for the meantime*.

He Has Stopped Playing Vint

Apollon Apollonovich is lonely.

He is not getting there. And the arrow of his circulars does not penetrate the districts: it breaks. Only here and there, pierced by an arrow, does an Ivanchevsky fly down; and the Kozlorodovs organize a round-up of the Sverchkovs. From Saint Petersburg, the Palmyra of the North, Apollon Apollonovich bursts out with a paper cannonade, – and (of late) misses.

Ordinary men in the street long ago christened these arrows with a name: soap bubbles.

The hurler of arrows, – in vain did he send down the toothed lightning of Apollo; history has changed; no one believes in the ancient myths any more; Apollon Apollonovich Ableukhov is not the god Apollo: he is Apollon Apollonovich, a Petersburg civil servant. And in vain did he shoot at the Ivanchevskys.

The circulation of papers has been diminishing these past few days; a countervailing wind has blown: paper that smells of typographic print has begun to undermine the Institution – in the form of petitions, accusations, unlawful threats, and complaints; and so on, and so forth: with that kind of treachery.

Well, and what kind of loathsome behaviour towards the authorities was circulating among the ordinary men in the street? A proclamatory tone had appeared.

And – what did this mean?

A very great deal: the impenetrable, unreachable Kozlorodov, the assessor, had, somewhere out there, turned insolent; and had set out from the provinces against the Ivanchi-Ivanchevskys: at one point in space the crowd had torn a wooden palisade into its separate stakes, and . . . Kozlorodov was absent; at another point the windows of the Tax Institution proved to have been smashed out, and Kozlorodov – was absent again.

From Apollon Apollonovich came projects, came counsels, came orders: the orders were showered in salvos; Apollon Apollonovich had sat in his study with a swollen temporal vein all these past weeks, dictating order after order; and order after order went rushing off like arrow-shaped lightning into the provincial darkness; but the darkness was advancing; before it had only threatened from the horizons; now it was flooding the districts and had surged into Pupinsk, in order thence, from Pupinsk, to threaten the provincial centre, from where, flooded in darkness, Ivanchevsky had flown down into darkness.

Just then, in Petersburg itself, on the Nevsky, the provincial darkness had appeared in the form of a dark Manchurian hat; that hat had swarmed together and was amicably strolling through the prospects; on the prospects it excited itself with a red calico rag (that was the kind of day it had turned out to be): on this day the ring of many-chimneyed factories ceased to belch out smoke.

Apollon Apollonovich was turning the enormous wheel of a mechanism, like Sisyphus; up the steep slope of history he had rolled the wheel ceaselessly for five years; the powerful muscles were bursting; but ever more frequently from under the muscles there stuck out a skeleton that was not involved in any of it, or rather, what stuck out was – Apollon Apollonovich Ableukhov, who lived on the English Embankment.

Because he really did feel like a bare, picked skeleton from which Russia had fallen away.

To tell the truth: even before this fateful night, Apollon Apollonovich had seemed to some of the high officials who had observed him somehow ragged, consumed by a secret illness, skewered through (only on the last night did he swell up); every day he threw himself with his heaps into a carriage the colour of a raven's wing, wearing a coat the colour of a raven's wing and a top hat – the colour of a raven's wing; two black-maned steeds bore Pluto away.

Over the waves of Phlegethon they bore him to Tartarus: here, in the waves, he floundered.

At last, – with many dozens of catastrophes (alternations, for example, of Ivanchevskys and events in Pupinsk) the Phlegethontic waves of paper struck against the wheel of the enormous machine which the senator was turning; in the Institution a breach opened up – the Institution of which in Russia there are so few.

And when there occurred a scandal without like – as people said later on – the Genius winged its way out of the mortal body of the wearer of diamond insignia within twenty-four hours; many were even afraid that he had gone off his rocker. Within twenty-four hours – no, within some twelve hours, no more (from midnight to midday) – Apollon Apollonovich Ableukhov swiftly flew down the rungs of his civil service career.

He fell in the opinion of many.

People said later that the cause of it was the scandal with his son: yes, he arrived at the Tsukatovs' soirée a statesman of national importance; but when it was discovered that it was his son who had fled from the soirée, all the senator's shortcomings were also discovered, starting with his cast of thought and ending with his diminutive stature; and when in the early morning the damp newspapers appeared and the newspaper boys went running along the streets with cries of 'Secret of the Red Domino', there could be no doubt whatsoever.

Apollon Apollonovich Ableukhov was in no uncertain terms struck off the list of candidates for a government post of exceptional importance.

As for the ill-famed newspaper report – well, here it is: 'It has been established by officials of the criminal investigation department that the rumours about the appearance on the streets of Petersburg of an unknown domino are based on incontrovertible facts; the hoaxer's trail has been found: suspicion has fallen on the son of a highly placed official who occupies an administrative post; measures have been taken by the police.'

From this day began the twilight of Ableukhov.

Apollon Apollonovich Ableukhov was born in 1837 (the year of Pushkin's death); his childhood was spent on an old aristocratic estate in the province of Nizhny --gorod; in 1858 he graduated from the School of Law; in 1870 he was appointed Professor of P– L– at the University of St Petersburg; in 1885 he became deputy director of the Ministerial Department of X, and in 1890 became its director; in the following year he was appointed by the highest decree to the Governmental Senate; in 1900 he became head of an Institution.

That is his curriculum vitae.

Charcoal Pills

Here already was the greenish lightening of morning, and Semyonych had not closed his eyes all night! In his little cupboard of a room he had groaned, turned, fidgeted about; he had attacks of yawning, itching and – forgive our sins, O Lord! – sneezing; and, in addition to all this – reflections of the following kind:

'Anna Petrovna, your mother, has come back from Shpain – she's on a visit . . .'

Concerning this, Semyonych said to himself:

'Yes, sir . . . I opened the door . . . I saw a lady I thought were a stranger . . . One I didn't know, and dressed in a foreign get-up . . . And she said to me . . .

'Aaaa . . .

'And she said to me . . .'

And the yawns came weighing down.

Now the Tetyurin chimney (of the Tetyurin factory) was speaking; now the little steamboats whistled, too; there was electric light on the bridge: a puff – and it was gone . . . Throwing off the blanket, Semyonych sat up: he grazed the floor-covering with his big toe.

He began to whisper to himself:

'And I said to him: "Your Excellency, *barin*, sir" – so on and so forth . . . And his honour said: "yes . . ."'

'He paid no attention . . .

'And he's just a little *barin*: hardly rises off the floor, he doesn't . . . And – forgive our sins, O Lord! – he's a white-toothed puppy and a milksop.

'They're not *barins*, they're just Hamlets . . .'

Thus did Semyonych snuffle to himself; and – put his head back under the pillow again; the hours passed sluggishly; small, pinkish clouds, ripening in the sun's radiance, fleeted high above the ripening radiance of the Neva . . . And warmed by the blanket, Semyonych kept muttering miserably:

'They're not *barins* but . . . swindlers . . .'

And that door banging there, echoing there down the corridor: was it burglars? . . . Avgiev the merchant had been burgled, Avgiev the merchant had been burgled.

They had come to cut the Moldavian Khakhu's throat.

Throwing the blanket off, he stuck out his head, which was covered in perspiration; quickly putting on his long johns, he jumped out of his warm bed with an air of fussed offence, and a chewing jaw, and shuffled in his bare feet into a spatial expanse that was full of mystery: the black corridor.

And – what was this?

A bolt clicked down there outside . . . the water closet: His Excellency, Apollon Apollonovich, the *barin*, was pleased to proceed thence, with lighted candle, to – his bedroom.

The dark blue expanse of the corridor was already turning grey, and there was light in the other rooms; and the crystal was sparkling: it was half past seven; the bulldog was scratching itself and pawing at its collar, and touching its back with a grinning, tiger-like muzzle.

'Merciful Lord, merciful Lord!'

'Avgiev the merchant was burgled! . . . Avgiev the merchant was burgled! . . . Khakhu the chemist nearly had his throat cut! . . .'

. . . .

Rays flashed furiously across the crystal, resonant, the blue sky.

Throwing off his little trousers, Apollon Apollonovich Ableukhov began to get clumsily tangled up in crimson tassels as he invested himself in his little quilted, mouse-coloured, semi-threadbare dressing-gown, poking his unshaven chin (which was, as a matter of fact, smooth even the day before) out of the bright crimson lapels, studded all over with a dense and prickly, completely white stubble, as though by a hoar frost that had fallen overnight and marked out both the hollows of his eyes and the hollows under his cheekbones, hollows which – we shall observe for our part – had grown greatly enlarged overnight.

He sat with his mouth open, his chest exposed and hairy, on his bed, taking a long time over drawing in and jerkily breathing out the air that did not penetrate his lungs; every moment or two he felt his pulse and looked at the clock.

He was evidently tormented by incessant hiccups.

And in no wise thinking about the series of most alarming telegrams that rushed towards him from all sides, nor about the fact that a governmental position was slipping away from him for ever, nor – even! – about Anna Petrovna, – he was probably thinking about what one thought about when looking at a small, open box of blackish pills.

That is to say – he was thinking that the hiccups, the jolts, the stoppages and cramped breathing (the yearning to drink in air), which as always brought on colic, a mild tickling of his palms, were caused not by his heart but – by the development of gases.

About the ache in his left arm and the shooting pains in his left shoulder he tried, all this time, not to think.

'Do you know what? It's all simply caused by the stomach!'

Thus once had the chamberlain Sapozhkov, an old man in his eighties, who had recently died of pectoral angina, tried to explain it to him.

'The gases, you know, make the stomach swell up: and the diaphragm contracts . . . That is what causes the jolts and the hiccuping . . . It's all the development of gases . . .'

Once in the Senate recently, while discussing a report, Apollon Apollonovich had turned blue, begun to wheeze and been helped out; when he was urgently exhorted to consult a doctor, he had explained to them all:

'It's the gases, you know . . . That's what causes the jolts.'

A dry, black pill that absorbed the gases sometimes helped him, but not always.

. . . .

'Yes, it's the gases,' – and off he went to . . . to . . .: it was – half past eight.

This was the sound that Semyonych had heard.

Soon after that – a door in the corridor had banged, echoing, and from afar another had boomed; removing his striped plaid from his frozen knees, Apollon Apollonovich Ableukhov again set off, approached the closed door of the bedroom, opened that door and stuck out a face that was covered in perspiration, in order to collide in that very same doorway – with another face, also covered in perspiration:

'Is it you?'

'Yes, sir . . .'

'What do you want?'

'I'm about on my errands here, sir . . .'

'Aa: yes, yes . . . But why so early . . .'

'I've got to go round everywhere keeping an eye out . . .'

'What is it, tell me? . . .'

'? . . .'

'Some kind of noise . . .'

'And what was it?'

'There was a bang . . .'

'Oh, that.'

Here Semyonych gripped the edge of his very wide long johns, and shook his head disapprovingly:

'It's nothing . . .'

. . . .

The fact was that ten minutes earlier, Semyonych had noticed with astonishment: a blond head had stuck itself out of the door of the young *barin*'s room; had looked to the right and looked to the left, and – disappeared.

And then – the young *barin* had flitted like a grasshopper to the door of the old *barin*'s room.

Had stood, breathed, shook his head, turned round, not noticing Semyonych, who was pressed up against a shadowy corner of the corridor; had stood, breathed again, and put his head – to the keyhole that let light through: yes – he was glued there, could not take his eyes off the door! The young *barin*'s curiosity was not *barin*-like, there was something wrong – something not right . . .

So he was a snoop, was he? And then, too – it was almost indecent.

It was not as though he was watching some stranger who might have hidden away – he was watching his own dear papa, his own flesh and blood; perhaps he was watching to see how his health was; but, then again: he had a feeling that this was no matter of a son's concern, but simply: for the sake of idleness. And so it had turned out: he was a rascal!

He was no lackey – but the son of a general, educated in the French manner. Here Semyonych began to clear his throat.

The young *barin* – how he jumped!

'Brush my frock-coat right away . . .' he said, angry-like.

And from the door of his papa's room he went to his own: simply some kind of rascal!

'Yes, sir,' Semyonych said, chewing his lips disapprovingly, all the while thinking to himself:

'His mother's come back, and all he can say is: "Brush my frock-coat".

'It's not good, not decent!

'They're just some kind of Hamlets . . . Oh, merciful Lord . . . spying through the keyhole!'

. . . .

All this had begun to creep about in the old man's brains as, gripping the edge of his trousers that were falling down, he shook his head disapprovingly and muttered ambiguously down his nose:

'Eh? . . . That? . . . Yes, there was a bang: that's right . . .'

'What made the bang?'

'It's nothing, sir: please don't trouble yourself . . .'

'? . . .'

'Nikolai Apollonovich . . .'

'Eh?'

'Banged the door as he went out: he went out early . . .'

Apollon Apollonovich Ableukhov looked at Semyonych, prepared to ask a question, and kept silent, but . . . chewed his mouth in a senile fashion: at the memory of the most unsuccessful talk he had had with his son here not long before (this was, after all, the morning after the soirée at the Tsukatovs'), little bags of skin hung down offendedly from the corners of his lips. This unpleasant impression rather sickened Apollon Apollonovich: he drove it away.

And, losing his confidence, gave Semyonych a pleading glance:

After all, the old man had seen Anna Petrovna . . . Had – one way or the other – talked to her . . .

This thought fleeted past intrusively.

Anna Petrovna had probably changed . . . grown thinner, aged; and, he would not wonder, gone grey: acquired more wrinkles . . . he ought to ask about all that carefully, in a roundabout way . . .

But – no, no! . . .

Suddenly, the sixty-eight-year-old *barin*'s face fell unnaturally apart in wrinkles, his mouth bared its teeth to the ears, and his nose receded into the folds.

And the man in his sixties became some kind of man a thousand years old; with a strained effort that bordered on shrillness, this grey ruin began forcibly to squeeze from itself a little pun:

'Er . . . em-em-em . . . Semyonych . . . Are you . . . em-em . . . barefoot?'

Semyonych gave a start of offence.

'Excuse me, your exc –'

'No, I . . . em-em-em . . . don't mean that,' said Apollon Apollonovich, trying to compose the little pun.

But he did not manage to compose the little pun and stood staring into space; then he drooped the merest bit, and then he fired off a monstrous remark:

'Er . . . tell me . . .'

'?'

'Do you have yellow heels?'

Semyonych took offence:

'No, *barin*, I don't; it's those Chinamen with long pigtails that have yellow heels, sir . . .'

'Hee-hee-hee . . . So they're pink, perhaps?'

'Human, sir . . .'

'No – yellow, yellow!'

And Apollon Apollonovich, a thousand years old, trembling, squat, stamped his slippers insistently.

'Well, and what if my heels were, sir? . . . They're covered in corns, your excellency . . . When you put your shoe on, they bore you and burn you . . .'

While all the time he thought:

'Oh, what's all this about heels? . . . Are heels what matter, then? . . . Look at you, you old mushroom, you haven't closed your eyes all night . . . And she herself is here, in an expectant position . . . And your son is a Hamletist . . . And there you go on about heels!

. . . Will you listen to it – yellow ones . . . You've got yellow heels yourself . . . You're a "person" too! . . .'

And got even more offended.

But Apollon Apollonovich, as always, in puns, in nonsense, in little jokes (as was always the case) simply manifested a kind of bullheadedness: sometimes, trying to keep his spirits up, the senator would become (in spite of it all – real privy councillor, professor and wearer of diamond insignia) – a fidget, a flutterer, a pesterer, a teaser, at those moments resembling the flies that get into your eyes, your nostrils, your ear – before a thunderstorm, on an oppressive day, when a grey thundercloud is wearisomely climbing above the lime-trees; such flies are squashed in their dozens – on hands, on moustaches – before a thunderstorm, on an oppressive day.

'And a young girl has – hee-hee-hee . . . A young girl has . . .'

'What does a young girl have?'

'Has . . .'

Oh, what a fidget!

'What does she have?'

'A pink heel . . .'

'I've no idea . . .'

'Well, take a look, then . . .'

'You're a queer fellow, that you are, *barin* . . .'

'They're made pink by her stocking, when her foot perspires.'

And without finishing his sentence, Apollon Apollonovich Ableukhov – real privy councillor, professor, head of an Institution – stamped off back to his little bedroom in his slippers; and – click: locked himself in.

There, on the other side of the door – he sat down, grew calm, and softened.

And began helplessly to look at himself: oh, but how he had shrunk! Oh, but how round-shouldered he had become! And – it looked as though one of his shoulders were higher than the other (as though one shoulder had been knocked out of shape). Now and then his hand pressed itself against his thumping, aching side.

. . . .

Yes, sir! . . .

The alarming reports from the provinces . . . And, you know –

his son, his son! ... Yes – he disgraced his father ... A dreadful situation, you know ...

Someone fleeced that old fool of a woman, Anna Petrovna: some scoundrelly mountebank, with cockroach moustaches ... Now she has come back again ...

No matter, sir! ... Somehow! ...

An uprising, the ruin of Russia ... And already they're preparing: they've made an attempt ... Some school-leaver or other with eyes and a little moustache bursts into an old, respected aristocratic house ...

And then – the gases, the gases!

Here he took a pill.

. . . .

A spring that is overloaded with weights ceases to be resilient; to resiliency there is a limit; to the human will there is also a limit; even an iron will melts; in old age the human brain grows watery. Today frost falls – and the firm, snowy heap is sprinkled with a luminescent sparkling; and sculpts from the frosty snowflakes a gleaming human bust.

The thaw comes rustling – the heap turns brown, is eaten away: it goes all flabby and slimy; and – slumps down.

Apollon Apollonovich Ableukhov had frozen in his childhood: frozen and struck root; beneath the frosty night of the capital city his gleaming bust looked sterner, stronger, more terrible – luminescent, sparkling, rising above the northern night above all until that dampish wind that had felled his friend, and which in recent times had flamed into a hurricane.

Apollon Apollonovich Ableukhov rose up to the hurricane; *afterwards*, too ...

Solitary, long and proud did Apollon Apollonovich Ableukhov stand beneath the flaming muzzle of the hurricane – luminescent, frozen, strong; but a limit is set to all things: even platinum melts.

In one night Apollon Apollonovich Ableukhov grew round-shouldered; in one night he collapsed and hung his great head; he too, resilient as a spring, drooped; and formerly? Only recently on the uncreased profile, challengingly thrown under the heavens towards the disasters, the red tongues of flame had quivered, that might . . . set light . . . to Russia!

But only a night passed.

And against the fiery background of the burning Russian Empire, instead of the strong, gold-uniformed man of state there was – a haemorrhoidal old man standing with his jerkily breathing, hairy chest exposed – unshaven, uncombed, perspiring – in a robe with tassels – he could not, of course, steer the passage (over potholes, bumps, ruts) of our tottering wheel of state! . . .

Fortune had betrayed him.

And of course – it was not the events of his personal life, not that out-and-out scoundrel, his son, and not the fear of falling to a bomb, as a simple fighter in the field falls, not the arrival there of some Anna Petrovna or other, a person of whom he knew little, and who had succeeded in no walk of life whatsoever – not the arrival there of Anna Petrovna (in a darned black dress and with a reticule), and above all not a red rag that had turned the wearer of flashing diamond insignia into a plain melted heap.

No – it was time . . .

. . . .

Have you seen men of state, who are falling into childhood but are none the less eminent – old men who for half a century have warded off so many blows – white-curled (but more often bald) leaders who have been hardened in the iron of battle?

I have seen them.

In assemblies, at meetings, at congresses they have clambered up to the rostra in their snow-white starched linen and gleaming tail-coats with padded shoulders; round-shouldered old men with drooping jaws, with false teeth, toothless –

　　　– I have seen them –

　　　　　– they have continued, out of habit, to strike the
　　　　　hearts of others while on the rostrum keeping
　　　　　their self-possession.

And I have seen them at home.

Hurling painful, obtuse witticisms into my ear in a whisper, with weak-minded commotion, in the company of their hangers-on, they trailed into their studies and boasted slaveringly about a little shelf of collected works, bound in morocco leather, which I too once read now and then, and with which they regaled both me and themselves.

I feel sad!

. . . .

At exactly ten o'clock the doorbell rang: it was not Semyonych who opened the door; someone came in and passed through – into Nikolai Apollonovich's room; he sat there, and left a note there.

I Know What I am Doing

At exactly ten o'clock Apollon Apollonovich had his coffee in the dining-room.

He usually ran, as we know, into the dining-room – icy, stern, shaven, spreading a scent of eau-de-Cologne and proportioning coffee with chronometer; today, however, scratching the floor with his slippers, he came trailing in for his coffee in his dressing-gown: unscented, unshaven.

From half-past eight until ten o'clock in the morning he sat sequestered.

He did not look at his correspondence, did not respond to the greetings of the servants, as he customarily did; and when the bulldog's slavering muzzle placed itself on his knees, his rhythmically mumbling mouth –

> He calls for me, my Delvig dear,
> Companion of my lively youth,
> Companion of my mournful youth –

– his rhythmically mumbling mouth merely choked on the coffee: 'Er . . . listen: take the dog away, will you . . .'

Tweaking and crumbling a French croissant, he stared at the black grounds of coffee with eyes that were turning to stone.

At half past eleven, Apollon Apollonovich, as though remembering something, began to fuss and fidget; his eyes darted restlessly, in a manner reminiscent of a grey mouse; he leapt up – and with tiny footsteps, trembling, quickened his pace towards the room that was his study, revealing the half-fastened long johns beneath the open skirts of his dressing-gown.

Soon the lackey looked into his study in order to remind him that the horses were ready; looked in – and stopped on the threshold as though rooted to the spot.

With amazement he watched as Apollon Apollonovich wheeled a heavy bookshelf ladder from shelf to shelf over the velvet rugs that were there strewn everywhere – moaning, groaning, stumbling, perspiring – and climbing up the ladder, clambering his way to the top, at risk to his own life, testing the dust on the volumes with his finger; catching sight of the lackey, Apollon Apollonovich chewed his lips disdainfully, and made no reply when reminded that it was time for him to leave.

Knocking a binding against a shelf, he asked for some rags.

Two lackeys brought him the rags; they had to be delivered to him on an upraised floor-brush (he would not allow anyone to go up to where he was, and would not come down himself); the two lackeys each took a stearin candle; the two lackeys stood on either side of the ladder with upwards-stretched, rigid arms.

'Raise the light, will you . . . No, not like that . . . And not like that . . . Er, yes – higher: a bit higher . . .'

By this time ragged clouds had billowed up from behind the buildings on the other side of the Neva, their gloomy, felt-like billows came to the attack; the wind beat against the panes; semi-twilight reigned in the greenish, frowning room; the wind howled; and higher, higher stretched two stearin candles on either side of the ladder, receding towards the ceiling; there, from a cloud of dust, from the very ceiling itself swirled the mouse-coloured skirts and the crimsonish tassels dangled.

'Your ex'cy!

'Is this any task for you? . . .

'You are pleased to trouble yourself . . .

'My goodness . . . Whoever heard of such a thing . . .'

Apollon Apollonovich Ableukhov, real privy councillor, could not hear what they were saying at all from the cloud of dust: what did he care! Forgetting everything, he was wiping the spines with a rag, banging the volumes violently on the rungs of the ladder; and – at last burst out sneezing:

'Dust, dust, dust . . .

'Look at it . . . look at it! . . .

'Well, now I shall wipe it . . . with the rag: like that, sir, like that, sir, like that, sir . . .

'Very good, sir! . . .'

And hurled himself at the dust with the dirty rag in his hand.

The telephone rang worriedly: that was the Institution calling; but the telephone's worried ring received as reply from the yellow house:

'His excellency? . . . Yes . . . He is having his coffee . . . We will tell him . . . Yes . . . The horses are ready . . .'

And the telephone rang a second time; and the second time the telephone rang the answer came a second time:

'Yes . . . yes . . . He's still at table . . . Yes, we have told him . . . We will tell him . . . Yes . . . The horses are ready . . .'

To the third, now indignant ring of the telephone they replied:

'On no account, sir!

'His honour is busy arranging the books . . .

'The horses?

'They are ready . . .'

The horses, having waited, went back to the stable; the coachman spat: to curse he did not dare . . .

. . . .

'I shall give them a good wipe!'

'Ai, ai, ai! . . . Will you look at his honour!'

'Ah-choo!'

And the trembling yellow hands, armed with volumes, hammered against the shelf.

. . . .

In the vestibule the doorbell began to tinkle: it tinkled sporadically; silence spoke between the two jolts of tinkling; like a memory − a memory of something forgotten, familiar − this silence flew through the space of the lacquered room; and − entered the study without being asked; here was something old, old; and − it was coming up the staircase.

An ear protruded from the dust, a head turned:

'Do you hear? . . . Listen . . .'

Who could that be?

It might turn out to be: Nikolai Apollonovich, that most dreadful scoundrel, profligate and liar; it might turn out to be: Hermann Hermannovich, bringing papers; or Kotoshi-Kotoshinsky; or, perhaps, Count Nolde; it might even, as a matter of fact, turn out to be – em-em-em – Anna Petrovna . . .

There was a jingling.

'Don't you hear it?'

'Your excellency, of course we hear it: I expect someone is opening up . . .'

Only now did the lackeys respond to the tinkling; rigid as stone, they still continued to shine their candles.

Only Semyonych, who was wandering about the corridor (always muttering, always miserable), enumerating out of boredom the directions in the wardrobe that contained the accoutrements of the *barin*'s toilet: 'North-East: black ties and white ties . . . Collars, cuffs – East . . . Watches – North' – only Semyonych, who was wandering about the corridor (always muttering, always miserable), only he pricked up his ears, became alarmed, cocked his ear in the direction of the tinkling sound; and pattered off to the study.

Thus does a faithful battle horse respond to the sound of the horn:

'I take the liberty of observing: someone is ringing . . .'

The lackeys did not respond.

Each held out his candle – to the ceiling; from the very ceiling itself, from the top of the ladder, a bare head peeped forth surrounded by clouds of dust; a cracked, agitated voice responded:

'Yes! I heard it too.'

Apollon Apollonovich, tearing himself away from a fat, bound volume – he alone responded:

'Yes, yes, yes . . .'

'You know . . .'

'Someone is ringing . . . the doorbell . . .'

Here they both seemed to sense something unutterable but comprehensible, for they both – started: 'Be quick – run – hurry! . . .'

'It's the *barynya* . . .'

'It's Anna Petrovna!'

Be quick, run, hurry: there's the tinkling again!

Here the lackeys put down their candles and came pattering out into the dark corridor (Semyonych pattered there first). From the very ceiling itself, in the greenish light of the Petersburg morning, Apollon Apollonovich Ableukhov – a black, mouse-like heap – darted his eyes uneasily; beginning to sigh, somehow he began to crawl down, groaning, leaning his hairy chest, his shoulder and his stubbly chin against the rungs of the ladder; crawled down – and then he set off at a quick-tapping pace in the direction of the staircase with a dirty dust rag in his hand and the skirts of his robe wide open, flapping in the air like a fantastic flight of birds. Now he stumbled, now he got up again, began to breathe heavily and felt his pulse with his finger.

. . . .

While up the staircase came a gentleman with downy side-whiskers, in a tightly-buttoned uniform with a drawn-in waist, with dazzlingly white cuffs, with the star of Anna on his breast, being reverentially escorted by Semyonych; on a small tray that barely trembled in the old man's hands lay a shiny visiting card with a nobleman's crown.

The skirts of his robe closed up now, Apollon Apollonovich fussily peered out from behind the statue of Niobe at the august, downy old man.

He truly did resemble a mouse.

You Will, Like a Madman

Petersburg is a dream.

If you have visited Petersburg in one of your dreams, you will doubtless know the heavy entrance porch: there are oak doors with mirror-like panes of glass; the passers-by see these panes; but behind these panes they have never been.

A heavy-headed copper mace shone soundlessly from behind the mirror of those panes.

There is a sloping, octogenarian shoulder: it has been dreamt about for years by the casual passers-by, for whom everything is a dream and who are a dream; on to this octogenarian old man's shoulder falls a dark tricorne; the octogenarian doorman gleams brightly in there in his gold braid, resembling an employee from a funeral train office in the discharge of his duties.

Thus it is always.

The heavy copper-headed mace rests peacefully on the octogenarian doorman's shoulder; and, crowned in his tricorne, the doorman falls asleep for years over the *Stock Exchange Gazette*. Then the doorman gets up and opens the door wide. Whether it is afternoon, morning or evening when you pass that oak door – afternoon, morning or evening you will see the copper mace; you will see the gold braid; you will see – the dark tricorne.

With amazement you will stop before this vision. You saw the same thing the last time you came here. Five years have now passed: events have gone turbulently by in the distance; China has awoken; and Port Arthur has fallen; the Amur region of our country is being flooded by yellow-faced people; the legends of the iron horsemen of Genghis Khan have come to life.

But the vision of the years of old is unaltering, continuous: an octogenarian shoulder, a tricorne, gold braid, a beard.

A moment – and if the white beard should stir into motion behind the glass, if the enormous mace should sway, if the silvery gold braid should dazzlingly flash like the poisonous streams that rush from the gutters, threatening the resident of the basement with cholera and typhus, – if all that should be so, and the old years change, you will, like a madman, whirl about the Petersburg prospects.

The poisonous stream from a gutter will wash you in the dank cold of October.

If there, behind the mirror-like entrance porch, the heavy-headed mace swiftly flashed, then doubtless, doubtless cholera and typhus would not float around here: China would not be in tumult; and Port Arthur would not have fallen; the Amur region of our country would not be flooded by slant-eyed people; the horsemen of Genghis Khan would not have risen up from their graves many centuries old.

But listen, listen closely: the thud of hooves . . . The thud of hooves from the steppes beyond the Urals. The thud of hooves is approaching.

It is the iron horsemen.

Freezing for years above the entrance porch of the black-grey, many-columned house, the porch's caryatid still hangs: a thick-bearded, stone colossus.

With a sad, thousand-year-old smile, with the dark emptiness of eyes that penetrate the day he has hung for years: has hung agonizingly; for a hundred years the cornice of the balcony ledge has been falling on to the back of the bearded man's neck and on to the elbows of his stone arms. Hewn from the stone with a vine leaf and bunches of stone grapes, his loins have grown. Firmly against the wall his black-hoofed, goat-like legs have pressed.

Old, bearded man of stone!

Many years he has smiled above the noise of the street, for many years has raised himself a little above the summers, the winters, the springs – with the rounded curlicues of ornamental moulding. Summer, autumn, winter: again – summer and autumn; he is the same; and in summer he is porous; in winter, covered in ice, he bled pieces of ice; in the spring from those pieces of ice and those icicles' drops flowed. But he is the same: the years pass him by.

Time itself comes up to the caryatid's waist.

Out of hard times, as above the line of time, he has bent above the straight arrow of the prospect. A crow has settled on his beard: has cawed monotonously at the prospect; this slippery, wet prospect gives off a metallic sheen; in these wet flagstones, so cheerlessly illumined by the October day, are reflected: the greenish swarm of clouds, the greenish faces of the passers-by, the silvery streams that flow from the babbling gutters.

The bearded man of stone, raised above the whirlwind of events, has supported the entrance porch of the Institution for days, weeks and years.

. . . .

What a day!

From morning on the droplets began to beat, to chirr, to whisper; from the seashore a grey, misty felt pressed; in pairs the clerks walked in; the doorman in the tricorne opened the door for them;

they hung their hats and damp garments on hooks and ran up the stairs of red cloth, ran through the white marble vestibule, raised their eyes to the minister's portrait; and walked through the unheated halls – to their cold desks. But the clerks did not write: there was nothing to write; no paper was brought from the director's office; there was no one in the office; the logs crackled in the fireplace.

Above the stern, oak desk no bald head tensed the veins at its temples; it did not look sullenly from where in the fireplace cornflowers of coal gas flowed over an incandescent heap of crackling will-o'-the-wisps: in that solitary room idly in the fireplace cornflowers of coal gas continued to flow over an incandescent heap of crackling will-o'-the-wisps; they exploded, tore themselves free and burst – red cockerels' combs, flying swiftly away up the smoky chimney, in order to merge above the rooftops with the fumes and the poisoned soot and to hang permanently above the rooftops in a suffocating, corroding gloom. There was no one in the office.

On this day Apollon Apollonovich had not stalked his way to the director's office.

Now they were tired of waiting; from desk to desk a bewildered whispering fluttered; rumours hovered; and – dark things were imagined; in the deputy director's office the telephone receiver rattled:

'Has he left? . . . It's not possible? . . . Tell him that his presence is required . . . it's not possible . . .'

And the telephone rattled a second time:

'Have you told him? . . . Is he still at table? . . . Tell him that time will not wait . . .'

The deputy director stood with trembling jaw; he was lifting his hands in bewilderment; an hour or an hour and a half later he descended the velvet stairs in a very tall top hat. The doors of the entrance porch opened wide . . . He jumped into a carriage.

Twenty minutes later, as he ascended the stairs of the yellow house, he saw in amazement Apollon Apollonovich Ableukhov, his immediate superior, fussily peeping out at him from behind the statue of Niobe in a repulsive, mouse-coloured dressing-gown, the skirts of which were drawn about him.

'Apollon Apollonovich,' cried the grey-haired knight of Anna, catching sight of the senator's stubbly chin from behind the statue, and he hurriedly began to adjust the large neck decoration beneath his tie.

'Apollon Apollonovich, so here you are, here you are! But I've been, we've been — ringing you, telephoning you. Waiting for you . . .'

'I . . . em-em-em,' the round-shouldered old man said, beginning to chew his lips, 'am rearranging my library . . . Forgive me, my dear fellow,' he added peevishly, 'for being dressed like this, in domestic fashion.'

And with his hands he pointed to his tattered dressing-gown.

'What is it, are you ill? Er, er, er – why, you seem to have swollen . . . Er, is it oedemata?' the visitor said, respectfully touching a dust-covered finger.

Apollon Apollonovich dropped his dirty dust-rag on the parquet floor.

'Why, you've chosen the wrong time to fall ill . . . I've brought you some news . . . I congratulate you: there's a general strike – in Morovetrinsk . . .'

'What are you talking about? . . . I . . . em-em-em . . . There's nothing wrong with me.' Here the old man's face fell apart into wrinkles of displeasure (he received the news of the strike with indifference: evidently nothing could surprise him any more) – 'And I'm sorry: a lot of dust has gathered, you know . . .'

'Dust?'

'So I'm wiping it off with a rag . . .'

The deputy director with the downy side-whiskers now respectfully bowed to this round-shouldered ruin and tried to set about explaining an exceedingly important paper which he unfolded before him on the mother-of-pearl table in the drawing-room.

But Apollon Apollonovich again interrupted him:

'Dust, you know, contains the micro-organisms of diseases . . . So I'm wiping it off with a rag . . .'

Suddenly this grey ruin, which had just sat down in an Empire armchair, leapt swiftly to its feet, supporting itself on the arm with one hand; the other hand swiftly jabbed a finger at the paper.

'What is this?'

'As I was telling you only just now . . .'

'No, sir, wait, sir . . .' Apollon Apollonovich pressed himself frantically to the paper: he grew younger, whiter, turned – pale pink (he was no longer capable of being red).

'Wait! . . . But have they gone out of their minds? . . . My signature is necessary? Under a signature like that?'

'Apollon Apollonovich . . .'

'I won't give my signature.'

'But sir – it's a revolt!'

'Give Ivanchevsky the sack! . . .'

'Ivanchevsky has been given the sack: have you forgotten?'

'I won't give my signature . . .'

With a face that had turned younger, the skirts of his dressing-gown indecently open, Apollon Apollonovich was now shuffling to and fro about the drawing-room, his hands behind his back, his bald patch bowed low: going right up to the astonished visitor, he sprayed him with spittle:

'How could they think of such a thing? Firm, administrative authority is one thing, but the violation of strict, lawful procedures . . . is another.'

'Apollon Apollonovich,' the knight of Anna tried to reason with him, 'you are a man of firmness, you are a Russian . . . We have relied on you . . . No, of course you will sign . . .'

But Apollon Apollonovich began to twirl a pencil that had come to hand between two bony fingers; he stopped, gave the paper a keen glance: the pencil broke with a snap; now he was fastening the tassels of his dressing-gown in agitation, his jaw trembling angrily.

'My dear fellow, I am a man of the school of Plehve . . . I know what I am doing . . . You can't teach your grandmother to suck eggs . . .

'Em-emem . . . I won't give my signature.'

Silence.

'Em-emem . . . Em-emem . . .'

And he blew out his cheeks like a balloon.

The gentleman with the downy side-whiskers descended the staircase in bewilderment; for him it was clear: the career of Senator Ableukhov, which had been built up over the years, had disintegrated into rubble. After the deputy director of the Institution had driven away, Apollon Apollonovich continued to pace about among the Empire armchairs in intense anger. Soon he withdrew; soon appeared again; under his arm he lugged a heavy folder of papers to the mother-of-pearl table, pressing the folder and his shoulder against his side, which still ached; placing this folder of papers before him, Apollon Apollonovich rang for service and gave instructions that a fire be lit in front of him.

From behind the nota benes, the question marks, the section marks, the dashes, from behind the work that was *now the last*, a death's head rose towards the fire in the hearth; its lips muttered of themselves:

'It doesn't matter, sir . . . It's just so . . .'

The fire-breathing heap began to seethe and snort, giving off boiling cracklings and glitterings – crimson, gold; the logs were mixed with coals.

The bald head rose towards the fireplace with a sardonic, an ironically smiling mouth and screwed-up eyes, as it imagined the infuriated, dedicated careerist flying away from it through the slush, having offered him, Ableukhov, what was nothing more than a sordid bargain, without a stain on his conscience.

'I, my good sirs, am a man of the school of Plehve . . . And I know what I am doing . . . Yes, indeed, my good sir . . .'

The acutely sharpened little pencil – now it leapt in his fingers; the acutely sharpened little pencil fell on the paper with flocks of question marks; for this was his final task; in an hour's time that task would be ended; in an hour's time the telephone in the Institution would ring: with a piece of news that the mind could not take in.

. . . .

The carriage flew up to the caryatid of the entrance porch, but the caryatid did not move – the bearded man – old, made of stone, supporting the entrance porch of the Institution.

The year 1812 freed him from the scaffolding. The year 1825 raged with the days of December; they raged past; the days of January raged past so recently: it was the year 1905.

Bearded man of stone!

Everything happened beneath him and everything ceased to happen beneath him. What he saw, he will not tell anyone.

He remembered how the coachman reined in his pair of thorough-breds, how the smoke billowed from the horses' heavy rears; a general in a tricorne, in a winged greatcoat trimmed with fur, gracefully jumped out of the carriage and, to cries of 'hurrah', ran in through the open door.

Later, to cries of 'hurrah', the general trod the floor of the balcony ledge with a foot of white elk. His name is kept secret by the bearded man who supports the cornice of the balcony ledge; the bearded man of stone knows that name to this day.

But he will say nothing of it.

No one ever will he tell about the tears of today's prostitute who took shelter for the night beneath him on the steps of the entrance porch.

He will tell no one of the minister's recent flying visits: the latter was wearing a top hat; and in his eyes there was a greenish depth; the greying minister, as he got out of his light sleigh, stroked his sleek moustache with a grey Swedish glove.

Then he swiftly ran in through the open door, in order to fall into reflection by the window.

The pale, pale blotch of his face, pressed to the panes, protruded – from over there; the casual passer-by, looking at that blotch, would not have been able to guess that that pressed-up blotch – the casual passer-by would not have been able to guess that that pressed-up blotch was the face of a commanding person who guided from up there the fate of Russia.

The bearded man knows that; and – remembers; but as for telling, he will not tell – anyone, ever! . . .

> It's time, my friend, it's time . . . For peace the heart is asking.
> Day runs after day. And every day that's passing
> Takes with it particles of life. Together you and I
> Intend to live some more. Look yonder – and we die.

Thus was the greying, solitary minister, now gone to eternal rest, in the habit of speaking to his solitary friend.

> And he is gone – and Russia has abandoned,
> That he exalted . . .

And – peace to his ashes.

But the doorman with the mace, falling asleep over the *Stock*

Exchange Gazette, knew the exhausted face well: Vyacheslav Konstantinovich was, God be praised, still remembered in the Institution, while Emperor Nikolai Pavlovich, of blessed memory, is no longer remembered in the Institution; the white halls, the columns, the banisters remember . . .

The bearded man of stone remembers.

Out of hard times, as above the line of time, has he bent above the straight arrow of the prospect, or above a bitter, salty, alien – human tear?

> There is no happiness, but there is freedom, peace . . .
> Much I have long desired stays in my dreams:
> Long, weary slave, my flight from here I've planned
> To work's and pure contentment's far-off land.

. . . .

The bald head raises itself slightly, – the Mephistophelean, faded mouth smiles in senile fashion at the flashes; in the flashes the face is coloured crimson; the eyes are still aflame; and they are still stony eyes: blue – and in green hollows! His gaze is cold and astonished; and – empty, empty. The seasons, the sun and the light were kindled by dark things. The whole of life is only a dark thing. So is it worth it? No, it is not worth it:

'I, my good sirs, am of the school of Plehve . . . I, my good sirs . . . I – em-em-em . . .'

The bald head falls.

. . . .

In the Institution whispers were fluttering from desk to desk; suddenly the door opened: a clerk with a completely white face ran to the telephone.

'Apollon Apollonovich . . . is retiring . . .'

Everyone leapt to their feet; the head of desk, Legonin, burst into tears; and all this arose: an idiotic hubbub of voices, the uneven trampling of feet, a voice, from the deputy director's room, trying to persuade; and – the rattle of the telephone (to the Ninth Department); the deputy director stood with trembling jaw; the telephone receiver seemed to dance in his hand: Apollon Apollonovich Ableukhov was really no longer the head of the Institution.

A quarter of an hour later, in a tightly buttoned uniform with a drawn-in waist, the grey-haired deputy director with the star of Anna on his chest was already giving orders; after another twenty minutes, he bore a countenance freshly shaven and young with excitement around the halls.

Thus was the event of indescribable importance accomplished.

A Loathsome Creature

The seething waters of the canal rushed to the place where from the unbridled expanses of the Field of Mars the wind crashed into the thicket's groaning branches: what a terrible place!

The terrible place was crowned by a magnificent palace; with its upwards-stretched tower it resembled a whimsical castle: pink and red, of heavy stone; the crown-bearer lived within those walls; this did not happen now; that crown-bearer is no more.

In thy kingdom remember his soul, O Lord!

The summit of the pink and red palace protruded aloft out of a roaring, thick mass of knotty branches that were completely without leaves; the branches stretched there to the sky in wild rushes and, as they swayed, tried to catch the fleeting flocks of the mists; cawing, a crow shot aloft; soared, swayed above the flocks, and came plunging down again.

A carriage was crossing that place.

Two small red houses flew towards it, forming the likeness of a gate-arch on the square in front of the palace; to the left of the square the heap of trees kept up a threatening roaring; and it was as if the careening summits of the trunks were engaged in an attack; the high spire jutted out from behind the foggy flocks.

An equestrian statue stood out blackly and unclearly on the foggy square; passing visitors to Petersburg do not give this statue any attention; I always stand before it for a long time: it is a magnificent statue! It is only a pity that some wretched mocker had put gilt paint on its socle when last I drove past it.

The autocrat and great-grandson had raised this statue to his illustrious great-grandfather, the autocrat had lived in this castle; here too, he had ended his unhappy days – in the pink stone castle; he did not languish long here; he could not languish here; his soul was torn apart between a petty tyrannical vanity and fits of nobility; from this torn soul the infant spirit flew away.

Probably the snub-nosed head in white curls appeared in the embrasure of the window more than once; that window up there – was it not from that one? And the head in white curls painfully surveyed the expanses beyond the window panes; and the eyes luxuriated in the pink fading of the sky; or: the eyes revelled in the silvery play and the seethings of the moon's reflections in the dense-leaved thicket; by the entrance porch stood a Pavlovsky sentry in a three-cornered hat with a broad brim, presenting arms to a gold-chested general wearing the order of St Andrew,[8] as he proceeded to a gilt carriage decorated with aquarelles; a flaming red coachman loomed up from the raised box; on the footboard at the rear of the carriage stood thick-lipped Negroes.

The Emperor Pavel Petrovich, having cast a glance at all this, returned to a sentimental conversation with a lady-in-waiting in muslin and gauze, and the lady-in-waiting smiled; on her cheeks there were two sly dimples, and – a black beauty spot.

On that fateful night the moon's silver flowed in through those same panes, falling on the heavy furniture of the imperial bedchamber; it fell on the bed, gilding a sly little spark-throwing cupid; and on the pale pillow a profile that seemed to be sketched in Indian ink was outlined; chimes were sounding somewhere; footsteps could be detected coming from somewhere . . . Not three moments passed – and the bed was rumpled: in place of the pale profile, the impression of a head was shadowed; the sheets were warm; the sleeper was not there; a little group of white-curled officers with drawn swords were inclining their heads towards the empty bed; people were trying to break down the locked door at the side; a woman's voice was weeping; suddenly the hand of a pink-lipped officer raised the heavy window blind a little; from behind the lowered muslin, there, in the window, in transparent silver – a thin, black shadow trembled.

And the moon continued to stream its light silver, falling on the heavy furniture of the imperial bedroom; it fell on the bed, gilding the little cupid who gleamed from the head of the bed; it also fell on the profile, deathly pale, as though traced in Indian ink . . . Somewhere chimes were sounding; in the distance footsteps were padding closer from every side.

. . . .

Nikolai Apollonovich vacantly surveyed this gloomy place, not noticing at all that the shaven physiognomy of the second lieutenant who was giving him the ride turned now and then to face his, if one might be permitted to observe, neighbour; the gaze with which second lieutenant Likhutin surveyed the victim he was giving a ride to, seemed full of curiosity; he kept turning restlessly all the way; all the way he kept nudging his side into him. Little by little, Nikolai Apollonovich guessed that Sergei Sergeyevich found it unbearable to touch him ... even though it were only his side; and now he elbowed him, awarding his fellow traveller a fine rain of jolts.

Just then the wind tore off Ableukhov's Italian broad-brimmed hat, and with an involuntary movement the latter caught it on Sergei Sergeyevich's knees; for a moment he also touched Sergei Sergeyevich's stiff fingers, but those fingers twitched and suddenly leapt to the side with the most manifest loathing and alarm; the angular elbow began to move. Second lieutenant Likhutin now probably had the sensation of touching the skin not of a familiar and, it might be said, bosom companion of his childhood, but ... of a loathsome creature, of the kind that is ... struck dead ... on the spot ...

Ableukhov noticed that gesture; he in his turn began to study the companion of his childhood, with whom he had once been on *thou* terms; this *thou*, Seryozhka – Sergei Sergeich Likhutin, in other words – had since the time of their last conversation become younger, yes, really – by some eight years, having turned from being Sergei Sergeich into Seryozhka; but now this Seryozhka did not harken with servility to the soarings of Ableukhov's thoughts, as he had done in *those days*, in the elder grove, in his grandfather's old park some eight years ago; and the eight years had altered everything: the elder grove had been chopped down long ago, while he ... – he looked with servility at Sergei Sergeich.

Their unequal relations had been stood on end; and everything, everything had gone in reverse direction; the idiotic appearance, the little coat, the jolts from the angular elbow and the other gestures of nervousness that Nikolai Apollonovich read as gestures of contempt – all, all this led him into melancholy reflections on the vicissitudes of human relations; this dreadful place had also led him into melancholy reflections: the pink-red palace, the wildly howling garden with its crows shooting into the sky, the two small red houses and the equestrian statue; though as a matter of fact, garden, castle and statue were now behind their shoulders.

And Ableukhov grew pinched and haggard-looking.

'Are you leaving the service, Sergei Sergeyevich?'

'Eh?'

'The service . . .'

'As you see . . .'

And Sergei Sergeyevich gave him a look as though until today he had not known Ableukhov; he looked him up and down from head to foot.

'I'd advise you to raise your collar a bit, Sergei Sergeyevich: you've a cold in your throat, and in this weather it's really very easy to . . .'

'What?'

'Easy to catch a quinsy.'

'And all because of a matter that concerns you,' Likhutin barked out hollowly; his agitated snorting was heard.

'?'

'Oh, I'm not talking about my throat . . . I'm leaving the service *all because of a matter that concerns you*, or rather, not that, but: thanks to you.'

'A hint,' Nikolai Apollonovich very nearly started to exclaim, and caught the look again: people never look at a friend like that, but rather, perhaps, at an unprecedented, outlandish wonder, the proper place for which is in the Cabinet of Curiosities[9] (not in a carriage, and even less on the prospect . . .)

With such a look do passers-by cast their eyes at the elephants that are sometimes led late at night in the city from railway station to circus; they roll their eyes, stagger back, and – do not believe their eyes; at home they will say:

'Would you believe it, we met an elephant in the street!'

But everyone laughs at them.

That was the kind of curiosity Likhutin's gaze expressed; there was no indignation in it; there was, perhaps, loathing (as from proximity to a boa constrictor); after all, creeping loathsome creatures do not provoke anger – they are simply struck dead, with whatever comes to hand: on the spot . . .

Nikolai Apollonovich was thinking about the words the second lieutenant had muttered about his leaving the service – solely because of him; yes – Sergei Sergeich Likhutin would lose the opportunity of working in the service of the state after what was soon going to happen between them both; the little flat would obviously be empty (in it the *loathsome creature* would be crushed) ... Something, something was going to happen ... here Nikolai Apollonovich felt afraid in good earnest; he began to fidget on the spot and – and: all his ten fingers, trembling, cold, gripped the second lieutenant's sleeve.

'Eh? ... What is it? ... Why are you doing that?'

Here a small house loomed past, a small house the colour of blancmange, which was surrounded from top to bottom by grey moulding work: rococo curlicues (which had once, perhaps, served as a refuge for that same lady-in-waiting with the black beauty spot and two sly little dimples on her lily-white cheeks).

'Sergei Sergeich ... Sergei Sergeyevich, I ... I must confess to you ... Oh, how sorry I am ... It's extremely, extremely sad: my behaviour ... Sergei Sergeich, I've behaved ... Sergei Sergeyevich ... shamefully, lamentably ... But Sergei Sergeyevich, I have an excuse: yes, I do, I do have an excuse. As an enlightened, humane man, as a bright spirit, not some ... Sergei Sergeyevich, you will be able to understand it all ... I couldn't sleep last night, or rather, I mean, I am suffering from insomnia ... The doctors consider me' – now he stooped to lying – 'or rather my condition – to be very, very dangerous ... Exhaustion of the brain with pseudohallucinations, Sergei Sergeyevich' (for some reason Dudkin's words came to mind) '... What do you say?'

But Sergei Sergeyevich did not say anything: he looked without indignation; and in his gaze there was loathing (as from vicinity to a boa constrictor); after all, loathsome creatures do not provoke anger: they are ... struck dead ... on the spot ...

'Pseudohallucinations ...' Ableukhov repeated beseechingly, frightened, small, clumsy, seeking out the other's eyes with his own eyes (the eyes did not reply to one another); he wanted to explain himself immediately; and – right here, in the cab: to explain himself here – not in the little flat; and now that fateful entrance porch was not far away; and if he was unable to come to an agreement with the officer before they got to the entrance porch, then – everything, everything: would be finished! Fin-ished! There would be a murder, or an outrageous action, or simply a disgraceful fight:

'I . . . I . . . I . . .'

'Out you get: we're here.'

Nikolai Apollonovich looked before him with leaden, unblinking eyes – looked at the shreds of bluish mist, from which drops squelched, spinning metallic bubbles on the surface of the gurgling puddles.

Second lieutenant Likhutin, having leapt down to the pavement, threw the money to the cab driver and now stood before the carriage, waiting for the senator's son; the latter seemed to dally.

'Wait, Sergei Sergeyevich: I had a stick here with me . . . Ach! Where is it? Did I drop my stick?'

He really was looking for the stick; but the stick had disappeared without trace; Nikolai Apollonovich, completely pale, turned beseeching eyes uneasily in all directions.

'Well, then?'

'But my stick.'

Ableukhov's head had receded deep into his shoulders, and his shoulders swayed; while his mouth crookedly moved apart; Nikolai Apollonovich looked before him with leaden, unblinking eyes at the bluish shreds of the mist; and – did not move.

At this point Sergei Sergeich Likhutin began to breathe angrily and impatiently; gripping Ableukhov by the sleeve, discreetly but firmly began the careful process of extracting him from the carriage, arousing the manifest curiosity of the house's yardkeeper – began to extract him like a sack stuffed full of goods.

But, once extracted, Nikolai Apollonovich fairly clutched at Likhutin's hand with his fingernails: for in the darkness, once they got through that door, the hand might perhaps assume an unseemly pose with regard to his, Nikolai Apollonovich's, cheek; in the darkness he would not be able to jump aside; and – all would be over: the bodily movement would be accomplished; the Ableukhov family would be disgraced for ever (they had never been physically beaten).

Now second lieutenant Likhutin (the devil!) seized with his free hand the collar of the Italian cloak; and Nikolai Apollonovich turned whiter than linen.

'I'm coming, I'm coming, Sergei Sergeich . . .'

He instinctively dug his heel into the side of the entrance-porch step; however, he at once thought the better of it, in order not to be made a laughing-stock.

The entrance-porch door slammed shut.

Outer Darkness

Outer darkness engulfed them in the unlit porchway (thus it is in the first moment after death); at once in the darkness the second lieutenant's panting and puffing was heard, accompanied by a minute tracery of exclamations.

'I . . . stood right here: here, here – this is where I stood . . . I was just standing, you know . . .'

'Do you say so indeed, Nikolai Apollonovich? . . . Do you say so indeed, my good sir? . . .'

'In a complete nervous attack, in the grip of morbid associations of ideas . . .'

'Associations? . . . But why aren't you coming? . . . What do you mean – associations? . . .'

'The doctor said . . . Oh, but why are you pulling me? Don't pull me: I can walk by myself . . .

'And why are you clutching my hand? . . . Don't clutch it, please,' came the voice from higher up, now.

'I don't mean to . . .'

'You're clutching it . . .'

'I tell you . . .' came from even higher up . . .

'The doctor said – the doctor said: it's a r-rare – brain disorder, called such-and-such: the domino and all the rest of it . . . A brain disorder . . .' came a squeak from somewhere above now.

But somewhere even higher up, a sudden, well-fed voice exclaimed loudly:

'Hello!'

This was right outside the door of the Likhutins' flat.

'Who is here?'

From the most complete darkness, Sergei Sergeich Likhutin raised his voice in displeasure.

'Who is here?' cried Nikolai Apollonovich, raising his own voice in the most enormous relief; at the same time he felt: the hand that had been clutching him fell away; and – a match struck reassuringly.

The unfamiliar, well-fed voice continued to proclaim:

'Well, I've been standing here . . . I've rung and rung – and no one comes to open. And, how do you like that: familiar voices.'

When the match was struck, some downy-white fingers appeared, carrying a bunch of the most luxuriant chrysanthemums; while behind them, in the murk, the stately figure of Verhefden also appeared – for some reason he was here at this hour.

'What? Sergei Sergeich?

'You've shaved your beard off? . . .

'What? . . . you're in civilian clothes . . .'

And pretending only now to have noticed Ableukhov (Ableukhov, we should observe, noticed this at once), Verhefden struck a match and with eyebrows raised high began to look out at him from behind the chrysanthemums that were swaying in his hand.

'And Nikolai Apollonovich as well? . . . How are you, Nikolai Apollonovich? . . . After last night I must confess I thought . . . You weren't yourself, were you? . . . You left the ball with a bit of a stir? . . . Since last night I've . . .'

Another match was struck; two mocking eyes stared out of the flowers: Verhefden knew perfectly well that Nikolai Apollonovich was not well received in the Likhutins' home; seeing him so manifestly drawn towards the door, from considerations of social politeness Verhefden began to hurry:

'I'm not in the way, am I? The fact is that I just dropped by for a moment . . . And in any case, I have no time . . . We are up to our eyebrows . . . Apollon Apollonovich, your dear father, is waiting for me . . . By all the signs it looks as though a strike is expected . . . We're up to our eyebrows in work . . .'

They did not have time to reply to him, because the door opened swiftly; an over-starched linen butterfly appeared from the doorway – a butterfly sitting on a bonnet.

'Mavrushka, is this a good time for me to call?'

'Yes, sir, the *barynya* is at home . . .'

'No, no, Mavrushka . . . You had better give these flowers to the *barynya* . . . It is a debt I owe,' he smiled to Sergei Sergeich, shrugging his shoulders in the way that a man shrugs his shoulders and smiles to another man after a day spent together in the society of ladies . . .

'Yes, it is a debt I owe to Sofya Petrovna – for a number of "fifis" I uttered . . .'

And again he smiled: and – caught himself:

'Well then, goodbye, my friend. Adieu, Nikolai Apollonovich: you look overtired, nervous . . .'

Footsteps went pattering down the stairs; and from there, from the lower landing, came once again:

'And it's not right to read books all the time . . .'

Nikolai Apollonovich very nearly shouted down:

'Herman Hermanovich, I also . . . It's also time I went home . . . Aren't we going in the same direction?'

But the footsteps receded, and – bang: the door slammed shut.

At this point Nikolai Apollonovich again felt lonely; and again – that he had been seized; yes – this time good and proper; seized in front of Mavrushka. On his face was written horror, while on Mavrushka's, it was – bewilderment and alarm, while a kind of open, satanic joy was quite distinctly written on the face of the second lieutenant; bathed in perspiration, with his free hand he drew out his handkerchief from his pocket – with his other free hand squeezing, pressing against the wall, pulling, drawing away and nudging the small, unwilling figure of the student.

In its turn: the small, unwilling figure proved to be as slippery as an eel; in its turn, this small figure, defending itself, jumped away from the door – away, away; when it was nudged – it pushed itself and squeezed itself away; thus, when we put our foot in an anthill, we instinctively jump aside at the sight of thousands of small red ants that busily rush about on the heap that has been crushed by our foot; and from the heap then comes a repulsive rustling; had the house once so attractive to him really become for *Nicolas* Ableukhov – an anthill crushed by his foot? What could the astonished Mavrushka make of that?

All the same, Nikolai Apollonovich was pushed inside.

'There we are now, if you please . . .'

All the same, he was pushed inside; but in the entrance hall, observing the last crumbs of dignity, surveying the familiar yellow oakwood coat-rack and surveying the same old upholstered handle on the drawer in front of the mirror, commented:

'Actually . . . I've only dropped in . . . for a short visit . . .'

And he very nearly gave his cloak to Mavrushka (ugh – the heat and the smell of the steam heating); and – there was the pink kimono! . . . A satin piece of it fluttered through from the entrance hall into the next room: a piece of Sofya Petrovna; or, more precisely – of Sofya Petrovna's dress . . .

There was no time to think.

The cloak was not surrendered, because Sergei Sergeich Likhutin, turning to Mavrushka and taking her arm, said in a hoarse and jerky voice:

'Go to the kitchen . . .'

And without observing the elementary decorum of a cordial host, Sergei Sergeyevich shoved the broad-brimmed hat and flying coat straight into the room with the Fujiyamas. There is no need to add that under the broad-brimmed hat and under the folds of the flying cloak the owner of the cloak, Nikolai Apollonovich, flew too.

As he flew into the dining-room, Nikolai Apollonovich saw, for one instant, running in at the door: a kimono; and then – the door slammed on a piece of the kimono.

Nikolai Apollonovich was transported through the room with the Fujiyamas, and noticed no essential change in it, noticed no traces of plaster on the striped, multicoloured rug; it had been trodden underfoot – *after the incident*; afterwards the rugs had been cleaned; but the traces of plaster remained. Nikolai Apollonovich did not notice anything: neither the traces of plaster, nor the damage that had been done to the fallen ceiling. Turning a frightened grin at the executioner who was dragging him along, he suddenly noticed . . . –

The door opened – and from Sofya Petrovna's room a head was thrust out of the narrow opening: Nikolai Apollonovich could only see – two eyes: in horror the eyes turned on him out of a flood of black hair.

But hardly had he turned to face the eyes, when the eyes turned away from him; and there was an exclamation:

'Ai, ai!'

Sofya Petrovna saw: through the alcove the second lieutenant, covered in perspiration, was dragging his way across the rugs and parquetry with a winged victim (in the cloak Nikolai Apollonovich looked as though he had wings) who was also covered in perspiration, – with a victim from under the wings of whose cloak a green trouser leg dangled most indecently, treacherously betraying a trouser strap.

'Trrr,' his heels went, as they dragged across the rug; and the carpet was covered with little wrinkles.

Just then, Nikolai Apollonovich turned his head, and, catching sight of Sofya Petrovna, he shouted to her tearfully:

'Leave us, Sofya Petrovna: this is a matter that must be settled between men,' – and as he said it, his cloak flew off and fell sumptuously on the small couch like some fantastic two-winged creature.

'Trrr,' his heels went as they dragged across the rug.

Feeling an enormous jolt, Nikolai Apollonovich hung for a moment in space, his legs jerking, and ... – with a soft slap, the broad-brimmed hat detached itself from his head. He himself, his legs jerking, describing an arc, went crashing into the unlocked, but firmly closed door of the little study; here the second lieutenant resembled a sling, and Nikolai Apollonovich a stone: like a stone he crashed into the door; the door opened: he disappeared into the unknown.

An Ordinary Man

At last Apollon Apollonovich stood up.

Calmly somehow, he began to look around him; tore himself away from the little bundles of parallel-positioned dossiers: nota benes, section marks, question marks, exclamation marks; sinking, his hand trembled and jumped with its little pencil – over the yellow sheet of paper, over the small mother-of-pearl table; the frontal bones were tensed in a single intense effort: to understand, no matter what, at whatever cost.

And – he understood.

The lacquered carriage with the coat of arms would no longer fly up to the old, stone caryatid; out there, behind the panes, towards him would not come: the octogenarian shoulder, the tricorne, the gold braid and the copper-headed mace; Port Arthur would not be restored from the ruins; but – China would rise up in disturbance; hark – listen: one seems to hear a distant trampling; that is the horsemen of Genghis Khan.

Apollon Apollonovich listened: a distant trampling; no, it was not; it was Semyonych, traversing the cold magnificence of the gleaming rooms; there he entered, looked around him, walked through; saw – the cracked mirror: across it a silver arrow had glimmered in zigzags; and – frozen for ever.

Semyonych walked past.

Apollon Apollonovich did not like his spacious apartment with its unaltering view of the Neva; out there the clouds rushed in a greenish swarm; from time to time they thickened into a yellowish smoke that descended towards the seashore; the dark, watery depths beat close against the granite with the steel of their scales; into the greenish swarm a motionless spire receded . . . from the Petersburg Side. Apollon Apollonovich began to look round him uneasily: these walls! Here he would settle down for a long time – with a view of the Neva. Here was his domestic hearth; his official career was over.

Well, and what of it?

The walls were snow, not walls! A little cold, it was true . . . What of it? Family life; in other words: Nikolai Apollonovich, – the most dreadful, so to speak . . .; and – Anna Petrovna, who had in her old age become . . . simply God knows what!

Em-em-em . . .

Apollon Apollonovich clutched his head tightly in his fingers, letting his gaze escape to the crackling and fire-breathing hearth: an idle cerebral game!

It escaped – escaped beyond the borders of consciousness: there it continued to rise into swarms of chaotic clouds; and Nikolai Apollonovich remembered – a small sprout of a lad with searching blue eyes and a mass (one must be fair) of the most various intellectual interests, all impossibly tangled up with one another.

And – he remembered a girl (this had been about thirty years ago); a swarm of admirers; among them a man still comparatively young, Apollon Apollonovich Ableukhov, now a state councillor and – a hopeless sigher after the ladies.

And – the first night: horror in the eyes of the female companion who was left with him – an expression of revulsion and contempt, hidden by a submissive smile; that night Apollon Apollonovich Ableukhov, now a state councillor, performed a loathsome act sanctioned by form: he raped the girl; the rape went on for years; and on one of those nights Nikolai Apollonovich was conceived – between two different smiles: between a smile of lust and a smile of submissiveness; was it any wonder that Nikolai Apollonovich subsequently became a combination of revulsion, fear and lust? They would have had to immediately set about educating the horror they had brought into the world: to humanize the horror.

But instead they inflated it . . .

And inflating the horror to extreme limits, they had each run away from the horror; Apollon Apollonovich – to direct the fate of Russia; Anna Petrovna – to gratify her sexual urge with Mantalini (an Italian *artiste*); Nikolai Apollonovich – to philosophy; and from there – to meetings of the graduates of non-existent institutions (to all those small moustaches!) Their domestic hearth now turned into a desolation of abomination.

Into this desolation of abomination he was now going to return; in place of Anna Petrovna he would merely find a locked door that led into her apartments (if Anna Petrovna did not conceive a desire to return – to the desolate abomination); he had the key to her apartments (he had only ever visited that part of the cold house twice; to sit there; on both occasions he had caught a cold).

While in place of his son he would see a blinking, evasive eye – enormous, empty and cold: the colour of cornflowers; not quite that of a thief; and not quite utterly frightened; the horror would hide itself there – that same horror that had flared up in the newly-wed woman on the night when Apollon Apollonovich Ableukhov, the state councillor, had for the first time . . .

And so on, and so forth . . .

After he had left government service these smart rooms would also probably be closed up one after the other; that meant that the corridor, with adjoining rooms for himself and his son, would remain; his very life would be bounded by the corridor: he would shuffle about there in his slippers; and – there would be: the reading of newspapers, the discharge of the organic functions, the place that had no comparison, the writing of his memoirs before he died, and the door that led to his son's rooms.

Yes, yes, yes!

To look through the keyhole; and – to jump away, having heard a suspicious rustling; or – no: in the corresponding place to bore a little hole with an awl; and – expectation would not deceive: his son's life on the other side of the wall would be revealed to him in the same precision with which a dismantled clock mechanism is revealed to the gaze. In place of his governmental interests, new interests would greet him – from this observation point.

All this would happen:

'Good morning, Papa!'

'And good morning to you, Kolenka!'

And – they would each go off to their rooms.

And – then, and – then: having locked the door, he would apply himself to the perforated hole, in order to see and hear and from time to time tremble, start jerkily – at the sight of the burning secret made manifest; be depressed, and afraid, and eavesdrop: as they opened their souls to each other – Nikolai Apollonovich and that stranger with the small moustache; at night, throwing the blanket from him, he would thrust forth a head covered with perspiration; and, as he reviewed what he had heard, he would sigh from the jolts of his heart, which were tearing that heart to pieces, take some pills and run ... to the place that had no comparison: shuffle in his slippers all the way to ... another morning.

'Good morning!'

'Indeed, Kolenka! ...'

There was the life of an ordinary man!

. . . .

An unmasterable urge drew him into his son's room; timidly the door creaked: the reception room was revealed; he stopped on the threshold; utterly – small and old; pulled with a trembling hand at the crimsonish tassels of his robe, as he surveyed the nonsense: the cage with the green budgerigars, the Arabian stool with incrustations of ebony and copper; and he saw – an absurdity: winding down from the stool in all directions, the boiling red folds of a domino cape, that had fallen sumptuously, like throbbing lights and streaming deer's antlers – straight under the head of a spotted leopard that lay prone on the floor with a grinning head; Apollon Apollonovich stood for a while, chewed his lips, stroked his chin that seemed strewn with hoar frost, and spat with revulsion (after all, he knew the story of that domino); buffoonish and headless, it sprawled its satin skirts and armless sleeves; a small mask was hung on a rusty Sudanese arrow.

To Apollon Apollonovich the room seemed airless: instead of air, the atmosphere contained lead; as though dreadful, undendurable thoughts were being meditated here . . . An unpleasant room! . . . And – a heavy atmosphere!

Here was the martyred, grinning mouth, here were the eyes of cornflower hue, here was the hair that stood bathed in light: invested in a uniform jacket with an exceedingly thin waist and clutching a white kid glove in one hand, Nikolai Apollonovich, clean shaven (and perhaps scented), a sword at his side, suffered from behind the frame: Apollon Apollonovich looked closely at the portrait that had been painted in the spring that had recently passed, and – strode into the next room.

The unlocked writing desk struck Apollon Apollonovich's attention: a small drawer in it had been pulled out; Apollon Apollonovich conceived an instinctive curiosity (to examine its contents); with quick footsteps he ran over to the writing desk and snatched up – an enormous photograph that had been left forgotten on the desk, and turned it this way and that in the deepest reflectivity (his absent-mindedness distracted his thoughts from the contents of the little drawer); the photograph depicted some lady or other – a brunette . . .

His absent-mindedness proceeded from the contemplation of a certain lofty matter, because this matter had unfolded into a train of thought which the senator went rushing after; this train of thought had nothing in common with his son's room, nor with the fact he was standing in his son's room, which Apollon Apollonovich had probably entered in mechanical fashion (an unmasterable urge is a mechanical action); mechanically he then lowered his eyes and saw that his hand was turning, not the photograph, but some sort of heavy object, while his thoughts were surveying that type of state functionary who in common parlance is called a careerist, a representative of which species he had recently had the misfortune to talk to: when the deceased minister had been alive, they were in solidarity with him, but now they were going to do something to him, Ableukhov . . .

What were they going to do?

The heavy object resembled a sardine tin in shape; it had been extracted by the senator's hand mechanically; mechanically had Apollon Apollonovich snatched up the cabinet photograph, and had woken from his thoughts – holding a round-ended object: and inside it something jangled; least of all at this point did the senator think about the abyss (we often drink coffee with cream over the abyss), but rather examined the round-ended object with the greatest attention, inclining his head over it and listening to the ticking of the clock: the clock mechanism inside the heavy sardine tin . . .

He did not care much for the object . . .

He took the object with him for more detailed examination – through the corridor into the drawing-room, – inclining his head over it and resembling a grey, mouse-like heap; as he did so he was still thinking about the same type of state functionary; men of this type protect themselves from responsibility with the most empty phrases, like 'as is well known', when nothing is yet known, or: 'science teaches us', when science does not teach (his thoughts always sprayed poison at the inimical party) . . .

Apollon Apollonovich ran with the object to the end of the drawing-room where the small, incrusted table rose on its leonine legs; primly there rose the long-legged bronze; he put the object on a lacquered Chinese tray, inclining his bald head, above which the shade of the lamp expanded with pale violet glass, delicately patterned.

But the glass was growing dark with time; and the delicate pattern was also growing dark with time.

. . . .

He Did Not Quite Explain Himself

As he flew into Likhutin's small study, Nikolai Apollonovich's heels crashed on the floor at full weight; this impact was transmitted to the back of his head; the tendons shook; he involuntarily fell to his knees, ramming the unpleasantly slippery parquetry with dark green cloth; and – bruised himself.

Fell and . . . –

> – at once leapt to his feet, breathing heavily and limping, rushed in fright to the heavy oakwood armchair, cutting a clumsy and rather ridiculous figure with a trembling jaw, manifestly trembling fingers, a single instinctive urge – to get there in time: to get to the armchair in time and grasp it, so that were he to be attacked from behind he could quickly run round the armchair, flying hither and thither away from his hither-and-thither-flying, merciless adversary, all of whose movements resembled the convulsions of a rabies sufferer; to get to the armchair in time, and to grasp it!

Or else, arming himself with that armchair, to knock his adversary down and, as the latter began to struggle under the heavy oakwood legs, to rush to the window as fast as possible (better to crash from the second floor down to the street, smashing the window-panes, then remain alone with . . . with . . .) . . .

Breathing heavily and limping, he rushed towards the oakwood armchair.

Scarcely had he reached it, however, than the second lieutenant's hot breath burned his neck; turning round, he managed to glimpse a pale, twisted mouth and a five-fingered hand, ready to fall on his shoulder: a face crimson with rabid fury, the face of an avenger, stared at him with swollen veins and eyes of stone; in that hideous face no one would have recognized the second lieutenant's soft face, steadily emitting 'fifi' after 'fifi'. The five-fingered paw – it was not a hand – would certainly have fallen on Ableukhov's shoulder, breaking it; but he jumped over the armchair in time.

The five-fingered paw fell on the armchair.

And the armchair cracked; the armchair crashed to the floor; in his ears there resounded – a unique, inhuman sound, the like of which had never yet been heard:

'Because here a human soul is doomed to perish!'

And the angular body flew after the small figure that darted away; from an oral orifice that sprayed spittle there escaped, bubbled and burst in a bundle of cracking wheezes the tones of a cockerel – voiceless and somehow red . . .

'Because . . . I . . . have got involved . . . do you understand? In all this affair . . . This . . . affair . . . Do you understand? . . . This affair is the kind of affair that . . . does not concern me . . . Or rather, no: it does concern me . . . Now do you understand? . . .'

And the crazed second lieutenant, catching up with his victim, raised above the small figure that was cringing in expectation of three deaths, waiting for the blow, two trembling palms (the small figure was still endeavouring to protect its sweaty head beneath its stooping back), nervously clenched his fists, hanging with his whole torso over the little lump of muscles that was fidgeting beneath his hands; while the *little lump* twisted and bowed with a cowardly, grinning mouth, repeating all the rhythms of the hands and trying to protect his right cheek with his palm:

'I understand, I understand . . . Sergei Sergeich, please calm yourself,' the little lump squeaked, 'and be quieter, quieter, I beseech you: my dear fellow, I beseech you . . .'

This little lump of body (Nikolai Apollonovich was backing away, bent unnaturally) – this little lump of body went mincing away on two crooked legs; and not towards the window, but away from the window (the window was cut off by the second lieutenant); at the same time the little lump saw in the window – (though it may seem strange, this was still Nikolai Apollonovich) – the funnel of a steamboat sticking up; on the other side of the canal he saw – the wet roof of a house; above the roof was an enormous, cold emptiness . . .

He backed away to the corner and – imagine: the leaden five-fingered paws fell on his shoulders (one hand, slipping across his neck, burned his neck with a forty-degree fever); so that he sank – squatting into the corner, bathed in a perspiration as cold as ice.

He was already preparing to screw up his eyes, to stop his ears, in order not to see the mad, crimson countenance and not to hear the crowings of the cockerel-like, voiceless voice:

'Aaa . . . An affair . . . where any decent man, where . . . aaa . . . any decent man . . . What did I say? Yes – decent . . . must get involved, without regard for propriety or social position . . .'

It was strange to listen to the incoherent alternation of none the less intelligent words accompanied by the absurdity of every feature, every movement; Nikolai Apollonovich thought:

'Should I not shout, should I not summon?'

No, what would he shout; and whom would he summon; no – it was too late; he must close his eyes, his ears; a moment – and all would be ended; bang: a fist struck the wall above Ableukhov's head.

Here he opened his eyes for a moment.

Before him he saw: two legs were placed wide apart (he was squatting, after all); a dizzying thought – and: without debating the consequences, his mouth open in a cowardly grin that seemed like a laugh, with dishevelled, flaxen-white hair Nikolai Apollonovich swiftly crawled between the two legs that were set wide apart; leapt to his feet, – and without further thought, rushed straight towards the door (the pewter edge of the roof flickered in the window), but . . . the five-fingered paws, burning with contact, seized him shamefully by the tail of his frock-coat; tugged: and the expensive material began to tear.

A piece of the torn-off tail flew away to the side somewhere.

'Wait . . . Wait . . . I . . . I . . . I . . . am not . . . going to kill you . . . Stop . . . You are not threatened with violence . . .'

And Nikolai Apollonovich was rudely thrown aside; his back struck the corner; he stood there in the corner, breathing heavily, almost weeping with the painful outrage of what had taken place; and it seemed that his hair was not hair, but some kind of bright radiance on the crimson background of the study's soot-grimed wallpaper; and his eyes that were usually a dark cornflower blue now seemed black with enormous, cold fright, because he had realized: the person who was raving above him was not Likhutin, not the officer he had insulted, not even an enemy, choking with vengeful fury, but . . . a violent madman, with whom it was impossible to talk; this violent madman, who was possessed of colossal muscular strength, was not at present throwing himself at him; but was probably about to do so.

And this violent madman, turning his back (now would have been the time to clap him one), moved on tiptoe to the door; and – the door clicked: on the other side of the door sounds were heard – something between a weeping and a shuffling of slippers. And – all was quiet. Retreat was cut off: there remained the window.

In the closed-up little room they both began to breathe in silence: the father-murderer and the lunatic.

. . . .

The room with the collapsed plaster was empty; in front of the slammed door lay a soft broad-brimmed hat, while from the small couch hung the wing of a fantastic cape; but when the armchair was overturned with a hollow crash in the little study, the door on the opposite side, the door to Sofya Petrovna's room, flew open with a creak; and from there Sofya Petrovna came pattering in her slippers in a cascade of black hair that fell behind her back; a transparent silk scarf that resembled a flowing radiance trailed after her; on Sofya Petrovna's little forehead a frown was quite manifestly visible.

She crept up to the keyhole; she squatted down by the door; she looked and saw: only two pairs of shifting legs and two . . . trouser straps; the legs thudded into the corner; the feet could not be discerned anywhere, but from the corner, bubbling, burst quiet wheezings and a throat seemed to gurgle: a unique, cockerel-like, inhuman whisper. And the legs thudded again; right next to Sonya Petrovna's eye, on the other side of the door, the metallic sound of the lock being clicked shut was heard.

Sofya Petrovna began to weep, jumped away from the door and saw – an apron and a bonnet: behind her back Mavrushka was covering her face with a clean, snow-white apron; and – Mavrushka was weeping:

'What is going on? . . . My dear *barynya*? . . .'

'I don't know . . . I don't know anything . . . What is going on? . . . What are they doing in there, Mavrushka?'

. . . .

It is half past two in the afternoon.

In its lonely study the bald head, that had lain on a hard palm, raises itself above the stern oak desk; and – looks sullenly to where in the fireplace the cornflowers of coal gas flow in a playful flock above the red-hot pile of crackling coals, and where they escape, explode and burst – the red cockerels' combs – pungent, light, flying swiftly up the chimney, in order to merge above the roofs with the fumes and the poisoned soot, and to hang there permanently in a suffocating, corroding gloom.

The bald head raises itself – the pale, Mephistophelean mouth smiles senilely at the flashes; the flashes turn its face crimson; and yet the eyes are still on fire; and yet the eyes are still made of stone: blue – and in green hollows! From them peered a cold, enormous emptiness; it adhered to them, looked out of them, never tearing itself away from the dark things; like a dark thing this world spread itself before it.

A cold, astonished gaze; and – empty, empty: the seasons, the sun and the light have been kindled by dark things; from the ages history has run right up to the moment when –

> – the bald head, that has lain on a hard palm, has raised itself above the stern oak desk; and – looks sullenly to where in the fireplace the cornflowers of coal gas flow in a playful flock above the red-hot pile of crackling coals. The circle has closed.

What was this?

Apollon Apollonovich remembered where he was, what had happened between two instants of thought; between two movements of his fingers with the little pencil that had turned in them; the acutely sharpened pencil – there it danced in his fingers.

'It's not important . . . It doesn't matter . . .'

And the sharpened pencil falls on the paper with flocks of question marks.

. . . .

Muttering God knows what, the madman still continued to lunge about; muttering God knows what, he continued to stamp: continued to stride in a diagonal through the small, airless study. Nikolai Apollonovich, spread-eagled against the wall, in the shadowy corner over there, continued to observe the movements of the poor madman, who was none the less capable of becoming a wild beast.

Every time a hand or an elbow lunged out with a sharp movement, he shuddered; and the madman – ceased to stamp, paused, lunged out of his fatal diagonal: two paces from Nikolai Apollonovich a dry and menacing palm began to sway again. Here Nikolai Apollonovich threw himself back: the palm touched the corner – drummed on the corner wall.

But the second lieutenant who had gone mad (pathetically rather than fiercely) was no longer pursuing him; turning his back, he dug his elbows into his knees: this made his back bend, and his head withdrew into his shoulders; he sighed deeply; he reflected deeply.

What escaped was:

'Lord!'

And again, the groan:

'Save and have mercy!'

Nikolai Apollonovich cautiously took advantage of his lull in the raving.

Quietly he got up and, trying still not to make any sound, he – straightened up; the second lieutenant's head did not turn, but then it did nothing but turn and turn, risking – yes, truly! – becoming unscrewed from his neck; a furious paroxysm had evidently broken out; and – now it waned; then Nikolai Apollonovich, limping somewhat, hobbled soundlessly to the desk, trying not to let his shoes creak, trying not to let the floorboard creak – hobbled, cutting a rather ridiculous figure in his elegant uniform jacket . . . with its torn-off tail, in new rubber galoshes and the muffler he had not removed from his neck.

He crept forward: paused by the little desk, listening to the beating of his heart and the quiet, muttered prayers of the sick man who was now calming down: and with an inaudible movement, his hand stretched out to the paperweight; but there was the rub: a little stack of writing paper lay on top of the paperweight.

If only his sleeve did not get caught on the paper!

Unfortunately his sleeve did catch on the little stack; there was a tell-tale rustle, and the little stack of paper scattered on the desk; this swish of paper awoke the second lieutenant, who had withdrawn, to life again; the paroxysm that had broken out and was now calming down broke out again with renewed vigour; the head turned and saw Nikolai Apollonovich standing with arm outstretched, armed with the paperweight; Nikolai Apollonovich's heart sank: he leapt away from the desk, while the paperweight remained in his fist – for the sake of precaution.

In a leap and a bound, Sergei Sergeich Likhutin flew up to him, threw his hand on his shoulder and began to press it: in a word – he took up his old refrain:

'I must ask forgiveness . . . Forgive me: I lost my temper . . .'

'Calm down . . .'

'All this is most unusual . . . Only, please – do me a favour and don't be afraid . . . Well, why are you trembling? . . . I seem to inspire you with fear? I . . . I . . . I . . . tore off the tail of your coat: I . . . I . . . couldn't help that, because you, Nikolai Apollonovich, manifested the intention of avoiding an explanation . . . But you must understand that it's impossible for you to leave me without an explanation . . .'

'But I'm not trying to avoid it,' Nikolai Apollonovich implored at this point, still clutching the paperweight in his hand. 'I myself began to tell you about the domino cape when we were down in the entrance porch: I myself seek an explanation; it is you, Sergei Sergeyevich, it is you who are delaying: you are not giving me a chance to give you an explanation.'

'Mm . . . yes, yes . . .'

'Would you believe it, the domino is explained by nervous exhaustion; and it is in no way the breaking of a promise: I did not stand in the entrance porch voluntarily . . .'

'So forgive me for the coat-tail,' Likhutin said, interrupting him again, and merely proving that he really was crazy (he was for the present leaving Ableukhov's shoulder in peace) . . . 'Yours shall be sewn back on; if you like, I myself . . . I have needles and thread . . .'

'This is all that was needed,' flickered through Ableukhov's head: he was studying the second lieutenant with astonishment, trying to make sure by visual means that the paroxysm really had passed.

'But that is not what it's all about: not needles and thread . . .

'Sergei Sergeyevich, in essence . . . That is nonsense . . .'

'Yes, yes: nonsense . . .'

'Nonsense with regard to the principal subject of our explanation: with regard to your standing in the entrance porch . . .'

'But it's got nothing to do with my standing in the entrance porch!' the second lieutenant said, with a vexed wave of his hand, proceeding to stride in the same direction as before: in a diagonal through the small, airless study.

'Well, is it about Sofya Petrovna, then . . .' said Ableukhov, coming out of the corner, now noticeably bolder.

'No . . . no . . . it's not about Sofya Petrovna . . .' the second lieutenant shouted at him: 'you haven't understood me at all! . . .'

'Then what is it about?'

'This is all nonsense, sir! . . . Or rather, not nonsense, but nonsense with regard to the subject of our conversation . . .'

'But what is the subject?'

'Look – the subject,' said the second lieutenant and, coming to a standstill before him, brought his bloodshot eyes up to Ableukhov's eyes that were wide with fright . . . 'Look, the essence of it is all to do with the fact that you are locked in . . .'

'But . . . Why am I locked in?' And the paperweight was again clutched in his fist.

'Why have I locked you in? Why have I dragged you in here, so to speak, by semi-forcible means? . . . Ha-ha-ha: this has absolutely nothing to do with either the domino cape or Sofya Petrovna . . .'

'He really has gone mad: he has forgotten all the reasons, his brain is subject only to morbid associations: and me he is actually planning to . . .' flashed through Nikolai Apollonovich's head, but Sergei Sergeyevich, as though he knew what he was thinking, hurried to reassure him, something that seemed more like mockery and cruel taunting:

'I repeat, you are safe here . . . There is only the coat-tail . . .'

'You are taunting me,' thought Nikolai Apollonovich, and through his brain shot a thought that was also, in its own way, mad: to whack the second lieutenant on the head with the paperweight; having stunned him, to tie his hands, and by this violent act save his own life, which he needed even if only because . . . the bomb . . . in the desk . . . was ticking! . . .

'Look: you're not going to leave here . . . And I . . . I am going to leave here with a letter dictated by me – with your signature . . .

I'll go to your place, to your room, where I was this morning, but where no one noticed me ... I shall turn all your things upside down; if my search proves completely fruitless, I shall warn your father ..., because' – he wiped his forehead – 'it's not a question of your father; it's a question of you: yes, yes, yes, sir – of you alone, Nikolai Apollonovich!'

He rammed a hard finger into Nikolai Apollonovich's chest, and now stood with raised eyebrow (only one eyebrow).

'This will not happen, do you hear? This will not happen, Nikolai Apollonovich – it will not happen, ever!'

And on the shaven, crimson face played:

'?'

'!'

'!?!'

An utter madman!

But it was a strange thing: Nikolai Apollonovich listened closely to this utter raving; and something inside him quivered: was this really raving? It was rather hints, incoherently uttered; but hints – at what? Were they hints at ... at ... at ...?

Yes, yes, yes ...

'Sergei Sergeyevich, what *is* all this about?'

And his heart sank: Nikolai Apollonovich felt that his skin did not enwrap his body, but ... a heap of cobblestones; instead of a brain he had a cobblestone; and there was a cobblestone in his stomach.

'What is it about? ... Why, the bomb, of course ...' – Sergei Sergeyevich retreated two paces, astonished in the extreme.

The paperweight fell from Ableukhov's unclenched fist; an instant before, it had seemed to Nikolai Apollonovich that his skin wrapped not his body, but – a heap of cobblestones; but now the horrors passed all bounds; he felt something cutting into the heavy masses of quintillions (between the zeros and the unit); the unit remained.

While the quintillion became – zero.

The heavy masses suddenly burst into flames: the cobblestones that crammed his body, becoming gases, spurted in the twinkling of an eye through the orifices of all the pores of his skin, and wound again the spirals of events, but wound them in reverse order; they twisted his body itself into a receding spiral; thus the very sense of his body became – a *zero* sensation; the contours of his features were traced sharply and acquired an incredible degree of meaning, revealing in the young man the face of a patriarch in his sixties; were sharply traced, acquired meaning, became as if carved; the face – white, pale white – became a luminescent countenance, bathed in luminescent boiling water; while, on the other hand: the face of the second lieutenant turned a bright carrot colour; his shavenness made him look even more stupid, while his little too-tight jacket became even smaller and tighter . . .

. . . .

'Sergei Sergeyevich, I am surprised at you . . . How could you believe that I, that I . . . ascribe to me consent to an act of dreadful villainy . . . While I am – not a villain . . . I, Sergei Sergeyevich – do not think I am yet an out-and-out scoundrel . . .'

Nikolai Apollonovich was evidently unable to continue; and he – turned away; having turned away, he turned round again . . .

. . . .

Out of the shadowy corner, as though it had swarmed into shape, emerged the proud, bent and round-shouldered figure that consisted, or so it appeared to the second lieutenant, of nothing but flowing radiances – with a martyred, grinning mouth, with eyes of cornflower hue; his flaxen-white hair, bathed in light, formed a transparent, almost halo-like circle above his gleaming, ultra-high brow; he stood with his palms raised aloft, indignant, insulted, magnificent, somehow raised on the blood-red background of the wallpaper: the wallpaper was red.

He stood – his muffler dangling from his neck and only one coattail: the other had – alas – been torn off . . .

Thus he stood: from the enormous hollows of his eyes a cold, enormous emptiness stared incessantly at the second lieutenant; adhered and chilled to ice; here second lieutenant Likhutin somehow felt that for all his physical strength and health (he thought he was healthy) and, moreover, his nobleness of character – he was only a looming phantom; so that Ableukhov had only to approach the second lieutenant with that scintillant aspect, and the second lieutenant, Sergei Sergeyevich, began manifestly to retreat from him.

'But I believe you, I believe you,' he said, beginning to flap his hands in bewilderment.

'Look, you see' – now he was really embarrassed – 'I was never in any doubt . . . Actually, I feel ashamed . . . I am agitated . . . My wife told me . . . She had this note slipped into her hands . . . She read it – of course, she opened it by mistake,' he lied for some reason, and blushed, and lowered his eyes . . .

'Once the note was opened, and I could read it' – the senator's son seized maliciously on this opportunity – 'then . . .' he shrugged his shoulders, 'then Sofya Petrovna was, of course, entitled (here there was a note of irony) to tell you, as her husband, its contents' – Nikolai Apollonovich muttered in a most haughty manner; and – continued to advance.

'I . . . I . . . lost my temper,' said Likhutin in self-defence: his gaze fell on the ill-fated coat-tail, and he seized hold of the coat-tail.

'Don't worry about this coat-tail: I will sew it back on myself . . .'

But Nikolai Apollonovich, his mouth just, just barely smiling – luminescent, elegant – reproachfully continued to shake his hands in the air:

'You knew not what you did.'

His dark cornflower, dark blue eyes and light-bathed hair expressed a dim, unutterable sadness:

'Then go: inform on me, do not believe me! . . .'

And turned away . . .

The broad shoulders began to move jerkily . . . Nikolai Apollonovich wept unrestrainedly; at the same time: Nikolai Apollonovich, freed from his rude, animal fear, became altogether fearless; and what was more: at that moment he even wanted to suffer; thus at least did he feel at that moment: felt like a hero given up to torment, suffering publicly and shamefully; his body was in its sensations a tortured body; while his feelings were as torn as his very 'I' was torn; but from the tearing of his 'I' – so he expected – a blinding torch would flash and a familiar voice would speak to him from there, as always – speak within him: for him alone:

'You have suffered for me: I am standing over you.'

But there was no voice. Nor was there any torch. There was – darkness. The feeling itself had probably arisen from the fact that only now had he understood: from the encounter on the Neva until this most recent moment he had been undeservedly insulted; he had been brought here by force, been hauled – dragged into the little study; and here, in the little study, the tail had been torn off his frock-coat; why, even as it was, he had suffered ceaselessly for twenty-four hours: so why on top of that must he experience terror in the face of insults inflicted by action? Why was there no reconciling voice saying 'You have suffered for me'? Because he had not suffered for anyone: had suffered for himself . . . Had, so to speak, reaped the consequences of the mess he himself had made from outrageous events. That was why there was no voice. And why there was no torch. In the place of his former 'I' there was darkness. That he could not endure: his broad shoulders began to move jerkily.

He turned away: he wept.

'Truly,' he heard behind his back, in a tone both reconciling and meek, 'I was mistaken, did not understand . . .'

There was in this voice none the less a shade of vexation: of shame and . . . vexation: and Sergei Sergeyevich stood painfully biting his lip; perhaps the newly reconciled Likhutin was now regretting that he had been mistaken, that now he could not strike his enemy dead: neither with his fist, nor with nobility; precisely thus does a mad bull, teased by a red handkerchief, rush at his adversary and – attack the iron bars of the cage: and stand, and bellow, and not know what to do. The second lieutenant's face displayed the struggle of unpleasant memories (the domino, of course) and most noble feelings; while his adversary, still with his back turned and weeping, kept saying unpleasantly, over and over again:

'Taking advantage of your physical superiority, you have . . . dragged me in the presence of a lady, like . . . like . . .'

The rush of most noble feelings got the upper hand; Sergei Sergeich Likhutin crossed the little study with outstretched hand; but Nikolai Apollonovich, turning (a tear trembled on his eyelid), in a voice that was choked by the frenzy that had seized him and – alas! – by a self-respect that had arrived too late, articulated jerkily:

'Like . . . like . . . a chicken in the yard . . .'

Had Nikolai Apollonovich stretched out his hand to him, Sergei

Sergeich would have considered himself the happiest of men: complete contentment would have played over his face; but the rush of noble feeling, just like the rush of frenzy, was immediately corked up within his soul; the rush of noble feeling fell into empty darkness.

'Did you want to make sure, Sergei Sergeyevich? . . . That I am not a father-murderer? . . . No, Sergei Sergeyevich, no: you should have thought of it earlier . . . You just hauled me like . . . like a chicken in the yard. And – tore off my coat-tail . . .'

'The coat-tail can be sewn back on again!'

And before Ableukhov had time to regain his wits, Sergei Sergeyevich rushed to the door:

'Mavrushka! . . . Black thread! . . . A needle . . .'

But the opened door very nearly struck Sofya Petrovna, who was just then eavesdropping on the other side of it; caught in the act, she jumped aside, but – too late: caught in the act, and red as a peony, she had nowhere to run; and at them – at them both – she threw an indignant, annihilating gaze.

Between the three of them lay the tail of the frock-coat.

'What? . . . Sonechka . . .'

'Sofya Petrovna! . . .'

'Have I disturbed you? . . .'

'Just imagine . . . Nikolai Apollonovich . . . You know . . . tore off his coat-tail . . . He ought to . . .'

'No, don't trouble yourself, Sergei Sergeich; Sofya Petrovna – please . . .'

'He ought to have it sewn back on.'

But Nikolai Apollonovich, his mouth twisted because of the stupid situation, wiping the tell-tale eyelashes with his sleeve and still limping on one leg, had already made his appearance in the room with the Fujiyamas . . . in a torn frock-coat, with one dangling tail; lifting up his Italian cloak, he raised his head and, seeing the damage that had been done to the ceiling, turned his twisted mouth, for the sake of propriety, towards Sofya Petrovna.

'Tell me, Sofya Petrovna, there seems to be some kind of change in your flat: in your ceiling there is some kind of . . . Some kind of disrepair: have painters been working?'

But Sergei Sergeyevich interrupted:

'That was me, Nikolai Apollonovich . . . I . . . was mending the ceiling . . .'

But all the while he was thinking:

'What? how do you like that: last night I didn't hang myself properly; and now I haven't explained myself properly . . .'

Nikolai Apollonovich, leaving, limped across the hall; falling from his shoulder, his fantastic cape trailed after him like a black train.

. . . .

From behind the nota benes, the exclamation marks, the section marks, the dashes, from behind what was now the *final* work the bald head raised itself; and – fell back again. The fire-breathing heap – crimson, golden – began to seethe and snort, giving off seething cracklings and gleamings; the logs were scattered with coals, – and the bald head rose towards the fireplace with a sardonically smiling mouth and screwed-up eyes; suddenly the lips straightened in alarm.

What was this?

In all directions red, seething torches unwound – throbbing lights and streaming deer's antlers: they began to branch out and lick from every side – tree-like, golden, transparent; they were hurled one by one out of the red crater of the fireplace; were hurled at the walls: the fireplace fleeted and expanded, turning into a stone, dungeon-like sack, where they froze (now stood up, now died away), all the flowing radiances, the flames, the dark-cornflower-coloured carbon gases and combs: in light made transparent – there a figure swarmed together, raised slightly beneath the receding vault and stoopingly extended; the red, five-pawed hands stretched out – scorching with the touch of the fire.

What was this?

– Here was the martyred, grinning mouth, here were the eyes of cornflower hue, here was the hair bathed in light: enwrapped in the fury of the fire, with arms spread wide, nailed by sparks in the air, with palms upturned in the air – palms, that were pierced through, –

Nikolai Apollonovich, spread out in the shape of a cross, was suffering there out of the radiance of the light and indicating with his eyes the red sores on his palms; while from the sundered heavens the cool, broad-winged archangel poured dew for him – into the red-hot furnace . . .

'He knows not what he does . . .'

Suddenly . . . a dizzying crack, a hissing, a snorting: the bright radiances, suddenly hesitating, exploded into pieces, sweeping the martyred figure away in cascades of sparks.

. . . .

A quarter of an hour later he gave instructions for the horses to be harnessed; forty minutes later he strode forth into the carriage (this we saw in the previous chapter); an hour later the carriage stood amidst the festive crowd; and – was it only festive? . . .

Something had happened here.

A space of less than an inch, or the wall of the carriage, separated Apollon Apollonovich from the rebellious crowd; the horses snorted, and through the panes of the carriage Apollon Apollonovich could see nothing but heads: bowlers, service caps and, above all, Manchurian fur hats; saw a pair of staring, indignant eyes fixed on him; saw too the contorted mouth of a ragged fellow; a singing mouth (they were singing). Seeing Ableukhov, the ragged fellow shouted coarsely:

'Get out, hey, look: you can't drive through here.'

The voices of other ragged fellows joined the ragged fellow's voice.

Then Apollon Apollonovich Ableukhov, in order to avoid unpleasantness, was obliged by the crowd to open the door of his carriage; the ragged fellows caught sight of the old man climbing out with lip a-tremble, holding on to the edge of his top hat with his glove: Apollon Apollonovich saw before him bawling mouths and a tall flagstaff: tearing themselves away from the wooden staff like crests in the air, lightly-whistling blades of red calico cloth exploded, fluttered and tore – splashing into the void;

'Hey, you, take your hat off!'

Apollon Apollonovich removed his top hat and quickly began to squeeze his way towards the pavement, abandoning carriage and driver; soon he was mincing in a contrary direction to the swarming mass; here small black figures flowed one by one out of the shops, the courtyards, the side prospects, the inns; Apollon Apollonovich strained himself to the point of exhaustion: and – found his way into the empty side prospects, from which . . . flew . . . Cossacks . . .

. . . .

Now the detachment of Cossacks flew past; the place became empty; one could see the backs of the Cossacks rushing towards the red cloth; and one could also see, swiftly running, the back of a little old man in a very tall top hat.

A Game of Patience

A samovar was boiling on the table; from an *étagère* a completely new, completely polished little samovar cast a metallic lustre; but the samovar that was boiling on the table was unpolished, dirty; the completely new little samovar was used when there were guests; when there were no guests, something that was quite simply a lopsided monster was placed on the table: loudly it wheezed and snorted; and from time to time red sparks shot out of the little holes in it. Someone's untrained hand had rolled some pellets of white bread; and they had been flattened on the crumpled, stained table-cloth; beneath an unfinished glass of sour tea (sour with lemon) a slovenly stain showed damp; and there was a plate with the remains of a cold cutlet and some cold puréed potato.

Well, and where was the luxuriant hair? In their place, a pigtail stuck out.

It was probable that Zoya Zakharovna Fleisch wore a wig (when there were guests, of course); and – we may observe in passing: it was probable that she made shameless use of make-up, because we saw her as a luxuriant-haired brunette, with skin that was enamelled and too smooth; while now before us was quite simply an old woman with a sweaty nose and a rat-like pigtail; she was wearing a blouse: and, again, it was dirty (probably a bed-jacket).

Lippanchenko sat half turned away from the small tea table, presenting both to Zoya Zakharovna and to the samovar his square, somewhat stooping back. Before Lippanchenko was a half laid-out game of patience, making one suppose that after supper

Lippanchenko had engaged in his normal evening pastime, which had a beneficial effect on his nerves, but that he had been disturbed: reluctantly, he tore himself away from the cards; a prolonged conversation took place, in the course of which the glass of tea, the game of patience and all the rest were, of course, forgotten.

After this conversation, however, Lippanchenko had turned his back: turned his back on the conversation.

He sat without his starched collar, with his jacket off, his belt, which had evidently been pressing his stomach, unfastened, making the tail of his uncomfortably starched shirt peep out in tell-tale fashion between his waistcoat and his shrinking trousers (still the same dark yellow ones).

We caught Lippanchenko at the moment when he was reflectively contemplating the black blotch of a cockroach that was creeping away from the clock with a rustle; they were to be found in the little dacha: enormous, black; and were to be found in abundance − in such unendurable abundance that, in spite of the light from the lamp, there was a rustling in the corner, and from time to time a small whisker protruded from the crack in the sideboard.

Lippanchenko was torn away from his contemplation of the creeping cockroach by the tearful lamentations of his life companion.

Zoya Zakharovna moved the tea tray away from her with a rattle, making Lippanchenko start.

'Well? . . . And what is going on? . . . And why is it going on?'

'What?'

'Don't you think that a woman who has been faithful, a woman in her forties, who has devoted her life to you, − a woman such as I . . .'

And her elbows fell to the table: one elbow was torn, and through the tear one could see old, faded skin and on it what was probably a scratched fleabite.

'What are you muttering about over there, little mother: speak more clearly . . .'

'Don't you think that a woman such as I has a right to ask? . . . An old woman' − and she covered her face with her palms: only her nose stuck out, and her two black eyes dilated.

Lippanchenko turned in his armchair.

Evidently her words had affected him; for a moment the semblance of a nagging pang of conscience appeared on his face; with
something that was halfway between a languid timidity and quite
simply a childish caprice, he blinked both small eyes; he evidently
wanted to say something; and evidently – was afraid to; he seemed
to be slowly deliberating something – perhaps what kind of response
this terrible confession would provoke within his companion's soul;
Lippanchenko's head was lowered; he breathed heavily and looked
out from under his brow.

But the urge to truthfulness suddenly ceased; and truthfulness
itself fell into the remote depths of his soul. He resumed his game
of patience:

'Hm: yes, yes . . . the five on the six . . . Where is the queen? . . .
Here is the queen . . . And – the jack is blocked . . .'

Suddenly he cast a searching, suspicious look at Zoya Zakharovna, and his short fingers with their golden fur moved a little
heap of cards: from a little heap of cards – to another little heap of
cards.

'Well, I've got a nice little game of patience . . .' he said, angrily
continuing to lay out the rows of cards.

Zoya Zakharovna carefully brought a clean-wiped cup to the
étagère, limping in her slippers.

'Well? . . . And why be angry then?'

Now, limping in her slippers, she began to move about the room;
a shuffling could be heard (the cockroach whisker hid itself in the
sideboard crack).

'But I'm not angry, little mother,' – and again he cast a searching
look at her: folding her arms on her stomach and letting her
uncorseted and considerable stomach protrude, as she walked her
hanging chin trembled; and quietly she went up to him, and quietly
touched him on the shoulder:

'You would do better to ask why I am asking you . . . Because
everyone is asking . . . They're shrugging their shoulders . . . So
now I think,' she leaned both her stomach and her breasts on the
armchair, 'I had better know . . .'

But Lippanchenko, biting his lip, went on laying out the cards
row by row, with an uneasily businesslike air.

He, Lippanchenko, remembered that the following day was of

unusual importance for him; if tomorrow he were unable to justify her in front of them, unable to shake off the menacing weight of the documents that had fallen about his ears, then it was checkmate for him. And, as he remembered this, he merely snuffled through his nose:

'Hm: yes-yes . . . Here is an opening . . . There's nothing for it: put the king in the opening . . .'

And – he could restrain himself no longer:

'You say they're asking? . . .'

'Did you think they wouldn't?'

'And they come in my absence? . . .'

'Yes, they do, they do: and they shrug their shoulders . . .'

Lippanchenko abandoned the cards:

'It won't come out: the twos are blocked . . .'

He was evidently agitated.

Just then from Lippanchenko's bedroom there came a plaintive clanking, as though the window was being opened in there. They both turned their heads towards Lippanchenko's bedroom; both were cautiously silent: who could it be?

Probably Tom, the St Bernard.

'But you must understand, you strange woman, that your questions' – here Lippanchenko, sighing, got up, – either in order to ascertain the cause of the strange sound, or in order to get out of replying.

'Violate Party . . .' – he gulped down a swig of the completely sour tea – 'discipline . . .'

Stretching, he walked through the open door – into the depths, into the darkness . . .

'But what kind of Party discipline can there be with me, Kolenka,' Zoya Zakharovna retorted, propping her face in her palm, and lowering her head, continuing to stand over the armchair that was now empty . . . 'Just think about it . . .'

But she fell silent, because the armchair was empty; Lippanchenko went thudding off in the direction of the bedroom; and she ran absent-mindedly through the cards.

Lippanchenko's footsteps approached.

'There have never been any secrets between us . . .' She said this to herself.

Then at once she turned her head towards the door – towards the darkness, the depths – and she began to say excitedly to the footsteps that were thudding closer:

'Why, you yourself did not warn me that in essence you and I have nothing to talk about' (Lippanchenko appeared in the doorway), 'that you have secrets now, and so I . . .'

'No, it's all right: there's no one in the bedroom,' he said, interrupting her.

'They annoy me: well, I mean – the looks, the hints, the questions . . . There have even been . . .'

His mouth was torn apart in a yawn of boredom; and as he unfastened his waistcoat he grumpily muttered down his nose:

'Oh, what are these scenes for?'

'There have even been threats concerning you . . .'

There was a pause.

'Well, so it's understandable that I ask . . . Why did you start shouting? What have I done, Kolenka? . . . Do you think I don't love you? . . . Do you think I'm not afraid for you?'

Here she twined her arms around his fat neck. And – whimpered:

'I'm an old woman, a faithful woman . . .'

And he saw her nose right before him: a hawk-like nose; or rather – a hawk-shaped one; it would have been hawk-like, had it not been for its fleshiness: a porous nose; these pores glistened with sweat; two compact spaces in the form of sunken cheeks were covered with indistinct folds of skin (when neither cream nor powder were used) – skin that was not exactly flabby, but – unpleasant, stale; two creases were manifestly cut from the nose beneath the lips, and drew those lips downwards; and her eyes stared at his little eyes; one could say that those eyes bulged and moved around persistently – like two black, two greedy buttons; and there was no light in them.

They simply moved about.

'Oh, stop it . . . Stop it . . . That's enough . . . Zoya Zakharovna . . . Let me go . . . I suffer from shortness of breath: you will choke me . . .'

Here he seized her arms in his fingers and removed them from his neck; and sank into the armchair; and began to breathe heavily:

'You know how sentimental and weak-nerved I am ... And again I ...'

They were both silent.

And in the deep, the heavy silence that fell after their long, joyless conversation, when everything had already been said, all the misgivings before words overcome and there remained only a dull submissiveness, – in the deep silence she washed the glass, the saucer and the two teaspoons.

But he sat on, half turned away from the tea table, presenting his square back to Zoya Zakharovna and the dirty samovar.

'Threats, you say?'

She fairly jumped.

She thrust herself forth: from behind the samovar; her lips curled back again: her anxious eyes very nearly leapt out of their sockets; anxiously they ran over the tablecloth, clambered up on to the fat chest and forced their way into the little, blinking eyes; and – what had time done?

No, what had it done?

These light brown little eyes, these little eyes that had still shone with humour and sly merriment at the age of twenty-five, had grown dim, sunken, and were covered by a menacing shroud; they had been overcast by the smoke of all the most filthy atmospheres: dark yellow, yellow-saffron; to be sure, twenty-five years was no small span of time, but all the same – to have faded so, to have shrunken so! And under the little twenty-five-year-old eyes dull fatty bags had formed; twenty-five years was no small span of time, but ... – why this Adam's apple forced out from beneath the round chin? The pink complexion of the face had grown yellow, oily, faded – made a horrifying impression with its grey corpse-like pallor; the forehead had grown too large; and – the ears had grown in size; yet there are old men who are decent? But he was not an old man ...

What had you done, time?

The fair-haired, rosy, twenty-five-year-old Paris student – the student Lipensky – swelling up like a delirious dream, turned stubbornly into a forty-five-year-old, indecent spider's belly: Lippanchenko.

Unutterable Meanings

A bush seethed . . . On the sandy shore here and there small lakes of salt water wrinkled.

From the gulf white-maned stripes came flying; the moon illumined them, stripe after stripe foamed in the distance and thundered there; and then fell, flying right up to the shore in ragged foam; from the gulf the flying stripe spread over the flat shore – submissively, transparently; it licked the sands: it cut the sands – corroded them; like a thin blade of glass, it rushed over the sands; here and there the glassy stripes splashed into a salty lake; filled it with a salt solution.

And then ran back. A new thunder-foaming stripe threw it again.

A bush seethed . . .

This way – over here, that way – over there, there were hundreds of bushes; at a certain distance from the sea the black and dryish arms of bushes stretched out; these leafless arms rose into space with insane gestures; a rather black little figure with no galoshes or hat was frightenedly running between them; in the summer, sweet and quietly wafting murmurs had come from them; the murmurs had dried up long ago, and now gnashing and groaning rose from this place; the mists came from here; and the dampness came from here; while fallen stumps stretched – out of the mist and the dampness; out of the mist and the dampness a gnarled arm began to wave, covered in bare branches like fur.

Now the little figure bent towards a tree-hollow – into the shroud of black dampness; here it reflected bitterly; and here into its arms it dropped an unsubmissive head:

'My soul,' rose up from the heart: 'my soul, – you have gone away from me . . . Respond, my soul: I am wretched . . .'

From the heart arose:

'Before you I will fall with a life torn apart . . . Remember me: I am wretched . . .'

The night, pierced through by a sparkling dot, was coming to a radiant end; and the scarcely perceptible little dot quivered right out on the horizon; apparently a trading schooner was approaching Petersburg; from the hole that had been pierced in the night a spark was ripening, bathed in light, like a ripening ear of grain whiskered with sunbeams.

Now it had turned into a wide, crimson eye, producing behind it the dark hull of a vessel and above it – a forest of rigging.

And above the small black mournful figure, towards the flying ghost, the wooden, many-branched arms flew under the moon; the bushy, gnarled head stretched forth into space, swaying a mesh of small black branches like a cobweb; and – it swayed in the sky; the weightless moon became entangled in that mesh, began to tremble, to flash more dazzlingly: and seemed to melt into tears: the airy intervals between the branches were filled with a phosphorescent glow that made plain inexpressible things, and from them a figure formed; – there it formed, there it began: an enormous body, burning with phosphorus, with a cloak of vitriol hue, flying away into a foggy smoke; an imperious hand, pointing into the future, stretched in the direction of a light that blinked over there from the small garden of a dacha, where the supple branches of the bushes struck at the trellis.

The small figure stopped, and beseechingly it stretched towards the phosphorescent intervals between the branches, that formed the body:

'But wait, wait; it cannot be like this – by suspicion alone, without explanation . . .'

Imperiously the hand pointed to the lighted window that shot rays through the black and gnashing boughs.

Here the blackish little figure uttered a cry and ran off into empty space; while after it darted the black, many-boughed outline, forming itself on the sandy shore into that strange whole that could squeeze from itself monstrous, unutterable meanings that did not exist anywhere; the blackish little figure struck its chest against the trellis of some garden, climbed over the fence and now slipped soundlessly, its feet catching in the dewy grasses, – towards that grey little dacha, where it had been so recently, where now everything was not as it ought to be.

Carefully it stole towards the terrace, put its hand on its chest; and soundlessly, in a leap and a bound, it ended up outside the door; there was no curtain on the door; then the little figure pressed itself to the window; there, through the windows, light expanded.

There they sat . . . –

> – On the table stood a samovar; beneath the samovar stood a plate containing the remains of a cold cutlet; and a woman's nose looked out with an unpleasant, disconcerted, slightly crushed appearance; her nose looked out timidly; and – timidly it hid: a nose – with a short pigtail; this pathetic head hung on a curved neck. Lippanchenko was leaning one elbow on the table; his other hand lay free on the back of the armchair; coarse – the palm of his hand opened and closed; one was struck by its breadth; one was struck by the shortness of its five fingers, that looked as though they had been lopped off, with hangnails and brown dye on the nails themselves . . . –

>> – In a leap and a bound, the small figure flew away from the door; and – found itself in the bushes; it was seized by an impulse of indescribable pity; out of the tree-hollow a browless, large-headed lump rushed, beneath two branches, towards the little figure; the winds began to moan in the rotted bell-mouth of the bush.

And the little figure began to whisper desperately near the bush:

'Why, one cannot simply . . . How can one . . . Why, nothing has been proved yet . . .'

A Swan Song

Turning the whole of his body away from the sighing Zoya Zakharovna, Lippanchenko stretched out his hand – well, just imagine! – to a violin that hung on the wall there:

'A man has all kinds of unpleasantnesses to deal with on the side . . . He comes home, to rest, and then – see what he gets . . .'

He fetched the rosin: with what was quite simply a kind of

ferocity, that exceeded all bounds, – he threw himself on the piece of rosin; with pleasure he took the piece of rosin between his fingers; with the guilty little grimace that was in no way appropriate either to his position in the Party, or to the conversation that had just taken place, he proceeded to rub his bow on the rosin; then he took the violin:

'One could say – he is met with tears . . .'

He pressed the violin against his stomach and bent over it, resting its broad end against his knees; the narrow end he pushed under his chin; with one hand, enjoying it, he began to tighten the strings, while with his other hand – he extracted a sound:

'Plunk!'

As he did this, his head bent and inclined to the side; with a questioning look that was not quite buffoonish and not quite sorrowful (childish, when all was said and done), he looked at Zoya Zakharovna and smacked his lips; it was as if he were asking:

'You hear?'

She sat down on a chair: with a questioning, half-tender, half-desperate expression she looked at Lippanchenko and Lippanchenko's finger; the finger tried the strings; and the strings – tinkled.

'That's better!'

And he smiled; she smiled; both nodded to each other; he – with rediscovered youthful ardour; she – with a hint of shyness that betrayed both a vague pride and her former adoration of him (of Lippanchenko?), – she exclaimed:

'Oh, what a . . .'

'Tinkle-tinkle . . .'

'Incorrigible baby you are!'

And at these words, in spite of the fact that Lippanchenko looked every bit like a rhinoceros, with a movement of his left wrist that was both swift and dexterous, Lippanchenko turned his violin around; its broad end moved with the speed of lightning into the angle between his enormous shoulder and his head that had inclined towards it; the narrow end remained in his fleeting fingers:

'Here you are, then!'

The hand with the bow flew up; and – weighed itself in the air: paused, and then touched a string with a most tender movement of the bow; the string moved across the strings; following the bow went – the whole arm; the arm was followed by the head; the head – by the fat body: they all went to one side.

The little finger bent with a flourish: it did not touch the bow.

The armchair creaked under Lippanchenko, who seemed to be straining in a single, intense, unmasterable, stubborn effort: to emit a tender sound; his rather hoarse and yet pleasant bass voice suddenly filled this room, drowning out both the snoring of the St Bernard and the rustling of a cockroach.

'Do not te-e-e-mpt me,' sang Lippanchenko.[10]

'Meee – without neee-eee . . .' the tender, quietly sighing strings chimed in.

'–eed,' – sang the sideways-bent Lippanchenko, who seemed to be straining a single, intense, unmasterable, stubborn effort: to emit a tender sound.

In the years of their youth they had spent a long time singing this old romance, which is not sung today.

. . . .

'Shhh!'
'Did you hear?'
'The window?'
'One ought to go: and take a look.'

. . . .

Dim shapes fleeted melancholically there in smoky green puffballs; the moon rose from behind a cloud; and everything that had stood there like dim shapes – distintegrated, fell apart; and the skeletons of the bushes showed black in empty space; and their shadows fell to the earth in shaggy tufts; the phosphorescent air revealed itself in the gaps between the boughs; all the airy blotches formed together – there it was, there it was: a body, burning with phosphorus; imperiously it stretched its arm towards the window; the little figure jumped towards the window; the window was not latched, and as it opened, it tinkled slightly; and the little figure leapt aside.

In the windows shadows moved; someone passed with a candle – in the curtained windows; this – unlatched – window was also illumined; the curtain was pulled aside; a fat figure stood for a moment and looked out there – at the phosphorescent world; it seemed that a chin was looking out, because – a chin was protruding; the little eyes were not visible; in place of the little eyes two eye sockets showed darkly; two hairless eyebrows gleamed unnaturally beneath the moon. The curtain moved; someone enormous and fat went back behind the curtained windows; soon all was quiet. The tinkling of the violin and the voice again issued from the little dacha.

The bush seethed. The large-headed, browless lump moved out into the moonlight in a single intense stubborn effort: to understand – come what may, at whatever cost; to understand, or – explode into pieces; from the small hollow tree trunk emerged this old, browless excrescence, overgrown with moss and scale; it stretched forth into the wind; it begged for mercy – come what may, at whatever cost. From the small hollow tree trunk the little figure detached itself a second time; and stole up to the window; retreat was cut off; one thing remained to it: to complete what had been begun. Now it hid itself . . . in Lippanchenko's bedroom it waited impatiently for Lippanchenko to come – to his bedroom.

. . . .

Scoundrels, too, have a need to sing their swan song, after all.

'To the dis-en . . . -cha-a-anted . . . are a-a-lien . . . all the cha-a-rms of former . . . da-a-ays . . . In assu-u-u-rances I trust no lo-o-onger . . .

'I no mo-o-re . . . believe in lo-ove . . .'

Did he know what he was singing? And – what he was playing? Why he was sad? Why his throat was constricted – to the point of pain? . . . Because of the sounds? Lippanchenko did not understand this, as he did not understand the tender sounds he was drawing forth . . . No, the frontal bone could not understand: the forehead was small, covered in transverse wrinkles: it seemed to be weeping.

Thus one October night did Lippanchenko sing his swan song.

Perspective

Well – so there!

He had sung, played; putting the violin on the table, he wiped his perspiring forehead with a handkerchief; slowly heaved his indecent, spider-like, forty-five-year-old belly; at last, taking the candle, he set off for his bedroom; on the threshold he turned once more, indecisively, sighed, and reflected on something; Lippanchenko's whole figure expressed a single vague, unutterable sadness.

And – Lippanchenko collapsed in the murk.

When the flame of the candle suddenly cut into the completely dark room (the blinds were lowered), the murk was cut apart; and – the pitch darkness exploded in yellow-crimson luminescences; along the periphery of the fierily dancing centre some pieces of darkness, in the form of shadows of all the objects, began to spin soundlessly in a circular movement; and in pursuit of the dark shoals, the shadows of objects, an enormous fat man, who burst out from under Lippanchenko's heels, and with a bustling movement quickened his pace in a circle.

The outrageous, soundless fat man was thrown between the wall, the table and the chair, broke against the shoals and exploded agonizingly, as though now he had experienced all the torments of purgatory.

Thus, having cast out its body as ballast no longer required – thus, having cast out its body, the soul is caught up by the hurricanes of all its psychic movements: the hurricanes rush through the psychic expanses. Our bodies are wretched little vessels; and they race across the psychic ocean from spiritual continent to spiritual continent.

'Yes . . .'

Imagine an infinitely long rope; and imagine that your body is bound at the waist by the rope; and then – the rope is wound round you; with frantic, with indescribable speed; tossed up, in expanding, ever growing circles, drawing spirals in space, you will fly into the atmosphere beyond the air with your head downwards, and your back advancing; and you will fly, a satellite of the earth, away from the earth into the immeasurabilities of the universe, overcoming the multi-millennial spaces – instantly, and becoming those spaces.

That is the kind of hurricane by which you will instantly be caught up, when the soul casts out your body as ballast no longer required.

And let us also imagine that each point of the body experiences a mad urge to expand without measure, to expand to the point of horror (for example, to occupy a space equal in diameter to the orbit of Saturn); and let us also imagine that we consciously sense not simply one point, but all the points of the body, that they have all swelled up – cut apart, white-hot – and go through the stages of the expansion of bodies: from a solid condition to one that is gaseous, that the planets and suns circulate quite freely in the interstices of the body's molecules; and let us also imagine that we have completely lost the sense of centripetal gravity; and in our urge to expand bodily without measure we explode into pieces, and that the only whole thing that remains is our consciousness: the consciousness of our exploded sensations.

What would we feel?

We would feel that our disjointed organs, flying and burning, no longer bound integrally together, are separated from one another by billions of versts; but our consciousness binds that crying outrage together – in a simultaneous futility; and while in our backbone, lacerated to the point of emptiness, we sense the seething of Saturn's masses, the stars of the constellations furiously eat into our brain; while in the centre of the seething heart we feel the incoherent, diseased joltings – of a heart so enormous that the solar streams of fire, flying out from the sun, would not reach that heart's surface if the sun were to move into that fiery, incoherently beating centre.

If we were able to imagine all this to ourselves bodily, before us would arise a picture of the first stages of the soul's life, which has thrown off the body; the sensations would be the more powerful, the more violently before us were our bodily constitution to disintegrate . . .

Cockroaches

Lippanchenko stopped in the middle of the dark room with the candle in his hand; the shadowy shoals stopped together with him; the enormous shadowy fat man, Lippanchenko's soul, hung head down from the ceiling; neither for the shadows of all the objects nor for his own shadow did Lippanchenko feel any interest; rather he was interested in a rustling – one familiar and altogether unmysterious.

He felt a sense of disgusted revulsion at the cockroach; and now – he saw – dozens of these creatures; they fled, rustling, into their dark corners, caught by the light of the candle. And – Lippanchenko was angry:

'Accursed things . . .'

And he thudded over to the corner to fetch the floor brush, which was a very long stick with a bristly mop on the end:

'Think you can get away? Just you wait! . . .'

He placed the candle on the floor; with the floor brush in his hand he clambered up on a chair; now his heavy, puffing body stuck out over the chair; his vessels were bursting with exertion, his muscles were tensed; and his hair was tousled; he pursued the creeping handfuls with the bristly end of the mop; one, two, three! and – cracking sounds came from under the mop: on the ceiling, on the wall; even – in the corner of the *étagère*.

'Eight . . . Ten . . . Eleven' – rustled the threatening whisper; and with cracking sounds, blotches fell to the floor.

Every evening before he slept he squashed cockroaches. Having squashed a good pile of them, he set off for bed.

At last, barging into his little bedroom, he locked the door with its key; and further: he looked under the bed (for some time now this strange custom had formed an indispensable part of his undressing), and before him he placed the guttering candle.

Now he undressed.

Now he sat on the bed, hairy and naked, with his legs apart; female-like rounded shapes were clearly marked on his shaggy chest.

Lippanchenko slept naked.

Obliquely across from the candle, between the window wall and the little wardrobe, in a dark, shadowy niche, an intricate outline emerged: of a pair of trousers that hung here; and formed the likeness of – someone looking out from there; Lippanchenko was for ever hanging his trousers in different places; and the result was always: the likeness – of someone looking out from there.

He saw this likeness now.

And when he blew out the candle, the outline trembled and emerged more clearly; Lippanchenko reached out his hand to the curtain on the window; the curtain was tugged aside: the receding calico rustled; the room shone with a greenish radiance of copper; there, from there: out of the white pewter of the clouds a flaming disc crashed across the room; and . . . –

Against the background of the completely green and as if vitriol-coloured wall – there! – stood a little figure in a wretched coat, with a frozen, chalk-white face: it looked like a clown, and its white lips were smiling. Lippanchenko went thudding in his bare feet in the direction of the door, but went, belly and breasts, smack into the door (he had forgotten he had locked it); at this point he was pulled backwards; a hot stream of boiling water splashed his bare back from shoulder-blades to buttocks; falling on to the bed, he realized that someone had cut open his back; cut it open as the hairless skin of a cold sucking-pig with horseradish sauce is cut; and no sooner had he realized this than he felt that stream of boiling water – under his navel.

And from there something hissed mockingly; and somewhere inside him he thought it was gases, because his belly had been sliced open; inclining his head over his heaving belly, staring senselessly into space, he slumped down in utter drowsiness, probing the flowing liquid with his fingers – on his belly and on the sheet.

This was his last conscious impression of ordinary reality; now his consciousness expanded; its monstrous periphery sucked the planets into itself; and sensed them as organs that had been disjointed from one another; the sun floated in the expansions of his heart; his backbone was made incandescent by the touch of Saturn's masses; in his belly a volcano opened.

All this time the body sat senseless with its head sagging on to its chest and its eyes staring at its cleft belly; suddenly it tumbled down – belly first into the sheet; the arm hung over the bloodstained rug, its fur showing reddish in the moonlight; the head with its sagging jaw was thrown in the direction of the door and stared at it with an unblinking eye; the eyebrows began to gleam browlessly; on the sheet emerged the imprint of five bloodstained fingers; and a fat heel protruded.

. . . .

A bush seethed: white-maned stripes came flying from the gulf; they flew close to the shore in ragged foam; they licked the sands; like thin blades of glass, they rushed over the sands; splashed into a salty lake, filling it with a salt solution; and ran back again. Between the branches of the bush one could see a sailing vessel rocking – turquoise, transparent; in a thin layer it cut the expanses with sharp-winged sails; on the surface of a sail a misty puff of smoke was growing denser.

. . . .

From the gulf white-maned stripes came flying; the moon illumined them, stripe after stripe foamed in the distance and thundered there; and then fell, flying right up to the shore in ragged foam; from the gulf the flying stripe spread over the flat shore – submissively, transparently; it licked the sands: it cut the sands – corroded them; like a thin blade of glass, it rushed over the sands; here and there the glassy stripes splashed into a salty lake; filled it with a salt solution.

When they entered in the morning, Lippanchenko was no longer there; there was a pool of blood; there was a corpse; and there was also a small figure of a man – with a white, leering face, beside itself; the figure had a small moustache; it was turned up at the ends; very strange: the man was sitting astride the corpse;[11] he was clutching a pair of scissors in one hand; he had this hand stretched out; across his face – over his nose, round his lips – the blotch of a cockroach crawled away.

He had evidently gone mad.

END OF THE SEVENTH CHAPTER

CHAPTER THE EIGHTH

and last

> The past moves by before me . . .
> Isn't long since it rushed by, full of events,
> In agitation, like the ocean?
> Now it is silent and peaceful:
> Few are the faces memory has kept for me,
> Few are the words that come down to me . . .[1]
>
> A. Pushkin

But First Of All . . .

Anna Petrovna!

We have forgotten her: Anna Petrovna had returned; and now she was awaiting . . . But first of all: –

– these last twenty-four hours! –

– these last twenty-four hours of our narrative have expanded and scattered in psychic space: in a most outrageous dream; and have blocked the horizon around us; and the author's gaze, too, has become entangled in psychic space; it has been shut off.

Anna Petrovna has been concealed along with it.

Like stern, leaden clouds, cerebral, leaden games have dragged themselves along in a closed horizon, along a circle that has been traced by us, – hopelessly, hopelessly, meticulously –

– in these last twenty-four hours! . . .

And through these sternly flowing and insalubrious events the news about Anna Petrovna has fluttered by with gleams of some kind of gentle light – from somewhere. Then we reflected sadly –

only for a single moment; and – forgot; while we ought to have remembered . . . that Anna Petrovna – had returned.

These last twenty-four hours!

A day and a night, that is: a relative concept, a concept that consists of a multivariety of moments, where the moment –

> – is either a minimal segment of time, or – something, well, different, psychical, able to be defined by the completeness of psychic events, – not by a figure; for if by a figure, it is precise, it is two-tenths of a second; and is in that case immutable; defined by the completeness of psychic events it is an hour, or a zero; the experience grows in the moment, or – is absent in the moment –

> > – where the moment in our narrative has resembled a full cup of events.

But Anna Petrovna's arrival is a fact; and – an enormous one; to be sure, there are in it no dreadful contents, as in other facts we have noted; that is why we, the author, have forgotten about Anna Petrovna; and, as is usually the case, the heroes of the novel have also forgotten about Anna Petrovna.

And yet all the same . . . –

Anna Petrovna had returned; the events we have described she did not see; she did not suspect, did not know about these events; only one thing that had happened troubled her: her return; and it must have troubled the persons I have described; these persons must after all have responded at once to this thing that happened; have showered her with notes, letters, expressions of joy or anger; but there were no notes or messengers for her: no one paid any attention to the tremendous thing that had happened – neither Nikolai Apollonovich, nor Apollon Apollonovich.

And – Anna Petrovna was sad.

. . . .

She did not go out; a hotel of magnificent fashion enclosed her within one of its small rooms; and Anna Petrovna sat for hours on the only chair, staring at the specks on the wallpaper; these specks got into her eyes; she moved her eyes to the window; and the window looked out on to an impudently staring wall that was some kind of olive tint; instead of the sky there was yellow smoke; all one could see, in a window over there, obliquely, was some piles of dirty plates, a washtub, and the rolled-up sleeves of arms through the gleaming of the panes . . .

Not a letter nor a visit: either from her husband or her son.

Sometimes she rang; some kind of giddy creature in a butterfly-shaped bonnet appeared.

And Anna Petrovna – for the umpteenth time! – was pleased to ask:

'A *thé complet* in my room, please.'

A lackey in black evening dress appeared, his linen starched, his necktie gleaming with freshness – with a most enormous tray, placed neatly: on his palm and shoulder; he surveyed the little room contemptuously, the clumsily mended dress of its occupant, the brightly coloured Spanish rags that lay on the double bed, and the shabby little suitcase; disrespectfully, but soundlessly, he plucked from his shoulders the most enormous tray; and without any sound the *thé complet* descended to the table. And without any sound the lackey withdrew.

No one, nothing: the same specks on the wallpaper; the same laughter and noise from the next room, the conversation of two chambermaids in the corridor; a grand piano – from somewhere downstairs (in the room of a visiting woman pianist who was preparing to give her recital); and – for the umpteenth time – she moved her eyes to the window, and the window looked on to the impudently staring wall that was some kind of olive tint; instead of the sky there was smoke, and all one could see, in a window over there, obliquely, through the gleaming of the panes, was . . .

> – (suddenly there was a knocking at the door; in sudden confusion, Anna Petrovna splashed her tea on the ultra-clean napkins of the tray) –

> > – all one could see, in a window over there, obliquely, was some piles of dirty napkins, a washtub, and the rolled-up sleeves of arms.

The maid came flying in and handed her a visiting card; Anna Petrovna blushed all over; she got up noisily from behind the table;

her first gesture was *that* gesture, the one she had acquired in her girlhood: a swift motion of the hand, adjusting her hair.

'Where is the gentleman?'

'He's waiting in the corridor, miss.'

Blushing, moving her hand from her hair to her chin (a gesture she had acquired only recently and was probably caused by shortness of breath), Anna Petrovna said:

'Ask him to come in.'

She began to breathe quickly and to blush.

There were heard – the laughter and noise from the next room, the conversation of the two chambermaids in the corridor, and the grand piano from somewhere downstairs; footsteps swiftly-swiftly running to the door were heard; the door opened; Apollon Apollonovich Ableukhov, not stepping across the threshold, was vainly making an effort to make something out in the semi-twilight of the little room; and the first thing he caught sight of proved to be a wall that was some kind of olive tint, staring outside the window; and – smoke instead of the sky; all one could see, in a window over there, obliquely, through the gleaming of the panes, was some piles of dirty plates, a washtub, and the rolled-up sleeves of arms that were washing something.

. . . .

The first thing that rushed at him was the meagre furnishings of the cheap little room (the shadows fell in such a way that Anna Petrovna was somehow pushed into the background); a room like that, and – in a first-class hotel! What of it? There was nothing to be surprised about there; there are little rooms like this in all the first-class hotels – of first-class capital cities: each hotel has one of them, many have two; but there are advertisements for them in all the guidebooks. You read, for example: 'Savoy Premier ordre. Chambres depuis 3 fr.' This means: the minimum price for a tolerable room is not less than fifteen francs; but for appearance's sake, you will unfailingly find in the attic storey an uninhabited corner, untidied, dirty – in all the first-class hotels of first-class capital cities; and it is of it that the guidebooks say: 'depuis trois francs'; this room is left in neglect; it is impossible to stay in it (instead you will end up in the fifteen-franc room); for the room that is 'depuis trois francs' lacks both air and light; even the maid would shun it, never mind you, the *barin*; furnishings and everything else are also lacking; woe betide you if you stay in it: the numerous staff of chambermaids, waiters and bellboys will view you with contempt.

And you will move to a second-class hotel, where for seven or eight francs you will rest in cleanliness, comfort and honour.

'Premier ordre – depuis 3 francs' – the Lord preserve us!

Here are a bed, a table and a chair; scattered in disorder on the bed are a small handbag, straps, a black lace fan, a little cut-glass Venetian vase, wrapped – just fancy – in a long stocking (of the purest silk), a plaid, straps and a clump of loud, lemon-coloured Spanish rags; all this, in Apollon Apollonovich's opinion, must have been travelling accessories and souvenirs of Granada and Toledo, which had in all probability once been valuable and had now lost all their show, all their lustre, –

> – and the three thousand silver roubles that had so recently been sent to Granada must evidently not have been received –
>
>> – why, it was simply embarrassing for a lady *in her social position* to be carrying these old rags around with her; and – his heart was wrung within him.

At this point he caught sight of the table, gleaming with a pair of ultra-clean napkins and gleaming with a *thé complet*: a hotel accessory, carelessly left here. From the shadows a silhouette emerged: his heart was wrung a second time, because on the chair –

>> – and yet no, not on the chair! –
>> – getting up from the chair he saw – was it her? – Anna Petrovna, who had grown sunken, put on weight, and – had a very strong streak of grey in her hair; the first thing he realized was a most deplorable fact: during the two and a half

years of her stay in Spain (and – where else, where?) – a double chin more plainly stuck out from beneath her collar, while a rounded stomach more plainly stuck out from beneath her corset; only the two azure-filled eyes of her once handsome and recently beautiful face shone there as they used to; in their depths the most complex emotions now ran high: timidity, fear, anger, sympathy, pride, humiliation at the furnishings of the wretched room, concealed bitterness and . . . fear.

Apollon Apollonovich could not endure this gaze: he lowered his eyes and crumpled his hat in his hand. Yes, the years of her sojourn with the Italian artiste had changed her; and where had her sedateness, her inborn sense of dignity, her love for neatness and order got to? Apollon Apollonovich let his eyes run over the room: scattered in disorder were – small handbag, straps, black lace fan, stockings and clump of lemon-yellow rags, probably Spanish.

. . . .

Before Anna Petrovna . . . – but was it he? The two and a half years had changed him, too; two and a half years earlier she had seen before her for the last time a face sharply carved from grey stone, coldly looking at her over the mother-of-pearl table (during their final talk); each little feature had cut into her sharply like an icy frost; but now, in his face – there was a complete absence of features.

(For our own part let us say: features were there not long ago; and we outlined them at the beginning of our narrative . . .)

Two and a half years ago Apollon Apollonovich, it was true, had already been an old man, but . . . there had been something ageless about him; and he had looked – like a statesman; but now – where was the man of state? Where the iron will, where the stony gaze, that streamed nothing but whirlwinds, cold, infertile, cerebral (not feelings) – where was the stony gaze? No, it had all retreated before old age; the old man outweighed it all: his position in the world and his will; what struck her was his terrible thinness; what struck her was his stooping posture; what struck her were the trembling of his lower jaw, and his trembling fingers; and above all – the colour of his little coat: never when she had been around had he ordered garments of this colour.

Thus did they stand facing each other: Apollon Apollonovich, – not stepping across the threshold; and Anna Petrovna – over the little table: with a trembling and half-spilled cup of strong tea in her hands (she was spilling the tea on the tablecloth).

At last Apollon Apollonovich raised his head to her; he chewed his lips and said, faltering:

'Anna Petrovna!'

Now he saw her completely (his eyes had grown accustomed to the semi-darkness); he saw: all her features lit up handsomely for a moment; and then again her features were covered by little wrinkles, puffinesses, fatty little bags: they surrounded the clear beauty of her childlike features with the coarsening of old age; but for an instant all her features lit up handsomely, and precisely – when with a sharp movement she pushed away the tea she had been served; and seemed positively to dart towards him; yet all the same: did not move from the spot; and merely threw to the old man with her lips from behind the little table:

'Apollon Apollonovich!'

Apollon Apollonovich ran towards her (thus had he run towards her two and a half years earlier, in order to thrust forth two fingers, tug them away and throw cold water); ran towards her, as he was, through the room – in his little coat, with his hat in his hand; her face inclined towards his bald pate; the surface of the enormous cranium, as bare as a knee, and the two protruding ears reminded her of something, and when his cold lips touched her hand, which was wet with the spilt tea, the complex expression of her features was replaced by an unconcealed sense of contentment: imagine, if you will – something childlike flared up, played and hid in her eyes.

And when he straightened up, his small figure stood out before her even with an exceeding distinctness, overhanging the trousers, the little coat (of a colour never seen before) and a large quantity of fresh wrinkles, with two eyes that tore his entire face apart and seemed to be new; these two sticking-out eyes did not seem to her, as they had done before, like two transparent stones; what emerged from them were: an unfamiliar strength and firmness.

But the eyes were lowered. Apollon Apollonovich, his eyes darting, sought for the proper expressions:

'I, thou . . .' he thought, and ended: 'you know . . .'

'?'

'Have come to testify to you, Anna Petrovna, my respect . . .

'And congratulate you on your arrival . . .'

And Anna Petrovna caught a confused, bewildered, simply gentle-seeming, sympathetic look – of a dark, cornflower hue, like that of warm spring air.

From the next room were heard: laughter, noise; from behind the door – the conversation of the chambermaids, continuing; and the grand piano – from somewhere downstairs; scattered in disorder were: straps, small handbag, black lace fan, small cut-glass Venetian vase and clump of loud, lemon rags, which turned out to be a blouse; the specks on the wallpaper stared; as did the window that looked on to the impudently staring wall that was some kind of olive tint; instead of the sky there was smoke, and in the smoke was – Petersburg: streets and prospects, pavements and roofs; the sleet was settling on the tin-plated window-sill out there; cold rivulets plunging down from the tin-plated gutters.

'We have . . .'

'Won't you have some tea? . . .'

'A strike beginning . . .'

Swayed above the Pile of Objects . . .

The door flew open.

Nikolai Apollonovich found himself in the hallway from which he had fled very early that morning in such haste; on the walls shone the display of ancient weapons: here swords rusted; there – inclining halberds: Nikolai Apollonovich looked as though he were beside himself; with a sharp movement of his hand he tore off his broad-brimmed Italian hat; the cap of flaxen white hair softened this cold, almost stern exterior with engraved stubbornness (it is hard to find hair of this tint in adult persons; it is frequently encountered among peasant children – especially in Belorussia); drily, coldly, clearly emerged the lines of a completely white countenance, like one in an icon, when for a moment he reflected, directing his gaze over there, where beneath a rusty green shield a Lithuanian helmet shone with its spike, and the cross-shaped handle of a knight's sword sparkled.

Now he flushed; and in his wet, crumpled cloak, limping slightly, he flew up the steps of the carpeted staircase; why did he keep flushing from time to time, glowing red, something that never normally happened to him? And he was – coughing; and he was – panting; he was shaken by a fever: it is indeed impossible to stand out in the rain too long with impunity; the most interesting thing was that the cloth had been ripped away from the knee of the leg on which he was limping; and – rags fluttered; his little student's frockcoat had ridden up beneath the cloak, its back and chest hunched; between the whole tail and the torn-off tail, the belt stuck out; truly, truly: Nikolai Apollonovich looked lame, hunchbacked, and – as though he had a little tail, as he flew with all his might up the soft-stepped staircase, his cap of flaxen white hair wafting along – past the walls where a pistol and a six-pointed mace bowed.

Slipped in front of the door with the faceted crystal handle; and when he ran past the rooms that shone with lacquer, it seemed that around him there formed only the illusion of rooms; and then flew apart without trace, erecting beyond the limit of consciousness its misty surfaces; and when he banged the corridor door behind him and walked down the corridor stamping his heels, it seemed to him that the veins at his temples were hammering: the swift pulsation of those veins plainly marked a premature sclerosis on his forehead.

He flew, not himself, into his multicoloured room: and the green budgerigars shrieked desperately in their cage and began to beat their wings; this shrieking interrupted his flight; for a moment he stared before him; and saw: the multicoloured leopard, thrown at his feet with gaping jaws; and – began to rummage in his pocket (he was looking for the key to the writing desk).

'Eh?'

'The devil take it . . .'

'Have I lost it?'

'Did I leave it somewhere?'

'How do you like that?'

And he began to rush helplessly about the room, looking for the treacherous key he had forgotten somewhere, picking through quite inappropriate objects of furniture, seizing a three-legged gold censer in the form of a sphere with an opening pierced in it and a half-moon on top, and muttering to himself all the while: Nikolai Apollonovich, like Apollon Apollonovich, was in the habit of talking to himself.

In fright he rushed through into the next room – to the writing desk: as he went, his foot caught on the Arabian stool with the ivory incrustation; it crashed to the floor; he was struck by the fact that the desk was not locked; the drawer was sticking out in tell-tale fashion; it had been pulled half-way out; his heart sank: how could he have been so careless as to forget to lock it? He tugged at the drawer . . . And-and-and . . .

No: oh, no!

The objects lay in disorder in the drawer; on the table lay a cabinet photograph, thrown at an angle; but . . . the sardine tin was not there; furiously, savagely, frightenedly, above the drawer emerged the lines of a crimson countenance with blue around some kind of enormous black eyes: black from the dilation of the pupils; this did he stand between the dark green upholstered armchair and the bust: of Kant, of course.

He – went to the other desk. He – pulled out the drawer: the objects lay inside the drawer in perfect order: bundles of letters, papers: he put them all – on the table; but . . . there was no sardine tin . . . At this point his legs gave way beneath him; and, as he was, in his Italian cloak, in his galoshes – he fell to his knees, dropping his burning head into his cold, wet, rain-dampened hands; for a moment – like that, he froze: the cap of flaxen hair gleamed strangely, deathly pale there, motionless, like a yellowish stain in the semi-twilight of the room among the green upholstered armchairs.

Yes – up he leapt! Yes – to the bookcase! And the bookcase –

flew open; the objects went flying this way and that, to the carpet; but there too – there was no sardine tin; like a whirlwind, he began to rush about the room, resembling an agile little monkey both in the swiftness of his movements (like his elevated papa), and in his modest stature. Indeed: fate was playing a joke; from room to room; from bed (here he rummaged under the pillows, the quilt, the mattress) – to the fireplace: here he soiled his hands in the ash; from the fireplace – to the rows of book-shelves (and the silk that covered the bindings began to slide on little brass wheels); here he thrust his hands between the volumes; and many of them, with a rustling, with a crash, flew to the floor.

But nowhere was the sardine tin to be found.

Soon his face, soiled with ash and dust, swayed without any sense or meaning above the heap of objects, which had been swept into a senseless pile and had been picked through by long, spider-like fingers that ran out on trembling hands; these hands moved restlessly about the floor from the outspread Italian cloak; in this stooping pose, trembling and sweaty all over, with bulging neck veins, he really would have reminded anyone of a fat-bellied spider, a devourer of flies; thus, when an observer tears a delicate spider's web, he beholds a spectacle: disturbed, the enormous insect, which has been trembling on a silver thread in space from the ceiling to the floor, goes clumsily running about the floor on furry legs.

In just such a pose – above the pile of objects – was Nikolai Apollonovich taken unawares: by Semyonych, who ran in.

'Nikolai Apollonovich! . . . Young *barin*! . . .'

Nikolai Apollonovich, who was still squatting down, turned; seeing Semyonych, with a swift gesture of his cloak he covered the pile of objects that had been swept together in a heap – the sheets of paper and volumes with gaping jaws – resembling a brood-hen on her eggs: the cap of flaxen hair showed so strangely pale and motionless there – like a yellowish stain in the semi-twilight of the room.

'What is it? . . .'

'If I may make so bold as to report . . .'

'Leave me alone: can't you see that . . . I'm busy . . .'

Stretching his mouth to the ears, he looked every bit like the head of the multicoloured leopard that lay grinning there on the floor:

'I'm arranging these books here.'

But Semyonych could not calm down.

'But please, sir: you are . . . requested there . . .'

'?'

'A family joy: for the little mother *barynya*, Anna Petrovna, herself, has been so good as to grant us a visit.'

Nikolai Apollonovich got up mechanically; the cloak flew from him; on the ash-smeared contours of the icon-like countenance – through cinders and dust – like lightning a blush flared; Nikolai Apollonovich cut an absurd and comic little figure in his student's frock-coat that protruded in two humps and had only one tail – and with a dancing half-belt, when he – began to cough; hoarsely, through his cough, he exclaimed:

'Mamma? Anna Petrovna?'

'She is over there with Apollon Apollonovich, sir; in the drawing-room . . . She has just been so good as to . . .'

'Do they want to see me?'

'Apollon Apollonovich requests your company, sir . . .'

'Very well, in a moment . . . I'll be there in a moment . . . Just a second . . .'

. . . .

In this room, so recently, Nikolai Apollonovich had grown into a self-contained centre – into a series of logical premisses that flowed from the centre, predetermining everything: soul, thought and this armchair here; only recently had he been the sole centre of the universe; but ten days had passed; and his self-awareness had got shamefully bogged down in this heaped-up pile of objects: thus does the free fly, scuttling along the edge of a plate on its six little legs, suddenly get hopelessly bogged down, both leg and wing, in a sticky mass of honey.

. . . .

'Psst! Semyonych, Semyonych – listen,' – here Nikolai Apollonovich nimbly darted out through the doorway, catching up with

Semyonych, jumped over the upturned stool and caught hold of the old man's sleeve (goodness, those fingers were tenacious!)

'I say, I wonder if you've seen in here – the fact is, that . . .' he said, beginning to grow confused, getting down on the floor and pulling the old man away from the corridor door . . . 'I forgot . . . You haven't seen a sort of object in here? Here, in the room . . . An object like a toy . . .'

'A toy, sir . . .'

'A child's toy . . . a sardine tin . . .'

'A sardine tin?'

'Yes, a toy (in the shape of a sardine tin) – a heavy thing, that one winds up with a key: there's a little clock inside that ticks . . . I put it here: a toy . . .'

Semyonych slowly turned, freed his sleeve from the fingers that had clutched it, stared at the wall for a moment (a shield hung on the wall – a Negro one: it was made from the hide of a once-slain rhinoceros), thought for a moment and then snapped disrespectfully:

'No!'

Not even 'No, sir': simply – 'No' . . .

'Well, I just thought you might . . .'

Just imagine: good fortune, family joy; the *barin* is beaming there, the *minister*: for such an occasion . . . And then here: a sardine tin . . . a heavy one . . . that winds up . . . a toy: and one of his coat-tails is torn off! . . .

'So you will permit me to announce you, sir?'

'I'll be there in a moment, in a moment . . .'

And the door closed: Nikolai Apollonovich stood there, not understanding where he was, – next to the upturned dark brown stool, in front of the hookah; before him on the wall hung a shield, a Negro one, made from the thick hide of a rhinoceros and with a rusty Sudanese spear hung to one side of it.

Not understanding what he was doing, he hurried to exchange the tell-tale frock-coat for one that was completely new; as a preliminary, he washed his hands and face clean of ash; as he washed and changed, he kept saying:

'How can this be, what is happening . . . And really, where could I have hidden it . . .'

Nikolai Apollonovich did not yet realize the full extent of the horror that had assailed him, a horror that proceeded from the accidental disappearance of the sardine tin; it was just as well that it had not yet occurred to him that: *they had visited his room in his absence and, discovering the sardine tin with dreadful contents, had taken that sardine tin away from him as a precaution.*

The Lackeys Were Astonished

And precisely the same houses loomed up there, and precisely the same grey human streams flowed past there, and the same green-yellow fog stood there; the faces scuttled there with a look of concentration; the pavements whispered and shuffled – beneath a throng of stone houses like giants; towards them flew – prospect after prospect; and the planet's spherical surface seemed embraced, as in serpentine coils, by the blackish-grey cubes of the houses; and the mesh of parallel prospects, intersected by a mesh of prospects, expanded into the abysses of the universe in the surfaces of squares and cubes: one square per man-in-the-street.

But Apollon Apollonovich did not look at his favourite figure: the square; did not give himself up to the mindless contemplation of stone parallelepipeds, cubes; as he swayed to and fro on the soft cushions of the seat of the hired carriage, he kept glancing in agitation at Anna Petrovna, whom he himself was taking – to the lacquered house; what they had talked of there in the hotel room had remained for everyone an impenetrable secret; after this conversation they had resolved: Anna Petrovna would move to the Embankment tomorrow; while today, Apollon Apollonovich was taking Anna Petrovna – to a meeting with her son.

And Anna Petrovna was disconcerted.

In the carriage they did not talk; Anna Petrovna looked out of the carriage windows: it was two and a half years since she had seen these grey prospects: there, outside the windows, the street numbering was visible; and the traffic moved; there, from there – on clear days, from far, far away, had blindly flashed: the golden needle, the clouds, the crimson ray of the sunset; there, from there, on misty days – no one, nothing.

Apollon Apollonovich leaned against the walls of the carriage with unconcealed satisfaction, partitioned off from the scum of the streets inside this closed cube; here he was separated from the flowing human crowds, from the dismally wet red paper covers that were being sold over there at that crossroads; and his eyes darted; only now and then did Anna Petrovna catch: a lost, bewildered gaze, and imagine – one that seemed simply gentle: blue as blue, childlike, senseless even (had he lapsed back into childhood?)

'I heard, Apollon Apollonovich: you are to be made a minister?'

But Apollon Apollonovich interrupted:

'And where have you come from now, Anna Petrovna?'

'Oh, I have come from Granada . . .'

'Indeed, ma'am, indeed, ma'am, indeed . . .' – and, blowing his nose, – added . . . – 'Business, you know: unpleasant things at the office, you know . . .'

And – what was this? On his hand he felt a warm hand: he had been stroked on the hand . . . Hm-hm-hm: Apollon Apollonovich did not know where to look; he was disconcerted, seemed alarmed even; he even felt annoyed . . . Hm-hm; no one had treated him like that for about fifteen years . . . She had quite simply stroked him . . . He had to admit that he had not expected this from the lady person . . . hm-hm . . . (Apollon Apollonovich had after all for the past two and half years considered this lady person to be a . . . lady person of . . . loose . . . conduct . . .)

'You see, I'm going into retirement . . .'

Had the cerebral game that had divided them for so many years and had grown ominously more intense this past two and a half years, at last burst out of his stubborn brain? And outside his brain, had it now gathered in storm clouds above them? Broken in unprecedented storms around them? But in breaking outside his brain, it had exhausted itself inside his brain; slowly his brain had cleared; thus in storm clouds you will sometimes see an azure gap running from one side – through bands of rain; then let the downpour lash over you; let the dark masses of cloud burst rumblingly with crimson lightning! The azure gap is growing; soon the sun will look dazzlingly out; you are already expecting the end of the storm; when suddenly there is a flash and a bang: the lightning has struck a pine tree.

The greenish light of day was breaking through the windows of the carriage; the human streams ran there in an undular surf; and that human surf was a thunderous surf.

It was here that he had seen the *raznochinets*; here the eyes of the *raznochinets* had gleamed, recognized him – some ten days ago (yes, only ten days: in ten days everything had changed; Russia had changed!) . . .

The glidings and rumblings of carriages flying past! The melodic cries of motor-car roulades! And – a detachment of police! . . .

There, where only the pale grey dampness hung suspended, at first appeared lustrelessly in outline and then completely took shape: the grimy, blackish-grey St Isaac's . . . And withdrew back into the fog. And – an expanse opened: the depths, the greenish murk, into which receded the black bridge, where the fog curtained the many-chimneyed distances and from where ran the wave of the approaching clouds.

. . . .

Indeed: after all, the lackeys were astonished!

Thus later on in the entrance hall was it told by the sleepy young lad Grishka:

'Here I am, sitting and counting on my fingers: why, from the Protection to the Nativity of the Mother of God . . . That makes . . . From the Nativity of the Mother of God to St Nicholas in Winter . . .'[2]

'Tell me another: the Nativity of the Mother of God, the Nativity of the Mother of God!'

'What do you mean? The Nativity of the Mother of God is a feast day in our village – She is our patron . . . So it works out at: as I count it . . . Then I hear: someone's driving up; I go to the door. So I throw the door open: and – oh, sainted fathers! Because it's the *barin* himself, in a hired little carriage (and a bad one, too!), and a *barynya* with him, of respectable years and wearing a cheap waterproof.'

'Not a waterproof, you little rogue: people don't wear waterproofs nowadays.'

'Don't embarrass him: he's daft enough as it is.'

'In a word – wearing a coat. While the *barin* gets in a lather: from the cab – phoo, the carriage – he jumps down, stretches out his arm to the *barynya* – smiles: like a cavalier, like, shows her every assistance.'

'Get away with you . . .'

'It's true . . .'

'I don't think they've seen each other for two years,' voices were heard saying all round.

'Stands to reason: the *barynya* gets out of the carriage; only thing is, I can see that the *barynya*'s embarrassed about this *event*: she's smiling there – not her full proper self; to give herself courage: she's holding on to her chin; well, and she's dressed real poor, like; there's holes in her gloves; her gloves aren't darned, I can see: perhaps there's no one to darn them; maybe in Spain they don't do no darning . . .'

'Tell us another, that will do now! . . .'

'It's like I'm saying: and the *barin*, our *barin*, Apollon Apollonovich, gave up all his finery; stood by the carriage, over a puddle, under the rain: the rain – oh my Lord! The *barin* hesitates, seems to start running on the spot, his feet stamping up and down on the spot; and when the *barynya*, getting down from the footboard, leaning right on his arm – for the *barynya*'s quite heavy – our *barin* even sagged right down; the *barin*'s tiny; well, I thought to myself, how could he hold up a heavy woman like that? He doesn't have the strength . . .'

'Don't weave fancy stories; tell us what happened.'

'I'm not weaving fancy stories; I'm telling you like it was; and anyway . . . Mitry Semyonych will tell you: they met in the entrance hall . . . What is there to tell? The *barin* just said to the *barynya*: welcome, he said, come in, Anna Petrovna . . . That was when I recognized her.'

'Well, and so what then?'

'She's aged . . . At first I didn't recognize her; but then I did, because I still remember how she used to give me sweets.'

Thus did the lackeys talk afterwards.

. . . .

But really!

A sudden, unforeseen fact: it was about two and a half years ago that Anna Petrovna left her husband for an Italian artiste; and now, two and a half years later, deserted by the Italian artiste, from the splendid palaces of Granada across the chain of the Pyrenees, across the Alps, across the mountains of the Tyrol, she came rushing back in an express train; but what was more remarkable was that the senator had found it impossible to breathe a word about Anna Petrovna not only for the past two and a half years, but even two and a half days ago (only yesterday he had bristled up!); for two and a half years Apollon Apollonovich had avoided even the thought of Anna Petrovna (and yet had thought about her); the very sound-combination 'Anna Petrovna' broke against his eardrums like a firecracker thrown at a teacher from under a school desk; except that a schoolteacher would bang his fist angrily on the desk; while Apollon Apollonovich merely tightened his lips contemptuously at this sound combination. But why at the news of her return did the customary tightening of his dry lips burst apart in an agitatedly wrathful trembling of the jaws (the night before – during his conversation with Nikolenka); why had he not been able to sleep that night? Why for a period of some twelve hours had that anger evaporated somewhere and been replaced by an aching anguish, bordering on anxiety? Why had he not been able to endure the wait, himself gone to the hotel? Had talked her round; brought her home. Something had happened there – in the hotel room; Anna Petrovna had forgotten her stern promise: she had made that promise to herself – here, yesterday: here in the lacquered house (having visited it and found no one at home).

Had made the promise: but – had returned.

Anna Petrovna and Apollon Apollonovich had been agitated and embarrassed by the explanation they had had with one another; and so when they had entered the lacquered house they had not exchanged abundant outpourings of emotion; Anna Petrovna looked at her husband askance: Apollon Apollonovich began to blow his nose ... beneath the rusty halberd; emitting a trumpet-like sound, he began to snort into his side-whiskers. Anna Petrovna graciously deigned to reply to the lackeys' deferential bows, displaying a restraint we have not seen in her before; only Semyonych did she embrace, and seemed to want to cry a little; but, casting a frightened, bewildered look at Apollon Apollonovich, she regained her self-control: her fingers stretched towards the little handbag, but did not take out her handkerchief.

Apollon Apollonovich, standing above her on the stairs, commandingly cast stern glances at the lackeys; he cast such glances at moments of bewilderment: but at ordinary times, Apollon Apollonovich was scrupulously polite and prim with the lackeys to the point of offensiveness (apart from when he was making his jokes). While the servants were standing there he maintained a tone of indifference: nothing had happened – until now the *barynya* had been living abroad, for the sake of her health; that was all: and now the *barynya* had returned . . . What of it? Oh, it was all very fine! . . .

There was, however, a lackey here (all the others had been fired, with the exception of Semyonych and Grishka, the young lad); this lackey remembered what he remembered: remembered the manner in which the *barynya* had made her departure abroad – without any warning to the domestic staff: holding a little travelling bag (and this – for two and a half years!); on the eve of her departure had locked herself in, away from the *barin*; while some two days before her departure *that fellow with the moustache* had been there in her room all the time: their black-eyed visitor – oh, what was his name again? Mindalini (his name was Mindalini), who sang some kind of un-Russian songs at their house: 'Tra-la-la . . . Tra-la-la . . .' And he never tipped.

This same lackey, remembering something, kissed the exalted hand with especial respect, feeling guilty about the fact that the details of the escape – the departure, that is – had not been effaced from his memory; for he was seriously afraid that the days of his sojourn in the lacquered house were numbered – on the occasion of the happy return of their excellencies to the lacquered house.

There they were – in the reception hall; before them the parqueted floor shone, like a mirror, with little squares: this room had seldom been heated during the past two and a half years; the expanses of this enfilade of rooms provoked an unaccountable melancholy; Apollon Apollonovich spent most of the time sitting locked in his study; he kept fancying that someone familiar and melancholy was about to come running to him, that now he was not alone: not alone would he stroll about the little squares of the parqueted floor here, but . . . with Anna Petrovna.

It was seldom that Apollon Apollonovich strolled about the little squares of the parqueted floor with Nikolenka.

His arm bent like a ring-shaped roll, Apollon Apollonovich led his guest through the reception hall: it was just as well that it was his right arm he presented; his left one twinged and ached with the impetuous, restless joltings of his heart; and Anna Petrovna stopped him, led him over to the wall and, pointing to a pale-toned painting, smiled to him:

'Ah, still the same old paintings! . . . Do you remember this fresco, Apollon Apollonovich?'

And – looked ever so slightly askance at him, blushed ever so slightly; her cornflower-coloured eyes were fixed on two eyes that were filled with azure; and – their gaze, their gaze: there was in it something charming, old-fashioned, ancient, something that everyone had forgotten but had forgotten no one and stood *in the doorway* – something of this kind suddenly arose between their gazes; it was not in them; and did not emerge in them; but stood – *between them*: as though wafted by the autumn wind. Let the reader forgive me: I shall express the essence of this gaze in a most banal word: *love*.

'Do you remember?'

'Of course, my dear: I remember . . .'

'Where was it?'

'In Venice . . .'

'Thirty years have passed! . . .'

A memory of the misty lagoon, of an aria sobbing in the distance, seized him: thirty years ago. Memories of Venice seized her, too, and divided: thirty years ago: and two and a half years ago; here she blushed at the inopportune memory, which she drove away; and another surged in: Kolenka. During the past two hours she had forgotten about Kolenka; her conversation with the senator had forced out everything else prematurely; but two hours before that she had thought only of Kolenka, and thought of him with tenderness; with tenderness and vexation that she had had no greeting, no reply from Kolenka.

'Kolenka . . .'

They entered the drawing-room; heaps of porcelain baubles rushed from every side; little leaves of incrustation shone – mother-of-pearl and bronze – on the little boxes, the little shelves that came out of the walls.

'Kolenka, Anna Petrovna, is all right . . . he's fine . . . is getting on splendidly,' – and he ran away, somehow to the side.

'And is he at home?'

Apollon Apollonovich, who had just fallen into an Empire armchair, on the pale azure satin seat of which little garlands twined, rose reluctantly out of the chair, and pressed the bell button:

'Why has he not come to see me?'

'Anna Petrovna, he . . . em-em-em . . . was, in his turn, very, very . . .' the senator said, getting strangely confused, and then took out his handkerchief: with sounds almost like those of a trumpet, he blew his nose for a very long time; snorting into his side-whiskers, he took a very long time about stuffing his handkerchief back into his pockets:

'In a word, he was overjoyed.'

A silence ensued. The bald head swayed over there beneath the cold and long-legged bronze; the lampshade did not flash with a violet tone, subtly painted: the secret of this paint had been lost by the nineteenth century; the glass had grown dark with time; the delicate pattern had also grown dark with time.

At the sound of the bell, Semyonych appeared:

'Is Nikolai Apollonovich at home?'

'Precisely so, sir . . .'

'Mm . . . listen: tell him that Anna Petrovna is with us: and that she asks him to come and see her . . .'

'Perhaps we shall go to him,' said Anna Petrovna, beginning to grow agitated, and with a swiftness unusual for her years she rose from her armchair; but here Apollon Apollonovich, turning sharply towards Semyonych, interrupted her:

'Em-em-em . . . Semyonych: I want to tell you . . .'

'I'm listening, sir! . . .'

'The wife of a Chaldean – I wonder – what is she?'

'I suppose she's a Chaldean, sir . . .'

'No – a *khalda*! . . .'³

. . . .

'Hee-hee-hee, sir . . .'

. . . .

'I'm not very pleased with Kolenka, Anna Petrovna . . .'

'Oh, why is that?'

'For a long time now, Kolenka has been behaving – no, don't be upset – been behaving: downright – no, don't be upset – strangely . . .'

'?'

The gilded pier-glasses in the window-piers devoured the drawing-room from all sides with the green surfaces of the mirrors.

'Kolenka has become somehow secretive . . . Cahuh, cahuh,' – and, in a fit of coughing, Apollon Apollonovich drummed his hand on the little table, remembering something private, frowned, and began to rub the bridge of his nose; he quickly recovered himself, however: and with extreme joviality he almost shouted:

'But as a matter of fact – no: it doesn't matter, my dear . . . It's nonsense . . .'

Between the pier-glasses the small mother-of-pearl table gleamed from everywhere.

There Was Utter Senselessness

Nikolai Apollonovich, overcoming a most intense pain in his knee joint (he had really taken quite a knock), was limping slightly: he was running down the booming expanse of the corridor.

A meeting with his mother!

Whirlwinds of thoughts and meanings overwhelmed him; or not even whirlwinds of thoughts and meanings: simply whirlwinds of meaninglessness; thus the particles of a comet, penetrating a planet, do not even cause an alteration in the planet's composition, flying past with staggering swiftness; as they penetrate the heart, they do not even cause any alteration in the rhythm of the heart's beats; but let the comet's speed slow down: then hearts will burst: the planet itself will burst: and everything will become a gas; if we could stop the spinning, senseless whirlwind in Ableukhov's head even for a moment, that senselessness would deck itself out in stormily swollen thoughts.

And – here are those thoughts.

The thought, in the first place, of the horror of his situation; a dreadful situation had now been created (as a consequence of the sardine tin's disappearance); the sardine tin, or rather the bomb, had disappeared; it had quite clearly disappeared; and therefore: someone had taken the bomb away; but who, who? One of the lackeys; and – therefore: the bomb had fallen into the hands of the police; and – he would be arrested; but this was not the main thing, the main thing was that Apollon Apollonovich himself had taken the bomb away; and had taken it away at the very moment when the matter of the bomb had been settled; and – he knew: knew everything.

Everything – what was that? Why, it was nothing; a plan of murder? There was no plan of murder; Nikolai Apollonovich firmly denied this plan: this plan was a loathsome slander.

There remained the fact of the bomb having been found.

Since his father was summoning him, since his mother wanted to see him – no, he could not possibly know: and he had not taken the bomb out of his room. And as for the lackeys . . . The lackeys would have discovered everything a long time ago. But no one had said anything. No, they did not know about the bomb. But – where was it, where was it? Had he really put it away in this desk, had he not put it somewhere under a rug, mechanically, by chance?

Things like that happened to him.

In a week it would be discovered of its own accord . . . Though in fact, no: it would announce its presence somewhere today – with a most dreadful roar (the Ableukhovs decidedly could not endure such roars).

Somewhere, perhaps, – under a rug, under a pillow, on a shelf, it would announce its presence: would roar and burst; the bomb must be found; but he had no time for searching now: Anna Petrovna had arrived.

In the second place: he had been insulted; in the third place: that mangy little Pavel Yakovlevich – he seemed to have only just seen him, returning from his little flat on the Moika; while Pepp

Peppovich Pepp – this was the fourth thing: Pepp was a dreadful expansion of the body, a distension of the veins, boiling water in the head . . .

Oh, it had all got confused: the whirlwinds of thoughts span with inhuman swiftness and roared in his ears, so that there were not even any thoughts: there was utter meaninglessness.

And now, with this meaningless boiling water in his head Nikolai Apollonovich ran along the booming corridor, without adjusting his little frock-coat in his haste and appearing to the gaze like some hunchbacked cripple, limping on his right leg with its painfully aching knee joint.

Mamma

He opened the door to the drawing room.

The first thing he saw was . . . was . . . But what can one say: he saw his mother's face from the armchair, and two arms stretched out: the face had aged, and the arms trembled in the lace of the gold street lamps, which had just been lit – outside the windows.

And he heard a voice:

'Kolenka: my own, my loved one!'

He could hold out no longer, and rushed to her:

'Is it you, my boy . . .'

No, he could hold out no longer: sinking to his knees, he seized her figure in his tenacious arms; he pressed his face against her knees, broke into convulsive sobs – sobs about what, he knew not: unaccountably, shamelessly, uncontrollably his broad shoulders began to heave (for let us remember: Nikolai Apollonovich had experienced no caresses these past three years).

'Mamma, Mamma . . .'

She also wept.

Apollon Apollonovich stood there, in the semi-twilight of a niche, fingering a little porcelain doll, a Chinaman; the Chinaman was swaying his head; Apollon Apollonovich came out from the semi-twilight of the niche; and quietly he groaned; with short little footsteps he moved across to that weeping pair; and suddenly he began to boom above the armchair:

'Calm yourselves, my friends!'

It must be admitted that he could not have expected these feelings from his cold, reserved son – in whose face these past two and a half years he had seen nothing but little grimaces; a mouth torn apart to the ears, and a lowered gaze; and then, turning round, Apollon Apollonovich ran anxiously out of the room – in search of some object or other.

'Mamma . . . Mamma . . .'

The fear, the humiliations of all these days and nights, the sardine tin's disappearance and, last but not least, the sense of complete insignificance – all this, whirling round, was coming untwisted in momentary thoughts; was drowning in the moisture of the meeting:

'My darling, my boy.'

. . . .

The icy touch of fingers on his arm brought him back to his senses again:

'Here you are, Kolenka: have a little sip of water.'

And when he raised from her knees his tear-stained countenance, he saw again what seemed to be the *childlike* eyes of an old man of sixty-eight: little Apollon Apollonovich stood there in his jacket with a glass of water; his fingers were dancing; he was more trying to pat Nikolai Apollonovich rather than actually patting him – on the back, the shoulder, the cheeks; suddenly he stroked the flaxen white hair with his hand. Anna Petrovna laughed; quite irrelevantly, she adjusted the collar; she transferred her eyes, which were intoxicated with happiness, from Nikolenka – to Apollon Apollonovich; and back again: from him to Nikolenka.

Nikolai Apollonovich slowly raised himself from his knees:

'I'm sorry, Mamma: I just . . .

'It's, it's – the unexpectedness . . .

'I'll be all right in a moment . . . It's nothing . . . Thank you, Papa . . .'

And he drank some water.

'There.'

Apollon Apollonovich put his glass on the little mother-of-pearl table; and suddenly – burst into senile laughter at something, the way little boys laugh at the antics of a merry *uncle*, nudging one another with their little elbows; two old, familiar faces!

'Indeed, sir . . .

'Indeed, sir . . .

'Indeed, sir . . .'

Apollon Apollonovich stood there by a pier-glass, which a golden-cheeked little cupid crowned with his little wing; beneath the cupid laurels and roses were perforated by the heavy flames of torches. But memory cut like lightning: the sardine tin! . . .

How could it be? What had happened? And a paroxysm broke within him again.

'Just a moment . . . I'm coming . . .'

'What's the matter, my dear?'

'It's nothing . . . Let him be, Anna Petrovna . . . I advise you, Kolenka, to be alone with yourself . . . for five minutes . . . Yes, you know . . . And then – come back again . . .'

And, the merest bit simulating the paroxysm that he had just had, Nikolai Apollonovich tottered, and somewhat theatrically let his face fall into his fingers again: the cap of flaxen hair looked so strangely pale there, in the semi-twilight of the room.

Tottering, he went out.

The father looked at the happy mother in surprise.

. . . .

'To tell you the truth, I didn't recognize him . . . These, these . . . These, so to speak, feelings,' – Apollon Apollonovich ran over from the mirror to the window-sill . . . 'These, these . . . paroxysms,' – and patted his side-whiskers.

'They show,' – he turned sharply, and raised the toes of his shoes, balancing for a moment on his heels, and then leaning with his whole body on the toes as they fell to the floor –

'They show,' – he said, putting his hands behind his back (under his little jacket) and turning them behind his back (making the little jacket begin to wag); and it looked as though Apollon Apollonovich were running about the drawing-room with a little wagging tail:

'They show that he has a naturalness of feeling and, so to speak' – here he shrugged his shoulders for a moment – 'good qualities of character . . .

'I never expected it at all . . .'

A snuffbox that was lying on the little table struck the attention of the renowned statesman; and wishing to impart to it a more symmetrical aspect in relation to the little tray that was lying there, Apollon Apollonovich very quickly walked up to that little table and snatched . . . from the tray a visiting card, which for some reason he began to turn between his fingers; his absent-mindedness proceeded from the fact that he had at that moment been struck by a profound thought, which was unfolding into a receding labyrinth of some kind of subsidiary discoveries. But Anna Petrovna, who was sitting in her armchair with a look of blissful bewilderment, observed with conviction:

'I always said . . .'

'Yes, dear, thou know . . .'

Apollon Apollonovich rose on tiptoe with his little jacket tail slightly raised; and – ran from the little table to the mirror:

'You know . . .'

Apollon Apollonovich ran from the mirror into the corner:

'Kolenka has surprised me: and I must admit – this behaviour of his has reassured me' – he creased his forehead – 'in relation to . . . in relation to,' – took his hand from behind his back (the edge of the little jacket was lowered), and drummed his hand on the table:

'M-yes! . . .'

Sharply interrupted himself:

'It's nothing.'

And fell into reflection: looked at Anna Petrovna; met her gaze; they smiled at each another.

And a Roulade Thundered

Nikolai Apollonovich went into his room; stared at the upturned Arabian stool: followed with his eyes the incrustation of ivory and mother-of-pearl. Slowly he went over to the window: there the river flowed; and a boat rocked on it; and the tide splashed; from the drawing-room, somewhere in the distance, peals of roulades filled the silence of the room; thus had she played in the old days:

and to these sounds, once upon a time, had he fallen asleep over his books.

Nikolai Apollonovich stood over the heap of objects, thinking in agony:

'But where is it . . . How can it be . . . Where on earth did I put it?'

And – could not remember.

Shadows, shadows and shadows: the armchairs showed green from the shadows; a bust emerged from the shadows over there: of Kant, of course.

At this point he noticed on the table a sheet of paper that had been folded in four: people who do not find the master of the house at home generally leave sheets of paper folded in four on the table; mechanically he took the piece of paper; mechanically he saw the handwriting – it was familiar, Likhutin's. Yes – that was it: he had completely forgotten that in his absence, this morning, Likhutin had been here: had dug and rummaged (he himself had spoken of it during the unpleasant meeting) . . .

Yes, yes, yes – he had ransacked the room.

A sigh of relief escaped from Nikolai Apollonovich's breast. All was instantly explained: Likhutin! Well – of course, of course; he had quite certainly rummaged around here; had sought and found; and, having found, taken away; had seen the open desk; and had glanced into it; the sardine tin had caught his attention with its weight, its appearance, and its clock mechanism; the second lieutenant had taken the sardine tin away. There was no doubt.

With relief, he lowered himself into an armchair; just then the silence was filled again by peals of roulades; thus it had been in the old days: roulades had come from there; nine years ago; and ten years ago: Anna Petrovna had played Chopin (not Schumann). And it seemed to him now that there had not been any events, since it had all been explained so simply: the sardine tin had been taken away by second lieutenant Likhutin (who else could it have been, unless one assumed, but . . . – why assume it?); Aleksandr Ivanovich would do his best about all the rest (during these hours, let us remember, Aleksandr Ivanovich Dudkin was having his explanation with Lippanchenko, now lately deceased); no, there had been no events.

There, outside the windows, Petersburg pursued and chased with its cerebral play and tearful spaciousness; there rushed onslaughts of wet, cold wind; enormous clusters of diamonds showed mistily there – beneath the bridge. No one – nothing.

And the river flowed; and the tide splashed; and the boat rocked; and a roulade thundered.

On the other side of the Neva's waters colossi arose – in the outlines of islands and houses; and cast amber eyes into the mists; and they seemed to be weeping. A row of shore lamps dropped fiery tears into the Neva: the surface burned with seething flashes of radiance.

A Watermelon is a Vegetable . . .

After two and a half years the three of them dined together.

The cuckoo on the wall cuckooed; the lackey brought in a steaming soup tureen; Anna Petrovna shone with contentment; Apollon Apollonovich . . . – incidentally: looking at the decrepit old man only this morning, you would not have recognized this ageless statesman, who had suddenly straightened up in his bearing, had sat down here at the table and taken a napkin with a kind of springy movement; they were sitting at soup, when a side door opened: Nikolai Apollonovich, lightly powdered, clean shaven, trim, hobbled along from it and joined the family in a tightly buttoned student's frock-coat with a collar of the most elevated proportions (resembling the collars of the Alexandrine epoch, now past).

'What is the matter, *mon cher*?' Anna Petrovna asked, throwing her pince-nez on to her nose in an affected manner. 'You are limping, I see?'

'Eh? . . .' Apollon Apollonovich cast a glance at Kolenka and seized the pepper-pot. 'Indeed . . .'

With a kind of youthful movement he proceeded to overpepper his soup.

'It's nothing, *maman*: I stumbled . . . and now my knee aches . . .'

'Shouldn't you put Goulard water on it?'

'Indeed, Kolenka,' Apollon Apollonovich said, bringing a spoonful of soup to his mouth, and looking from under his brows, 'these bruises of the knee joint are not to be trifled with; these bruises can play up . . .'

And – swallowed the spoonful of soup.

'Maternal feeling is a remarkable thing' – and Anna Petrovna put her spoon on her plate, and her large, childlike eyes stared as she pressed her head into her neck (making her double chin rise from under her collar) – 'a remarkable thing: he is already grown-up, and yet I still worry about him as before . . .'

She appeared quite naturally to have forgotten that for two and a half years she had not troubled about Kolenka at all: Kolenka's place had been taken by a stranger, swarthy and long-moustached, with eyes like two black prunes; naturally – she had forgotten just over two years ago she had used to tie this stranger's necktie, there in Spain, every day: a violet one, made of silk; and every morning for two and a half years she had given him a laxative – Hunyadi – Janos.

'Yes, maternal feeling: you remember – when you had dysentairy . . .' (she said 'dysentairy').

'Of course, I remember perfectly . . . You mean the slices of bread?'

'That's right . . .'

'It would appear, *mon ami*, that you are suffering from the consequences of dysentery right now?' – Apollon Apollonovich muttered from his plate, placing a stress on the final y.

And swallowed a mouthful of soup.

'It's not good . . . for you . . . to eat berries at such a time, sir,' the content voice of Semyonych was heard to say from behind the door; his head peeped through: he was looking from over there – was not serving.

'Berries, berries!' Apollon Apollonovich boomed in a bass voice and suddenly turned right round to face Semyonych: or rather, to the chink in the door.

'Berries.' And began to chew his lips.

Here the lackey who was serving (not Semyonych) smiled in anticipation, looking as though he wanted to announce to them all:

'Something special is on its way!'

And the *barin* screamed.

'Tell me, Semyonych: is a watermelon a berry?'

Anna Petrovna turned only her eyes towards Kolenka: condescendingly and slyly she concealed a smile; transferred her eyes to the senator, who had frozen in the direction of the door and had, it seemed, completely withdrawn into expectation of an answer to his absurd question; with her eyes she said:

'Is he still up to his old games?'

Nikolai Apollonovich embarrassedly grasped for his knife and fork until, impassively and distinctly, a voice darted out, not surprised by the question:

'A watermelon, your excellency, is not a berry at all, it's a vegetable.'

Apollon Apollonovich quickly turned right round, and suddenly fired off – ai, ai, ai! – his impromptu:

> Correctly, Semyonych,
> You old curd bread, –
> You've worked this out
> With your bald-topped head.

Anna Petrovna and Kolenka did not raise their eyes from their plates: in a word, it was – like the old days!

. . . .

After the scene in the drawing-room Apollon Apollonovich showed them by his appearance: everything had now returned to normal; with appetite he ate, joked and attentively listened to the stories about the beauties of Spain; something strange and melancholy rose in his heart; as though there were no time; and as though it had all happened yesterday (Kolenka thought): he, Nikolai Apollonovich, was five years old; attentively he listened to the conversations his mother had with the governess (the one Apollon Apollonovich had shown the door); and Anna Petrovna – exclaimed ecstatically:

'Zizi and I; and behind us again there will be *two tails*; we'll go to the exhibition; with our *tails* behind us, to the exhibition . . .'

'No, what brazenry!'

Kolenka saw before him an enormous room, a crowd, the rustle of dresses and so on (he had once been taken to an exhibition): and in the distance, hanging suspended in space, enormous, black-brown *tails* floating out of the crowd: as a child, Nikolai Apollonovich had never been able to understand that Countess Zizi called her social admirers *tails*.

But this absurd memory of tails hanging suspended in space provoked within him a suppressed sense of alarm; he must go and see the Likhutins: make sure that it was really . . .

That what was 'really'?

In his ears he kept hearing the ticking of a watch: ticky-tock, ticky-tock; the hand ran round in a circle; only of course it did not run here – in these gleaming rooms (under a rug, for example, where any of them might accidentally place a foot on it . . .), but – in a black cesspool, in a field, in a river: kept up its 'ti-cky-tock'; the hand ran round in a circle – until the fateful hour . . .

What nonsense!

All this came from the senator's dreadful joke, which was a truly grand one . . . in its tastelessness; everything had come from that: the memory of the black-brown tails, floating out of space, and – the memory of the bomb.

'What is it, Kolenka, you seem distracted: and you're not eating your cream? . . .'

'Ah, yes-yes . . .'

. . . .

After dinner he strolled through this unlighted hall; the hall glowed faintly; both with moonlight and with the lace of a street lamp; here he strolled about the little squares of the parqueted floor: Apollon Apollonovich; with him – Nikolai Apollonovich; they stepped across: out of the shadow – into the lace of the street lamp's light; stepped across – out of this bright lace – into the shadow. With an unaccustomed trustful gentleness, his head inclined low, Apollon Apollonovich said: half to his son, and half to himself:

'You know – thou knowest: it is a difficult position – to be a man of state.'

They turned around.

'I told them all: no, promoting the import of American sheafing-machines is not such a trifling matter; there is more humanitarianism in it than there is in windy speeches . . . Public law teaches us . . .'

They walked back over the little squares of the parqueted floor; they stepped across; out of the shadow – into the lunar gleaming of shoals.

'All the same, we need humanitarian principles; humanism is a great cause, achieved through much suffering by such intellects as Giordano Bruno, as . . .'

For a long time yet did they wander here.

Apollon Apollonovich spoke in a cracked voice; sometimes he took his son by a button of his frock-coat with two fingers: he moved his lips right up to his son's ear.

'Kolenka, they're windbags: humanitarianism, humanitarianism! . . . There is more humanitarianism in sheafing-machines: we need sheafing-machines! . . .'

Here he put his free arm around his son's waist, drawing him over to the window – into the corner; muttered and swayed his head; they no longer took him into account, he was not needed:

'Thou knowest – they've passed me by!'

Nikolai Apollonovich did not dare to believe his ears; yes, how naturally it had all happened – without explanation, without a storm, without confessions: this whispering in a corner, this fatherly caress.

Then why all these years had he . . . – ?

'Yes, Kolenka, *mon petit ami*: you and I shall be more frank with each other . . .'

'What did you say? I can't hear you . . .'

Past the windows flew the crazy, piercing whistling of a small steamer; brightly the fiery lantern at its stern, almost obliquely, disappeared into the mist; ruby-coloured circles expanded. With trustful gentleness, his head inclined low, Apollon Apollonovich spoke: half to his son, and half to himself. They stepped across: out of the shadow into the lace of the light from the street lamp; stepped across: out of this light lace – into the shadow.

. . . .

Apollon Apollonovich – small, bald and old, – illumined by the flashes of the dying coals, on the small mother-of-pearl table he began to lay out a game of patience; it was two and a half years since he had laid out a game of patience; thus had he become

imprinted on Anna Petrovna's memory; this had been two and a
half years ago: before their fateful conversation; the bald little figure
had sat at this same table and at this pack of patience.

'The ten . . .'

'No, my dear, it's blocked . . . And in spring – you know what: I
think we might go to Prolyotnoe, Anna Petrovna.' (Prolyotnoe was
the Ableukhovs' family estate: Apollon Apollonovich had not been
in Prolyotnoe for some twenty years.)

There, beyond the ice, the snow and the jagged line of the forest
he had, by a stupid accident, nearly frozen to death, some fifty years
ago; at that hour of his lonely freezing it had been as though
someone's cold fingers had stroked his heart; the icy hand had
beckoned; behind him – the centuries had receded in immeasurability: ahead of him – the hand revealed: immeasurabilities; the immeasurabilities flew towards him. The icy hand!

And – now: it was melting.

For Apollon Apollonovich, as he relieved himself of his post,
remembered for the first time: the melancholy district distances, the
smoke of the hamlets; and – the jackdaw.

'What do you say, let us to Prolyotnoe: there are so many flowers
there.'

And Anna Petrovna, getting carried away again, spoke excitedly
of the beauties of the palaces of the Alhambra; but in her transport
of ecstasy, it must be admitted, she forgot that she was going off
key, that she was saying 'we' instead of 'I', and 'we' meant:
'Mindalini – (Mantalini⁴ – so it would appear) – and I'.

'*We* arrived in the morning in a charming little carriage drawn by
donkeys; *our* team, Kolechka, had these large pompons; and you
know, Apollon Apollonovich, *we* got used to them . . .'

Apollon Apollonovich listened, moved the cards about; and –
abandoned them: he did not finish the game of patience; he sat
hunched and round-shouldered in his armchair, illumined by the
bright purple of the coals; several times he grasped at the arm of
the Empire armchair, preparing to jump to his feet; yet he evidently realized in the nick of time that he would be committing an
act of indiscretion, were he to interrupt this verbal flood in mid-
sentence; and fell back into the armchair again; now and then he
yawned.

At last he tearfully observed:
'I must admit: I'm tired . . .'
And moved from the armchair – into a rocking chair.

. . . .

Nikolai Apollonovich offered to see his mother to her hotel; as he came out of the drawing-room, he turned round to face his father; from the rocking chair – he saw (so it seemed to him) – a melancholy gaze, fixed upon him; sitting in the rocking chair, Apollon Apollonovich swung it slightly with a nod of his head and a motion of his foot; this was his last conscious perception; he did not see his father again; and in the country, at sea, and in the mountains, in cities – in the dazzling halls of important European museums – he remembered that gaze; and it seemed: Apollon Apollonovich was consciously saying farewell – with a nod of his head and a motion of his foot: that old face, the quiet creaking of the rocking chair; and – the gaze, the gaze!

The Watch

Nikolai Apollonovich accompanied his mother to the hotel; and after that, he turned on to the Moika; there was darkness in the windows of the little flat: the Likhutins were not at home; there was nothing for it: he turned and went off home.

Now he hobbled into his bedroom; for a moment, he stood in the most complete darkness; shadows, shadows and shadows; the lace of the light from the street lamp cut the ceiling; out of habit, he lit a candle; and took off his watch; absent-mindedly he looked at it: three o'clock.

Now it all rose up again.

He realized that his fears had not been overcome; the certainty that had endured all that evening had disappeared somewhere; and everything had become – unsteady; he wanted to take a bromide; there was no bromide; he wanted to read 'Revelation'; there was no 'Revelation'; just then a distinct, troubling sound flew to his ears: 'ticky-tock, ticky-tock' – he heard softly; was it the sardine tin?

And this thought took hold of him.

But it did not torment him; something else did: his old sense of delirium; forgotten by a day; and emerging by night:

'Pepp Peppovich . . . Pepp . . .'

It was he; swelling into a colossus, from the fourth dimension he was penetrating the yellow house; and was rushing about the rooms; sticking with invisible surfaces to his soul; and his soul was becoming a surface: yes, the surface of an enormous and rapidly growing bubble, swollen into Saturn's orbit . . . ai-ai-ai: Nikolai Apollonovich felt distinctly cold; winds wafted against his forehead; after that, everything began to burst: became simple.

And – the watch ticked.

Nikolai Apollonovich reached towards the sound that exasperated him; sought the location of the sound; his boots creaking, he softly crept towards the table; the ticking was growing louder; but right by the table – it disappeared.

'Ticky-tock,' – he heard softly from the shadowy corner; and he crept back again: from the desk to the corner; shadows, shadows and shadows; the silence of the grave . . .

Nikolai Apollonovich began to pant, rushing about with candle outstretched amidst the dance of the shadows; he kept trying to detect the fluttering sound (thus do children pursue a little yellow butterfly with nets).

Now he took the right direction; the strange sound revealed itself; the ticking could be heard distinctly: in a moment he would intercept it (this time the butterfly would not get away).

Where, where, where?

And when he began to seek the point from which the sound was spreading, he immediately found that point: in his own stomach; indeed: an enormous heaviness was pulling his stomach.

Nikolai Apollonovich saw that he was standing beside the night table; and at the level of his stomach, on the surface of the little table, ticked . . . the watch he had taken off; he looked at it absent-mindedly: four o'clock.

He returned to his old idea (second lieutenant Likhutin had taken the bomb away); the sense of delirium was disappearing; so too was the heaviness in his stomach; quickly he threw off his frock-coat and trousers; with pleasure unbuttoned his starched linen: collar, shirt; he pulled off his long johns: on his leg, where the knee was, a bloody bruise was conspicuous; and the knee had swollen; now his legs had gone down into the snow-white sheet, but – he reflected, leaning on his arm; the features of the icon-like countenance stood out white upon white.

And – the candle went out.

The watch ticked; complete darkness surrounded him; and in the darkness the ticking began to flutter again like a little butterfly taking off from a flower: now here; now there; and – his thoughts ticked; in different parts of his inflamed body – the thoughts throbbed like pulses: in his neck, in his throat, in his arms, in his head; even in his solar plexus.

The pulses ran across his body, chasing one another.

And, lagging behind his body, they were outside his body, forming a throbbing and conscious contour to every side of him; half an arshin away; and – more; here he quite distinctly realized that it was not he who was thinking, or rather: it was not his brain that was thinking, but this throbbing, conscious contour outlined outside his brain; in this contour all the pulses, or projections of pulses, were instantly transformed into thoughts that concocted themselves; a stormy life was, in its turn, progressing in his eyeballs; the ordinary points that were visible in the light and projected in space – now flared up like sparks; leapt out of their orbits into space; began to dance around him, forming a tiresome tinsel, forming a swarming cocoon – of lights: half an arshin away; and – more; this was what the pulsation was: now it flared up.

This was also what the swarms of thoughts that thought themselves were.

The spider's web of these thoughts – he realized – did not at all think what the owner of that web would like to think, or rather, not at all what he tried to think with the help of his brain, and that – it ran away from the brain (to tell the truth – the brain's convolutions merely strained; there were no thoughts in them); only the pulses thought, as they showered diamonds – of sparks and little stars; over this golden swarm ran a kind of photopod, reverberating in it like an affirmation.

'But it's ticking, it's ticking . . .'

Another one ran past . . .

What thought itself was an affirmation of the situation that his brain rejected, and with which it obstinately struggled: the sardine tin was here, the sardine tin was here; the hand was running round it; the hand had grown weary of running: it was running to the fateful point (that point was already near) . . . Now the luminous, fluttering pulses showered frantically, like the sparks of a bonfire if you gave the bonfire a good bang with a cudgel – now they showered: beneath them a kind of blue insubstantiality revealed itself, from which a flashing centre instantly pierced the perspiration-covered head of the person who had lain down here, with its prickly and trembling lights resembling a gigantic spider that had run here from other worlds, and – reflecting itself in his brain: –

> – unendurable roars would resound, roars you might not be able to hear, because before they struck your eardrum, you would have a shattered eardrum (and a few other things as well) –
>> – The blue insubstantiality had disappeared with it – the flashing centre beneath the onrushing luminous tinsel; but with a mad movement Nikolai Apollonovich flew out of bed at this point: the current of thoughts that were not thought by him instantly turned into pulses; the pulses attacked and throbbed: in his temple, his throat, his neck, his arms, and . . . not outside these organs.

He thudded on bare feet; and ended up in the wrong place: not at the door, but in a corner.

It was getting light.

Quickly he threw on his long johns and thudded into the dark corridor: why, why? Oh, he was simply afraid . . . He had simply been gripped by an animal instinct for his precious life; but he did not want to go back from the corridor; he did not have the courage to look into his rooms; he had neither the strength nor the time to go searching for the bomb again; everything in his head had got mixed up, and he could remember neither the minute nor the hour when the time would expire: any moment could turn out to be the fatal one. What remained was for him to shiver here in the corridor until it was properly daylight.

And withdrawing into the corner, he squatted down.

Meanwhile the moments were slowly expiring within him; the minutes seemed hours; many hundreds of hours had already flowed by; the corridor turned dark blue; the corridor turned grey: proper daylight was beginning.

Nikolai Apollonovich was more and more convinced of the nonsensicality of the thoughts that thought themselves; these thoughts were now inside his brain; and his brain coped with them; and when he decided that the time had long ago expired, the version of the sardine tin's having been taken away by the second lieutenant somehow diffused itself of its own accord around him in the vapours of the most blissful images, and Nikolai Apollonovich, squatting down in the corridor – whether out of a sense of safety, or out of tiredness – well, well: he took a nap.

He came to when something slippery touched him on the forehead; and, opening his eyes, he saw – the slavering muzzle of the bulldog: in front of him the bulldog was snorting, and wagging its tail; indifferently he fended off the bulldog with his hand and was about to resume what he had been doing before: to continue something over there; twirl some vortices to the end, in order to make a discovery. And – suddenly realized: why was he on the floor?

Why was he in the corridor?

Half asleep, he trudged off back to his room: as he approached his bed, he was still twirling his sleepy vortices to an end . . .

– There was a roar: he understood everything.

. . . .

– Afterwards, on long winter evenings, Nikolai Apollonovich often returned to the heavy roar; it was a peculiar roar, not comparable with anything else; deafening and – not sharp in the slightest; deafening and – hollow: with a metallic, bass, oppressive quality; and after it, everything died away.

. . . .

Soon voices were heard, the uneven thud of bare feet and the quiet howling of the bulldog; the telephone began to rattle: at last he opened the door of his room; a jet of cold wind burst against his chest; and the room was filled with lemon-yellow smoke; in the jet of wind and the smoke, he stumbled quite incongruously over some kind of splintered thing; and he more sensed than understood that it was a piece of the shattered door. There was the pile of cold bricks, there were the shadows, running: out of the smoke; singed shreds of rugs – how had they got there? Now one of the shadows, thrusting itself through the pall of smoke, barked rudely at him.

'Hey, what are you doing here: can't you see there's been a disaster in the house?'

And another voice rang out there; and – one heard:

'The scoundrels, they all ought to be . . .'

'It's me,' he ventured.

He was interrupted.

'A bomb . . .'

'Ai!'

'Yes, a bomb . . . it exploded . . .'

'?'

'In Apollon Apollonovich's room . . . in his study . . .'

'?'

'Thank God, he's unharmed and all right . . .'

Let us remind the reader: Apollon Apollonovich had absent-mindedly taken the sardine tin out of his son's room into his study; and had forgotten about it altogether; he was, of course, in ignorance as to the sardine tin's contents.

Nikolai Apollonovich ran over to the place where the door had been only a moment before; and where – there was now no door: there was an enormous gaping hole, from which clouds of smoke were coming; if you had looked into the street, you would have seen: a crowd was gathering; a policeman was pushing it back off the pavement; and gawpers gaped, their heads thrown back, as from the black holes of the windows and from the crack that had been cut across the house, yellowish-lemon clouds ominously gushed out.

. . . . , . . .

Nikolai Apollonovich, himself not knowing why, went running back away from the gaping hole; and ended up he knew not where –

– on the snow-white bed (right on the pillow!) sat Apollon Apollonovich, pressing his bare legs against his hairy chest; and he was in his undershirt; embracing his knees in his arms, he was unrestrainedly – not sobbing, but roaring; in the general hubbub he had been forgotten; with him there was no lackey ... not even Semyonych; there was no one to comfort him; and there, all on his own ... to the point of strain, of hoarseness ... –

– Nikolai Apollonovich rushed towards this helpless little body as a nurse rushes in the middle of the roadway towards the three-year-old mite that has been entrusted to her, and which she has forgotten in the middle of the roadway; but this helpless little body – the mite – at the sight of the son running towards it – leapt up from the pillow and – waved its arms: with indescribable horror and with an unchildlike sprightliness.

· And – how he launched himself into flight, leaping into the corridor!

With a cry of 'Stop him!', Nikolai Apollonovich ran after him: after this mad little figure (though actually, which of them was mad?); they both rushed into the depths of the corridor past the smoke and the rags and the gestures of thundering persons (some fire or other was being put out); the flickering of these strangely bawling little figures was eerie – in the depths of the corridor; the undershirt fluttered in flight; their heels thudded, fleeted; Nikolai Apollonovich launched himself in pursuit, hopping, limping on his right leg; he gripped his falling long johns in one hand; while with his other hand he strove to grasp hold of the fluttering hem of his father's undershirt.

He ran, shouting:

'Wait ...

'Where are you going?'

'But stop!'

Having run all the way to the door that led to the place that had no comparison, Apollon Apollonovich caught hold of the door with a cunning inaccessible to the mind; and in a most rapid fashion found himself in that place: bolted into that place.

For a moment, Nikolai Apollonovich shrank back from the door; for a moment, distinctly engraved were: the turn of the head, the sweaty brow, the lips, the side-whiskers and the eyes that shone like molten stone; the door slammed shut; everything vanished; the door catch clicked; he had bolted into that place.

Nikolai Apollonovich hammered desperately at the door; and beseeched – to the point of strain, of hoarseness:

'Open up . . .

'Let me in . . .'

– And –

'Aaa . . . aaa . . . aaa . . .'

He collapsed in front of the door.

He dropped his arms to his knees; threw his head into his hands; at this point he lost consciousness; with a thudding of feet, the lackeys came running towards him. They dragged him into his room.

Here we shall place a full stop.

We shall not enter into describing how the fire was put out, how the senator, in a most violent fit of palpitations, explained himself to the police: after this explanation there was a conference of specialist doctors: the doctors found him to be suffering from a dilation of the aorta. And yet: during all the days of the strike, in the chanceries, offices, ministerial chambers he made his appearance – exhausted and thin; his powerful little bass voice rumbled persuasively – in the chanceries, offices, ministerial chambers – with a hollow, oppressive quality. We shall merely observe: he succeeded in proving something. Someone out there was arrested; and then – was released because of insufficient evidence; connections were brought into play; and the case was dropped. No one else was apprehended. Throughout all these days his son lay in attacks of nervous fever, never once recovering consciousness; and when he came to, he saw that he was alone with his mother; there was no longer anyone else in the lacquered house. Apollon Apollonovich had moved to the country estate and stayed there all that winter amidst the snow, taking an indefinite vacation; and from that vacation went into retirement. Before doing so, he prepared for his son: a passport for foreign travel, and money. Ableukhova, Anna Petrovna, accompanied Nikolenka. She did not return until the summer: Nikolai Apollonovich did not return to Russia until his father's decease.

END OF THE EIGHTH CHAPTER

EPILOGUE

The February sun is on the wane.[1] Shaggy cactuses are scattered here and there. Soon, soon from the gulf to the shore, sails will come flying; they fly: angularly winged, swaying; a small cupola has receded into the cactuses.

Nikolai Apollonovich, in a blue gandurah,[2] in a bright-red Arabian chechia,[3] freezes in a squatting position; an extremely long tassel falls from his chechia; his silhouette is distinctly sculpted against the flat roof; beneath him are the village square and the sounds of a tom-tom: they strike the ears with a hollow, oppressive quality.

Everywhere there are the white cubes of the wretched little village houses; a bellowing Berber is driving on a little donkey with shouts; a heap of branches shows silver on the donkey; the Berber is olive-coloured.

Nikolai Apollonovich does not hear the sounds of the tom-tom; and he does not see the Berber; he sees what is standing in front of him: Apollon Apollonovich – bald, small, old – sitting in a rocking chair, swinging the rocking chair with a nod of his head and a motion of his foot; he remembers this movement . . .

In the distance an almond tree shows pink; that jagged peak is bright violet and amber; that peak is Zaghouan,[4] and that cape is Cape Carthage. Nikolai Apollonovich has rented a cottage from an Arab in a coastal village near Tunis.

. . . .

Beneath the weight of sparkling, snowy caps, the fir boughs have sagged: shaggy and green; ahead is a five-columned wooden building; snowdrifts have flung themselves over the railings of the terrace-like hills; there is on them the pink reflection of a February sunset.

A small, round-shouldered figure has appeared – in warm felt boots, mittens, leaning on a stick; its fur collar is raised; a fur hat is pulled down over its ears; it is making its way along a cleared path; it is being helped along by the arm; the figure that is doing the helping has a warm rug in its hand.

Spectacles have appeared on Apollon Apollonovich in the country; they have steamed up in the frost and through them neither the jagged forest distances nor the smoke of the tiny villages, nor the jackdaws have been visible; shadows are visible, and more shadows; between them are the lunar gleaming of shoals and the little squares of the parqueted floor; Nikolai Apollonovich is tender, attentive, sensitive – with his head inclined low, he steps across – out of the shadow – into the lace of the light from the street lamp; steps across: out of that bright lace – into the shadow.

In the evening the little old man sits at the table in his room amidst round frames; and in the frames there are portraits: of an officer in buckskin breeches, of an old woman in a satin head-dress; the officer is his father; the old woman in the head-dress is his deceased mother, née Svargina. The little old man is scribbling his memoirs, so that they may see the light in the year of his death.

They have seen the light.

Those most witty memoirs: Russia knows them.

. . . .

The sun's flame is impetuous: it burns crimson in your eyes; you turn away, and – it strikes you frenziedly in the back of your neck; it makes even the desert seem greenish and deathly pale: as a matter of fact, life is deathly pale; it would be good to remain here for ever – by the deserted shore.

In a thick pith helmet with a veil that has come unwound in the wind, Nikolai Apollonovich has sat down on a heap of sand; before him is an enormous, mouldering head – very soon now it will collapse into sandstone thousands of years old; – Nikolai Apollonovich has been sitting before the Sphinx for hours.

Nikolai Apollonovich has been here for two years; he is studying in the museum at Bulaq.[5] The 'Book of the Dead'[6] – and the writings of Manetho[7] have been interpreted wrongly; here, for the searching eye, there is a wide expanse: Nikolai Apollonovich has vanished in Egypt; and in the twentieth century he foresees Egypt;

all culture is like this mouldering head: everything has died; nothing has remained.

It is good that he is thus engaged: sometimes, tearing himself from his schemes, it begins to seem to him that not everything has yet died; there are some kind of sounds; these sounds roar in Cairo: it is a peculiar roar; it resembles – that same sound: deafening and – hollow: with a metallic, bass, oppressive quality; and Nikolai Apollonovich – is drawn to mummies; that 'incident' has led him to mummies. Kant? Kant is forgotten.

It has begun to be evening: and into the sunsetless twilight the piles of Gizeh[8] stretch monstrously and threateningly; everything is expanded in them; and everything expands from them, in the dust that hangs in the air, dark brown lights begin to burn; and – it is stiflingly oppressive.

Nikolai Apollonovich has leaned reflectively against the dead side of a pyramid.

. . . .

In an armchair, in the full blaze of the sun, the little old man sat motionless: he kept looking at the old woman with his enormous cornflower-coloured eyes; his legs were wrapped in a rug (he had evidently lost the use of them); on his knees bunches of white lilacs had been placed; the little old man kept stretching towards the old woman, leaning out of the armchair with his whole body:

'You say he's finished it? . . . Then perhaps he'll come?'

'Yes: he's putting his papers in order . . .'

Nikolai Apollonovich had finally brought his monograph to an end.

'What is it called?'

And – the little old man beamed:

'The monograph is called . . . em-em-em . . . "On the Instruction of Duauf".'[9] Apollon Apollonovich forgot absolutely everything: forgot the names of ordinary objects; but that word – Duauf – he firmly remembered; Kolenka had written about 'Duauf'. One throws back one's head and looks upwards, and there is the gold of green leaves: stormily it rages: blue sky and fleecy clouds and a little wagtail was running along the path.

'He's in Nazareth, you say?'

Oh, and the thick mass of the bluebells! The bluebells were opening their lilac jaws; right there, amidst the bluebells, stood a movable armchair; and in it a wrinkled Apollon Apollonovich, with unshaven stubble showing silver on his cheeks – beneath a canvas sunshade.

. . . .

In 1913 Nikolai Apollonovich still continued to stroll about the fields, the meadows, the forests for days on end, observing the work in the fields with morose indolence; he had a peaked cap on; he wore a camel-coloured sleeveless jacket; his boots squeaked; a golden, wedge-shaped beard had changed him strikingly; while a lock of perfect silver stood out distinctly in the cap of his hair; this lock had appeared suddenly; his eyes had begun to ache in Egypt; he began to wear dark blue spectacles. His voice had grown coarser, while his face was covered in sunburn; his speed of movement was gone; he lived alone; he never invited anyone to see him; he never visited anyone; he was seen in church; it is said that of late he had been reading the philosopher Skovoroda.[10]

His parents were dead.

THE END

NOTES

1 **Our Russian Empire ... et cetera**: this is a parody of the official title of the Russian Tsar, which included about sixty names of the lands and territories he ruled, and ended 'et cetera, et cetera, et cetera' (*i prochaya, i prochaya, i prochaya*). Rus is an archaic form of the name for Russia.

2 **downgraded**: in Russian, *zashtatny*. A bureaucratic term that meant that a town was no longer the centre of an administrative district.

3 **Tsargrad**: the Old Russian name for Constantinople. Nineteenth-century Russian nationalists liked to assert Russia's claim to Constantinople, and Bely is making an ironic comment on this.

4 **right of inheritance**: the Right of Inheritance was founded on the cultural and political relations between Russia and Byzantium.

5 **Piter**: the popular and colloquial name for Petersburg is derived from the Dutch, Pieter. Pieterburg is actually a Dutch name, which Peter the Great intended to vie with Amsterdam, the city on which its design and planning were modelled.

6 **for the public**: in Russian, *publichnyi dom* (literally, public house) means brothel. There is some obvious ironic humour here.

7 **It only seems to exist**: here Bely is following the tradition, established by Gogol and continued by Dostoyevsky, of depicting Petersburg as an unreal city.

CHAPTER THE FIRST

1 **It was a dreadful time**: these lines are from Pushkin's long poem *The Bronze Horseman*, though Bely quotes them in a slightly altered form (*O nei* instead of *Ob nei*).

2 **the very progenitor of the Semitic, Hessitic and red-skinned peoples**: this is sheer wordplay, delivered in the humorous tradition of the eighteenth-century English novel, to which this opening paragraph pays tribute. 'Hessitic' is an invention, and 'red-skinned' has an ironic connotation here.

3 **the Kirghiz–Kaisak Horde**: the name given to the nomadic Kirghiz people during the eighteenth and nineteenth centuries. The Kirghiz were related to the Mongols who had once subjugated Russia. Russian noblemen (including the eighteenth-century poet Derzhavin) liked to trace their ancestry back to real or imaginary Mongol antecedents.

4 **Anna Ioannovna**: niece of Peter the Great, and Russian empress from 1730 to 1740.

5 **Mirza Ab-Lai**: probably a reference to the sultan and khan of the Middle Kirghiz Horde, Ablai (d. 1781). Bely may also have derived the name Ableukhov from the ancient Russian Obleukhov family, two descendants of which came to occupy a prominent position in Russian literary life at the turn of the century. N.D. Obleukhov was the editor of the weekly periodical *Znamya* (1899–1901) and other conservative publications, while his brother, A.D. Obleukhov, was a poet who translated Alfred de Musset. The Obleukhovs were well known in the symbolist circles that Bely frequented.

6 **Ukhov**: in Russian, *ukho* means ear.

7 *Heraldic Guide to the Russian Empire*: *Obschii gerbovnik dvoryanskikh rodov Vserossiiskoi Imperii, nachatyi v 1797 godu*, a publication that gave illustrations and descriptions of noble coats of arms.

8 **the blue sash**: the blue sash was worn with the medal of Andrei Pervozvanny – one of the most important decorations that could be bestowed by the Russian Empire.

9 **rejected in the appropriate quarters**: an allusion to the fierce resistance offered by Konstantin Pobedonostsev (head of the Russian Holy Synod) to any attempts at liberal reform.

10 **the Ninth Department**: a Department was a section of a higher government institution. Gogol mentions one in his story 'The Overcoat' (1841), and it is this link with Gogol that Bely is consciously trying to establish here.

11 **the head of that department**: a reference to Vyacheslav Konstanti-

novich Plehve (1846–1904), Minister of the Interior and Chief of the Gendarmes, who was assassinated with a bomb on 15 July 1904 by the Social Revolutionary E.S. Sazonov.

12 **My senator**: the members of the Senate – Russia's highest legislative and administrative organ – were drawn from the three highest ranks in the government and military service. Their uniform consisted of gold-trimmed jacket and white trousers.

13 **a humorous little street journal**: the events of 1905 gave rise to the publication of a very large number of small political and satirical journals. In his memoirs, Bely mentions caricatures of Witte, and 'Pobedonostsev's green ears'.

14 **real privy councillor**: the second highest rank in the Table of Ranks, established by Peter the Great.

15 **Count Doublevé**: Count 'W', i.e. Count Witte. Sergei Yul'yevich Witte (1849–1915) was Minister of Finance from 1892 to 1903, and was one of Alexander III's closest advisors. He was largely responsible for many bourgeois reforms in pre-revolutionary Russian society, and in many ways may be seen as a liberal. He headed the Russian side of the peace negotiations that concluded the Russo-Japanese War and were held in Portsmouth, New Hampshire, USA, in the summer of 1905.

16 *borona*: the Russian word is pronounced baranáh – making the pun more obvious.

17 **the islands**: Kamenny, Krestovsky and Yelagin Islands, which are enclosed by the two arms of the Bolshaya Nevka river. Bely also includes the large and mostly working-class Vasily Island in this expression.

18 **yellow house**: in Bely's novel, as in Dostoyevsky's *Crime and Punishment*, yellow is the prevailing colour. It is the colour of central Petersburg, its residences and its official buildings. In Bely's case, however, the matter is somewhat complicated by the fact that the yellow colour also symbolizes the Asiatic East, which has invaded the Europeanness of Peter the Great's creation.

19 **tramcars ... 1905**: the first tramline in Petersburg was opened on 15 September 1907.

20 **the equestrian monument of the Emperor Nicholas**: the monument to Nicholas I on Mariinskaya Square, designed by Montferrand and

executed between 1856 and 1859 by the sculptors Klodt, Ramazanov and Zaleman. At this and other monuments to Russia's former rulers, a soldier stood on guard.

21 **the ending of life's way**: an ironic comment on the fact that so many senior government officials were assassinated by terrorists between 1901 and 1907.

22 **the gold needle**: the spire of the Admiralty building, referred to as the 'Admiralty needle' by Pushkin in *The Bronze Horseman*. The needle is a constant motif throughout the novel, and 'The Admiralty Needle' was one possible alternative title considered by Bely.

23 **the Flying Dutchman**: this image of the legendary sea-captain eternally doomed to roam the stormy seas with his ship merges in Bely's novel with the image of Peter the Great – the connection is made plausible by the fact that Peter lived for a time in Holland.

24 **German Sea**: the older Russian name for the North Sea.

25 **Noses**: here, and in the passage that follows, Bely introduces a reminiscent allusion to Gogol's short story 'The Nose' (1835). There is also possibly a reference to a popular rhyme that was current among the Petersburg public in 1905 concerning the president of the Executive Committee of the Soviet of Workers' Deputies, G.S. Khrustalev-Nosar (1877–1918) – his surname translates as 'Noser' – and the Prime Minister, Witte, whose nose, according to the writer Yu. P. Annenkov, was 'unnoticeable in profile, like that of Gogol's Major Kovalyov':

> Of premiers the Russians have acquired
> An inventory rich and rare:
> One premier has no nose at all,
> The other premier is Nosar.

26 *raznochinets* (plural, *raznochintsy*): the Russian word means 'an individual of no definite social rank', and was used to describe intellectuals who did not belong to the gentry. Turgenev's Bazarov (in *Fathers and Sons*) is perhaps the best-known example of such a type in Russian literature.

27 **The parallel lines ... Peter**: Vasily Island was built and planned by the architect Trezini, following instructions from Peter the Great. There were to have been parallel canals, on the model of the canals of Amsterdam, but the project was never brought to completion, and the unrealized canals were subsequently called lines.

28 **Stolovaya**: public dining-room.

29 **the past fateful five years**: the first five years of the twentieth century, which Bely viewed as the watershed between two historical eras.

30 **China . . . fallen**: a reference to the Boxer Rebellion of May 1900, and to the conclusion, in January 1905, of the Russo-Japanese War, which dealt a humiliating blow to Russia's national pride.

31 **Coursistes**: in Russian, *kursistochki*, the diminutive form of *kursistki*, who were young women attending classes at universities and other places of higher learning. Women were not formally accepted as students at the Russian universities.

32 **the *plaisirs* of Peterhof's nature**: a reference to the Summer Palace, 'Mon Plaisir', built at Peterhof (Peter the Great's summer residence outside Petersburg) from 1714 to 1723.

33 **picon**: a kind of essence that was added to alcoholic drinks.

34 **Konstantin Konstantinovich**: Grand Duke Konstantin Konstantinovich Romanov (1858–1915), Nicholas I's grandson, and a poet who published verses under the initials K.R.

35 **And he is not**: a quotation from Pushkin's unfinished Lyceum poem 'There was a time . . .' (*Byla pora . . .*).

36 **Vyacheslav Konstantinovich**: Vyacheslav Konstantinovich Plehve.

37 **And now it seems**: a quotation from Pushkin's Lyceum poem 'The more often the Lyceum celebrates . . .' (*Chem chashche prazdnuyet litsei . . .*, 1831).

38 **And o'er the earth**: another quotation from *Byla pora . . .*

39 **Panteleimon**: sometimes referred to as Pantaleon, 'The All-Merciful'. A medieval physician who became one of the patron saints of physicians, and is much revered in the Russian Orthodox Church, where his name is invoked in prayers for those who suffer from 'demonic possession' and mental illness. His bones are interred at the monastery on Mount Athos.

40 **What is truth?**: the question addressed by Pontius Pilate to Christ (John 18:38).

41 **Our Bat**: Pobedonostsev was frequently depicted in satirical caricatures as a bat or nocturnal bird.

42 **collegiate registrar**: according to the civil service Table of Ranks, a collegiate registrar belonged to the last, or fourteenth class, while a state councillor belonged to the fifth class.

43 **Liza's shadow**: a reminiscent allusion to a scene from Tchaikovsky's opera *The Queen of Spades* (1890). Abandoned by Hermann, Liza throws herself into the Winter Canal.

44 **Hercules and Poseidon**: sculptures that ornament the façade of the Winter Palace.

45 **Nikolayevka**: a greatcoat with a pelerine, of the kind that became fashionable during the reign of Nicholas I.

CHAPTER THE SECOND

1 **I myself, though in books**: the epigraph to this chapter is taken from Pushkin's unfinished long poem *Yezersky* (1832).

2 **the *Comrade***: a Petersburg radical newspaper, though it was not published there until 1906.

3 **Daryalsky**: the hero of Bely's novel *The Silver Dove*, who is killed by sectarians.

4 **the Chernyshev Bridge**: a bridge across the Fontanka.

5 **Angel Peri**: the name is derived in an ironic manner from a poem by Zhukovsky, 'The Peri and the Angel' (*Peri i Angel*, 1821), which is a translation of the second part of Thomas Moore's long poem *Lalla Rookh*. **Peri**: 'evil genius, malevolent elf or sprite ... one of several beautiful but malevolent female demons employed by Ahriman to bring comets and eclipses, prevent rain, cause failure of crops and dearth, etc.; in mod. Persian, poetically represented as a beautiful or graceful being (cf. *fairy* in Eng.) ... In Persian mythology, one of a race of superhuman beings, originally represented as of evil or malevolent character, but subsequently as good genii, fairies, or angels, endowed with grace and beauty' (*Oxford English Dictionary*). In nineteenth-century England, Europe and Russia, 'Peri' was often used as a complimentary epithet addressed to a woman of high society, in the sense of 'fair one'.

6 **Hadusai**: the great Japanese painter and graphic artist Katsushika Hokusai (1760–1849).

7 **Duncan and Nikisch**: Sofya Petrovna uses the French pronunciation of the names of Isadora Duncan (1878–1927), the American dancer, and Arthur Nikisch (1855–1922), the celebrated Hungarian orchestral conductor. According to received Russian pronunciation, the stress would fall on the first syllable of each surname.

8 **meloplastics**: *meloplastika*, a word invented by Bely as a humorous slip for *mimoplyaska* (mime-dance), a term invented in 1908 by the ballet critic Nikolai Vashkevich, with reference to Duncan's dancing. Sofya Petrovna's confusion is made all the more grotesque by the fact that *meloplastika* also suggests *metalloplastika* (metalloplastics), a craft taught to Russian schoolgirls that involved the tracing of designs with a heated needle on specially treated metal plates.

9 **Henri Besançon**: Angel Peri's mind has concocted a somewhat grotesque compound of Henri Bergson and Annie Besant (the theosophist author of *Man and His Bodies*).

10 **the Gregorian Regiment**: the regiment is a fictitious one, though it is given verisimilitude by being placed under the patronage of a foreign monarch – and one of the royal hussar regiments in Russia was in fact headed by King Chakrabon of Siam.

11 *khokhol*-**Little Russian**: i.e. Ukrainian. *Khokhol* is the derogatory Russian name for a Ukrainian, while 'Little Russian' means the same thing – the two expressions form a tautology.

12 **Lippanchenko**: this character is probably modelled on the real-life composer S.V. Panchenko (1867–1937), who was a friend of the poet Blok's wife, Lyubov' Dmitrievna, with whom Bely was for a time infatuated, believing her to be an incarnation of the Holy Sophia invoked in the apocalyptic writings of the philosopher Vladimir Solovyov. Panchenko was obviously perceived by Bely as a rival.

13 *dushkan*: darling (Ukr.).

14 *brankukan, bran-kukashka* or *brankukanchik*: more Ukrainian endearments.

15 **The Red Buffoon**: Bely's image of the 'red buffoon' or 'red jester' is derived from Edgar Allan Poe's short story 'The Masque of the Red Death' (1845). Bely also wrote a verse ballad entitled 'The Buffoon' (*Shut*, 1911) in which a hunchbacked figure in a satin cape is the central character.

16 **Freak, frog**: possibly a reference to another story of Poe's, 'Hop-Frog' (1849).

17 **the Ciniselli Circus**: an indoor circus, housed in a stone building on the Fontanka, that performed during the winter months.

18 **civil servants of the fourth class**: according to the Table of Ranks, these included real state councillors, ober-procurators, master heralds, major generals (in the army) and junior admirals (in the navy).

19 **the fields of bloodstained Manchuria**: most of the fighting in the Russo-Japanese war took place in Manchuria.

20 **crowds inundated ... clergy**: a reference to the funeral of Prince Sergei Nikolayevich Trubetskoy (1862–1905), a noted liberal campaigner. His funeral acquired the character of a political demonstration both in Petersburg and in Moscow.

21 **Peter's little house**: in Russian, *Petrovskiy domik* – Peter the Great's Summer Palace, designed by Trezini and built in the Summer Garden, 1710–1712.

22 **Torricellian vacuum**: the Italian physicist and pupil of Galileo, Evangelista Torricelli (1608–47), devised the mercury barometer, demonstrating the ability of air pressure to support a finite column of mercury. A Torricellian vacuum is an airless space formed above the surface of a liquid in a closed vessel.

23 **Morzhov**: a comical name in Russian, suggesting a walrus. The name also has obscene connotations.

24 **Gregory of Nyssa**: bishop of Nyssa, who lived *c.* 335–94 AD, and one of the Cappadocian Fathers, the younger brother of St Basil the Great. A Platonist, Neoplatonist and ascetic thinker.

25 **Ephraem Syrus**: a fourth-century Christian Church father and ecclesiastical writer (*c.* 306–73).

26 **the Apocalypse**: the Church Slavonic name for 'Revelation', the book of St John the Divine.

27 **academist**: a student of the Ecclesiastical Academy.

28 **Harnack**: Adolf Harnack (1851–1930), German Protestant theologian who preached a Christian morality based on universal brotherhood.

29 **schemonach**: a monk who has taken the *schema*, the highest monastic

rank in the Orthodox Church, demanding the fulfilment of a number of exacting tasks and statutes.

30 **Narodnaya Volya**: the 'People's Will' movement, a populist revolutionary organization.

31 **St George's medal**: a military decoration established by Catherine the Great, and extended to the lower ranks in 1807.

32 **Yakutsk region**: a region of north-eastern Siberia. Many political exiles were sent there.

33 **I was brought out in a pickled cabbage barrel**: an episode from the life of the Socialist Revolutionary activist Grigory Andreyevich Gershuni (1870–1908).

34 **Helsingfors**: the Swedish – and Imperial Russian – name for the capital of Finland, until 1917 a Grand Duchy under the protection of Russia, and a part of its Empire. The city is now called Helsinki (though still known as Helsingfors among the Finnish–Swedish minority).

35 **Kaigorodov**: Dmitry Nikiforovich Kaigorodov (1866–1924), the Russian botanist, entomologist, birdwatcher and pedagogue, whose most famous work was 'From the Kingdom of Our Feathered Friends' (*Iz tsarstva pernatykh*, 1892).

36 **Yesterday the eyes had looked**: there is an apparent inconsistency in Bely's text here: Dudkin's encounter with the senator on Nevsky Prospect and their subsequent meeting in Ableukhov's house take place on the same day.

37 **A certain gloomy building**: probably St Petersburg University.

38 *phytin*: a medicinal preparation that was used in the treatment of nervous disorders, hysteria, et cetera.

39 **the perennial Horseman**: Falconet's equestrian monument to Peter the Great (1782), situated on Senate Square. It cost 450,000 roubles.

40 **Finnish granite**: the base of the monument is a large slab of Finnish granite.

41 **lower your hooves**: the images here are drawn from Pushkin's poem *The Bronze Horseman*.

42 *shaking of the earth*: Bely uses the archaic Russian word for earthquake – *trus*.

43 **Nizhny, Vladimir and Uglich**: Nizhny is also known as Nizhny Novgorod. All three towns are situated north-east of Moscow and represent Russia's medieval past.

44 **Tsushima**: the naval battle at Tsushima on 14–15 May 1905 ended with the complete destruction of a Russian squadron.

45 **Kalka**: the tributary of the river Kalmius at which the Russian Princes and their Cuman allies were defeated by the Mongol–Tartar forces on 21 May 1223.

46 **Kulikovo Field**: the site of the battle between the Russian forces, under the leadership of Dmitry Donskoi, and the Mongol–Tartar army, on 8 September 1380. The battle ended in victory for the Russians.

47 **Mongol mugs**: this is a reference to the Japanese delegation that visited Petersburg in 1905 in order to conclude the peace treaty between Russia and Japan.

48 **Styopka**: Styopka, the son of the shopowner Ivan Stepanov, is a character from Bely's novel *The Silver Dove* (1909). *Petersburg*, which was intended as the second part of the trilogy, contains a number of references to him. In *The Silver Dove* he leaves his native village and disappears into the unknown.

49 **Bessmertny**: the name means 'immortal'.

50 **Tselebeyevo**: the village in which the action of *The Silver Dove* takes place.

51 **strange people**: the mystical sectarians who are the 'doves' in the earlier novel.

52 **a visiting *barin***: a reference to Pyotr Daryalsky, the principal character in *The Silver Dove*. Styopka relates various elements of the novel's plot.

53 **"The First Distiller"**: Lev Tolstoy's folk comedy of the same title (1886), illustrating the evils of drink.

54 **temple**: probably the Buddhist meeting-house in Staraya Derevnya (then a Petersburg suburb), the construction of which lasted from 1909 until 1915, and had the support of the Dalai Lama.

55 **Philadelphia**: in Greek, 'brotherly love'. A town in Lydia, Asia Minor, named after its founder Attala II Philadelphos. It was the seat of one of the seven churches of Asia mentioned in the Book of Revelation (2–3), and offered certain promises for the future there (3:7–13). The

Philadelphian Christians believed that they would be saved from the temptation that would affect the whole world, and their church survived in isolation in the midst of Muslim lands.

56 **the cult of Sophia**: the Greek word σοφία means 'mastery, knowledge, wisdom', a concept associated with the idea of the semantic completeness and organization of things. In the philosophy of Vladimir Solovyov it came to stand for the eternal feminine which he perceived to lie at the base of divinity, the collective mystical body of Logos, and the ideal man. It was closely associated with the Solovyovian concept of the 'universal soul'. Solovyov's poem 'Three Encounters' (*Tri svidaniya*, 1898) describes the philosopher's meetings with the 'eternal friend' – one of these takes place in the reading room of the British Museum.

57 **the Nizhny Novgorod female sectarians**: a reference to Anna Nikolayevna Schmidt (1851–1905), the Nizhny Novgorod mystic who wrote a treatise entitled 'The Third Testament'. She corresponded with Vladimir Solovyov, and Bely met her at the home of the philosopher's brother, M.S. Solovyov, in 1900.

58 **1912**: Bely believed that years ending in 12 played a decisive and mystical role in Russia's fate and history.

59 **Even so, come, Lord Jesus**: cf. Revelation 22:20.

CHAPTER THE THIRD

1 **Though he's an ordinary sort of fellow**: the epigraph is from Pushkin's poem *Yezersky*. Line 6 of Pushkin's original reads *Khot' chelovek on ne voyennyi* ('Though he's no military man'). Bely either misquotes, or uses a non-standard text. Many editions of *Peterburg* have a misprint in line 2, where *Ne* (No) is given as *No* (But).

2 **A Holiday**: 5 October was the name-day of the Tsarevich Alexei, heir to the Russian throne. But the holiday could also have been occasioned by Witte's being made a count after his conclusion of the peace negotiations with the Japanese, which were accounted a great diplomatic success. The official state reception for this event was also on 5 October.

3 **a shot was fired**: the daily cannon-shot from the Peter and Paul Fortress at twelve noon.

4 **from the third class to the first class inclusive**: according to the Table of Ranks established by Peter the Great, there were fourteen classes for each rank.

5 **cavalier of St Anne**: originally a Holstein military decoration, included in the Russian list of honours by Paul I in 1797.

6 **White Eagle**: a Polish military honour, included in the Russian list of honours in 1815.

7 *likhach*: a smart cab and its driver.

8 *bogatyr*: a hero in Russian folklore.

9 **My devachanic friend**: in Sanskrit, Devachan is 'the place of the gods' – for theosophists, the name of heaven.

10 **opoponax**: an aromatic resin with a musky odour, obtained from the plant of the same name.

11 **and from the kingdom of necessity create the kingdom of freedom**: these words originate from a passage in Friedrich Engels's *Anti-Dühring*.

12 **Noble, slender, pale**: there is an obvious similarity between Varvara Yevgrafovna's poem and Pushkin's poem 'Once a poor knight there did live' (*Zhil na svete rytsar' bednyi*, 1829), in its revision of 1835:

> Full of a pure love,
> Faithful to a delightful dream,
> A.M.D. [Ave Mater Dei, tr.] with his blood
> He traced upon his shield.

Dostoyevsky makes much play with these lines in his novel *The Idiot*, and they were also used by Blok as the epigraph to one of his poems ('A.M. Dobrolyubov', 1903).

13 **Apperception**: a Leibnizian term, denoting the transition from a lower to a higher state of consciousness. In Russian, *appertseptsiya* (apperception) and *perets* (pepper) sound very close to each other.

14 **Cohen's *Theorie der Erfahrung***: the book *Kants Theorie der Erfahrung* (1871) by the German philosopher Hermann Cohen (1842–1918), founder of the Marburg School of Neo-Kantianism.

15 **Kant, Comte**: in Russian, the two names differ by only one letter (Kant = *Kant*, Comte = *Kont*).

16 **Mill's *Logic***: John Stuart Mill's *System of Logic* (1843) was a formative influence on nineteenth-century Russian social thought.

17 **Sigwart's *Logic***: the two-volume work (1873–8) by the German Neo-Kantian philosopher Christoph von Sigwart (1830–1904).

18 **professor of the philosophy of law**: an allusion to the life of Pobedo-nostsev, who graduated from the Imperial Law School in 1846 and subsequently occupied the chair of Civil Law.

19 **Bundist-socialist**: the Bund was a national Jewish political organization.

20 **Sow the useful**: an inexact quotation from Nekrasov's poem 'To the Sowers' (*Seyatelyam*, 1876).

21 **a mystical anarchist**: the doctrine of 'mystical anarchism' was developed by the writer Georgii Chulkov in his book *On Mystical Anarchism* (1906), and had a certain following among the Russian Symbolists, though Bely was firmly opposed to it, seeing in it a 'profanation' of Symbolist tenets.

22 **Tam**: a 'musical' exclamation – but the word also means 'there' in Russian.

23 **Gazing at the rays of purple sunset**: a romance by the composer A.A. Oppel, to words by Kozlov. In the original, the second line reads 'We stood upon the bank of the Neva.'

24 ***The Queen of Spades***: Tchaikovsky's opera, based on Pushkin's short story, with its hero, Hermann.

25 **the Code of Laws**: *The Code of Laws of the Russian Empire*, a systematic code of pre-1917 Russian law, published in sixteen volumes.

26 ***tabes dorsalis***: a form of neurosyphilis, affecting the spinal cord.

CHAPTER THE FOURTH

1 **Grant God that I may not go mad**: the epigraph is the first line of an untitled poem by Pushkin (1833) that was never published in the poet's lifetime.

2 **a statue by Irelli**: there is no such statue in the Summer Garden. Bely

may have inadvertently written Irelli instead of Rastrelli – whose equestrian statue of Peter the Great (1743–4) is to be found on Horse Stable Square, near the main entrance of Mikhailovsky Palace.

3 **Maison Tricotons**: possibly the ladies' fashion shop, Maison Annette, at No 25 Nevsky Prospect.

4 **Krafft's**: Krafft's chocolate factory was situated at No 10/5 Italyanskaya Ulitsa.

5 **Ballet's**: a confectioner's shop at No 54 Nevsky Prospect.

6 **rust-red palace**: the Winter Palace in Petersburg, built 1750–61. The palace's original blue-white tint was replaced in the nineteenth century by a dark brown one.

7 **Yelizaveta Petrovna**: daughter of Peter the Great, Empress Elizabeth of Russia (1741–61).

8 **Aleksandr Pavlovich**: Tsar Alexander I (1801–25).

9 **Aleksandr Nikolayevich**: Tsar Alexander II (1855–81).

10 *zemstvo* **official**: a *zemstvo* was an elective district council in pre-1917 Russia.

11 **the editor of a conservative newspaper, the liberal son of a priest**: apparently a reference to the essayist, writer and publisher Aleksei Sergeyevich Suvorin (1834–1912).

12 **Charleston**: Charleston, Virginia, USA, where an influential Masonic lodge was based. Its head was called the 'antipope'. The reference here is to Léo Taxil (see note 17).

13 **liberal professor**: the 'professor of statistics' is, by Bely's own admission, a caricature of the Constitutional Democrat politician Peter Struve, though in his memoirs Bely claimed that he had not consciously intended to reproduce Struve's features.

14 **the Boxers in China**: a reference to the Boxer rebellion of 1900, a revolt by the Society of the Righteous and Harmonious Fists, encouraged by the Dowager Empress Tzu Hsi against foreign domination.

15 **Who art thou**: this quatrain, like the entire scene being described, is closely connected with Bely's poems 'Masquerade' (*Maskarad*, 1908) and 'The Festival' (*Prazdnik*, 1908), which depict the appearance of a fateful red domino at a festive masquerade.

16 **a rustling stream of confetti**: Bely appears to have confused *konfetti* (*confetti*) with *serpentin* (paper streamers).

17 **Taxil**: Léo Taxil, a French anticlerical writer; his real name was Gabriel Antoine Jogand-Pagès (1854–1907). He 'exposed' devil-worship among the Freemasons, but later confessed that his activities had been a hoax.

18 **Palladism**: the highest circle of Freemasonry, and supposedly also of devil-worship.

19 **terrible vengeance**: an allusion to Gogol's story of the same name.

20 **like a sheaf of ripe grain**: this entire passage presents an image of the white domino as a symbol of Christ, standing in opposition both to political terror (the red domino) and to autocracy (the Bronze Horseman).

21 **Vanka**: a familiar name for a cab driver (short for Ivan).

22 **And the light did not shine**: there are overtones here of the Gospel according to St John (1:5).

23 **Word and deed!**: this expression meant, from the fourteenth century until the reign of Catherine II, that the person who uttered it had an important matter to relate concerning a person of state. Thereupon he became involved, as an informer, in the investigation of a political plot by the Secret Chancellery.

24 **From Finland's icy cliffs to fiery Colchis**: a quotation from Pushkin's poem 'To the Slanderers of Russia' (*Klevetnikam Rossii*, 1831).

25 **It's time, my friend**: the words are loosely taken from Pushkin's poem of the same title (1831).

CHAPTER THE FIFTH

1 **When morning and its star doth gleam**: the epigraph is taken from Pushkin's verse novel *Eugene Onegin* (Chapter 6, Lensky's poem), with a slight alteration in line 3.

2 **Aa-ba-a-ate un-re-est of the paa-aassions**: the words are from Glinka's romance 'Doubt' (*Somnenie*, 1838), and form a leitmotif in Bely's 'Fourth Symphony'.

3 **Allasch**: a clear spirit flavoured with thyme.

4 **Oh, do not suppose that those ties ... shedding of blood**: there is an evident allusion here to the conversations between Raskolnikov and the investigator Porfiry Petrovich in Dostoyevsky's *Crime and Punishment* – one of the many instances in *Petersburg* where Bely invokes that novel.

5 **Illegitimate ... seamstress**: there is perhaps a hint here of Part IV, Book 11, Chapter 8 of Dostoyevsky's *The Brothers Karamazov*, where Smerdyakov tells Ivan about the murder.

6 **Colours of a fiery hue**: the verses are Bely's own.

7 **a lawless comet**: an echo of a line from Pushkin's poem 'The Portrait' (*Portret*, 1828).

8 **arshin, vershoks**: 1 arshin was equal to 0.71 metres, 1 vershok was equal to 4.4 centimetres.

9 *petit-jeu*: parlour games – charades, forfeits, epigrams, et cetera.

10 **Karolina Karlovna**: the name of Bely's first nursery-governess, who spoke German, and looked after him in January 1884.

11 **the logic of Dharmakirti with a commentary by Dharmottara**: Dharmakirti was a seventh-century Indian philosopher, and Dharmottara a ninth-century one. Bely read Dharmakirti in the Russian translation of F.I. Shcherbatskoy, published by the Academy of Sciences in 1904.

12 **a *Chronic* aspect**: a pun on chronic and Chronos.

13 **Turanian**: Turanians were non-Semitic and non-Aryan nomads who supposedly came to Europe and Asia before the Aryans. Rudolf Steiner believed that logic was invented during the supremacy of the Turanians and Mongols.

14 **Saturn**: according to Rudolf Steiner's anthroposophical teaching, the first stage in the evolution of the cosmos.

15 *bogdykhan*: the traditional Russian name (derived from Mongolian *bogdokhan*) for the Chinese emperors.

CHAPTER THE SIXTH

1 **Behind him always**: the epigraph is taken from Pushkin's *The Bronze Horseman* (V, 148).

2 **insect powder**: in Russian, *persidskiy poroshok*, literally 'Persian powder'. The 'Persian' theme is established here.

3 **Serafim of Sarov**: an elder at the Orthodox monastery of Sarov who lived from 1760 to 1833. He imposed penances of awesome severity on himself, once standing for a thousand nights in continuous prayer.

4 **on the corner of Anichkov Bridge**: a reference to the sculpted groups of young men with horses that adorn the Anichkov Bridge in St Petersburg.

5 **credit bill**: i.e. a banknote.

6 **Potapenko**: Ignaty Nikolayevich Potapenko (1856–1928), a *belle-lettriste* and playwright who was popular in the Russia of the 1880s and 1890s. In 1905 he produced a play called *The New Life*.

7 **Shemakha**: a city in Azerbaijan.

8 **Young Persian**: this group does not seem to have existed as such. Bely invents it on the model of 'Young Turks', to denote the supporters of constitutional reform in Persia.

9 **In fear of God and in faith proceed**: words proclaimed by the deacon during the Orthodox liturgy.

10 **if one had raised their lids**: a reference to Gogol's story 'Viy', and the monster's long eyelids.

11 **Some girls**: these verses, like the ones that follow it, are entirely Bely's own creation – they are modelled on the Russian *chastushka*, a relatively modern form of humorous folk song.

12 **in a Helsingfors coffee house**: the images of Dudkin's hallucination stem partly from the real-life mental illness of Bely's friend and acquaintance S.M. Solovyov in 1911. On 26 November 1911 Bely wrote to Blok: '... all that you write to me in veiled hints is *more than familiar: the yellow fascination*: succumb to it and – the motor car, the Tartars, the Japanese visitors, and also – Finland, or *"something"* that is in Finland, also – Helsingfors, Azev, the revolution – it is all the same gamut of emotions ... What happened to Seryozha has affected me dreadfully,

for two weeks I have suffered with Seryozha: for one of the ideas that now persecutes him is the face of an Oriental.'

13 **Apachés**: Paris thugs and hooligans who took part in street demonstrations.

14 **St Basil the Great's prayer, the admonitory one, to devils**: what is intended here is an allusion to the 'Prayer of Exorcism for those Suffering from Devils' in the Russian Orthodox *Trebnik*, or 'Prayer Book'. There appears, however, to be a confusion with the subtitle of Vladimir Solovyov's poem of 1898, 'An Admonitory Word to Sea Devils' (*Das Ewig-Weibliche*).

15 **Dr Inozemtsev's drops**: an opium-based infusion used as a painkiller in the treatment of intestinal diseases, and proposed by the Russian physician F.I. Inozemtsev (1802–69) as a treatment for cholera.

16 *Enfranshish*: a number of explanations have been offered for the word-play surrounding this verbal hallucination, which gives rise to the 'Persian' name Shishnarfne, in particular that it is derived from the French words '*En franchise*' written on the containers of a brand of insect ('Persian') powder sold in Russia before 1917. There is also an obvious connection with the Russian word *shish*, meaning fig (as in not a fig), or nose (as in *pokazat' shish*, to pull a long nose). Bely himself compared the Enfranshish episode with Gogol's story 'The Portrait', in which a sinister figure leaps out of a portrait in order to put an end to the hero, Chartkov.

17 **Yevgeny's fate**: Yevgeny is the hero of Pushkin's *The Bronze Horseman*.

18 **Petro Primo Catharina Secunda**: the Latin inscription on the Finnish granite base of the Bronze Horseman statue.

CHAPTER THE SEVENTH

1 **Weary am I, friend**: the epigraph is taken from Pushkin's poem 'It's time, my friend, it's time! The heart asks peace' (*Pora, moi drug, pora! pokoya serdtse prosit*, 1834). The first line has been altered by Bely.

2 **Gaurisankars**: Gaurisankar is a Himalayan mountain situated near Mount Everest. Until 1913 it was erroneously believed to be the same mountain as Everest, and therefore the highest in the chain.

3 **Nokkert**: the real name of Bely's governess from 1886 to 1887.

4 **Acathistus**: in the Orthodox Church, a hymn of praise to Jesus Christ, the Mother of God and the Saints, performed by the congregation standing up.

5 **Section marks**: the typographical sign ¶ – in Russian, its name is *paragraf*, or paragraph.

6 **Konshin**: Aleksei Vladimirovich Konshin, director of the Russian State Bank; his signature was reproduced on Russian banknotes.

7 **vint**: a card game.

8 **the order of St Andrew**: the highest order of the Russian Empire, established in 1698.

9 **the Cabinet of Curiosities**: *Kunstkamera* – the first Russian public museum, founded by Peter the Great. In 1718, Peter issued a ukase commanding that all human and animal 'monsters' were to be sent to the museum.

10 **Do not te-e-e-mpt me**: 'Do not tempt me without need' (*Ne iskushai menya bez nuzhdy*), the romance by Glinka, an 1825 setting of Baratynsky's poem 'Dissuasion' (*Razuverenie*, 1821).

11 **the man was sitting astride the corpse**: Dudkin sits astride the dead Lippanchenko in an obvious and grotesque parody of the Bronze Horseman.

CHAPTER THE EIGHTH

1 **The past moves by before me**: the epigraph is taken from Pushkin's tragedy *Boris Godunov* (1825) (VII, 17), Pimen's monologue. The last line has been changed slightly by Bely.

2 **the Protection in Winter**: the Orthodox Feast of the Protection (*Pokrov*) is on 1 October; the Nativity of the Mother of God is from 7 to 12 September; 'St Nicholas in Winter' (*Nikolai zimniy*) is the day of the decease of St Nicholas the Miracle Worker, 6 December.

3 **khalda**: the Russian word for 'a brazen hussy'.

4 **Mantalini**: the name of a frivolous and sentimental character in Charles

Dickens's novel *Nicholas Nickleby* (1839). Bely was very fond of Dickens's work, which he read often. 'Mindalini' has overtones of 'almonds', being derived from the Russian word *mindal'*.

EPILOGUE

1 **The February sun is on the wane**: Bely lived in Tunisia during January and February 1911.

2 **gandurah**: one of Bely's own definitions of this word reads: 'The gandurah is an Arabian coloured shirt that comes down to below the knees; the Arabs wear it under a cloak.'

3 **chechia**: 'a round Tunisian fez with a very long tassel'.

4 **Zaghouan**: a Tunisian mountain range.

5 **the museum at Bulaq**: a museum of Egyptian antiquities, opened in 1858, and situated in Bulaq, a port of Cairo.

6 **The 'Book of the Dead'**: a collection of 150 spells meant to be recited by a dead man to protect himself from injury in the world beyond.

7 **Manetho**: Manetho of Sebennytos, an Egyptian scholar and priest who lived around 400 BC and wrote a description of the Egyptian royal houses.

8 **the piles of Gizeh**: the pyramids outside Cairo.

9 **Duauf**: Duauf, or Dauphsekrut, an Egyptian king of the Middle Kingdom (20–18 centuries BC) whose letter to his son ('The Instruction of Duauf') is a celebrated work of ancient Egyptian literature.

10 **Skovoroda**: Grigory Skovoroda, the eighteenth-century Ukrainian philosopher and poet (1722–94), a Neoplatonist and moralist.